DARK STRANGER

THE TRILOGY

I. T. LUCAS

NOTE FROM THE AUTHOR:
This is a work of fiction!

Names, characters, places and incidents are products of the author's imagination or are used fictitiously and are not to be construed as real. Any similarity to actual persons, organizations and/or events is purely coincidental.

TABLE OF CONTENTS

DARK STRANGER
THE DREAM

I. T. LUCAS

PRELUDE: SYSSI

Premonitions are tricky.

And although Syssi had been having them for as long as she could remember, she could never predict how they'd come to pass.

Yet in one way or another, they always did.

It was a curse.

Knowing something was coming, but not the when or the how, left her perpetually anxious.

Lately, she sensed a dark shadow descending over the world, a malevolence that had an oddly familiar flavor to it. An old and powerful force was on the rise, readying to plunge the world into darkness. Yet again.

It alarmed her.

So much so that she dreaded watching the news or reading a newspaper. To witness global events unfold according to her predictions only fueled their potency. And like one of those biblical prophets of doom, the foreknowledge she was burdened with was too vague to heed—even if anyone cared to listen.

And yet, although the portents were mounting, it seemed as if no one was concerned. Blinded by one trifling thing or another, most of her friends were convinced that their future was secure.

As if weapons of mass destruction were not threatening to annihilate the world, and the slaughter of thousands in Africa and in North Korea and in other godforsaken dictatorships wasn't happening. Not to mention that hunger was still a serious problem in parts of the globe, and basic human rights were rapidly eroding in those and other parts: specifically, those of women.

It weighed on her.

Being a powerless observer sucked.

There was nothing she could do.

Except, some small part of her was rebelling against this perceived helplessness, whispering in her mind that she was wrong. It was like an itch, a nagging suspicion that she was forgetting something important, and that just around the corner, a life-altering adventure awaited.

Perhaps it had something to do with the dream that had been tormenting her for months. Infrequent at first, lately it had been a nightly occurrence, and she would wake up gasping, sweaty, shaky, and with a mean headache.

The dream always began in the midst of a heart-pounding pursuit.

Out of breath and desperate, she was running for her life through a dark wood—a pack of vicious wolves on her heels. With the hellhounds' terrible red-glowing eyes and snarling muzzles never far behind, her panting breaths were the only other sounds to disturb the quiet of the night.

What am I doing here?

Why are they chasing me?

Dear God, I'm going to die—horrifically—they are going to tear me apart.

Her eyes darting frantically in search of help, Syssi could see nothing besides the elusive shadows the moon was casting on her path.

She was losing hope, her legs threatening to give out, when up ahead in the distance she discerned what looked like a silhouette of a man. She couldn't be sure, though. The tall shape was barely visible below the limbs of a large tree—it might've been just another shadow.

It remained a mystery. She'd never reached him, not even once, always waking up before getting close enough to find out if he'd been real.

Trouble was, Syssi didn't know what to make of the dream. Was the dark stranger friend or foe? Was she supposed to run to him? Or from him?

On that, her premonition remained undecided, churning up a strange mix of contradicting feelings: a sense of trepidation, but also excitement.

Yes, her premonitions were definitely tricky.

CHAPTER 1: SYSSI

"Watch out!" Syssi threw a hand out, bracing against the Porsche's front panel.

Her new boss, the most talked about professor on campus, Dr. Amanda Dokani, was going to get them killed.

"Would you chill?" Amanda cast Syssi an annoyed glance before accelerating again to take advantage of an opening in the next lane over.

Syssi held her breath. The space didn't look big enough for a motorcycle. The Porsche was a small car, but not that small. When Amanda managed to slip it into the tiny space without causing an accident, Syssi sagged in relief.

Would telling her boss she was driving like a maniac get her fired?

Nah. Not after all the trouble Amanda had gone through convincing Syssi to come work for her. Besides, they were friends. Sort of. "You're dangerous. I'm never going to hitch a ride with you again."

Amanda snorted. "I don't know what your problem is. I'm an excellent driver."

If she wasn't holding on to the dashboard for dear life, Syssi would've crossed her arms over her chest and huffed. "Why can't you stay in one lane? Do you really think all that weaving between cars will get you there faster? And anyway, what's the rush? You have plenty of time until your first class starts."

Amanda let out a resigned sigh. "Fine, I'll slow down. But you need to tell me what's gotten into you. Yesterday, you had no problem with my driving."

True. But that had been before the disturbing foretelling that had forced itself into Syssi's mind this morning. Amanda was in danger, the premonition had been clear on that, but the details had been fuzzy.

"I had a premonition about you."

"Aha, I knew it. Let's hear it." Amanda looked excited as she peered at Syssi with a pair of big blue eyes that seemed to be glowing from the inside. It must've been a trick of the light—a reflection from contact lenses—because people's eyes didn't emit light. Though, it sure as hell looked like it.

Syssi shook her head. This wasn't the first oddity she'd noticed about her new boss. Not that any of it was a big deal, just small things.

3

Was Syssi the only one who noticed that there was something peculiar about the professor?

Probably.

Amanda's students were too busy gaping and admiring to actually listen to her lectures, let alone notice that there was something off about her.

Tall and lean, with dark, glossy, short hair, deep blue eyes, and full, sensuous lips that were red without the benefit of a lipstick, Amanda's beauty bordered on the surreal. Distracted by her looks, most people could see nothing beyond it, and at first, Syssi had been no different. But with each passing day, since she had first walked into Amanda's lab a little over two months ago, it was getting easier see the person inside and ignore the cover.

Upon discovering that Professor Dokani was conducting experiments on extrasensory perception, Syssi had volunteered to be a test subject. What better way to explore her ability to foresee glimpses of the future than having a neuroscientist examine it?

Her results had been so exceptional that even though neuroscience hadn't been her field of study, Amanda had pestered her to join the research team.

Syssi had politely declined.

She had an internship lined up with a wonderful architect. Tragically, though, the poor man had died of a heart failure a few days before she'd been supposed to start. So here she was, working at the lab and getting valuable insight into an ability that had haunted her, her entire life.

At least until she could find another architect to intern with.

"It was vague, as they all are, so I didn't want to worry you for nothing, but I sensed that something major was going to happen to you—not life threatening, but life changing."

Amanda smirked. "Hey, maybe the groundbreaking paper we are working on will get published in *Nature*? That would be major and life changing."

Syssi shook her head. "The premonition wasn't bleak but it wasn't sunny either. Besides, we are not ready. Even I know we have to do a lot more experiments before we can prove your hypothesis."

Tapping a long-nailed finger on the steering wheel, Amanda frowned. "I know. Tell me something, are you still getting those nightmares? The ones with the wolves?"

Syssi blushed. "Yeah, almost every night." She'd told Amanda about the dreams, but not about the recent changes in their nature. Last

Saturday, she'd gotten a little closer to her would-be dream rescuer, and closer yet each night since. His facial features were still obscured by the shadows, but she could tell that he was tall, exceptionally so, and that his body was beautifully built—lean and strong like that of an athlete's.

Even though it was only a dream, his proximity was doing all kinds of weird things to her, affecting her in a most disturbing way. The man was like the epicenter of a force field, emitting some kind of attractant she was powerless to resist.

The way he held himself, his entire body language exuding an aura of power and confidence, was calling to everything female in her. Syssi yearned for her dream guy like she'd never yearned for any real man.

To be with him would differ from any sexual experience that she'd ever had or even fantasized about. Before the dreams had taken on this new twist, her fantasies had been quite tame, as well as the men starring in them. Kind of like her ex-boyfriend, or perhaps just a little more exciting. Gregg had been as far removed from intense as it got.

Not this guy.

He would demand nothing less than her complete and utter submission.

The shocking part was that she found herself yearning for his dominance. The concept was so foreign to her that she should've found it abhorrent, and certainly not titillating. Still, it was hard to argue with the very physical evidence her dream arousal was leaving behind.

Wet panties weren't a big problem first thing in the morning, but the arousal carried over to her waking hours. Syssi could've banished it, forcing it off her mind, but the truth was that she didn't want to. It made her feel alive. There was something naughty and delicious about her constant state of arousal, her yearning for the forbidden sensation, and she refused to give it up.

Not yet, anyway.

She would cast these fantasies aside once she started dating again and had a real guy in her life. It didn't require a degree in psychology to figure out that there was a connection between the dreams and her extended dry spell.

Amanda cast her a sidelong glance, no doubt puzzled by Syssi's blush. "The dreams are affecting you, and this is why you see trouble lurking in every corner. I think you are mixing up real premonitions with a bad mood."

"Not likely. I know the difference. A premonition has a very distinct feel to it." Syssi sighed. "I'm just tired. All I need is one good night's sleep to regain my sunny predisposition." One without disturbing dreams about a sexy dark stranger.

"What you need is to get laid. One good tumble and the nightmares will go *poof*. Isn't a handsome guy part of the dream? You need to catch up to him and turn that nightmare into something naughty instead of scary; something fun like several screaming orgasms." Amanda squirmed in her chair. "I could use some myself." She winked at Syssi, the seductive smile on her beautiful face so sinful it had Syssi squirm a little herself. Amanda was such a sexual creature that it was impossible to remain unaffected. Especially given Syssi's already elevated state of arousal.

If it were anyone else other than Amanda, Syssi would've been freaked out, thinking she was that transparent and that everyone could figure out what her dreams were about. But the woman had sex on her mind twenty-four seven. She would've turned a dream about a trip to the supermarket into something sexy.

But even though Amanda was very open about her sexuality, sometimes shockingly so, Syssi didn't want to share this with her boss. She hid her discomfort with a shrug. "I don't know if he is handsome or not because I never get close enough to see him. It's not that kind of a dream."

Liar, liar, panties on fire.

CHAPTER 2: AMANDA

"Where the hell is he?" Amanda murmured and took another quick glance at the time before fixing her gaze back on the lecture hall's door.

From her elevated vantage point on the podium, there was little chance she could miss Kian. At six foot four and with two distinctive bodyguards at his side, he wasn't exactly inconspicuous, or easily overlooked.

She was just anxious for him to show up.

At last, after endless nagging and cajoling, her brother—the all-important Regent and head of her clan on the American continent—was making the time to come see her teach.

He should be here already. Kian was punctual to a fault. *Unless, he isn't coming after all.*

Snatching her phone out of her purse, Amanda turned her back to the class.

Where are you? I have to start in a few minutes, Amanda texted, then waited, tapping her heeled shoe on the podium's hardwood floor.

Don't get your knickers in a twist. Parking the car. Be there in two.

Letting out a relieved breath, she smiled and texted back. *Knickers? Really? What century are you stuck in? It's a thong now. Get with the times, old man. And unless you can fly, you won't make it in two.*

Old man walking as fast as he can while texting. Stop bugging me.

Amanda chuckled, but as she shifted her attention back to the rapidly filling classroom, her eyebrows dipped with worry. At this rate, Kian might not find an empty seat, let alone three, which might provide him with a perfect excuse to leave.

"Professor Dokani, I just wanted to tell you that I love your lectures," called out a brave soul sitting in the first row.

Gutsy boy.

She smiled and gave him the thumbs-up.

The room, already one of the largest in the department at one hundred and fifty seats, was nearing full capacity. Amanda's class, "Mind: The Final Frontier", was quickly becoming a favorite of the student body. Not that she had any illusions as to why her class was so popular.

It wasn't due to a sudden interest in the philosophy of neuroscience, or appreciation for the title's reference to *Star Trek*. And sadly, it wasn't due to her fascinating lectures or her amazing teaching skills either. No, the course's popularity had mainly to do with her looks.

Owing to her exceptional hearing, Amanda couldn't help but overhear her students' murmurs; most of which were flattering, though some were not just rude but outright derogatory. She would've loved nothing more than to slap those boys around for talking like that about a woman, any woman. Unfortunately, she couldn't. Not only would it get her fired from the university, but it would expose her supernatural hearing and uncommon strength.

Amanda sighed. Beauty wasn't all that it was cracked up to be. What most people didn't realize was that it was both a gift and a curse. No one bothered to look past the cover to see what was on the inside.

Even Amanda herself hadn't been immune. For most of her life she'd let this exquisite exterior define her, but lately it just wasn't enough. She wished to be admired for her skill as a teacher, and not the looks her unique genetic heritage had bestowed upon her.

"Just look at her," she heard one of the boys whisper. "She looks like something straight out of an anime illustrator's fantasy."

Nice. But although what he'd said was flattering, and not vulgar like some of the other comments she'd heard, Amanda had to disagree. Unlike the nearly naked anime beauties, she was dressed, modestly and impeccably.

Still, at the back of her mind, shoved into a hidden corner she managed to ignore most of the time, Amanda often felt like an anime character: an exaggerated exterior masking a hollow interior. But then she covered it up well, projecting a confident attitude and dressing the part.

This morning she'd taken particular care, choosing an outfit to best fit the role she was playing: a distinguished and respected professor, yet a hot one. The slim-fitting black trousers and blue silk blouse revealed very little skin, leaving the job of accentuating her figure to the exquisite cut of the luxurious fabrics.

Amanda didn't own a single article of clothing that wasn't a top designer label or cost less than most folks' monthly mortgage payments. Not that she could afford that kind of stuff on a professor's pay; that wouldn't have covered her shoe budget alone. But her shares in the clan's extensive holdings ensured she could buy whatever struck her fancy without ever needing to work for it.

The research she was conducting had a higher purpose than earning her income or even prestige.

Still, she liked feeling important for a change. And besides delighting in her students' reactions—amusing and thrilling as they were—she had to admit that she truly enjoyed teaching and was surprisingly good at it.

With a thinly veiled smirk, Amanda watched the young men—some freezing in place, awestruck as they stared at her, others tripping over their own feet as they tried to find a seat without taking their eyes off her.

Some tall, some short, some pale, some dark. Most were average-looking. A few were worth a second glance.

Yummy, so many to choose from.

She loved their attention, their lust. Drinking it in, Amanda was in her element: the hunter in a field of ogling prey.

Mortals, with their weak, malleable minds, were easily snared, their memories of the hook-ups easily erased, and the men themselves just as easily forgotten.

Regrettably, it was a modus operandi for her kind.

Repeatedly thralling partners messed with their brains, while hiding her true nature for extended periods of time was tiresome and carried the risk of exposure.

Long-term relationships were simply impossible.

Those of her kin who'd tried had gotten burned; most figuratively, some literally.

Case in point; the witch hunts.

In days past, a woman like her might have been called a femme fatale, a succubus, or even a vamp. Nowadays, there was a new term, cougar, which she liked better. It didn't carry such negative connotation and was, in fact, closer to the truth.

Not that anyone would dare think of her as an older woman. Amanda shuddered at the thought.

She was a beautiful, young female.

Her fake birth certificate stated that she was born on the sixth of May, 1984. It got the sixth of May right, but the actual year of her birth was 1773.

Amanda was over two hundred years old.

The funny thing was, for a near-immortal she truly was young. Kian was four years shy of two thousand—the old goat. Compared to the life spans of mortals, though...

Well, what they didn't know didn't hurt them. She was what she was—what biology and her kin's traditions made her—a lustful, hedonistic, near-immortal.

Amanda liked who she was, and she loved her life. Most of it anyway.

At last, as the classroom began to settle down, she spotted Kian, flanked by his trusted sidekicks—number one and number two as she nicknamed Brundar and Anandur. The three headed for the back row, where seats immediately became available, vacated by their occupants who scurried to find a place elsewhere.

Good.

Amanda would never admit it, but Kian's approval meant a lot to her. Being that much older, he fulfilled both the roles of the father she'd never had and a big brother.

Lately, the clan's holdings were increasing at a staggering pace, and managing their family's extensive affairs was taking up most of Kian's waking time. It had taken relentless nagging to pry him away for a couple of hours to come see his baby sister teach.

CHAPTER 3: KIAN

Kian was taken by surprise when the lecture reached its end with a lively discussion concerning free will. Enchanted by Amanda's rendition of the mysterious nature of consciousness and the brain's uncharted neural pathways, he had lost track of time just like the rest of her students. Even Brundar and Anandur, who'd expected to be bored out of their minds, had been listening—riveted throughout the entire class.

"It's time to go," Kian whispered, motioning for them to follow as he pushed to his feet. Leaving Amanda's mesmerized audience behind, they sneaked out of the lecture hall unnoticed, which in itself served as another testament to her skill. More often than not, the three of them attracted a lot of unwanted attention; be it admiration from females, or apprehension from males.

Then again, establishing their headquarters in a big city that was home to the film and music industry had its perks. On the streets of Los Angeles—with all of its actors, musicians, and wannabes of the same—a bunch of tall, good-looking men wasn't an unusual sight.

Once outside, Kian squinted at the glaring sun and pulled on his custom-made, heavy-duty sunglasses. Unlike his native Scotland, it rarely got cloudy enough here for him to forgo the shades. And at this time of year in particular, the bright orb's glare was brutal on his over-sensitive eyes.

Not that it got significantly better during what passed for winter in Southern California.

Pulling up to the curb, his black SUV with its dark-tinted windows attracted the interest of the few people on the street. Thankfully, no one lingered to gawk.

"She's really good. Even I got it," Anandur remarked as he opened the passenger door for Kian.

With a slight nod, Brundar seconded his brother's opinion.

"I still hate the idea of her being so publicly exposed. It's risky. All it will take is for some nosy reporter to go digging into her fake dossier, and all hell will break loose." His temper on the rise, Kian slammed the SUV's door.

He had to admit, though, Amanda had had her students spellbound. Some of it was no doubt due to her beauty, and some due to her special ability to influence. But as he was immune to both and had still found the lecture fascinating, he had to give her the credit she was due.

"Where to, Master?" his driver asked, easing into traffic.

"We are having lunch at Gino's."

Mindful of the amount of work still waiting for him, Kian pulled out his phone and began scrolling through the avalanche of emails and texts that had managed to accumulate during the two-hour class. He'd barely gotten through a fraction of them when his driver parked the SUV in front of Amanda's favorite place for lunch.

Gino's was a short drive away from campus, close enough for her to grab a quick bite to eat during her lunch break, but too far for her students to get there on foot. Which meant the risk of her bumping into one of them was low. She'd discovered it two years ago when she'd gotten her first job at the university.

A generous grant provided by one of the clan's subsidiary corporations ensured Amanda had free rein to test her ideas. But even though Kian was funding her research, he didn't put much stock in her achieving her main objective. His reasoning was that even if Amanda failed to find anything useful for the clan, her research could potentially benefit humanity, which, of course, was the ultimate goal and justified the substantial monetary investment.

"Is it we, as in you and Amanda, or are we invited as well?" Anandur asked as they stepped out of the vehicle.

"No. I will have you guys stand sentry, salivating while Amanda and I eat. This is not the Middle Ages, and I didn't do so even then. Really, Andu, sometimes I wonder if it's part of your act or are you really that thick."

Brundar chuckled, a jab directed at his obnoxious brother never failing to bring a rare smile to his austere face.

"What I mean, ladies... are we all sitting together as one big happy family, auntie and uncle with their beloved nephews? Or Amanda and you upstairs, while we guard from a safe distance—out of hearing range—downstairs?" Anandur arched both of his bushy red brows.

"I don't know. It's up to Amanda. I'm not sure what she has in mind." Kian frowned, remembering she'd mentioned that there was something she wanted to talk to him about.

"Aha, you don't know. So I'm not so thick, am I?" Anandur smirked.

Kian shook his head but smiled despite himself. Anandur liked to act the big brainless oaf. At almost six and a half feet tall and about two hundred and fifty pounds of muscle, he looked like a pro wrestler. Add to that a head full of crinkly red hair, a bushy red beard and mustache, and he could play an extra in a Viking movie.

In contrast, Brundar looked almost feminine. A little over six feet, he wasn't short, but his lean build, pretty angelic face, and his choice of hairstyle—keeping his pale blond stick-straight mane so long it reached the small of his back even when bound with twine—made him look delicate. Metrosexual.

Their appearances couldn't have been more misleading. Of the two, Brundar was the deadlier force—cold, calculated, and skilled. A true master.

Anandur's reliance on his brute strength, though, didn't mean that he could be easily fooled or manipulated. He was a keen observer, capable of quick and accurate assessments of sticky situations, never acting on impulse. The big oaf act fooled his opponents into underestimating him, which naturally was the whole point.

Together the brothers, who'd been serving as his bodyguards for centuries, were deadly to anyone posing a threat to Kian or the clan.

As expected, Gino's was packed with customers waiting in line on the sidewalk to be seated. The few round bistro tables on its narrow veranda were all taken; some by young mothers with their strollers blocking whatever little space remained, and others by business types from the nearby offices.

Bypassing the crowd, Kian took the worn stairs leading directly from the back entrance up to what Gino called his VIP section. It was a small room on the second floor reserved for his special guests—those who for various reasons didn't want to mingle with the rest of the clientele, or members of his large, extended family.

The room looked like an old lady's parlor. Old-fashioned wallpaper in green and yellow hues covered walls which were decorated with the fading portraits of stern matriarchs and patriarchs posing in their Sunday best—their disapproving expressions staring from their frames. Six upholstered chairs surrounded a round dining table in the center, and the serve ware came from a peeling sideboard laboring under the weight of piles of china.

Looking at it, Kian imagined that one of these days the thing would collapse, and Gino's heirloom collection would be history. But each time he'd mentioned it, Gino had just smiled, saying not to worry; his grandmother's sideboard had held for the past fifty years and would keep on holding for at least that many more.

With another glance at the wood's widening cracks, Kian shrugged and sat down. He would hate to tell the guy; *I told you so,* when it eventually fell apart.

As he peered at the street through the open French doors that led to the tiny balcony overlooking the front, the lacy curtains fluttered in the light, warm breeze.

Feeling his tension ease, Kian realized he liked it here. It was cozy and intimate, despite the tacky decor, or perhaps owing to it.

CHAPTER 4: ANANDUR

"Hey, Gino!" Anandur waved the proprietor over. "How are you doing, buddy? Life treating you well?"

"Can't complain. Business is doing good, the family is good, so I'm good. Eh? What can I do for you, gentlemen?"

For some reason, Gino was always nervous around them, despite the fact that since Amanda had gotten the job at the university, they were eating here at least twice a month and leaving extravagant tips. Anandur had often wondered if it was the small guy's instinctive wariness of men their size, or Gino suspecting them of being Mafia goons.

Calling Kian boss certainly didn't help matters. But what the heck, Anandur liked messing with the old man.

"The boss is upstairs. Could you please set us a table down here next to the stairs?" Anandur leaned down to Gino's ear. "We need to watch both entrances. If you know what I mean," he whispered, pausing for effect. "Oh, and the lady is going to join him shortly, so it will be two upstairs and two downstairs for lunch today."

"The lovely Ms. Amanda?" the small man breathed, wiping his spotless hands on his pristine apron, his mostly bald head glistening with perspiration.

"The one and only." Anandur chuckled. "And speaking of the devil, here she is in person, the beautiful Dr. Amanda Dokani." He pointed at the front door.

"Hi, boys!" Amanda sauntered into the restaurant, causing a momentary halt in the chatter. She hugged Brundar, then stretching to reach, kissed Anandur's cheek. "Kian is upstairs?"

"Yep, he is waiting for you. But before you go, I just wanted to say, you totally rocked today!" Anandur high-fived her. "I didn't snooze even once." He pulled her into a hug.

"Congratulations on the promotion," Brundar added, for once not skimping on words.

Gino was still wiping his hands, waiting for her to acknowledge him.

Amanda turned, flashing him her megawatt smile. "Gino! Sweetheart!" She leaned to give him a hug.

"*Bellissima!*" He blushed the color of beets, returning the hug and planting a kiss on each of her cheeks. "So happy to see you again."

"You always brighten my day, Gino. The way you say bellissima... Makes a girl swoon. Be a darling and bring me my wine upstairs? I'm in the mood to celebrate. You still stock it, I hope?"

"I keep it just for you, bellissima!" He beamed.

Amanda's favorite wine, a 2005 Angelus, was too rich for Gino's regulars, but he always kept a bottle just for her. Excusing himself, Gino scurried to the kitchen to fish out the bottle he was hiding behind the onions in the pantry. The unmistakable scent always clung to the bottle, and Anandur wondered if Amanda could smell it as well. Female immortals' sense of smell wasn't as acute as that of the males, but still, this one was quite pungent.

Starting up, Amanda paused mid-stair. "Aren't you coming?" She arched her brows.

"Sorry, princess, we are on guard duty, keeping an eye out from down here. The two of you together in public always makes me twitchy." Anandur waved her off and dragged a chair to the small table the waiter had placed near the stairs.

"As you wish." Amanda shrugged and kept climbing.

CHAPTER 5: AMANDA

Amanda wasn't about to argue. The conversation she was planning to have with her brother required privacy.

Argh, he is going to fume and rant, she cringed.

For a good guy, he sure had a very short fuse. But this needed to be done, and giving up was not an option.

The future of their clan depended on it.

"I'm so proud of you!" Kian got up and pulled her into a hug.

"It's about time someone was!" Lingering in the comfort of Kian's warm embrace, Amanda sniffled, blinking back the tears that were threatening to ruin her carefully applied makeup. "The naughty party girl is finally making a contribution." She chuckled.

Nine years ago, Amanda had decided to enroll in college, surprising everyone, most of all herself, with how brilliant she'd turned out to be. In just seven years, she'd earned a Ph.D. in the Philosophy of Neuroscience, and was now hailed as a new and fresh thinker, a leader in her field. Her papers were published in the most respected scientific journals.

"Oh, sweetheart, when you look ahead to a lifespan of thousands of years, two centuries of partying seem like nothing at all. And after the sorrow you had endured, you deserved all the joy you could find."

Why the hell did Kian have to bring it up?

Her day had been going so well until he opened the trapdoor on the old pain she'd buried deep down behind thick walls and a moat. Surfacing, it dragged its serrated edge through her insides. "You know I don't talk about it!" She pushed away from him, wiping the few tears that found their way out despite her best efforts.

In the silence that followed, the sound of Gino's light footfalls echoing from the stairwell announced his arrival. A moment later, he rushed in with a loaded tray in one hand and a folded stand in the other. Setting it up by the table, he proceeded to pull out a chair for Amanda. "My lady?" He gestured for her to take a seat.

Donning her well-practiced cheerful mask, Amanda did what she'd always done when unpleasant thoughts intruded. She pushed them back into their little jail, redirecting her train of thought to a happier place; like whether Gino insisted on always serving them himself because he coveted their generous tips, or because he believed they were celebrities. "Thank you, Gino." She sat down, sneaking another discreet swipe at her eyes before offering him a bright smile.

Gino removed the red-checkered napkin from the basket of freshly baked rolls, letting the steam out, then fussed with the placement of the wine glasses. Once he was satisfied with how everything looked, he proceeded to make a big production out of opening the bottle and pouring Amanda's wine.

As he pulled out two menus from his apron pocket and was about to hand them out, Kian stopped him with a chuckle. "Please, we have no need for these. Unless new items have been added since our last time here, I can recite your menu verbatim. I'll have a Caesar salad and the vegetable lasagna, please."

"The garden delight fettuccine and your delicious house salad, *per favore.*" Amanda smiled at Gino and reached for one of the fragrant rolls.

"Very well!" His face beaming with satisfaction, Gino puffed out his chest and stuffed the menus back in his apron pocket. "I'll be back with your salads momentarily."

Sipping her wine, Amanda stole a furtive glance at Kian to assess his mood as she thought of a way to broach the delicate subject she needed to discuss with him.

"You're plotting something." Kian narrowed his eyes. "I know that contemplating look, the one you have when you want to tell me something you know I'm not going to like. Let's hear it then and get it over with so I can bite your head off, and we can eat in peace."

Amanda pouted. "You could be nice and agreeable for a change."

"Spill!"

"I want you to meet Syssi," she blurted in a hurry, cringing in preparation for his retort.

"Syssi?" He arched a brow.

"Yes, Syssi, my research assistant, remember? I mentioned her before." Amanda looked hopefully at Kian. He didn't seem angry. Yet. Maybe this would go easier than she had expected.

"Last I heard you mention that girl, you were blabbering about an architecture graduate who excelled at predicting coin tosses."

"I hired her," Amanda said while trying to look remorseful.

"And what credentials did she bring to the job? Arranging the Functional MRI machines in an aesthetically pleasing manner? Painting the lab in designer colors? I understand you wanted to test her, but why hire the girl?"

Kian's level of aggravation was rising with each sentence. He had this tendency to fuel his own temper over minor issues. And yet, when things hit critical mass he somehow managed to be as cool as a cucumber.

"Syssi is an amazing person; smart, dedicated, and hard working. The internship she had lined up bummed. The poor schmuck died of a heart attack on a fishing trip of all places. I needed a research assistant, and she was both available and the best test subject I had to date. She is off the charts, Kian. And it's not only the coin tosses, which in itself is beyond impressive; she guesses with eighty-seven percent accuracy. The random-computer-selected-images test? You know which one I'm talking about?"

When he nodded, she continued. "She was spot on, or close to the correct image in ninety-two out of a hundred pictures. She has the strongest precognition ability of any mortal I've ever tested. I'm telling you, Syssi is a Dormant, Kian. I just know it." Amanda could barely contain her excitement.

Kian ran both hands through his hair. "I can't do it, Amanda. It's just wrong. Pick another male. It doesn't have to be me."

"I don't know what your problem is, Kian. You bang random women you pick up at clubs and bars, and I know for a fact that you've even paid for it on occasion. So why not Syssi? Why not someone who has the potential to change your life and give hope to the rest of us? We know there must be Dormants out there; carriers of our unrealized genes who can be turned into near-immortals like us. Potential mates we could bond with for life. And I think I finally found a way to identify them. You know why I started this research in the first place, searching for anomalies, paranormal abilities. Once we realized DNA testing was useless, instead of giving up, I took a different approach. Don't you want children, Kian? Immortal children? Don't you want a life mate?" Amanda was exasperated. If it were up to her, she wouldn't even pause to think. But only males possessed the venom necessary to activate the dormant DNA.

It was a cruel twist of fate, or as Kian believed, the work of a crazy geneticist. Only the immortal females contributed the special genetic material to their offspring. And only males could activate it in a Dormant.

An immortal mother and a mortal father produced mortal offspring who possessed the dormant immortal genes and could be activated by venom. If not activated, the dormant genetic material would remain inert but still pass from mother to daughter, and so on. It wouldn't pass to the sons, though.

The immortal heredity was matrilineal.

To facilitate the activation of a Dormant, an immortal male would have to inject the latent with his venom. When sexually aroused, the male's fangs elongated and venom was produced in specialized glands; the need to bite and release it into the female's system congruent with the need to ejaculate.

Aggression toward other males triggered a similar reaction. Though the venom produced for the purpose of immobilizing or even killing an opponent was obviously more potent and carried a different mix of chemicals. A large amount of it, pumped into the victim's system, paralyzed the body and stopped the heart. Even in immortals.

Kian just stared at her, looking stunned by her audacity. But she did not back down. Holding his stare, she challenged him to pick up the gauntlet.

"You really want to know what the big deal is? I'll tell you. I hate it! I hate what I have to do. I feel like a drug addict; needing, craving the release sex provides and despising the need. I wish I could abstain, or at least have the luxury human males have of taking matters into their own hands, so to speak. But I can't bite myself, can I? If I could put my hands on the sick ████ who designed us this way, I would kill ███████████ slowly." Kian took a fortifying breath in an obvious attempt to calm down, then continued in a quieter voice.

"I use these women. I don't remember their faces or their names. They are all interchangeable in my mind. Not to feel like a jerk, I try not to objectify them, giving them as much pleasure as I can, and when tampering with their brain I leave the memory of pleasure intact, erasing only the biting part and replacing my features with those of another. That's all I can do to ease my conscience. But there is nothing I can do for myself, for the way I feel, as if I'm a ████damned animal with no control over my baser needs."

Reaching over and taking Kian's hand, Amanda purposely kept pity out of her expression. "I had no idea it got so bad for you."

She did not understand his misery. She loved sex. Loved the variety of partners. Perhaps it was different for the females of the clan because supposedly, there was a purpose to their sexual appetite. Conception was extremely rare for her people, and pregnancy was hailed a miracle. With the females of the clan holding the key to its continuity, as only their progeny could turn immortal, they were encouraged to seek a variety of human partners in the hopes of conceiving.

Their plight was not as bad as that of the males. The possibility of having a child to share their long life with, to bear witness to their journey, made the lack of a life-mate tolerable. But for the males there was no such solace. If their dalliance with a human resulted in a child, that child was mortal, with a mortal's short lifespan and vulnerability. But wasn't that exactly what she was trying to rectify? Find Dormants that were descendent from other matrilineal lines?

As all members of her clan were the progeny of one immortal female, they were forbidden to one another.

A taboo.

Kian took her hand. "You're still young, Amanda, so it's still fun for you. But I bet it will get old by the time you reach my age."

Amanda looked into his eyes and spoke softly. "Forgive me for pushing. But I still don't get what all of that has to do with you attempting to activate Syssi. If she turns out to be a dud, all you did was have sex with another faceless, nameless female. But if she is the real deal, isn't it worth a try?"

As his handsome face hardened, Kian pulled his hand away, leaned back in his chair, and crossed his arms over his chest. "Here is the thing, sister of mine. She will not be another faceless, nameless girl. We don't know how long it takes to turn an adult woman. Don't pimp me out like I'm some man-whore." He uttered that last bit acidly, his expression turning to menacing.

She had known her holier-than-thou brother would find her request objectionable, but she hadn't expected him to be that adamant about it. Nevertheless, she had to give it another go. Tempt him. Too much was at stake. Shaking off her despairing mood, Amanda straightened her back and leaned forward. "Syssi is beautiful, Kian, and smart. You're going to love her..." She paused, realizing that the word love did her a disservice in the context of this conversation. "I mean, it's not like you'll be suffering. She is exactly your type. She is blond, very pretty, with a deliciously curvy figure. I'm sure you'll find her attractive. And engaging. Did I mention already how smart she is? And nice?"

"I'll take your word for it, but I'll pass. Ask someone else. If she is so wonderful, I'm sure you'll have no shortage of volunteers." There was a finality to his tone that would have deterred a lesser opponent. But Amanda remained adamant.

"I'm not going to choose someone else," Amanda hissed, then hushed as she heard Gino climbing the stairs.

Sensing the heavy tension in the room, Gino's smile faded. "Here are your salads, and more rolls. Enjoy!" He turned and beat a hasty retreat.

Amanda waited till Gino was out of earshot before resuming her offense. "You are my only brother, and what's more, you're our mother's only living son. You're the closest to a pureblood male the clan has. Your venom's potency is Syssi's best chance of turning. And when she turns, she will have the potential to create a new matrilineal line. Don't you want to be the one who creates it with her? Who knows if I will ever find another one? Maybe she is the one lucky shot? Are you willing to bet on it? To forfeit your one chance because of pride and arrogance?" Amanda was practically huffing with righteous indignation.

Kian regarded her coolly, still leaning back in his chair with his arms crossed over his chest. "Nice speech, Amanda. One problem, though. The 'when', is an 'if'. If she turns and if I were a betting man, I would not put my money on this one. And the answer is still no."

Amanda set her elbows onto the table, dropping her forehead on her hands. "You are such a stu… stubborn old goat. Just sleep on it. Don't decide anything yet. Maybe when you meet her, you'll change your mind."

"I don't think so, princess." Kian's tone got a shade warmer as he leaned in and patted her cheek as if she was a petulant child. "Look, you will have similar chances of success using another male. The only thing I'm spoiling for you is your romantic fantasy. It's not a big disaster. Put on your big-girl panties and deal!"

Amanda smiled at his feeble attempt at levity. Despite his stubbornness and gruffness and bad temper, she knew that he loved her. "If I were leaning that way, I would have snatched Syssi for myself in a heartbeat. I like her that much." She pouted.

Kian rolled his eyes and dug into his salad, letting her know that as far as he was concerned, this discussion was over.

CHAPTER 6: SYSSI

"Why Amanda thought I could do this is beyond me," Syssi muttered as she stared at yet another printout. The freaking computer had been spouting nonsensical results all morning, and she was no closer to finding the error than she'd been five hours ago.

Taking a hammer to the thing was looking more and more enticing.

Heaving a sigh, she ran her fingers through her hair. Again. Sticking out in all directions, it was tangled and knotted from the number of times she'd pushed her fingers through it.

I probably look like Einstein, and not because of what's under my cranium.

It was time for a break, the hollow feeling in her belly reminding her she hadn't eaten yet.

The two espressos, one cappuccino, and eight cups of coffee she'd consumed before lunch—which was excessive even for a caffeine addict like her—didn't qualify as nutrition.

It crossed her mind that she reached for coffee the way other people reached for alcohol. When agitated or worried, or just in need of a break, the ritual of making it, pouring it, and stirring in the precise amount of sweetener relaxed her.

Drinking a truly good cup of coffee was her idea of bliss.

Pushing up from her chair, she stretched her back, listening for the familiar popping sound. A stretch wasn't as satisfying without it. When it came, she did a couple of side to side twists and then turned toward the two postdocs. "I'm going to grab a sandwich. You guys want anything?"

Hannah shook her head, pointing to the empty protein shake container on her desk. Her latest diet craze consisted of protein shakes, protein bars, and water. Nothing else.

David, the other postdoc, smiled his creepy smile and took a big bite of his salami sandwich.

Ugh, she must have been really engrossed in her work not to notice the nauseating stench.

"I can bring cookies."

Hannah made a sad face. "Rub it in, why don't you. Waving sweet, delicious carbs in front of the fat girl. Meanie!"

"Fine, so no cookies."

"Hey, what about me? I want something sweet..." David leered.

"In solidarity with Hannah, no dessert." Syssi pretended not to get it—her usual line of defense against unwanted advances.

David was a jerk. He didn't flirt or tell jokes, or any of the other things guys usually did to get Syssi's attention. He ogled, made inappropriate comments, and habitually invaded her personal space, believing for some inexplicable reason that he was God's gift to women everywhere. His delusional beliefs aside, his problem wasn't that his features were unappealing, David was an average-looking guy, but that he was schlumpy and unkempt. More than his personal hygiene or taste in clothes, it was his personality that needed a major makeover.

In the lab's kitchenette, Syssi slapped together her favorite sandwich of goat cheese, tomatoes, and basil on whole wheat, then ate it leaning against the counter.

She wasn't ready to go back yet.

Out there, she would have to deal with David. And unfortunately, as she'd learned from experience, he wasn't done. Once David started with his idiotic comments, he'd be on a roll for the rest of the day.

Oh, the joy...

"Good afternoon, darlings!" Syssi heard Amanda make her grand entrance. "Missed me terribly, I hope? And where is my girl Syssi?"

"Over here!" Syssi called over a mouthful.

Amanda poked her head into the kitchenette, then stepped in and leaned against the counter next to Syssi. "What's up? You look troubled."

"I'm dying out there. I can't find what's wrong with my programming. The computer has been spouting nonsense all morning, and I'm ready to go at the thing with a sledgehammer."

"Why didn't you ask David for help?" Amanda crossed her legs at her ankles and her arms over her chest.

Syssi cast her boss a sidelong glance. "Are you serious? He will never let me live it down, probably demand a hookup as payment. The creep."

Amanda's expression turned serious. "I know you don't like David, heck, I don't like him either. But he is very good at what he does, and you need to use him. There will always be people like him trying to mess with you, but if you let them, you'll find it damn hard to accomplish anything. You need to be forceful and refuse to take shit from anyone. Sometimes a girl needs to be a bitch not to get pushed around. Be a bitch, Syssi! You might even enjoy it." Amanda winked, her gorgeous face returning to its usual brightness.

"Thank you for the advice, mommy."

Joking aside, Amanda was right. Syssi needed to deal with David, or working in the lab would become intolerable.

What puzzled her, however, was Amanda's admission that she didn't like David either. She was the boss and no one dictated to her who she should employ and who she should not. With a frown, Syssi asked, "What I don't understand, though, is why you hired him if you don't like him?"

"He was the best applicant for the job. And besides, I hired him *because* I don't like him."

"So am I to assume that you don't like me either? Since you hired me..." Syssi pretended offense.

"No, my dear, sweet Syssi, I adore you. You know that!" Amanda slapped her cheek playfully, then kissed it. "I hire females I like and males I don't."

Searching her face, Syssi realized Amanda wasn't joking. Her boss seemed sincere. "I don't understand."

"Better shun the bait, than struggle in the snare," Amanda quoted, looking down at her stiletto-clad feet.

"Oh, Amanda, you're not that bad. I don't buy the whole femme fatale act."

"Who said it's an act? I am bad. You have no idea how bad!" Amanda made a wicked face.

"You witch!" Syssi laughed, mock-punching Amanda's shoulder.

Amanda shrugged, pushed away from the counter, and headed for her desk with the sensual saunter of a practiced temptress.

Syssi didn't buy Amanda's sex-on-a-stick act. It was nothing more than the theatrics of a drama queen. Being so strikingly beautiful, her boss naturally expected to be the center of attention wherever she showed her face.

Except, was it possible that she really was as sexually active as she claimed to be? Maybe.

And why not? Amanda wasn't married—didn't even have a boyfriend—she could and did as she pleased.

Good for her!

Reflecting on her own nonexistent love life, Syssi cringed. She hadn't been on a single date since things had finally fallen apart with Gregg. For two lonely years, she'd mourned a relationship that had been dying a slow death long before it had ended. Though, in retrospect, she realized it was the sense of failure more than any lingering tender feelings that had her stuck on the sidelines while everyone around her was having the time of their lives, or at least pretending to.

Syssi had met Gregg her first week of college, and they'd stayed together until his graduation four years later. Being her first serious boyfriend, and her first and only lover, there had been this expectation that their relationship would lead to marriage. Except, when he had moved to Sacramento for a job, it had been a relief for both of them.

So why was she still alone? Syssi had no good answer for that. Men found her attractive, and she didn't lack propositions, but there was no one she found even remotely enticing. Except the guy from her dreams, that is, but he didn't count.

Her relationship with Gregg had left her wary of starting a new one. For some reason, being with him had dimmed her spirit, and two years later it hadn't bounced back yet.

Most of the time he probably hadn't been aware of acting like a jerk, never actually saying or doing anything that could have been perceived as outright offensive or belittling.

Instead, he'd just always managed to twist things around and blame her for everything that hadn't been working to his satisfaction. His grades falling short of spectacular had been her fault because she had taken too much of his time. They hadn't gone out enough because she hadn't scheduled and planned it. They hadn't had enough friends because she hadn't been outgoing enough... and so it went.

But the worst part had been the sex. There had been no intensity to it, no excitement, it'd felt like a chore. Was it a wonder then, that she hadn't been looking forward to it? And of course, it had been all her fault. She hadn't initiated enough, she hadn't excited him enough. She hadn't been hot enough.

Blah, blah, blah...

Logically, she knew he had been full of shit. Where had been his contribution? Had he been just a bystander in their life together, waiting for her to do everything? But on the inside, in that irrational place where her fears and insecurities hid, she sometimes thought that maybe he had been right. Maybe she really wasn't assertive enough, outgoing enough, sexy enough...

Lacking... She felt lacking.

Syssi shook herself. *That's definitely enough self-pity for one day.*

And besides, not all of it had been bad. Gregg had stood by her side in her time of need. He had been loyal, and apart from the never-ending complaining, a pleasure to talk to.

But when the relationship had ended, she'd focused on the negatives; the bad parts had been vividly remembered and endlessly reexamined, while the good parts had been marginalized, forgotten.

It was time to move on, though. Maybe she should try some of the blind dates her friends were trying to set her up on. Or even look into those dating sites Hannah had suggested. But although Syssi had promised herself she would do it, she still hadn't taken a single step in this direction. Tomorrow, next week…

"Yo! Syssi! Your cell phone is ringing!" Hannah called from the other room.

"Coming!" Syssi hurried to retrieve her phone from her purse. But by the time she fished it out, her brother's call had already gone to voice mail. And if that wasn't frustrating enough, David's salami breath assaulted her as he bent over her shoulder to look at her screen, invading her personal space.

"Amanda said you needed my help," he breathed into her ear. "For a kiss, I'm willing to do you a favor," he added with a smirk, amused by his own wit.

"Cut it out, David, and please move your salami breath away from me. You know I can't stand the smell of meat," Syssi snapped. Pushing to her feet, she almost toppled her chair backward, forcing David to back up.

His eyes widened. "That was such a bitchy retort, so unlike our polite, proper Syssi. It was hot!" He leered before taking the seat she'd vacated.

"You want me. I know you do. That's why you're so flustered." He winked and started scrolling through the program. "Don't worry, sweetheart. I'll take good care of you." His hands flew over her keyboard, his concentration not at all affected by his sorry attempts at flirting.

She had to hand it to him. David had a way with computers that he definitely lacked with women.

With his face almost touching the screen, he kept going, "Nothing turns me on like a strong, assertive woman. I'll scrub my mouth with thorny roses for a kiss from you." Riding on a wave of his fetid breath, David's whispered poetic attempt did nothing but trigger Syssi's gag reflex.

She couldn't believe it. Instead of discouraged, he seemed even more determined.

"Look, David, I'm going to return this call, and you are going to find out what's wrong with my program. Not as a favor, but because it's your job. Amanda hired you for your programming skills. It sure as hell wasn't for your charming personality!"

"Oh, baby, you have no idea how hot you look when you're angry."

"Ugh! I'm going to strangle him!" Syssi kicked the leg of the chair he was sitting in.

Snorting, Hannah shook her head.

"It's not funny!" Syssi barked and walked out the door.

She hated confrontations. Especially futile ones like this. But at least David was going to fix her programming. Except, what would it take to fix him? For some reason, a vet with a scalpel came to mind.

Leaning against the wall, she banged her head. Today was such a shitty day, with her shortcomings and insecurities popping up like teenage zits. Just when she thought she was rid of them for good, they returned sprouting white heads. More than the confrontations themselves, she hated how ill-equipped she was to deal with them. Why the hell was it so hard for her to assert herself or show her temper?

Even now, her hands were still shaking, and she had to take a long calming breath before returning her brother's call. If Andrew detected her agitation, he would start a full-blown interrogation. And she was so not in the mood for that.

He answered on the first ring. "Hi, Syssi, how's the new job?"

"It's okay. Though I really suck at programming. Other than that, Amanda is a great boss and the work is interesting." Syssi paused before plunging. "You really should come visit. The woman is a stunner, and I would pay good money to see your jaw drop when you see her. The great Andrew Spivak will be speechless!"

Syssi was joking. Nothing ever fazed Andrew. But he was single and so was Amanda. Who knew what might happen if the two got together...

"You have piqued my curiosity. Though I doubt she's all that. Anyway, I spoke with Dad today."

"Yeah? How are they? What are they up to?"

Their parents were volunteering in Africa. Her mother, Dr. Anita Spivak, a retired sixty-six-year-old pediatrician, was working twelve-hour shifts in the harsh conditions of the ravaged region, providing much needed medical care to its children. Syssi's father, who had spent his professional career as a pharmaceutical sales rep and later as an executive, was enjoying his retirement; photographing nature and wildlife while helping his wife.

They rarely called.

Syssi wished she could blame Africa for that, but it was nothing new. Her parents had always been too busy with their careers, their social life... each other.

Andrew had been the responsible adult in their household, practically raising Syssi and their younger brother, Jacob.

Their mother had had Andrew at twenty-eight, and had given up on conceiving again when long years had gone by and nothing had happened. It hadn't been a big heartbreak. With her workload, raising even one child had been difficult. Lucky for Andrew, their grandparents had stepped in, providing the care he had needed. Syssi's arrival had been a miracle, the pregnancy taking Anita by surprise at the age of forty-two. A year later, she had been blessed again with another miracle. Jacob.

The two babies had been welcomed and loved but left mostly to the care of nannies. By the time they had arrived, their parents had been too established in their routines to make any changes for their sake.

"Dad sends their love. He says he has enough material to publish his first book, and he promises to send us the files to look through and choose the pictures we like most."

"I wonder when that will happen. You know him; lots of promises and little delivery." Syssi could not help sounding bitter. Their dad had been promising to drag their mother away from her work for a few days back home. Syssi was still waiting... two years later. She had hoped they would at least show up for her graduation, wishing they'd surprise her at the last minute. How naive of her. They never had.

"How are you doing, Andrew? Still bored at your desk job?"

It had been a while since he'd been sent away on one of his assignments abroad, and being stuck in the office usually made him restless.

Syssi had often wondered about Andrew's frequent trips. After retiring from a hush-hush Special Ops unit, he had joined the Internal Antiterrorism Department—supposedly as an analyst. Why then, had he been spending months at a time abroad? Doing what? Research?

"Actually, I'm swamped with work here, and truth be told, I'm tired of living out of a suitcase. I think you'll have to tolerate my annoying presence in your life for a little longer this time."

Andrew sounded happy to stay home... Intriguing... Was it possible he'd finally met someone?

"There must be a woman involved. I can think of no other reason for you to sound so cheerful about staying put. So tell me, who is she? Did you find someone special?" Syssi asked hopefully.

Andrew chuckled. "No, there is no one special. Who's crazy enough to stick around me?"

"You're a great guy, Andrew. Someday, you'll make some lucky girl very happy."

"I doubt it."

"You'll see. I have a feeling... Soon."

When Syssi had a feeling, those who knew her listened. Her premonitions had a freakish tendency to come to pass.

"I hope you're kidding because if you're not, you are scaring the shit out of me. You know I'm not built for anything serious!"

It was funny how scared he sounded. The brave warrior afraid of being snared by some mystery woman. "Nah, just messing with you," she lied.

"Wow! You had me there for a moment." Andrew took a deep breath and exhaled it forcefully, exaggerating his relief... Or maybe not.

"I have to let you go. I have to get back to work and deal with a pesky problem." Syssi sighed.

"Need me to come beat that problem up? I will, you know..."

"I just might take you up on that offer," Syssi answered, not sure she meant it as a joke. "Bye, Andrew."

* * *

Andrew leaned back in the swivel chair and laced his fingers behind his head. He wondered what Syssi wasn't telling him. The pesky problem was probably a guy, he smiled knowingly.

Nothing new there.

Syssi was so lovely, there would always be some poor schmuck making a pest of himself over her.

Maybe he should visit that lab after all, and not just to admire the infamous Dr. Amanda Dokani.

CHAPTER 7: AMANDA

"Promise me that you are not going to drive like a lunatic." Syssi put her hands on her hips and glared at Amanda.

Folding her tall frame into the driver seat of her Porsche, Amanda buckled up and lowered the passenger side window. "Would you get in already? You're jumpy because of the nightmares, not my driving."

With a frown, Syssi opened the door and leaned against the frame. "If you don't promise, I'm not getting in. I'd rather walk."

"I'll be good. But only until I drop you off. After that I'm going to drive this baby like it should be driven."

Syssi got in and turned to look at her, worry lines furrowing her forehead. "You should be careful. Remember my premonition?"

Amanda shrugged. "You don't know what or when or how. I'd rather live dangerously than not at all."

With a wince, Syssi looked away.

Oh, shit, she shouldn't have said it. Hurting the girl's feelings hadn't been her intention. "I'm sorry. I didn't mean it like that. Please don't take it personally."

"No, you're right. I'm too cautious. I don't go on dates because I'm afraid the guys will end up being jerks, or boring. Worse, I'm anxious about having to tell a guy that I don't want another date even before I went on the first one. Pathetic. My money is in a savings account, earning zero interest, because I don't want to chance losing any of it in the stock market. I could've doubled what I have if I trusted my gut and bought Apple stock even though it was already high." She let out a sigh and slumped in her seat.

"What you need is a pattern interrupt. Something to zap you out of your comfort zone and force you into action." Amanda knew exactly what that something was, or rather who, but he'd refused to cooperate.

She needed to come up with a plan of how to get these two together in the same room. Kian was basically in the same situation as Syssi.

His days consisted of work and his nights of meaningless hookups. Day in and day out. He'd never taken a vacation, had never gone to see a concert or a play, and he'd been to the movie theaters exactly once. Kian wasn't living, he was functioning. He just wasn't aware of it.

Amanda was betting that once Kian and Syssi laid eyes on each other, the encounter would shock both of them out of their stagnation. It was only a gut feeling, but it was a strong one. She just knew that they would make each other happy.

But she was getting ahead of herself. One thing at a time.

First she needed to get them together, then let nature take its course on the express lane to the nearest bedroom. After that was accomplished it was a matter of waiting to see if Syssi transitioned.

Amanda believed she would.

Leaving the university grounds, she accelerated, and the Porsche glided along at what she considered an excruciatingly slow pace. It was late, and most of the rush-hour traffic was over. There was no reason to go so slow. With a quick glance at Syssi, Amanda let her foot press down on the gas pedal a little. The girl didn't notice a thing. She was busy looking out the window and moping.

Amanda kept accelerating until she was cruising at a more reasonable speed.

Turning her head toward her forlorn passenger, she was about to tease Syssi about her bad mood, when suddenly a stupid suicidal squirrel decided that it was a good day to die.

The furry thing jumped from a low hanging tree branch, right in front of her car. Amanda slammed on the brakes and the car swerved, skidding out of control. She managed to right the Porsche a split second too late, hitting a water hydrant head on.

Metal groaned, Syssi cried out, and Amanda held her breath, waiting for the airbags to deploy and the hydrant to erupt in a geyser. But the impact hadn't been powerful enough to cause either. Evidently, she'd managed to slow down sufficiently to avoid more serious damage.

Throwing the door open, Amanda unbuckled and got out, rushing around to open Syssi's door. "Are you hurt?" The impact had been mild, but humans were so damn fragile.

Syssi tried to shake her head, then winced, rubbing the spot where the seatbelt had cut into the skin of her neck.

"Hold on, darling. I got you." Amanda leaned inside and unbuckled her.

"What happened?" Syssi asked.

"A good for nothing stupid squirrel. I should've just ran him over."

"Don't say that!"

"Just kidding. But I'm mad as hell. I have plans for tonight." Amanda went over to the front and examined the damage. "Not as bad as I thought. It's just cosmetic." She got inside and turned on the ignition. "It's good that the Porsche's engine is in the back. Get inside, Syssi."

"What about the hydrant?"

"It's fine. Let's go."

Amanda waited for Syssi to buckle up before backing away from the hydrant and easing into traffic.

She'd better call Onidu and tell him to get her a loaner. Pressing a button on the steering wheel, she called home.

"Onidu, darling. I had an unfortunate fender bender with a hydrant. I need you to get me a rental."

"Of course, Mistress. Are you well? Do you require medical attention?"

"I'm perfectly fine. But my beautiful car isn't. Would you take care of it for me?"

"Naturally, Mistress."

"Thank you." Amanda ended the call.

"Who was it?" Syssi asked.

"Onidu? He is my butler."

"Figures," Syssi murmured under her breath, thinking Amanda couldn't hear her.

When they reached Syssi's place, Amanda parked next to the curb and turned to her personal seer. "So that was it, I guess," she said.

"That was what?"

"The bad thing you were predicting was going to happen. I was in danger and it wasn't life-threatening. To either of us." She winked. "Case closed."

Syssi shook her head and winced, rubbing her neck again. "I don't think so. Not unless parting with your Porsche for a couple of days is a monumental, life-changing event for you."

"So what is your advice, my sage oracle?" Amanda asked as Syssi stepped out onto the sidewalk.

"Just be careful and watchful. There isn't much else you can do."

CHAPTER 8: MARK

"To us!" Mark saluted.

Mark's team from SDPD was celebrating their latest breakthrough at Rouges.

The local bar catered to a mixed crowd: students from nearby Stanford, young professionals from Palo Alto, and the occasional riffraff. Most days of the week a live band provided entertainment. Except tonight.

Tuesdays, the band was off, so the place was not as packed and not as loud. Which was why they had chosen tonight for their celebration.

"Peace, love, and rock 'n' roll!" Logan downed a shot.

To outsiders, SDPD stood for Software Development Programming Department. Only those on the inside were privy to the special programming that the firm masquerading as a gaming developer was really working on.

In fact, the Strategic Defense Programming Division was a civilian outlet serving the federal government, its substantial pool of genius tasked with the development of viruses that could disable enemy weapon systems—specifically, WMDs—weapons of mass destruction.

Top programmers, gifted hackers, and brilliant mathematicians were secretively lured into its fold. Some were seduced by promises of big money, others by a chance of changing the world, and a few were simply blackmailed.

Once in, they were never let out.

Not that anyone really wanted out.

Realizing the significance of what they were working on, they knew there couldn't be a higher calling or a greater purpose for their skills.

They were literally saving the world. Regrettably, as anonymous heroes.

"To Mark!" Armando raised his sixth shot of tequila. "Our boy genius. The one and only. The king of hacking. May he keep producing more fine lines of code!" He downed the shot, his cheering friends banging the table as they tossed back their drinks.

Mark felt a ripple of apprehension course through him. The salute was generic enough not to divulge anything specific and yet, potentially, it could have clued someone in.

SDPD, and Mark in particular, had provided the basis for the most famous computer virus in history. The virus that had infiltrated and damaged a dangerous rogue regime's nuclear facilities.

It was just the beginning.

They were well on their way to developing something even better. Soon, there would be no advanced weaponry that they couldn't disable, providing a safety net for the US and its trusted allies.

Naturally, some governments and terrorist organizations didn't appreciate their work, therefore Mark's life and that of his coworkers depended on their anonymity.

They were supposed to be invisible.

Heck, they were not supposed to even exist.

They were all drunk.

Well, everyone except for Svetlana, who was a bottomless pit. The tiny Russian mathematician had an off-the-charts IQ and a not-so-secret crush on Mark.

Holding her shot glass, she stood up to her full height of five feet nothing and saluted; "To Mark!" Then downing the straight shot of Absolut vodka she favored, proceeded to drop herself onto his lap, wiggling her tiny butt to get more comfortable or perhaps stir something up.

Mark tensed. Wrapping his arm around her waist to steady her, he held her in place, preventing her from burrowing further.

The girl took it as a sign of encouragement. Turning to face him, she planted a wet kiss on his lips.

The guys went wild, whooping and whistling. "Svetlana! Svetlana! Svetlana!" They cheered her on.

Getting bold, she straddled him, took his cheeks in both hands, and licked his bottom lip with her small pink tongue, urging him to let her in.

Gently, not wishing to offend her, he pushed her away and rearranged her position so she remained seated only on one of his thighs. Holding on to her waist, he reached for his drink and saluted. "To the team!"

"To the team!" the guys shouted.

Dejected, Svetlana pushed up from his thigh, and the sad look she pinned on him made him wince.

It was a shame that she chose him as her object of desire. Any of the other guys would've loved for her to get frisky with them. Svetlana was a pretty little thing, with skin so white it seemed translucent, huge, pale blue eyes, and long, wavy, white-blond hair. She was just a kid, really, barely over the minimum drinking age.

Mark liked the girl, just not in the way she liked him.

Winking at her, he playfully smacked her butt. As he had intended, Svetlana perceived the gesture as him flirting back. Smiling, the hurt look gone from her big blue eyes, she turned and went back to her seat.

Mark exhaled quietly. Being gay wasn't a big deal to anyone anymore, but he was a product of a different era and preferred to keep it private.

No one needed to know.

He didn't flirt with other gays or go to gay bars. Instead, he'd found a lucrative escort service that provided partners to affluent men like himself. As these establishments went, it was discreet, costly, and offered a good selection of prime healthy studs.

For Mark, it was the perfect solution. He made shitloads of money he didn't need; his shares in the family business were more than enough to keep him in style. So why not spend it on his insatiable appetite? Safely and prudently.

He even had a tryst scheduled for later tonight and needed to leave soon to get ready.

Mark was excited.

Jason's web profile had been promising. The guy was young, handsome, and a student at Stanford, which promised he wouldn't be a complete dolt. Mark had no patience with stupidity. To him, it was as big of a turn-off as an offensive body odor or a potbelly.

At nine o'clock, Mark excused himself claiming a headache. He left after a round of cheerful, drunk hugs from his friends and a lingering one from Svetlana.

As he waited outside the club for the cab that would take him home, he sought to sober up in the night's cool air. Except, his buzz was more about the thrill of anticipation than any lingering intoxication.

He got home with twenty minutes to spare—just enough time to grab a quick shower, decide on a flattering pair of slacks and a button-down shirt, and set his living room to the right atmosphere. His guest being a paid escort, the effort wasn't necessary. Nevertheless, as this was the extent of his love life, Mark was determined to get the most out of it.

Thinking about the wicked seduction he had planned for tonight, Mark paced around his living room impatiently.

At the sound of a knock, he took a deep breath, and with a last quick glance at the mirror by the front door, hurried to open it for his guest.

The young man standing on his front porch looked nothing like the guy in the picture on the escort service's website.

Mark's neck tingled. Something was wrong.

"You're not Jason," he said, debating if he should slam the door in the guy's face.

"Sorry, Jason could not make it tonight. I'm Gideon, his replacement." The man forced a fake smile that did not reach his eyes.

Something was definitely off.

The guy was handsome enough; tall, with broad shoulders and muscular arms, but he wasn't gay. Mark had centuries of experience and an innate sense about these things. He could sniff out a gay man from a mile away.

Gideon, if this was his real name, definitely wasn't one.

There was something oddly familiar about the guy's aggressive vibe, though, and Mark's sensation of dread grew worse. A moment later, an adrenaline surge tightened his gut as he finally recognized it for what it was. His body's natural alarm system had been triggered by the presence of another immortal male.

Except, this one wasn't a member of his clan. And as the only other immortals Mark knew of were his clan's mortal enemies—the Doomers—this man meant him harm.

Terrified, he tried to slam the door closed, but the guy blocked it with his shoulder and with a brutal punch to the face sent Mark staggering backward. Following with his own body weight, the assassin brought Mark down.

When they hit the floor, Mark struggled to get free. But he was no match for the strength and skill of his assailant. In mere seconds, he found himself pinned face down to the floor with the immortal's fangs sinking deep into his neck.

All struggle ceased the moment the assassin's venom hit his system—the euphoria blooming in his mind and the languid feeling spreading through his body effectively paralyzing him.

He felt the venom being pumped into his bloodstream, pulsing in sync with his heartbeat. Although still aware enough to understand that he was about to die, in his drugged state he couldn't bring himself to care.

Eventually, the assassin withdrew his fangs and licked the puncture wounds closed. Mark knew that his near-immortal body would heal the bruising in a matter of minutes, and shortly thereafter, the venom paralyzing him would stop his heart, then disintegrate.

There would be no trace left of any wrongdoing, and heart failure would be determined as the most probable cause of death.

The family would obviously know. Besides blowing it to pieces, the only way to stop a near-immortal's heart was to inject the body with loads of venom.

His Advanced Decision Card listed Arwel's phone number as his next of kin.

The paramedics would call him.

Arwel would know what happened.

"This is for giving your corrupt western pets your stolen technology, you queer scum! This is for the computer virus!" the murderer hurled, then spat at Mark's face. "You brought the war to your own doorstep. Fighting by proxy is over!" he hissed through clenched teeth.

Mark was only dimly aware of what the Doomer was saying, hearing the words but not truly comprehending them. Through the drugged haze of his mind, he heard two more sets of footsteps entering his home. Conversing in short, clipped sentences, the men were speaking in some foreign language he didn't recognize.

It didn't matter. Nothing mattered anymore.

As he drifted away, he wondered if there was anything beyond this reality. Would his soul go on to some kind of heaven? Was there anything besides dark oblivion waiting for him?

If there were, he wished other souls would be there, so he wouldn't be alone. The thought of spending an eternity of incorporeal existence aware, and yet with no one to communicate with and nothing to do, terrified him more than fading into nothingness.

CHAPTER 9: KIAN

Kian woke up with a start, his sweat-saturated hair sticking to the back of his neck and his heart still pounding from the nightmare. Filled with an intense sense of dread, all he could remember was the endless running and getting lost in a maze of strange staircases that had led nowhere, and being turned around in corridors that had twisted on themselves in impossible ways.

What had he been running from? Who had been chasing him? Why had they been chasing him?

It was just a dream. Kian tried to shake off the uneasy feeling. Nothing more than his mind rearranging bits and pieces of thoughts and memories to create an action horror flick with him in the starring role.

Yeah, that's all it was.

Unlike his mother and sisters, he didn't place much stock in dreams or premonitions. Ordinary, everyday reality was strange enough without throwing that into the mix.

Kian flung off the damp duvet, pushed off the tangled sheets and dropped his feet to the floor. Sitting on the bed with his elbows on his thighs, he let his head drop as he waited for his heartbeat to slow down.

After a moment, the smell of freshly brewed coffee wafting from the kitchen was just the incentive he needed to shrug it off and jump into the shower. At first, he'd planned to be quick about it, but with the hot water jets pounding his skin from all six showerheads, it just felt so good that he allowed himself to linger.

It was absurd that a man surrounded by so much luxury got so little use out of it. There was always too much to do and not enough time to do it. He was rushing everything; his showers, his meals, his interactions with others. And yet, there were always some tasks left undone and issues unattended to.

Most of the time Kian didn't mind the intense pace and the heavy mantle of responsibility. It kept him far too busy to dwell on the fact that he was lonely, although rarely alone. Or that his very long and productive life felt futile, despite all of his accomplishments.

Just once in a while he would have liked to slow down. Savor life. Smell the coffee.

Coffee, he could really use some right now, followed by Okidu's decadent waffles, topped with fresh fruit and smothered in coconut whipped cream. It wasn't the healthiest of breakfasts, but what the heck. It was good!

He was fortunate to have Okidu as his cook, his butler, his cleaner, his chauffeur, and his companion. Lots of hats for one person to wear, but then again, Okidu wasn't really a person. Quite often, Kian had trouble remembering that his butler wasn't a living breathing man.

Okidu was a marvel of ingenuity; a biomechanical masterpiece posing as a person. He didn't require sleep, didn't require maintenance, was self-repairing, and could survive on garbage. He could even morph his form from male to female and vice versa by adjusting his facial features and body shape; sometimes alternating between the two just for the sake of entertainment, and sometimes because circumstances favored a particular gender. Inherently, Okidu had none. No reproductive system or sex organs to define him one way or the other.

No one knew who'd created Okidu, or how, or when. There were only seven of his kind known to exist. A priceless masterpiece that could not be replicated or replaced. Over five thousand years ago, the seven had been a wedding gift to Kian's mother, a token of love from her groom. They had been believed to be an ancient relic even then.

Kian couldn't remember a time without Okidu being around. Since he was a little boy, Okidu had been there to ensure his safety, to feed him, to dress him, and to keep him company.

Though uncomfortable thinking of Okidu as a possession, as such, he was Kian's most valued one. Regrettably, Okidu couldn't be a friend or a confidant, he just didn't function that way. With his decision-making ability limited to a preprogrammed set of instructions within which he could learn and adapt, he was incapable of feeling true emotions. Nevertheless, he easily fooled the casual observer by approximating the appropriate tone and facial expressions.

"Good morning, Master!" Okidu exclaimed with a happy face and a perfect British accent as Kian entered the kitchen. Lately, he had taken to acting out his favorite mini-series on BBC, featuring an aristocratic British family and their household staff. Okidu had been alternating between mimicking the snobby butler, the hurried maid, and the cockney driver. Lacking a personality of his own, he must've calculated that mimicking cliché characters would make his passing for a human likelier.

It had been amusing at first. The exaggerated gestures, the different costumes, the accents. It was like having a private comedy show—every day, all day long, for weeks on end. It became annoying, and this morning it really grated on Kian's nerves.

Furthermore, there were only two waffles left, with Anandur and

Brundar ogling them like a couple of hungry wolves.

"I saved the last two for you, Master!" Okidu chimed.

Kian felt like punching something, or someone, or rather two someones. Pinning the two with a hard stare, he barked, "Do I have to see your sorry faces every morning before I've even had my coffee? And then you wolf down my waffles? Don't you have food in your place?"

The brothers had an apartment two stories down from Kian's penthouse, and though every Guardian had one in the family's secure high rise, they preferred to stay together and share one.

Smack in the middle of downtown Los Angeles, the building he had built for the clan's American arm was a luxurious dig. To preserve appearances, some of the lower floor apartments were time-shared by international corporations in need of lodging for their visiting executives. The upper floors and an extensive underground facility served the clan. A private parking level, with elevators that required a thumbprint to open their doors, ensured his family could come and go safely and discreetly.

It took hiding in plain sight to a whole new level.

"Sorry, boss, but our kitchen doesn't come equipped with Okidu. And to be honest, between Brundar and me, we can't even fry an egg." Anandur was still eyeing the surviving waffles.

Kian sighed. "Resistance is futile," he murmured and poured himself a cup of coffee. Leaning his butt against the counter, he took a satisfying first sip of the hot brew.

"Please make some more waffles for the kids, Okidu. You have underestimated their appetite."

"Coming right up, sire!"

"It smells heavenly in here." Kri, their only female Guardian, poked her head into the kitchen.

Tall and athletic, his young niece was a kick-ass kind of girl, which got her the approval of the male Guardians. And although muscular and wide shouldered, she still managed to look feminine.

As always, her long tawny hair was pulled away from her pretty face and woven into a tight braid. Today, the heavy rope was draped over the front of a red workout shirt.

"Okidu made waffles, and no one called me? I'm deeply wounded." She walked in and planted her rear on a stool.

"Come in. Why the hell not? It's a goddamn party!" Kian dropped a plate in front of Kri and poured her a cup of coffee.

He couldn't tell her to go away now, could he? She had as much right, or lack thereof, to invade his kitchen as the other two.

"Thank you, Kian. As always, you're so kind." Kri accepted the mug. Holding it in both hands, she took a sip. "Ugh, bitter, I need sugar." As his stern look made it perfectly clear that he was done serving her, Kri got up to get it herself. "I know. I've already used up my quota of hospitality."

"What are you doing here, Kri?"

"I thought I'd stop by on my way to the gym and see if you wanted to join me for a workout." Avoiding his eyes, Kri looked down at her cup.

The girl had a silly crush on him and was using every excuse as an opportunity to spend more time with him.

Kian ignored it.

Descending from the same matrilineal line, they were considered closely related despite the many generations separating them.

A serious taboo.

Not that he would have ever considered anything even if that wasn't the case. In his mind, Kri would always be his little niece.

He figured she'd get over it.

Being only forty-one years old, Kri was barely a teenager in near-immortal terms, and like a mortal teenager, he assumed she suffered from a case of transitory, immature infatuation.

One she would laugh off later in life.

Kian glared at her, then turned to glare at the guys. "From now on, no one comes up here before nine in the morning, *capisce*?" He regarded their despondent faces. "And I want you to knock and wait to be allowed in. No more waltzing in whenever you feel like it. This is not the ▓▓damn subway station!"

They had the same exchange every couple of weeks. Like spoiled kids, they'd behave for a while, then go back to pissing him off.

That was the trouble with employing family. What could he do? Couldn't fire them, couldn't smother them either. It would upset their mothers.

Kian sighed.

"But the waffles, Kian! The waffles!" Kri lamented in mock despair.

"Get the ▓▓▓▓▓ recipe!"

A loud knock announced another member of the team. Okidu rushed over to open it for Onegus, the head of the Guardians.

Taking one sniff of the tantalizing aroma, Onegus smiled his Hollywood smile, and, what a surprise, immediately beelined for the kitchen.

At least the SOB was actually supposed to show up for his morning meeting with Kian.

"Oh no you don't! Everybody out! Let's move the party to the other room!" Kian passed through the butler's pantry into the dining room, which was never used for its primary function. Kian ate at the kitchen counter and never had the kind of guests he wanted to invite to a sit-down dinner.

He liked to work from home, though, so when needed, he used the room for informal meetings. Not that this was a meeting.

More like a home invasion...

His home office was his quiet place to work, and he didn't want the gang invading it and messing with his neatly arranged stuff.

On some level, the fact that the whole force could fit easily inside his dining room was depressing. The number of Guardians had shrunk in recent years, and with only seven of them remaining, their duties were limited to providing security detail, mainly to him as Regent, and internal policing—enforcing the clan's laws.

Back in the old country, when the force had still been the size of a small battalion, Kian had led it into more battles than he cared to remember. In the days of hand to hand combat, when the Guardians had been tasked with protecting and guarding the clan's turf, the force had numbered between sixty and eighty warriors. But as times had changed—the USA becoming a relatively safe place for them to live and hide in—it had dwindled down, its defense services no longer needed.

Kian, as the clan's American Regent, was in charge of the Guardians as well as heading the local clan-council. And that was in addition to managing the clan's huge business empire.

He snorted as he remembered thinking that acting as Regent, over what were now two hundred eighty-three people, would be an easy job. It wasn't.

With their business empire growing and branching into various industries, Kian was working harder and longer than ever. There simply weren't enough damned hours in the day. Was it a wonder then that he was short-tempered and irritable?

He couldn't remember the last time he had some time off.

Just as his uninvited guests, and Onegus, were preparing to plant their butts on the chairs surrounding his long dining table, Kian's cell phone vibrated.

He pulled it out and glanced at the caller's name before answering. "Arwel. What's up in the Bay Area?"

There was a moment of silence, then a sigh.

Kian felt a ripple of anxiety rush down his spine. "Talk to me!"

"Mark was found dead in his home this morning." Arwel paused.

Kian remained silent, stunned by the impossible news.

"His cleaning lady found him on the floor of his living room and called 911. He had my number on his Advanced Decision Card, listing me as next of kin."

Arwel's speech faltered. It had been a while since a member of their family had been killed. The security and anonymity the clan enjoyed in their adopted home made them complacent. The pain of loss had faded into distant memory. Facing it once again was hard, more so for Arwel.

The poor guy had enough trouble coping with life as it was, with his over-receptive mind bombarded relentlessly by the emotions of others. To protect himself, he often drank excessively. Though he sounded sober now.

"His body was intact. The paramedics declared heart failure as the probable cause of death. Obviously, we know what that means—fangs and venom. We checked his house for clues." There was another pause. "Doomers got him, Kian. They are here and have somehow found Mark."

As Kian's mind processed the implications, the chill that had started in his heart upon first hearing the disturbing news spread out to encompass his entire body.

DOOM—the Devout Order Of Mortdh Brotherhood—was his clan's ancient enemy. Sworn to annihilate every last member of his family and destroy any and all progress Annani was helping humanity achieve, they sought to plunge the world back into ignorance and darkness.

Theirs wasn't an idle threat.

Time and again, the order had manipulated mortal affairs by planting seeds of hatred, triggering wars, and dragging humanity down—successfully halting and reversing social and scientific advancement all too often.

The DOOM Brotherhood was a relentless scourge.

It was Kian's worst nightmare made manifest. He had believed that hiding in plain sight among the multitudes of mortals would keep his family safe from this powerful enemy. And yet, the Doomers had somehow gotten to Mark.

"Are you sure he was murdered by Doomers?"

"They left a message taped to his computer screen."

"What did it say?"

"Nothing and everything. It's a drawing. Two sickle swords crossed at the handle, flanking a disk. Their ▓▓▓▓ emblem. I took a photo of it."

"Send me the picture."

"Hold on."

Kian switched screens. The image of the crude drawing was blurry, but there was no mistaking the DOOM's emblem.

As grief and impotent rage warred for dominance over his emotions, he pushed up from his chair and began pacing.

As a man of solution-driven action, Kian felt an irrational, overbearing need to do something, anything, that would make this all go away. Except, there was no action that would bring Mark back. No going back in time and changing the decisions that had led to this.

The only thing left for him to do was to mourn the dead and safeguard the living.

"Bring our boy home... Take the jet and bring him here," he told Arwel, then paused to realign his mental gears and get them in motion.

"Check his body and make sure they didn't plant any tracking devices on him. The bastards know we'd bring Mark home for a proper service. Can't risk them following you here. Go through his place again, see if anything is missing. Check for any clues that can point to us; letters, photos, personal mementos, and the sort. If you find anything like that, bring it here. I'm sure his mother will want to have it. Pay attention to details. I need to know if they found anything."

"I'm on it!" Arwel was about to hang up.

"Arwel! I'm not done. I want all clan members from your area evacuated. Have Bhathian contact them and explain the gravity of the situation. Provide each one with a different route and mode of transportation. I don't want a mad rush to the airport. They are to take nothing and tell no one. Just get up and go. We'll take care of the details once everyone is safe."

"They are not gonna like it, boss."

"I know, but until we figure out what went down, they'll be chilling their butts over here. I'd rather have them pissed than dead."

Kian ended the call and turned to the Guardians. By the look of their somber faces, they were ready to hear the bad news, waiting for the boulder to start rolling and come crashing down on them.

It was one of those moments everyone dreads; the unexpected disaster striking out of nowhere, destroying the illusion that you're in control, and shoving the cruel reality in your face.

Shit happens! Deal with it!

Squaring his shoulders, Kian delivered the grim update. "As you've probably figured out, we have a situation. Mark, son of Micah, was murdered in his home last night." Kian lifted his phone to show them the DOOM emblem. "This was left behind, taped to his computer screen."

Damn

"~~Fuck~~!" was the only response from Anandur. Brundar and Onegus looked ready to kill, and Kri sniffled, trying to hold back her tears.

None of them knew Mark very well, but they knew of him; the clan's genius programmer. His loss was devastating not only on a personal level but also as an asset that would be difficult to replace.

Kian sat down and dropped his elbows on the table, then hung his head on his fisted hands. "It's all my fault. I take full responsibility," he admitted, the guilt eating at his gut.

With a curse, Onegus brought his fist down on the table. "How could it be your fault, Kian? Beyond your usual spiel of being Regent and responsible for everyone and everything. Yadda, yadda, yadda."

"It is my fault. I might as well have placed a neon sign, pointing to his head and blinking: Here I am. Come get me! Anyone with half a brain could've figured out that a code this sophisticated couldn't have been developed with current knowhow."

Kian had known he was taking a big risk by allowing Mark to leak too much info too soon. But he had felt he had no choice. The risk of WMDs in the hands of power-hungry despots outweighed the risk of exposure. And besides, he had never imagined that the Doomers would come after Mark. He'd assumed that if they'd retaliate, they'd do it the same way they had always done, using the mortals under their influence against those the clan was helping.

Kian continued, "After so many years with no casualties, we've become complacent. And even before, the few of us the Doomers managed to snare were random cases of a male being in the wrong place at the wrong time. They've never been able to hunt us down successfully; there are just too few of us, and we hide too well. Except now, I feel like I've drawn the ~~Doomers~~ a ~~goddamned~~ damned yellow brick road!"

"Maybe they just got lucky with Mark?" Kri suggested. Which earned her the condescending you-don't-know-what-you're-talking-about look from the others.

"No, guys, just hear me out. Think of how the Doomers always retaliated before. They went after our humans or helped theirs against ours. Suppose the Doomers were seeking revenge on the team that worked on that code. They somehow find them, identify Mark as the top programmer, and decide to take him out; send us a message. I bet they didn't even know he was one of us."

Kri got more animated. "We never used to work so close with mortals. We'd supply a bit of information and back off, let them work on it, figure it on their own. Then we'd supply some more, so it would look legit—home grown. No way the Doomers were expecting to find an immortal working on the same team with mortals. No freaking way!" Kri stared them down, daring them to try and refute her logic.

"She might have a point," Onegus admitted.

"Even if Kri is right, that doesn't change the outcome. Doomers still found and murdered Mark. And now that they have a clue as to what to look for and where, they might find more of us." Kian pushed to his feet and walked over to Kri. "Good thinking, though. You're a smart girl." He squeezed her shoulder.

At any other time, under different circumstances, Kri would've been ecstatic to receive this kind of praise from Kian. Now, she just nodded and reached for his hand on her shoulder, squeezing it back.

"Sire, the waffles are ready!" Okidu chose that moment to bring in a loaded platter. He placed it carefully on the sideboard, then scurried away, expecting a stampede. But the food was ignored.

"Thank you, Okidu," Kian dismissed him. "Actually, I need you to do one more thing. Make sure we have four clean, vacant apartments ready, and if you could, please air Amanda's penthouse. We are about to have overnight guests."

"Certainly, sire!" Okidu bowed.

"Thank you." Kian nodded to Okidu and faced the Guardians.

"Onegus, I want you to call an emergency council meeting for nine in the evening today. Don't tell them what it's about. I don't want anyone calling Micah to offer condolences before I see her. No one should get news like that over the phone. We'll meet in the big council room. Instruct everyone to wear their ceremonial robes. I'm going to demand sequestering for all council members, which they will surely bitch and moan about. But we don't have enough manpower to provide security detail for each of them separately. I need them here, protected. Hopefully, the formalities will impress upon them how serious I am about this. That will be all."

Kian's eyes followed his people as they pushed away from the table and silently trudged toward the living room. Onegus pulled open the front door, and with a slight nod, left followed by the somber brothers. Kri remained behind, looking lost.

Walking up to her, Kian took her in his arms and let her burrow her nose into his neck, hugging her for a long moment. Being so young, she had never faced the loss of a friend, and unlike the men's emotions which had been deadened by centuries of countless battles, hers were still raw with pain and grief. When she sighed and let go of him, he looked into her eyes, making sure she was okay.

But there was a reason he'd taken Kri on as a guardian. Squaring her shoulders, she pushed her chin up, and the determination he saw in her eyes proved to him that she really was the hard-ass he'd hired.

"Go, I need time to plan." He dismissed her with a pat to her back.

Alone, Kian allowed himself to drift on the waves of guilt and dread for a few moments, letting his mind go in different directions, envisioning every foreseeable danger and coming up with creative if not feasible solutions. It was an old and tried technique of his. Like purging out the pus from a malignant wound; eventually the blood would run clean, and healing would start.

Regrettably, other than the steps he'd already taken, he came up with nothing.

First thing on his agenda was persuading his sister to move into the keep. Out of all the council members, he expected her to give him the most trouble. He'd better talk to her before the meeting and prepare her. It would save him the public drama. Besides, getting Amanda to safety was a priority.

Good luck with that.

Preparing for battle, he pulled out his phone and called her.

After the initial shock over the news had worn off and her sniffles had subsided, she protested, "I can't just abandon my lab or not show up for classes.

Kian cut her short. "So come to the meeting and vote against!"

"You know how the vote will go!" she hissed.

"Yes I do. And if you had an ounce of wisdom in that brain of yours, you wouldn't be fighting me over this. More than your life is in danger. If they find you, they wouldn't kill you, you'd just wish they had."

Amanda huffed. "You're overestimating the risk. They are not going to find me. And if you're that concerned about my safety, assign a couple of Guardians to watch over me."

"You know we are short on Guardians. That's why I'm calling for the sequestering of all council members. I just can't keep everyone safe unless they are all in one location."

"Find a solution. I'm not leaving my work." She ended the call.

Kian sighed and ran the fingers of both hands through his hair, smoothing back the flyaway strands. He'd have to go over to her place himself and convince her it was the smart thing to do.

Or, what was more likely, drag her out kicking and screaming.

CHAPTER 10: KIAN

It was oppressively quiet in the SUV on the way to Amanda's lab. The Lexus's almost soundproof interior filtered the outside traffic noise, leaving Brundar and Anandur's tight-lipped silence undisturbed.

Kian craved a cigarette, desperately, and a shot of whiskey or two.

He'd quit smoking years ago, but here and there the craving returned with gusto. Like it did now. It wasn't concern for his health that had prompted him to get rid of the habit, after all, his kind didn't get cancer or heart disease. He just hated smelling like an ashtray. The way the stench had used to cling to his hair and clothing had disgusted him.

Though he would kill for one now.

Comforting the devastated Micah had been excruciating. It had left him empty and deflated. There was no good way to deliver this kind of news to a mother. You offered your sympathy, said how sorry you were, offered your help in anything and everything.

Blah, blah, blah... The words hadn't even registered. In the end, he'd just held her while she'd cried.

And in the aftermath, he'd been left with no energy to deal with Amanda.

Heaving a sigh, Kian gazed out the window and watched the cars passing them by. He wondered what kind of sorrows their mortal occupants were hiding behind their impassive expressions.

There was so much anguish in their short, miserable lives, and family dying on them was such an integral part of their experience that it defined the whole of their existence. He suspected humans coped with the depressing certainty of their own mortality by keeping it out of their thoughts in any way they could. It sucked.

To lose a loved one was the worst experience ever. He wouldn't allow that to happen to him.

Not again.

There was nothing he could've done to prevent Lilen's death all those centuries ago, but he'd be damned if he'd let anything happen to his obstinate sister.

Not on his watch.

Fisting his hands, he felt his lips curl in a snarl as his resolve hardened. He would march into that lab, throw Amanda over his shoulder, and carry her to the SUV. And he didn't give a damn if he had to do it while she was kicking and screaming the whole way. To keep her safe, he'd even lock her in one of the underground cells.

Yeah, that sounds good. Easiest way to deal with the brat.

Kian took a deep breath. Okay... *like that will fly.*

He needed to chill.

Patience is a virtue, he repeated. *Patience is a virtue.*

Yeah, it just wasn't one of his.

Let someone else get that merit badge. Kian didn't plan on applying for sainthood anytime soon.

Taking the elevator down to Amanda's lab, he wondered if it just happened to be in the basement of the research facility or had Amanda chosen it because she preferred working underground.

It seemed to be a natural default, an unconscious preference for his kind. The older ones, like him, still suffered from some sensitivity to harsh light, but it was nothing a pair of quality sunglasses couldn't handle, and certainly nothing that bothered the younger immortals.

Still, the original race of gods had truly shunned the sunlight. Their sensitive eyes had to be covered in protective goggles to filter even the little light that could infiltrate through the sides of a more ordinary protective eyewear.

There had been no windows in their dwellings. Instead, shafts positioned diagonally through the thick walls had provided airflow while minimizing sunlight.

The flip side of this handicap had been an excellent night vision, which near-immortals shared to some degree with their ancestors. The gods had been nocturnal creatures, more comfortable in the relative darkness of the night when the soft glow of the moon and stars replaced the harsh sunlight. So much gentler on their sensitive eyes and skin.

Not for the first time, it crossed his mind that his ancestors must've been at the source of the outrageous vampire myths.

Creatures with fangs that sucked blood and burned in sunlight...

Right.

Mortals and their wild imaginations running amok with exaggerations and embellishments.

They got the fangs and sunlight part right, even the mind control was spot on, but where had the blood-sucking part come from? Or the red eyes for that matter? An immortal's eyes tearing up from too much exposure to the sun's harsh light? A careless one forgetting to lick the puncture wounds closed?

Who knew?

The truth was that the gods of old were at the source of many intriguing stories, with the vampire lore being one of the most imaginative. In his opinion, however, the legends of the snake people were more fitting. What was it about bats that so fascinated mortals that they preferred them to snakes? Not that he was all that fond of reptiles himself. Besides, the things couldn't fly, and as this particular ability was part of what made the vampire stories work, the bats kind of made sense.

His bodyguards were still uncharacteristically quiet as they made their way down the corridor, the rhythmic beat of their boots on the concrete floor the only indication that they were still with him.

He wasn't expecting Brundar to be chattering away, but Anandur's silence bothered him. Kian turned to look back at the brothers. Though grimly focused, their eyes were following their feet instead of scoping the place.

Not good.

"Snap out of it, guys! And stay alert! You think it's safe down here just because there are people all around us?"

"What jumped and bit you on the ass, Kian! You think I don't pay attention? I have been doing the same shit for how long now? A millennium? I can do it sleepwalking." Anandur sounded more pissed than offended.

"Yeah, yeah. You may kiss my ass to make it all better, lick it clean too!" Kian jumped sideways to avoid the punch Anandur aimed at his shoulder.

At least the guy was smiling now.

Brundar shook his head and kept going, leaving them behind.

Stopping at the junction of corridors that terminated at the one leading to Amanda's lab, Kian called him back. "Stay here. This is a good spot. You can see everyone coming this way from either direction." He pointed to where he wanted them to stand guard.

"I'm going in by myself. The hellion is not going to like an audience."

Not exactly. Amanda loved drama. It was Kian who could live without it. "Try not to attract any attention to yourselves, and stay alert!"

CHAPTER 11: ANANDUR

Leaning against the wall next to his brother, Anandur smirked as he watched Kian duck into Amanda's lab. The guy was in for one hell of a fight, and if Kian thought it would go down easier without an audience, he was deluding himself.

"Man, I would've loved to see that," he told Brundar.

His brother ignored him, as usual not interested in talking.

Anandur shook his head and turned his attention to the sparse foot traffic. A trio of giggling girls was heading his way, and he had to admit that staying out in the corridor was proving to be quite entertaining.

The girls were eyeing him and his brother with unabashed interest, smiling and sauntering as they got closer.

Gutsy, forward minxes.

Evidently, it was easier said than done for him and Brundar to avoid attracting attention.

Not that he had a problem with that.

With what they were wearing, or rather not wearing, he got himself a healthy eyeful of young female flesh. In addition to the painted-on, torn jeans all three were wearing, the tall brunette's T-shirt was open at the sides with her purple lace bra showing, while her friend's sported so many slashes that there was hardly any of it left to cover anything. And the one with the spiky pink hair wore a tiny thing with a Mickey Mouse picture on it that looked like something she'd swiped off her kid brother.

Got to love this generation, Anandur thought as he flashed them his best seductive smile and winked.

Their response to his blatantly masculine charm was as immediate as it was predictable, and his nostrils flared as the unmistakable, sweet smell of female arousal reached him, triggering his predatory instincts.

Brundar wasn't doing much better. Growling quietly beside him, his brother's body tensed as he got ready to pounce.

Adjusting himself, Anandur wrapped a restraining arm around Brundar's shoulders, holding on tight and squeezing hard while smiling at the girls.

"Damn, why are the good-looking guys always gay? It's so unfair!" the tall one whispered to her friends.

Anandur chuckled, his hearing more acute than the girls could ever suspect. Squeezing Brundar even harder, he kissed the top of his brother's head.

"I'm going to break your ▓▓▓▓▓ arm if you don't let go," Brundar hissed.

Frowning, Anandur released his brother with a pitying sidelong glance. The poor guy suffered from a crippling lack of a sense of humor.

When the disappointed trio disappeared behind a corner, turning into another corridor, Brundar hastily cast a shrouding illusion around Anandur and himself. Obscuring their presence from any mortal passerby, his illusion made them appear part of the wall—undetectable unless someone bumped straight into them.

CHAPTER 12: SYSSI

Syssi focused on the images flashing at evenly spaced time intervals on the screen: square, circle, star, triangle, star, circle, triangle, square...

The shapes were popping randomly in a never-ending sequence, and her task was to guess which one would flash next and hit the appropriate key—before the image appeared.

It was mind-numbingly boring, mainly since she'd been at it for the past couple of hours.

Any other day, she would've just quit. After straining her mind for so long, the test results were iffy anyway, but not today.

Syssi had never seen Amanda in such a bitchy mood before. The woman was scary. Something or someone must have pissed her off big time during her lunch break because she'd come back sullen and practically snarling at everyone.

Hannah and David had done the smart thing and had left an hour ago... Ran for their lives was more like it.

But not Syssi, no, Amanda's precognition experiments favorite test bunny had to stay behind.

Soon, she'd have to stop. Her eyes were tearing and her headache was blooming into a full-blown migraine. In a few minutes, she'd have to tell Amanda she couldn't take it anymore.

Sighing, she rubbed her blurry eyes as the lab's door opened with a creak.

Curious to see who it was, Syssi peeked between one flashing symbol and the next...

And lost her concentration.

Or rather had it blown to pieces.

The man closing the door was breathtakingly handsome; tall, broad-shouldered, and perfectly proportioned under the conservative charcoal suit he was wearing. The suit looked expensive, and it had been probably custom made for him, but she was sure it wasn't hiding any flab. The guy looked like he was all muscle.

Holding himself regally as he scanned the lab, his posture was somewhat stiff, until he found Amanda and loosened marginally.

As he glared at her, his deep blue eyes were hard and sad, making him appear angry, or frustrated.

He smoothed back his chin-length tawny hair in what seemed like a nervous habit, brushing the curling ends with his fingers and forcing them away from his angular, beautiful face.

Holding her breath, Syssi felt faint, her heart racing wildly and her legs turning to rubber. With an effort, she pulled air into her oxygen starved lungs and rubbed her tingling arms.

"You can save your breath, Kian. I'm not going to let you drag me away to your lair. There is nothing you can say that will persuade me to abandon my work. It's too important, so turn around and go home." Amanda circled her finger and pointed it at the door.

When he didn't budge, she crossed her arms over her chest and narrowed her eyes, staring him down while tapping her high-heeled shoe on the concrete floor.

So, this is Kian, Amanda's brother. Wow.

He looked nothing like Syssi had imagined he would. On the few occasions Amanda had mentioned her brother, she'd referred to him as the old goat, or the stupid old goat, painting in Syssi's mind an image of an older guy sporting a goatee and thinning, wispy hair.

In her wildest dreams, Syssi couldn't have imagined him as the magnificent Greek-god-facsimile standing before her. Although, with Amanda as his sister, she should have known better. A stunning woman like her boss just couldn't have an unattractive man for a brother.

Syssi felt like an ugly duckling next to these beautiful swans. Who wouldn't? No mere mortal could achieve this level of perfection.

Forcing her eyes away, she tried to do a disappearing act by sliding down in her chair and hiding behind her computer screen. Too shook up to continue the experiment, she went through the motions and pretended to be working, using it as an excuse to stay out of sight.

There was no way she was attracting attention to herself. If she were lucky, Kian would leave without ever noticing her.

Syssi didn't think she could survive an introduction.

Her reaction to him was so immediate and so overpowering that she had no idea what to do with it. She'd never responded like this to a man.

Syssi had never been one of those girls who idolized movie stars or rockers, and their big muscles and gorgeous faces had left her indifferent. Looks just hadn't been all that important to her. All she'd wanted was a nice, intelligent guy who was decent looking.

And yet, here she was, yearning with terrifying intensity for a man that could never be hers. Men like him didn't exist in her world.

He was beautiful, yet all male, there was nothing feminine about his perfect features. And his sophisticated business suit didn't fool her. Kian exuded a kind of primitive power and dominance that terrified her.

Because instinctively she felt compelled to submit to it.

Where the hell were these thoughts coming from? Even the terminology was foreign to her. What was happening to her?

Oh, God, just make him leave already.

She was going to take these embarrassing thoughts with her to the grave. No one, and she meant absolutely no one, would ever find out that such absurdities had ever flitted through her mind. She might not be a bra-burning feminist, but she would never let anyone dominate her either.

"Why are you being so stubborn? Did I really need to drop everything and come over here because you wouldn't listen to reason? There is real danger out there, and I can't let you—" Kian stopped mid-sentence as Amanda held a finger to her lips, shushing him, and pointed toward the back of the room.

"Syssi, stop hiding and come meet my brother Kian." Amanda was getting closer, waving her hand in invitation.

Syssi remained glued to her chair, hoping the floor would split open and swallow her up.

"Come out, girl. He doesn't bite... much." Amanda's snort sounded like a cackle.

Syssi shrunk away from her. The woman's sarcastic tone sounded positively evil, evoking in her imagination an image of the beautiful swans morphing into ugly vultures.

"Stop it, Amanda! You're scaring the girl with your idiotic comments!" Kian snapped.

Syssi felt like laughing—a crazy, cackling laugh. She wasn't scared of them. Why would he think that? What really scared her was her own reaction to Kian. She was intimidated out of her freaking mind, and now Amanda was forcing her to show herself.

No guy had ever terrified her like that. On occasion, she'd felt awkward, a little uncomfortable, and her accursed uncontrolled blushing had always been an impediment to her romantic life. But this was so out of her realm of experience that it was panic attack inducing.

As Kian's footsteps got closer, sweat broke out over her face and her stomach roiled. And then he was standing right beside her, extending his hand to help her up.

No-no-no-no!

Except, what choice did she have?

Lifting her head, Syssi thanked providence, her cursed foresight, and whatever else that had prompted her to take a little extra care with her looks this morning. She had blow-dried her hair, put on a little makeup, and worn nice pair of pumps that added three inches to her height.

At least she wouldn't look like a complete midget troll standing next to all that perfection.

But then, as her eyes made it all the way up to his face, her heart skipped a beat. This spectacular man was looking down at her with uncensored male appreciation.

Enthralled by the hunger in his eyes, she took his offered hand, the jolt of energy passing through her body bringing on such strong blast of desire that it stunned and shamed her at the same time.

If her legs felt like rubber before, now her knees dissolved completely. She was holding onto his hand for dear life, her whole weight leaning on it. "Sorry, my legs must've gone numb from sitting too long," she managed in a hoarse whisper.

In the silence that followed, the hunger she saw in Kian's expression burned like an inferno before abruptly turning into scalding ice.

The change was startling.

As he straightened, his posture stiffened, his eyes hardened in disapproval, and his mouth narrowed.

He looked angry again. Forget angry, he looked savage, cruel. But this time his displeasure was directed at her, and not at Amanda.

Syssi felt her face heat up. She must've misinterpreted his expression, and her response had been totally inappropriate. Worse, her attraction to Kian must have been blatantly obvious for him to notice it, and he decided he wanted nothing to do with her.

Oh, God.

A guy like that probably had women throwing themselves at him constantly; prettier women, elegant, sophisticated, assertive. He was so far out of her league, he might as well have been from a different planet.

Mortified, she lowered her eyes.

CHAPTER 13: KIAN

Kian had been ready to chew Amanda's head off for shushing him, but then she'd pointed her finger at the girl hiding behind a large computer screen.

Curious, he'd dipped his head.

All he had seen under the desk were jean-clad, long legs and a pair of slender, heeled feet, but his enhanced senses had registered the girl's rapid heartbeat and the acrid aroma of her fear.

The two of them snarling at each other's throats like a couple of feral beasts, they must've scared the girl. And then Amanda had made it even worse with her sarcasm, sounding like a wicked witch and fueling the girl's fear instead of trying to ease it.

Intending to rectify the situation, he'd crossed the short distance to the girl, when it had suddenly dawned on him that Amanda had called her Syssi.

The same girl she wanted him to seduce.

Amanda's schemes aside, though, he needed to do something before the poor thing fainted. And at any rate, he was intrigued.

Extending his arm to help her up, he was curious to see her face, but it was hidden behind a curtain of wavy blond hair. It wasn't exactly blond, though. Several shades of light browns, blonds, and gold intertwined to create a spectacular whole. Taking a sniff, he knew it wasn't the kind that came out of a box. There was no residual smell of chemicals—just the light flowery scent of her shampoo. Not that he would've minded one way or another. Amanda colored her hair from time to time to change her looks, and it wasn't only about keeping her identity secret. She simply enjoyed it.

With a little sigh, the girl seemed to gather enough courage to look up at him.

Kian was dumbstruck.

Syssi was beautiful.

Staring at her lovely, blushing face, he was entrapped by her guileless gaze. The man who'd bedded thousands of women was rendered speechless by one blushing girl.

Kian couldn't explain it if he tried.

Yes, she was lovely, beautiful, with pale, flawless skin, and a small straight nose, and those perfectly shaped, plump, pink lips that were utterly kissable.

But what had delivered that gut-crunching punch was her big, bright, blue-green eyes.

In that brief moment, when their eyes had first met, he'd gotten a glimpse of her soul.

Startled, he kept staring, captivated, feeling as if he knew her—was coming home to her after being lost for a long time. It was all out there in her sincere, open face: the intelligence, the kindness, the shadow of sadness that shouldn't have been there.

And a hesitant, hopeful expression.

So sweet.

The girl was attracted to him, and she wanted him to like her.

Her lashes dropped over her expressive eyes, and she bit down on her lower lip before taking his offered hand.

Incredibly, that one small innocent touch stunned him, igniting an incinerating erotic current that burned a path straight from her fingers down to his groin.

What the hell?

Cursing the traitor in his pants, Kian was grateful for his suit jacket covering the evidence of his response. The girl looked flustered enough without getting a gander of that, and besides, he hated giving Amanda the satisfaction of being right.

Syssi was all that Amanda had claimed her to be and more.

Now that he got her standing, Kian could also appreciate her deliciously curved body as Amanda had so aptly put it. Skintight jeans hugged long slim legs, the gentle curve of her hips narrowing into a small waist. Perfectly shaped breasts, substantial but not too big, strained her T-shirt, stretching it across her chest. And through the split neckline, he got a delightful glimpse of the rounded tops.

Damn! Amanda had been right. Syssi was exactly his type.

And she was blushing!

What girl blushed these days? None that he'd encountered lately, and for sure none so gorgeously delicious.

That demure demeanor just floored him.

Combined with the slight whiff of her arousal intermingled with that of her anxiety, the potent elixir cranked the dial of his lust all the way up, turning it into a burning need. His venom-glands began pulsating, swelling and dripping venom droplets down his elongated fangs into his mouth. The damned razor-sharp things were threatening to punch out over his bottom lip.

Kian pressed his lips tight. He could just imagine the sight of him flashing these beauties, a monster straight out of a horror flick. He'd bet Syssi's arousal would be gone in a flash. She would run screaming, and that hopeful infatuated look would be gone for good.

But oh, man, how he wanted her.

His imagination ran amok with the things he wanted to do to her, the erotic scenes flashing rapidly through his mind.

First, he'd tighten his grip on her hand and yank her to him, holding her sweet curves flush against his front, then grab her nape to tilt her head up and catch her lips, kissing the living daylight out of her. When he'd gotten her all breathless and panting, he would lower her to the desk and peel those tight jeans off her...

Yeah.

Kian shook himself. He had to stop that train wreck before it crashed and burned. Reining in his runaway libido, he shackled it with the steel cables of his tight self-control.

Bloody immortal hormones.

This whole thing was absurd. If that little chit had anything special about her, it was her ability to turn both his sister and him into blabbering, romantic dolts. He was too old and too experienced for these kinds of teenage fantasies.

Recognizing her...

Feeling like coming home to her...

He couldn't believe this kind of nonsense even crossed his mind.

It must've been just plain old lust.

For the past couple of nights, he had not gone prowling, and his sex-starved body was kicking his hormones into overdrive and making him stupid.

Sensing the change in him, Syssi pulled her hand out of his grasp and lowered her eyes, blushing again.

Oh, crap, her timid response just threw more gasoline on the fire of his arousal, spurring on the predator in him.

Taking a deep breath, Kian hissed as he pulled it through his clenched teeth.

Oh, great, now he was hissing... charming.

He had to get out of there.

As he turned away from her to face his smirking sister, he felt the girl's hurt gaze burning holes in his back.

"Now, who has his knickers in a twist? Dear brother of mine." Amanda mocked his agitation. "Don't pay any attention to his foul mood, Syssi. It has nothing to do with you. It's just the way he is: An. Old. Grouchy. Goat." Amanda walked over to Syssi and wrapped a supportive arm around the girl's shoulders.

It was a ridiculous standoff, with Kian brooding on one side, and the two women forming a united front against him on the other.

When had he become the villain here?

He just wanted to get it over with, haul Amanda home and get that smoke and drink he was so desperately craving.

CHAPTER 14: BRUNDAR

Out in the hallway, Brundar leaned his shoulder against the wall, twisting his dagger between his fingers as he observed the sparse foot traffic of mortals passing him by.

There was a common pattern to the way they talked, walked, the stuff they wore and the things they carried.

They fit a certain profile.

Some were leaving, walking in chatty groups of twos and threes, heading to the cafeteria or some other joint for their evening meal and making plans for later on. Others, holding on to their coffee mugs and their laptop cases, were coming in to do some late work at the labs.

Behind him, Anandur chuckled.

His brother was passing the time by entertaining himself with stupid YouTube clips on his phone, oblivious to the fact that he was on guard duty and was supposed to be invisible.

Idiot.

Brundar rolled his eyes as he imagined the ghost stories Anandur's disembodied chuckles might start. Glancing both ways, he checked to see if any of the students walking by them had overheard his idiot of a brother.

A girl clutching her laptop hurried by him without a glance, and another walked away walked away, too busy talking on her phone to notice anything. But something about the three guys coming his way made the hair on the back of his neck tingle in alarm.

Snapping to attention, Brundar palmed the hilt of his dagger.

The men didn't fit the mold he'd discerned.

With no coffee or laptops, the young men were built like linebackers and marched purposefully with the gait of trained warriors.

They were heading straight for Anandur and him, staring right at them as if they weren't at all affected by his concealing illusion.

They shouldn't have been able to penetrate his shroud... unless...

Unsheathing his second dagger, Brundar assumed a fighting stance. Next to him Anandur did the same while speed-dialing Kian, proving he hadn't been as distracted as he'd appeared to be.

"Doomers in the hall. About to engage," he said when the shit hit the fan.

CHAPTER 15: SYSSI

As Kian ended the call and returned the phone to his pocket, his face turned from brooding to grim to determined, and his body seemed to swell with aggression.

Something was up.

"Is there another way out of here?" he barked, confirming Syssi's suspicion.

"We can pass through the kitchenette to the adjoining lab; its front exit door faces a parallel corridor." Amanda hurried to grab her purse and laptop. "Syssi, take your stuff, we are leaving!" She was already in the kitchen.

Kian urged Syssi to follow.

"What's going on?" she asked while trying to walk as fast as Kian's hand on the small of her back was propelling her to. His stride was so long that she was forced to jog to keep up.

"Some unwanted company I'd rather avoid is coming this way," was his cryptic reply.

Syssi was afraid to ask any more questions.

Kian looked like he was ready to commit murder, and what's worse, she sensed that with him it wasn't just an expression. Which didn't really make sense considering the guy was supposedly the CEO of an international conglomerate. But her gut had an opinion of its own, and it didn't match the one her mind was comfortable with.

Come to think of it, he reminded her of Andrew. When her brother got like that, she knew to stay clear of him and keep quiet. In his line of work shit happened, a lot, and it didn't matter if he was on leave. Dealing with it, the last thing he needed was to be distracted by his little sister's curiosity.

Trotting behind Amanda, she wondered what she had gotten herself into. Who were these people? Was she in real danger? Or was it her imagination?

Except Amanda looked scared, she wasn't imagining that. And in addition to deducing it from her companions' urgency, Syssi felt it in her gut, which in this case was in agreement with her brain, confirming that something dangerous was coming their way.

Rushing through the adjoining lab, they exited into a corridor on the other side of the basement. But instead of heading for the elevators farther down the hallway, Amanda opted for the nearby emergency stairs. She threw open the door, and they ran up. While Amanda and Syssi's heels played a staccato beat on the metal stairs, Kian was somehow managing the climb soundlessly—his considerable weight not hindering his silent treads.

Interesting, what the mind focused on in an emergency.

Once outside, they hurried toward an SUV that had been conveniently waiting for them in front of the building, and the three of them crammed themselves into its back seat.

Had Kian summoned the car? When? She hadn't noticed him calling anyone. Had she been too preoccupied?

Duh, running scared from some unspecified danger would do that to a person.

The driver turned his head to face them, smiling a weird, fake-looking smile; the kind usually molded on the faces of store mannequins.

"Where to, Master?"

Master?

The situation was becoming creepier by the minute, and Syssi was going into a full fight-or-flight mode, or rather a fright and flight.

What did she really know about Amanda and her brother? Nothing. They might be the dangerous ones, and not whoever they were running from. Or perhaps she should be scared of both.

There were just too many things that didn't add up about Amanda and Kian. Though if asked, Syssi would not have been able to point to a single thing that would look suspicious to someone else.

They were just too good-looking, unnaturally so. Amanda had a butler who called her mistress, and Kian had a driver who called him master. Kian, who must've weighed well over two hundred pounds, could climb stairs soundlessly, and sometimes Amanda's eyes shone as if they were illuminated from the inside. Separately, each item on her list could be explained away, but taken together they painted a picture that was slightly off.

Or a lot.

"Drive for a few blocks then park. I need to check on the guys."

Sitting squeezed between Kian and Amanda, Syssi clutched her purse with trembling hands, trying to hide how shaken she was—feeling like Alice in Wonderland right after she had fallen down the rabbit hole.

"Don't worry, sweetie, we're going to Kian's place and we will have a good laugh about this whole silly episode over drinks." Amanda hugged her stiff shoulders and patted her cheek.

Why the hell was Amanda treating her like a child?

But instead of feeling offended or at least peeved, for some inexplicable reason, Amanda's words had a calming effect. Syssi's tension eased, and she felt herself relax, becoming comfortable, even languid.

How is it possible?

Her rational mind refused to accept the unexplained change. Except, Amanda's hand kept stroking her hair and it felt so wonderful that Syssi's eyelids began drooping.

She was so tired...

How come? Syssi wondered again and tried to resist, but she couldn't fight the sudden compulsion to sleep.

CHAPTER 16: KIAN

Amanda kept her mouth shut until Syssi's eyes closed and she slumped into the back seat, leaning against Kian's arm.

"She's out. So what's going on? And if this was all a trick to get me to come with you..."

Not deigning to respond, Kian only cast her an incredulous glare, then dipped his head to look at Syssi.

She was leaning against his bicep, her wild mane of hair covering half of her face and most of her upper body. Gently, he brushed it away from her cheek and tucked it behind her ear. Holding her carefully, he shifted so her cheek came to rest on his pectoral and wrapped his arm around her.

Syssi sighed contently but didn't wake. Tucked under his arm, her soft, small body felt as if it belonged there.

But Kian craved more.

In her sleep, she'd relaxed the death-hold she had on her purse, and her delicate hands were resting gracefully in her lap. Taking one small palm, he placed it on his thigh, savoring the added sensation. For now it would have to do.

Like hell...

Closing his eyes, he dipped his head to her hair and inhaled her fresh, sweet scent, then inched down to sniff at the soft skin in the hollow between her neck and shoulder.

Divine... So inviting...

Not surprisingly, his fangs distended and begun throbbing with venom. Struggling against an overwhelming urge to sink them into the smooth, creamy column of her neck, he forcefully leashed the monster inside and pulled back.

With a wicked smirk, Amanda was eyeing him from Syssi's other side, no doubt debating between taking advantage of the opportunity to needle him some more and letting him enjoy the moment.

For now she kept quiet, but knowing his sister, she was patting herself on the shoulder. Observing his reaction to Syssi being exactly what she had predicted, she was basking in the success of her brilliant matchmaking.

Still, patience not being one of Amanda's virtues any more than it was his, a few moments later she asked again, "Seriously now, what's going on?"

"Anandur called from where I left Brundar and him to guard the hallway leading to your lab. Doomers showed up, and they were about to fight them off, giving us time to get away. That's all I know for now. It was right outside your door, Miss 'I'm in no danger,'" Kian bit out, glaring at her, his fury rising as the implications of what had just happened, or rather had almost happened, began sinking in.

"Because of your obstinacy, Anandur and Brundar are fighting for their lives." Throwing the accusation at her was unfair, but Kian was livid. If he had arrived just a few moments later, she would have been taken.

Imagining what horrific things those monsters would have done to her, he felt as if acid was slowly sliding down his throat and into his gut.

Amanda crossed her arms over her chest and shrugged, pretending she wasn't shaken. But she wasn't fooling him, not for a moment. Kian knew her too well. Amanda was just too proud to admit it, but the truth was written all over her face—she was distraught.

Taking a deep breath, he calmed his tone to something a little more human-sounding than a growl. "Was there anything important left in the lab? Something that might be useful to the Doomers?"

She shrugged again. "All the data from my paranormal research is on my laptop, and the lab's computers have only the standard university stuff. So no, I don't think they will find anything useful there. What I wonder, though, is how did they know where to find me?" She was trying to sound unaffected and matter-of-fact, but the slight tremble in her voice betrayed how rattled she was.

"It must have been something they found at Mark's place. Them showing up at your doorstep a day after his murder can't be a coincidence. Probably something about your work. Unless they hit your home as well." Kian glanced down at his phone again, anxious for news from his men.

"Onidu would've called if they did." Amanda had no reason to worry for her Odu; he was practically indestructible. But she pulled out her phone and called anyway.

"Onidu, darling, did we have uninvited guests today?"

"No, Mistress. Should I be expecting anyone?"

"Our enemy showed up in the lab and I wanted to check on you and give you a heads-up."

"You wish to give me heads, Mistress? What should I do with them?"

Kian chuckled. The Odus were very literal.

"Never mind. Just be watchful."

"Of course, Mistress."

CHAPTER 17: BRUNDAR

The fight in the hallway would've been epic—if anyone had been able to see it.

Brundar was keeping the area shrouded in such a thick illusion of dread that anyone passing by hurried away, avoiding the turn into the short side corridor as if it were the anteroom to the fiery pits of hell.

The Doomers attacked with surprising skill, and they were strong and determined. But then, Brundar and Anandur had spent centuries honing their fighting techniques, and the younger immortals were no match for them.

The skirmish was over almost before it began. Daggers stabbed and slashed, most of them parried, some penetrating tissue, some only tearing at clothes. Punches and kicks found their targets with meaty thuds, eliciting strained grunts.

In the end, Anandur was choking the air out of one assailant, while Brundar had his dagger buried in another's chest.

The third managed to escape.

Brundar dropped his gasping opponent, the guy's body hitting the concrete floor and jerking up from the force of it. The impact put an end to the gurgling sounds of his desperate struggles for air.

For a split second Brundar contemplated giving chase, but instead he sent his other dagger flying after the running man, nailing him between the shoulder blades.

The guy slowed only to yank the thing out and kept running.

Brundar had to let him go.

He couldn't maintain the shroud over the fight scene and at the same time cast another around the pursuit.

Unfortunately, Anandur's pitiful illusionist ability was limited to shrouding himself only, and even that was not done particularly well.

Brundar checked himself for injuries, satisfied that his many cuts and bruises were already healing. In a few moments, the bloodstains drying on his shredded clothes would be the only evidence left of the pounding he'd taken.

A glance at Anandur reassured him that his brother was just as banged up but no worse. The concrete floor where their downed opponents lay crumpled like ugly rag dolls was splattered with blood, and though some of it must've been his or Anandur's, most of it came from the Doomers.

Looking down at the incapacitated immortals, Brundar figured it wouldn't be much longer before their bodies repaired the damage.

It presented him with a dilemma.

Clan law prohibited injecting a fallen enemy with a deadly dose of venom. It was akin to execution, which neither he nor Anandur were authorized to carry out. Of course, the rules were different if it happened in the heat of battle; all was fair when fighting for your life. But in this situation, the boss had to give them the green light.

Anandur pulled out his phone. "Kian, we have two down and one escaped. What do you want us to do with the two we got? We don't have much time before they resurrect."

"Bring them to the brink, but leave them in stasis. How are you guys doing? Everything okay?"

"Nice of you to ask, but truly, it offends me that you do, boss." Anandur was right. He and Brundar were invincible; the Doomers hadn't stood a chance.

"My offer from before stands. You can kiss my ass. Stay where you are. I'm sending a clean-up crew." Kian hung up.

Anandur pocketed his phone and grimaced as he turned to Brundar. "You heard the boss, we inject to the brink. Though I'll be damned if I know why he wants the scum alive. Maybe he plans to make hood ornaments out of their ugly carcasses." He chuckled. "I wonder who he's going to send to do the clean-up. Can you imagine Okidu in his suit with a white apron over it, on his knees, scrubbing blood from the concrete?" Anandur chuckled again.

He lost his smile as he glanced at the purple-faced, nearly dead male lying crumpled at his feet. "I don't believe I have to put my mouth on this filth." Anandur's face twisted with utter disgust.

He cast a quick glance at the other Doomer whose bleeding heart was already on the mend, slowly pushing out the knife embedded in it. "You'd better hurry." He crouched down and immediately turned his head sideways. "Whoa! Mine stinks."

Brundar was ready, his fangs were already fully extended from the heat of the fight, dripping venom and primed to go. Grabbing the male by the hair and twisting the guy's head, he exposed the neck and hoisted it up to his mouth. With a loud hiss, he sank his needle-sharp fangs into the Doomer's flesh, keeping them embedded as the venom pulsated, invading the man's bloodstream.

Injecting to the brink was a precise art. Too little did diddly-squat, and too much meant a permanent address in a hole in the ground. Listening carefully to the immortal's heartbeat, Brundar waited until it slowed down to almost nothing, then pulled his fangs out and sealed the puncture wounds.

The man could still die, but if he did, it was no sweat off Brundar's brow. He'd done what he'd been ordered to do. If he'd miscalculated, then oh, well; he'd done his best.

Anandur was still at his prey's throat, the man's undamaged heart taking longer to slow down. When he was done, he licked the wound closed and spat out.

"I need to rinse out my mouth after this shit!"

Anandur kept spitting out and wiping his mouth on his sleeve in between fits of spitting.

Eventually, Brundar took pity on him and handed him the flask of whiskey he had hidden in his jacket's inner pocket.

"Thanks, bro, you're a lifesaver."

Anandur took a big swig of the Chivas, gargled it in his mouth a few times and then spat it out. After the second and third swig had gone down his throat, he handed the flask back.

Brundar cranked his neck back and emptied what remained of the whiskey down his own throat. As his adrenaline level began dropping, Brundar's aches and pains made themselves known, and the beating his body had taken became hard to ignore. Slumping down to the floor, he propped his back against the cold concrete wall and let his head drop back.

Now, with their gruesome task done, all that was left was to wait for the clean-up crew. Until then, they had to maintain the shrouding and guard their prey.

Brundar felt tired, yet energized.

It was good to be fighting again, to feel the adrenaline rush, to use the skills he had practiced and perfected over the centuries.

Lately, he'd been feeling almost useless. What was the point of being a perfect killing machine if you never got to kill anymore?

As he reveled in the sense of power and utility, there was a small tinge of guilt in all that satisfaction. The enemy was attacking his family, but instead of the dread he should've been feeling, Brundar felt invigorated from the rush he'd gotten from the fight.

It was good to be needed; to carry out tasks only he and his Guardian brethren could.

Perhaps now, with this new danger looming over the clan, they could call in some of the others, those who had left the Guardian force for lack of purpose.

With a rare, fond glance at Anandur, he reminisced about their stormy past in the force. The battles, the brotherly revelry when they had come back home victorious, the pride of accomplishment, the gratitude of the clan.

Closing his eyes, Brundar welcomed the visions of his glorious past and smiled wistfully.

He missed those halcyon days.

CHAPTER 18: SYSSI

Syssi's cheek was resting on something hard and smooth that smelled amazing.

Strong fingers caressed her cheek. "Wake up, sleepyhead. We're here." The deep, masculine voice reverberated through her rib cage.

Who? Where?

Suddenly, it all came rushing back.

Kian.

He was holding her tucked against him, caressing her and talking to her as if he gave a damn.

She stiffened, attempting to sit up and shake his arm off, but the sudden movement made her head spin, and she had to lean back against the seat... and his arm.

"Take it easy, beautiful, give yourself a minute; there's no rush." He kept stroking her cheek with his thumb.

They were in what seemed to be an underground parking structure, still sitting in the same car, supposedly still in the same universe.

Who are you, and what did you do with Kian the grouch?

The man sitting next to her had more mood swings than a hormonal teenager. She needed to tell him to cut it out, but it felt so good to be held like that. Syssi kept still, allowing herself a few moments of bliss to enjoy this surreal break in reality. Maybe she was still dreaming? And in her dream this gorgeous man was caring, kind, and warm, and called her beautiful.

She didn't want to wake up.

Just a few moments longer.

Then Amanda had to ruin it by sounding the wake-up call. "Syssi, if you're still sleepy, you can lie down on Kian's couch. I'm done sitting in the car. Let's go!" She opened the door and got out.

Nope, no dream.

Kian extracted his arm from around her shoulders and opened the other door. Unfolding his tall body, he stepped out of the SUV.

As soon as he left her side she missed him; his warmth, his closeness, his scent. Standing by the door, he offered her his hand—being gentlemanly, or perhaps thinking she needed help getting out.

As a matter of fact, she did.

Still woozy, she felt weak as if she'd been awakened too early from a very deep sleep, or perhaps had too much to drink. But neither of those applied.

What was happening to her?

She wasn't sick, wasn't hungry...

So why was she feeling like this?

Trying to make sense of why she felt so off-kilter, Syssi concluded it must've been the aftermath of all that adrenaline leaving her system.

Taking Kian's offered palm, she stepped out of the car and let him walk her to the elevator.

Once they reached the penthouse level, the three of them and Kian's driver stepped out into a beautiful vestibule. A round granite table stood in the center of a mosaic-inlaid marble floor, holding a huge vase of fresh flowers. Across from each other, two sets of double doors led to what she assumed were two separate penthouse apartments.

Kian's driver opened the one to their left, ushering them inside with the flair of a seasoned butler.

The place was beautiful.

If Syssi were to design her own dream home, she would make it look just like that.

The first thing that caught her attention was the wall of glass opposite the entry door, overlooking the magnificent, unobstructed cityscape. To its right, another glass wall opened to an expansive rooftop terrace, complete with a lush garden, a long narrow lap pool, and an elegant assortment of lounge furniture.

The living room decor was magazine-perfect.

Over the dark hardwood floor, a bright area rug delineated the sitting area. Three espresso-colored leather sofas surrounded a stone coffee table that must've been at least eight feet wide on each side. Vibrant, large-scale art covered three of the cream-colored walls, while a big screen topping a contemporary-style fireplace occupied the fourth.

To complete the perfectly put together room, vases filled with fresh flowers were strategically scattered throughout.

Syssi could think of nothing she would've changed. She loved the way Kian had managed to make the space warm and inviting despite its size and opulence.

Come to think of it, it made more sense that someone else had done the decorating...

A woman...

Of course Kian would have someone in his life, maybe even living with him, she had no reason to assume he was single.

Syssi rubbed a hand over her sternum, calling herself all kinds of stupid as she tried to soothe the sudden ache in the center of her chest.

Walking toward the glass wall overlooking the city, she decided to discreetly fish for information. "Wow, this is beautiful. You have an amazing taste, Kian," she complimented.

Kian took the bait. "Can't take credit for it. This is all the work of our interior decorator, Ingrid. My only input was no clutter and no museum pieces, just a comfortable, livable space. Ingrid came up with all the rest on her own, and I basically approved most of her suggestions." He shrugged and walked over to the bar. Pouring himself a Scotch, he asked, "What can I offer you, ladies?"

"I'll have gin and tonic," Syssi called from her spot next to the glass wall, where she was pretending to look out at the view.

The relief she'd felt upon hearing his answer was just plain stupid. Even if there was no woman sharing his home, it didn't mean he didn't have one. And besides, he wasn't hers, and never would be. She had no business feeling jealous or possessive over him.

But oh, God, how she wished she did.

Kian unsettled her on so many levels, Syssi doubted she could have an intelligent conversation with the guy. Hiding her powerful attraction to him was taxing. Her acting skills weren't that good. The sooner she said goodbye the better, before she slipped and made a fool of herself by letting her insane desire for him show.

"Same for me." Amanda joined her at the view wall, slanting her a knowing glance.

"House! Open terrace doors," Kian commanded the smart-home system, sending the mechanized glass-panels sliding almost soundlessly into the wall.

Outside, Syssi chose one of the loungers next to the pool and sat down. This high up, the sound of the bustling city was nothing more than a distant hum, the drone disturbed only by the occasional car horn.

Tilting her head back, she gazed at the darkening sky, its wispy clouds illuminated by the orange and red hues of the setting sun.

"Beautiful, isn't it?" Amanda plopped next to her. Lying back with her palms tucked under her head, she joined Syssi in gazing at the color display in the sky.

"Yes, it is," Syssi agreed.

A glass in each hand, Kian stepped out and sat sideways on the lounger facing Amanda and her.

Even seated, he looked so big and so damn beautiful that he took her breath away. And what's more, with his jacket off and his white dress shirt's top buttons open, she glimpsed the outline of all those hard muscles she'd felt when he'd held her close in the car.

Syssi stared, not quite gaping, but still her lips were slightly parted, and she felt her face reddening. With an effort, she shifted her eyes away from him and glanced up at the sky, discreetly observing Kian from the corner of her eye.

After handing Amanda and her the chilled beverages, Kian pulled a gold lighter and a pack of Davidoffs from his trouser pocket. Taking a cigarette out, he held it between his thumb and forefinger, lit it, and inhaled deeply.

His lids dropped over his eyes as he took several long drags, and the tension that was etched on his handsome face seemed to ease. With his craving assuaged, he lifted his eyelids a little, peering at Syssi from behind a column of smoke.

"Pew! Kian, you said you'd quit!" Amanda crinkled her nose in distaste, waving a hand in front of her nose.

Ignoring Amanda, Kian's eyes stayed trained on Syssi. "It doesn't seem to bother you, Syssi, does it?" he asked on a stream of smoke.

"No, I like the smell of cigarettes, even cigars. I find it relaxing." Taking little sips from her drink, Syssi inhaled, enjoying the smell of tobacco mixed with Kian's cologne.

It reminded her of her grandpa. When she was little, she used to sit cuddled on his lap while he'd read to her. His clothes had always smelled of cigars and cologne. No wonder she associated the mix of these scents with safety and love.

After a long moment of staring into her glass and swishing the ice cubes around, she squared her shoulders and turned to Amanda. "Would anyone care to explain what's going on?"

Amanda pushed up from the lounger and walked a few steps away, distancing herself from the offending smell. "There are those who believe that what we do in the lab is evil or unnatural, the work of the devil or some other nonsense like that. A certain religious sect declared war on our work, sending us nasty messages and threats. Luckily, Kian took it seriously and decided to post guards around the lab, believing the nuts may become violently incensed and actually carry out what they've been promising to do. As much as it pains me to say, it seems Kian was proven right. The guards called him to let him know they spotted suspicious characters in the hallway, and Kian decided not to take any chances with an unnecessary confrontation. The guards called again to say they were able to scare the thugs off, so hopefully this is the end of it."

Turning to Kian, Amanda smirked. "Anyhow, I'm going to leave you two lovebirds alone and head across the hallway to my place. I need to call Onidu and have him bring over my stuff. I have nothing here." Blowing a kiss at Kian, she winked at Syssi and walked away.

Syssi blushed down to the roots of her hair.

Did she really say it? Lovebirds?

She swore she was never going to forgive Amanda for embarrassing her so.

"I probably should be going too; it's getting late. I should call a taxi. I usually walk home from the lab, it's only about twenty minutes away on foot, so I leave my car at home to save on the parking fees. Sometimes Amanda insists on picking me up in the morning and then driving me home after work." Syssi was blabbering but couldn't stop herself.

So embarrassing. Now he'd think she was an idiot.

Not to mention that he might get the impression that she was stingy, or poor. She was neither. Syssi was frugal, preferring a hefty bank account to frivolous spending. Her girlfriends from the lucrative private high school she'd attended used to roll their eyes at what she considered fiscal responsibility, and some even had gone as far as calling her a tightwad. While they had been flaunting their parents' money, competing for who had the latest and most expensive things, she'd never developed a taste for it.

Syssi had no idea where this propensity had sprouted from. Growing up as she had in an affluent home, she knew her parents could afford all those things that had been so important to her friends, and they had never refused any of her requests. Syssi had never lacked for anything. But even as a kid she'd preferred getting money rather than toys or other trinkets as birthday presents, and had been thrilled to watch her bank account grow with every new deposit. Maybe it had been her mother's dislike for shopping that had influenced her. Anita simply hadn't had the time or the inclination for it. She'd ordered what she needed from catalogs. After all, her mother had spent most of her days wearing a lab coat and had deemed what was under it inconsequential.

That being said, Syssi didn't think it had been intellectual snobbism that had her sneer at unnecessary spending. Syssi valued independence almost above all else, and a big part of being independent was having her own money—and plenty of it—with the caveat that it had to be earned.

Her parents had covered tuition as well as room and board throughout undergrad and architecture school. But she'd refused to accept anything else. Syssi worked for her spending money as an SAT tutor. She was quite proud of the fact that her services had been in such high demand, she'd even managed to put away a good chunk of what she'd been making into her saving account.

Listening to her make a fool of herself, Kian smiled, but it wasn't the comforting kind, more the amused expression of a predator ready to pounce on his cornered prey.

And what do you know... that blast of desire hit her again even harder than before.

Come kiss me, she beckoned him mentally. *Touch me. Do something. Can't you see I'm burning?* Quickly averting her eyes, Syssi prayed Kian couldn't read her expression.

She wished she was the type who could actually voice these thoughts, or even act upon them. But she never would. Even intoxicated, she could never be that brazen.

Sighing, Syssi cursed her romantically debilitating shyness. She could lust after Kian on the inside, but she'd never make the first move.

Braving a glance, she expected Kian's expression to be smug. Men like him were used to women fawning over them. They were empowered by it, expected it. Instead, he surprised her.

His beautiful eyes were full of regret.

With a resigned sigh, he pushed up from where he sat and offered her his hand. "Come on, beautiful, let me take you home," he said quietly.

Ignoring his hand, Syssi kept looking at him with wide questioning eyes, perplexed by the mixed signals he was sending her. "Why do you keep calling me that?" she blurted.

Usually, she was good at reading people, but Kian's mercurial behavior was impossible to figure out. One moment he looked like he wanted to do all kinds of naughty and exciting things to her, the next he regarded her as if she was a nuisance that he wanted nothing to do with. Then calling her beautiful again.

Make up your mind! Syssi wanted to scream at him.

"That's because you are beautiful." Kian's face softened, but his smile remained tight-lipped. Pulling her up to her feet, he held on to her hand as he led her out. At the front door, he paused to call to his butler, "Okidu, I'm taking Syssi home. I'll be back shortly."

The squat man rushed out of the kitchen. "Let me drive the young lady, Master. You do not have to burden yourself thus." Okidu was already putting his driver hat on.

"It's okay, Okidu. It would please me to take Syssi home myself." Kian held the door open for her.

"But, Master—" The guy seemed distraught.

Kian pinned him with a hard stare. "That's enough."

She wanted to tell Kian that she'd rather have the butler drive her, but after a quick look at his face she reconsidered. That hard, determined expression of his reminded her of Andrew, and she knew Kian wouldn't budge. She had enough experience arguing with her brother to know it would be futile to try.

It's gonna be torturous. Syssi grimaced, imagining the awkward silence that would most likely stretch between them on the drive to her home. Kian didn't seem like the kind of guy who did small talk, and neither was she. Hopefully, traffic would be merciful and the drive short.

She'd been right.

Starting with the elevator, through the car ride, it was just as awkward as she had imagined it would be. Kian drove stone-faced and quiet. She was stiff and nervous, anxious for it to be over.

It felt like a first date gone all wrong. Except, it wasn't even a date! Just two people who rubbed each other the wrong way, or perhaps the right way, which was even scarier.

As they got closer to her place, she began to worry. There was no doubt in her mind that Kian would insist on walking her to her door and not leave till she was safely inside. And after seeing the grandeur of his place, she hoped he wouldn't think that her tiny guesthouse-apartment was a dump.

Right behind her landlady's home, the converted garage was cozy and safe. And the rent was no more than what she would've paid at the dorms, while offering her more privacy and quiet. But compared to his penthouse it looked like a hovel.

Damn, sometimes being frugal and independent backfired. If she'd accepted her parents' offer to pay for a decent apartment, she wouldn't be fretting now about Kian getting the wrong impression about her.

He insisted not only on walking her to the door but on checking the interior for any possible threats as well. Thankfully, though, he didn't seem to mind or even notice the old secondhand furniture, or the mess. Syssi, on the other hand, added it to her long list of Kian-related embarrassments.

Standing like a doofus by the door, she waited for him to be done.

It took Kian all of thirty seconds, and even that took as long only because he decided to include the bathroom in his sweep.

Her neighbor's cat decided to take advantage of the open door and perform an inspection of his own. Walking around the small space, his tail held high in the air, he gave Kian serious competition for the whole aloof, regal, everyone-is-beneath-me look.

Crossing paths, the two males stopped to face and size each other up, and granting each other their royal approval, continued on their way.

Syssi cracked up.

Add snorting laugh to the list, she admonished herself, but it was just too funny. It was a shame she hadn't recorded the exchange, it would've gone viral on YouTube.

"What's so funny?" Kian regarded her like she was short of a screw.

Covering her mouth with her hand to try and suppress the giggles, Syssi just pointed at him and then at the cat—who, sitting on his hind paws, waggled his tail in agitation, apparently disapproving of the giggling as well.

"Whatever it was, I'm glad my feline friend and I were able to make you laugh. It was our distinct pleasure to amuse you." Kian bowed theatrically, his hand almost touching the floor.

Some of Amanda's flair for the dramatic must've rubbed off on her brother.

Suspecting he didn't get to be this way often, she found his unexpected playfulness endearing. It made him seem more approachable, easing some of the discomforting effect he had on her.

Syssi realized she liked him, and not just for his amazing body and his beautiful face.

Blushing, she lowered her eyes. But then his silence compelled her to lift them back up, and her breath caught.

Kian was looking at her as if he was dying to kiss her. Except, it wasn't the predatory look from before. His eyes were soft and full of longing—a deep want that for some reason was shadowed by dark clouds of sorrow and regret.

Gazing into those sad blue eyes, she knew he wasn't going to do it, and she would forever wonder what kissing him would've felt like.

It's better to live dangerously than not live at all. Amanda's words echoed in her head.

On impulse, Syssi brought her palms up to his cheeks, touching them lightly with her fingertips. Kian closed his eyes and leaned into her caress. Bending his considerable frame to just the right height, he all but invited her to stretch up on her toes and kiss him.

Her kiss started soft, gentle, with their bodies barely touching. Kian held her almost reverently; one hand cradling the back of her head, the other around her waist.

It was a nice, sweet kiss, but it wasn't what she wanted. What she needed. Underneath his reserve and his tenderness, Syssi sensed the wild beast he was holding back.

She wanted it unleashed.

Pressing herself closer to him and feeling the hard ridges and planes of his powerful body, she wanted more of him. With her hands streaking into his soft hair, she grasped fistfuls of it and pulled him closer, a soft moan escaping her throat.

It was all the encouragement he needed.

In a split second, Syssi found herself pressed against the wall, the hand at the back of her head fisting her hair, the other cupping her butt and lifting her up. Kian positioned her so their bodies aligned, grinding his hard length against her pelvis.

Hot, demanding, powerful.

As his tongue pushed past her lips—exploring and dueling with hers, retracting and invading in a blatant imitation of the act of sex—she felt her core bloom for him, flooding with wetness.

Now, that was a kiss! Syssi acknowledged with the few brain cells still functioning. Raw and intense, it ignited a burn that was about to burst into an all-out fire.

Touch me, she implored Kian silently, her breasts tight and heavy, craving his touch.

With her silent plea ignored, she resorted to rubbing herself against his chest, hoping the friction would provide some sort of relief. But all too soon he retracted, leaving her bereft.

Both palms cradling her cheeks, he touched his forehead to hers and closed his eyes. For a moment, they both panted breathlessly, waiting for their racing hearts to slow down.

As Kian lifted his head and looked into her eyes with that sad and resigned expression from before, her heart sank. The odd roll of her stomach portended that Kian was leaving and wasn't planning on ever coming back.

The one time she was actually considering taking a guy she'd just met to her bed, he didn't want her.

Syssi shut her eyes against the pain, concentrating on memorizing the feel of Kian's thumb caressing her cheek. He waited until she reluctantly opened her eyes to look at him.

An odd light shone in his dark blue eyes as he kept her mesmerized with that intense gaze. "Good night, sweet Syssi, you had a long day, and you're very tired, you need to get some sleep."

She was... so very tired... so confused...

Shuffling her feet, Syssi barely made it to her bed before collapsing on it—fully clothed with her shoes still on.

CHAPTER 19: KIAN

Syssi was out for the night.

Standing next to the bed and watching her, Kian sighed and raked both hands through his hair.

The girl was proving difficult to resist.

She'd wanted him from the start, and even if he hadn't been able to scent her desire, it had been all over her expressive face—sweet and innocent in her shyness, still young and hopeful, so different from him.

He'd been tempted, breaking protocol and not taking his bodyguards with him so he could be alone with her. For a few moments, he'd even managed to convince himself that he was doing it for the clan.

Their future dependent on finding Dormants.

Except, he would've never forgiven himself if he'd taken her. It would've been deceitful, dishonorable. Kian had sacrificed enough of himself for the clan, for his family; the one thing he refused to give up was his self-respect, his honor.

As much as he craved her, he couldn't take what she so freely offered. The decent thing to do was to stay away.

Except, how could he?

When she had smiled at him, after his ridiculous bow, that radiant smile had transformed her from sweet and beautiful to spectacular, and he'd wanted to vow that he'd always make her smile like that. Even if it meant making a fool of himself, it would be well worth it just to hear her laugh and giggle, carefree and unreserved.

Gazing at her beautiful face, he wanted to stay. Not for sex, although he wanted that too, but to embrace her and hold her tightly, caress her hair and whisper sweet nothings in her ear. To amuse her, to make her happy.

Just one kiss, he'd thought a moment before she'd kissed him—she wouldn't remember it anyway.

He couldn't allow it.

Knowing he would be leaving soon and erasing himself from Syssi's memories—most likely never to see her again—had twisted a knot inside him, bringing on a sense of loss and resigned sadness.

But it was the right thing to do.

For Syssi's sake.

His thrall had buried and muddled her memory of the day's events, starting from the moment he'd entered the lab. All she'd remember tomorrow would be going home with a headache and collapsing on her bed. If at all, the memory of him might surface in her dreams, nothing more.

With a sigh, he removed her shoes and tucked the blanket around her, making sure her feet were covered.

And still, he couldn't make himself leave.

Looking down at her lovely face, he brushed a strand of hair away from her damp forehead.

What an inferno blazed beneath that shy, reserved exterior of hers. So much so that Kian could almost believe Syssi harbored some sweetly dark desires—the kind he would've been more than happy to fulfill.

He'd never find out, though, would he?

Was he foolishly stubborn, just as Amanda had accused?

Why was he fighting this so hard?

Was he truly doing the decent thing and being chivalrous?

Kian wished he had someone he could talk to. Someone to help him clear his head and sort through all these conflicting and confusing emotions. Except, there was no one he was comfortable enough with, or close enough to.

With one last brush of his fingertips against her smooth cheek, he headed for the door. And as he closed it quietly behind him, Tim Curry's "Sloe Gin" lyrics echoed in his head. *I'm so* ▨▨▨▨ *lonely.*

Kian shook his head as he walked down the long driveway back to his car, the cool air helping clear his head. He didn't have the luxury of allowing himself to wallow in self-pity. Even if a relationship with Syssi were possible, though he had no idea how such thing could've worked with a human, there was no place for it in his life. Running the clan's international business conglomerate and keeping his family safe from the Doomers required his full and undivided attention.

Unbidden, his thoughts drifted back to how this never-ending war had begun.

CHAPTER 20: KIAN

The story was one Kian had heard his mother tell many times. With each retelling, the details would change a little; some new tidbits added, others omitted. As a child, Kian had thought her forgetful, or fanciful. Only later, he'd realized that she'd been tailoring her story to her audience.

Besides, it wasn't as if anyone would've dared to accuse a goddess of forgetting, or making things up.

By now he had it memorized.

The tale would've sounded familiar to most mortals, as its distorted echoes had been recorded in the traditions of several of their cultures. Written in various languages, the names of the players had been changed and the story adapted to fit different agendas, different moralities, different sets of beliefs.

It had become a myth.

But as all timeless myths go, it had at its core a true story.

There had been a time when the gods lived among the mortals— bestowing their benevolence, providing knowledge and culture and helping humanity establish an advanced, moral and just society.

In gratitude, the people had worshiped the gods, expressing their adoration with offerings of their best goods and their freely donated labor.

Obviously, these gods hadn't been actual deities. Still, whether they had been the survivors of an earlier, superior civilization or refugees from somewhere else, his mother wouldn't say. She either didn't know or was keeping the knowledge to herself. Annani took her godly status very seriously and made sure everyone else did as well.

Perhaps she sought to elevate her grandness, as if it was needed or even possible, by shrouding her origins in mystery.

The gods had unimaginable powers. They could cast illusions so powerful that they fooled the minds of thousands. Their power over the human mind was so strong that their illusions not only looked and smelled real but even felt real to the touch. They could project thoughts and images into the unsuspecting, inferior minds of mortals, influencing everything from moods, to moral conduct, to a call to battle, all the way to divine revelation and inspiration.

Physically, they were perfect. Stunningly beautiful. Their bodies never aged or contracted diseases, and healed injuries in mere moments.

But they could still die.

Even the gods couldn't survive decapitation or withstand a nuclear blast. For which, unfortunately, they had the means.

They were few.

The limited gene pool combined with an extremely low conception rate prompted the gods to seek compatible mates among the mortals. Those unions proved to be more fruitful, and many near-immortal children were born. But when those children took human mates, their progeny turned out to be mortal.

Upon closer examination, their scientists found a way to activate the dormant, godly genes, but only for the children of the female immortals. The children of the males were sadly doomed to mortality.

Annani, one of the few pureblood children born to the gods, and the daughter of the leading couple, became the most coveted young goddess.

The one fortunate enough to mate her would become their next ruler.

The chain of events following her coming-of-age wasn't surprising. A fierce competition ensued between two suitors. Mortdh, the son of her father's brother and, therefore, the first in line for her hand, was her intended. And Khiann, the son of a less prominent, though wealthy family, who on the face of things didn't stand a chance.

But Annani was very young and impetuous, and she chose the one she loved and who loved her back. Not the one she was promised to, who never really cared for her and had already numerous concubines and children of his own.

Mortdh was infuriated and demanded she mate him, as was his right. But his right was superseded by her choice. The gods' code of conduct clearly stated that any mating, even one with a lowly mortal, had to be consensual.

Madly in love, Khiann and Annani were joined in a grand ceremony.

Both gods and mortals were so infatuated with the great love story that they wrote hymns and created myths to commemorate it.

Khiann and Annani's love was the story everyone loved to tell.

The tale of love's triumph.

It drove Mortdh insane. In his mind, he lost not only his one chance for sovereignty, but the respect of all.

And it was: All. Her. Fault.

His hatred of Annani, and by extension of all women, burned with rabid intensity. He detested the females' right to choose a mate, he abhorred the matrilineal tradition of the gods. He vowed to seize power and change all of that. Under his rule, women would have no rights. They would become property, to be purchased and sold like cattle. Heredity would cease to be matrilineal, the chains of power would become patriarchal.

In his hatred and madness, Mortdh did the unthinkable; an atrocity so great that it shook the ancient world.

He murdered Khiann.

He murdered a god.

Savagely took the life of Annani's one great love.

The laments sung to mourn Khiann's passing and to grieve for the great love so tragically lost would become a ritual to be performed every year on the anniversary of his death.

Annani's father called for the big assembly to decide Mortdh's fate. His crime was the gravest of all. To kill a god was so unthinkable, their law did not even contain a punishment severe enough for what he had done. As executing a god was not allowed, the most terrible sentencing in their code was entombment. And the full assembly of all gods was needed to sentence one of their own to that horrific fate.

A god would not perish in the tomb; slowly his body would cease to function, going into a kind of suspended state. But it took a long time, a very long time, until consciousness faded.

A decision of that severity required a unanimous vote.

Mortdh fled to his stronghold in the north. Together with his near-immortal son Navuh, he assembled an army of mortal soldiers and his other near-immortal progeny. In his deranged mind, he concluded that if he could not rule the gods, he would eliminate them.

Lording supreme over mortals and near-immortals would suffice.

The assembly of gods listened to all the undisputed evidence and voted unanimously to pass the sentence of entombment. Mortdh's parents planned to plead for their son. However, upon hearing the damning testimony, the cold cruelty of the premeditated murder, they realized they had no choice but to vote with the rest. Their son had become insanely dangerous and had to be stopped.

Annani sat on the council's deliberations, frozen in her grief. The only thing keeping her from collapsing into a despondent stupor was her need for vengeance. She had to hold on until the voting was done. She listened to the proceedings with her tears flowing down her cheeks and onto her lap. But when at last the voting was done and the sentence was passed, she felt no satisfaction.

She felt nothing but pain.

Annani wished she could die. Without her love, she had no reason to go on. There was nothing that could have filled the horrific void in her heart, and the agony of grief was more than she could endure.

Death would have been a mercy.

But as snippets of the debate pierced through the haze of her desperation, she forced herself to focus on what was being discussed, and was alarmed by what she heard. Apparently, the council had no clue how to detain Mortdh in order to execute the verdict.

Rumors of forces gathering under his banner suggested a war was brewing, and there was talk of assembling a force of their own. They were deliberating whether to go on the offensive and try to capture Mortdh, or remain in their stronghold and defend it against his attack.

From experience, Annani knew that the talk would go on endlessly, producing no definite action. What was the point of the sentencing if it could not be executed? How would her justice be served? Who would capture Mortdh? What if he attacked first and won?

If he ever captured her, her fate would be worse than death. Of that she had no doubt.

True to her nature, Annani did not hesitate long before deciding on a course of action.

She was going to run away.

She would take her flying machine and her love's precious gift of seven biomechanical servants and fly to a distant land the gods had never graced.

Mortdh would never find her.

Untouched by the gods, it would most likely be a primitive place, one without culture or an established society.

She would have to start a new civilization.

To accomplish that, she would need a set of instructions and a trove of knowledge. But then again, Annani knew exactly where to get it. She would steal her uncle's library, which contained much of her people's science and culture and was stored on a tablet she had seen him read often. He had even let her borrow it on occasion.

That decision and its prompt execution saved her life and the future fate of humanity.

That same night, while the gods still deliberated, Mortdh flew his aircraft over the council's fortress and dropped a nuclear bomb.

The only weapon guaranteed to kill the gods.

The devastation was so widespread that over half of the region's population died along with their gods. The nuclear wind carried the fingers of death far and wide, decimating everything alive on its way.

Including Mortdh.

Out of the ashes and ruins, humans and near-immortals rose and tried to survive on what was left. Nothing grew, and those the nuclear wind spared, hunger took.

The human population kept dying.

The near-immortals, as children of the gods, had bodies that could survive longer and heal faster and should have fared better. Some of them must have made it to distant lands and built new lives.

Annani sincerely hoped that indeed that was the case. Though over the next five millennia she encountered none.

The only part of the region unaffected by the nuclear devastation was its northern tip. Mortdh's stronghold. With Mortdh's death, his eldest son Navuh took over leadership of his people; several hundred mortal and near-immortal warriors along with their female broodmares.

Most of the unfortunate women had been mortal, but a few must have been Dormant or near-immortal because Navuh's immortal army had kept growing through the millennia, and with it, his power and his sphere of influence.

Navuh had sworn to uphold his father's vision of the new world order. And with his tight grip on the region's leaders, he had succeeded in plunging that part of the world into darkness and oppression the likes of which had never been known before.

It had been worse for the women.

They had become cattle: to be owned and sold by their fathers or brothers, to be bought by their husbands and discarded at their whim. They had been stripped of all personal rights. For all intents and purposes, women had ceased to be considered people. They had become things. Patriarchy had been born and was there to stay.

Annani fled to the far, desolate and frozen north. She never stayed in one place long, always fearing she would be found. Slowly, though, rumors of the disaster that befell Mesopotamia found their way up to her icy hideout, and she learned she was the last of her kind.

The only remaining goddess alive.

By now, all traces of the carefree young woman she used to be were gone. With her heart frozen just like her new home, she was numb and emotionless and lacked the motivation to do aught but get by.

And yet, she had to survive, for she was the custodian of a treasure: the knowledge, culture, and ideology of her kin.

The future of humanity was in her hands.

Without her, Navuh's darkness would spread until it consumed everything decent in the world.

She could not, would not, allow that to happen.

For five years, Annani ran and hid and survived with the help of her servants who made sure she at least had food and shelter.

Eventually, her grief and pain subsided sufficiently to allow her to move on. Not to forget, and not to stop hurting—that was never going to happen—but to start on her monumental task.

During her self-imposed stasis, she spent a lot of time thinking and realized she couldn't do it alone. She needed to create more of herself.

Annani knew of only one way to achieve that.

She had to procreate.

Except, she vowed never to love again. Her heart would forever belong to her one true love. Her soul would remain faithful to Khiann's memory.

To produce offspring, she would share her body with her mortal lovers, but nothing more.

She took many, using them and discarding them in short order. After the deed, she would fuddle her partner's mind, leaving behind a dreamlike memory of a heavenly encounter.

For the males it was no hardship to be used like that; after all, she was the most beautiful woman in the world. And to her surprise, Annani discovered it was not a great hardship for her either.

Her heart might have been frozen, but her body roared to life with insatiable heat.

Over the next five millennia, Annani was blessed with five children. Her first child was born after three thousand years, during which she almost despaired of ever conceiving.

Alena, her eldest, proved to be a blessing beyond measure. For an immortal, she was a miracle of fertility, delivering thirteen wonderful children in the span of five hundred years.

Kian was next, born only a few decades after Alena. Annani named her firstborn son in memory of her lost love. Except, she changed it a little as to not bait the fates. Kian would become the most instrumental in her quest to enlighten humanity.

A millennium later, sweet Lilen arrived. He grew to become a kind and brave man, well-liked by everyone. His tragic loss in battle plunged his mother back into the depths of despair, where she lingered till the birth of her daughter Sari pulled her out of that dark vortex.

Last but not least of the children was Amanda. The very young, and until recently, wild party-girl. The princess, as everyone called her.

Annani had never revealed the identity of the fathers, but she'd described them in detail, alleviating her children's natural curiosity.

They had been the most magnificent men. She had chosen the strongest, the smartest, and most handsome males. They had been the fiercest warriors and natural leaders among their kind.

Kian wondered if the image she had painted for her children hadn't been exaggerated. Mere mortals were not that great. Had she done it for her children's sake? Her own? Had she even known whose seed had taken root? Or perhaps, she had just believed them to be so sublime because she had never stayed long enough to get to know them all that well.

With the human population growing and spreading to new and distant lands, Annani's clan needed two geographically strategic centers of operation. Kian had moved with some of the clan from Scotland to America, and Sari had taken over the European center, becoming his counterpart in the old country.

Annani's influence in the Western Hemisphere had grown. The gods' knowledge and wisdom had been slowly trickled to the mortals, helping them to evolve into the advanced society they would one day become. But the progress had been slow, thwarted time and again by Navuh's destructive power.

The Devout Order of Mortdh, as Navuh called his army of ruthless killers, was a formidable foe.

Lacking the intellectual resources Annani had stolen must have chafed terribly, as the Doomers had made a religion out of destroying and halting any progress she had helped mortal society achieve, whether scientific or social. Their dark sphere of influence had encompassed at times the majority of the civilized world. And each time, it had taken Annani and her clan centuries to recoup and push back the evils of ignorance and hate.

Annani's clan was small, numbering in the low hundreds, its slow growth limited by its single matrilineal line.

The Doomers, on the other hand, were legion.

As far as Kian could ascertain, they had an advantage from the start, with Navuh inheriting a few near-immortal or Dormant females from his father.

They must've guarded these females fiercely, as none had ever made it out of the Doomers' clutches.

Heavens knew, Kian and his nephews had searched near and far for centuries. They had followed rumors and fantastic tales of witches, nymphs, succubi, and other mythical creatures, in the hopes of finding an immortal female at the source of the stories. But as time and again the clues had led to nothing, they had eventually stopped looking; reluctantly accepting their fate.

Outnumbered and outmuscled, the clan's best strategy had always been to hide.

They had lived quietly and unassumingly, avoiding any undue attention. Of course, the ability to create illusions and erase memories had been instrumental in that effect.

Taking advantage of their sophisticated knowledge base, slowly but surely, they had developed a shrouded economic empire.

Owned and operated under myriad identities and entities, the clan's holdings included land, coal and ore mines, banks, manufacturing facilities, hotels and other real estate all over the world, adding in modern times a trove of patents and technology-based enterprises.

Occasionally, the Doomers had managed to snare a clan member, and several males had been lost that way. Kian shuddered at the prospect of the Doomers ever catching a clan female.

In their hands, she would long for an end that would never come.

Now, as the rules of the game had been irrevocably changed, Kian would have to reevaluate the clan's time-trusted strategy.

Annani was safe in her Alaskan shrouded fortress. The place was extremely well hidden under a manufactured dome of ice; undetectable even with the help of satellites. The only way in and out was on a specially designed aircraft, piloted by one of her trusted Odu servants. Even Kian couldn't find the place on his own.

Sari and the European clan should be fine as well. They all lived in their Scottish stronghold, which was defended with the help of the best surveillance equipment there was and clouded by its occupants in a perpetually maintained illusion.

That left his people.

They were scattered all over California and trusted their safety to living unseen among millions of mortals.

This would have to change.

Kian grimaced, imagining the hell they'd give him when he suggested moving them all into his secure keep: first the council members, and then the rest.

Unfortunately, he couldn't just order it; every major decision required a vote. And wasn't that a damn shame. But then again, he had an ace up his sleeve that guaranteed the vote would go in his favor.

CHAPTER 21: ANDREW

"What do you think?" Andrew's boss leaned over his shoulder to look at the photos attached to the file Andrew was reading.

"Apparently, business is booming in Maldives, judging by the sudden increase in visitors from that country over the last couple of weeks."

Arriving within days of each other, three groups of "businessmen" from that tiny country had entered the United States through the Los Angeles International Airport.

His boss tapped the top row of photos. "What alerted security, beyond Maldives being a godforsaken bunch of insignificant islands with no industry to speak of, was that each group consisted of four young male members. Too young to be businessman, and too heavily muscled. Besides, these bushy beards are an excellent disguise. They will be unrecognizable once they shave them off."

Airport security had used this oddity as an excuse to forward the information to their department without the risk of being accused of profiling. Looking at the security camera photos of the twelve young men, Andrew grimaced. Businessmen. What kind of businessmen looked like that? None that he had ever met. Not that he had met that many.

Be that as it may, it was a shame that airport security needed an excuse to report characters that would've raised the suspicion of anyone with half a brain. In his opinion, outlawing profiling was a perfect example of political correctness gone too far.

The vast majority of terrorists were young men between the ages of eighteen to twenty-five. In fact, most violent crimes were perpetrated by the male members of this age group. Seventy-year-old grandmothers and five-year-old girls posed a very remote security risk, so did families with small children. By considering everyone an equal opportunity threat, Homeland Security was wasting its limited resources and increasing the risk of missing the real thing.

Like these boys.

"I wonder what kind of trouble they are up to." His boss straightened and pulled his pants up over his hefty belly. It was hard to believe that once upon a time the guy had been a warrior in an elite unit.

Andrew smirked. "The bunch wouldn't have raised suspicion if

Maldives were happening to compete in an international pro-wrestling tournament, and these impressive specimens were the team members."

The men exuded health and vitality, the kind that came from strenuous physical activity, and their straight and sure postures were those of well-trained soldiers.

The boss was of the same opinion. "They look like Marines."

The guys were all tall and seemed to be of several different ethnicities. One was Asian—a tough-looking fellow, and two looked like they were of Scandinavian descent—handsome, blond, blue-eyed devils. They kind of reminded Andrew of his Special Ops buddies and the way the motley bunch had looked coming back from a mission with their suntanned faces covered by several weeks' worth of growth.

"Find out where they are staying and what they are doing. The report mentions three different hotels the men listed for their stay."

"I'll follow up on this tomorrow and see if they ever checked in."

The boss clapped him on the shoulder. "You do that. Now get your ass out of here and go home."

As was his habit, Andrew was the last one in the office. The other agents had families to go home to, but there was no one waiting for him at his house. Tonight, though, he had plans; a date with his sparring partner down at the gym, and if she was in the mood, a romp later on.

Susanna was another *analyst* in his department, which meant that she still went on missions abroad same as he. What had started as an easy camaraderie, had quickly turned into a "friends with benefits" arrangement.

At first, he had been wary of taking their friendship to the next level. According to conventional wisdom, a workplace fling was a disaster waiting to happen. But it had worked out fine. Neither had any expectations or treated it as an exclusive arrangement. They were just scratching each other's itch.

Andrew couldn't allow for anything more and neither could she. Not as long as they were still going on active missions. For him, the party was going to end soon. He was about to hit the dreaded forty. Susanna still had time before the powers that be chained her to a desk.

When he got down to the gym, Susanna was the only one there.

"You're late," she said from behind the punching bag she was practicing her kicks on. The woman was one hell of a martial arts enthusiast.

"Sorry about that. I just had another file dropped on my desk. The boss wanted me to take a quick look at it."

She delivered a punch and followed it with a kick. "Anything interesting?"

"I don't know yet. Tomorrow, I'll know more. It might be nothing, just a bunch of kids touring the States."

She slanted him a knowing look. "But you have a hunch they are up to something."

Andrew rubbed his neck. "Yeah, a gut feeling. By the look of them, they are either athletes or soldiers, but I'm betting on the second one. Their postures give them away. Put uniforms on them and they can easily impersonate Marines."

She chuckled. "You mean they look like they have sticks up their butts?"

Andrew narrowed his eyes at her. "Watch it. I was a Marine once."

Susanna executed a series of quick jabs. "And how long did it take you to lose that posture so it wouldn't give you away?"

Andrew snorted. "Months. I don't know why they bother to recruit from the Marines when they want guys who can blend in."

"I guess because of the training and the stamina." Susanna took off her gloves and sauntered up to him. "Talking about stamina, how about we skip the workout and check out what you've got?"

Andrew grinned and wrapped his arm around her muscular shoulders. "I'm all for it."

"I thought you would be."

CHAPTER 22: KIAN

A little after eight, Kian closed the file on a property in Maui he'd been trying to read for the past half an hour and walked out of his home office.

"Do you have my robe ready?" he asked Okidu.

"It is freshly ironed and hanging on a hook by the front door. Let me get it for you, Master."

"Thank you."

As Okidu handed him the robe, Kian draped it over his shoulders and headed for the underground complex.

Once he reached the Grand Council Hall, Kian flicked on the lights and took a good look around. He hadn't seen the amphitheater-style auditorium since he'd inspected the newly completed building four years ago.

The room's opulence and grand size was reminiscent of a bygone era of indulgence, representing Kian's largest splurge on the clan's headquarters. Working from what he'd remembered of his mother's descriptions, he'd tried to replicate the gods' council chamber as best he could.

Semicircle rows of comfortable red-velvet seats formed a horseshoe pattern, and large columns held graceful arches with murals and plaster reliefs depicting mythical scenes. Exquisite detailing adorned mosaic-inlayed marble floors, and the staircase leading to the second-floor balcony featured elaborate plaster moldings and brass rails.

At four hundred seats, the council hall could accommodate all of his clan's American members with room to spare. And just to be on the safe side, the currently unfurnished second-floor balcony could house an additional two hundred seats if needed.

Kian had no idea what had possessed him to build it on such a grand scale. Between his two hundred and eighty-three, Sari's one hundred and ninety-six, and his mother's seventy-two the whole clan numbered five hundred fifty-one members. What were the chances of all of them gracing his keep at the same time?

Probably none.

But he liked to plan big and prepare for all conceivable contingencies. Perhaps in the future a monumental event, hopefully a celebration, would require the presence of each and every clan member.

The chamber had turned out exactly as he had envisioned it. Well, with the exception of the council members' seats that were still just as ugly as the first time he had seen them, and were proof that contrary to what everyone thought of him, he had the capacity for compromise.

Sitting on the raised platform, arranged in an arc to face the audience, the thirteen throne-like monstrosities had been Amanda's choice. She'd somehow managed to convince Ingrid the interior designer to back her up, and so despite his protests the ostentatious gaudy things had stayed.

Some battles were just not worth fighting.

Still, as he sat on his regent seat, stretching his long legs and bracing his arms on the heavy armrests, Kian had to admit that the thing, albeit an eyesore, was comfortable. His seat was in the center, with the six council members to his right and the six Guardians to his left. Onegus, as chief guardian, sat on the council side.

Glancing behind him, he made sure that the two large movable screens at the back of the stage were at the optimal angle for teleconferencing Mark's service. After he had talked it over with his mother and Sari, it had been agreed that tomorrow night all members of the clan would take part in the ceremony.

Satisfied with the screens, he shifted his focus to the multiple rows of plush seats. Damn, the room was huge. Too big for the small council meeting he'd called for.

Reaching under the robe's voluminous folds into his pants pocket, he pulled out his phone and called his secretary. "Shai, we need a smaller room for future council meetings. Call Ingrid, have her choose a suitably sized room and prepare a design for it. I want it on my desk by tomorrow morning."

"It shall be done." Shai clicked off.

With a sigh, Kian pushed to his feet and walked over to the six light switches located near the entry doors. Flipping each one on and off, he eventually figured which one controlled what and turned off the lights over the audience section, plunging it back into the shadows.

Walking back to his seat, it suddenly dawned on him that he was micromanaging everything.

Did he really care how the new small council room would look? He should delegate the whole thing to Ingrid and give her free rein to do as she pleased, trusting her to do it right.

Yeah, like those ▓▓damn awful chairs.

Except, this was the whole point, wasn't it. If he wanted to free up any of his time, he'd have to deal with these kinds of insignificant petty annoyances. His obsessive need to control each and every detail had worked in simpler times. Now it was hindering his performance.

He had to rethink the way he was doing things.

Some of his workload would have to be relinquished to others. Though knowing himself, trusting them to do it well and then living with the consequences would be tough.

Kian planted his ass on his throne and waited in the empty auditorium for his people to arrive—not because anyone was late, but because he'd gotten there early to make sure everything was in order.

Just another example of his OCD...

As if Shai couldn't have done it for him.

Tapping his fingers on the armrests, he watched the door, expecting the Guardians to get there first.

Tradition dictated that the council's meeting place had to be secured and protected prior to the arrival of its distinguished members. Though with safety not being an issue in the bowels of the keep, the men would be upholding the custom more out of respect, or maybe habit. Still, he had no doubt they would be arriving soon.

Besides Kri, their most recent female addition, the six men were seasoned warriors who'd been serving in this capacity for centuries and were likely to stick to doing things the way they had always been done.

Anandur and Brundar were the oldest, serving with him for over a thousand years. Born of the same mother and two very different sires, they were nothing alike.

Besides both being deadly, that is.

On the surface of things, Anandur appeared charming and easygoing, always ready to jest and pull pranks. But as a stalwart defender of the clan, the guy was a ruthless slayer of its enemies. His tactic of projecting a demonic visage of himself into his opponents' minds and scaring them shitless was his kind of a cruel joke. They either ran for their lives or died believing they were going to hell.

Brundar was still an enigma after all the long years he had been serving as Kian's bodyguard. Besides his brother, no one really knew him, and Kian wondered how well even Anandur did. Brundar was aloof, secretive and somber. Rumors hinted he had a sadistic streak, others that he was a masochist. One had to wonder, though, how someone that couldn't stand being touched could enjoy being at the mercy of another.

Brundar looked like an angel; a vengeful, deadly angel of wrath. Possessing unparalleled skill and agility, he had perfect aim with any kind of projectile weapon and complete mastery with any kind of blade.

Just as Kian had expected, the brothers made it first, Onegus walking in right behind them.

"Good evening, Kian," Onegus said. The brothers nodded their greeting.

As Brundar climbed the three stairs and took his seat, Anandur stopped for a curtsy, lifting his robe's tails like a lady's gown and batting his red eyelashes at Kian.

The guy just couldn't help his compulsion to clown around, despite it being highly inappropriate considering the circumstances that had brought them here.

Nevertheless, for once Kian was grateful for the comic relief.

Onegus, on the other hand, didn't share his leniency, flicking the top of Anandur's head. "Show some respect!" He pinned the redhead with a hard stare before taking his seat.

It was doubtful Anandur had felt the flick through the cushion of his crinkly hair, but he rubbed at his scalp as he looked at his superior. "It's not my fault that you have no sense of humor."

"Oh, just shut up." Onegus was clearly not in the mood to carry on with the guy, and rightfully so.

What often started with Anandur goofing around, ended up with a sparring match at the gym where the big oaf ruled as an undisputed champion. So unless Onegus wanted to pull rank, he was smart to nip the thing in the bud.

An inch or two shorter than Anandur, Onegus was still quite tall but not as burly, more on the lean, athletic side. With smiling brown eyes, curly blond hair, and a million dollar smile, he claimed to be more of a lover than a fighter, which, of course, was total crap. Still, it was true that he often used that charm as a weapon in his diplomatic capacity on Kian's behalf and to his own benefit with the ladies.

"I'm telling you; the assholes didn't know he was one of us!" Kri's agitated voice turned Kian's attention away from the guys. He glanced at the door as she entered the room while arguing with the stoic Yamanu.

For all intents and purposes, Kri was as good as invisible next to that guy. Yamanu had this effect on people, his startling looks commanding everyone's attention to the exclusion of everything else. Which might have been the reason Yamanu hardly ever left the keep. Except, that raised another important question... How the hell did he manage to get any sex without prowling the clubs and bars?

Not that he would have had to work hard for it, towering as he did at six and a half feet and built like a sculptor's fantasy of how a male body should look. And as if that was not enough, Yamanu wore his shiny, black hair in a straight curtain that fell down to his waist.

His most startling feature, though, were his hypnotic, pale blue eyes, strange and out of place in his dark, angular face.

Yamanu was a master illusionist with an ability as powerful as that of the gods of old. His illusions could alter the perception of reality in thousands of mortal minds, providing a sense of touch, smell, and sound, in addition to sight. On more than one occasion, this unique talent of his had saved the clan from serious trouble.

With hordes of mortals attacking anything in their path, Kian's small force of warriors hadn't stood a chance, and though his people were hard to kill, a sword could sever a mortal's or immortal's head with the same ease. Even worse, the thought of what those savages could've done to the females if they had gotten past his warriors' defenses... and the children...

Hell, he'd better not go there if he wanted his head clear for the meeting.

The last Guardians entering were the somber duo from the Bay Area; Bhathian and Arwel.

The two looked worn out and miserable, but the sad truth was that it hadn't been the recent tragedy that had caused their misery. It had just amplified it.

Bhathian always looked pissed off. If not for the unpleasant vibe emanating from him, the big guy could've been considered handsome. His tall muscular frame and strong face were certainly attractive. As it was though, his angry expression and sheer size made him look more like an ogre. And Arwel, with his out-of-control empathetic ability, was wearing a perpetually tormented expression.

Regardless of their disparate physiques and temperaments, Kian had to admit that the seven Guardians formed an impressive, unified front in their formal ceremonial attire. Onegus's robe as both Guardian and councilman was white with a double edge of black and silver, the others were black with a single silver edge.

Kian's, in his opinion, was ridiculous. Made of blood-red velvet and edged in black, silver, and white it looked like a glitzy monarch's costume. The despotic getup was only missing a crown and scepter. But be that as it may, he had no intention of arguing with his mother over her choice of formal robes. Not that it would've done him any good.

The doors pushed open again as Shai and the four council members he was escorting entered the room. Acting as if he'd designed the place himself, Shai flicked all the lights back on. Pointing proudly, he explained the chamber's features and decor, "...we have four hundred seats down here, and two hundred more can be added on the balcony. The room is decorated in the Neo-Grecian style…"

Kian tuned Shai out, focusing on the council members instead.

Bridget, the local clan's only MD, had her medical and research facilities located in the building's underground, and they bumped into each other on occasion.

Kian liked and respected the pretty redhead, with her pleasant and unassuming demeanor. It never ceased to amaze him that a woman so petite could break and reset badly fused broken bones with ease. It was one of the few things a near-immortal needed medical care for; delivering babies and sewing up the more serious wounds being the other two. All were rare occurrences, which left Bridget with plenty of time to research their kind's unique biology.

Edna, a brilliant attorney and an expert on clan law, oversaw the legal aspects of their business transactions and presided over clan members' trials.

Besides her sharp mind, Edna was a tough cookie, which was the main reason Kian had chosen her as his replacement in case something happened to him. He could trust her to handle the job. That didn't mean that the rest of the clan would be happy with her at the helm. She was known as a harsh and unforgiving judge, and though respected, wasn't well liked.

Kian couldn't remember seeing the woman ever smiling, and her looks matched her austere attitude. Edna didn't bother with making herself pretty. If anything, the opposite was true. It must have been a deliberate effort for her to look so plain. Her brown hair was tied in a severe knot on her nape, she wore no makeup, and the ceremonial robe was a big improvement over her daily wardrobe of ill-fitting pantsuits.

Edna's one saving grace was her eyes. They shone with intelligence and the kind of understanding that delved into the most hidden places of her victims' souls, reaching behind their mental shields and baring all of their nasty secrets. It was quite unnerving, as Kian remembered from personal experience. It was also a rare ability. Normally, immortals couldn't penetrate each other's minds, only those of humans. Annani could, but then she was a full-blooded goddess.

Because of her unique talent, Edna was nicknamed the Alien Probe.

William, the Science Guy as everyone called him, was the opposite. Good-natured and bubbly, he looked like a chubby bear, proving that even superior genes couldn't combat the consequences of a big appetite. William liked to eat a lot, while sitting in front of the computer, or the television, or with company. He was the go-to guy for all things technological—one of the few smart enough to translate and comprehend the technical information contained in the ancient gods' tablet.

Walking between Edna and William, the suave Brandon stood out like a peacock amongst ducks. In charge of culture and media, his job was to promote books, movies, TV shows, and magazine stories; advocating the gods' social agenda—starting with democracy, through equal rights, to education and research—the list was long.

By portraying the desired state as an expressed ideal, enacting it in stories, plays, and movies, mortals assimilated the message. To strive for something better, people had to imagine it first to be aware of the possibility.

Understanding this dynamic, oppressive regimes denied their people free access to these sources, fearing the exposure to new and better ideas would promote social unrest. Demonizing the cultures that produced the dangerous materials served as a deterrent to their ignorant and brainwashed masses against seeking the corrupt, immoral, evil, etc. sources of information.

Unfortunately, there was little Kian could do to bring enlightenment to those closed-off regions, and their populations were falling further and further behind the Western world.

He often asked himself what came first: Navuh finding fertile ground for his propaganda in these places, or his propaganda creating the atmosphere in which oppressive regimes could gain power.

The fact remained, though; wherever women were marginalized, considered inferior, and denied rights available to men, the society as a whole lagged behind.

No exceptions.

"Would someone please open for me?" Amanda called for help while kicking the doors.

As Shai rushed over to let her in, she handed him one of the two Starbucks trays she had been carrying. Besides the trays, she also managed to hold onto a paper bag full of bottled drinks, her robe, and her purse.

"Sorry I'm late, everyone. I had to have coffee and stopped at Starbucks, but then figured it would be rude to be the only one with a cappuccino, so I brought some more."

Brandon relieved her of the other tray and the bag, then together with Shai they passed the drinks around.

"Thank you, guys." Amanda put on her robe and took a look around. "Kian, this is so not the place to have a small council meeting in; it's huge! We need a small room, one with a table to put our drinks on." She took the last vacant chair next to Onegus.

Kian shook his head. It was so like Amanda to ignore everyone and everything and just say whatever popped into her head.

"Already on it. Can we begin now?" he asked as he pushed to his feet and turned to face the council.

"Hold for one more second, I'm starting the recording!" Shai called from his command station at the controls of the sophisticated equipment.

Kian waited for the guy to give the thumbs-up before he began again.

"Okay. This is council meeting?" He had forgotten to check the number of the last session.

"Four hundred and twelve!" Shai supplied.

"Thank you." Having a secretary with eidetic memory was definitely convenient.

"This is council meeting four hundred and twelve. All members present." Kian recited the standard opening sentence meant for record keeping.

Taking a deep breath, he addressed the council. "Last night, Mark son of Micah, was murdered by the DOOM Brotherhood in his own home." Kian paused for a moment, waiting for everyone's shocked responses of disbelief and sorrow to settle down.

"We were dealt a monumental blow. Beyond losing a beloved family member, the loss of his incredible talent will hinder our progress in developing the software that could potentially save the world by disabling the weapons meant for its destruction." Looking at their worried and pained expressions, he added in a softer tone, "Bhathian and Arwel brought his body home, and the service in his honor will be held tomorrow at midnight." Kian looked at their faces as each member gave him a somber nod of agreement.

His next request wouldn't meet with such easy acquiescence. Bracing for the inevitable argument, Kian gripped the lapels of his robe and fixed the council with a hard stare.

"Until the level of threat is ascertained, I move to seclude all council members in our secure building. We can't afford to lose any of you, and we don't have enough Guardians to provide each member with a security detail. You'll have to cancel any appointments you had scheduled for the time being. I'm sorry for the inconvenience, but I see no other option."

"I don't know how anybody can find us among the mortals, there is nothing pointing to us," Brandon protested. "We can't be prisoners in your glass tower; you know we need to consort with mortals for obvious reasons."

Kian had been expecting someone to raise that objection. "At this point, we don't know how much the Doomers know. Mark's laptop and sat-phone are missing. We can only hope they don't have anyone capable enough to break through his firewalls. And besides, there might have been other clues at his house that can lead to us. I'm not willing to take unnecessary risks. As to being prisoners, you can still go to clubs, bars, restaurants, and whatever random places you like. I just don't want you anywhere near your habitual meeting or workplaces."

"If they try to break into his laptop, it will self-corrupt all info. Same for the phone, I'm not worried," William offered.

"What if they have someone of Mark's caliber?" Kian kept playing the devil's advocate.

William snorted. "Then we're screwed, but they don't. No one has."

"Did you inform Mother and Sari?" Amanda looked at Kian with her big, sad eyes, ignoring the whole seclusion discussion. She'd already expressed her opinion about this idea earlier. Hopefully, she wouldn't stir things up and embarrass him in front of the entire council.

"I called them shortly after Arwel delivered the news. Tomorrow during the service both of them, together with their people, will be with us via teleconferencing. The whole clan will take part in Mark's final journey."

"Thank you," she said in a small voice.

He was glad she hadn't argued with him about the seclusion, but it pained him to see Amanda's usually animated face look defeated as she sank back into her chair.

"I think you're being overly cautious, but let's vote on it!" Edna went straight to the point, probably under the assumption that the council would vote against Kian.

But he had an ace up his sleeve.

"As this is a security issue, the Guardians will take part in the vote."

This was another advantage of keeping the council members in the dark about the subject of this meeting. Edna hadn't thought to check the emergency bylaws. Not that she could've done anything to stop him if she had known. The council members had no chance; they were as good as tied and locked.

The Guardians always voted with Kian.

"Let's see then. All in favor of seclusion, raise your hands!" he called.

The Seven Guardians and Kian all raised their hands, and so did Bridget. Not a big surprise since she already lived in the keep. Defeated, William and Edna joined the show of hands.

That left two.

Brandon shrugged. "Well, what do you know, vacation time for me! I'll finally get to see all the *Battlestar Galactica* episodes."

Kian glanced at Amanda, expecting her to argue, but she didn't. Evidently, the experience at the lab had scared her into compliance.

CHAPTER 23: SYSSI

The nightmare was back.

Terrified, Syssi was running away from a pack of snarling wolves. With the moon obscured by dark clouds and the dense canopy of tall trees, the barely visible trail was illuminated only by a darting speck of light. Following it, Syssi prayed she wouldn't stumble and fall.

All alone in the foreboding darkness, the huge monsters' red glowing eyes and sharp fangs never far behind, she was defenseless.

Soon, she wouldn't be able to run anymore, and they'd get her. Rip her apart.

How did I get here?

Why are they chasing me?

Desperate tears streaming down her cheeks, Syssi kept running, when up ahead in the distance she glimpsed something that gave her a glimmer of hope. Hidden under the dark shadows cast by the thick limbs of a tree was a silhouette of what looked like a tall man.

"Help me!" Syssi called to him.

There was no response.

Was he even real? Or was her mind playing tricks on her? Desperately searching for a pattern in what was nothing more than rocks and bushes loosely resembling a human form?

But what choice did she have?

It was either find help or die a horrific death.

She had nothing to lose by changing direction and running toward him. If there was nothing there, she would just keep on running. Until she could run no more.

But as she got closer, and it became apparent that the man wasn't a figment of her imagination, hope and relief bloomed in Syssi's chest.

"Help!" she yelled again. But he ignored her, his gaze fixed on the pursuing red eyes.

"Help me! Damn you!" Syssi shook his arm, forcing him to look at her.

Finally he turned, shifting his intense eyes to her. "No need to yell, Syssi. Get behind me." He turned back to stare at the rapidly approaching wolves.

How did he know her name? Did she know him? She would've remembered someone like him. The man was stunningly beautiful.

What a strange thing to notice at a time like this.

Never mind. He is going to help me.

Hiding behind his large frame, she watched the wolves burst out of the tree line and circle them, snarling; their horrid yellow fangs dripping with fetid saliva.

The man raised his hands and snarled back at the wolves, exposing a pair of huge, acid-dripping fangs.

Acid?

What made her think it was acid?

Oh, right, the dirt sizzled where drops of it fell.

The wolves began backing away with their tails curled under their bellies, still snarling and drooling at her rescuer as they made their retreat.

"Run! You mangy cowardly dogs! Not so brave now, are you?" she taunted the wolves from her safe spot behind the guy's back.

The wolves turned and ran into the thicket, leaving her alone with the stranger.

"Thank you. You saved my life. I don't want to think what would've happened if you weren't here to help me." Syssi smiled at him. The guy was so tall that she had to crank her neck way up to look at him.

"You should keep on running, Syssi. There is a reason the wolves fear me, I'm a monster too." He flashed his fangs.

Was he trying to scare her off? She wasn't afraid of him.

"Why aren't you running?" he asked when she didn't budge.

"How can you say that? You're not a monster. You're a hero!" Syssi stretched up on her toes and kissed him on the lips.

"Are you crazy? What are you doing? You'll get burned by the acid!" The man brought his thumb to her lips and wiped them vigorously.

"Your acid is harmful only to the demon wolves. It tastes good to me." She licked her lips and smiled, coyly inviting another kiss.

"You have no idea what you're asking for," he growled, looking at her menacingly and flashing his sharp fangs again.

But then a small, terrible smile curled his lips, and his lids dropped halfway over his eyes. "Do you want these fangs piercing the skin of your neck? Do you want me to bite you?" It sounded more like a promise than a threat.

"Will it hurt?" Syssi asked in a small voice.

"Yes, it will. But it will also bring you intense pleasure. Do you feel adventurous?" He dipped his head and brought his lips to the base of her neck. Not touching. Threatening.

"Then I want you to," Syssi whispered, brushing her hair away to give him better access. And yet, despite her brave words her heart began beating faster and she closed her eyes, her excitement tinged by fear.

"Why?" he whispered in her ear, brushing his lips lightly against her neck.

Shocking herself, Syssi blurted throatily, "Because I want you to make love to me."

Hey, it's my dream...

Yes, she realized—this was only a dream.

Good. Inside her own head, she could be as brazen as she wanted to.

"Would you?" she asked.

"I don't know how." He turned away from her.

Incredulous, Syssi gasped. "Have you never done it before?" There was no way a man like him wasn't constantly propositioned by women. His celibacy could only be explained by religious prohibition, perhaps priesthood. Or maybe he was a monk. Except, he didn't seem like either.

"It was so long ago, I forgot how." He sounded dejected.

At least he wasn't a virgin. But she was curious about his decision to abstain. "Did you take a vow of celibacy? Join a monastery?"

But then, as she thought more about it—

Wait! There could be another explanation. What if he can't? What if he has a condition, and I'm making it so much worse for him?

Talk about putting one's foot in one's mouth.

With a sinister smile on his beautiful face, he dipped his head to look into her eyes. "No, I didn't abstain, I had plenty of sex, just not the kind that qualifies as lovemaking," he said sarcastically.

"Oh..." What was she supposed to say to that? Suspecting she knew the answer, she asked anyway. "What's the difference?"

The way his expression turned predatory seemed familiar for some reason. Had they met before? She would have remembered him. Really not the kind of guy she could've ever forgotten.

"One is the gentle lovey-dovey kind a girl like you likes, the kind you have with someone you care about. The other is just a fuck, rough and intense, so much so that it sometimes hurts. But you don't give a damn because it hurts so good. Not something a good girl like you knows anything about or wants." He gave her a haughty, condescending look.

Who did he think he was? Assuming things about her? Even if they were true? Still, he had no right.

"How would you know? You know nothing about me," she protested. "Don't presume what I know or what I want."

"Fair enough, although I'm in your head, so I should know. But I'll ask anyway; what do you want, Syssi?"

Now, wasn't that the million dollar question. What did she want?

Thinking, she bit down on her bottom lip and looked down at her feet, when out of nowhere a memory surfaced, flooding her with intense desire.

Syssi remembered being pressed against a wall, a man's hand fisting her hair, pulling just hard enough to provide the smidgen of pain that was driving her wild. He was kissing her, grinding himself against her, his ferocity and intensity making her wet and needy. She'd urged him to do more, but he'd withdrawn, leaving her unsatisfied.

It had been him! The same guy...

Why couldn't she remember his name?

Was it Cain? Kaen?

"I remember you. You kissed me. It was exactly like you said; rough, intense, a little painful. It was an amazing kiss and I was desperate for more. But you stopped and left me hanging. Except, you looked as if you regretted letting me go. And I know that you cared."

Wow, who was that woman that possessed her and spoke out of her mouth so blatantly?

Cain, or whatever his name was, eyed her like a tasty treat, smiling and flashing his fangs. "So, you like a little pain with your pleasure, don't you, naughty girl?"

Syssi paused to think. "I guess it's like sprinkling spice on a dish that is otherwise bland... I don't like bland food."

Okay, saved by a metaphor; no way she was spelling it out for him. Not even in a dream.

"That is something we have in common. I don't like bland food either."

Was he mocking her? She glanced up, checking his expression. No, he wasn't. If possible, he looked even hungrier for her. And his blatant lust ignited a fire within her.

Syssi felt herself grow wet, dizzy, dimly aware that she'd never understood what swooning was all about before experiencing it herself.

As her legs nearly went out from under her, he saved her from falling by grabbing onto her waist and holding her against his body in a tight embrace. For a long moment, he just looked into her eyes, his gaze so hungry and yet unsure, his lips so close and yet out of reach.

She'd die if he didn't kiss her.

Or scratch his eyes out for teasing her like this.

One of the two.

"Don't you dare…" she started.

Misinterpreting her words, he pulled his head away.

"Kiss me!" she commanded.

A small smirk brightened his fearsome expression. "Make up your mind, sweet girl. Do you want to be kissed or not?"

"Don't you dare not kiss me."

His brows lifted and he grinned. His long fangs on full display, he looked absolutely evil. She should've been frightened, but she wasn't. If anything, the sight of them sent a blast of desire down into her core.

He inhaled, his eyelids dropping over his eyes for a moment as if he'd just smelled something delicious. "Lustful little thing, aren't you? And so demanding."

Oh, for heaven's sake, was he going to make her beg?

Whatever, it was just a dream, right? No one would ever know if she did.

"Please, kiss me…," she breathed and parted her lips in invitation.

His arm still wrapped securely around her, he tangled his free hand in her hair. Grabbing a fistful, he held her in place and lowered his lips to hers.

Time slowed down as Syssi watched him close the distance in slow motion. Breathing was impossible, and her heart felt like it had stopped beating. She was going to die. Right here, right now, in this dream. But she didn't care. Besides this man and the way he was making her feel, nothing mattered. She needed him more than her next breath. Or her next heartbeat.

When their lips finally touched, the relief was so profound that she felt dizzy with it. Though the part of her that was still capable of thought suggested that it might've been the lack of oxygen in her lungs.

At first, his touch was gentle as he took possession of her mouth, even unexpectedly sweet, but it lasted no more than a second.

She felt, rather than heard, the hungry growl that started deep in his throat. And as he let it loose, his restraint snapped and he attacked—his tongue invading her mouth, the hand fisting her hair tightening, pulling at the roots, and the fingers of the other one digging deep into her flesh. It should've been painful, uncomfortable, but her body was somehow transforming it into erotic heat.

Syssi's eyes rolled back and the husky moan that escaped her mouth was like no sound she'd ever made before. It should've been embarrassing, but she couldn't care less.

Her dark stranger was turning her into a mindless puddle of need.

"I better finish what I've started then. It'd be very ungentlemanly of me to leave a lady hanging, wouldn't you agree?" he whispered as he lowered her to the ground... laying her... on a bed?

Oh, the wonders of dreamscape.

Propped on his elbow, he loomed above her, looking into her eyes as his hand snaked under her shirt, finding her achy nipple and circling it slowly with his thumb.

Syssi arched her back, her shirt and bra performing a magical disappearing act as she offered him more.

Holding his eyes locked on hers, he dipped his head and took the offering in his lips, suckling gently as he moved his thumb to rim her other nipple.

The pleasure was so intense, she felt as if a tight coil was winding inside her, and at any moment it would spring with an explosive force.

Syssi was panting, her hips undulating, her juices flowing. *More,* she begged soundlessly, *I need more.*

As if to answer her silent plea, she felt his teeth graze the bud he was suckling, and then gently close around it. And yet, no alarm bells sounded in her head; there was no fear. She trusted her dream lover not to hurt her...well, that wasn't entirely true... she trusted him to hurt her just right.

Applying light pressure to her achy nipple with his blunt teeth, he pinched her other one between his thumb and forefinger and tugged.

She whimpered, the zing of pain opening the floodgates down below. She couldn't remember ever being so wet—her panties soaked through and her juices running down her thighs. And yet, there was no embarrassment, no anxiety.

Instead, unexpectedly, there was joy.

The joy of discovering that she was capable of experiencing such pleasure, that there was someone, even if only in a dream, who knew the secret code to unlocking her hidden desires.

Looking at her with hooded eyes, he kept the pressure steady, then began gradually increasing it until it became too much...

Exploding, Syssi screamed, her hips arching off the bed, her climax rippling powerfully, shaking her whole body.

When the tremors subsided, she reached for Kian, trying to bring him down to cover her trembling body with his warmth and his strength.

To connect.

Kian, that was his name. She remembered it now.

"Shh... it's okay." He resisted her pull, caressing and licking her tender nipples, easing the hurt away.

As he lifted his head, the hard planes of his face looked softer, his gaze appreciative. Stroking her damp hair, he bent down and kissed her lips softly, sweetly. "You're a treasure, beautiful girl," he said, his features blurring, dissipating...

"Wait! Don't go!" Syssi panicked. "Don't leave me alone... I want to give you pleasure too..."

He was almost gone now...

"You did, my sweet Syssi..."

She woke up gasping, her face flushed, her body sweaty, her panties soaking wet.

It had been just a dream.

It hadn't been real.

As a deep sense of loss and disappointment enveloped her, Syssi curled upon herself, hugging her knees.

The most amazing sex she'd ever experienced had been nothing but a dream, a fantasy.

God, if the foreplay had been enough to bring about such a reality-altering orgasm, what would the actual act have been like?

Could she even imagine it?

Dream it?

Probably not.

How could she?

Without experiencing this little taste of how it could be, she wouldn't have known to yearn even for this, let alone more.

Was it even attainable in the real world?

She would never know, would she?

Heavens, how she longed for her fantasy lover: the man from her dream.

If she were lucky, she would dream of him again. It was the most she could hope for.

CHAPTER 24: KIAN

Back at his apartment, Kian dropped the ceremonial robe on one of the kitchen counter stools and walked over to the bar. Too wired to go to bed, he poured himself a drink and took it outside to the terrace. Getting comfortable on a lounger, he pulled out a cigarette from the pack he had left there, lit it, and inhaled gratefully.

As he watched the smoke curl up and dissipate into the dark sky, his thoughts wandered to Syssi. Her innocent, hopeful expression when he had first seen her face emerge from behind the curtain of her wild hair. The way her body had felt tucked against his when she'd slept in the car, her cheek resting on his chest.

That kiss...

After spending such a short time with Syssi, getting a taste for her, her absence already felt like something vital was missing from his life, and he had an inkling that he could never go back to the numb state of existence he had been living in for so long.

Except, what choice did he have? He had to stay away and somehow try to forget her. Unfortunately, it wasn't going to be as easy for him as it had been for her. After all, he couldn't thrall away his own memories.

With a sigh, he took another drag from his cigarette and wondered if she was still sleeping, and if she was, was she dreaming about him?

As memories could never be truly erased, just pushed below the barrier separating the conscious mind from the unconscious, she might remember him in her dreams. Or maybe conjure him in her fantasies. He hoped she would.

He'd be thinking and dreaming about her. Of that, he was certain.

* * *

Sometime later, Kian woke up miserably cold and achingly hard. Apparently, he had fallen asleep on the lounger outside.

It was one hell of a dream.

The way she flew apart from so little...

Only in your dreams, buddy... you're not that good, he chuckled.

But it had felt so real...

She had felt so real...

So good.

The girl was haunting him even in his dreams.

He needed to get rid of this obsession with a woman he could never see again. If he wanted to retain a shred of self-respect and one untainted spot on his dark soul, he would stay away from her.

Damn, sometimes it seemed like the cost of doing the right thing was too steep. Except, to succumb to his craving and take her would be the equivalent of a hit and run. Or more accurately, a screw and run.

He had enough on his guilty conscience as it was.

Hell, he had enough guilt to fill up a lake.

Kian hung his head and let out a sigh, his breath misting in the cold air. If only Syssi weren't so sweet and naive, if she were one of those girls he went out looking for hookups in the nightclubs he frequented, he would've taken her without a second thought and then forgotten about her the next day. But then, that sweetness and that naiveté were exactly what made her so irresistible to a man like him.

A dark-souled killer.

Heaven knew how many had breathed their last breath at his hands. And it didn't matter that he had killed only to protect his family.

At first he'd had nightmares, but with each subsequent kill another part of his soul had shriveled and died, until one day he'd realized that ending a life no longer bothered him—it left him indifferent.

There was a dark void in his soul that craved Syssi's light. Trouble was, the vacuum was so big that it would've devoured her whole and still hungered for more, long after depleting all that she had to give.

He couldn't do it.

Syssi was a forbidden fruit.

A fresh, sweet, succulent fruit.

He'd better stick to the somewhat overripe, often even rotten variety he was used to. Not as tasty, but with less guilt attached.

Except a glance at his watch revealed it was four twenty in the morning; too late to go prowling for sex in bars or clubs.

Resigned, he made his way inside, not looking forward to the cold shower he was about to take.

CHAPTER 25: DALHU

"I'm sorry, sir. I've done the best I could. These Guardians were invincible. I've never seen anyone fight like this. I would've stayed and fought to the death, but I thought you would like to know what happened." The guy was about to piss himself, and rightfully so.

In the failed attempt to grab the professor, Dalhu had lost two out of the three men he had sent to retrieve her. And the worthless coward who had managed to escape and come back to report the fiasco was still alive only because Dalhu was down to ten warriors including himself, and he couldn't afford to lose one more.

"You've done well. Dismissed." He managed to get the words out without his rage spilling out, then waved the worthless piece of shit away.

He should've sent more men. Hell, he should've gone himself.

If you want something done, do it yourself, as the saying went.

Three men should've been more than enough to abduct one female.

One very beautiful, immortal female...

Dalhu lifted the framed article that his men had found at the programmer's home. Staring at the professor's stunning face, he commended the scientific journal's editor for choosing to dedicate most of the page to her beautiful image and only a few paragraphs to describe her research. Smart man.

The fact that she'd autographed her picture with "To my darling Mark" had tipped off Dalhu that Dr. Dokani might be another immortal. A quick Internet search had yielded only a few references to the little-known scientist and her specialized and not that popular field of study, proving that Dr. Amanda Dokani wasn't some famous celebrity. Which had led Dalhu to believe that the woman must've been someone important to the guy. Otherwise, it made no sense for the programmer to value the autographed article enough to frame it and place it on his desk, where he would have been staring at it whenever he'd sat down to work. And as the bastard had been gay, it sure as shit hadn't been his girlfriend or a case of infatuation with a pretty face.

The professor was family.

Besides, encountering Guardians at her lab had been a nasty surprise, but it had served as proof positive that his hunch had been right. Dr. Dokani was an immortal female of Annani's clan. Not only that, but to warrant the protection of Guardians, she was someone of vital importance.

 He should have gone himself.

With the bitter taste of failure souring his exuberant mood over yesterday's victory, Dalhu's face contorted in a nasty grimace. If he had better fighters at his disposal, she would have been in his possession now. But the inferior stock he had to work with had been no match for the superior warriors protecting her.

Well, screw it.

It wasn't as if anyone else had ever succeeded in snatching one of the clan's females. Being such a priceless commodity, they were fiercely guarded by their males, and as they were also almost impossible to detect, none had ever been captured by the Order.

Nonetheless, it felt like such a failure. A once in a lifetime opportunity squandered.

Absconding with the professor would've been the ultimate coup...

Dalhu felt his anger gain momentum, bubbling up from the churning fire always on a low simmer in his gut. Damn it, he had to douse it before it exploded into a full-out rage, pushing logic and reason out and turning him into a mindless beast.

With a curse, he slammed the seat cushion beside him, his fist tearing into the fabric. Taking several deep breaths, he fought the overwhelming urge to strike again.

Breathe in through the nose, breathe out through the mouth, in and out... He counted to ten, focusing on his breathing as he made a deliberate effort to unclench his fists.

Calm down, identify the problem, think of a solution, he recited the three steps of anger management that he'd learned from an Internet course. It had taken a couple of minutes, but eventually the red haze of rage began to recede, and a semblance of logic returned. His mind was taking the slow road back to sanity.

It didn't matter. It wasn't even a setback.

As it was, this mission had turned out to be far more successful than he had expected it to be. What had begun as a simple retaliation strike, designed to cripple the Americans' progress in their war on weapons of mass destruction in the hands of Navuh's protégés, had given the Order their first clan hit in centuries.

Taking that immortal programmer out had been a sheer stroke of luck.

It was Dalhu's triumph.

His kill.

It had happened on his watch.

Dalhu's position in the Brotherhood of the Devout Order of Mortdh was about to get a serious boost.

With smug satisfaction, he reclined on the elaborately carved sofa and propped his booted feet on the dainty coffee table. He could already taste Navuh's praise, even though it irked him that he was craving it from the lying, manipulative son of a bitch.

Stretching his arms and lacing his fingers behind his head, Dalhu pushed out his chest, filling it with so much air it was a wonder his shirt buttons didn't pop. With the pendulum of his emotions back on the upswing, he was once again soaring on the wings of his success.

Man, it feels good to be top dog.

Taking a satisfied look at the elegant room he was in, Dalhu no longer felt like an interloper in all that opulence. The Beverly Hills mansion he had rented for this mission was spectacularly plush; Persian rugs in every room, impressive reproductions of famous art, and fake, dainty French antiques that were covered in miscellaneous shit. Definitely not the right scale for his massive body. But he liked it nonetheless. He could get used to that; a king of his own castle.

It was a nice change from the training facilities and battlefields he was accustomed to. Regrettably, the lavish accommodations were temporary.

Not that their current home base was lacking in any way... If he could disregard the ~~constant~~ lack of privacy, and that besides his clothes and his weapons nothing really belonged to him.

Navuh provided for his army of mercenaries well. They were well paid, well housed, well fed, and well ~~fucked~~.

The small tropical island, indistinct from the many other tiny land pieces scattered throughout the Indian Ocean, provided them with a perfect setup. Its thick jungle canopy hid the training grounds from view of passing aircraft and satellites, and with their quarters as well as the rest of their facilities built underground, no one suspected that thousands of immortal warriors called it their home.

Steep, rocky cliffs prevented approaching their side of the island by boat, and the jungle made landing an aircraft there near impossible. The only way in or out of their base was a secret tunnel road connecting it to the island's other side.

The underground passage terminated in a small airport that was operated by mortals. It served the men leaving for or returning from missions, as well as the oblivious tourists visiting the other side.

For obvious reasons, the mortal pilots were thralled within an inch of their lives, and Dalhu often wondered how safe flying with them really was.

The planes shuttling people and cargo on and off the island had no windows, and apart from the pilots flying them, no one other than Navuh and his sons knew the island's exact location.

The secret was safe with the flyers. The compulsion they were under was so strong that there was no chance in hell they would talk. No matter what was done to them.

Given enough pressure, their brains would just blow a fuse, and they'd either end up brain dead, or dead period.

It was just the way it needed to be. For the island to serve its dual purposes, its location had to be extremely well guarded.

Known to the select few as Passion Island, the other side was home to a very exclusive and luxurious brothel. Young and beautiful prostitutes, junkies, and runaways were abducted from all over the world and brought to serve the rich, famous, and depraved... as well as Navuh's men.

It was pure genius.

Navuh made shitloads of money out of the girls while providing an in-house brothel for his army's needs.

Dalhu hated to admit it, but the son of a god was a brilliant businessman.

To make the place the success it was, its money-generating assets were well taken care of. Good food, good medical care, supervised drug and alcohol use, plus careful monitoring, in all likelihood prolonged the girls' otherwise compromised life expectancy.

But it was slavery nonetheless.

The only alternative the girls had to prostitution was to serve as maids, waitresses, or cooks. The only way off the island was a one-way ticket to either heaven or hell, leaving their corporeal bodies behind.

Given the choice between manual work and prostitution, most opted to work on their backs; lured by the nice private rooms and the patron gifts that paid for their drugs and their drinks and other small luxuries.

The service personnel, on the other hand, got only the basics, worked twelve-hour shifts, six days a week, and slept four to a room.

Between the illusion of having a choice, the promise of rewards, and the fear of punishment, the girls did their best to provide outstanding service, earning them a reputation for being the best money could buy.

Navuh was a master at the art of motivation, or rather manipulation.

Come to think of it, the soldiers didn't fare much better than the whores. Probably worse, as their servitude was indefinite. The only way out was the same as the girls'. Except, final exit options for immortals were limited by the nature of their near indestructibility.

The fastest way for a Doomer to die was to get blacklisted by Navuh and executed, either fighting to the death gladiator style, with a lethal dose of venom, or a beheading.

Dalhu couldn't remember anyone actually choosing to end things that way. Although over the years, he had witnessed enough pitiful bastards succumb to that fate.

Hell, they all knew they lived or died at their Exalted Leader's whim.

It was what it was. As long as they served Navuh well and kept their heads down, the soldiers had nothing to worry about.

And nothing to show for it either.

Looking back to his own nearly eight hundred years of service, his compensation had been mainly room and board and the use of prostitutes.

As he saw it, his rewards were the ones he had given himself. The things he had accomplished. The things he had learned. He had done it all without any guidance or help. Even literacy had been something he had accomplished on his own, teaching himself to read and write not that long ago.

For most of his life, Dalhu had lived in ignorance.

But not anymore.

To most Doomers, the money they were paid for their services seemed great, but Dalhu was smarter than that. Although his account in the Order's bank held millions, he knew the amount was meaningless. He could never take it out.

He charged his expenses to the Brotherhood's American Express that was covered by his account, but as it was routinely monitored, all he could use it for was to buy himself fancy shit and pay for his use of the island's whores. Cash withdrawals were limited to no more than five thousand dollars at a time, and only when going on missions. A detailed account of what he spent it on was required upon his return.

To most of Navuh's fighters, it was more than enough. The simple-minded, brainwashed morons couldn't conceive of using the money for anything else.

Navuh's system was brilliant.

He paid his soldiers well so they felt rewarded and stayed loyal. But by limiting their access to their own money, he ensured they always had to come back. If they didn't, they were presumed dead and the money reverted to him.

Win-win for Navuh.

Dalhu lifted his hand and stared at the Patek Philippe watch on his wrist and the five-carat diamond ring on his index finger. Just these two pieces alone were worth in excess of one hundred and fifty thousand dollars. He had another Patek Philippe and two Rolexes, each in the hundred thousand range.

Strutting around and showing off the stuff, he pretended to be a consummate connoisseur of fine jewelry... Dalhu couldn't have cared less for the ostentatious shit.

But it provided the means to an exit in case he needed one.

Like a cunning mistress to a rich man, he was accumulating a wealth of marketable goods under the guise of vanity. He had to be smart about it, though, waiting years between each purchase to avoid suspicion. Navuh executed men at a mere hint of sedition or suspected desertion.

It wasn't much, and Dalhu wasn't planning anything yet. But he liked to be prepared as best he could for anything life might throw at him; be it an unforeseen calamity or a great opportunity.

One never knew what tomorrow might bring.

"Sir, we are ready to place the call." Edward, his second, bowed politely, jarring Dalhu from his thoughts.

Pushing off the couch, he stretched his big body, then jutted his chest out and his chin up. Dalhu was ready for his reward; the rare praise from Navuh.

As he entered the mansion's sophisticated media room, Dalhu nodded to the assembled men and walked over to the equipment, making sure the wiring had been set up correctly for the scheduled teleconference.

Inspect, don't expect—was a good piece of advice for any leader, more so if one had morons for underlings.

The equipment worked fine and everything else was ready as well. His men had already cleared a large carpeted area in front of the screen by pushing the overstuffed recliners all the way against the side walls, and were now taking their places on their knees in a compulsory show of respect and devotion to their master; Lord Navuh.

Dalhu took hold of the keyboard and knelt facing the screen with his men at his back, watching the electronic clock on the side of the screen. He made the call at the precise time it had been scheduled for, sending the request and waiting for it to be acknowledged.

Several long minutes passed before the face of Navuh's secretary finally appeared. "Greetings, warriors, please get in position for his Excellency, Lord Navuh."

The men prostrated themselves with their foreheads touching the floor and their hands beside their heads, palms down.

"Our exalted leader; Lord Navuh," the secretary announced, signaling they could begin the devotion.

Ten strong voices sounded the chant.

Glory to Lord Navuh the wise and the just
In his guidance and mercy we put our trust
With his bounty we thrive
By his will we live and we die
We are all brothers in
the Devout Order of Mortdh
In his name we wage this Holy War

As always, the devotion was repeated three times. When it was done, the men held their position while Dalhu pushed up to his knees and faced his leader.

"Was your mission successful, warrior?" Navuh asked.

Addressing Dalhu by the generic term probably meant that Navuh hadn't bothered to learn his name. Anger flared, but he managed to keep his expression impassive and his tone respectful.

"It was, my lord, an unparalleled success. We infiltrated the enemies' secret organization and took out their number one asset, effectively halting any further progress their technological mastery could produce for the foreseeable future. But the victory was even greater than the one we set out to win. The programmer we killed was an immortal. At long last we succeeded, taking out one of our true adversaries. I believe we are closer than ever to uncovering the hornet's nest. It would be a great honor for my team and myself if your lordship would allow us to stay and hunt them down." Dalhu bowed his head, touching his forehead to the carpet as he anxiously awaited the praise that was his due.

"You have done well, as is befitting of my scions. It is a great victory in our ancient war against the corruption and depravity of our mortal enemies. You are to be commended for your bravery and your loyalty to the Holy War. May Mortdh strengthen your hands and harden your hearts, to go forth and deliver his vengeance to the vile and the wicked."

Basking in Navuh's lavish praise, Dalhu and his men commenced the devotion.

Glory to Lord Navuh the wise and the just
In his guidance and mercy we put our trust
With his bounty we thrive
By his will we live and we die
We are all brothers in
the Devout Order of Mortdh
In his name we wage this Holy War

As the screen went blank the men rose to their feet, embraced, and clapped each other's backs.

Dalhu joined in reluctantly. As their leader, it was unavoidable, even though he didn't share in their revelry. He was already thinking and planning ahead, something the simpletons were incapable of doing.

It was the Doomer way. A commander was the brain and his underlings were his feet and his arms. He led and they followed. He wasn't one of them, not in his heart or his mind. They were beneath him. His to use or dispose of.

Navuh had not asked about casualties, and Dalhu hadn't volunteered the information—it wasn't important—no one cared. But he was short on fighters if he was to go on a hunt for immortals.

Their kind was notoriously hard to find.

In close proximity, an immortal male was relatively easy to detect by the tingling awareness that alerted the males to each other's presence; a built-in warning mechanism that competition was near.

A female, on the other hand, was nearly impossible to discern.

Dalhu had never met one. He heard rumors, though. Supposedly, when aroused, an immortal female emitted a unique scent that was distinctly different from the one produced by mortal women. But that necessitated that he found her while she happened to be in that state, and what were the chances of that?

No wonder one had never been caught.

How was he going to do it? Where would he start looking?

He had deduced already that the enemy had a presence in California; in the Bay Area as well as in Los Angeles. The programmer and the professor had to be part of a larger nest. But both areas were huge and densely populated by millions of mortals.

He needed more clues.

Tomorrow, he would go and check out the professor's lab himself. Not that Dalhu was expecting to find her there. Spooked by the failed abduction attempt, the professor wouldn't dare come back to the university. But others would, and he could ask them some questions. Perhaps someone knew where she lived.

If they knew nothing, he would check with human resources. The university must have a physical address for her, not the post office box listed everywhere else he'd checked.

CHAPTER 26: SYSSI

The morning came all too soon for Syssi.

Tossing and turning for hours after waking from that dream in the middle of the night, she had finally fallen asleep when the sun had come up. Her alarm had gone off in what seemed like only a few minutes later.

She felt groggy.

The headache that had begun in the lab must've developed into a full-blown migraine, complete with the symptomatic confusion that accompanied it. As hard as she tried Syssi couldn't remember how she had gotten home.

There was a vague memory of Amanda driving her, and she must've collapsed on her bed straight away because she was still wearing the clothes from the day before.

Shuffling to the bathroom, Syssi took them off and dropped them in a dirty pile on the tiled floor, then stepped into the shower. With her head hung low, she let the water soak her hair.

What the hell is wrong with me?

That numbness refused to wash away. Feeling as flat as the two curtains of dripping wet hair at the sides of her face, Syssi found it a strain even to reach for the shampoo. Going through the motions, she worked it into her scalp and watched the foaming clumps wash down the drain. The laborious process of shampooing her mane had to be done twice, then came the conditioning, once, then soap, then towel.

Blow-drying all of that hair was exhausting as well. She loved her luxurious mane, but sometimes it was just too much work. Chopping it off would have made her life so much easier.

Right. Like there was a chance in hell she'd ever do it. It was the one feature that she was positive was beautiful. The rest? It depended on her mood. Some days she thought she looked pretty good; others? Not so much.

Her deflated mood meant that today was going to be one of the "not so much." Not a big deal, she was fine with being just okay and not spectacular.

Like Amanda.

Syssi wouldn't have wanted it. Amanda's beauty was a burden. It was too much, too intimidating, too restrictive, too isolating. With her confidence and her dramatic flair, Amanda carried it well, but Syssi could have never pulled it off. The stares alone would have sent her running for shelter.

Syssi shivered. How was Amanda dealing with all that leering, the envy? How did she feel about intimidating the hell out of everyone she came in contact with?

Being somewhere on the spectrum between okay to pretty was exactly where Syssi was comfortable.

Eyeing the pile of jeans, she grimaced—too constricting. Shifting her gaze to the comfy yoga pants, she grabbed them instead. Not exactly stylish or appropriate for work, but whatever, she had no energy for anything tight.

Finishing her unprofessional attire with a plain T-shirt, Syssi plodded barefoot to the stretch of counter that was her kitchen and made herself coffee.

As she sat at her dining table, still feeling lethargic from the lack of sleep, the prospect of leaving the house and walking to work seemed daunting. She couldn't bring herself to get going. For some reason, there was an unpleasant feeling churning in her gut, warning her to stay away from the lab.

It had something to do with Amanda. Maybe it was about her boss's bitchy mood yesterday. The prospect of spending another work day with a grumpy tyrant was not appealing.

Still, it might not be about work at all. The sense of loss that had come on the heels of her dream still clung to her, weighing her down like a wet, sticky sludge.

Except, it couldn't explain the foreboding. The only thing that made sense to her was that it had something to do with her premonition about Amanda.

Her phone rang, and Syssi jumped, answering without bothering to check the caller ID. "Hello?"

"Syssi, darling, I wanted to tell you that I'm not coming to the lab today." Amanda produced a very fake sounding cough. "I must've caught something. I need you to take over my test subjects for me. I'll email you the schedule." Another fake cough.

"Sure, no problem. I hope you'll get well soon."

"Thank you, darling. Me too. Hopefully by Monday, I'll be as good as new. A weekend in bed will surely help. Thank God it's Friday, right?"

Syssi laughed. "Absolutely. Feel better and don't forget to stay hydrated."

"Of course. Love you, darling. Have a good one."

"Love you too."

Amanda had been faking it big time. One of the odd things Syssi had noticed about her boss was that she never got sick. Heck, the woman never got tired. She was a work horse. The last flu epidemic had the entire lab surviving on Dayquil and cough drops, but not Amanda. She'd attributed her resilience to the flu shot she'd gotten, but so had everyone else at the lab.

Her boss was probably arranging a long weekend for herself. Except, why did she feel the need to lie to Syssi about it?

It had to be guilt. She was leaving Syssi to deal with a double load of test subjects. Not a big deal, she could handle it. But not before she had another cup of coffee, or two.

Sipping on the fresh cup she'd poured, Syssi popped open her laptop and started going through her emails, when images from the dream tried to push their way into the forefront of her mind. She pushed them back. It was best to ignore them. What was the point of dwelling on something that could never be? The fantasy was better forgotten; else real life would always pale by comparison.

That erotic dream had come out of nowhere, shaking her conviction that she wasn't all that sexual.

Syssi sighed, she couldn't remember the last time she'd felt even a spark of desire for a man. Was it possible that she had been repressing her needs while subconsciously yearning to be touched?

Oh, well, she didn't have time for all that self-analytical nonsense. She needed to get going or else she'd be late.

Reluctantly, Syssi closed her laptop and pushed up from her chair. She rinsed out her mug in the sink and then headed to her closet for shoes. But as she reached for a pair, she froze, suddenly seized by an overwhelming sense of dread.

Something dark and dangerous was looming out there. But what?

What the hell? Her heart started pounding a crazy beat against her ribcage.

Trying to overcome her panic attack, she looked for a reasonable explanation for what might've triggered it. The wolves chasing her in the dream, the grueling workday she had yesterday, the headache...

But all along Syssi had known none of these were the real reason. That kind of panic had seized her only once before.

On the night her brother Jacob had died.

She had been living in the dorms at the time. Jennifer, her roommate, and Gregg had been there when the panic attack had struck.

Syssi still remembered that when her phone had rung, she had had her head down between her knees struggling to breathe. Knowing with complete certainty that nothing would ever be the same once she answered that call, she'd let it ring, trying to postpone the inevitable.

Eventually, Jen had answered it for her...

"Syssi, sweetheart, it's your brother..." Jen handed her the phone.

Andrew's voice was pained... "It's Jacob...," he managed to croak through his choked-up throat. "That damned motorcycle... he was killed on the spot..."

Syssi sat there, frozen, not really listening to the rest of his words. Her eyes staring into nothing, she felt like her life force was draining out of her, and the cold was spreading from the center of her heart to the rest of her shaking body.

She was going into shock.

It had happened over four years ago, and she had spent most of the first two crying.

It still hurt like hell. Heaving a sigh, Syssi wiped away the few tears that escaped her tightly squeezed eyes.

If it hadn't been for Gregg, she wouldn't have made it. He had been wonderful throughout that ordeal, a real lifesaver. Syssi shivered as she imagined going through all that pain without his help. He had held her for hours while she'd cried, had arranged for someone to take notes at the classes she'd missed, had fed her, had talked to her, and somehow had managed to pull her out of the dark vortex she had been sucked into.

She wondered if it hadn't been too much for him to bear at such a young age. Maybe the erosion in their relationship had started then. Could she really blame him? What twenty-year-old wanted a girlfriend who was perpetually sad? Was it possible that he had stayed as long as he had out of pity? Or some misplaced sense of guilt?

Be that as it may, she would forever be grateful to him for standing by her side in her time of need.

This was what Andrew failed to understand when he'd accused her of being a softie. After the breakup, she'd been so down that her brother had been convinced Gregg was the worst kind of scumbag. Syssi had no doubt that Andrew would've gone after Gregg had she not warned him to leave him alone. But contrary to what Andrew believed, she'd done it not because she was a pushover, but because when it had really mattered, Gregg had been there for her. Everything else that hadn't worked between them, all her grievances, paled in comparison.

So yeah, he'd been a jerk at times, and his behavior had left her with some emotional scars. But those weren't the kind that wouldn't eventually heal.

She knew they would. They were there only because she had let them form in the first place. If she'd been stronger, Gregg's petty jerkiness would've bounced off her.

Forgiveness hadn't come easy, and it hadn't happened right away. This wisdom had taken her a long time to acquire.

She'd been angry for months.

But letting go of all that anger had been one of the best things she had done for herself. It had been therapeutic. And realizing that Gregg had earned her forgiveness in the best possible way had been instrumental in that healing.

Syssi wished him nothing but happiness.

Hopefully, one day he would find his perfect someone, and when he did, she hoped he would invite her to his wedding. And she would go, gladly, and celebrate with him. After all, they'd shared each other's lives for four years and parted on good terms. Syssi no longer harbored resentment toward him, and she believed that the same was true for him also.

Would she invite him to her wedding? Maybe.

Syssi wasn't sure Gregg had reached enlightenment the same way she had.

To be angry was poisonous to the soul, and forgiveness wasn't easy. But she'd found a way to do it, and not only with Gregg.

Often, there was at least one good thing or quality that deserved gratitude. Finding this one thing and focusing on it was helpful, it allowed letting go of resentment with ease.

Syssi chuckled. This was another thing she should be grateful to Gregg for. If not for him, she wouldn't have learned this valuable lesson.

She had a feeling that she would have to put this technique to the test again. Letting go of anger was something she would have to deal with in the future.

Unfortunately, it wasn't a philosophical conclusion. More like a premonition.

Great.

Plopping down on the couch, Syssi covered her eyes with her hands, and taking a deep breath, thought back to all of her other premonitions— big and small. There were none she could remember that in one way or another hadn't come to pass.

Pushing up to her feet, she walked over to the kitchen counter and snatched the phone off its cradle.

"What's wrong?" Andrew answered right away.

It was such a relief to hear his voice that she plopped back on the couch. "Nothing yet. I had a bad feeling and wanted to check that if you were all right."

"Phew, you got me scared. A call from you this early, I thought you heard something from Mom and Dad."

"No, but I'm going to call them next. Are you at work already?"

"Yes. Why?"

"Are you going to be there all day?"

"Yes."

"Good. Call me before you head home. Will you remember?"

"No problem. Can you do me a favor and text me after you talk with Mom and Dad?"

"I will."

Next, she called her father's sat phone. Everything was fine over there. They were getting ready for bed. And no, they had no plans to visit anytime soon. She texted the update to Andrew.

Okay, who else?

Amanda?

The premonition must've been about her. She was probably going on some last minute romantic getaway with one of her boy-toys, and something was going to happen to her. Syssi needed to call Amanda back, caution her again, and hope her boss would heed the warning.

"Yes, darling," Amanda answered, all traces of her pretend sickness gone from her voice.

"I just wanted to remind you to be careful. Remember that bad feeling I had? I was just hit with another wave of it."

Amanda was silent for a few seconds, and when she answered, she no longer sounded as cheerful. "Staying in bed over the weekend seems like a good strategy to avoid risk, don't you think?"

"If that is what you're really going to do."

"I don't plan on going anywhere."

"Promise?"

"Yes."

"Okay. Stay safe, and get well."

"I will."

The good news was that the panic had eased. Whatever Amanda had decided to do following Syssi's call would keep her safe.

Otherwise, Syssi knew the panic would not have ebbed.

CHAPTER 27: AMANDA

Amanda ended the call and put her phone back in her purse. Syssi's premonition must've been about what had happened in the lab yesterday. And the bad feeling persisted because of the traumatic experience.

She hadn't spoken with Kian since leaving him alone with Syssi yesterday, but Amanda was sure he'd thralled the girl before sending her home with Okidu.

Syssi's conscious mind didn't remember what had happened, but her body and her subconscious did. It took time until the elevated levels of hormones released during fight-or-flight went back to normal.

She should question Okidu about Syssi's state of mind when he'd taken her home. It was possible that the girl's powerful mind had helped her resist the thrall. Kian might have been able to submerge her memories of him and what had happened in the lab, but perhaps not as deeply as he thought he had.

Pulling on a pair of leggings under her sleep shirt, Amanda didn't bother with shoes before padding across the vestibule to Kian's penthouse, and she didn't knock before entering either.

If he wanted her so close under his nose, she would make sure that it tickled.

There was no one in the living room or the kitchen, but she knew Kian was home. His office was the last room at the end of the long hallway, but even though she couldn't hear him, she sensed his presence.

Except, she wasn't looking for her brother. Not yet.

"Okidu, dear, where are you?"

One of the doors along the hallway opened, and the butler hurried out to greet her.

"Mistress Amanda, how can I be of service?"

Good question. It wasn't as if Okidu could describe Syssi's emotional state.

"When you took Syssi home yesterday, did she say anything to you on the way?"

"Master Kian took Mistress Syssi home. I offered to save him the trouble, but he said it was his pleasure to drive her himself."

Oh, this was good. Amanda smiled. Very, very good. Kian never bothered getting his thralled partners back home, he sent Okidu, same way she did with hers, having Onidu take care of getting them back safely, either to their home or to the club she'd picked them up at.

Kian must've felt something for the girl.

"Do you know if he thralled her before taking her home?"

"No, Mistress, he certainly did not. I must assume he did it later at her place of residence."

Fantastic.

Amanda should thank the Doomers for helping her plans along. Without their surprise visit, Kian would not have been forced to spend time with Syssi.

What surprised her, though, was that Syssi had gotten under Kian's skin in such a short time, and that was without doing a single thing to encourage him or even show him that she was interested. Not that it hadn't been obvious.

Amanda wanted to dance a victory dance around Kian's living room.

But there was another piece of information she needed before she could celebrate. "Okidu, could you tell me what time it was when Kian took Syssi home, and then when he returned?" The Odu had an internal clock that recorded everything. He could provide her with the exact timing of anything he'd witnessed.

"Certainly. Master Kian left at six twenty-four and returned at seven fifteen."

Amanda tapped a finger on her lips. Not enough time for a hookup, but possibly some kissing. She had to find out. If Kian had managed not to touch Syssi at all, she would have to reconsider her assessment of their compatibility.

Him driving her home was a good start, but something along the lines of not being able to keep their hands off each other would've been better.

According to her mother, true love mates were always desperate for each other—more so than other horny, run of the mill immortal couples.

But she was getting ahead of herself. Kian would've said that she was letting her romantic fantasies cloud her good judgment. There was no guarantee Syssi was even a Dormant, let alone Kian's true love mate.

"Thank you, Okidu. That will be all." She dismissed him before heading down the corridor.

He rushed after her. "Mistress Amanda, Master Kian is working with Master Shai, he asked not to be disturbed."

She put a hand on his shoulder. "Thank you, Okidu. But it doesn't apply to me."

"Yes, Mistress." Okidu bowed.

Kian's closed door didn't even slow her down. Amanda pushed the handle and entered.

"Good morning, gentlemen."

Kian looked over her attire, or lack thereof, and grimaced. "Go back to your place and put something on, Amanda."

There were two chairs in front of Kian's desk. Shai occupied one, and Amanda took the other while casting them both haughty glances. "What's the matter, don't you like my fashion statement?"

Keeping a straight face while watching their confused expressions was a struggle. They didn't know if she was being sarcastic or serious.

Smart man that he was, Kian knew when he was out of his element and changed the subject. "What can I do for you, Amanda?"

She smiled. "I wanted to talk to you about your date with Syssi yesterday."

Shai's head snapped around, and he gaped at Kian. "A date?"

Kian waved his hand. "There was no date. It's just Amanda's twisted sense of humor. Would you excuse us for a few moments, Shai? I'll call you when I'm done."

His voice had sounded cultured and polite, but both she and Shai had heard the menacing undertones. The difference was, Shai got scared and scurried away, while Amanda smiled sweetly and got ready to spar with her brother.

Let the games begin.

She was going to get details out of him, and she wasn't going to stop until she did. Kian had no idea what he'd brought upon himself by insisting she move into the keep.

When the door closed behind Shai, Kian dropped the polite mask and growled, "I don't care what fashion statement you're trying to make, but this is a working office. You will dress appropriately when you come in here during working hours. Is it clear?"

She batted her eyelashes. "Of course. But you'll need to post a schedule on the door. As far as I know, it's always working hours for you."

Kian's lips lifted in a little smirk. "Then I guess you always need to dress appropriately when you come in here."

"I don't know what your problem is, Kian. There is no one here that is not family. Why should you or anyone else care what I wear?"

"According to your logic, I can spend my workdays in boxer shorts, or better yet, naked."

Amanda couldn't help the snort that escaped her throat. Imagining her stuck-up brother working in the nude was just too much. "Okay, I agree."

Kian lifted his hands. "Hallelujah. For once, I win an argument with you."

Let him think that. It would put him in a more compliant mood. "You see? I can be reasoned with. By the way, how did it go with Syssi yesterday?"

Immediately, his expression closed off. "Fine."

Damn, she would have to pull it out of him one crumb at a time.

"Did she stay long after I left?"

"No."

"What did you guys talk about?"

"Nothing. I took her home a few minutes later."

Ugh. "Why did you take her home yourself instead of letting Okidu do it?"

"Where are all these questions leading, Amanda? I have work to do and you're wasting my time."

Well, if he wanted her to get to the point she would. "Did you like her?"

A shade of melancholy flitted over Kian's harsh features. His eyes were trained on her, but there was a faraway look in them. Amanda held her breath. Kian wouldn't lie to her, but he was perfectly capable of refusing to answer and kicking her out.

"Yes, I did." He pushed his hair back, racking his fingers through it. "I erased myself from her memory along with everything that happened in the lab and after." He sighed. "I wish I could do the same for myself. She will be difficult to forget."

Poor Kian. He was drawn to Syssi but fighting it with all he had. And for what? For some misguided sense of honor? For upholding a definition of right and wrong that he himself had written?

Or was the formidable Regent afraid of feeling something after nearly two millennia of feeling nothing—of burying himself in work and duty while clinging to a code of honor in an effort to anchor himself to something and not disappear completely?

The task she'd undertaken was going to be even tougher than she'd anticipated. Both Syssi and Kian had built themselves an armor made out of routine and habit. Feeling safe and at home inside the little bleak cubicles they had crawled into, they were terrified of venturing out.

There were only two ways to force them to change. Blow up their safe zone, or tempt them with something they couldn't resist.

CHAPTER 28: DALHU

So this was what a university looked like.

Dalhu strolled along the winding pathways between grassy lawns and flower beds, observing the small groups of young humans sprawled on the grass. Books open, laptops propped on upturned knees, they were socializing more than studying.

A ping of envy coursed through him. He'd never had the opportunity to devote time to learning, or to socializing for that matter. He didn't know how to relate to people other than as a soldier to commander or a commander to soldier. He knew how to take orders and issue them, but not how to conduct a conversation.

Not entirely true.

The other thing he was an expert on was seduction. Lucky for him it didn't involve much talking. His kind exuded powerful pheromones females found difficult to resist. He didn't know it for a fact, but it made sense. Otherwise the ease with which he entrapped women would have been hard to explain.

Even here, in the open air, he could scent the surge of lust his appearance induced in the young females he was passing by. Perhaps after he was done with what he came here to do, he would pick up one of them and take her home with him.

No, this was a really bad idea. He would take her to a hotel instead. Bringing a lone girl into a house full of horny immortal males was asking for trouble. Human females were fragile. They could barely satiate one immortal male and survive it. Even hookers had trouble keeping up. If he ever brought a woman to the Beverly Hills mansion, he would make sure to bring one for every one of his men as well.

Hire a whole damned whorehouse for a night.

"Excuse me." He forced a smile for the girl he'd stopped. "Could you please point me toward Dr. Amanda Dokani's laboratory?"

The girl pushed her glasses up her nose as she looked up at him. Way up. He tried to smile again.

"Are you volunteering for her extrasensory tests?"

"Yeah, that is exactly what I'm here for."

"What's your talent?"

Killing. He was really good at that, but as far as he knew he had no other talents. "I don't have any."

She shrugged. "Oh, well, you never know. Anyway, you see that gray building over there?" She pointed.

He nodded.

"The labs are on the lower level. There should be a directory near the entry."

"Thank you, miss." Dalhu bowed his head.

She cast him a perplexed look. "You're welcome."

He'd messed up again. To humans, he looked no older than a man in his early thirties. He should pay better attention to how they interacted with each other, and make sure he was responding the way someone his perceived age should. Tonight, he was going to watch American television and absorb their contemporary culture. Apparently, the movies he'd watched in preparation for this mission were outdated.

When he got to Professor Dokani's laboratory, Dalhu found it underwhelming. It wasn't big, or fancy looking, and it was one of many. The entire basement level of the building was comprised of various labs, and the place was teeming with activity. There was a lot of research going on in the neuroscience department, and Dr. Dokani was just one of many other researchers.

"Can I help you?" A chubby girl with a pretty face gave him the once-over. He did one of his own. It was hard to estimate her height from behind the desk she was sitting at, but she wasn't short. A big plus. Dalhu liked his women tall, and had no problems with generous curves either. On the contrary. Perhaps she was the one he would take with him after he was done with his investigation.

"I'm looking for Professor Amanda Dokani."

"I'm sorry, she is not in today. Is there anything I can do for you? I'm Hannah, her research assistant." She offered him her hand and he shook it, holding on as he gazed into her eyes.

"Do you know where she lives?"

Caught in his thrall, the girl's pupils dilated, but she was fighting it. Hannah shook her head and pulled her hand out of his grip. "I don't. You may want to check with Human Resources."

He looked at her with new appreciation. The girl was both pretty and smart. Only those with powerful minds could resist his thrall.

Still, he couldn't leave without erasing her memory of him. Bracing his hands on her desk, he leaned forward, putting his face very close to hers.

"You are a very pretty girl, Hannah. But I need to tell you

something." He leaned even closer. "Your hair is messy." Dalhu smiled as he pushed full force into her mind.

Hannah's hand shot to her head and she finger-combed her chin-length curls.

"You need to go to the bathroom and brush it."

With her pupils completely dilated, Hannah's eyes turned almost all black, only a thin brown border remaining. "Excuse me, I need to go brush my hair." She reached for the strap of her purse, lifting it from where it hung on the back of her chair, and pushed up to her feet.

In a few minutes, she would have one hell of a headache. His thrall had been forceful and not exactly surgical. There would be more than just him missing from her memory.

Alone in the lab, he walked over to the small office he'd noticed on the other side. Several framed diplomas hung on the walls. Among them, was an enlarged copy of the article his men had found at the programmer's home.

Dalhu stood transfixed in front of the professor's picture, unable to pull his eyes away from her. She was so beautiful that it hurt. His hand went to his chest and he rubbed at his sternum.

"Excuse me, you're not supposed to be in here."

Dalhu tore his gaze away from the framed article and pivoted on his heel.

A petite blonde, with a thick mane of hair like that of a lion, was standing with her hands on her hips and glaring at him with a pair of blue-green eyes. She wasn't fooling him with her bravado, though, he could hear her heartbeat thundering behind her ribcage. She was scared of him. As she should be, and not only because he towered more than a foot over her.

"I'm sorry. I was looking for Professor Amanda Dokani, and I thought I would find her here. Then I got stuck reading this article." He pointed at the wall.

She followed his eyes and smirked. "Yeah, I'm sure it was the article."

Dalhu flashed her what he hoped looked like a bashful smile. "Okay, you caught me. I was staring at the picture. She is very beautiful."

Her heartbeat slowed as she relaxed and smiled back. "That she is. But she is not here today. You can try again on Monday."

Dalhu stepped out of the professor's office and leaned against the wall, sliding down so he could look into the girl's eyes. "Do you know where she lives?"

She frowned. "Why? Are you a friend of hers?"

What was it with the kids in this place? Were they all brainiacs? This one seemed even more resistant to thralling than Hannah.

"Yes, I am. What's your name?" He tried a different approach. If he primed her with questions she didn't find suspicious she might relax her resistance.

"Syssi."

"Have you been working here long?"

"No, it's my second week. Why?"

"No reason. Just being friendly. Would you like to have a cup of coffee with me?" He wasn't really interested. Not because she wasn't pretty, the girl was beautiful in her own way, but she was too small. Dalhu preferred his women tall. Besides, she was blond when he craved a brunette. A very particular brunette. After gazing at the professor's face, no other woman could compare.

He extended his hand but she didn't even look at it. Her pupils were dilated, and she couldn't move her eyes away even though he could see she struggled to. "No, thank you, I can't," she whispered her refusal.

It seemed he couldn't compel her to do as he said, but maybe he could compel her to tell the truth.

"Why?"

"Because you scare the crap out of me." Her eyes widened in horror and she slapped a hand over her mouth. "I'm sorry. I don't know what came over me," she mumbled behind her fingers.

Dalhu laughed. "It's okay. I scare a lot of people. It's the size." He waved a hand over his body.

Syssi shook her head. "Maybe. Do you want me to tell Amanda that you stopped by? What's your name?"

"No, I want to surprise her. I'll come back Monday. It was nice meeting you, Syssi." Again he offered her his hand, and this time she took it. Holding on, he repeated what he'd done with Hannah.

Rubbing her temples, the girl was still standing in the same spot Dalhu had left her when he closed the lab's door behind him.

"Could you please point me in the direction of Human Resources?" he asked the first guy he saw in the corridor.

"Sure. I'll show you where it is."

The young man walked with him all the way to the building housing the department he was looking for.

"Thank you. I appreciate it."

"No problem, dude."

In the office, Dalhu found an elderly woman whom he thralled easily to search the database for the professor's address.

"Here you go, dear." She handed him the scrap of paper she'd scribbled it on.

"Thank you." He thralled her again to forget he was ever there.

CHAPTER 29: SYSSI

Syssi held up a card, the picture side facing her and the back facing her test subject. "What am I looking at?"

"A rabbit." Michael didn't hesitate before guessing correctly.

She picked another card from the stack and lifted it up. "Okay. What am I looking at now?"

"A locomotive. Can we stop now? I think I've proven my telepathic ability many times over. I'm bored."

She couldn't blame him. Michael was a powerful telepath, but the purpose of this experiment was to find out if his ability diminished over time.

With most talents it did, as Syssi could attest from her own experience. She could guess the first ten coin tosses correctly, but her accuracy diminished with each subsequent toss until after the hundredth she was no better than someone with no paranormal talent at all.

"Let's keep going until you start making mistakes. I want to find out at what point you start losing concentration."

"Okay, shoot."

She lifted another card.

"House."

It was a flower. Syssi rolled her eyes. "I know you're doing it on purpose. Come on, Michael, you are getting paid by the hour and you are mine for the next thirty-five minutes."

Michael waggled his brows. "I can think of more pleasant ways to spend those minutes."

He was such a flirt. Michael was cute and he knew it, but he was just a kid. A twenty-year-old business major who also played on the football team and had the muscles to show for it.

"Me too, but I'm getting paid by the hour as well." She lifted another card.

"A man's face."

After another fifteen cards Michael started making mistakes, real ones, and after another ten he wasn't getting any of them right.

"Okay, I think you're done." Syssi glanced at her watch. Michael still owed her fifteen minutes, but he was useless at this point.

He leaned back in his chair and stretched his long legs. "When are we going to try real thoughts? I'm tired of the pictures."

There was a sequence she needed to follow, but Michael was spent. "We have a few minutes left, but I doubt you'll be able to do anything. Your brain is fried."

"Try me."

Syssi closed her eyes and thought about coffee. She was tired, had a headache, and wanted to go home and take a nap. But with Amanda missing in action, she had to stay. And later on she had another obligation.

"You want to take a break and go have a cup of coffee with me."

"Close. I was thinking about coffee but not about having one with you."

Syssi frowned.

Something bothered her about this exchange and it wasn't Michael's flirting. She had a weird sense of déjà vu, as if she'd had the same conversation with someone else today. An image flitted through her mind. A giant of a man, dark, scary, smiling at her and asking her out.

Syssi shook her head. She was losing her mind. As if the dreams weren't enough, she was now having waking hallucinations. Maybe it was the headache's fault. She'd been having a lot of those lately. She should get it checked out.

Or maybe she just needed to start getting out more, preferably to do something outdoorsy. The two things she was short on were guys and fresh air. Combining the two sounded like a plan.

"You know what? Why not? Let me invite you to a cup of cappuccino."

Michael's eyes widened in surprise. "Really? You're not just saying it?"

Syssi smiled. "Nope. How do you like it? Lots of milk or lots of foam?"

He looked confused. "Are you going to order it?"

"I'm going to make it. We have a cappuccino machine in the kitchenette. So, how do you like it?"

"However you make it is fine." The disappointed look on his handsome face tugged at her heart. She shouldn't have teased him like that. But they were playing a game. It wasn't as if Michael believed she would ever say yes.

"Come on, you can watch me prepare it."

Making her way to the kitchen, she stopped by Hannah's desk. The postdoc was slumped in her chair, eyes closed, rubbing at her temples.

"You have a headache too?"

Hannah nodded.

"We need to call maintenance and have them check the ventilation in here. I've been getting way too many of those lately."

Hannah opened her eyes. "I think you're right. I never get headaches, and this one came out of nowhere. It was right after that guy left."

Syssi narrowed her eyes. "What guy?"

Hannah frowned. "I don't remember. Now that I think about it, there was no one here. I must've imagined it."

Syssi got an uncomfortable feeling in her gut. "Was your imaginary guy huge?"

"How did you know?"

That uncomfortable feeling had just gotten worse. "A lucky guess."

Syssi continued to the kitchen with Michael following closely behind. "What's going on, Syssi?"

She waved her hand dismissively. "Nothing." This was too weird even for a place that dealt with paranormal phenomena and extrasensory perception.

Michael put a hand on her shoulder. "I can sense your feelings, Syssi. You can't hide it from me. You're worried about something. Spit it out. There is nothing that would freak me out at this point."

She was tempted. After all, as a fellow talent, he wasn't going to think she was crazy or make fun of her. And it wasn't as if she had many opportunities to talk about her premonitions with others.

"It might be a coincidence, but I don't think it is. If it were only me, I would've blamed lack of sleep, or poor ventilation. But both Hannah and I have a headache, and we both have a vague impression of a huge guy visiting the lab but can't remember it. The more I try to focus on that fleeting image, the more it dissipates."

Michael closed his eyes, his forehead furrowed in concentration.

"What are you doing?" she asked after long moments had passed and he didn't even twitch.

"Feeling." He opened his eyes and sighed. "Sometimes, I can sense a residual of intentions. There is something here, I can feel it. But it could've been left by anyone; even you or Hannah or Professor Dokani. Not David, I can always feel his imprint clearly and it doesn't belong to him. The guy is genuinely full of himself. None of his posturing is a front."

"What is it, then?"

"A powerful yearning."

"Yearning for what?"

Michael shrugged. "I don't know. It just feels like a need. It's kind of sad. Lonely."

Shit, was it her?

It wasn't Amanda's, that was for sure. Most of the time the woman was upbeat and cheerful. It couldn't have been Hannah either. The postdoc was a social animal with tons of girlfriends and more guys chasing after her than she knew what to do with. And it wasn't David, who thought he was all that. So it had to be either one of the test subjects, or the mysterious visitor who had or hadn't been there.

Or maybe it was her.

Syssi had thought she'd managed to get over the melancholy that had assailed her this morning. But apparently, the yearning she'd felt for her dream lover hadn't gone anywhere.

CHAPTER 30: DALHU

Dalhu couldn't believe how easy it had been to obtain the professor's address.

Too easy.

For centuries, the clan had been hiding from Navuh's vengeance, keeping their existence secret and leaving no trail that could lead back to them. Until this recent stroke of luck with the programmer, the Brotherhood hadn't been able to locate any of their hideouts.

It would have been careless of the professor to have her address recorded in a database that was so easily accessible. Then again, the programmer had been easy enough to find. As long as their true nature remained hidden, Annani's clan members could live and work among the humans, trusting that their anonymity would keep them safe.

His gut churning with anticipation, Dalhu parked his rented Mercedes in front of the Santa Monica condominium complex. It looked exactly like a type of place a wealthy clan member would choose. Only a few blocks away from the ocean, the luxurious complex was gated, and there was a guard on duty.

A weak thrall sufficed for the guy to let Dalhu inside the complex grounds.

The door to the professor's residence was naturally locked, and as far as he could tell there was no one inside. Perhaps the professor had gone out.

He could wait for her to come back.

The problem was how to enter without breaking the door or the door knob. He needed her to enter her home without suspecting anything was wrong. Any sign of trouble would send her running.

Dalhu circled around, jumping the six foot gate leading to the condominium's backyard with ease. First, he checked for alarm sensors in the windows. There was no wiring in the screens, but it didn't mean that there were no sensors on the window frames. His best bet was to find a fixed window. It wouldn't have a sensor, and if it wasn't visible from the front door, he could break the glass to get in and still have the element of surprise.

From the back, the only access was a sliding door that for sure had a sensor on it. He found what he needed on the wall facing the side yard.

One of the bedrooms had a window that was made of three panels, with only the one in the center openable. The two on the side were fixed glass and although narrow, they were big enough for him to slide through.

Picking up a good-sized rock, he tapped the glass with it, counting on the heavy drapery hanging on the inside to absorb the sound of the falling shards.

The window cracked. When no alarm sounded, he took care of the rest of the glass with a few more taps. The opening was low, and Dalhu stepped over the sill, careful around the jagged edges protruding from the frame.

As Dalhu pushed the drapery aside, he found that the bedroom he stepped into was vacant. No furniture at all. The next room over was the same, and when he reached the living room, Dalhu had to concede defeat.

The professor hadn't been careless, she'd been smart. She might have owned this condominium, but she obviously didn't live there.

He needed to go back to that lab and search Dr. Dokani's office until he found something. Anything. A receipt from the dry cleaner or a car mechanic was all he needed to find her real residential address. Chances were that the professor had her laundry delivered home and her car picked up for service and returned.

Tonight, he would send men to search the lab and go over every piece of paper they could find.

CHAPTER 31: SYSSI

At four o'clock, Syssi collected her purse and waved to the postdoc. "Bye, Hannah, have a great weekend."

"How is your headache?" Hannah asked.

"Better, but it's still there. How about you?"

She shrugged. "I'll live. Are you going to the old people's house?"

"Of course. It's Friday, and my girls are waiting for me."

The *girls* ranged in age from late eighties to mid-nineties, and yet she often thought of them more as girlfriends than grannies.

Syssi chuckled. They sure as hell didn't behave like anyone's grandma.

Toward the end of her life, her Nana had lost her eyesight, and Syssi had been reading to her whenever she'd visited. Her Nana's three friends had soon joined, and Syssi had found herself reading to the four of them. With few exceptions, she'd been visiting the *Golden Age Retirement Home* every Friday afternoon for the past three years, even after her Nana had passed away.

The three had become her substitute grandmas. Hattie was the oldest and fully blind, but she didn't let her disability slow her down and was the ringleader of the group. A gutsy and spunky Holocaust survivor, she had enough stories to fill the pages of at least twenty books.

Clara was the youngest. She could see well enough to move around but not to read or even watch television. Leonora was sweet and motherly and could see just fine, but she loved hearing Syssi read even though she was partially deaf. Which meant that Syssi had to be real loud.

Embarrassing as hell, given the types of books the three loved to hear her read; raunchy romances with lots of explicit sex scenes.

They'd even made her read *Fifty Shades of Grey* to them.

All three books.

She had to admit that it had been fun, though. The old girls had laughed so hard she'd feared for their lives, and eventually she'd loosened up and laughed with them.

It was easy to forget that two generations separated her from the three. Sitting in one of the girls' rooms, door closed, Syssi often felt like she was in a college dorm, having a good time with her friends.

"Hello, ladies." She tried to peek at the book Leonora was holding in her lap. "What are you hiding in there?" Not that anything could be worse reading out loud than *Fifty Shades*. Other than straight up erotica, that is. Hopefully the old loons wouldn't go that far.

"Sit down, girl, and tell us about your week first," Clara said, patting a spot beside her on Hattie's bed.

Syssi dropped her purse on the night stand and with a sigh flopped down next to Clara. Sometimes she suspected the girls were looking forward to this part of their get together more than the reading. Nosy busybodies.

"Nothing special. The new job is exciting and challenging. I'm learning new things every day."

"How is that boss of yours treating you? Is she nice?" Hattie asked. Out of the three, it seemed she had taken Syssi's Nana's dying wish most seriously; looking after Amelia's granddaughter as if she was her own.

"I have no complaints. Most of the time she makes me feel like I'm her darling. There was this one day, though, that I saw another side of Amanda. When someone pisses her off, she can get bitchy as hell."

Clara patted her knee. "Everyone gets moody from time to time. What you need to keep in mind is that it is probably not about you, and there is no reason for you to get upset. The best thing you can do is to get out of the line of fire. You don't want to get hit just because you are there and make an easy target."

"Amen to that," Leonora said.

"I know, and I didn't take it personally. It was just such a departure from her usually upbeat, cheerful personality."

Clara sighed. "Don't be fooled by appearances, girl. Lots of folks put on a happy face to cover for a sad heart."

"Mm-hmm." Hattie nodded in agreement.

Was Amanda sad? Not likely.

Her boss was too excited and optimistic about her research, too busy being dramatic, and too sexed up to have an inclination toward melancholy.

"I don't think she is a sad person. She just got mad over something. Not a big deal."

As Leonora leaned closer and smiled, Syssi knew what was coming next.

"Now that we've covered work, we want to know if you met a nice young man, or even better, a naughty one." Leonora winked, an exaggerated one complete with a twisted mouth like some character from an old gangster movie.

"Someone to get your heart pounding and your blood pumping?" Clara added and waggled her brows.

Syssi shook her head.

"Anyone at all?" Hattie asked.

She was going to disappoint them the same way she did every Friday since she'd broken up with Gregg. "No."

In unison, the three let out a sigh and sagged.

Leonora shook her head. "I was so sure that this week you were going to meet someone and finally end your self-imposed celibacy. In my days, a girl had to get married if she wanted some action between the sheets. But women today have the pill and all the other contraptions to keep them from getting nasty surprises. Get out there and have fun, girl. It is time." Last Friday, Leonora had read Syssi's future in her tarot cards, like she had been doing every other week or so, and had decided Syssi was about to meet someone. "All three cards were there. You had the lovers, the two of cups, and the ten of cups."

Syssi had agreed to Lenora's readings for the fun of it, not because she really believed that cards could predict her future. But evidently Leonora felt differently. Still, arguing the point with a ninety-year-old was not only futile but potentially hazardous to the woman's health. It was much better to just roll with it. "Maybe the timing was wrong, or maybe I met him but didn't realize that he was the one. And besides, the week isn't over yet."

That seemed to mollify Leonora, who was holding her hand over her heart as if she was experiencing chest pains. The old woman crossed her arms over her ample bosom. "That must be it. My cards don't lie."

Syssi glanced at the others, expecting them to snicker at Leonora's proclamation, but found the two nodding solemnly. She loved them, but they were all loony.

"Are you sure no handsome boy made your heart flutter?" Clara asked, flapping her old hands up and down.

Did a dream flutter count?

Whatever, she could make them happy with that one. If the old bats believed in tarots, chances were that they also believed in dreams. She would just skip the parts that were not so innocent.

"I kind of met a handsome guy, but he wasn't real. I dreamt of him."

Hattie snickered. "What kind of a dream?"

For once the blush that crept up Syssi's cheeks didn't embarrass her. Not only were two of the women vision-impaired, but she didn't mind even if they could've seen it. During their long lives the three had experienced more than she could ever dream of or imagine. Her naughty dream would have amused them. Not that she was going to give up any details.

"I don't remember much," she lied. "It was a nightmare, and I was running away from a pack of wolves. The guy who helped me chase them off was very handsome."

The three smiled knowingly.

Syssi stifled a relieved sigh. Now that she'd given them something to be happy about, they would stop asking about her nonexistent love life.

Pulling out the book that had been lost in between the folds of her skirt, Leonora handed it to Syssi. "I'm sure you had enough of us old crows pecking at you. How about you read to us now?"

As Syssi lifted the book, her breath caught. On the cover, a couple was kissing passionately against a dark and ominous background. A pale moonlight cast light on the tall man and the petite woman, while the tree branches encroaching on the small clearing looked like monsters, their gnarled branches tipped with taloned fingers.

The title, though, was what caused goose bumps to rush all over her skin. In bold white letters, it read: *Dreams of a Dark Lover*.

CHAPTER 32: KIAN

Kian watched the mourners as they made their way into the clan's large council room, each stopping by Micah, her brother Otto, and their mother. The three were seated on the raised stage next to Mark's beautifully carved sarcophagus.

Wearing their traditional mourning robes made of brown jute, the clan members waited their turn to approach the small grieving family one by one, then kneel beside them, hugging or clasping their hands.

Nothing was said, as there were no words that could ease the pain of Mark's immediate family. It was more about sharing their energy, their warmth, and their love with those who were in desperate need of it.

The overhead screens showed the other clan members in Scotland and Alaska arriving at their respective council rooms and taking their places for the ceremony.

Looking at the screens, Kian waited for Annani and Sari's arrival, grateful for the marvel of modern technology that made it possible for the whole clan to participate, and for his mother to lead the dirge.

The goddess's voice would accompany Mark on his journey to the other side, honoring his memory with her song.

Once everyone was seated and the doors closed in all three chambers, Annani made her grand entrance. And though they all knew her and had seen her before, some still gasped and oohed before a respectful hush fell over them all.

The awe and reverence the clan felt for their matriarch was palpable.

She was small and slender, a mere inch or two over five feet, her delicate, otherworldly beauty misleadingly youthful. But there was no mistaking the awesome presence. Fiery red hair cascaded in thick waves over her shoulders all the way down to her hips, and every bit of her exposed skin radiated with white luminescence. Her big green eyes, so old and so wise, shone tonight with an inner light that was bright enough to illuminate an auditorium and inspire reverence.

Raising her glowing arms, Annani pulled the brown hood of her mourning robe over her head, then tucked her hands inside the robe's sleeves, effectively cutting off her luminescence in a show of respect for the dead.

Lowering her head, she began the lament.

Her voice was angelic, pure and strong. It resonated inside the hearts and souls of her audience, touching their sadness and tugging at its strings. As a chorus of voices joined her, the lament was magnified by the hundreds of voices coming from the sea of brown robes swaying to the mournful sounds.

When Annani reached the last bars of her sad song, Shai activated the hovering platform under the sarcophagus, raising it a couple of inches above the floor.

Kian, together with the seven Guardians, stepped up to the platform. They formed two lines, four on each of its sides, and guided the ornate coffin down the steps. The rest of those present joined the procession behind Mark's family, accompanying him on his final journey to his resting place in the catacombs.

Once there, Shai raised the sarcophagus higher, and the Guardians helped guide it into the niche that had been selected for him in one of the largest chambers. The same artist who'd made the beautiful sarcophagus had been tasked with carving the inscription into the stone right under the niche.

Kian waited until the chamber was filled, and the last of the mourners entered before addressing the crowd.

"Mark will be missed and remembered, not only by his immediate family but by each and every one of us." He pointed to the plaque. "It says here, 'Mark, beloved son of Micah, nephew of Otto, grandson of Jade, great-grandson of Annani.' But the truth is that Mark is not inside this beautiful sarcophagus. What's left behind is just the vessel that carried Mark's eternal soul for as long as he walked the earth. I hope that his journey to the other side was peaceful and that beyond the veil he found love and joy awaiting him. And yet, even though we must believe Mark's new reality is the mythical heaven, and that he's well, it's of little comfort to those who are left behind. We miss him, and his absence will always feel like a vacuum, an open wound in our hearts that will not heal until the day we join him on the other side. Regrettably, the veil which keeps us apart from him and the others we've lost and miss is impossible to pierce. In the meantime we, the ones on this side of the divide, must draw strength and courage from each other. Our task of providing enlightenment and holding evil and darkness at bay will never be done as long as the Devout Order Of Mortdh Brotherhood is still out there. We are a family, we stand together, and we will not be defeated, for the simple reason that we cannot. Without us, humanity's future is doomed to eternal darkness."

As his people responded with grim nods and quiet murmurs of approval, Kian demonstrated by embracing first Micah then her mother and lastly Otto. When the family left the chamber, Kian and the Guardians took their places on both sides of the empty hovering platform and guided it out. A path was cleared for them, and then the procession reformed behind them.

When the last of his people left, Kian removed his robe, folded it and draped it over his arm. Alone in the penthouse's dedicated elevator, he could finally let go of the strong posture and reassuring expression he'd been forced to keep up all evening long. With a sigh, he let his shoulders sag and hung his head.

CHAPTER 33: SYSSI

Immersed in the story, Syssi hadn't noticed how long she'd been reading until her sore throat started protesting. A glance at her watch confirmed that it was late. She lifted her head to glance at the window.

It was getting dark.

Any other Friday, she would've paused for a cup of tea and some gossip with her girls and then continued reading for another hour. Today, however, she didn't feel safe driving home alone at night. The uneasy feeling that had been troubling her lately persisted, and it cautioned her to play it safe.

She closed the book and lifted her head. "I'm afraid this will be all for today. It's getting dark and I want to get home before nightfall."

There were some murmurs of disappointment, but none of the women voiced a protest. They didn't like her going home while it was dark outside either.

"You'll have to come back tomorrow, then. I can't wait until next Friday to hear the rest," Hattie said.

Syssi agreed, she didn't want to wait either. The book was amazing, and she was just getting to the good parts. "I know, I'm dying to find out how it ends. I'll come tomorrow morning. But not too early. I like sleeping in on the weekends."

Clara clapped her on the back. "Don't worry about it. It's not like we are going anywhere. And take the book with you. You can finish it tonight."

Syssi was tempted. It wasn't as if she had anything else planned, and reading beat watching the tube any day. "But it's not fair to you girls. You'll have to wait until tomorrow." She offered the book to Leonora.

The woman pushed it back into Syssi's hand. "It's okay, child, we know how the story ends." She winked. "And they lived happily ever after. That's the beauty of romances; predictable endings that are always happy."

True, that was why Syssi liked them too. It was light, feel-good reading, and God knew she needed it given the dark clouds always looming on her horizon.

"Thank you." She kissed Leonora's cheek, then Hattie's, and lastly Clara's. "I'll see you tomorrow. Good night."

Twenty-five minutes later, Syssi parked her car in front of her landlady's house. It wasn't completely dark yet, but it was getting close. Clutching her keys in one hand and the book in the other, Syssi rushed down the long driveway to the guesthouse. She opened the door and locked it immediately after getting in, securing the chain.

The thing was a joke, she knew that—a strong kick and the chain would detach from the wood it was screwed to—but it made her feel just a little bit safer.

Her dinner consisted of a bag of mixed greens topped with stir-fried tofu, and she washed it down with a Coke Zero which was the only poison she allowed herself in her otherwise healthy diet.

Being good about every little thing was boring. A girl needed to be bad about something.

Giddy with anticipation, she got ready for bed and crawled under the blanket with her book. Pathetic, really, that this was what got her excited these days.

But whatever, it wasn't as if she had anything to prove to anyone. Living an adventure by immersing herself in the pages of a romance novel was much safer than going for real thrills, and it suited her just fine.

Two-thirds into it, her eyelids started drooping and she fell asleep without finding out if the lovers found a way to be together.

Her brain supplied an alternative ending all of its own.

The woods were as dark as they always were in her nightmares, but no wolves were chasing her this time. Unafraid, Syssi strolled leisurely along the familiar path, her eyes trained on the massive tree in the distance. Her lover awaited her there, and she was safe because he would never let anything happen to her. She was precious to him.

He'd told her so.

Feeling the soft fabric of her long white dress caress her thighs and her calves as she walked, Syssi felt sexy, desirable. On her feet, she had simple, flat sandals, but in her dream her modest height didn't bother her. She felt confident even without the benefit of heels making her taller. Her lover found her beautiful as she was.

With a frown, she tried to recall his name, but even though it felt as if it was on the tip of her tongue, it kept slipping away. She remembered figuring it out the other night, so why for heaven's sake was it eluding her now?

How was she going to greet him? Hello, my dream lover?

Syssi chuckled as funnier ideas flitted through her mind. She could call him her handsome dude, or hunky hunk hunk. Or she could borrow Amanda's lingo and just call him darling, or sweetheart, or honey. Men did it all the time when they couldn't remember a woman's name. She could do it too.

But it felt distasteful.

She had every intention of continuing what they had started the other night—with a man whose name she didn't know.

Bad girl, Syssi. Shame on you.

When she got closer, she saw him standing in exactly the same position as the other night. Unmoving, he was looking at something in the direction she was going, but she couldn't see what it was.

"Hi." Now that she was so close to him that she could smell him, her confidence faltered and her voice quivered. The man smelled absolutely delicious. Fresh pine and something wild yet safe.

He turned, his intense blue eyes mesmerizing her. "Hello, beautiful. How come you're here? Did I summon you?"

This was embarrassing. Hadn't he been waiting for her?

"Are you disappointed that I came?"

Faster than she thought possible, his arm looped around her and he pulled her against his big, hard body. "No. I'm glad you're here. You're braver than me. I was afraid to come for you."

Him? Afraid? Impossible. He was so big and so strong. He made her feel safe.

Lifting her face up, she brought a hand to his cheek and cupped it gently. "I can't imagine what can scare a man like you."

He lowered his lips to hers and kissed her lightly. "You do."

Her eyes widened. "Me? No one is scared of me. I'm a nice person. I would never harm anyone."

"I know, sweet girl. Not intentionally. But you are very dangerous. I'm afraid that you're going to tear out my heart from my chest and hold it in the palm of your hand—my life at your mercy."

Ugh, not romantic. Not at all.

"That sounds awful."

He smiled, his fangs not as long or terrifying as they'd been the other night. "You see? I'm bad at this. I don't know the right things to say."

So that was what scared a big guy like him. He wasn't big on words. Well, what she wanted from him didn't require a lot of talking. He might feel more confident with the doing.

Good thing it was a dream and she wasn't encumbered by her overpowering shyness. It was such a good feeling, to just say what was on her mind. Get it out.

"Make love to me. You're good at that."

He chuckled. "That, I am."

The bed appeared out of nowhere, a four poster monstrosity covered with white fluffy pillows and a white down comforter that looked like it was a foot thick.

Should she climb on top of it?

It wouldn't be graceful. The mattress was at least three feet off the ground, and Syssi would have to either hop or scramble to get there. Neither of which could've been done in a sexy or alluring manner.

As dreams went, she wasn't doing a good job at creating the right environment for a romantic atmosphere.

He solved her dilemma, swinging her up into his strong arms in one fluid motion, and sitting on the bed while still holding her tight.

Not sure what to do next, Syssi brought her hands to the row of small buttons at the front of her dress and started fumbling with the first one.

He grasped her hands and brought them to his lips for a kiss. "Let me, sweet girl, you keep your hands down by your sides."

The unmistakable tone of command in his voice did something to her. Syssi felt her nipples draw tight and her panties grow damp. A flush bloomed on her face and on her chest, the white dress contrasting and accentuating the redness. But it wasn't embarrassment that had caused it. It was the heat of excitement.

The only other time Syssi had felt passion that intense had been the night before. With the same man: Her dream lover.

She should ask him for his name.

Later.

Done with the top portion of the buttons, he parted the two halves of her dress, stealing her ability to think let alone talk or ask questions.

Her back arched of its own volition, thrusting her chest up. She couldn't wait to feel his big hands on her naked breasts. What a shame she was wearing a bra. Unlike the other dream, though, she didn't dispense with it with a thought. She wanted him to do it at his own pace. Having him in charge of her pleasure was exactly how she wanted it.

In a dream, social conventions and her own ideas of how a woman should act were of no consequence.

This was about pure pleasure.

She couldn't help a frustrated whimper as his fingers brushed lightly over her lacy bra, barely touching her stiff peaks.

With eyes that were smoldering with passion, he went back to the buttons, opening each and every one until the two halves of her dress slid open. Her body was fully on display for him, with nothing other than a sheer white lacy bra and matching panties.

"You're beautiful," he whispered, placing his palm over her soft tummy. Fingers splayed, his palm spanned the entire width of her.

A thought drifted through her mind that a man that big would be proportionally endowed. It gave her pause. What if she was too small?

She had a thing for tall guys, but this man was exceptionally tall. Maybe the disparity was too much?

Except, this was a dream. Her dream. And she could make sure that everything fit perfectly.

The hand on her tummy moved lower, and Syssi held her breath in anticipation. She was burning with desire, clutching her teeth together to stifle the needy whimpers that threatened to escape her mouth. When his palm finally made contact with her heated center, engulfing it in its entirety, she closed her eyes and let her head fall back.

"Look at me, sweet girl," he commanded. "Watch me pleasure you."

Lifting her lids halfway, she obeyed, watching his hand as he pushed her panties aside and slid his fingers over her engorged folds.

"You're so wet for me," he hissed out, and the smoldering look in his eyes turned luminescent.

He was casting light on her.

She'd seen something like that before. Amanda's eyes were the same. Maybe that was where her brain had taken the idea from.

The last vestiges of her lucidity flew away when she felt the tip of his finger press against her opening. Gently, he gathered moisture before pushing his finger a little farther, then retreated to do it again.

He treated her like a virgin, and in a way she was. It had been so long that she might as well have turned back into one.

Slow, maddeningly slow, he was getting her accustomed to his touch. Not expecting such gentleness and consideration from a man as dominant as him, Syssi felt her heart swell with gratitude.

Hell, it was more than that.

Her heart was swelling with love for her dream lover.

A man she'd conjured in her mind.

And how devastatingly sad was that?

CHAPTER 34: AMANDA

Amanda's phone was dancing the jig on her kitchen counter, buzzing and chiming at the same time. Reaching for it, she smiled at Onidu's quirky face on the screen.

The picture had been taken during last year's trip to Hawaii, capturing perfectly his look of repugnance at the shorts and T-shirt she had insisted he should wear in place of his habitual suit. It was the best picture she had of him; with his expression so close to the real thing, she could almost believe it was genuine.

"Yes, darling."

"I have grave news, Mistress. It seems your laboratory has been ransacked by vandals. All is in disarray, with pieces of equipment strewn about and loose wires dangling precariously from what is left standing. Every last drawer has been pulled out of its place and its contents lie torn to pieces, littering the floor. But the worst are the disgraceful, hateful words—which I am too much of a gentleman to repeat—scribbled all over the walls. It is terrible! What should I do, Mistress?"

Onidu sounded truly distraught, and Amanda had to remind herself that it was nothing more than his programming providing the appropriate tone for the situation at hand.

"Onidu, sweetie, can you record what you see with your phone and send it to me?" Amanda knew it was no use trying to persuade him to recite the graffiti. His programming prevented the use of profanities; her mother's work no doubt.

"Yes, Mistress, right away."

WHORE, SLUT, HARLOT, TART, DIE... were some of the endearments scribbled with a black sharpie on the walls, and a sloppy drawing of the Doomers' emblem ensured she knew whom the message was from.

Very creative boys. Nice vocab. Amanda's face tightened with distaste as she turned off the phone and dropped it on the granite counter. Shaking her head, she crossed the kitchen to pour herself more brew. But then, as she lifted the carafe, she froze with the thing suspended in midair.

What if she had left something behind? The thought sent a cold shiver of unease up her spine. What if the Doomers had found something?

Chewing on her lower lip, she tried to remember if there had been anything left in the lab that the Doomers could use. The test results from her pet project were safely stored on her laptop, which she remembered taking with her. And the small notebook with her hastily jotted ideas and random thoughts was always in her purse, ready for whenever and wherever inspiration struck...

That uneasy feeling gaining sudden momentum, Amanda raced to her bedroom and started rummaging through the multitude of pockets in her purse. Getting frustrated, she upended it, emptying the whole thing on her bed.

The notebook wasn't there.

Running back to the living room, she repeated the routine with her laptop case.

It wasn't there either.

Oh, shit, shit, shit... Amanda raced back to the kitchen for her phone.

"Kian, we've got a big problem," she said the moment he answered.

"What's going on?" He tensed, picking up on her urgency.

"I left something behind in the lab, and if the minions-of-all-that-is-evil have found it, we are in deep shit!" She relayed Onidu's report, telling Kian about the break-in and the graffiti.

Kian wasn't interested in the details. "What did you leave in the lab, Amanda?"

"Look, I'm sorry! I thought I had it in my purse, but I didn't... I must have left it somewhere." She was on the verge of tears.

"Just tell me what the hell it is, Amanda!" Obviously, Kian had lost his patience.

"I can't find my notebook, the one with all my great ideas and all the other stuff I like to keep handy. The thing is, I wrote in it the first names and cell phone numbers of all my paranormal test subjects." She sighed. "And the rankings I assigned to them. Most are between one and three, Syssi is a ten, and another boy is an eight. If the Doomers have half a brain between them, they'll go after these two, but if they are all morons, they might go after each person on that list."

Amanda paused, waiting for Kian to explode. When all she heard was his heavy breathing she continued, offering what she believed was a slight glimmer of hope. "It's only first names and phone numbers, maybe it's not enough for the Doomers to go by?"

"Oh, that's plenty enough. It may take them some time and some cash to find someone to dig through the phone records, but when they do, it will be child's play for them to zero in on your subjects' cellular signal and locate them. We are probably out of time already. Call Syssi and tell her not to leave her home. I'm going to pick her up myself. Text me the info for the boy. I'll send Guardians for him as well."

The line went dead.

"Damn." Amanda searched for Syssi's contact, pressing call before it crossed her mind that the girl was probably still sleeping. Six o'clock on a Saturday morning was too early to call a human.

Syssi picked up after several rings. "Hello?" As Amanda had expected, her voice was groggy from sleep.

"Good morning, sweetie. I'm so sorry to wake you. I wanted you to do something for me and didn't realize how early it was. Are you planning on going anywhere in the next couple of hours?"

"No. But later I'm going to the retirement home. Why? What do you need?"

Explaining the whole mess to Syssi while she didn't remember a thing was too much. Better leave it up to Kian. Shit, she wouldn't remember who he was either.

"I'll call you later, after you had a few cups of coffee. I know you don't function before your third one."

Syssi yawned. "Thanks."

CHAPTER 35: KIAN

"Meet me down in the garage, and bring your weapons," Kian barked into his phone, then shoved it in his back pocket as he rushed out the door.

It had never crossed his mind that the Doomers might pose a threat to Syssi. The only one he'd been concerned about was Amanda. Frantic with worry for the girl, he punched the button for the elevator over and over again, and when he finally stepped inside, he couldn't wait for it to descend fast enough.

His body pulsing with pent-up aggression, Kian wasn't surprised at what he saw when he caught his reflection in the mirror. He looked like a killer. Eyes glowing and fangs protruding over his lower lip, the face staring back at him didn't look even remotely human—the vicious expression reflecting his murderous intent.

Damn, he would have to calm down before showing up at Syssi's doorstep. One look at him and the girl would drop in a dead faint. Which could actually work to his advantage. She wouldn't resist when he picked her up in his arms and took off with her.

Not the best way to go about it, but Kian doubted that he'd be able to calm down enough to pass for a human during the short drive to her place, leaving him no other choice.

As he raced through the parking level toward the Lexus, Anandur's and Brundar's heavy boots pounding behind him, he was inundated with gruesome images of Syssi in the hands of his enemies. Like snippets out of a nightmare, they were flashing in his mind one worse than the next.

"What's going on, boss?" Anandur called from behind him.

"The Doomers have Amanda's list of paranormals. They will go after at least two of them. We are picking up her assistant, Syssi. She tops the damn list."

Snarling, his lips peeling away from his elongated fangs, he vowed that if anything happened to her, if the sick bastards laid a finger on her, hell had not known the fury he'd unleash on them.

As he turned on the ignition, Amanda's text came in, reassuring him that Syssi was home and wasn't planning on leaving anytime soon. It had done little to calm him down. He wouldn't relax until he had her in the safety of his keep.

Ranting and cursing at LA's goddamned traffic, Kian drove recklessly, speeding and weaving in between cars. It was a miracle he hadn't gotten pulled over yet. He prayed his luck would hold, not because he was concerned with getting a ticket, but because of the delay it would introduce.

With his anxiety for Syssi growing worse with each passing moment, constricting his chest and twisting his gut, the pain he was feeling was more than physical—the unfamiliar sensation one he hoped never to feel again.

Shaken by the ferocity of his reaction, Kian was forced to admit that she'd awoken in him something he believed had been long dead. Feelings that he had sworn off long ago because experience had taught him that they were nothing but a prelude to disaster.

Kian had loved once.

It had been so long ago, the memory of the actual events had faded, but he still remembered the pain of it ending.

Her name was Lavena, a beautiful seventeen-year-old mortal girl. He had just turned nineteen. Too young and too inexperienced to know better, he fell head over heels in love with her. And as the young often do, he believed himself invincible; there were no obstacles he couldn't overcome, no difficulties great enough to deter him from his beloved.

Disregarding his mother's dictum, he ran away and married the girl. They loved each other passionately, and as he tended to the small farm he'd bought for them, and she to their modest home, for a short time they lived in simple bliss.

Slowly, though, Lavena's mind began showing the effects of the frequent thralls he was forced to subject her to. Even as impetuous as he was, he knew he had to make sure she never found out what he was.

Lavena grew distraught, believing she was losing her mind; finding herself time and again spacing out and forgetting where she was or what she was doing.

In his effort to lessen the damage, Kian refined his thralling technique to a level of fine art, doing his best to keep it minimal, but the episodes kept coming. By the time he realized the fairy tale had to end, it was too late. They were expecting a child.

Their life together became a nightmare.

At first, he tried to abstain as much as he could. When it became clear he couldn't hold back his raging immortal hormones, he resorted to the use of prostitutes.

Kian hated himself, hated what he was doing to the girl he loved, hated the kind of twisted life he was forced to live.

Lavena became distant and mistrustful. No longer blinded by her adoration, she began noticing that he never got sick and that his scrapes and bruises would disappear just as soon as he got them. She began to fear him, believing he wielded some kind of dark magic.

He had to leave.

It was easy to fake his own death. All it took to convince Lavena and the rest of the villagers that he had been mauled by wild beasts was for his torn, bloodstained tunic to be found in the woods. With no body to bury, his wife buried that shirt.

Shrouding himself, he watched from a distance as Lavena mourned his death, as she delivered their beautiful, healthy daughter, as she got better, as she married a widower with four kids of his own.

Kian kept coming back. He watched his child get married and have children of her own. He watched them live their lives, get old and die, while he remained unchanged; their lifetimes but a blink of an eye on the horizon of his own.

Years upon years of gut-wrenching sorrow and regret.

Kian had vowed never to be that stupid or careless again.

He had kept that vow for nineteen hundred and seventy-six years.

CHAPTER 36: SYSSI

Syssi cursed, burying her face in a pillow. Amanda's call had woken her up from the most amazing dream way before she'd been ready for it to be over. Heck, if it were up to her, she would've been happy staying in that dream world with her dream lover forever.

Like the other night, he'd brought her to an earth-shattering climax, moments before the dream had abruptly ended. This time, by an annoying ringing.

Worse, she had no name to go with the memory of his gorgeous face.

And yet, the big difference was that this morning she wasn't consumed by melancholy. The thing that kept the sadness at bay was hope that she would dream of him again. Two nights in a row was the beginning of a pattern.

As she showered and dressed, Syssi wondered what brought on the dreams. Last night it had obviously been the paranormal romance novel she'd been reading. It could explain the fangs. Except, the leading guy's, or rather vampire's, description didn't match that of her dream lover. Besides, the book couldn't explain the night before. Nothing could. Except perhaps for her subconscious trying to tell her the same thing as the three wise old ladies; that it was time to end her self-imposed celibacy and take a chance on life.

Trouble was, just thinking about it made her anxious.

She wasn't ready for the dating world. Hell, she had never been ready. Syssi hated the whole process of sifting through numerous guys in the hopes that one of them would turn out to be the one. She hated the awkward dates and having to say it was nice but no thank you.

Out of nowhere, an image of a huge and scary man flitted through her mind. Vaguely, she remembered someone like that asking her out, but it didn't feel like an actual memory, more like a dream. Not a good one, though. Perhaps she'd dreamt it before dreaming of her imaginary lover.

Except, she had a nagging suspicion that there was more to it. Not a premonition, not exactly, but a gut feeling that something dark and dangerous was lurking outside, waiting for her to make the wrong move. It was the same feeling that had prompted her to leave the retirement home early and avoid driving in the dark. And she was pretty sure it was somehow connected to her premonition about Amanda.

Great, now she was anxious, and feeding off her thoughts the fear was gathering momentum. She needed a distraction before it turned into a full blown panic attack.

Syssi turned on the television and made herself a fresh cup of coffee, spiking it with Kahlua to help calm her down.

After two more spiked coffees and an old episode of *Friends*, she felt her anxiety ebb.

Until the startling screech of tires brought it back.

Syssi ran up to the window to see if anyone was hurt.

Trouble was, her guesthouse was all the way at the end of the driveway in the back of the lot, and only a small section of the street was visible from where she was standing and peeking from behind the curtain. The main house was blocking the rest.

She didn't see a car, but clearing the side of the main house were three large men. One rushed down her driveway, leaving the other two at the curb.

What was going on?

Fear gripping her, she let the curtain drop back into place, taking a step sideways to get out of his line of sight. As he kept getting closer, the sound of his pounding boots thundering in the quiet of the peaceful morning, her fear morphed into panic.

Tall and muscular, the guy looked like a menacing predator closing in for the kill—that is, until his beautiful face came into focus.

Recognizing him, Syssi's hand flew to her mouth and she gasped.

It couldn't be. Backing away from the window, she lifted her hand to her forehead.

Was it possible the dream had been a premonition? Or had all that Kahlua addled her brain and she was seeing things; superimposing the face of her dream lover on that of a stranger?

Not sure she had the guts to find out, Syssi took another step back.

The man must've seen her backing away and figured he was frightening her. Slowing down, he stopped several feet away from her front door.

"Syssi, it's me, Kian...," he called out. "Amanda's brother. Don't be afraid. Please open the door."

With her hand on her heaving chest, Syssi moved back to the window and pushed the curtain aside to take a better look.

Kian? Amanda's brother?

Her frantic heartbeat had slowed down a bit, but her hands were still clammy and shaky.

What was Amanda's brother doing in my dream? What is he doing here? Is Amanda okay? Why didn't she mention him when she called?

Suddenly worried about her friend, Syssi rushed to open the door. "What happened? Is Amanda okay?"

"Amanda is fine. I'm sorry to have given you a fright, but we have a bit of a situation. Everything is under control, no need to panic, but I do need to talk to you. May I come in?" he asked and stepped closer.

Now that he was standing right in front of her, she could appreciate how really tall he was. To look at his strikingly beautiful face, she had to crank her neck way up. But even though her worry for Amanda had been assuaged, and she was feeling calmer, she was still scared of this man. Or rather of what his appearance on her doorstep at six thirty in the morning could mean.

Syssi swallowed nervously.

Amanda's brother was even more intimidating than her conjured dream lover. With all those muscles coiled and ready to pounce, he looked like a killer—the tension and menace radiating from him a sure sign that the situation was not as trivial as he'd tried to make it sound.

God, all this gorgeous maleness was turning her head into mush.

He was gazing at her intently as if expecting her to say something.

Oh, that's right, she was supposed to invite him to come in. Damn, Syssi felt her cheeks redden. Not only was she acting like a moonstruck teenager, but her place wasn't as tidy as she would've liked when inviting someone like him inside. There was nothing that she could do about it, though. She couldn't just leave him standing outside when he'd so politely asked if he could come in.

"Yes, of course, please." Syssi smiled a tight little smile, gesturing for him to follow her while doing her best to pretend as if he wasn't making her nervous and awkward as heck.

The stranger that wasn't a stranger...

Following her, he walked in and closed the door. Her place seemed to shrink with him in it, and suddenly she felt trapped, struggling to get air into her lungs as if Kian had somehow consumed all of the breathable air. And yet, as she felt the heat rolling off of him at her back, a rush of awareness coursed through her body, tightening it all over in some places, while loosening it in others. She had to take a breath if only to inhale his scent.

Unable to bear the tension, she whipped around only to find herself a fraction of an inch from his solid chest. Afraid of what she might see, she hesitated a moment before looking up at his face.

Syssi inhaled sharply. His eyes were the most intense shade of blue she had ever seen. She felt enthralled by them. Hypnotized.

Wow, waking up must have been a dream within a dream, and she was still sleeping, still dreaming, and conjuring this gorgeous man, those amazing eyes.

She wondered if he would feel real if she touched him. Except, remembering how very real he had felt in her dream... well, that obviously offered no proof one way or the other.

Syssi waited for him to say something, or at least kiss her senseless, but he did neither. Instead, he was boring into her eyes, holding her captive.

It felt as if he was pushing at some mental barrier inside her head, the pressure at her temples getting progressively worse until the barrier shuttered and a flood of submerged memories came barging to the forefront of her mind.

As Syssi struggled to process and assimilate the influx, she was aware of Kian's hard eyes watching her intently.

At first, Syssi felt as if her head was about to explode from the tremendous pressure, but as it eased and the memories rushed in, she was certain she was losing her freaking mind.

Kian at the lab, the danger, rushing to the car, the penthouse, that kiss, the dreams.

What was real?

What was a dream?

Searching his eyes for answers, Syssi found her own burning desire mirrored. Except, his seemed more like a predatory hunger, one she'd experienced before. She remembered him standing in this exact spot, looking at her with the same ravenous expression on his handsome face.

This hadn't been part of her dream. It had happened.

Overwhelmed, she took a step back.

Kian looked so intimidating as he loomed over her like a mountain of a sex-starved man. And yet, curiously, now that she remembered him, she was no longer afraid. Excited, anxious, needy, awkward... yes... but not afraid. For some reason, she felt she could trust him. Kian would protect her.

Syssi had no reason to question her infallible instinct. It had never steered her wrong before.

Which brought back the issue of what the heck he needed to protect her from, and what really was going on?

"What...?" she began.

Kian cut her off, gesturing for her to stop.

Clearing his throat as if trying to bring some moisture into his dried-out mouth, his voice came out sounding like gravel. "I need you to pack a bag, you're coming with me," he commanded and then waited for her to do as she was told.

"Really? Just like that?" Syssi cocked an eyebrow.

"I'll explain everything on the way. The situation I mentioned before makes it dangerous for you to stay. We need to get out of here, ASAP. Please hurry up and pack only what you'll need for a couple of days." Kian took hold of her shoulders and turned her around toward the bedroom, playfully smacking her butt as if to hasten her on her way.

Taken by surprise, Syssi jerked her head back, giving him the what-the-hell-do-you-think-you're-doing look before strutting to the bedroom.

But as soon as her face was turned away, she smiled.

What was it about this man that she would allow him to do that? Delivered by his hand, a move that she would've found offensive coming from anyone else, had brought her a delicious tingle of arousal.

He had a lot of nerve, though—playing around as if they were an item and as if nothing was going on, without bothering to explain what the hell it was.

Rushing, she opened drawers and threw items of clothing on the bed; yesterday's bizarre events and this morning's panic attack enough to convince her that she needed to get away. But from whom or what?

She'd soon find out. Kian had promised he'd explain.

Pulling her overnight bag from under the bed, Syssi thought about her strange memory loss and its sudden return. She shook her head. At least one mystery had been solved. The erotic dreams hadn't come out of nowhere. They had been the result of her attraction to Kian. She hadn't remembered him consciously, but her subconscious had done a marvelous job of choosing this incredibly handsome man to star in her sexy dreams.

She had a feeling Kian had something to do with her memory loss. But what? Had he hypnotized her? And if he had; when? How? Why?

Could she trust him if he had?

Was she a complete idiot if she did trust him?

Syssi was packed and ready to go in a matter of minutes, hurrying to brush her hair, apply a little eyeliner, and step into her platform slides. She was ready to step out of her bedroom when her eyes fell on the romance book lying face down on her nightstand. Unzipping her bag, she added it to the few things she was taking with her.

Five inches taller, with her hair falling in thick, shiny waves down her back, she left her bedroom more confident in her looks but less so in the soundness of her mind.

That extra minute spent had been so worth it.

As she walked back into the room with her duffle bag slung over her shoulder, Kian's eyes widened, and the heat in them made her feel feminine and powerful.

Sexy.

Wanted.

Walking toward him, she even swayed her hips a little. But then her confidence faltered, and she searched his eyes, hesitantly gauging his reaction.

As if guessing what she was looking for, Kian gave her an appreciative once-over, his hooded gaze letting her know how much he liked what he saw.

She smiled, wordlessly thanking him for his mute admiration. But then she lost her nerve and lowered her eyes, her momentary bravado replaced by an embarrassed blush.

In two quick strides, Kian closed the distance between them and reached for the duffle bag. Slinging it over his shoulder, he wrapped his arm around her waist and pulled her close against his side.

Syssi stiffened momentarily, not sure what to make of the possessive move. It definitely wasn't the casual type between friends. It was something more. And though she didn't want to read too much into it, it felt incredibly good just to go along and lean into him as if it was the most natural thing for her to do.

As they walked out the door with their arms around each other, she sensed it was a new beginning. But of what? And as they kept going down the long driveway, the feeling intensified, shaping into a strong premonition that she was never coming back.

She didn't know the why or how of it, or if it was good or bad.

Regrettably, it was in the nature of premonitions to be vague; revealing only a hint of an outcome and very little if any of the particulars.

Syssi wondered if there was anything she would terribly miss. The furniture belonged to her landlady, all her photos were safely stored on her laptop, and the rest of her stuff could be replaced with as little as a thousand bucks. Except her Precious, of course.

Her BMW convertible was the only luxury she had accepted from her parents, and she loved that car. Precious would go wherever she went. Leaving it unattended on the street was out of the question.

"What about my car?" She turned to Kian.

By then they had reached the curb, joining the two imposing men standing guard. One was a huge redhead, the other a slightly smaller, gorgeous blond. Both were looking her over with unabashed male curiosity and appreciation.

Tucking her closer against his side, Kian tightened his hold. "Give me the keys." He held out his palm, staring daggers at his companions.

Puzzled by his abrasiveness, she lifted her eyes to look at his angry face. "Aren't you going to introduce us?"

Pointing dismissively at the men, he barked, "The big red oaf's name is Anandur, and Rapunzel's name is Brundar." Partially blocking their view of her with his body, he finished the introduction. "And this is Syssi, Amanda's assistant."

Sidestepping Kian, the one named Anandur smiled and brought his lips down to her offered hand for a kiss. "Enchanted."

Was she imagining it, or did Kian just hiss?

Brundar bowed his head without saying a thing, but his lips curled up slightly, suggesting he was suppressing a smile.

This time, there was no hiss.

"Which one is yours?" Kian asked, closing his fingers over her keys.

"The blue BMW over there." She pointed.

He tossed the keys to Anandur, who caught the dangling thing midair, and mock-saluting Kian walked over to her car.

"Brundar, you're driving," Kian ordered and opened the SUV's back passenger door for Syssi. Motioning for her to scoot over, he joined her in the back seat, and settling close to her, placed a proprietary hand on her thigh.

With the thick curtain of her hair hiding her face, Syssi smirked. She wasn't sure what to make of Kian's behavior. He was acting like a jealous boyfriend.

On the other hand, it was entirely possible that he was always rude to these guys, or that the animosity between them lingered from something that had happened before. In either case, it had nothing to do with her.

Still, whatever the reason, Syssi didn't mind the feel of his body pressed against her side, or his fingers closing around her knee. On the contrary, it felt nice. It had been so long since she had enjoyed this kind of closeness.

Suddenly overcome by an intense yearning for it, her gut twisted with a sense of loss as she realized how improbable it was for something meaningful to develop between them.

She was such an idiot.

One hot kiss and two erotic dreams didn't constitute a relationship or even a fling.

What was she thinking?

Syssi sighed. Wishing for it wasn't going to make it so.

But in the meantime, she could pretend a little and enjoy the warmth of togetherness. Even if it was all an illusion. For the duration of this adventure, she decided she would let it unfold and deal with the consequences later.

CHAPTER 37: KIAN

Holding Syssi close, Kian savored the feel of her. Still worried about how haggard she had looked when he had first gotten to her place, he glanced down, but her face was hidden behind her hair.

Damn! The girl had looked ashen as if she had been sick or tired from a sleepless night, and her pretty face had been pinched with worry and fear.

It was his fault.

He must've harmed her somehow with his thrall the other night, and this morning had scared her out of her mind, galloping down that driveway the way he had. The fact that he had no choice did nothing to ease his guilt.

He wanted to make that tired look go away, to enfold her in the shelter of his arms and ease her fears and worries, to cocoon her in safety and warmth and undo whatever damage he had unwittingly done.

But this was not the right time for this. And besides, he would probably freak her out. As it was, his body didn't get the message that it was okay to power down yet, and with the way he was still primed for a fight, he could just imagine how threatening he must seem to her.

Forcing in a deep breath, Kian tried to relax his coiled muscles.

He was so grateful that he had made it in time. His original plan had been to thrall Syssi again to get her to cooperate, but he was glad he had decided against it and had restored her memory instead. It had confused the hell out of her, but at least he hadn't compounded the damage to her brain.

Yeah, keep telling yourself that.

The truth was, he wanted Syssi to remember him; and all other plans had flown out the window once he had seen her again and his hormones had taken over, doing his thinking for him.

Kian smirked, remembering how following her inside, he had zeroed in on that shapely behind of hers.

Lucky for him, she hadn't caught him ogling it.

But oh, boy, those form-fitting leggings she was wearing outlined her ass so perfectly and left so very little to the imagination, he'd had to fight the urge to cup them with his hands, and after giving them a nice squeeze, run his fingers along that center seam all the way down to her core.

When she had turned around and found him almost pressed against her, he had wanted to kiss her, bad. It was good that he had learned some restraint over the years because with the way she had gazed at him, wanting him to do just that, he had to remind himself that there was no time and that he had to restore her memories and get her out of there first. The kissing had to wait. Though he had managed to get away with that little slap on her delicious ass, thankfully, without getting in trouble.

She might've even liked it.

Perfect, the girl was absolutely perfect.

Sexy, sweet, beautiful.

His.

Sitting next to Syssi, feeling her warmth radiate through their clothes, smelling her delicious scent, Kian wondered what it was about her that stirred these unfamiliar cravings in him. The lust was to be expected; Syssi was beautiful and sexy and it was in his nature to want her body. But the possessiveness, the protectiveness, the tenderness he felt toward her, these were new.

He hugged her closer and caressed her knee lightly, reluctant to spoil the moment and upset her with the explanation he had promised. But it needed to be done.

Taking a deep breath, he shifted so he could look into her eyes and took her hand, squeezing it gently.

"Remember the people we were trying to avoid the other day in the lab?" Kian used the most reassuring tone he could muster, hating that he had to scare her again. "They came back last night and ransacked the lab— wrote hateful things on the walls."

Syssi's hand flew to her chest and the color drained from her face. "Oh my God! Poor Amanda, she must be so upset!"

Well, that hadn't worked as well as he had planned; the girl had turned as pale as a ghost.

And he hadn't even gotten to the punch line yet.

"She is distraught, but not over the damage. That is easily fixed... Amanda had a notebook. Among other things, it contained a list of all her paranormal subjects by their first name, phone number, and the ranking she assigned them. That notebook is missing, and we believe the vandals got it and may try to harm those on the list."

"Why?" Syssi kept rubbing her chest as the bad news kept piling.

"Why do they do all the evil deeds they do? Hate, fear, ignorance, greed, envy. Take your pick. They may believe special abilities are evil, the mark of the devil or some other nonsense like that. The why doesn't matter, just know that they will. You are the highest ranked on Amanda's list, which makes you their number one target."

Just talking about it had blown his hard-won composure away. The idea of anyone or anything posing a threat to Syssi had him seething with rage. "Can I have your cell phone? We need to get rid of it. The ~~fuckers~~ can track you by its signal." He held out his palm. "Don't worry. I'll buy you a new one."

Syssi handed him the device and scooted away, putting some distance between them. Kian knew he'd sounded vehement delivering his little speech, and with her already being scared, his dark mood must've added a layer of anxiety.

Pulling her back to him, he plastered her against his side and squeezed her shoulders reassuringly, tightening his fingers on her cold, sweaty hand. "Don't worry, sweet girl. I'd never let anything happen to you. I'd rip to shreds each and every one of those bastards with my own bare hands before I let anyone lay a finger on you. You are safe with me." Kian finished his gruesome pledge with a kiss to the top of her head.

Except, it didn't seem to help with her anxiety. The poor girl remained silent and rigid.

Way to go calming her nerves, moron.

At this point, she must've been as scared of him as she was of the looming threat.

Opening the window just a crack, he sent her phone flying straight into a construction curbside trash bin.

Now the ~~fuckers~~ A-holes could follow it to the damp.

CHAPTER 38: SYSSI

"You could stumble and twist your ankle wearing these insane shoes," Kian bit out as Syssi wavered and gripped his bicep for support.

Walking from the car to the elevators, she felt a little lightheaded. Was it the Kahlua? Perhaps. Though it also could've been whatever Kian had done to her head. But then, being scared out of her freaking mind might've had something to do with it as well.

"It's not the shoes, they're actually pretty sturdy. I'm just a little dizzy. I might be still tipsy from all the Kahlua I had this morning. Or, what's more likely, the weakness and lack of balance are the results of all the excitement. I was so scared..." Embarrassed, she glanced his way before looking down at her feet.

Some of the dark shadows had lifted off his handsome face, and he no longer looked as frightening as he had in the car. Though judging by his stiff posture, he was still tense.

"Tipsy? Before lunch? Somehow you don't strike me as the type." A smile tugged at his lips as he wrapped his arm around her waist, propping her against his side so she was almost floating, her feet barely touching the ground.

"No, I'm not, I hardly ever drink. I've been feeling anxious for the past few days. The bad feeling was so strong that I couldn't shake it off." Syssi looked up at Kian with a sad smile, deciding to tell him the truth about herself. After all, Amanda had probably already told him all about her and her questionable talent. "I learned from experience to listen to that cursed foresight of mine and not disregard it as nothing. When I feel something bad is going to happen it almost always does. So anyway, long story short, I spiked my coffee with some Kahlua to soothe my rattled nerves."

Kian kissed the top of her head and squeezed her shoulder. "I'm grateful for your foresight, and you should be too. It's a good warning mechanism that might've saved you from something very nasty. But enough of that, I don't want you thinking about it anymore. You're safe now."

Parting ways with Brundar at the elevators, they stepped into the one going up to the penthouse.

"How many of those spiked cups did you have?" Kian asked as the doors opened to the vestibule.

"Three, but there wasn't that much alcohol in them. It's just that I'm a really lightweight drinker." She grimaced. "Half a glass of wine makes me woozy."

"You'll feel better after you eat. This dizziness is probably the result of stress combined with alcohol and an empty stomach. I'll have Okidu whip up something." Kian dropped her duffle bag by the entry and headed for the kitchen.

Hesitating, Syssi wasn't sure if she was to follow him or wait by the door. Looking around and twisting her hands as she reacquainted herself with the place, she wondered if Kian planned for her to stay with him.

She should've thought of asking him to drop her off at Andrew's.

Truth be told, though, she'd let him lead her like a goose and hadn't been thinking at all. It seemed that her brain took a hiatus whenever Kian was near, mistakenly assuming they were an item and letting him take care of her as if she was his. Except she wasn't, which explained why she felt so awkward and displaced coming home with him. Besides, she was an independent woman who didn't need anyone to take care of her. Except until recently, it had meant earning a decent income and paying her own bills.

Defending herself from crazy cult members wasn't something she'd ever anticipated dealing with.

Syssi wasn't a warrior, she had never even taken a self-defense class, and she had a feeling calling the police wouldn't have done her any good. She needed someone like Kian or her brother to keep her safe from them. Posturing her independence and insisting on staying home would've been just stupid. Sometimes, a girl needed to acknowledge her limitations and accept help.

Taking a deep breath, she put one foot in front of the other and followed Kian to the kitchen.

CHAPTER 39: KIAN

The sound of Okidu chopping vegetables greeted Kian as soon as he opened his front door. The thing was, the speed at which his butler was performing the simple task would've seemed unnatural even for an experienced sushi chef. He hurried to the kitchen and put a hand on Okidu's shoulder. "Good, I'm hungry, and so is Syssi," he said, letting Okidu know that they had company he should be mindful of.

The speed slowed immediately.

"It seems we both skipped breakfast." He turned around and motioned for Syssi to join them in the kitchen, then reached under the counter and pulled out a stool for her.

Okidu paused his chopping and turned around with a big welcoming smile already plastered on his face. "Of course, Master, and good day to you and the lovely lady. It is a pleasure to see you again, madam." He wiped his hands on a dish towel and bowed.

"May I serve breakfast in the dining room, Master?" He intercepted Kian as he was about to pull out another stool for himself.

"Yes, good idea, the dining room..." Kian pushed back the stool and redirected Syssi toward the formal dining room.

Good save.

Thankful for Okidu's intervention, Kian shook his head. As ridiculous as it was for someone his age, he didn't have much practice at being a host. Besides the Guardians, he never had guests over—not that the guys qualified as such or required special treatment.

If not for his butler, it would've never crossed Kian's mind that there was anything wrong with inviting Syssi to eat brunch at the kitchen counter. Not that there was, necessarily, but she deserved a little courtesy, and the truth was that he wanted to impress her.

Never mind that what Okidu had been programmed to consider as proper etiquette no longer applied to this day and age. Kian, however, was a product of a different era.

Damn, it had been such a long time since he had treated a woman like a real lady. Problem was, he would've been laughed at if he tried it with any of the mortal women he typically interacted with—in any capacity.

Kian grimaced as it crossed his mind that his mother would've been appalled to see him behave like this. If she ever decided to grace his home with her presence, he'd have to brush up on the good manners she had attempted to instill in him all those centuries ago.

Regrettably, he didn't have much use for even a fraction of those manners with the kind of company he kept. Curiously, though, it hadn't bothered him before. His nightly prowls required little if any effort or finesse on his part. He'd show up, zero in on his chosen prey, and the females usually took it from there.

Easy...

He had never brought any of them home.

If he hadn't ~~fucked~~ _screw_ ed them against a wall in a dark alley or some other secluded corner, he would bring them to one of the timeshare apartments on the lower levels, or a hotel. Later, Okidu would make sure that Kian's thralled and confused partners found their way back safely.

He had never spent the night with any of them.

"I don't mind eating at the kitchen counter," she said in a small voice.

Kian leaned to whisper in her ear, "I don't mind either, but it will upset Okidu to no end, and he'll act pissy for the rest of the day. I'd rather humor him." He was such a rotten liar. But Syssi looked uncomfortable and he wanted to put her at ease.

She smiled. "I wouldn't want to upset the poor guy. Lead the way."

Walking her toward the dining room, Kian put his hand on the small of her back—his touch eliciting a slight shiver. Syssi was attracted to him, but so were most of the women he came in contact with. He wanted more from her even though he shouldn't. There could be nothing between them other than some harmless flirting, and he was pushing the limits of that too.

As he pulled a chair out for Syssi, he was acutely aware of how different she was from his nightly fare.

The women who tended to take his bait were the hardened, disillusioned types frequenting the bars and clubs, looking for some good times. Just like him.

No questions asked and no expectations.

Most times he hadn't even asked for their names.

Syssi seemed so innocent and fragile in contrast, sitting there like a proper lady with her back straight and her hands in her lap, looking nervous.

Her eyes darting around, she looked at everything and anything in the room just to avoid meeting his eyes.

So shy... so reserved... so sweet...

She wouldn't make it easy on him. She would expect him to woo her, be romantic.

Kian's brows drew tight as it dawned on him that he didn't know how to do that. He had never felt the need to make that kind of an effort before.

Living the way he did, and with hardly the time or patience to watch or read anything romantic, he didn't even have the benefit of learning by example from fiction.

Yeah, he had the finesse of a bulldog and was just as charming.

He would have to improvise, and hopefully, manage not to blunder too much. Because even though he expected to have Syssi for only a few days, he wanted those days to be special, different.

CHAPTER 40: SYSSI

Kian was acting like the perfect gentleman. It started with him pulling the chair out for her, then waiting for her to be seated before gently pushing it toward the table. When Okidu brought a pitcher of orange juice, Kian insisted on pouring it into her glass, and when the salad arrived, he loaded her plate himself.

No guy had ever doted on her like this. In fact, she'd only seen such manners in a period movie, or read about it in a historical romance novel. Although Kian looked to be in his early thirties, he was old-fashioned like a man at least double his age.

Which reminded her.

"I forgot to ask Anandur to bring me the keys to my car. Could you please call him?" She glanced at her watch. "I have an appointment later today that I can't miss."

Kian frowned. "Could you reschedule?"

Syssi shook her head. "I could, but I would hate to do it. I promised three dear old friends that I'd come back and finish reading a book to them today. They'll be very disappointed if I don't. We were just getting to the good parts yesterday, but it was getting late, and I didn't want to drive home at night."

He looked doubtful. "Is this some new thing? Friends reading together?"

Syssi chuckled. "No. The three were my grandmother's friends. Toward the end of her life she lost her eyesight, so I read to her whenever I came to visit, which was every Friday afternoon. Her friends always joined us, and after she passed away, I didn't have the heart to stop the visits. They kind of adopted me as their granddaughter. Besides, I enjoy their company. They are lots of fun."

As she thought about the kinds of books the ladies had her read, Syssi felt a blush creeping up. After all this time, she should've been cured of the damned blushing. Was it possible that her grandmother's friends sought to help her get over it by making her uncomfortable on purpose?

If they did, then it wasn't working. The bane of her existence was incurable.

Perhaps she should use a heavy foundation, the kind actors used on stage. Because nothing else could cover it up. It was such an embarrassment to have her feelings show when she would've preferred to keep them to herself.

For a private person like her, it felt awful to be exposed like that. It had gotten to the point that she avoided talking about anything that might cause her discomfort, which unfortunately included talking with guys she was interested in. Not that there had been many. But there had been one or two instances when she would've liked to start a conversation but hadn't out of fear that her flaming cheeks would advertise her interest.

Kian was no exception. The only difference was that she was stuck with him and had nowhere to run.

He clasped her hand. "That's very nice of you."

She tried to shrug it off. "It's nothing. As I said, it's not a big sacrifice. I enjoy doing it."

Kian nodded. "I'll have one of my guys drive you."

"I would hate to inconvenience anyone. I have a car and no one knows I visit the Golden Age Retirement home. I'll be perfectly safe."

"Perhaps. But I'll be going out of my mind with worry. I'll feel so much better knowing you have someone to protect you in case of trouble."

Syssi narrowed her eyes at Kian. He was a sneaky one, guilting her into agreeing. "I know what you're doing."

He smirked. "Is it working?"

"What do you think?"

"Good. It's a huge relief. I meant every word of it." He sounded sincere. "When do you need to be there and how far away is it?"

"I didn't tell them an exact time, but I think ten will be perfect. The drive there shouldn't take more than twenty to twenty-five minutes."

Kian seemed happy with that. "Excellent. That means we have plenty of time to have coffee out on the terrace. It's a beautiful sunny day and it would be a shame to spend all of it inside."

"I would love that."

Okidu prepared a tray and Kian carried it outside despite the butler's protests.

"He is awfully bossy, isn't he?" Syssi said as they stepped outside.

Kian lowered the tray onto a mosaic-inlaied bistro table. "It's not that he is bossy, it's that he is programmed to assume responsibility over all domestic duties, and whenever I do something that he considered as his domain, he gets rattled."

Syssi arched a brow. "Programmed?"

Kian paused in the middle of pouring coffee into one of the small porcelain cups Okidu had put on the tray. "Set in his ways, that was what I meant. We all have habits we cling to. Sugar?"

"Yes, please. One cube."

Kian dropped it in. "Creamer?"

"A little bit... That's enough."

He stirred it all together and handed her the cup. "Any habits that you have and don't like anyone to disturb?" he asked.

Syssi took a sip, relieved that it had come out the way she liked it. "I'm very particular about how I like my coffee. I was gritting my teeth when you did it for me. But it came out good."

"Why didn't you tell me?" Kian poured a cup for himself and didn't add anything to it. "I would've left your coffee alone to fix any way you wanted."

She shrugged. "It would've been rude. But you asked."

"I appreciate the honesty."

She nodded. "It's one of the things I value most about people. I'll take rude and honest over polite and deceitful any day. But I know I'm odd that way. Most people prefer polite even if it involves some white lies."

Kian flinched as if she hurled an insult at him. Did he think she was insinuating that he'd lied about something?

Perhaps he had. But about what?

He seemed to recover fast. "Yeah, most people are too touchy to hear the brutal truth."

That was probably what had caused the flinch. He'd been reminded of hurting someone's feelings. The guy was doing his best, but he seemed like the type who wasn't all that attuned to other people. Under his good manners and sophisticated veneer, she sensed a rough edge. Even danger. Curiously, it didn't scare her. On the contrary, it was titillating.

Syssi shook her head. There must be something wrong with her. She'd never understood the appeal of bad boys, thought herself above such silliness, and yet here she was, pining for a man who was hiding something dangerous just underneath the surface.

The thing was, she also sensed that Kian was a good guy. He wasn't as full of himself as she would've expected from someone so good-looking and successful, but he carried himself with the confidence and self-respect of an honorable man. A decent man. The whole package was quite irresistible. Except, he could loosen up a little; the guy was too serious, too somber. She wanted to see him smile more.

"I wasn't completely honest before." She smirked.

Kian arched a brow. "Oh, yeah? How so?"

"If you ever see a huge zit on my nose, and I ask you if it looks horrible, I expect you to lie and say that nothing can detract from my beauty." She made a face, scrunching her nose and forcing her eyes to cross.

Kian didn't laugh, not even a chuckle. Instead, he leaned back in his chair and pinned her with a stare that was hard to read. "I'll remember that. But I wouldn't be lying."

"Oh, you're smooth, very smooth."

He seemed offended again. "That's the honest truth. You could be covered in pimples and still look beautiful to me."

Anddd... the blush was back.

What was she supposed to say to that?

Silly girl, just say thank you. Hattie's voice sounded in her head.

"Thank you, that's very sweet."

Kian chuckled. "Believe me, Syssi, there is nothing sweet about me."

CHAPTER 41: KIAN

Kian wanted to kick himself. Syssi looked like she wanted to hide under the table and it was all his fault. It had been going so well, she was loosening up and smiling more around him, and then he had to throw in that last remark, flustering her again.

She was so easy to read. A pretty blush would be the first indicator that she was feeling uncomfortable, then she would dip her head and let her long hair fall forward to hide her face.

She had done both after his last remark.

A change of subject was needed. Something neutral. "How are you enjoying working at the lab?"

Syssi shrugged, still not looking at him. "I like the research and I like working with Amanda, but this is temporary, just until I find another internship."

"You studied architecture, right?"

She nodded, finally lifting her eyes to his and smiling a little.

It was progress. "I know a thing or two about it. Not from the design side, but from the development and construction sides. Our family owns several development companies. In fact, most of the high rises on this street are ours." Why the hell was he telling her that?

It would be just another thing he would need to erase from her memory once it was safe for her to return to the old converted garage she called home. He needed to have a talk with Amanda about the wages she was paying the girl. As far as he could remember, the budget for her research assistant's salary was generous. Syssi should be able to afford a decent apartment.

"I didn't have a chance to get a good look, but from what I've seen so far your building is gorgeous. Who's the architect? Anyone well known?"

Kian chuckled. "Not really. She is a cousin of ours. I can ask if she has a need for an intern." Amanda was going to kill him if he helped Syssi get away from her, but he would be doing them all a favor. The girl had a knack for messing with Amanda's and his heads.

Syssi blushed again. "I wasn't fishing for a job recommendation. Besides, I'm more into designing single family homes and would like to intern with someone that does that."

"I'll ask around. I'm sure an internship will pay more than what my sister is paying you." It was so unlike Amanda to take advantage of the girl and pay her less than the job had been budgeted for, just because she hadn't been trained in neuroscience.

A quiet snort escaped Syssi's throat. "I doubt that. Amanda pays me very well. I'm going to have to settle for much less as an intern."

So why the hell was she living the way she did? Kian ran his fingers through his hair. It could be that she was burdened with student loans. He'd read an article about it last weekend. It said that the cost of tuition had doubled in the last ten years and students were drowning in debt. Or maybe she didn't want to make any adjustments to her lifestyle because this well-paying job was temporary.

"It could be a good idea for you to stay at the lab longer and pay down some of your student loans before taking an internship with lower pay."

She cast him a puzzled glance. "I don't have any. My parents paid for my schooling."

Her parents must've been well to do. That would explain the expensive car. He'd wondered how she could've afforded it while living so modestly.

"In that case you can save up some money for when the budget gets tighter."

Kian knew the exact moment she realized the reason for his suggestions.

Syssi's ears turned crimson and she lowered her head. She didn't look at him, and if his hearing weren't as good as it was, he would not have heard what she said. "My place is close to the university and offers privacy. That's why I rent it. I don't need anything fancy. I prefer putting money in the bank rather than spending all I make."

He was such an ass, making her uncomfortable again.

Crap and double crap, he needed to fix it. "Of course, I understand perfectly. It's very wise of you."

Lifting her head a little, she glanced at him from behind the curtain of her hair. He must've passed her scrutiny because her head went all the way up and she thrust her chin out. "I'm glad you think so. Most people think I'm stingy, and I'm so tired of defending my choices. There is nothing wrong with being frugal. It brings me peace of mind."

Kian couldn't help reaching for her hand. "I admire your financial acumen. A rare quality for someone as young as you. More than that, I admire you for sticking to your wise decisions even though they are unpopular. It requires guts."

That brought a real smile to her beautiful face. "Thank you." It was like someone had flipped a light inside her and she shone like a brilliant star—her inner beauty even brighter than the physical one.

Kian wanted to kiss her so bad that it hurt. Hell, he wanted to do much more than kissing. But he'd promised himself he wouldn't do it again. The taste of that one kiss he'd allowed himself when he'd thought he would never see Syssi again had been his undoing. One more and he would be forever lost.

This beautiful girl, this amazing person, could never be his, not even for one night of passion. Morality aside, he knew that one time with her could never be enough.

He'd better get out of there before his control snapped.

"I need to go and take care of some business, but I'll send up one of my guys to escort you to the retirement home. Will you be okay here by yourself for a few minutes?"

"Yes, of course. I don't want to take any more of your time."

She was disappointed, he could smell it, but he needed to put some distance between them. Fast. "I'll see you when you come back." He squeezed her hand lightly before getting up.

"Thank you, Kian. I appreciate all that you're doing for me. But I don't want to impose. I can stay with my brother, or at a hotel."

"We'll discuss it later. I need to run." He forced a tight smile and walked away, pulling his phone out of his pocket the moment he closed the door behind him.

There was no way he was letting her go anywhere. She wasn't safe out there. But he'd fight this battle later when he was better composed.

Thinking of who to assign as her bodyguard, he immediately ruled out Anandur. The guy was a flirt and a ladies' man. Alone with Syssi, he would seduce her in no time. Brundar was a safer choice. Kian made the call.

"Yes, boss."

"I need you to escort Syssi to an appointment. She is waiting for you out on the terrace. She'll give you the details when you get there."

"No problem. When?"

"Now."

"I'm on my way."

Kian pushed the phone back in his pocket and wondered what to do with himself next. There was always paperwork that needed attention; reports to go over, profit analysis of acquiring new properties to read, the list was long. In fact, it was endless, and he was in no mood to tackle any of it. Besides, the files were in his home office. His other option was to go down to Shai's office in the basement. His assistant kept copies of everything.

Easier said than done.

The fifty feet or so separating him from Syssi already felt like too far. Kian rubbed his sternum. It felt as if his heart was made out of a magnet, and it was pulling him toward the one in Syssi's chest. The difference was that instead of the pull weakening, the farther away he got, the stronger it became.

Damn. He didn't want her going out without him, and it had nothing to do with her safety. Brundar was an army of one and a much better fighter than Kian.

A true master.

Kian just wanted to be near her. Keeping it platonic would be hell, but he was discovering that staying away from her was worse.

He was losing his ██████ mind.

CHAPTER 42: SYSSI

Syssi took another sip of her cold coffee and nibbled on a biscuit. She was glad that Kian was too busy to accompany her. Imagining him listening to her read that romance book to the ladies was enough to send her running the other way. She wouldn't have agreed to go on with it, and the girls would've been disappointed.

Besides, what did she expect? That he would be her driver? Her bodyguard? He had people on payroll for that.

Kian felt responsible for her because of Amanda, and he was being a gracious host, but that didn't mean he wanted to spend any more time with her than he absolutely had to.

A high caliber businessman, Kian was a very busy guy.

A guy who for some reason had run off like his tail was on fire, leaving her alone with his butler.

Had she said something to offend him? Had he been under the impression that he'd offended her?

Probably the second one.

Truth be told, she'd been more embarrassed than offended. He was right, she wasn't a student anymore, and that guesthouse was a bit shabby for someone who was making decent money. She should move somewhere nicer.

The thing was, he'd actually done her a favor. Talking about her shitty apartment had been infinitely better than obsessing about Kian's sexy lips and piercing eyes and thinking about how he'd made her feel in her dreams. She would have looked like a freaking tomato.

God, how she wished there was a cure for that awful impediment.

If not for that damn blushing giving her away, she could've pulled off looking cool, sophisticated. She envied those women who could pretend disinterest even when they were internally drooling over a guy. The lack of this elementary ability, one that others took for granted, was causing her endless grief.

Pushing up to her feet, Syssi walked over to the glass railing and glanced at the adjoining buildings, trying to guess which belonged to Kian's family. Two across the street were a similar style, but it was difficult to take a look at those that were on the same side as the one she was in.

"Ready to go?"

Syssi jumped and turned around, bumping into Kian's solid chest. His arms shot around her to keep her from falling. "I'm sorry I startled you."

"How do you do that? Do you have silencers on your shoes or something?" She glanced down, hiding the spike of desire his hands on her body brought about.

He chuckled. "You were just preoccupied. That's why you didn't hear us come in."

Heck, she hadn't even noticed Brundar standing a few feet away, looking like a silent assassin. Syssi shook her head. Sometimes her imagination took flights of fancy, producing the weirdest thoughts.

An assassin? Really?

"Let me just grab my purse." She tried to push out of Kian's arms, but he held on, letting her go a second later.

The man was surely sending mixed signals, and she had no idea what to make of them. One moment he seemed to be attracted to her, the next he was treating her like a random acquaintance. And since the second one was more fitting to their situation, it was safer to assume that this was the extent of his feelings for her. But then he'd do something like he'd done a moment ago; hold her for a second too long like he didn't want to let her go.

The thing was, if Kian was interested in her, what the hell was stopping him from making a move? There was no way a guy like him was shy, and unless he were blind and stupid, which he wasn't, he must've realized she was attracted to him. With all that damned blushing, a twelve-year-old would've already figured that out.

Was he waiting for her to make the first move?

Without an audience, Syssi would've snorted. Kian would be waiting until he grew old because that wasn't going to happen. Not because she didn't want to, but because she couldn't.

With a sigh, Syssi walked over to retrieve the book from her duffle bag, dropping it inside her purse.

"I'm ready." She turned to the two men.

Kian took her elbow. "Let's go."

She cast him a sidelong glance. "Are you escorting me down to the car?" He was taking this host thing too seriously.

"I'm escorting you all the way to your destination and staying until you're done." Kian stopped in front of the elevators and pressed his thumb to the scanner.

Syssi's heart gave a little flutter. "I thought you had work to do."

"I do." He shrugged. "But I'd much rather spend time with you than with my paperwork."

He's done it again. Talk about mixed signals.

A soft ping announced the elevator, and a moment later the doors slid open. As the three of them stepped in, Syssi was grateful for Brundar's stoic presence. Without him there, she might have taken off one of her platform slides and bashed Kian over the head with it for driving her crazy.

Maybe that would've prompted him to do something, shaken him out of whatever was holding him back, and he would've finally made his move. Kissing her, touching her, like he'd done in her dreams.

A quick glance at the mirror confirmed that her cheeks were red and she turned sideways, hiding her face.

Don't think about that. Think disturbing thoughts.

Not a problem, Syssi had plenty of those, but it was a weapon of last resort she dreaded to use. All she had to do was open the floodgates on the bad shit swirling in her head. Earthquakes, wars, famine. This dark vortex was always there in the back of her mind, lurking, waiting to pull her down, and it took a constant, conscious effort to keep these disturbing thoughts at bay.

She hated letting the darkness in, but it was the only thing that could get rid of her blush almost instantly. The difficult part was getting rid of the crap later.

"What's wrong?" Kian's arm wrapped around her and he pulled her into his arms. There was nothing sexual in the gesture. He was comforting her.

How the hell could he have known what she'd been thinking about? Did she look upset?

"Why do you ask?"

"You seemed sad suddenly. Is there anything I can do to help?" His palm was rubbing circles on the small of her back.

Yes, you can keep holding me like this forever.

"It's nothing. I just remembered a sad story I read in the newspaper." Reluctantly, she wiggled out of his embrace and cast a furtive glance at Brundar.

Motionless, his stare fixed on the elevator's doors, the guy looked like he was made from stone—so unobtrusive that it was easy to forget he was even there.

It was the same on the drive. Brundar sat in the back, silent and watchful, while Kian and Syssi talked.

"Before meeting Amanda, have you tried to research your paranormal abilities?" Kian asked.

Had she ever. "Naturally. I've read anything and everything I could find about the subject."

"Anything interesting?"

"Lots of things, but very little that is substantiated by solid research."

"Tell me about it."

Thinking back to the books she'd read, she searched her mind for something he would find interesting. "Do you know that some dogs have a telepathic connection to their owners?"

He cast her a sidelong glance. "No, I didn't know that."

"There was an experiment conducted where owners left their dogs in a care facility and were told to come visit them at random times. The dogs would start getting excited as soon as the owners were on their way. Some even before that. They sensed their owners were coming for a visit as soon as the people made the decision, before they even got in a vehicle."

"Fascinating. Any other animals with special abilities?"

"Parrots. In one instance a talking parrot was able to tell what his owner was looking at in another room."

"What about people?"

"Amanda can probably tell you more about this than I can. We ran all kinds of experiments. Like the random shapes guessing, which I hate. She once had me do it for two hours straight. I felt I would go insane if I had to look at another square or triangle or circle."

He winced. "Sounds boring."

"It is."

Kian turned into the retirement home parking lot, and a few minutes later the three of them were standing in front of the reception desk.

"Hi, Syssi, who are your friends?" Gilda, the receptionist, had her eyes glued to Kian and was practically drooling. Fred, one of the orderlies, was eyeing Brundar.

Syssi made the introductions. "Can we go in?"

Gilda shook her head. "You can go in. But not the men. I'll have to call Leonora and ask her if it's okay to bring male visitors into her room."

Kian leaned over the counter and smiled at her. "I'm sure the ladies will be fine with us visiting them. Syssi's friends are always welcomed."

Gilda's eyes glazed over and she nodded. "Of course. Syssi's friends are always welcomed."

What was that? Did he just hypnotize the woman? Had he done the same to her to make her forget about what had happened in the lab?

As soon as they were buzzed in and the door closed behind them, Syssi whispered, "What have you done to her? And don't tell me nothing, because Gilda would've never allowed someone new inside without checking who they were."

Kian shrugged, but his shoulders remained tense. "A little mental suggestion, that's all."

"Like hypnotism?"

"Yeah, exactly like that."

"Where did you learn how to do it? And did you use it on me?"

He winced. "It's a useful trick, that's all. I figured you'd sleep better if you forgot all about those lunatics. I thought that this was the end of it. But evidently I was wrong."

They'd reached Leonora's room and Syssi knocked.

"Come in!" Hattie answered.

Syssi opened the door just a crack and peeked in. "I have two guys with me. I think it would be better if you ladies came out and met us at the salon."

The door swung open and Leonora filled the frame. She looked Kian and Brundar over, top to bottom and then back up. "Well, hello, handsome boys." She turned around. "I wish you could see them, Hattie. Mm-hmm, gorgeous!"

"I'm sorry about that," Syssi whispered. "After a certain age it seems that people think they have the right to say whatever is on their minds."

Kian chuckled and patted her back. "It's quite alright. They are having some harmless fun. Brundar and I are more than happy to be the objects of their excitement and give the old girls something to talk about. Am I right, Brundar?" Kian clapped his friend on the back.

Brundar responded with a grunt.

Leonora's room wasn't big enough for all of them, especially the two tall guys, but they managed. Brundar went back out to the hallway and brought two more chairs.

Hattie got up and bee-lined straight for Kian as if her eyesight was perfectly fine. "I'm blind, but I can see with my hands. Do you mind if I touch you?"

"Not at all, go ahead." He took her hand and brought it to his face. Hattie cupped his cheek than added her other hand to the exploration.

She nodded. "I approve."

Kian chuckled softly. "I'm glad I passed your test, my lady."

"Ooh, he called you a lady." Clara clapped her hands. "Such a polite young man."

Brundar shifted in his chair, and Syssi caught him frowning before he quickly schooled his face into its usual stoic mask.

"Brundar is very handsome as well, Hattie. Don't you want to see him too?"

Kian looked like he was barely stifling a laugh. "Yes, Lady Hattie. You should check him out."

Hattie shook her head and waved a finger at Kian as if he was a naughty boy. Shuffling back to her chair, she stopped by Brundar and gave his shoulder a light pat. "You don't like to be touched, son, I understand."

How the hell could she have known that about him?

Syssi cast a quick glance at Brundar. Hattie was right. The guy looked relieved to be spared a touching session. She had misunderstood his frown. It wasn't that he'd felt left out, he'd been afraid of getting included.

Leonora poured everyone tea and handed each of them a small porcelain cup. "Did you bring the book, dear?"

Syssi pulled it out of her purse and handed it to Leonora. "I don't think I'll be reading to you today. The guys will be bored by a silly romance novel."

"Let me take a look." Kian snatched the book from Leonora's hands. "*Dreams of a Dark Lover*, a vampire romance novel. Sounds fascinating. I would love to hear it. How about you, Brundar?"

The guy shrugged.

"It's decided then." Kian thrust the book at Syssi's hands. "Everyone wants to hear you read."

She was going to die.

"I can't. It's too embarrassing. Have you ever read a romance novel?"

"Can't say that I have. That's why I'm curious. But if it's too difficult for you, I can read it instead."

That would be infinitely better. "You're my hero," she blurted before thinking how it would sound. "I mean, thank you. I appreciate it." She rolled her eyes. "More than you can imagine."

With a big grin splitting his face, Kian flipped the book open to the page with the folded corner. "My pleasure."

CHAPTER 43: KIAN

Two chapters into the story Brundar had excused himself, preferring to wait outside. Five chapters into it, Kian had to cross his legs to hide a massive hard-on.

"As Bernard's fingers skimmed Vivian's breasts, a bolt of desire hit her core, the heat spreading over her trembling body—"

He had no idea how explicit the story would be. Reading about hot sex between a vampire and a human was half the trouble, though. What was killing him, minute by excruciating minute, was the scent of Syssi's arousal. If not for the ironclad control he'd honed over centuries, he would've pounced on her and taken her on the bed she was sitting on— audience and all.

Given the satisfied expressions on their wrinkled faces, the three crones weren't oblivious to what was going on. He'd caught them stealing glances at Syssi and him, smirking and nodding to each other as if this was all some grand scheme they had orchestrated between them and were overjoyed to see it come to fruition.

Thankfully, the last few chapters were dedicated to a big wedding and to tying up miscellaneous loose ends in the plot, giving him a much needed reprieve from all the sexual tension.

Closing the book, he released a puff of breath and forced a tight smile. "Aren't romances supposed to end with and-they-lived-happily-ever-after? I must've missed it." He flipped through several of the final pages, pretending to look for the phrase.

Clara started clapping and the other two joined her. "Bravo, Kian, you've done a marvelous job," she said. "Thank you."

Kian bowed his head. "My pleasure." More like torture.

Leonora patted Syssi's back. "This one is a keeper. You've done well, girl."

Syssi blushed. "Kian and I are just friends. He is my boss's brother."

"Of course, dear," Hattie said in a mocking tone.

Kian pushed up to his feet and handed Leonora the book. "Ladies, thank you for allowing me the privilege of reading to you, but Syssi and I must be on our way."

As Syssi hugged Leonora goodbye, Hattie shuffled up to him and put a hand on his chest. "Take care of this girl, Kian. She is precious to us."

"I will." He clasped her gnarled, small hand, sensing traces of power in her. Unable to resist, he delved into her mind to see what it was, but somehow she was blocking him. The woman was either highly intelligent or suspicious by nature. Most likely both.

Some humans were resistant to thralls, but his was particularly powerful. Kian seldom encountered a human who could block him so quickly and effectively.

It'd taken several more minutes until Syssi and her friends were done hugging and saying their goodbyes, and he had promised to each of them separately that he was going to take good care of Syssi.

Once they were out on the hallway, Kian took Syssi's hand. "These three are something else." He chuckled.

She dipped her head. "I know. And today they've really outdone themselves. I would've never agreed to you coming in with me if I had known how they were going to behave. I'm sorry if they embarrassed you."

Kian brought her hand up for a kiss. "They didn't. I want to take care of you." He was a masochist, for even holding her hand, let alone kissing it. Every touch was electrifying, and yet he couldn't help himself, needing at least this little contact with her.

She cast him a quizzical look. "What do you mean?"

Damned if he knew. His heart was telling him to take Syssi home with him and never let her go, to do all he could to keep her safe and make her happy. But it was like wishing for the moon. He couldn't keep her because she was a human, and he couldn't make her happy even if he found a way to keep her. What he could do, however, was keep her safe.

"I'm going to make sure that no harm comes to you. And I want to help you find a great internship with an architectural firm that handles the kind of projects you like."

"Thank you, that's very sweet of you." She snorted. "I'm sorry, not sweet, very manly." She deepened her voice, imitating him.

Adorable. Especially when she was like that, playful, not fearful.

Outside, leaning against the Lexus's side, Brundar was watching the front door. "You want me to drive?" he asked as they came out.

Kian tossed him the keys. Sitting in the backseat together with Syssi wasn't a smart idea, but then he had already proven that he was stupid when it came to her. He forced himself to leave some space between them.

For a couple of minutes, they rode in silence.

"Kian." She turned to him. "Could you please take me to Andrew?

My brother? I really should be staying with him."

He shook his head. "They will look for you at his place. It's not a stretch to assume that you will run to hide at the home of the only relative you have nearby."

"Not in this case. Andrew works for the government and his address is registered under a different name."

She had no idea how easily the Doomers could get this information. "These people have resources you wouldn't believe."

Her brows lifted. "A group of crazy fanatics?"

"There is more to it than that. It's an international organization and they have massive financial backing."

"How about a hotel, then?"

Brundar nodded as if agreeing that it was a good idea.

Maybe it was. Bringing Syssi to the keep hadn't been the smartest thing to do. He hadn't been thinking straight this morning, the worry and anger clouding his judgment.

It wasn't just the issue of him keeping his hands off her when she was so near. Even if he had Syssi move into Amanda's place, thralling away the memory of an extended stay could be potentially harmful to her. The more memories there were, the more intrusive and widespread the thrall had to be. Especially in the case of a highly intelligent woman like Syssi.

"Fine. Brundar, take us to the Four Seasons."

Her eyes widened in surprise, then in alarm. "Not the Four Seasons. I was thinking along the lines of a Sheraton or a Holiday Inn. I can't afford the Four Seasons."

Kian harrumphed. "Don't be ridiculous. I'm paying for it. We need a two-bedroom suite because I want Brundar to stay with you. I'm not leaving you unprotected. Besides, how did you think to pay for it? With your credit card? You would've led them right to you."

That shut her up, literally. Syssi opened her mouth to say something and then closed it, crossing her arms over her chest and frowning.

Unbelievable, he'd actually won an argument with a woman. His mother and sisters, except perhaps for Sari who was the most reasonable, never conceded this quickly.

He clasped Syssi's hand. "Thank you."

"For what?"

"Not arguing about it."

She chuckled. "That's because I'm still thinking about another solution. I don't like that you're paying for my hotel. I've caused you enough trouble as it is."

"No, you didn't. You are a victim in all of this, and none of it is your fault. If anyone is to blame, it's Amanda. And if it makes you feel better, I can charge the room to her credit card."

"Do you want me to get fired?" Syssi looked horrified by his idea. "And how can it be her fault?"

"If she didn't forget her notebook in the lab, no one would have known about you. But I was joking about charging her. It's not a big deal for me. Can we leave it at that?"

She nodded. "For now."

Good enough.

"What about my things? I left them at your place."

Kian pulled out his phone. "I'll have my butler deliver your luggage. Anything else you need?"

"No, as long as I have my laptop I can keep myself busy."

"Good. By the time we are done eating lunch your things will be there."

Kian texted Shai, asking him to make reservations for the two-bedroom presidential suite and for lunch at *Culina*, the Four Seasons' restaurant.

CHAPTER 44: SYSSI

Syssi held the menu in front of her face, hiding as she read through the list for the third time. It wasn't that she was overly picky about what she wanted to eat, she just needed a little time to compose herself.

Surviving the visit to the three evil witches masquerading as nice old ladies was proof that she was much tougher than she thought she was. Between listening to Kian reading sex scenes, with his deep bedroom voice and watching his beautiful lips, while imagining those lips doing things to her that had nothing to do with reading, Syssi had been so close to climaxing that one touch would've sent her flying.

At some point she'd been tempted to follow Brundar's example and excuse herself, but not to wait outside.

A one minute visit to the bathroom would've been all she needed to bring herself release and come back in a much calmer state. The thing was, Syssi had a feeling the witches would have known what she was doing and she would've died from embarrassment.

Even thinking about sad things hadn't done the trick this time. In desperation, she'd closed her eyes, pretending she was testing her precognition with the damn random images projector. After a while, the square, triangle, circle, etc., had done it, and she'd been able to breathe normally.

Sort of.

Until she'd gotten in the car with Kian, Syssi had been able to hang onto her composure, but sitting so close to him it had become a desperate struggle. She had to fight her hormonal body all the way from the retirement home to the restaurant. Hopefully, Kian would leave her at the room he'd rented for her, and she could get a cold shower and a change of underwear.

Leaning sideways to peek from behind the menu, she glanced at Kian, and saw him frown. Poor guy, he was probably hungry and she was taking her sweet time. "What do you recommend?"

"Tell me what kinds of foods you like."

"I can't decide. Everything sounds delicious in Italian." Not that she knew the language, but throughout her life she'd spent enough time in Italian restaurants to learn the names of dishes and ingredients. "Between the pera vegana and the pomodoro e basilico, which one is better?"

"If you're not too hungry, the pera vegana. It's a salad, so it's not overly filling."

"Perfect."

As soon as she closed her menu, the waiter rushed over to take their orders. Kian ordered the pasta dish that was her second option, and Brundar ordered the hamburger Italiano with a side of patate prezzemolate.

Syssi wondered what the guy's story was. It was obvious that Kian didn't treat Brundar as an employee, even though he barked commands at him left and right. Besides, there was a vague family resemblance between them. Brundar's face was more delicate, beautiful in an almost feminine way, but not really. He was all man behind his angelic features and long pale hair.

A dangerous man.

"How long have you been working with Kian, Brundar?" she asked to start a conversation.

He cast a sidelong glance at his boss. "Ages."

Syssi laughed. Brundar looked to be about her age. He couldn't have worked with Kian for more than a few years unless he'd started as a kid.

"Brundar and Anandur are my cousins. We've been inseparable since a very young age," Kian solved the puzzle for her.

"That explains it."

When the food arrived, the guys didn't seem in the mood for conversation, and she let them be, watching them eat. Both had impeccable table manners.

A rarity for men their age.

After lunch, Kian escorted her up to the fanciest hotel suite she'd ever seen.

"Kian, this must cost a fortune." She wanted to grab her duffle bag, which had been delivered sometime during their lunch, and walk out.

He waved his hand. "If you don't want to share a room with Brundar, we need two bedrooms."

She opened her mouth to say that she didn't mind, but Kian put a finger on her lips. "Let's put it this way. *I* don't want you to share a room with Brundar."

There was no arguing with him. She would stay the one night and check out tomorrow. A suite this big in a hotel this fancy must've cost thousands of dollars. Just thinking about it gave her heart palpitations and not the good kind. If someone wanted to throw around that much money, they should give it to charity instead.

He caressed her cheek. "Just try to enjoy yourself. I wish I could stay, but I need to have some work done today. I'll try to stop by tomorrow morning."

"You work on weekends?"

His chuckle was sad. "I work each and every day. On the weekends I work a little less."

"That's not healthy."

"I know." He leaned down and brushed her lips lightly with a barely there kiss. When he lifted his head, his eyes were closed as if he wanted to savor it, memorize it.

"Goodbye, Syssi." He turned around and marched out of the room.

Brundar sat down on the couch and grabbed the remote, flipping channels until he found a wrestling competition.

Syssi picked her bag up and swung it over her shoulder. "I'm going to take that one." She pointed at one of the doors.

Brundar nodded.

Walking into the bedroom, she continued straight into the adjacent bathroom and dropped her luggage on the floor. After a quick appraisal of the amenities, Syssi decided to forgo the bathtub, even though it was nice and deep, and go into the shower.

She needed to cool down first with a splash of cold water.

People did things like that in books and movies, but it had been a remarkably stupid idea. The freezing water had done nothing for her. After all, the mess was in her head and not on her skin. She turned the knob all the way to the other side and waited, shivering, for the hot water to arrive.

Better.

Okay, time to do some thinking.

She was attracted to Kian, big time, and he seemed to be attracted to her, but not as strongly. Which made sense. He was amazing. Not only handsome and smart but also generous and gracious.

On a scale of one to ten, he was a twenty.

In comparison, she was an eight. Okay, maybe an eight and a half. She was pretty but not spectacular like Kian. And she was short. At five feet and five inches, she was almost a foot shorter than him. As to smarts, she wanted to believe that they were on an equal footing. She'd always excelled at school. There was the issue of an age difference, but it wasn't huge. Six years at the least and ten at the most.

The biggest divide was the disparity in achievement. She was just starting out, while Kian was managing a multimillion corporation.

Sadly, he was out of her league.

Unless he suddenly showed not only interest but clear intent, she was going to try to play it cool around him.

But what if he actually made the move? Would she go for it, knowing that it could only be a short fling? Syssi shook her head. If she let him in, Kian would break her heart. Not on purpose, of course, he seemed like a decent guy, but because he would regard it as a casual fling and she couldn't. She just wasn't built that way.

Letting him past her defenses was risky.

Having Kian in her dreams, where she could submit to him sexually and yet remain in full control of the situation, was one thing; having him in real life was another. She couldn't allow herself such vulnerability. Besides, no real flesh and blood man could compare to a fantasy, and disappointment was almost guaranteed.

Coward, stop being so cautious. Living means taking chances.

Syssi wished she could borrow some of Amanda's chutzpah. If there was one thing she was envious of, it was her boss's confidence.

The woman's beauty was almost a handicap, too much to handle, and money didn't impress Syssi. She liked having it because it provided her with a safety net, but she never wished for the kind of fortune Amanda and Kian had.

Syssi liked being average and attracting as little attention as possible to herself.

God, she was so boring.

CHAPTER 45: KIAN

Leaving the hotel had tested the limits of Kian's willpower. Somehow, Syssi had become an addiction, an all-consuming and unhealthy one. It was like an affliction that had taken root in no time. He hadn't even had sex with the girl for heaven's sake.

Maybe that was the problem.

He should get her in bed and get this out of his system.

Hell, he felt like the worst kind of jerk even considering doing something so dishonorable. It was one thing to seduce women who were looking for a commitment-free hookup and didn't expect anything more from him, and a different thing altogether to seduce a girl that held herself to a different standard and was quite obviously developing feelings for him. Not to mention the dishonesty of it all.

If he made love to her, because with Syssi it wouldn't be just a screw like with the others, he would be doing Amanda's bidding. He would be sinking his fangs into her and pumping her with his venom, attempting her activation without her consent or even knowledge of the possibility. And it didn't matter that he was convinced nothing would happen. It would still be unethical and immoral.

Allowing this thing between them to drag on was only going to prolong their misery. He would save both of them unnecessary heartache by ripping the Band-Aid off. Getting out and staying out was the right thing to do.

Breaking an addiction was tough, but it had to be done. The only way to sever her mystifying hold on him was to go cold turkey.

* * *

Four hours and twenty-two minutes later, Shai closed the file they'd been working on. "I think we should call it a day."

Kian had to agree. He couldn't concentrate because his head was miles away, mulling over a decision that should have been a done deal.

For the first time that he could remember, Shai had to repeat to him the results of a cost analysis. The proposed military-grade drone factory represented an investment in the tens of millions. Not the kind of decision he should be making in his current state of mind. Problem was, Kian suspected that unless he had Syssi sitting right next to him, he wouldn't be able to have any work done anytime soon.

"Yeah, you're right. Let's continue tomorrow."

"No problem." Shai looked relieved.

Kian was well aware that he was using his lack of concentration as an excuse to go back to her, nonetheless, he found himself calling Anandur.

"Meet me next to the car in ten minutes and bring an overnight bag."

"Oh, thank you, that's so kind of you. Are you taking me on a romantic vacation?" Anandur used a high-pitched valley girl tone.

Kian sighed. "Exactly. You and Brundar and me. Bring a change of clothes for your brother as well."

Unfortunately, protocol demanded that he didn't leave the keep without taking two bodyguards with him, or one when there was no other choice. Kian had already broken the rules by leaving Brundar at the hotel to guard Syssi and returning to the keep by himself.

His punishment was having to bring the ladies-magnet along.

Perhaps he should tell Shai to come too and work with him at the hotel. Maybe he'd be able to get some work done.

Not a bad idea, but Shai had looked so glad to be done that Kian had no heart to call him back. Instead, he collected the files Shai had prepared for him and stuffed them into an antique briefcase that he rarely used. It served more as a decorative piece in his office than as something to carry work in. Fortunately, the metal hinges and latches still worked.

In a way, it was good that Brundar and Anandur would stay in the hotel suite with him and Syssi. Their presence would help him behave and stay away from her bedroom. After all, he wouldn't seduce her with the brothers in the next room.

In his closet, Kian added to his briefcase a change of underwear, a brand new pair of sleep pants he'd never used either, and one of the travel kits of toiletries Okidu kept ready and stocked for Kian's last minute business trips.

"Where are we going, boss?" Anandur said as Kian tossed him the keys.

"The Four Seasons."

Anandur got behind the wheel. "Oh, goodie, so you are taking me on a romantic vacation after all."

"Hardly." Kian got inside and closed the passenger door. "I put Syssi up in a hotel suite and left Brundar to keep her safe."

Anandur lifted a bushy brow. "And you think one Guardian is not enough? Especially Brundar who is an army of one?"

Kian had a hard time explaining it to himself and had no desire to share his reasoning, or lack thereof, with Anandur. "I have my reasons and they are none of your business."

"Aha. So it's like that." Anandur seemed way too happy with himself.

~~Screw~~ it, let him think what he would.

For the rest of the drive Kian pretended to work, which kept Anandur's flapping mouth shut.

"Kian?" Brundar opened the presidential suite's door.

"Good evening." Kian pushed by him without answering the implied question of what he was doing there. Mainly because he had no good answer for that.

"Hello, brother." He heard Anandur clap Brundar on the back.

Syssi was nowhere in the living area. "Where is she?" Kian turned to Brundar.

"In her bedroom."

"Sleeping?"

"No."

Kian walked over to where the trail of her scent led and knocked on the door. "Syssi? Are you sleeping?"

"Give me a moment," she answered.

He heard the patter of bare feet and a moment later the clunking of high-heeled shoes on the hardwood floor.

Syssi opened the door. "Kian, I wasn't expecting you back this evening. What happened?"

He would answer her when his tongue unfroze in his mouth. She was stunning. Curiously, she was always more beautiful than his memory of her, surprising him anew each time he saw her again. Instead of the form-fitting leggings she had on before, she changed into a pair of jeans that molded to her legs and her hips in the same way the leggings had, and she was wearing a white T-shirt with a deep neckline that exposed the very tops of her breasts.

Mouthwatering.

Kian shrugged, pretending as if she hadn't rendered him momentarily speechless. "I thought I'd come over and keep you company." He leaned closer to whisper in her ear. "Brundar is not much of a conversationalist. Spending time with him is as fascinating as watching paint dry."

Syssi stifled a chuckle. "I see that you brought reinforcements," she said as she saw Anandur sharing the couch with Brundar.

"Yeah. In case I'm not entertaining enough, Anandur is a sure bet. The guy missed his calling; he should've been a comedian." He took her hand and led her toward the dining table where he'd left his briefcase.

She shook her head. "He is too big and too muscular for a comedian. On the other hand, even if he is not that funny, I'm sure he will have an audience. Girls will go wild for him."

Kian barely managed to keep down the growl bubbling up from some primitive place in his gut. If Syssi didn't stop talking about how good looking Anandur was, he was going to lose it.

Oblivious, she kept going. "His brother is also gorgeous. If he smiled a little, the girls would have been all over him too. That hard expression on his face is kind of intimidating."

Gritting his teeth, Kian pulled out a chair for her. "My lady?"

"Thank you." She blushed a little.

"Have you eaten already?"

"Yes. I ordered room service for Brundar and myself. The prices they charge here are outrageous. I tried to pick the least expensive items, but Brundar wanted a hamburger and it wasn't like a guy his size could do with an appetizer portion—"

Kian lifted his hand. "Would you stop fretting over costs? Trust me, I can afford it."

Syssi flinched. "Of course, you can. I wasn't implying that you can't."

Damn, he'd sounded too aggressive and impatient, and it had nothing to do with her concern over expenditure and everything to do with the two handsome Guardians.

He turned to them. "I'm going to order dinner, you want anything?"

Anandur lifted a finger. "I ate before we left, but some munchies and a bunch of beers would be much appreciated, boss."

Kian nodded. "Syssi? What about you? Maybe dessert?"

"I would love some ice cream, if they have it. And a cappuccino. There is a coffeemaker in the kitchen and I made myself some, but I didn't like how it tasted."

For some reason, it made him stupidly happy that she'd asked for something, obliterating the anger over her previous remarks. Providing her with what she was craving felt satisfying. Especially since she never asked for anything and balked at every dollar spent.

He ended up ordering two of each appetizer on the menu, beers for the guys, a dinner for himself, and cappuccinos for Syssi and himself. He also ordered each and every flavor of ice cream the restaurant offered.

"Don't you think you overdid it a bit?" Syssi said once he was done with the order.

"Nope. You've seen Brundar eat, and he is nothing compared to that one." He pointed at Anandur. "He can demolish a mountain of food on his own."

She giggled. "Yeah, a big guy like that needs a lot of fuel."

Apparently, the girl wasn't a good judge of character because she was clueless as to what her comments about Anandur were doing to him. Frankly, though, his reaction was totally uncalled for, and she couldn't possibly suspect the kind of jealous monster lurking behind the sophisticated façade he was fronting. Not only that, but he had no right. It wasn't as if he'd done anything to indicate he was interested in her, or had given her the option to encourage him or conversely tell him to go to hell.

The smart thing to do was to steer the conversation to a safer subject. "What have you been doing while I was gone?"

Syssi let out a puff of air. "Amanda gave me a list of neuroscience papers she wanted me to read to get better acquainted with the subject. And let me tell you, scientists are horrible writers. The one I was trying to crack all afternoon was so dense, so obtuse, that I was starting to question my intelligence. In the end, I realized it wasn't as complicated as it seemed. It was just badly written. I made a summary, using clear wording, and I'm going to suggest to Amanda to give her students the summary to read instead of the original paper. It will save them hours upon hours of frustration."

He could watch her talk for hours.

Syssi was so lovely when she got excited and animated. Her eyes sparkling and her hands gesticulating, she let loose of the stiff posture and the guarded look.

If there was a way to get rid of those for good, he would've loved to know what it was. Despite his efforts to appear polite and agreeable, Syssi was intimidated by him, and he didn't know what else to do to make her comfortable.

Liar, you know perfectly well what she needs.

At his core, Kian was a simple man, with simple solutions and even simpler needs. The sexual tension between them could be relieved only by giving it an outlet.

Problem was, it was out of the question.

CHAPTER 46: SYSSI

After Kian had finished his dinner, and Syssi had demolished most of the ice cream, they drank their cappuccinos and talked a little more, while the brothers watched one sports game after the other.

He'd told her about the drone factory he was thinking of building, and she'd told him some more about paranormal phenomena and the prevalent theories concerning it.

It had been a good conversation. She found that talking about interesting subjects and not looking directly into his eyes distracted her from Kian's mesmerizing sex appeal.

Except, she couldn't keep it up forever. She made the mistake of looking at his hands for a second too long, and her imagination went on a wild ride of what those hands could do.

A graceful and prompt retreat was in order.

"I'm sorry, I've blabbered on and on about all these weird subjects. You brought work to do, and I should leave you to it."

Kian grimaced. "I would much rather spend time listening to you talk than deal with this." He tapped his briefcase.

Syssi pushed up to her feet. "We all have to do what we have to do. I need to read at least one more article before going to sleep."

Kian caught her hand. "Bring your laptop out here. We can work together."

Yeah, right. As if she could concentrate on anything with him around. "I'm sorry, but I get easily distracted. I need to work in a quiet place."

Holding on to her hand, Kian pinned her with his intense blue eyes, and it took all she had to pull away and not melt into a puddle at his feet.

"Good night, Kian. Good night, guys." She waved at the brothers and trotted to her bedroom as fast as her high-heeled mules allowed.

Once her door was closed and locked, Syssi collapsed on the bed, face down. Kian was killing her. Except for that one look at the end before she'd gone to her room, he hadn't shown any interest in her as a woman.

He was friendly, and it could've been a pleasure talking to him if not for her out of control hormonal state.

Time for another cold shower?

No, enough of that. Mind over body.

She needed to take control and beat that attraction into submission. Another boring, badly written scientific paper was the hammer she would do it with.

Barely keeping her eyes open, Syssi read page after page of data collected from tests done on monkeys, including the indecipherable math that had been applied to the results. She was good at math, but not this kind. Many of the symbols she hadn't even seen before today. In the end, she surrendered and let her eyes close, promising herself just a few moments of rest.

* * *

"What would it be, beautiful?"

Syssi opened her eyes and looked at Kian. He was leaning against her closed door, his arms crossed over his chest. Hadn't she locked it? She'd thought she had.

"What would be what? I don't understand what you're talking about." She glanced at the floor, looking for her laptop. Was it still on the bed? Syssi patted around but it wasn't there. She wasn't wearing her jeans and T-shirt either.

Instead, what she had on was a white, spaghetti-strapped satin nightgown. Problem was, Syssi didn't own anything like that.

"I'm dreaming again, ain't I?"

Dream Kian nodded. "So what would it be? Do you want me to make love to you or not?"

"You know I do. You're the one who's sending mixed signals, not me."

"I'm not the kind of lover you're used to."

She snorted. "God, I hope not."

He uncrossed his arms and sauntered toward the bed. "Are you sure?" He tugged on the blanket, pulling it off her an inch at a time.

"Yes." Syssi flung it to the side, exposing herself in one fluid motion.

Kian chuckled. "Tsk, tsk. So impatient."

"You think? I've been waiting for this for far too long."

He crawled on top of her, his lips almost touching hers as he held himself up and away from her body. "I need to make it good to be worthy of such honor."

"You are and you will. You're the one I've been waiting for."

His lips were soft when he kissed her, his tongue gentle in its inquiry as he waited for her to part her lips for him. The technique was perfect, but it lacked the fiery passion she knew lurked inside of Kian.

Obviously, since she was the one creating this scenario.

The one real kiss she'd shared with him was nothing like this polite, sweet thing.

"Kiss me like you did before," she whispered.

He lifted his head and looked at her with his glowing eyes. "Remember that you asked for it."

She nodded and he smiled, a wicked twist of lips that was the furthest thing from reassuring. In fact, it sent a shiver of fear down her spine. What the hell was she doing? Giving him a free pass to do as he pleased with her?

It's a dream, silly, it's not real. Let yourself go for once and enjoy.

With one large hand Kian cradled her head, entangling his fingers in her hair and using it as an anchor to hold her in place, while his other hand tugged on the nightgown. The thin straps snapped, and he pulled it off her in one swift motion, baring her to him.

"Beautiful," he hissed through his elongated fangs.

Stupid vampire romance was putting ideas in her head. But wait, Kian had fangs in all her dreams. Was her subconscious trying to tell her something?

But what? That he was dangerous? That she was craving danger?

She wanted to ask him about it, but as she opened her mouth Kian delivered on his promise and kissed her like she wanted to be kissed. With a light tug on her hair, he took ownership of her mouth, his tongue invading, his teeth nipping.

When his other hand palmed her breast, Syssi arched into it, remembering their first dream encounter and how he'd brought her to a climax with his lips and his teeth. Before that night, she hadn't known it was in her to orgasm like that; flying up and floating on a cloud before drifting back to earth.

She'd been on the receiving end of pleasure in both dreams and hadn't gotten to touch him, to explore him. She wanted to do it now.

"I want to see you naked," she whispered as he let her take a breath.

"Curious?"

"Dying. You're the most beautiful man I've ever seen. I want to see everything."

Kian flopped to his back and lifted his arms, tucking his hands under his head. "I'm all yours, sweet girl."

Syssi rose up to her knees, and appraised the mountain of man sprawled before her. His head was almost to the headboard and his feet reached the very end of the mattress.

"What should I go for first?"

Kian lifted his head a little and looked down at the large bulge in his pants, then waggled his brows.

She giggled, wondering if the real Kian would be as playful in bed. "Don't worry, I'll get there. But first, I want to explore this magnificent chest."

Leaning over him, she started at the top button of his shirt, wanting to go just as slow as he had done the previous night in her dream, but she was too impatient and in seconds had them all undone.

On an inhale, Syssi parted the two halves.

Smooth, with only the lightest smattering of hair on his chest, Kian was built perfectly. All lean muscle without an ounce of fat to be seen. He lifted up and shrugged off the shirt then returned to his previous pose with his hands tucked under his head. Not surprisingly, his arms and shoulders were amazing too. Not bulky like a body builder's, his lean musculature was athletic like that of a swimmer or a gymnast.

She ran her palms over his torso and whispered, "You're perfect, just as I've known you would be."

Kian hissed. "You'd better hurry up. I want to be the one doing the touching, and it's killing me to keep my hands away. I'm not going to hold back much longer."

His bunched muscles and strained face confirmed how hard it was for him to lie still and let her explore. In a moment, his patience was going to get rewarded.

With a quick flick of her fingers, she popped the button on his jeans, then carefully pulled the zipper down. He was so hard and his pants were stretched so tight over his bulge that she was afraid of hurting him.

She'd been right to be careful because Kian wasn't wearing any underwear, and his shaft came into view as soon as the zipper was halfway down, then sprang free when Syssi pulled it all the way.

She gasped. His manhood was as beautiful as the rest of him. Smooth and rigid, thick and long, and she couldn't wait to taste it.

With gentle fingers, she touched him, marveling at the velvety texture covering a rigid core. Kian inhaled sharply, then hissed as her hand closed around his shaft and she lowered her head to take it into her mouth.

The ringing started just as she was about to close her lips around it.

What the hell? Was it an alarm?

No. It was the damn bedside phone.

Ugh. Syssi wanted to hurtle the bloody thing against the wall, but of course, she didn't. Nonetheless, she was going to give whoever dared call her so early a piece of her mind.

"Who is it?" she barked.

"Good morning, beautiful. I'm ordering breakfast. What would you like?" Kian sounded awfully cheerful for such an ungodly hour.

With wicked satisfaction she thought that he wouldn't be as happy if he knew that his phone call had just cost him a blow job. The other him, but still.

"It's six in the morning, Kian."

"I'm sorry, is it too early for you?"

He didn't sound sorry at all.

"Coffee." She hung up and plopped back on the bed.

Naturally, she wasn't naked, she was still wearing the jeans and the T-shirt, and the laptop was open on the other side of the bed. The only reminder she had of the dream was another pair of wet panties.

So annoying. Syssi grabbed a pillow and shoved it over her face to muffle a frustrated groan.

CHAPTER 47: KIAN

"How long are we going to be stuck here?" Anandur asked after they'd finished their breakfast.

More than two hours had passed since Kian had woken Syssi up, but she was still a no-show. She was either mad at him for waking her up so early and had decided to stay in her room, or she had gone back to sleep.

"I'll try to convince her to come home with me today."

Anandur scratched his beard. "Do you think it's smart to take her to the keep?"

"No, but I can't spare even one of you to guard her. We don't have enough men." It was true, keeping them here because he was obsessed with the girl wasn't fair to the guys. They had other things to do, and at a time like this the keep's occupants needed its few Guardians to be there at all times. But that wasn't the only reason.

"Thrall her. It's quicker," Brundar suggested.

Maybe he should.

"I'm going to knock on her door." Anandur wiped his mouth with a napkin and pushed his chair back.

Not a bad idea. If she was still mad over the wake-up call, Kian preferred for Anandur to get hit with the brunt of her ire.

The Guardian rapped his knuckles on her door. "Syssi, it's time to get up."

There was a muffled, "Shit," and then a patter of small feet rushing to the door. She opened it a crack, hiding her lower half behind the door, and cranked her neck to look at Anandur. "God, you're tall." She shook a head of mussed hair that was sticking out in all directions. "I'm sorry, I overslept. I'll be out in ten minutes tops."

"It's okay. Take your time, there is no hurry."

"Thank you." She closed her door.

Anandur came back to the dining table and sat across from Kian. "She is such a cute little thing."

The seemingly innocent remark had Kian seeing red. "Keep your opinions to yourself."

A red brow lifted almost to the guy's hairline. "Someone woke up grumpy this morning."

Kian ignored him and signaled an end to the exchange by lifting the *Wall Street Journal* and hiding behind it. The thing was that Anandur was right. Syssi was adorable and sexy as hell.

There had been a good reason for him calling her up when he had. She must've been dreaming something naughty because he'd been awakened by the scent of her arousal.

Sometime around one in the morning, the brothers had retired to the other bedroom. Kian had stayed up to catch up on his work, going over the files he'd brought with him until the words had started to blur.

Lying down on the couch to catch a little shut-eye, he'd been alone in the living room when the enticing scent had hit his system. It had been a struggle not to go to her and take care of her need, and he'd been thankful for the two Guardians sleeping in the other room. Their presence had helped rein in his libido.

That didn't mean, though, that he would've allowed them to get a whiff of what belonged to him alone.

Waking her up had been the first thing he had done, so no more of the aroma would filter into the living room. Next, he'd opened every window, and lastly, he'd ordered breakfast, hoping that the scents of baked goods and freshly brewed coffee would mask the last traces of her aroma.

As promised, Syssi emerged from her room ten minutes later.

"I'm so sorry to have kept you all waiting. I fell asleep."

"No worries. Here, I have fresh coffee for you." Kian gestured to the dining table where he had saved a thermal carafe filled to the brim for her. It had been delivered together with their breakfast, but the container it was in would have kept it warm. Something to eat was another matter. What he'd ordered could've fed six people, but had been barely enough for the two Guardians.

Syssi sat across from him, avoiding his eyes. Was it about the dream? Or was she embarrassed about keeping them waiting?

He poured her a cup. "What would you like to eat?" He handed it to her.

"I'm not hungry yet, thank you." She took the cup and he handed her the container of assorted sweeteners.

"Did you sleep well?" He couldn't help asking.

Her head shot up and she looked at him with suspicious eyes. "Very well. How about you?"

He stretched and pretended to grimace in discomfort. "Not at all. I've worked until late, and when I finally lay down, I discovered that the couch is not comfortable." He was lying through his teeth. The couch was perfectly fine. Granted, not as good as his bed at home, but not as bad as he'd made it sound.

"Why didn't you go home? Two men to guard me are more than enough. You could've been sleeping comfortably in your own bed."

Crap, this didn't work. He needed another angle. Time to take off the kid gloves.

But wait? Did he really want Syssi to come home with him? Alone with her in his penthouse, there would be nothing to stop him from taking her. Other than his self-respect, that is, and Kian had a feeling that it would not be enough.

On the other hand, without her near him, he wouldn't be able to do shit, as he'd proven to himself yesterday.

This was so beyond messed up.

It was all Amanda's fault. If not for her matchmaking, he wouldn't be in such a bind. Except, he knew it wasn't true. Even if Amanda had never mentioned Syssi to him, he would not have reacted to her any differently once he'd met her.

He would need to think of a solution, but until then Syssi had to come home with him. A financial empire was at stake.

"We could've all been sleeping more comfortably. Anandur and Brundar in their own apartment, and you in a perfectly appointed guest room that is even nicer than the one in this suite. Not to mention the amount of money we could've saved." He was such a manipulator. Kian couldn't care less about the money, but he knew Syssi did. It was a low blow, hitting her where he knew it would hurt, but she'd left him no choice.

With a sigh, she nodded. "You're right. If you agreed to drop me at my brother's as I asked, you would have saved a fortune."

Stubborn woman. This wasn't the answer he was anticipating.

"As I've explained before, your brother's place is not safe. You would be putting both of you in danger by staying with him." That at least was true.

Syssi lifted her hands in defeat. "You win. I give up. Let's go to your place."

Hallelujah.

CHAPTER 48: SYSSI

Once again Syssi was about to enter Kian's penthouse, unsure about the wisdom of the move and feeling awkward. Not that she had a choice. The only option left to her was to buy an airline ticket and join her parents in Africa. There was little chance the fanatics would follow her all the way there.

Except, it was akin to curing a headache by chopping off the head. Too extreme a solution for the situation. In a few days, they would know if those crazies had made a move to capture her or Michael, and if they didn't, she could go back home to her old life.

Fearing her own attraction to Kian was not good enough of a reason to flee all the way to the other side of the world. Besides, she hated heat and humidity, mosquitoes and God knew what other bugs. How her mother was tolerating it was beyond her.

"Are you hungry yet?" Kian asked the moment they stepped inside.

"Yes, a little."

"Good. I'll ask Okidu to serve us brunch."

It seemed that the guy liked to feed her. Which must have meant that he cared at least a little. Or maybe not. Maybe he was just being hospitable. She really didn't know what to think anymore.

Kian was unlike any other guy she'd ever met, and not just because he was leagues above anyone she knew. The guy was full of contradictions. At times she'd felt certain he was going to make a move, kiss her again or tell her something that would indicate he was interested. At others she was convinced she'd imagined it, nothing but wishful thinking making her see interest where there had been none. Because there was no way a guy like him would go for a girl like her. His normal fare was probably celebrities, movie stars and models, not everyday people like boring lab assistants or architect's interns.

But then she remembered that one kiss, the real one, and the way he'd looked at her. Syssi shook her head. She was driving herself nuts. The best thing to do was to let things unfold and see where they led.

The tricky part would be not to let herself fall for the guy, not any more than she already had. Not that her infatuation with Kian meant that she was falling in love with him. She needed to keep telling herself that.

Play it cool and guard her heart.

Easy.

Right.

Same as yesterday, Okidu served their brunch in Kian's formal dining room. Two people sitting at a table large enough for eighteen was awkward in itself, and not having Brundar or Anandur as buffers didn't help either. And to top it off, she tended to overeat when nervous, which meant that she attacked the delicious meal as if she hadn't seen food in a week.

When she was done, Syssi dabbed at her mouth with a napkin, attempting to look ladylike despite the way she'd gobbled up everything on her plate. The truth was that it had been delicious, and remarkably it had also all been vegetarian. Glancing at her plate, she realized that there was nothing left but a few crumbs from the delicious eggplant sandwich. If no one were watching, she would've picked those up too and stuffed them in her mouth.

But someone was.

Syssi could feel Kian's eyes on her even without looking at him.

When Okidu came in with the coffee, she was granted a few moments' reprieve, but once he left, the silence between them felt like a vacuum begging to be filled.

With nervous fingers, Syssi folded and refolded her napkin, then braved a quick glance at Kian.

Her breath hitched.

Reclining in his chair and sipping on his coffee, he was watching her raptly. Not the casual friendly look from before, but one that was appraising and unnerving.

Averting her gaze, she cleared her throat. "Thank you for a wonderful meal. I've noticed, though, that everything was made with vegetables and mushrooms. You didn't order any meat dishes for yourself when we ate out either. Are you a vegetarian? Same as Amanda?"

Kind of lame. She'd already determined he was a vegan yesterday, but it was the best she could come up with under his unnerving stare.

"It's a healthier way to eat, not to mention kinder. I think most of us are instinctively reluctant to kill a living creature. If people had to actually hunt and kill their own food, I'm sure many would choose not to—not unless they had no choice because there was nothing else. I stay away from all animal products as much as I can, although when the alternative is starving, well... self-preservation and all that. Amanda tries, but you know her, she has to have her Brie or goat cheese from time to time." He smiled a tight-lipped smile.

Syssi had to agree. Amanda hated rules. Her boss was a rebel.

"Yes, I know what you mean. What puzzles me though, is your comment about eating meat as an alternative to starving. Have you ever been in such situation?" It took deliberate effort, but Syssi finally let go of the napkin, placing it beside her plate.

"There were times when there was nothing else, when I ran out of provisions, out in the wilderness or on a trek at some remote location. Hunting and killing for food was my only way to survive. Yeah, I've been in situations like that." He shrugged as if it was of no consequence, and yet, his sharp expression told a different story.

"Are you into the whole extreme-survival-camping thing? Lately, whenever I go channel surfing, I stumble upon one of those reality shows. The theme has become very popular. Obviously, the shows are staged, but I assume that for some it's a real form of recreation."

Kian didn't strike her as the type. He embodied the sophisticated, worldly CEO, not an extreme survivalist. And yet, she could sense that just under the surface there was something wild lurking inside him. Maybe he had served in the armed forces at some point, a commando unit like Andrew's. Except, he was too young to have done both.

"No, for me it wasn't a recreational choice. Let's just say there were times in my life when I was forced to fend for myself in a hostile environment." There was a finality in his grave tone that suggested he wouldn't appreciate any further questions on the subject.

Syssi figured he couldn't talk about it, or wasn't allowed—

Like Andrew.

Yep, the little he had said sounded like Special Ops. "I admire your ability to do so. If left alone in the wild, I would probably become the food. I have no survival skills whatsoever. No sense of direction either. I would be lost and defenseless." Syssi shivered, remembering the nightmare and her desperate run through the woods with the demon-wolves snarling at her heels.

Unbidden, images of what had followed slammed into her mind, sending a powerful flash of arousal through her. Erupting in her core, it spread up through her chest all the way to the nerve endings of her fingertips, making them tingle as if zapped with an electric current.

Oh, God, please, let it stop!

God didn't answer her prayer. If anyone did, it must've been the devil. Because following that first crack, the floodgates burst open, and every erotic moment she'd spent with Kian in her dreams rushed through her mind like a fast-forwarded movie.

She tried to stop the moan from escaping her throat, but despite her efforts a quiet whimper managed to get away. Mortified, Syssi blushed and looked down, desperately hoping Kian would attribute that embarrassing sound to her fear of getting lost in the wild.

CHAPTER 49: KIAN

Kian's body had reacted before his mind had time to process the torrent of sexual triggers slamming into him and knocking his breath out with the force of a battering ram.

Kind of like the one that had popped behind his zipper.

What the hell had just happened?

What had brought on that tortured moan? And why was Syssi suddenly emitting such strong scent of arousal tinted by fear? It was nothing like the soft kind he'd scented this morning. This was powerful. Overwhelming. A trigger he couldn't resist.

It wasn't as if Kian was a stranger to that particular combination. Sensing his predatory nature on a visceral level, most females responded to him that way; their lust and their apprehension combining to create one heady aphrodisiac.

His favorite.

But coming from sweet shy Syssi that explosive mixture fueled his lust like nothing before.

And as it grew stronger, his control grew weaker.

Taking over, the predator in him overpowered the thin layer of civilized behavior he struggled to maintain. Kian pounced. In one quick move, he had Syssi on his lap, trapped there in the cage of his arms.

Taken by surprise, she squeaked.

She must've felt his cock swell and twitch under her butt because her eyes widened and her lips parted on a sharp inhale, the flush on her cheeks climbing along with her arousal.

"You see, Syssi. If you were mine, I would have taken care of you, defended you, provided for you. You would have never been left alone to fend for yourself. The only wild beast to fear would have been me."

Even to his own ears, he sounded like a Neanderthal, but every word was true. All that was male about him craved this. He wanted to be everything to her, the only one to take care of her in every possible way, the only one she would ever want or need.

Searching his face, Syssi smiled a little, probably thinking he was only teasing. But as she looked into his eyes, sensing the kind of animal she was trapped by, her smile faltered.

With his palm closing gently around the back of her neck, he held her gaze as he drew closer to her mouth, slowly, deliberately, prolonging her breathless anticipation until she was panting with it.

Abruptly, he tightened his grip on her nape and closed the remaining distance between them, striking her soft lips with an almost bruising ferocity.

Syssi melted into the kiss, pressing herself against him, surrendering to his invading and probing tongue, flicking it and sucking it in.

So damn good.

As he withdrew, breathless, she followed, licking his lips and pressing her own little tongue into his mouth.

Reluctantly, he refused her entry.

By now, his fangs had fully descended, following the rest of his body in preparation for what it assumed was coming.

He couldn't allow her to find out that he wasn't who or rather what she thought he was. Not yet, anyway.

Entangling his fingers in her hair, he pulled her head back and nipped her bottom lip in warning, then licked it to soothe the small pain away.

"No, sweet girl, I can't have you do that. I need to be in charge when we are together like that." He tried to mask the implied command with gentle words and a soothing tone, then kissed her again, softly, tenderly—teasing, testing her compliance.

CHAPTER 50: SYSSI

Oh, God...

Syssi wanted, needed to intensify the kiss, but she needed to please Kian even more. Something in her craved his dominance, wanted to please him, wanted him to be in charge of her pleasure.

It turned her on like nothing had ever done before.

She was so aroused, her hardened nipples felt like they were pushing against her lacy bra and threatening to poke holes through the sheer fabric.

Mortified, she suspected Kian could feel not only her hard little nubs pressing against his chest but the wetness soaking through her stretchy pants as well. There was no way the scrap of her lacy panties could absorb all of what her arousal was pouring forth. Panting, she dipped her head, burrowing her forehead in his chest to hide her flaming hot cheeks.

A moment later, she sucked in a fortifying breath and tried to push off to get up, but he held her down, returning her head to his chest and stroking her hair as he leaned and kissed the top of it.

"Shh... It's okay, sweet girl. I've got you. I love how you respond to me. It's perfect, and it turns me on so much I'm afraid my zipper is not going to hold." Stroking her hair and running slow circles on her lower back, he waited for her to regain her composure.

On the one hand, she was even more embarrassed realizing Kian must've sensed how disturbed she was by her own reaction. But on the other, she appreciated his effort to ease her discomfort by admitting he was just as affected as she was.

Feeling the evidence of his arousal prod her butt, she chuckled and looked up hesitantly, not sure if Kian was joking or not.

His expression surprised her.

He regarded her as if she was special, precious, and not the disgrace to the feminist movement she'd felt like a moment ago.

Syssi didn't know what to say or how to react. Luckily, she didn't have to; his phone chimed, disrupting the sexually charged atmosphere.

Shifting his weight and wiggling to get the device out of his pants pocket, he kept his hold on her, delivering a quick peck to her forehead before answering the call. "Don't go anywhere," he whispered while covering the mic with his thumb.

As if she could.

With his hand drawing small circles on her back, and his hard muscular chest tempting her to rest her cheek on it, Kian's warmth and alluring smell lulled her into a hazy, dreamy state.

She heard him and the other guy talk, but the words didn't register.

The maelstrom of emotions and cravings were all new and uncharted territory for her. She had met the man just a few days ago for goodness' sake, and already she was dreaming about him, wanting him, needing him with an intensity bordering on desperation.

But what puzzled her even more was that despite his previous efforts to appear uninterested, he seemed to feel the same way about her. Was this crazy attraction the work of wild pheromones on steroids? Or was there more to it?

Words like destiny and fate floated through her mind, but she waved them away. Only fools and hopeless romantics believed in those.

Syssi didn't count herself as either.

Play it cool. Guard your heart.

Kian sighed as he returned the phone to his pocket. "As much as I hate to, I have to take care of a potentially combustible situation. Though believe me, I would've much preferred to stay here and stoke this one." Smiling suggestively, he quickly kissed her lips and lifted her off his lap.

"Make yourself at home. Okidu will show you around and help you get settled. Ask him for anything you need. I'll be back as soon as I can." He turned to leave.

"Wait. I don't think it's a good idea, Kian. I understand why I can't stay with Andrew, but I can join my parents in Africa. I'm sure I'll be safe there."

Moving into Kian's penthouse, even temporarily, would be a mistake. With the electrified currents sparking between them they might get carried away into doing something they would both later regret, albeit for different reasons. Hers would be a broken heart, his would be regret over breaking it.

Kian turned back and got in her face. With only scant inches between them, he took hold of her chin, tilting her head so she was forced to gaze into his hard eyes.

"You're not going anywhere. You're mine to protect, mine to take care of, and this place has the best security money and loyalty can buy. I will not trust anyone and anyplace else with your safety. So make yourself at home."

That predatory look that had made her heart flutter before was back, but as he smiled a tight-lipped smile, it transformed into something that was between sinister and lascivious. "We both know where this is heading, so why go through the pretense, Syssi? You might as well put your stuff in my bedroom. Anything else will be an exercise in futility."

Syssi tried to escape his hold and look away, but he wouldn't let go of her chin, forcing her to look into his eyes.

What a fool she'd been. The illusion she'd created in her mind, was just that, an illusion. The real Kian was a caveman, a big gorilla who thumped his chest and proclaimed all kinds of male bullshit.

Fueled by her deep disappointment in him, she felt her discomfort turn into anger. The polite, considered guy she had gotten to know was gone, and in his place was this rude, presumptuous jerk who thought he could order her around. Worse, who was under the impression she would be grateful he invited her to share his bed just because he was a great kisser.

The guy sure had an inflated ego, probably fueled by numerous too-easy conquests. Not that she showed a lot of resistance, or any for that matter.

The thought made her absolutely furious, mostly with herself.

That's it, Syssi. For the first time in your life, you earned the official title of slut.

As much as she craved him, she was not about to become another notch on his belt.

"You may be right. I'm not going to deny this thing between us, but you offend me by presuming I'm the kind of woman who jumps into bed with someone she just met. I'm grateful for your concern for my safety, but if I'm not leaving for Africa, I would at least appreciate having a room of my own." Unflinching under the intensity of his gaze, she continued. "Face it, Kian, this whole situation is temporary, and in a day or two I'll be back at my own place—it's not like I'm moving in permanently. So please, don't make it harder for me than it already is."

It was so unlike her to react so strongly. She hated heated confrontations and tried to avoid them at all costs. Walking away was more her style. Surprisingly, though, Syssi didn't feel as shaky or disturbed by this as she normally would.

For some reason, she trusted Kian to respect her wishes. And even though she was still angry, venting some of it helped her realize that although crude, Kian hadn't meant offense by his words. Like many guys, his communication skills were not that great.

But she needed to make a stand, else he would walk all over her.

His expression softened, and he let go of her chin to rake his fingers through his disheveled hair. "Forgive me, you're right. Whatever makes you comfortable is fine with me." He looked at her apologetically. "I wish I could be more charming and debonair for you, or even just patient, but that's not who I am. A rough around the edges, insensitive jerk, that's more my style." He smiled a little, still looking contrite.

Syssi felt relieved beyond words that her original assessment of him had been right. Kian was a good guy. A little intense, a little crude, but his intentions were not dishonorable. Well, maybe a little. But that wasn't a big deal. He was, after all, only a man.

With composure that surprised her, she smiled. "Now you're just fishing for compliments," she said to let him know that they were still okay. "I like you, Kian, just the way you are. I'll take blunt and honest over charming and deceitful any day, but that doesn't mean I'll tolerate it when you behave like a jerk." She rose on tiptoes and kissed his lips lightly. "Go, do whatever you need to do, I'll be fine." She grabbed his elbow to turn him around, and when he did, slapped his butt to send him on his way.

"Getting frisky, are we?" He laughed as he walked out.

"Just payback, smooth talker," she called after him.

So that was it.

There was no going back. She'd admitted to Kian that she liked him, basically giving him a green light. Perhaps not for a quick seduction, she would make him work for it because he wouldn't appreciate her otherwise, but she was finally ready to step outside her comfort zone.

To live, really live and not just go through the motions, she needed to start taking risks. Kian was a big one, but he was certainly worth it. Because if she gambled and won, it would be like winning first prize in the lottery of life.

Problem was, she had no idea what her odds were like. The stakes were high, that was for sure. Because if she lost, it would destroy her.

CHAPTER 51: KIAN

On his way out, Kian chuckled and shook his head.

Syssi defied characterization. How refreshing—a real person and not a facsimile of some preconceived set of attributes. She was different, and he liked that she didn't fit into any standard mold: shy and reserved in some situations, hot and wild in others. Taking her pleasure in yielding sexually, asserting her will otherwise.

She certainly stood up to him, as not many would, and even fewer could.

Reflecting on her spike of arousal at his little show of dominance, and how it had unsettled her, he suspected it had been the first time she'd experienced anything of that nature.

Syssi had no idea what to make of it, or how perfect he'd found her response to be. And although it had been only a tiny taste, Kian hoped to be the first and the only she would ever explore this further with. Regardless of how far she would let it go, he would love anything she would allow. He would go slow, introducing her to the pleasures of submission one little step at a time, careful not to overwhelm her, or frighten her.

A little fear was part of the game, but just a little. She needed to learn to trust him; to feel safe letting go with him.

Wait! Whoa... what was he thinking? There was no future for them.

And what a pity that was.

The more time he spent with Syssi, the more he realized how perfect she was for him. She was exactly what he wanted, just as Amanda had predicted he would, her courage to be honest and true to herself impressing him above all.

In contrast, Kian felt like a scumbag. A deceitful jerk. And the biggest joke was that she believed him to be an honest guy,

Trouble was, there was no way for him to come clean and tell her the truth, about anything really.

And that didn't sit well with him at all.

It had been a mistake—a momentary lapse of reason, a weakness—to start with Syssi something that could never be. He must've been possessed when he'd blurted that nonsense about her moving into his bedroom.

What the hell had gotten into him?

She didn't deserve to be talked to like that. Syssi was an amazing woman: smart, sweet, beautiful. In a few days, though, she'd go back to her old life, and he would have no choice but to scrub her memories once again.

This time for good.

For his own sanity, he needed to keep his distance.

Damn, he was deluding himself if he thought he could let her go. He'd become obsessed with her, needing her to be near him to function.

He was so screwed. What the hell was he going to do?

I'm an idiot for starting this in the first place.

And it wasn't as if he hadn't known better.

What had he been thinking? That he would use her and then get rid of her like all the others?

Even if he were willing to sink that low, let his honor and self-respect go to hell, fate or perhaps his bloody hormones had taken the choice out of his hands. For some inexplicable reason, he needed her worse than a drug addict his next fix.

Perhaps he should book that trip to Scotland he'd been putting off forever. He hadn't seen Sari and the rest of the gang in ages. But more to the point, it would take his mind off a certain sweet blond that was threatening to ruin what had taken him nearly two thousand years to achieve: Letting go of an impossible dream and accepting a fate of an endless, lonely life.

With a sigh, Kian stepped into the elevator and glanced at himself in the mirror. He looked miserable, tortured. If only he could talk to someone about this messed up situation, get some good advice, find a way to be with Syssi without ruining her life or his.

The trip to Scotland sounded like a good idea in theory, but the truth was that he didn't have time for that. He was drowning in work, and taking even a few hours off required careful planning. Taking a trip to see family was out of the question, while getting any work done without Syssi around seemed impossible too.

Man, he needed help.

Pulling out his phone, he called the last person who he thought could do that.

"Hello, Kian," Amanda answered cheerfully.

"Where are you?"

"Having my nails done."

That would explain the Vietnamese he heard in the background.

"When are you coming back?"

"Why? What do you need?"

Kian raked his fingers through his hair. "Could you invite Syssi to stay at your place?"

"Why? What have you done to her?" Amanda's tone had turned accusatory.

"Nothing. Yet. That's why I need you to take her away from me. She is driving me crazy. I can't be with her and I can't be without her. Maybe staying across the vestibule in your place will be a good compromise."

"Kian, Kian, Kian. Stop being such a sanctimonious prick and just have sex with the girl already. Be gentle, though. It has been a very long time for her."

"You have absolutely no morals, Amanda. And you claim to care for Syssi."

"I do, you idiot, and I care for you too. That's why I want you two to be together. You need each other."

"She is a human, Amanda. And the chances of her being a Dormant are nonexistent."

"You don't know that. You're just terrified of taking a chance. Stop being such a coward and take a risk. Live!"

"You're not helping."

"The hell, I'm not. I swear, if you don't do it, I'm going to involve Mother."

"You're bluffing."

"Try me!" She hung up.

████████ *hell*.

Kian hurled the phone at the mirror, watching the device bounce off and land on the floor. ████damned Shai had gotten him an indestructible cover after he'd pulverized the last one.

Now he had nothing to break. Unless he used his head. Banging it until it bled sounded like a plan. Maybe something would shift inside and he could go back to the way he'd been before.

With a sigh, Kian leaned his forehead against the cool glass. As much as he hated to admit it, Amanda wasn't completely wrong.

He wasn't living. He was functioning.

It dawned on him then that the only times he'd felt alive lately had been with Syssi.

Perhaps he needed to reevaluate his position. Take a chance. Maybe Syssi would turn out to be a Dormant after all, making him the happiest male on the planet.

He would never know unless he tried.

As the saying went; nothing ventured, nothing gained. He had to take a risk.

Problem was, unbeknownst to Syssi, she would be risking more than he, and unlike his sister, Kian believed that to do so was not only dishonorable but despicable.

CHAPTER 52: AMANDA

With a smirk, Amanda slipped the phone into her purse and leaned back.

"What you happy for?" the nail salon owner asked. Holding Amanda's hand and painting one of her long nails with bright red nail polish, she looked at her expectantly. There was nothing these hardworking women loved more than a juicy piece of gossip.

"I found my brother his future wife. He fought me hard on this, didn't want to even meet her."

The woman frowned. "Why? She ugly?"

"She is beautiful, and smart, and sweet. He doesn't know how lucky he is."

The woman harrumphed. "Men are stupid. You good sister, find him good wife."

"I know."

"But if he not want see her, why you smile?"

"I had a little help from Lady Luck, and now my stubborn brother has no choice but to spend time with her."

She should send a gift basket to the Doomer headquarters, thanking them for helping her matchmaking plans along. Inadvertently, by bringing Syssi and Kian together, they might have saved their enemy clan's future. Except, not all of it had been good. The clan had lost Mark in the process.

Amanda sighed. They hadn't been tight, but she loved her nephew and was going to miss him dearly.

The fates worked in mysterious ways, but they always demanded a sacrifice for bestowing their gifts. Had they taken his life in exchange for securing the clan's future?

It was a horrible thought to mull over, and therefore Amanda got rid of it as soon as it flitted through her mind.

The old woman smiled, her eyes sparkling with excitement. "You think he fall in love?"

"I'm sure of it."

The question wasn't whether they would fall in love with each other, but whether Syssi was a Dormant who Kian could turn into a near-immortal like them.

Amanda had a strong feeling that she was, but there was always a possibility that she might be wrong. It was a frightening prospect. Kian and Syssi's hearts were on the line. But there was no other way. The future of the clan depended on the success of this experiment.

DARK STRANGER
REVEALED

CHAPTER 1: SYSSI

"Wow, that was one hell of a kiss," Syssi breathed. More like a total meltdown.

She was grateful for the call that had interrupted what might have ended in Kian's bedroom. It had broken the spell. If not for the emergency that had required Kian's immediate attention, she would've let him take her to his bed and would've regretted it dearly.

Even though she was no longer mad at him, Syssi still refused to become another notch on his belt. She held herself to higher standards.

Oh, God, she wished she didn't.

Relinquishing her outdated standards for a morning of passion with Kian would've been worth the sacrifice. The fire he'd ignited in her was like nothing she'd ever experienced before and she craved more, wanted to explore it and find out where it led.

Still hot and bothered, she wondered how long he'd be gone. It depended on what kind of emergency it was. Must've been something major to bother the CEO on a Sunday morning. Unless he'd used it as an excuse to leave and cool down.

For some reason, Kian was fighting his attraction to her.

Did he deem her beneath him?

It wasn't as if he was some kind of an aristocrat while she was a pleb. The only things that defined social strata in the United States were money and political connections. Granted, she had none, but Kian didn't strike her as snob. Maybe it had something to do with her working for his sister. He might have regarded a relationship between them inappropriate because of his financial connections to the lab. According to Amanda, her research was funded by one of the corporations owned by their family.

Syssi shook her head and gathered the dirty dishes left over from their brunch. Guessing would bring her nothing other than a headache. She would have to grow a set and ask Kian what was his deal.

God, what a big mess her simple life had become.

As she carried the dishes to the kitchen and got busy at the sink, Syssi reflected on the recent upheaval in her orderly routine. In the span of less than twenty-four hours, she had been chased by a group of dangerous zealots, spellbound by her boss's gorgeous brother, and hypnotized by him to forget all about it, including meeting him, only to have Kian star in her most erotic dreams ever.

In the light of day, however, the real Kian was better than any dream, and to be wanted by a man like him was one hell of a heady feeling.

If she was wanted, that is.

The man was a puzzle she couldn't decipher, a mystery. Not a problem she'd encountered often. Most people were transparent to her, their motives clear.

That fact in itself was cause for alarm, and then there was her insane response to Kian.

Syssi didn't know what to make of that. Yes, he was gorgeous, intelligent and successful, but that shouldn't have been enough to induce such a profound transformation in her.

The woman who had thought of herself as not all that sexual had been turned into a mindless puddle of need. And even more shockingly, it seemed that her newfound passion had a somewhat kinky twist to it.

Who would have thought?

Embarrassed, Syssi felt her face heating and attacked the dishes with renewed vigor, soaping and scrubbing the already clean plates.

"Please, mistress, let me." Gently but firmly, the butler took the plate she was washing out of her hands, then led her away from the sink.

"I'm sorry, I just thought to make myself useful." The poor guy probably thinks I'm after his job. "I'm not the kind of guest who needs to be waited on. I like to help."

"Oh, but madame, it is my distinct pleasure to serve you. You would not wish to deprive an old man of his pride and joy now, would you?" He smiled his weird mannequin smile.

Manipulative butler.

"Well, of course not..." And although it was hard to tell, she hazarded a guess that he was in his early forties—hardly an old man. "But please, call me Syssi."

Okidu squared his shoulders. "I certainly will not." He affected indignation with a heavy British accent. "Let me show you the guest rooms, madame." He dipped his head and extending his arm motioned for her to precede him down the corridor.

There were four luxurious bedroom suites in addition to Kian's and the butler's, each decorated in its own unique color scheme and style.

Syssi chose the smallest of the four, snorting as she was reminded of Goldilocks in the Three Bears' House.

"May I unpack your luggage, mistress?" Okidu asked as he brought her duffle bag inside the walk-in closet.

"No, thank you. I'll do it myself."

"As you wish, madame." He bowed, then eased out of the room, gently closing the door behind him.

Syssi emptied her bag, fitting the few things she had brought with her all on one shelf, then moved on to the bathroom to deposit the Ziplock bag containing her toiletries and makeup on the vanity.

Eyeing the large jacuzzi tub, nestled within an intimate enclave with a big window overlooking the cityscape, she was tempted to try it out. Which reminded her that there was a lovely lap pool out on the terrace, and it would be a damn shame if she didn't take advantage of it while staying at Kian's amazing penthouse. The tub could wait for later.

Problem was, she didn't bring a swimming suit. Syssi was about to give up on the idea when a simple solution popped in her mind. In a pinch, a solid black bra and matching undies could pass for a bikini.

Still, on the remote chance that Okidu was more astute than most men and would guess it was underwear, Syssi wrapped a large towel around her makeshift swim attire.

The sun was warm on her skin as she stepped onto the terrace. Hopefully, the pool was heated and the water was warm as well. Dipping her toes, she was happy to discover that it was and jumped in. The pool felt heavenly, soothing away the remaining vestiges of her anxiety as she swam slow, lazy laps then rolled over onto her back and floated.

Sweeping her hands in circles to keep herself afloat, Syssi closed her eyes in bliss. It was like vacationing in some luxury resort, and to make the experience complete, Okidu even served her a piña colada smoothie, poolside.

Perfect.

Well, almost. Kian wasn't there, and she missed him.

A warm feeling suffused her. She really liked the big, arrogant oaf. He'd blundered badly, behaving like an ass, but any guy that was man enough to apologize and take responsibility for his mishaps, as well and as sincerely as Kian had done, was okay in her book. And anyway, the way the man got her heart pumping, she wasn't sure she wouldn't have forgiven him even if he had not.

Yep, I'm definitely turning into a horny, brainless floozy. She chided herself as she finished the last of the smoothie with a loud slurp.

Leaving the empty goblet by her towel, she glided into the center of the pool, turned on her back again, and paddled leisurely with her eyes closed.

"Hi, gorgeous!" Amanda startled her.

Splattering and splashing to right herself, Syssi soaked Amanda, who was squatting by the side of the pool and smiling like a Cheshire cat.

Served Amanda right for sneaking in on her like that. "Hi, yourself, I completely forgot you're next door." Syssi wiped her eyes. "Wait a minute, you told me you have a condo in Santa Monica. When did you move here?" she asked, twisting her hair to wring it out.

Amanda brushed water droplets off her jean-clad legs and got up. "Oh no, this is just temporary. I definitely did not move in here, although Kian keeps nagging me to. I love him, but living right under his nose would be a really bad idea. Anyhow, he keeps it ready for me in case I change my mind, and with those crazy fanatics on the loose, I decided to humor him." She winked.

"Kian told me what happened at the lab. I would've called you, but he threw away my cell phone, and I didn't remember your number. How are you holding up?" She could've asked Kian, but it hadn't even crossed her mind. She'd forgotten all about Amanda. Apparently, with him around, her hormone level skyrocketed, affecting her brain's ability to function properly.

"I'm fine. The whole thing will blow over in a few days, and by then the lab will be as good as new. I've already arranged for cleanup and for new equipment to be delivered. The only task remaining is repainting the walls and maintenance is on it."

"Have you given any thought to how we're going to continue the research until the lab is ready? I think you're overly optimistic assuming all of this can be done so quickly. I'd give it at least two weeks, if not longer." Syssi got out and wrapped herself in the large towel.

"We can do some of the work from here, going over the data we already have, maybe even start a new paper. Don't worry, I'll make sure you earn your pay. It won't be all swimming and lazing around... Just most of it." Amanda snorted as she plopped down on one of the lounges.

"What about Hannah and David, are you planning on bringing them here as well?" Wrapping the towel tighter against the cool breeze, Syssi sat down next to Amanda.

"Heavens, no! I called Professor Goodbow and explained the situation. He promised he'd find them something to do until this mess is cleared. And anyway, Kian doesn't allow strangers up here. Top floors are for family only."

"I'm not family..."

"Yeah, but you're special. Besides being the lunatics' top target, I think my stubborn brother finally capitulated and went after you. Am I right? I hope I'm right. Tell me I'm right!"

Syssi's cheeks heated. What the hell had Amanda done? Had she been talking with Kian about her and he had not been interested? That would explain a lot. Like his reluctance to engage with her.

Damn.

"What do you mean—finally capitulated?"

"Yeah, I know. It's just that I wanted to get the two of you together for some time, but Kian being Kian refused all of my matchmaking efforts. So I didn't tell you anything because what was the point? Right? But now that the fool finally met you, he likes you, as I told him he would. I'm going to have such a blast saying I-told-you-so. You guys are perfect together." Amanda smirked, all smug satisfaction over the success of her yenta schemes, or perhaps over the prospect of endlessly needling Kian.

Amanda pushed up from the lounger and stretched her long body, the bottom of her T-shirt still damp and clinging to her skin. "I'm going back to my place across the hall. If you need anything, you know where to find me." She bent down and gave Syssi a warm hug. "I'm really glad you're here, Syssi. Kian needs someone to take care of him. And being the loving sister that I am, I found him the perfect someone." Amanda kissed Syssi's cheek.

Surprised and touched, Syssi hugged and kissed her back. Knowing Amanda liked her was one thing, but this was above and beyond. "Thank you. It really means a lot, you thinking so highly of me. But Kian and I have just met, and I don't know if anything will come out of it. He is... well you know... he is really handsome... obstinate... controlling... endearing..." Syssi laughed as Amanda rolled her eyes and made the go-on gesture with her hand. "And he seems to like me, but we don't really know each other, so don't plan the wedding just yet. Okay?" she said, meaning it as a joke.

"I've got a good feeling about this, girl, and I hate being disappointed." Amanda poked a warning finger at Syssi's chest before turning to go inside.

Syssi shook her head. Bossy family.

Lying down on the lounger Amanda had vacated, she turned on her stomach and cradled her face in her arms. Tired from the day's excitement, the sun pleasantly warm on her back, she grew drowsy and closed her eyes.

"Mistress," Okidu said. "I brought you supper in case you were peckish."

Slowly, Syssi opened her eyes. There was a thick robe draped over her back, which explained why she felt so warm and toasty even though it was getting late.

It was so nice of the butler to cover her. With the two of them alone in the place, it couldn't have been anyone other than Okidu. "Thank you for the robe. It was very kind of you."

She slipped her arms into the overlong sleeves and looped the belt twice around her waist, then brought the lapels closer to her cheeks.

Kian's scent was all over the thing. Combined with the warmth of the thick terry fabric, it cocooned her in what felt like home—safe, hers. Syssi closed her eyes. She missed him, and his absence felt as if there was a hole in her heart.

Which was nuts.

"You are welcome, mistress. It was getting chilly, and I did not want to wake you. You looked so peaceful. But it is late, and the master would have not been happy if I failed to provide you with nourishment. Would you like to dine outside? Or should I take the tray inside?"

By now, it was indeed a little cold out on the terrace, but recalling yesterday's sunset, she wanted to watch it again. "Here would be great, thank you."

Syssi ate her dinner at the small bistro table, watching the clouds turn all shades of orange, red, and purple until they faded into darkness by the time she was done.

She couldn't help feel a bit disappointed that Kian had not returned in time to join her for dinner, and as she carried the tray to the kitchen, she wondered what was keeping him. He had been gone for hours. But then, he obviously couldn't just drop everything to be with her. Hopefully, he wasn't staying away because he didn't want her company.

A disturbing thought. But she couldn't allow herself to think like that.

Amanda had told her about Kian's insane workload and long hours, and so had he. Evidently they had not been exaggerating.

The little Syssi knew about Kian, she had learned from Amanda's complaints about how difficult it was to get him to come see her teach because he was always working; busy running the family business. He'd mentioned real estate, and a military grade drone factory that he was in the process of buying. Two completely unrelated businesses. Supposedly, Kian was running an international conglomerate, which meant that there were many more.

She should Google it. Maybe she could find out more about their financial empire. One thing was clear, though, big money was involved, on a scale that was hard for her to grasp even though she'd minored in business. Later, she could ask Kian about it. It was a safe topic, far removed from carnal thoughts.

But right now, a Jacuzzi tub with her name on it was waiting.

CHAPTER 2: DALHU

Dalhu paced the length of the mansion's opulent home office, contemplating his newfound knowledge. The professor's little red notebook had been an eye-opener on so many levels.

With a light knock, the old cook pushed the door open. "Your tea, sir," she said and shuffled in, holding a tray in her trembling hands. On her first day, Dalhu had thought the tremor was caused by fear. After all, cooking for twelve large warriors wasn't something the woman was used to. But after she'd served them three meals that day, with her old gnarled hands trembling no more and no less, he'd realized it was just age.

Dalhu took the tray from her, afraid she would spill the hot tea on her large bosom. The last thing he needed was a trip to the hospital. The woman was in her seventies—there was no way any of his men could produce venom to heal her with a bite. "Thank you, Miriam."

"Would you like something to eat, sir?" she asked. "I can make a special treat just for you." At least once a day, she would offer to pamper him with something special, and each time he would refuse. For someone her age, she already worked too hard.

"No, thank you. That will be all, Miriam." She looked disappointed, but he wasn't particular about his food and was fine eating whatever she made for the men.

When she left, he closed the door behind her and resumed his pacing.

It had taken him a while to decipher the professor's illegible handwriting and cryptic references, but eventually an interesting picture had emerged.

First and foremost, he had discovered that the enemy still adhered to the old taboos against procreating between members of the same matrilineal descent. Second, and not less important, that they had no Dormants of other lines.

He'd always assumed that they were a cowardly bunch; the kind who preferred running and hiding to honorably facing their enemies in battle. But as the real reason for their tactics became glaringly obvious—that there just weren't enough of them to offer a fight—he was grudgingly compelled to grant them respect.

How the hell had they managed to achieve so much—stolen knowledge notwithstanding—when there couldn't have been more than a few hundred of them?

Making tracks in the luxurious Persian rug, his mind went back to the issue of Dormants. Apparently, the professor believed that finding mortals with special abilities, of the paranormal kind, would lead her to potential Dormants.

Why?

None of his brethren had any of the various traits she had mentioned in her notebook. And certainly none of the Dormants he had encountered as a child had exhibited anything out of the ordinary—not his mother and sister, nor any of the other women in Navuh's "special harem."

Navuh's powers were to be expected, after all, he was the son of a god, and so were his sons' formidable abilities.

The rest of the men could thrall most mortals to some extent, but not all—the weaker the mind, the less it resisted manipulation—but that was it.

As to Dormants, they were a rare and precious commodity, guarded fiercely by Navuh for obvious reasons. And apparently, the despot was the only one to possess any.

Dalhu closed his eyes as his thoughts drifted back to his mother and sister. His mother had been a whore, as all the other Dormant women in Navuh's special harem—and the same fate had been awaiting his sister— he just hadn't been around to witness it.

After all this time, he had trouble remembering their features. The only clear memory that he still managed to hold on to was his mother's voice. Some nights, he still heard her singing to him in his dreams.

Dalhu had been taken away to the training camp and turned at thirteen, never to see his small family again. He hadn't been allowed. The one time he'd tried, he'd gotten off easy with a severe beating as punishment, only because he'd been so young. An older male would've been beheaded.

The group of Dormant women were Navuh's secret broodmares. Selling their bodies to serve wealthy mortals provided him with a source of income and male children for his army of near-immortal mercenaries.

The sons were activated and became soldiers, the daughters were not and were relegated to prostitution like their mothers before them. Neither was given a choice.

Once the boys were turned, they were never allowed near the Dormants again. Fornicating with one carried the death penalty for both.

The Dormants were to serve mortals only.

In the past, Dalhu, like the rest of the soldiers, had assumed that the women weren't turned because according to the teachings of Mortdh they were deemed inferior. It had taken him centuries to piece together the real reason behind the segregation. If turned by an immortal male's venom, an immortal female's chances of conceiving dropped to nearly nonexistent. And Navuh needed the women to bear as many children as possible, which they had, providing over the millennia thousands of warriors for his army.

The *special harem* had always been heavily guarded—nowadays even more so as a fenced-off enclave of *Passion Island.*

A selective breeding program was pairing Dormants with clients believed to possess the traits valuable to Navuh; mainly physical size and strength, with sociopathic tendencies a close second.

Navuh needed his soldiers to be strong and ruthless—nothing more.

Dalhu sat back at the desk and pulled out a quarter from his pocket. He tossed it up in the air and slammed it onto the desk when it came down. Repeating his experiment twenty times, he was assured of having no special precognition ability.

As expected, his predictions came true roughly half of the time.

"Edward!" he called his second.

The soldier came rushing in. "Yes, sir."

"Take this coin and flip it ten times. I want to see how many you can guess correctly."

Edward looked puzzled, but he did as he was told with no questions asked. He guessed right four out the ten.

"That will be all," Dalhu dismissed him.

Returning the quarter back to his pocket, he wondered if these abilities could be somehow developed, learned. He wouldn't have put it past Navuh to conceal this kind of information from his troops. As power hungry as Navuh was, the despot would not have wanted his divine status undermined by his lowly soldiers exhibiting even a fraction of his abilities.

Dalhu lifted the professor's small red notebook off the desk and leaned back in the heavy executive swivel chair. Flipping through the pages, he reached the one containing the list of paranormal subjects.

Interesting stuff really. Telepathy, both sending and receiving, or only one-way transmission. Remote viewing, past viewing, precognition, influencing—emotional and otherwise. The ability to cast illusions. Communication with the dearly departed.

Most of the test subjects exhibited dismal talent. Except two.

Syssi, the professor's assistant, was the sole recipient of the score of ten—the highest. Her talent was precognition. How ironic that he'd met the girl and hadn't realized what a priceless treasure she was. A seer. What a powerful tool she could be. Dalhu wondered what kind of predictions she could make.

The other interesting subject was a guy named Michael: a student on the same campus. His talent was telepathy—of the receiving kind—his ranking was eight. Not bad. Being able to read other people's minds could be a great asset too, probably a more useful tool than that of the female's.

Soon, Dalhu would have both to do with as he pleased.

The woman's address had been easy to find in the university's Human Resources database. The hacker he had hired hadn't had much difficulty retrieving her record, especially with that weird spelling of her given name. He could've sent one of the men to the HR office for that, but hacking worked faster.

The telepath posed a greater challenge, but it was nothing money couldn't overcome. His cell phone number was listed on his parents' account in Minnesota, so the phone bill was useless for finding his address. And there were five students named Michael Gross living on campus. He had to be located by his phone's signal.

The guy Dalhu had found to do it had been expensive but worth it. Unfortunately, he encountered some trouble, and had gotten the job done only late this evening, pinpointing the boy's location to a popular student hangout, a club not far from the dorms, which was currently teeming with people.

Dalhu had men in position at both locations.

The team at the woman's house was poised to snatch her as soon as she came home. Though if she didn't show up soon, he planned to fork out the money for the guy to track her cellphone as well.

The other team, dispatched to bring the telepath, was hanging outside the club. Without a picture to identify him by, they would wait for the boy to get out and separate from his friends. Regrettably, the acuity of the tracking device was limited to pinpointing the place, but not one individual out of a tightly packed crowd.

It wouldn't be much longer.

Soon, Dalhu's phone would be buzzing with the confirmations of their capture.

This wasn't what excited him, though. Catching the two potential Dormants was almost inconsequential in comparison to getting his hands on the beautiful, immortal professor.

Dalhu pulled out the auto repair shop's estimate he'd found tucked between the journal's pages. Apparently, the professor's Porsche was undergoing repairs at a Beverly Hills collision center specializing in luxury European automobiles, and it would be ready for pickup next Thursday. Luckily, the estimate included the car's license plate number.

This time, he wasn't going to send any of his underlings. Dalhu was going to be there himself, waiting all day until someone came to pick it up. If it were the professor, he would snatch her from there. But even if someone else showed up in her place or the shop delivered the car, he would just follow the Porsche to the professor's actual residence.

Next Thursday, the lovely Dr. Amanda Dokani would be his.

CHAPTER 3: KIAN

"Finally, it's done." Kian put down the phone and leaned back in Shai's chair. The deal had almost gone up in smoke. Several times he'd been tempted to let it go to hell, but Onegus had kept things going. His chief Guardian and negotiator was in Spain, ironing out the last details on the beach property Kian was trying to snatch before it even went on the market. But as often happened, a competitor had also learned of the deal and offered a better price.

Kian wondered who'd tipped them off. Perhaps his sniffer had double dipped, selling the information twice.

Who else could've known that the owner of the shabby hotel had just lost his wife to heart failure and wished to get rid of the place they had run together for years? The guy had told his son, who had told his girlfriend, who had met the sniffer at a coffee shop and had told him about it during a random conversation.

Unless the guy had also sold the information to Kian's rival, no one could've known the place was on the market.

With the bidding war getting out of hand, Kian had been about to give the thing up when the competitor bowed out. Not that he could blame the guy. With what he'd ended up agreeing to pay for the place, it would take much longer to realize profits, but Kian and the clan were in no hurry.

Time was on their side.

"You want to drink to that?" Shai opened his mini fridge and pulled out two Snake Venom beers—the world's strongest at almost seventy percent alcohol by volume, and the only beer immortals could get drunk on.

"Sure, why not." Kian accepted the bottle.

He needed something to take the edge off. Not an easygoing guy on a good day, which this one certainly wasn't, Kian was nearing melting point. It had started with Amanda's ultimatum, then continued with a deal that turned out to be not as sweet as he'd hoped, and now he had no more excuses and needed to decide what to do about Syssi.

"It's not such a bad deal. We'll still make good money." Shai mistook his grimace.

Kian wasn't going to correct him. Let the guy think he was disappointed with the numbers, not with his sister and her cavalier attitude, and not with himself and his crumbling resistance.

"Good job, Shai." He clapped his secretary on the back. "Let's call it a day. I'm out of here."

"Thanks. But I'm just the pencil pusher. You and Onegus have done all the work."

Yeah, right. That was Shai's favorite expression, when in fact he was indispensable. The guy could've taken on more, but he didn't want to. He was comfortable with his position and didn't strive for anything more. Something Kian couldn't for the life of him relate to. He always pushed himself to the limit, expected more of himself than others, and was incapable of giving up.

Except, it seemed that he was capable of giving in.

As he mulled over the situation in between the phone calls and the e-mails and the general hysteria that erupted around this ▓▓▓▓ deal, he realized that he was being a hypocrite.

He hadn't forbidden Amanda from using another male to try to activate Syssi. Did he count himself above the other males of his clan? Was it okay for another to act immorally while Kian prided himself on taking the higher ground?

The answer was obviously no. But the last straw that had done it for him, was thinking of some other male touching his Syssi. As soon as Amanda would realize he was not going to do it no matter what, she would rope another male in. None of the others would refuse her, not unless Kian issued an order prohibiting it.

He could still do it, but Amanda must've anticipated this move before he even thought of it and threatened him with involving their mother. There was no doubt in his mind that Annani would side with Amanda. The future of her clan was at stake, and she had no problem bending the rules when it suited her.

They had him cornered, which was a huge relief. Having no choice felt a lot better than admitting he couldn't control his craving for the girl.

Except, when he finally made it back to the penthouse, ready to pick up where he had left things off with Syssi, she wasn't there.

Searching, he poked his head into every room, checking even out on the terrace, but she was nowhere to be found.

Where the hell can she be?

He pulled out his phone and rang Amanda. "Is Syssi with you?" he asked without preamble.

"No, did you manage to scare her off already?" Amanda taunted.

With a grunt, he ended the call and shoved the phone back in his pocket.

The obvious conclusion was that she had left. Though, how she had managed to do that without a thumbprint access to the elevators, or security letting him know, baffled him.

Maybe Okidu had helped her, taking her down in the elevator. With that main obstacle out of the way, there would have been nothing preventing her from waltzing away.

And as the guys in security were more concerned with people coming into the building than leaving it, they would have thought nothing of her casually strolling out the front door.

With a vile curse, Kian kicked a planter, wincing as the thing toppled.

He had no one to blame but himself.

After all, he hadn't specifically forbidden her to leave, or informed security to detain her if she tried.

Walking back inside, Kian pulled out his phone ready to call Okidu when he heard a distant hum.

Jets.

Whirlpool tub's jets.

So that's where she is...

Relieved, he shoved the phone back into his pocket and followed the sound.

When he reached the room she was in, Kian shook his head. Syssi had chosen the smallest, most plainly furnished suite in the penthouse. It was so like her. Though how he knew that about her puzzled him. He just did.

With a sigh, he kicked off his boots and plopped down on the bed. It seemed that despite the long hours it had taken him to get back to her, his wait wasn't over yet.

Closing his eyes, Kian made a go at some shut-eye, but it was no use. Problem was, he kept imagining Syssi's gorgeous body soaking naked in that tub, the tips of her perfect breasts peeking above the soapy water...

Oh, hell. With that scenario doing all kinds of things to his male anatomy, he itched to barge in there and...

Yeah, as if that would end well...

"Not!" he muttered as he reached inside his pants, adjusting himself. But his damned cock was so distended that it jutted above his waistband.

Cursing, he covered it with his shirttails.

With all that had been going on lately, he hadn't had the time or the inclination to go prowling for sex. And the long stretch of abstinence was taking its toll.

His biology was demanding its pound of flesh.

Except, the thought of slaking his need with some cheapie he picked up at a bar, suddenly felt repugnant to him.

He craved Syssi. Her fresh, sweet innocence was calling to his tainted soul.

Soon.

She would get out from that bathroom and find him waiting for her like some creepy stalker, and realize that her time was up.

What the hell is taking her so damn long?

Kian was losing his patience. Now that the decision had been made, he could wait no longer.

As the tub began draining, his pulse sped up. Any moment now, she'd get out…

No such luck.

He growled deep in his throat. Then he heard her applying lotion. And more lotion. And just as his agitation was gaining critical velocity, he heard what sounded suspiciously like a moan.

What the hell?

Had the little minx rebuffed him just to go ahead and pleasure herself without him?

Oh, no, she didn't!

With a surge, Kian shot out of bed and was about to barge in on her, when he heard the hairdryer turn on. His palm a fraction of an inch away from the door handle, he barely managed to stop in time.

His body bursting with barely contained aggression, he plopped back down on the bed, crossed his arms over his chest, and ordered himself to calm the fuck down!

One deep breath after another, he kept talking himself down from the high tree branch onto which he had climbed.

Take it easy, moron. She has no idea you're lying in wait for her like a fucking perv.

He kept telling himself he needed to be patient, romantic, go slow…

Except, how the hell would he manage that when he was strung up tighter than a bow string?

Exasperated, Kian banged his head against the headboard.

CHAPTER 4: SYSSI

Syssi's fingertips were starting to prune.

As fun as the spa was, it was time to get out. Turning the whirlpool off, she stepped out of the tub and wrapped herself in one of the plush towels stacked by its side.

All during her soak, Kian's words from earlier had been playing over and over in her mind, providing a background soundtrack to the vivid images they were painting.

On one hand, all these new and intense sensations electrified her. It was like discovering a whole new world of pleasure she had never known existed. It was exhilarating. On the other hand, she was afraid that once she had gotten a taste for how it could be, she would do just about anything to get more of it.

Before, she had never understood what drove people to indulge in careless sex, despite the potential utter devastation it entailed. Unwelcome pregnancies, ruined marriages, family feuds, wars... Literature painted an abundance of catastrophic scenarios Syssi had used to believe were mostly fictional. After all, what was so difficult about keeping your pants on?

But now, as need gnawed at her like a hungry beast, she understood.

Standing on the cold marble and looking out the window at the dark sky, she grew nervous. Kian would be back soon. And then what? Was she strong enough to say no to him, or at least not yet? Or was she going to surrender to her longing and have reckless sex with a man she barely knew but wanted desperately?

Toweling the moisture off with the excessive vigor of her rising frustration, she questioned her indecision. What was really the point of delaying the inevitable? If not tonight, then the next, or the one after that. If Kian still wanted her, that is. He might have concluded that she was too much trouble, and go for the easy and available.

Everyone around her was talking about hookups and booty calls, instead of dates and relationships. People treated sex as casually as going to the movies or out for a drink. In this uninspiring, emotionally disconnected landscape, the pursuit of sexual gratification was the norm, and the rare relationship an exception. An oddity.

Still, she wondered if all these people were deluding themselves into accepting this sorry state of affairs as gratifying. Perhaps they were just desperately reaching out for any kind of connection, hoping something real would sprout from all that carnality.

She couldn't see herself living that way. Maybe she was old-fashioned, or just naive, but she needed at least the illusion of a relationship, if not the real thing, to get all hot and sweaty with a guy.

Oh, but Kian...

He was like an addiction, an obsession, calling to her, drawing her in like a moth to a flame. She knew she was going to burn, but at this point she didn't care.

She was going to do it, had to...

Catching her panicky reflection staring back at her from the mist-covered mirror, her hand flew to her chest.

Oh, God! She wasn't ready!

It had been so long since her last time, Syssi felt like a virgin all over again; nervous, insecure, frightened. So okay, it probably wasn't going to hurt like the first time had—thank heavens for small favors—but she felt anxious nonetheless.

What if she fell short of Kian's expectations, what if he found her unexciting... lacking...

What if, what if... stop it! She ordered the self-disparaging internal monolog to cease.

Rubbing lotion onto her hands, she decided a whole body rub would help with her jitters. Squirting a generous dollop of the stuff, she slathered it all over, watching her skin turn slick and soft.

She took a little longer than necessary to work it into the soft skin of her breasts, running her thumbs over her sensitive nipples and tweaking them lightly till they tightened into hard little knobs. It felt nice, but didn't come close to the kind of fire Kian's touch had ignited in her dream.

Would reality be as amazing as that fantasy? How would his hands feel? His lips? She closed her eyes, imagining, and as the slow simmer of arousal flared into searing heat, a quiet moan escaped her throat.

What am I doing? Syssi sneaked an embarrassed glance at the mirror as if catching herself red handed. Grimacing, she shook her head; how pathetic was it for someone her age to be so reserved. After all, she was by herself with no one to judge her one way or the other, but she still felt uncomfortable touching herself with the lights on and in the vicinity of a mirror.

With a sigh, she wiped her moist hands on the towel and began blow-drying her hair. Once she was done, she was ready to head out when a faint bang sounded from behind the closed door.

Cautiously, she opened it a crack.

It was dark, and coming from the brightly illuminated bathroom, it took a moment for her pupils to dilate enough to make out the large shape lying on her bed. As her eyes fully adjusted to the dim light, Kian's handsome but brooding features became clear.

He looks like the big bad wolf about to devour Little Red Riding Hood... Me. Syssi chuckled. Apparently, today was a fairy-tale day. First Goldilocks and the Three Bears, then Little Red Riding Hood, what next? Cinderella, or Beauty and the Beast?

Syssi leaned toward the second one. As gorgeous as Kian was, she had a feeling that he was more of a beast than a prince.

"Oh, my! What a big, strong body you have, Grandma!" Purring seductively, she sauntered into the room. But as Kian's expression turned from brooding to menacing, she chickened out, and cursing her inability to put a muzzle on her stupid mischievous streak, she turned to flee into the walk-in closet.

"All the better to pounce on you, my dear!" Kian took to the role play with gusto, and leaping off the bed with the swiftness and grace of a jungle cat caught her from behind before she managed to reach the closet. Holding her back against his chest, he lifted her up.

She jackknifed, kicking her legs and trying to get away while laughing nervously and clawing at the strong fingers clutching hers on the towel.

It was futile.

In one swift move he swung and tossed her on the bed, then pounced, looming above her as he caged her between his thighs and outstretched arms. Still panting from the laughter and exertion of her failed escape attempt, she couldn't fill her lungs.

Or maybe her shortness of breath had nothing to do with exertion and everything to do with Kian. The long strands of his wavy hair falling around his angular features, he was insanely beautiful...

And terrifying.

There was no humor in that hard beauty, only hunger.

Caught in the intense glow of Kian's eyes, she felt trapped like a deer in the headlights of an oncoming car. Fear trickled down her spine in liquid drops of fire that pooled at her core, wetting the insides of her naked thighs.

He caressed her cheek then kissed the hollow of her neck, gently soothing her before bringing his palm to rest over her fisted hand. "Let go of the towel, Syssi," he whispered. Except, coming through his clenched teeth, his words sounded hissed, rough and demanding.

Not ready to let go yet, Syssi shook her head.

He kept at it, stroking her straining knuckles with his thumb, until gently, one at a time, she let him pry her fingers open.

Gazing into his hungry eyes, she was still apprehensive but didn't resist when he entwined their fingers and stretched her arms over her head, holding them there as he brought his face down to shower her with featherlight kisses.

He kissed her eyelids, her eyebrows, her cheeks, her nose, the hollows at the sides of her neck. He kept kissing her like that until she began to relax; her body growing slack. Only then, he released his hold on her hands and leaned back on his haunches to stare hungrily at her body.

Under Kian's searing gaze, laid out like a bounty before him, Syssi stretched out ready to be unveiled. There were no more thoughts, no more hesitation, only a burning desire.

Slowly, carefully, as if unwrapping a precious gift, Kian peeled away one side of the towel and then the other.

"Damn! Just look at you... perfection." He swallowed, gazing at her with an expression full of awe, as if he'd never seen a woman as beautiful as her. No one had ever looked at her like that. She basked, for the first time in her life feeling truly desired. And not by any man, by Kian. The nearest male approximation of a god.

As his eyes lingered on her breasts, watching them heave with her shallow, panting breaths, Syssi felt her nipples stiffen. And when his tongue darted to his lip, her breath caught as she imagined him licking, sucking. Instead, he continued his tour of her body, his eyes traveling down until coming to a halt at her bare mound.

"Beautiful. All of you." He cupped her center.

With a strangled moan, her lids dropped over her eyes.

"Perfect," he whispered, bending to lightly kiss one turgid peak. "Magnificent." He kissed the other, then waited until she opened her eyes and looked at him.

"I want you so badly, I'm going to go up in flames if you won't have me," he breathed. Running his hands along her outstretched arms, he reached her hands and entangled their fingers. His face a scant inch from hers, he searched her wide open eyes.

Gazing up at his beautiful face, she saw her own raging need reflected in his eyes. "I want you, Kian, so much that it hurts," she whispered.

It was a terrifying thing to admit, and the only reason she'd mustered enough courage to speak the truth, was the way he was looking at her. There was no way he was faking it. Kian's soul was shining through his eyes, and he was baring himself to her just as much as she was baring herself to him.

He closed his eyes in relief, but only for a brief moment. Then with a measuring look, he asked again. "Are you sure?"

She must've seemed shell-shocked to him, lying underneath his big body with her eyes opened wide, panting.

And in truth, she was.

Still, she needed this like she needed to take her next breath.

"I need you," she whispered.

The change in his expression was lightning fast. Sure of his welcome, Kian's last vestiges of restraint shattered, and he descended upon her like a hungry beast; smashing her lips with his mouth, thrusting his tongue in and out, and growling as he nipped at her lips.

Swept in the torrent of his ferocity, Syssi arched her back, aching to feel the length of his body pressed against hers—to feel his weight on top of her.

Except, he remained propped on his shins, his bowed arms supporting the weight of his chest, their bodies barely touching.

But with her mouth under attack and her arms pinned, there was little she could do about it besides moan and whimper.

Kian's mouth trailed south, kissing and nipping every spot along her jawline and down her neck to her collarbone, then licking and kissing the small hurts away.

Syssi panted in breathless anticipation, her painfully stiff nipples desperate for his hands, his lips...

"Please...," she whispered, her need stronger than her pride.

He lifted his head, the hunger in his eyes belying his teasing mouth. "Tell me what you need, beautiful." He let go of one of her hands to caress her cheek, extending his thumb to rub over her swollen lips before pressing it into her mouth.

She sucked it in, swirling her tongue around it until he pulled it out to rub the moisture over her dry lips.

With the hand he had freed, she cupped Kian's lightly stubbled cheek, letting the last of her shields drop and allowing him to see in her unguarded expression all of the desire and adoration she felt for him.

He leaned into her tender touch. "My sweet, precious girl," he whispered, covering her hand with his own.

Holding her palm to his lips, he kissed its center before returning it to where it was before. "I like the way you look with your arms outstretched, surrendering to me, trusting me with your pleasure."

Hooded with desire, his eyes were pleading with her to give him that, promising only pleasure if she did.

Syssi felt powerless to deny him anything. Without a word she complied, stretching her arms and grabbing onto the headboard's metal frame.

How did he do that, she wondered, setting her body on fire— knowing what she needed better than she did herself.

To hell with precaution and consequences, she was done being careful. No more almosts, no more only ifs, no more maybe-next-times, this was it.

With Kian, she had finally glimpsed the path to the elusive bliss. And the only way she could traverse that road was with him in the driver seat. She needed to cede control to him. And to do that, she needed to trust him… which was scary.

It wasn't that she feared he'd hurt her physically, she knew he wouldn't. But to trust that he would not exploit the tremendous emotional vulnerability she was about to expose; that took real courage.

Or stupidity.

Still, she knew it was her one and only chance to take the plunge because there was no doubt in her mind that she would never even consider this with anyone but Kian.

Releasing a shuddering breath, she gazed into his eyes, and the way he looked at her, waiting breathlessly for her acquiescence, provided the final push.

She took the plunge.

"I don't know why I feel this way with you, trusting you to take control of my pleasure, but I do. I crave it," Syssi whispered, a rush of pure lust sweeping through her with the admission.

CHAPTER 5: KIAN

Kian groaned. "Do you have any idea how perfect you are? How much your trust means to me?" He dipped his head, pouring his gratitude and appreciation into a tender kiss.

Well aware that lovely, sweet Syssi was nothing like what he was accustomed to, and the set of rules she played by was different than his, he had to make sure she understood the rules of this new game he was introducing her to. But now that she had given him the green light, he was in serious trouble because there was nothing holding him back, and his damned instincts were screaming for him to rip off his pants, plunge all the way into her, and sink his fangs into her neck while he was at it.

Not going to happen. Kian took a deep breath and closed his eyes, forcing the beast to back the hell off.

First, he would make sure to take care of her pleasure.

Kissing and licking the column of her throat, he needed at least a moment between her thighs, even if only to feel her through the fabric of his pants. Pushing her knees apart, he aligned his erection with her sex, careful not to scrape her with his zipper as he rubbed against her.

Damn, it feels good.

With a groan, he slid farther down her body until his face was level with her stiff peaks. For a moment, he just looked at their sculpted perfection, watching them heave with each of her breaths. Until he heard her whimper.

Only then, he took one tip between his lips. He pulled on it gently, twirling his tongue round and round, while lightly pinching its twin between his thumb and forefinger and tugging on it in sync with his suckling.

As he kept alternating between the sensitive nubs, suckling them harder and grazing them lightly with his teeth, Syssi's moans and whimpers were getting louder and more desperate.

She was loving it. Her hips circling under the weight of him, she held on to the headboard with a white-knuckled grip.

Kian eased up, giving her a small reprieve. "Ask me to make you come, baby," he breathed around her wet nipple, lifting his eyes to her sweat-misted face.

"Please...," she whimpered.

"That's not good enough. You can do better than that."

Syssi arched her back, and as she turned her desperate eyes up to her tight grip on the headboard, he felt an outpour of wetness slide down her thigh.

"Oh, God! Yes! Please... Please make me come... Kian."

As his blunt front teeth carefully closed around one nipple, and his fingers around the other, Syssi erupted. And as he kept increasing the pressure, turning the slight ache into what must've been an almost unbearable hurt, her climax continued rippling through her—her beautiful body quaking with the aftershocks as she wailed until her voice turned hoarse.

That was it for him.

Unable to hold it off anymore, he came hard, erupting spasmodically inside his pants. Except, it did nothing to soften his erection, he was still as hard as before.

Releasing some of the pressure took the edge off, though. Now, with the wild beast raging inside him contained for a little longer, he could watch Syssi climax again and again.

He would never tire of seeing her like that. Her dazed, blissed out expression suffusing him with tenderness.

My beautiful, passionate girl.

Cupping her breasts with his palms, he soothed her tender nubs, waiting for them to soften under the warmth of his touch.

As her ragged breathing slowed down, Syssi mouthed, "Wow!" her cheeks flaming.

Kian smiled, peering at her from between the hands he had cupped over her ample breasts.

Releasing her hold on the metal frame, she took his cheeks between her palms and pulled him up for a kiss.

"Did I give you permission to bring your arms down, sweet girl?" he said before sealing his lips over hers. He then traced the line of her jaw with kisses and nibbles, all the way up to her earlobe, catching the soft tissue between his teeth.

Syssi squirmed. "No," she said in a small voice, caressing his stubble with her thumbs. "My hands have a mind of their own. I just had to touch you." She pouted, pretending contrition.

"Be a good girl and put your hands back up, or I'll have to flip you over and spank that sweet little bottom of yours." He tweaked her nipple and smirked, watching her eyelids flutter as a shiver of desire swept through her.

"Is that a promise?" Syssi taunted, whispering breathlessly as she lifted and tightened the aforementioned body part and pressed her pelvis up to his belly. Still, she hastened to obey his command, and stretching her arms, returned her hands to the headboard.

The hint of trepidation in her eyes hadn't been lost on him. Syssi wasn't sure if he was just teasing or intended to make good on that threat.

"Could you be any more perfect for me?" Kian said, shaking his head. "My little minx has some naughty fantasies I would be more than happy to fulfill. I promise. If you ask really nicely... or behave really badly, you can bet your sweet bottom on it." He winked, and with a surge, dived down and pressed an open-mouthed kiss to her wet folds.

Syssi squeaked, lifting and pulling away from him, but Kian gripped her hips and pulled her back down. Sliding both hands under her bottom, he lifted her pelvis up to his mouth and licked her wet slit from top to bottom and then back up, growling like a beast.

At first, she stiffened. But Kian kept at it even though he knew she felt scandalized. This was such an intimate act, demanding a level of trust and familiarity that must've been difficult for her. After all, he had her spread out naked, her sex soaking wet from her earlier climax, licking and feasting on it while he was still fully dressed.

He was pushing her, testing her limits, thrilled that despite her initial reluctance she was letting him have his way.

He loved that ceding control to him turned her on. The more he demanded, the more he pushed, the more she responded with wild abandon, rewarding him with her moans and whimpers and more of her sweet nectar pouring onto his greedy tongue.

He could go on like that for hours, savoring and exulting in the pleasure he was wringing out of her.

It wasn't about him being a selfless giving lover, not entirely. Having his pants on and not allowing her to touch him was the only way he could stay in control. His hunger for sex, for her, was so intense, he was afraid of what he'd do to her otherwise.

The beast in him wanted to impale her sex with his cock and sink his fangs into her neck in one brutal move. And then go on screwing her for hours, biting her and coming inside her over and over again. Rutting on her like the animal it was.

Traumatizing her.

It was true that she would have climaxed every time he would have sunk his fangs into her neck... or her breast... or the juncture of her thigh. The aphrodisiac in his venom would've made sure of that. And yes, her pain and bruising would've faded from its healing properties. And after he was done, he could easily thrall the nasty memory away.

Except, he was neither a sadist nor a mindless beast... well... not entirely, and not as long as he remained in control.

He cared too much for this girl to let go—even a little.

Before he slaked his need, he would make sure she was properly pleasured, sated, and soaking wet from multiple orgasms. And even then, he couldn't let loose the monster lurking inside him.

CHAPTER 6: SYSSI

The man is wicked.

Drawing lazy circles around her nether lips and scooping her juices with his tongue, Kian groaned with the pleasure of literally eating her up.

He'd been doing it for so long, keeping her at a slow simmer, skirting the spot where she needed him most, that she had to bite on her bottom lip to stifle the sounds she was making. Her needy groans sounded like angry growls.

"Please, I can't take it anymore!" she finally hissed.

Kian lifted his head. "Tell me what you need, baby." He smirked, licking her juices from his glistening lips.

Hanging on the precipice, she was beyond shame or reserve. "You... I need you inside me! Please..." She groaned—panting from parted lips as he pulled his hands from under her butt and lowered her back to the mattress. Eyes trained on her face, he tightened his grip on her hip, anchoring her down, and slid one long finger inside her slick core.

Her channel tightened, clutching and spasming around the thrusting and retreating digit. It felt so good. Syssi moaned, closing her eyes and letting her head drop back.

"Look at me!" Kian growled.

With an effort, she lifted her head and looked at him with hooded eyes, her lower lip pulsing, swollen from where she had bitten on it before.

Holding her gaze, he pulled out his finger and pushed back with two. She inhaled sharply at the amplified pleasure. A slight burn started, reminding her how long it had been for her, and for a moment she got scared. But then as he lowered his chin and slowly, deliberately, flicked his tongue at her most erogenous spot, a flood of moisture coated his fingers, turning the intrusion from slightly painful to blissfully pleasurable.

His fingers pumping in and out of her, in that slow, maddening way, Syssi was hanging by a thread—straining on the edge of the orgasm bearing down on her. She needed him to move just a little faster, or pinch her nipple with the powerful fingers of his other hand, and she would've gone flying.

But Kian had other ideas. Joining a third finger, he stretched her even wider. Again, there was a slight burn, but she couldn't care less.

Let it hurt, just let me dive over that edge.

She kept her eyes on his face, watching him as a wicked gleam sparkled in his eyes, just a split moment before he closed his lips around the tiny bundle of nerves at the apex of her sex and sucked it in.

"Kiannnnn!" Syssi erupted, mewling and thrashing as the climax came at her violently, jerking her body off the bed. Kian didn't let go, pumping his fingers and suckling on her, he prolonged it, squeezing every last drop of pleasure out of her.

A moment later, or perhaps it had been longer than that, she came down from floating in that semiconscious, postorgasmic space and opened her eyes. A gasp escaped her throat. Kian was suspended above her— gloriously naked. Giving her no time to ponder the how and when he had shucked off his clothes, or to admire his beautifully muscled body, he speared into her with a grunt.

Syssi cried out.

It hurt. Boy did it hurt, and not in a good way. Not an erotic pain. Just pain, hot and searing.

As her channel stretched and burned, struggling to accommodate Kian's girth, Syssi wanted to push him off; memories of her first time intruding on and marring what was supposed to be something wonderful— casting an unpleasant shadow over the bliss that he had brought her before.

Tears streaking from the corners of her eyes, she panted, waiting for the pain to subside.

"I'm sorry," Kian whispered, kissing her teary eyes, as he tried to pull out.

"No, just give me a moment." She clutched him to her. This wasn't going to end like that, no way.

He didn't move, not even a twitch. With muscles strained and eyes blazing in his hard face, he looked at her, holding his breath as he waited for her body to adjust to his invasion. Only when the pain started to ebb and she began to moan and undulate—her lust and her pleasure overriding her pain—did he began thrusting, carefully, gently, until she gasped again.

This time, in pleasure.

For what seemed like a long time, he moved inside her with infinite care, his thrusts slow and shallow, and eventually even the memory of pain was gone, there was only pleasure.

Syssi brought her palms to Kian's cheeks and pulled him down, kissing him softly. She was falling in love with this man, and there was little she could do about it. Right now she was overwhelmed with feelings of gratitude, for his patience, for his care. Kian was putting her pleasure first.

"I'm okay now. You can let go," she whispered against his lips.

His thrusts got a little deeper, but he kept going slow for a few moments, gauging her response. When she closed her eyes and moaned deep in her throat, he increased the tempo and force, gradually going deeper and faster until the powerful pounding rattled the bed, banging it against the wall and driving them both toward the headboard.

Kian braced himself by grabbing the metal frame above where she was holding on, his biceps bulging with the strain and sweat dripping down the center of his muscular chest.

As Syssi climbed toward another climax, Kian's grunts and her moans were accompanied by the sounds of the bed's feet sliding and screeching on the hardwood floor, and the headboard banging against the wall. A carnal soundtrack to the drama of their fierce coupling.

Forcing her eyes to remain open, Syssi stared at Kian's handsome face, awed. Straining, he was covered in sweat, his lips pressed into a thin line. And his eyes, those hypnotic blue eyes of his, were glowing with an eerie luminance.

I'm delirious, she thought, marveling at the sight.

Shifting those amazing eyes down to her neck, he dipped his head to suck and lick at her fast pulsing vein; strands of his soft hair caressing her cheek as he kept his relentless pounding.

On an impulse, Syssi turned her head sideways, startled to find herself silently pleading with him; *Bite me! Please…*

Oh, God!

The sharp pain of his fangs sinking into her flesh shocked her; the needlelike incisors clearly not human.

Fangs… He had fangs in my dream… was her last coherent thought as his seed jetted into her, and she fell apart, her climax erupting in waves of volcanic intensity.

The euphoria that followed left her boneless and exhausted. Unable to open her eyes, blissful and content, she sighed, surrendering to oblivion.

CHAPTER 7: KIAN

Kian retracted his fangs and closed the small incision points with a couple of licks.

Stroking Syssi's damp hair away from her temples, he looked at her peaceful, sleeping face, then pressed a gentle kiss to her parted lips.

He had exhausted the poor girl.

When he had entered her, he had not expected her to be so tight, and the look of pain on her face had startled him. After climaxing twice, she had been so wet, it should've been a smooth glide.

If he hadn't known better, he would have thought her a virgin.

He'd wanted to withdraw immediately, but Syssi had stopped him. Apparently, she was made from tougher stuff than he'd suspected. Still, he'd held himself in check. With his superior physiology providing stamina to match, he could've kept going. Except the same couldn't have been said about her. What was slow and gentle for him, had been a rough ride for Syssi.

She looked drained.

Pulling out, careful not to wake her, Kian remained suspended over her for a moment, and as he looked at her beautiful face, he was gripped by an intense craving to cleave unto her and make her his.

Heavens! How he wanted to come clean and tell Syssi everything: about himself, who he was, what he was... needing her to accept it all, accept him...

To love him.

His chest tight, he reluctantly prepared to perpetuate the deception, and with a heavy sigh, reached into her mind, carefully extracting the memory of his bite.

It had to be done.

Out of respect for Syssi, he resisted the temptation to take a peek and see himself through her eyes. It was selfish, but he hoped she was falling in love with him, even if just a little, because he couldn't help falling for her.

It was futile, and tomorrow he was going to exorcise these dangerous feelings by any means available to him, but tonight he would allow himself to feel. Just this once.

With one more kiss to her sweet lips, he got up and walked over to the bathroom, bringing back a warm washcloth for his girl.

Syssi didn't stir. Not as he gently wiped away their combined issue, nor when he climbed into bed, not even when he turned her sideways so he could spoon behind her.

Reaching for the crumpled comforter at the foot of the bed, he pulled it up to cover them both.

"Sleep tight, precious," he whispered.

Too early for him to fall asleep, Kian closed his eyes and focused on the sensation of Syssi's soft curves curled against his body. Ever since Lavena, he hadn't spent a night with a woman. Frankly, he hadn't been so inclined. But he would have loved to have Syssi pressed against him every night. There was a sense of peace, of rightness in having her there that he hadn't expected.

He wondered if Syssi had known it would be like this between them. She was a seer, so it was possible she'd gotten a glimpse of them together.

When his phone went off on the nightstand, Kian grabbed it quickly before the ringing woke her up.

"Yeah," he whispered.

Syssi didn't stir. Yep, exhausted.

"Why are you whispering?" Yamanu asked.

"Never mind that. Do you have news about the boy?"

He'd assigned Yamanu the job of retrieving Michael, the other talent on Amanda's list who was a potential target for the Doomers. But instead of picking him up right away, he had Yamanu and his team follow the kid around to see if Doomers showed up. There had been a couple of problems with that. Michael and his football team had traveled out of town for a game, while his phone remained behind.

"He is back and he has his phone. Someone found it and brought it to lost-and-found, but the battery was dead."

"Is he in the dorms?"

"Was, until about an hour ago. He went with a couple of buddies to a club."

"Wait until he gets back and you can pick him up the moment he's alone. We've wasted enough of your time already."

"Yeah, I figured you'd say that. But if the Doomers don't make a move, now that he has his phone back, he might be safe. One more day and we'll know for sure."

Kian chuckled. Yamanu was disappointed that no Doomers had shown up and there was no fight. Ever since Brundar and Anandur's report about the skirmish at the lab, he'd been eager to test his skills against some Doomers. The Guardian hoped he would still get his chance. "I'm giving you until tomorrow morning."

"Thanks, boss."

CHAPTER 8: MICHAEL

"I'm never going to get wasted like this again," Michael groaned.

Getting buzzed had been fun, but the aftermath was a bitch. He shouldn't have fueled up on all that crappy vodka before going to the club. But given the outrageous prices the place charged for drinks, Eddie's idea to buy the stuff cheap at the supermarket had been genius.

And besides, not being twenty-one yet, and getting in with a friend's ID, buying drinks at the club would have been pushing his luck unnecessarily, stupid. The guy at the door never paid close attention to the pictures, but the bartender had been known to occasionally double-check if something looked fishy to him.

Then again, it wasn't like his unfortunate shortage of cash had nothing to do with it...

Given his pitiful allowance, and not being that big on drinking to begin with, most nights Michael had been the one to volunteer as their triad's designated driver. But tonight they had flipped for it, and Zack had gotten to do the honors.

He had to admit, though, that there was something to be said for hitting the snooze button on his inhibitions—easier to flirt. Not that he suffered from a lack of confidence, but still, sometimes a dude needed something extra to go after the hottest girls everyone was hitting on.

"So, Michael, did you get Gina's number, or is she still moping after that douchebag boyfriend of hers?" His friend Eddie was too loud, too close, his voice pounding in Michael's ears.

"Shh... Eddie, you are drilling holes in my head. Don't you have any other volume besides loud and extra loud?" Michael rubbed his temples and increased the length of his strides, trying to put some distance between himself and his friend's booming voice.

The night was chilly, the light breeze carrying a faint smell of freshly cut grass, and if Eddie would've ever shut up, the ten-minute walk from the parking lot to their dorms might've helped with the headache.

"I'm not loud. You're drunk, bro... And back to the subject of Gina-the-football-player-slayer. If she's not interested in you, I might want to give her a try... If it's okay with you, that is... I don't want to infringe on your turf or anything."

"She is all yours. Just shut up already. You are loud." Michael walked even faster, the brisk pace helping sober him up.

Gina was hot, but she was dumb as a brick. And although she had given him her number, Michael wasn't sure he was going to call.

"Nice…" He heard Eddie from some distance behind him, and then Zack's snort from even farther away.

Michael was about to come up with some clever shit to say when he got a weird feeling that they were being watched. He'd been getting these strange vibes ever since they had returned from the game, but until now he hadn't sensed any malice radiating from whomever was watching him. Hey, it might have been Gina, or some other girl with a crush on him.

Right.

The thing was, this felt very different from before. Looking around the deserted campus, he slowed down then stopped as the sensation got stronger. The small hairs on the back of his neck prickled.

Crouching low with his elbows tucked at his sides—fists up— Michael scanned for the source of his alarm.

With his sudden halt, Eddie and Zack stopped themselves from knocking him over by throwing out their hands and bracing against his back. Being built like a truck, the force of the impact didn't budge him an inch.

"What the hell, man? What's wrong with you?" Zack growled.

"Shh… Shut up for a moment…" Michael raised his palm to signal for them to keep quiet. The feeling of being watched was just amplified by a hefty dose of a menacing threat when his receptive mind tuned into someone's nefarious, dark intentions.

The adrenaline rush sobering him instantly, he listened for the source.

As his friends finally caught on to his defensive stance and positioned themselves back-to-back with his, forming a triad, Michael wondered who might be dumb enough to jump three football players weighing in aggregate over seven hundred pounds.

Regrettably, he was pretty sure it wasn't the cheerleading team. He wouldn't have minded being ambushed by them.

The list of possible suspects included junkies, armed robbers, or members of a defeated team. Though, this time they had been the ones who'd lost, so it ruled out that.

Except, nothing stirred in the eerily quiet night.

Disturbed only by the remote hum of cars passing by, Michael had the impression that it was the quiet before the storm. He could feel the imminent attack down to his bones.

His nemesis, whoever he or they were, was about to attack.

"Get ready, boys. Shit is coming down," he whispered.

As the last word left his mouth, two groups of some of the biggest, scariest mother~~fuckers~~ he had ever seen, came running at them from opposite directions.

"We're history," Eddie whispered as they braced for impact.

Except, it never came.

The two groups collided... attacking each other.

Surprised and relieved, Michael watched as these titans fought hand to hand, performing the best martial arts moves he had ever seen, in fiction or elsewhere, their bodies so fast they blurred.

"~~Fucking~~ hell, what is that?" Zack's eyes darted left to right trying to follow the moves.

"We should scram..." For once, Eddie was the voice of reason. "Whoever wins will come after us next."

Except none of them moved, mesmerized by the spectacular show of combat skills.

Michael had the passing thought that they had somehow stumbled upon a movie shoot. No way anyone fought like that for real. Unfortunately, it wasn't only that the battle looked and sounded authentic, but the emotions he was picking up were of such deep mutual hatred, not even method actors could fake them so well.

"A gang war?" Zack suggested.

"On campus? Not likely," Michael whispered even though there was no need. The combatants were too busy fighting to pay them any attention.

Eddie nodded like he knew the answer. "Aliens. These ~~fuckers~~ guys are not human. No one can move so fast."

Yeah, right. Eddie had watched too many sci-fi movies. The thing was, Michael had no better explanation. Their speed was inhuman.

Even though he found it hard to follow the moves, the sounds told the story just as well. The fleshy thuds of fists and boots finding their targets, the metallic clank of knives clashing, and the grunts of pain and exertion of the combatants completed the picture.

CHAPTER 9 YAMANU

Following Michael and his friends from the club, Yamanu had gotten pulled over. Damn kids had been speeding while inebriated, and the idiot cop had let them go. It had taken Yamanu exactly two seconds to thrall the guy, but he'd lost at least three minutes while waiting for the cop to amble up to his window.

"Don't worry," Bhathian said. "Nothing can happen to him in two minutes."

Yamanu shook his head. When he caught up to the boys, he was going to box Michael's ears even though he wasn't the driver. The guy behind the wheel was probably just as drunk, and Michael shouldn't have gotten in the car with him. That's what Uber was for.

With his damn luck throwing obstacles at him at every turn, when he skidded into the dorm's ██████ parking lot, it was full. There was no time to drive around the damn place in circles, looking for a vacant spot. Instead, Yamanu jumped the curb and parked on the lawn, squeezing the car between two trees.

"Let's go." He threw his door open.

"What if we get towed?" Arwel slammed his door shut.

"I'll call a taxi to—" Yamanu tensed and lifted his palm, while beside him Arwel unsheathed his dagger. He had no problem picking up on the Doomers' presence, even though he wasn't as strong an empath as Arwel. Differentiating their pattern of aggression from the normal currents produced by the many students occupying the dorms around them, combined with the sudden wave of fear coming at him from the boys, he could trace the signals like a beacon pinpointing their location.

"Follow me!" Yamanu sprinted toward that beacon.

With Arwel and Bhathian running close behind him, they reached Michael and his friends at the same time the Doomers did.

Three Doomers against three boys and three Guardians.

The boys, though quite brawny for young humans, posed no challenge for the Doomers. But at the same time, the Doomers didn't pose a real challenge for the Guardians either.

Good odds.

He had to hand it to the young men though, they did good, proving that they had brains on top of brawn by forming a triad to protect each other's backs. Obviously, they didn't stand a chance against the Doomers' strength, training and weapons. But at least, they wouldn't have gone down without a fight.

As it turned out, though, Yamanu had underestimated the Doomers, and he realized his mistake as soon as he and his fellow Guardians engaged the fighters. Brundar had been right; this new breed of Doomers was nothing like those he had encountered in the past. Not only were they better trained and stronger, but the bastards fought with what seemed like suicidal desperation.

Still, the Guardians were better. It had taken a little longer than it should've, but eventually the Doomers started losing their momentum and making mistakes.

At that point, Yamanu detangled himself from the melee, confident in his companions' ability to finish the job without him.

Three sets of eyes moved away from the skirmish to focus on him and got even wider.

Yamanu chuckled. Any moment now their eyeballs would fall out.

As he approached them, Michael and his friends tensed, lifting their fists and readying for a fight.

"Calm down, boys. I'm not here to harm you, I'm here to protect you against these brutes." Mild term for what he thought about the Doomers, but the boys didn't know what kind of evil he and his friends had just saved them from, and it was better it stayed that way.

"Come with me," he commanded, motioning for them to follow as he threw an illusion over the scene, making it disappear from sight.

The boys didn't budge, staring frozen and slack-jawed at the spot where only a moment ago they had witnessed a fierce fight.

Damn, would he have to carry them to safety?

"Come on, girls, move it!"

That got their attention, but it seemed their feet were refusing to obey. Yamanu shrugged. He'd hoped to avoid unnecessary thralls, but it seemed there was no other way.

CHAPTER 10: MICHAEL

Michael watched the surreal scene unfolding right before his eyes, unable to reconcile what he saw with reality. And if things hadn't been weird enough before, featuring the clash of the titans Jackie Chan style, now the bizarre scene disappeared as if it never existed, leaving behind a dude that looked like something from a shroom hallucination.

Standing, at least, six and a half feet tall, the man's long black hair reached down to his waist, and his pale blue eyes looked eerie on his dark, angular face.

"Come on, girls, move it!" the dude said, shoving at Michael and his friends and forcing them to start moving.

Herded like sheep, with the tall dude pushing and prodding them to keep going, they made their way through a narrow alley between two buildings. When they came out on the other side, the guy found a bench and pointed to it.

"Sit!" he commanded.

Michael found himself obeying even though he tried to resist.

What the hell? Suddenly Eddie's aliens theory seemed like the best explanation of what was going on. They were being abducted by aliens who were going to do all kinds of weird shit to them, and he was helpless to do anything about it. The one in front of them was definitely using mind control.

"Look at me!" he commanded in a singsong cadence, compelling them to obey.

Michael closed his eyes, refusing to look into the guy's hypnotic ones. He was going to fight with everything he had. No alien motherfucker was going to mess with him.

He expected the guy to command him to open his eyes, or reach into his mind and compel him to do it, but it seemed that he was more interested in Eddie and Zack.

"What you've just witnessed was nothing. A bunch of drunk students got into a brawl. By tomorrow, you'll forget it ever happened. I want you boys to get up, go on to your rooms and go to sleep. Michael, you stay. I'm taking you to see your auntie. It's a family emergency."

How did the guy know his name? Did aliens perform background checks on their victims? But wait, he'd just sent Zack and Eddie to their rooms. Was Michael the only one the aliens were interested in? Why?

His friends rose to their feet and walked away without giving Michael a second glance; following the dude's command like a couple of zombies.

Carefully, afraid of what kind of alien shit he was going to find, Michael let his senses probe, checking on the guy's intentions. Amusement; the guy thought this was funny.

This alien was scaring the crap out of him, and he thought it was amusing?

Anger fueling his nerves, Michael asked, "How do you know my name? And what auntie? And what family emergency?"

"Good evening, Michael, I'm Yamanu." The stranger smiled and offered Michael his hand, his perfectly straight teeth flashing white in his dark face.

"Hi, normally I would have said nice to meet you back, but I'm not sure it is." Michael shook the frying-pan-sized hand. "And you know my name, how?" Again, Michael reached to feel the guy's emotions. Surprisingly, what he found was respect. What he didn't find, though, were malevolent intentions, or anything that would indicate the guy was an alien.

Yamanu smirked. "You have some balls on you, son; most guys would be a tad more polite in your situation."

"And what situation is that exactly? If you'd be so kind as to enlighten me?" Now that he knew the guy meant him no harm, Michael gathered the courage to stare into the guy's unnerving eyes, forcing himself not to flinch.

Yamanu threw his head back and let out a guffaw, the laugh reverberating through his massive body as he plopped down on the bench next to Michael.

Shaking his head, he wrapped his arm around Michael's shoulders. "I like you, son. Really big balls—coconut size." He gestured with his other hand as if weighing the big fruit. "Not many have the guts to stare down these peepers of mine." He pinned Michael with a stare. "So, I'll tell you what, let's say there are some weirdos out to get you." Yamanu chuckled at Michael's arched brow. "It has to do with the strange things you can do up here." He tapped Michael's forehead. "You ask me how I know," he continued, nodding at Michael's surprised expression. "Dr. Amanda Dokani is a good friend of mine, and she asked my friends and me to protect you. So here we are."

As if on cue, the other two showed up, looking like roadkill; bloodied, their clothes torn and dirty.

"Had a nice time chatting, girls? While we were doing all the dirty work, and the cleanup?" The shorter one of the two sounded only partially amused as he dropped tiredly onto the bench, resting his arms on its back and stretching out his legs.

The other one hesitated for about two seconds before shrugging and doing the same on the other side of the bench.

"Michael, this is Arwel, and that is Bhathian." Yamanu introduced his friends.

They each gave a nod when Yamanu said their name, looking too wiped out to respond. For a moment, the four of them just sat there saying nothing.

"What did you do with the Doomers?" Yamanu broke the silence.

"Sleeping peacefully, loaded and ready to go," Arwel said.

"We'd better get a move on, then." Yamanu rose, giving a hand to Arwel, who stood up groaning.

The guy held his side, leaning into his bracing hand. "I think I have a broken rib."

"You should go see Bridget when we get home, make sure that rib heals right," Bhathian advised while limping along. "I think I'll come with you. Something is wrong with my foot."

Michael walked beside Yamanu; shell-shocked.

Who or what the hell are Doomers? And what did Arwel mean when he said they were sleeping peacefully, loaded and ready to go... Was he talking about the guys they fought off? Was sleeping a euphemism for dead?

Glancing at his companions, Michael let his senses probe freely, but all he felt coming from them was their confidence in their strength and their ability to protect.

They meant him no harm, and they were friends of Dr. Dokani, not aliens. Now that he wasn't as scared, the whole notion seemed ridiculous. Aliens, really. Still, who were the weirdos that were after him, and why the hell did Dr. Dokani have friends who looked and fought like elite commandos?

He was intrigued by the powerful men. Who were these guys? How did they know Dr. Dokani? Were they some secret government agents? Special Ops? With his imagination churning up one fascinating scenario after another, by the time they reached the car, his head was pounding worse than before.

Sitting in the back with Arwel, Michael suddenly felt exhausted. And when Yamanu twisted back and looked at him, he felt compelled to let his eyelids slide shut.

Fighting the urge, he forced his eyes to remain open, hoping to see where they were taking him. But a few minutes into the ride, he lost that battle and passed out.

CHAPTER 11: SYSSI

The bedroom was still dark when Syssi opened her eyes, with only a smidgen of light coming through the bathroom's cracked door.

Still, it sufficed.

Looking down at the muscular arm draped around her middle, she drew in a deep breath, making an effort to exhale it as quietly as possible so as not to wake Kian. Not yet.

She needed a few moments to think and process what had just happened.

Oh, God. It had been real this time. And the proof was curled behind her back, his big body warm, and his chest rising and falling with each of his slow, rhythmic breaths.

He wasn't a figment of her imagination. She hadn't dreamt this.

Not that she could've imagined any of it if she tried. Syssi couldn't remember ever passing out after sex. But then again, she never had mind-blowing orgasms that left her boneless, breathless, and floating, either.

If she had known sex could be like that, she wouldn't have stayed celibate for two years. She seriously doubted, though, it could've been so good with anyone but Kian. He had been well worth the wait.

As memories of the experience replayed in her mind, she touched her hand to her neck, for some reason expecting it to feel bruised. But there was nothing there. No tenderness, no teeth marks, and her skin felt as smooth and as flawless as ever.

She must've dreamt the whole bite thing. What was she thinking, it's not as if something like that ever happened outside of fiction. That vampire romance novel had apparently left an impression.

But if that hadn't happened, what else hadn't been real?

Except, she remembered the rest vividly. Every delicious little thing—even that first painful thrust. It hadn't been pleasant, but what had followed had. At the memory, her channel tightened with desire—the feel of him inside of her, moving slowly, rhythmically, smooth velvet over a hard core...

Bareback! No condom!

Oh. My. God!

She had had unprotected sex with a man she had just met—

practically a stranger.

Pregnancy wasn't an issue, as she still had her IUD. But that wasn't the only thing to worry about, was it?

Well, there was nothing she could do about it now.

The good news was that she felt no foreboding, and with her special gift, she would've known if there was a reason for worry; her cursed foresight never failed to predict impending disasters.

Still, not using protection had been incredibly stupid.

In her defense, it had been so long since she'd been with a guy, and even then it hadn't been an issue since Greg had been her first, and they had stayed together for four years.

Except, she should have known better. He should've known better. Kian hadn't been living like a monk before taking her to his bed.

I'm an irresponsible floozy, she thought without any real conviction behind the self-reproach. But even though Kian was guilty of the same, it bothered her that he might think so. After all, she hadn't offered even a token resistance. And to think she had given him that speech about being presumptuous.

What a joke.

Still, as much as she tried, she couldn't feel guilty or even remorseful about the best sex of her life.

Stifling a chuckle, Syssi remembered her grandmother's old-fashioned advice, cautioning her to develop a friendship with a man before jumping into bed with him, or else he'd lose interest once he had his way.

Syssi didn't care.

Even if it had been a one-time deal, and she never got to see Kian again, she would've had her way with him anyway. The only problem was; no other man would ever compare. Syssi had a feeling that Kian had ruined it for her with anyone else.

With a heavy sigh, she turned in his arms to look at his sleeping face.

Beautiful.

She couldn't think of a better word to describe him. Handsome just didn't do him justice. It was more than that, though, a lot more. There was so much strength and honor in him. Kian was a leader in the best sense of the word. He led because he considered it as his duty, not because he was power hungry or greedy. The poor guy didn't have a life outside of work. And yet, he didn't complain. Giving it all he had, he was sacrificing himself, his health and his emotional well-being, for his family. What bothered her, though, was that it seemed they were taking it for granted. Even Amanda.

Kian needed more balance in his life. If he let her in, she would make sure of it.

Leaning into him, Syssi burrowed her nose under the long strands of his hair and sniffed at the crook of his neck.

His scent was intoxicating.

Warmed by the vapor coming off his skin, she lingered there for a moment, lulled by his scent and the rhythm of his steady pulse. But then as her fingers began tracing the ridges and valleys of his well-defined chest, she shifted to follow them with her eyes.

"Hi, gorgeous," Kian murmured as his hand began a leisurely descent of her back. Palming both of her butt cheeks with one large hand, he pulled her closer, pressing her against his erection.

Lifting her head, she looked at his sleepy face. "Back at you, handsome. I thought you were sleeping."

"Must've dozed off. I still have work to do tonight."

Poor guy. Working on a Sunday night was true slavery. "You know, even slaves got a day off."

"I'm a captive, which is worse."

She quirked a brow. "Whose?" It was impossible to envision anyone bossing Kian around.

"My own flawed character. I'm an obsessive compulsive workaholic." He smiled and bent his neck to cover her mouth in a tender kiss. "But not now. My time with you is the best I've had in ages. I'm not in a hurry to give it up and go back to the drudgery."

Palming the back of her head, he brought her closer so her cheek rested against his pectoral, then resumed his leisurely strokes.

With a content sigh, Syssi closed her eyes, wishing she could stay like that forever. Because nothing had ever felt that good before.

Not that the sex hadn't been out of this world, but this peaceful closeness was priceless.

Unfortunately, forever turned out to be less than a minute long, as a quiet knock on the door was immediately followed by the butler's hesitant inquiry; "Master? Are you there, master?"

Jerking out of Kian's arms, Syssi pulled the comforter over her naked breasts, afraid that the butler would open the door and poke his head in, looking for his master.

"Shh... It's okay. Come back here." Kian pulled her back down into his embrace. "It's only Okidu. Don't worry—he knows better than to come in."

"Yes, Okidu, what is it?" Kian asked.

"So sorry to disturb you, master. But Yamanu wished for me to inform you that the guest you were expecting has indeed arrived, and he— that is—Yamanu, is inquiring as to what to do with the young man."

"What is he doing now?" Kian asked.

"He is sleeping down in the guest suite, master."

"Let him sleep. Tell Yamanu I'll deal with the boy later." Kian dismissed him.

"As you wish, master." Okidu acknowledged so politely, Syssi imagined him bowing to the closed door. And maybe he had because it took a few seconds before she heard his light footsteps going back down the hallway.

With a relived sigh, she snaked her hand under the comforter, seizing him and stroking him lazily. She asked, "Who is the guest you were expecting?"

Kian's hand closed on her butt, and he gave it a light squeeze, then trailed his fingers down the valley between the cheeks reaching her wet folds from behind. With a feather-light touch, he circled her opening in sync with her up and down strokes, getting her wetter by the second. "It's not important. Keep stroking me like that and I'll be buried inside you in a flash," he slurred.

Syssi pushed back against his stroking fingers and tightened her grip around his length. "Is that a threat or a promise?"

"Stop." Kian gripped her wrist, stilling her hand. "You must be sore from before, and I don't want to hurt you, again." He winced.

She smiled at him sheepishly. "Would it offend you terribly if I said I wasn't sore?" Biting on her bottom lip, she looked at him from under her long lashes.

"To the contrary, I take pride in a job well done." Kian chuckled as he stretched himself on top of her, pinning her arms to her sides. "Are you sure?"

The confinement ratcheted her arousal, and she moaned deep in her throat. "I want you."

With his eyes locked on hers, Kian raised his hips and positioned himself at her opening. Nudging her entrance with just the tip of his shaft, he waited as she grew wetter before pushing in slowly.

This time, as he slowly eased into her tight sheath, stretching her, there was only pleasure, and she felt her inner muscles ripple along his length, pulling him in.

Kian closed his eyes, groaning as he rammed the rest of the way in.

Syssi gasped at the sudden invasion, more from the suddenness of it than any discomfort. He felt perfect inside her, and she pushed her thighs even wider apart, drawing him impossibly deeper.

They were both breathing heavily, their chests heaving, each inhale and exhale eliciting corresponding tightening and expanding in their sexes.

Kian retracted just a fraction, then slowly pushed back, repeating the shallow movements a few more times before wrapping his arms around her and flipping them over, positioning her on top.

Syssi pushed up to her knees and straddled his hips, bracing her hands on his chest. With her fingers splayed over his pecs, she rocked her hips, lifting and lowering herself on his shaft.

"You're so beautiful," she whispered and leaned to kiss his lips. But as she tried to lick into his mouth, he stopped her. Just as he had done before.

With his fingers pulling at her long hair, he took over and thrust his tongue into her mouth. Wrapping his other arm tightly around her middle, he held her down against his body as he pounded up into her with increasing ferocity.

On the verge of climax, her core tightening and rippling, Syssi whimpered.

Her response spurring his aggression, he fisted more of her hair, pulling on the roots and inflicting pinpricks of pain. As he pounded his hips up into her faster, harder—his penetration was so deep, he was hitting the end of her channel with every thrust.

Syssi's orgasm erupted in powerful spasms, her core tightening its grip around his thickening erection.

Battering into her, he came with a snarl, flooding her with pulsing spurts of seed.

She collapsed on top of him, her muscles going lax.

As they waited for their breaths to even out, Kian's hands were warm and tender as he stroked her hair and caressed her back—reassuring. Now that the storm was over, his gentleness seemed in stark contrast to his former aggression.

Her chest heaving in sync with Kian's and her cheek on his pec, Syssi listened to his strong heartbeat as it gradually calmed down. Impossibly, he began hardening again inside her. "You're a machine. I can't believe you're up again so soon."

"With you around, I'm afraid I'll be suffering from a case of perpetual hard-on." Kian smirked, but then his expression morphed into one of concern. "Are you okay?"

It seemed he wasn't over her pained reaction to his initial invasion. Apparently, it had been just as traumatic for him as it had been for her. The thing was, she had all but forgotten about it while he was still obsessing. Part of his nature, Syssi supposed, he'd told her so himself. It was sweet, though, the way he kept making sure. It showed that he cared.

"I'm more than okay. A little sore... wink, wink... but in a good way." She smiled coyly, pursing her lips for a kiss.

Flipping them sideways, he kissed her gently. "I have no words, Syssi. I'm afraid anything I'll say wouldn't do justice to the way you make me feel."

She cupped his cheek, caressing it and watching his eyes close in pleasure at her soft touch. "You don't have to say anything. Your body and your eyes tell me all I need to know. For now. Later, when you find the words, you'll tell me." She kissed each eyelid softly. "Don't fall asleep. We both need a shower." She traced his lips with her fingers.

"I'm not sleeping." Kian opened his eyes. "I would love to take a shower with you, but we better not. I wouldn't be able to keep my hands off of you, and you need time to recuperate." He kissed her fingers, then got out of bed and grabbed his clothes from the floor.

Syssi barely stopped herself from rolling her eyes. She was fine.

"I'll go shower in my room. There are a few things I need to do before I can turn in, but I'll come back and join you later... If it's okay with you?" He paused to look at her.

Syssi lay sprawled on the bed, unabashedly naked under his gaze. And why not? Kian made her feel sexy and desirable.

"You're so beautiful...," he breathed. "I'd better go before I jump you again." Belying his words, he remained rooted in place. With his clothes bundled under his arm, he gazed at her with longing.

Syssi smiled smugly, his praise infusing her with a rush of feminine power. "Just make sure you come back to me. I want to wake up in your arms."

"It's a promise." Kian winked, providing her with a perfect view of his sculpted ass and powerful thighs as he turned to leave.

Once he was out the door, Syssi lingered before getting out of bed. With the endorphins gone, she felt like a wreck; bone tired despite the little shut-eye she got after that first bout of sex with Kian. And it wasn't even eleven at night yet.

Her body protesting being moved, she winced as she shuffled to the bathroom and filled the tub with water—going for another soak to soothe her aching muscles and relieve the soreness she could no longer deny.

So strange that she hadn't been sore at all after the first time, when she should've been. There had been no pain, not even discomfort during the second time, Kian and she fit perfectly, and yet she was sore and achy all over.

Syssi shrugged. The simplest explanation was usually the correct one. After the first time, she'd been probably so high on endorphins that she couldn't have felt anything other than bliss.

CHAPTER 12: KIAN

Bracing his hands on the shower's marble wall, Kian let his head drop between his outstretched arms. With the hot water blasting him from multiple jets, he felt good, relaxed.

Syssi was a perfect fit for him. So much so that he doubted he could've been able to conceive of someone like her even if he tried. Without knowing her, experiencing her, he wouldn't have known what to ask for.

It was like she was made for him. And although he had just met her, he had yet to find even one thing he didn't like about her. But then, on some level he hoped he would. Some annoying habit, or a personality flaw that would make it easier to let her go.

It would be excruciating otherwise.

Just thinking about it brought on a tight, uncomfortable feeling in his gut, and he wished he could drop everything and get back in bed with her, even if only to hold her as she slept.

Except, the anticipated guest was the boy, Michael, and he needed to check on him and get an update from Yamanu.

As it was, he felt a twinge of guilt for forgetting all about the young man while indulging in mind-blowing sex with Syssi...

Making love, he corrected himself. That definitely was making love.

Sweet fates. All he wanted was to go back to her, wrap his arms around her, and lose himself in her.

Man! Was he in a shitload of trouble.

What had he done to annoy the vindictive fates that they would deal him such cruelty? Giving him a taste of heaven, showing him how perfect his life could be with Syssi, and then forcing him to give her up?

He'd been a good son and a good brother, he'd always tried to do the right thing. Why couldn't he get a break?

Unless, he was wrong and Amanda was right and Syssi was indeed a Dormant. In that case he was being rewarded rather than punished.

A fleeting sense of hope banished some of the darkness that had descended on his soul, giving him the burst of energy he needed to keep going and do what needed to be done.

Finishing up quickly, Kian got dressed and headed for the basement.

The guest suites were on the same level as Bridget's clinic and the large commercial kitchen. Getting out of the elevator, he heard Arwel's and then Bhathian's voice coming from the clinic.

Damn, they must've encountered Doomers if they were being treated by the doctor.

"What's going on, guys?" he asked as he entered through the door that had been left open.

Bhathian treated him to one of his ogre frowns. "Doomers, obviously."

"Did the boy get hurt?" Kian hoped the answer was negative. He'd risked the boy's life for the chance of capturing Doomers.

"No, we got there in time. Though barely."

"How are you doing?" Kian was dismayed to see them so banged up.

"On the mend." Arwel pulled down his T-shirt over his bandaged torso.

"Broken rib?"

"Yup."

"How about you, Bhathian?" It was worrisome that the Doomers had managed to get close enough to the guy to cause damage. Bhathian was a powerful and skilled fighter.

"A wrong move, that's all. Busted my ankle, but now it's fine. I'll be as good as new by tomorrow."

No doubt, but that didn't mean that the pounding the men had taken by a bunch of ██████ Doomers was not a cause for worry. Unless they had been outnumbered. "How many Doomers showed up?"

Arwel avoided Kian's eyes as he muttered, "Three."

"That's bad, guys. Three Guardians against three Doomers should've been a child's play for you."

Bhathian shook his head. "The ██████ have improved a lot since the last time we had a chance to fight them."

"Obviously. Where is Yamanu?"

"Getting a beer in the kitchen."

Beer sounded like a great idea. "You guys want some?"

Bhathian shook his head again. "I'm going to bed. Doctor's orders." He glanced at Bridget.

She patted his wide back like he was a schoolboy with a scraped knee. "To heal faster, they need to rest, and Bhathian needs to lie down with his leg up."

"Yeah, you're right. Go, get a good night's sleep and we'll discuss what happened out there tomorrow." Kian wanted all of his seven Guardians in top notch condition as soon as possible. Two down, even for one night, was worrisome.

He needed to talk to Yamanu. Kian found him in the kitchen, nursing a beer and demolishing a bag of potato chips.

"I heard you got your asses handed to you." Kian walked over to the fridge and pulled out a cold one for himself.

Yamanu smirked. "I wouldn't go that far, but it was a nasty surprise. They fought to the death."

Kian lifted a brow. "You killed all three?"

"No, they're in the crypt, together with the other two."

Kian popped the cap off the bottle and took a swig. "I wish you would've left one conscious for interrogation. We need to find out how many of them are here, and where are they staying. I'm so damn tired of being on the defensive. For once I would've loved to go after the bastards. Get to them before they got to us." Kian took another swig.

Yamanu shook his head. "That was the plan. But the Doomers fought a suicidal battle, and I had to leave Arwel and Bhathian to it and go take care of Michael and his friends."

"That's not good."

"We had no choice."

Kian nodded. "What about the boy? You said his friends were involved?"

Yamanu waved with his beer. "It's all taken care of. I thralled the other two and sent them to their rooms, then compelled Michael to sleep."

"Good."

"He is a fighter."

"Michael?"

"Yeah. His friends too, but they are human."

"So is Michael."

Yamanu nodded. "So you don't think Amanda is right about this?"

"No, I don't. But too much is at stake not to give it a try. We'll see how it goes."

"The kid has potential; courage, cool head, good instincts. Michael has all the makings of a good fighter. Guardian material."

"It's a little premature to talk about recruiting. First, we need to find out if he is one of us, which is doubtful."

"You're the boss." Yamanu saluted with the bottle.

Kian walked over to the suite adjacent to Michael and watched the kid sleep through the two-way mirror as he contemplated what do with him. Pulling out his phone, he rang Amanda.

"What?" She sounded agitated. Well, tough, he needed her help.

"We have Michael. I thought you would like to know as soon as he got here."

"Is he okay?"

"He is fine, the Guardians not so much." He heard Amanda gasp and quickly qualified. "A little banged up, that's all. They had a run in with Doomers."

"Damn, I should come home."

"Where are you?"

This was an improvement; Amanda calling the keep "home."

"Same as every night, I'm on the prowl."

"When can you be back?"

"Half an hour."

"Come down to the basement, I'm in the room next to Michael's, the one with the two-way mirror."

"Fine." The line went dead.

Michael's *guest room* was nothing but a fancy jail cell; complete with an en-suite bathroom, a big flat-screen, a PlayStation, and an assortment of DVDs and video games.

Very comfortable accommodations designed to keep guests for as long as needed; willing or not.

Finally, when the door banged open, more than an hour later, Kian didn't bother to look—recognizing his sister's signature dramatic entrance. He rolled his eyes; Amanda couldn't do "subtle" if her life depended on it. And instead of hi-how're-ya, the first words out of her mouth were, "I see you got the poor kid thralled."

"What did you want me to do? Tell him bedtime stories until you showed up? You said half an hour!" Annoyed, Kian waved his hand in the air.

"Oh, excuse me. Unlike my high and mighty brother who has a sweet, little hottie waiting for him in bed, some of us still need to go prowling."

"Watch your tone, Amanda. You sound like a petulant teenager, and just as inappropriate."

"I know, right?" Amanda ran her fingers through her short hair and shivered. "It's just that I had a sucky night. The guy I picked up... Ugh... big mistake."

Kian tensed immediately, ready to storm out and do some damage. "Did he hurt you?"

"Oh, please..." Amanda rolled her eyes. "As if a mortal could. Let's just say that if not for your call, I would have gone looking for the next one to erase the memory of the first one... Never mind; it happens. Thankfully, not often."

Crossing over to the two-way mirror, Amanda braced her palms against the glass. "What a shame this cutie is too young, just look at that body..."

Kian smirked. "I didn't know you had an age limit."

"I draw the line at twenty-one. If they can't drink..."

Kian walked over to stand next to her, shoving his hands in his back pockets. "There is always Mexico. I think the drinking age is eighteen over there. You could go for a visit."

"Ouch!" he exclaimed when she kicked his shin. "What was that for?"

"For being an ass." She smirked. "So tell me, how did it go with Syssi?"

"You want the long or the short version?"

"I want all of it. Spill!"

"I like her."

"Oh, come on! That's all you're gonna give me?"

"Yep."

"You mean, mean, old goat... I hate you!" She slapped his back, slanting her eyes at the smug smile he was trying to suppress.

"What do you want to do with the kid? We can't hold him down here forever." Kian returned to the subject at hand.

Amanda shrugged, crossing her arms over her chest. "We can try turning him, he is as good a prospect as Syssi, and we already got him here."

"It's not as simple as it is with Syssi... I can't believe I just said that... I'll rephrase... In some ways, it's even more complicated than it is with Syssi. He has to fight one of us aggressively enough for the guy fighting him to generate venom. How are we going to explain that?"

"Tell him the truth?"

"Are you out of your mind?"

"You can always thrall him later if it doesn't work."

"And what, keep him locked down here while we beat the shit out of him on a daily basis?"

"Just look at him!" Amanda pointed at Michael. "He is a football player... this kind of challenge will appeal to his testosterone-impaired, guy-brain. He'll probably think it's all a great macho test and love every minute of it."

"I don't know..." Kian rubbed the back of his neck, still unconvinced.

"Let's go to sleep. We'll decide how to do it in the morning. I'm bushed."

Leaving, Amanda leaned and kissed Kian's cheek. "Good night. Sleep tight. Keep Syssi's neck safe from your bite...," she singsonged on her way out.

* * *

As the bed sunk under his weight, Kian cursed silently. But Syssi just sighed and turned around. Lifting the comforter, he carefully slid behind her warm, sleeping body.

Bummer. She wasn't naked. And under the long T-shirt she wore as a nightgown, she was wearing panties as well—and not the thong kind.

How disappointing.

"Hi, what time is it?" she whispered groggily and yawned.

"It's late. Go back to sleep, sweet girl," he whispered and kissed her exposed neck.

"Hmm... that felt nice." Syssi sighed.

Smiling contentedly, he relaxed behind her, cocooning her with his body.

Good night, sleep tight, don't let the immortal bite. Amanda's little rhyme played in his head as he drifted off.

CHAPTER 13: DALHU

Dalhu paced the mansion's long upstairs gallery, seething with impotent rage. To say he was disappointed was the understatement of the century.

The team he had assigned to lie in wait for the woman had given up at sunrise, requesting permission to abandon post when it had become clear she wasn't coming home. The team he had sent after the guy had never come back or reported at all.

Their phones were dead.

The men were dead.

As capture wasn't an option for Doomers, they would've kept fighting until dealt a mortal blow. If struck down by mere mortals, they would've been left for dead, only to regenerate later and come back to base. But as none of the three had, he had to assume they had been taken out by Guardians. Just like the first two.

The Guardians were proving to be a real pain in his ass. He was down to six men.

Fisting his hands, Dalhu gathered his resolve. With the obvious presence of his enemy luring him like a vulture to the smell of carrion, there was no way in hell he was going to give up. He would just have to regroup and reevaluate his strategy.

It had been monumentally stupid of his men to ransack the lab and alert the enemy to the fact that they'd gotten their hands on that notebook—allowing the Guardians to take preemptive measures.

Those two potential Dormants should've been free for the picking, if not for the morons he had sent to the lab.

It should have been a stealth operation.

Lucky for them, those men were already dead. Taken out by the Guardians that had been protecting the telepath. Otherwise, he would have slaughtered them himself. Slowly.

Nevertheless, it was nothing but another setback.

He needed to come up with a plan. And to do so he had to make a list of all that he knew about the enemy; their strengths and weaknesses, patterns of behavior. How and where the few other immortal hits the Brotherhood had scored over the centuries had been accomplished. Only then he could figure out the right approach.

The next order of business would be to ask for reinforcements, which would be tricky. He would have to come up with a way to make the request without revealing the losses he had incurred. Reporting casualties, in the absence of results substantial enough to justify the losses, could have dire consequences for him.

Failure was not tolerated in Navuh's camp. Men lost their heads for less.

In the meantime, though, he had to boost morale among his remaining men. Not to mention his own.

The hookers he had reserved for tonight, or call girls as they preferred to be called, would be a step in the right direction.

Nothing like a night of debauchery to make everyone happy.

CHAPTER 14: KIAN

"Where are you going?" Syssi asked groggily.

"Go back to sleep, sweet girl. I'm going down to the gym. If I don't squeeze my workout first thing in the morning, I'll never get to it later." Kian kissed her warm, smooth cheek.

She turned, peering at him from under heavy lids. "What time is it?"

"It's five in the morning. Way too early for you."

"You slept even less than I did!" she protested, pulling on his hand to get him back in bed.

"I don't need as much sleep as you do, and you definitely need the rest." Kian winked and leaned to kiss her mouth.

Syssi shook her head, pressing her lips tightly together. "Morning breath," she mumbled through clenched teeth.

Kian cocked an eyebrow. "Mine or yours?" He smiled and kissed the corner of her mouth anyway.

Grabbing a pillow, she hid her face under it to escape his kisses.

Not discouraged by her antics, Kian leaned down to her other end, kissing the little bit of butt cheek protruding from her panties. Her skin there was so soft and her scent so sweet, he couldn't help himself and nipped a little.

"Stop that!" Syssi tugged on her nightshirt to cover her cute little butt.

"I can't help it. You're too tasty…" He pulled her shirt back up, and after another quick nip to her bottom, rushed out, dodging the pillow she threw at him.

* * *

Down at the gym, the activity was already going full swing when Kian walked in.

"Boss man! Over here!" Yamanu called from his station next to the racks of barbells, curling his bulging bicep.

Kian lifted a barbell as well and started his reps. "I'm surprised everyone is here so early. What's going on?"

"Finally seeing some action got everybody excited. There's nothing like the prospect of kicking some Doomer ass to motivate the guys to get back in top shape."

"And here I thought all of this time you were training hard to be ready for battle, when all along you were doing it only to look good for the ladies." Kian shot Yamanu a mocking grin.

The guy arched his brows and flipped Kian the bird before getting serious. "The SOBs are strong fighters. Last night, they managed to inflict some serious damage on us. That never happened in the old times. It shouldn't have been that difficult to subdue the mother~~futers~~. And regardless of whether they've gotten better or we've gotten weaker, we cannot afford to leave it at that." Yamanu paused as he switched hands. "We've been slacking off lately. It's time to get back in the game."

"It's good that you guys got some fire under your lazy asses, but I don't anticipate any more skirmishes." Kian switched sides as well. "As it is, we already have five undead in our crypt. At this rate, collecting more of their worthless carcasses will necessitate an expansion." Kian chuckled, taking a small rest before starting over on his left side.

Yamanu switched hands again, continuing the reps without rest. "What do you plan to do with them?"

Kian shrugged. "I don't know. It's not like we need to feed them. They just take up space. If it was up to me... well, you know my opinion on the subject. But Annani doesn't want them dead."

Kian had learned long ago that there was no point in trying to change his mother's mind once she made her decision. And as the head of their clan her word was final. Besides, more often than not, she had proven to be right in the end.

He had to wonder, though. Did she plan to keep the Doomers frozen like that indefinitely? Or did she delude herself that they could be redeemed; made to realize the evil of their ways and see the light.

She should know better than that.

Centuries of brainwashing and hatred couldn't be undone. Wishing it would not make it so.

Kian shrugged. "How is the boy doing, still asleep?"

"I didn't wake him, so he'll keep sleeping until I do. What's the deal with him? Do we keep him?" Yamanu shifted the barbell and began working on his triceps.

"Amanda wants to try turning him. I'm going to give him the option of giving it a try or having his memory scrubbed. Then we will need to figure out where to hide him so the Doomers can't find him, and what story to plant in his head so he can tell his parents he is alive. I don't want to ruin the kid's life. It's a messy situation."

"What about the other one? The girl?"

Damn. Anandur and his big mouth. He had probably told every occupant of the keep about Syssi. Not the way Kian wanted to play this.

"I don't know what I'm going to do with her. In the meantime, she stays with me. So hands off." The last thing he needed was for the Guardians to start sniffing around his woman. A potential Dormant was a huge deal, something every immortal male coveted; a beautiful potential Dormant was a cause for riots. Besides, he would rather not have to kill any of his nephews because they'd made a move on Syssi.

The way to solve it would have been to declare her his officially, but he couldn't do it, not before he told her everything and she accepted him as hers. The thing was, he couldn't tell her anything yet.

Yamanu flashed Kian his perfect smile. "Nice... Let me guess... You are in charge of turning the girl. You lucky bastard!"

Kian ignored Yamanu's big grin, doing like the three wise monkeys, and switched subjects back to Michael. "When you're done here, go wake the kid up. I'll get Amanda and we'll talk to him."

Kian replaced the barbell on the rack and walked over to the row of treadmills. Switching one on, he began pounding away at a clip pace.

CHAPTER 15: MICHAEL

"Time to get up, kid!"

Startled by a hand shaking his shoulder, Michael surged up. "What? Where?"

He had no idea where he was, but he recognized the tall, dark man staring at him with a pair of eerie pale blue eyes.

Yamanu—the dude from last night.

"Where am I?" Michael rubbed at his temples as he swung his legs down the bed's side, then looked at his socked feet. Someone had taken his Converses off. Luckily, his socks were relatively clean and free of holes. Getting dressed for the club last night, he realized that he had run out of clean ones and had pulled the least dirty pair out of his overflowing laundry bin.

With a quick glance around, he saw his brand-spanking-new Converse shoes lined up against the wall with their toes pointing in like two misbehaving brats sent there to serve penance.

"You're enjoying Dr. Dokani's hospitality. Five-star accommodations, including a change of clothes, a new toothbrush, and a razor. It's all in the bathroom. And when you're done there, your complimentary breakfast is waiting right here." Yamanu pointed to the covered tray on the coffee table.

As the appetizing smells registered in his sluggish brain, Michael salivated, suddenly feeling hungry as hell. No big surprise there. He always woke up hungry. But for once, there was something more pressing than food.

"When is Dr. Dokani going to see me? I really need someone to clue me in as to what kind of shit I'm in, and how deep."

"Go get cleaned. And better be quick about it, she'll be here shortly…" Yamanu scrunched his nose in distaste. "You stink."

Lifting his arm, Michael sniffed at his armpit. It wasn't that bad… "I don't know what you're talking about, dude. You're worse than my mom."

Yamanu shook his head as he turned to leave. "Just trust me on that."

Trust him… like he had a choice.

Taking off his clothes, Michael looked around the bathroom for a place to dump his dirty stuff, but there was nothing that looked like a laundry basket. And unlike his bathroom at the dorms, this one was nice and clean and smelled good. So instead of dropping them on the floor like he usually would, he folded them on top of the counter next to the new clothes Yamanu had left for him.

First, he used the razor to shave off his stubble. Some guys looked awesome with a little growth, but not him. Michael's square jaw was too big and too pronounced already to add anything to it. A shame, because he hated shaving every morning.

Next, he got into the shower and used the soap liberally, especially on his armpits. If Yamanu could smell him, so would Dr. Dokani, and he couldn't allow that. The professor wasn't the kind of woman any guy dared approach in a less than perfect state of grooming.

Not that he thought he had a chance with her, or anything ridiculous like that. The woman intimidated the hell out of him.

He actually preferred to come for testing when the professor wasn't there. Syssi was much more approachable, and he felt comfortable with her, enough to even flirt a little. He had no chance with her either, but at least she was nice about it, letting him get away with way more than anyone in her position would. It was a shame she was older. Not that he had a problem with that, but she obviously did.

After the shower, Michael got dressed quickly and headed back to the suite's small living room where his breakfast was waiting. Hopefully it was still warm.

When the knock came, Michael was about to inhale the last pastry on his plate. Stuffing it into his mouth and chewing quickly, he walked over to the door.

Opening the thing from the other side, Dr. Dokani walked in with an enviably good-looking dude.

Figures, Michael thought, *for a chick like her to have a boyfriend that looks like that.*

"Good morning, Michael, I hope you had a pleasant and restful sleep," she said.

Michael shook the hand she offered.

"This is Kian, my brother." She motioned to the guy.

He shook the dude's hand as well.

A brother then, not a boyfriend... As if it matters... Like I had a chance in hell, Michael thought while fronting like he was cool—confident.

"Let's have a seat, shall we?" She pointed to the couch and sat across from him on the chair. She was wearing a skirt. It wasn't short, but it must've ridden up a little as she sat down, because part of her thigh was showing and it was very shapely. In fact, it was so shapely that he had trouble looking away.

The brother cleared his throat, and Michael had no choice but to tear his eyes away from the professor's legs. The stern stare he encountered was enough to chill his overheating blood.

His butt dropped onto the sofa as if he'd been physically pushed. Sitting on the very edge, Michael planted his elbows on his knees and clasped his hands in front of him. Leaning toward the professor, he purposefully kept his eyes level with hers. "Dr. Dokani, what's going on?"

"Amanda... please call me Amanda. We are all friends here. Kian?" She turned to her brother who was still standing. "Would you like to be the one to explain?"

"No, sister mine. You do the honors, I insist." The dude pinned her with a hard stare.

Not fair, she mouthed at him.

He is your talent, he mouthed back.

"Guys? How about you clue me in? You're freaking me out."
What the hell?

How bad could it be, for these two to argue about who would deliver the grim news?

"Okay, I'll start." Amanda sighed and recrossed her long legs. Michael prided himself on keeping his eyes on her face and not taking a peek to see if her skirt had ridden even higher. And it had nothing to do with the intimidating brother who had sat down next to her in the other chair, facing Michael as well. Nothing at all.

"What I'm about to tell you will sound unbelievable, fantastic, and though I'm sure you'll have many questions, I ask that you just listen until I'm done."

Michael swiped two fingers over his lips in a zipping motion.

"Okay, then," Amanda said.

"Thousands of years ago, a species of nearly immortal people lived among humans, who believed them to be gods. Their bodies neither aged nor contracted disease. And as they healed and regenerated from most injuries quickly, they were almost impossible to kill. They also possessed special abilities, like the ability to create powerful illusions. These powers, along with their immortality, made them seem divine to the primitive people.

"They took mates from among the humans and many mixed children were born, possessing some of the powers as well. But as in any society, there were internal struggles for power, which eventually resulted in a nuclear catastrophe that wiped out the gods and a huge chunk of the mortal population.

"One lone goddess escaped the cataclysm, taking with her the advanced knowledge of her people. She had made it her mission to trickle this knowledge to humanity, and over the millennia guided it to become a more advanced, better society. But she had enemies.

"The scions of her nemesis survived the nuclear disaster and embarked on a road of destruction, vowing to eliminate her, her progeny, and any progress humanity achieved through her help.

"We, as her descendants, are helping her achieve her goals. Unfortunately, there are not many of us. We believe, though, that there are Dormant mortals, people carrying our genetic code that we can activate. To date, all our attempts at identifying Dormants have failed. I started my research on a hunch, believing some Dormants might exhibit paranormal abilities. Among all my test subjects, you and my assistant Syssi were the only ones talented enough to be considered potential candidates."

Amanda paused to take a breath. "Our enemies of old, the Doom Brotherhood or Doomers as we call them, got hold of parts of my research that contained information about Syssi and you. Being identified as potential Dormants, you became highly coveted targets for them. Luckily, we were able to get to you before they did. Now we face a dilemma. I'll let Kian explain."

Michael looked first at Amanda's serious face then Kian's, then back at Amanda's, waiting for them to crack and tell him they were pulling his leg. But as they held on to their serious expressions, gradually his mouth morphed into a smile. Clapping his hands and laughing he looked at the ceiling and the two-way mirror.

"I knew it. I've been punked! You have a camera crew behind that mirror. Damn!... For a moment, you got me there... unbelievable.... Okay, guys, you can come out now... you had your fun..." Michael looked at the door, waiting for it to burst open.

"Guys?" He looked at Amanda and Kian. "Oh, come on, how long are you going to drag it out? I'm on to you..."

"I think Michael needs a demonstration." Amanda turned to her brother.

"It would be my pleasure." Kian's evil smile should've warned Michael something other than a joke was up. Though later, when he would think about it, nothing could've prepared him for what came next.

Right in front of his eyes, Kian began morphing into a creature straight out of a nightmare. Somehow he was becoming larger—like in huge—his skin turning red, and black horns sprouted on top of his head. His eyes, which had been blue a moment ago, turned completely black, and long, sharp fangs protruded from that cruel mouth that was still smiling that evil smile.

But now it was absolutely terrifying.

"What the hell?!" With no way to escape other than going through that demon, Michael scrambled back and climbed the sofa's back, screeching like a chick.

The demon disappeared in a flash, and in its place Kian was back, with the same god-awful smile plastered on his smug puss. "Need some more convincing? I can do Bigfoot, King Kong... Ask me. It's the only time I'll take requests, so don't be shy," the jerk taunted.

"You put something in my food, drugged me, I know it..." Michael's heart was pounding in his chest louder than it did when he had faced those titans last night. He got so scared, his hands were shaking.

His hands had never done that before. Ever.

This must be what a bad trip feels like, he thought as he wiped his sweaty palms on his jeans. Zack had one, after trying some weird stuff the guys from the chemistry department had cooked, and he had sworn never to touch hallucinogenics ever again. Now Michael understood why.

"There was nothing in your food and you know it. You're just trying to rationalize the unbelievable, choosing to believe in something even more outlandish instead. Does that make sense to you?" Kian sounded like he was losing his patience.

Michael rubbed his chest as he tried to force his brain to stop misfiring so he could think for a moment. The demon from hell had appeared right after Kian had promised a demonstration. From the little he knew about how hallucinogenic drugs worked, it didn't make sense that the effect could have been so well timed.

But Amanda's story was just too out there.

Except, why would they go to all this trouble to deceive him? He was a nobody. What would they gain by messing with him?

"I'm listening...," Michael capitulated, figuring he had nothing to lose by hearing the rest of the story: incredibly scary guy getting pissed, notwithstanding.

"Good, so here is the dilemma. In order to activate your dormant genes, one of us has to inject you with venom... Yeah, venom. You heard me right." Kian raised his palm to stop Michael's what-the-hell?

"The males of our species have fangs that produce venom in two situations." Kian lifted his hand, two fingers up. "During sex, or when aggressing on other males. This venom is what facilitates the activation. We know this because that's how we activate our boys when they reach puberty. We treat it as a right-of-passage ritual. An older boy is chosen to fight the Dormant, who only has to fight well enough to generate the level of aggression needed for the older boy to produce venom and bite him. For a thirteen-year-old, in most cases one time is enough. In an adult male your size, we have no clue. We've never done it before. This means that you'll have to go through gladiator style matches every day until you turn or give up. If you turn, you gain immortality and become one of us. If you don't, we erase your memory of our existence."

"So what's the dilemma?" Michael asked. "It seems you've already decided what you want to do with me."

"First of all, no, it's up to you. You decide you don't want to get beaten bloody and pumped with venom every day—we erase your memory now. You choose to stay—I already explained what happens then. The problem is that out there Doomers are waiting to snatch you, either to kill you or somehow use you. You cannot go back to school or to your parents' home.

"We'll take care of you, of course; provide resources for relocation, new name, new school, whatever you need. Plant new memories in your mind, giving you some plausible explanation for the whole mess. But you need to make up your mind and decide if you're willing to give it a shot. I will not sugarcoat it for you. I don't think it will work. Amanda believes there is a chance and I'm willing to give it a try, but I don't want to give you false hope."

The room went quiet as Michael took a moment to think it through, which wasn't easy with Amanda and Kian staring at him. He felt like the poor schmuck on a game show, standing on a podium and sweating for the answer as the annoying music played in the background.

Michael suppressed a snort as it crossed his mind that Amanda and her jerk brother were certainly pretty enough to play as hosts on this freaky gameshow from hell.

"I'll do it." He broke the silence. "The way I see it, I'm screwed anyway. I can go into your version of a witness protection program now or later, it doesn't really matter. But on the remote chance that I can gain immortality, I'll say it's worth my while to stay here for a few weeks and give you guys a run for your money."

Kian nodded. "There is one more complication you need to consider. The longer you stay, the more memories we'll need to replace, and it may mess with your head. Besides the large chunk of missing time you will not be able to account for, you might remember bits and pieces of events, not knowing if you lived through them or dreamt them, and that's if you got away with no permanent brain damage. I want you to make an informed decision." Kian watched Michael, waiting for him to acknowledge that he understood.

"Yeah, well… I made up my mind. We'll need to come up with a good story to tell my parents, though. I don't want them freaking out when they can't find me at school."

"You come up with the story, we'll help with the details. One last thing; as long as we are running our little experiment, you will have to remain locked up down here. I can't have you wandering around with the knowledge of our existence and our location. I'm sure you can understand the necessity."

"I guess," Michael said in a small voice.

This was the hardest part of the deal for him. He liked being around people. Solitary confinement, even in a sweet dig like this, would be tough.

CHAPTER 16: SYSSI

Syssi had been disappointed when Kian had left her alone earlier in the morning. The bed felt cold and lonely without him. But she'd gone back to sleep and woke up a few hours later feeling wonderful. In fact, she stayed in bed long after waking, trapped by the tactile pleasure of the duvet's soft fabric and the thick fluffy down comforter it covered.

What a night, she sighed.

In her wildest dreams, she had never imagined she could be like that. Wanton, uninhibited, and what's more, with someone she had just met.

It defied how she defined herself.

Cautious, reserved, shy, risk-averse, was how she thought of herself. Well, she'd have to adopt some new adjectives. Not to replace the old ones, those still applied, but in addition or rather as qualifiers.

She could begin with wanton, though only with Kian... and that was true for uninhibited and a little kinky as well.

Still, it was a good start.

Stretching her arms and toes, she felt good, which considering the vigorous activities of last night was surprising. And it wasn't just the sense of physical wellbeing and vitality.

She felt content.

Such a simple and unassuming word—content.

Except, before experiencing it, she hadn't been aware of its lack. It took the absence of the uneasy hum always simmering below the surface of her awareness, for her to realize it had even been there.

Syssi wondered how long this I-am-at-peace-with-the-universe sensation would last. Better not to dwell on it, though, lest she hasten the hum's return. There were more pleasant things to contemplate. Like how comfortable she felt letting go with Kian, or how he seemed to enjoy everything about her.

He'd spent time with her, even though he was so incredibly busy. He'd listened to her talk as if she was fascinating. He'd made love to her, teaching her things about herself she hadn't known. He'd told her over and over again how much he loved the way she yielded to him, ensuring she felt good about it. There had been no artifice in any of it. He had no need. And yet he'd taken the time, showing that he cared.

Kian made her feel secure that way.

Except, was he like this only with her? Or was he making all of his partners feel special?

How many?

The sudden flare of jealousy blew away any remaining vestiges of her peaceful happiness; its shattered pieces lying like boulders on her chest, constricting her ability to draw breath.

She felt queasy imagining the line of gorgeous women coming and going through Kian's home.

His bed.

With that disturbing thought, Syssi was out of bed and in the bathroom in seconds.

Splashing cold water on her face helped. And as she attacked her teeth with the toothbrush, brushing so vigorously that her gums ached, she made up her mind to find out more about Kian.

The best candidate to pump for information was obviously Amanda. Except, protecting her brother, she might not cooperate. And anyway, it would be too awkward.

Okidu, on the other hand, was a different story. Syssi remembered reading somewhere that it was impossible to keep any secrets from the household staff. And if that was true, the butler must know everything that was going on.

With her mind made up, Syssi headed for the kitchen. She was going to have a little chat with the guy.

"Good morning, mistress," Okidu greeted her. "May I offer breakfast? I brewed a fresh pot of coffee and kept some of my famous waffles in the warming drawer for you." He was again smiling that fake-looking smile she had noticed before.

"Thank you, I would love some." Syssi pulled out a stool and sat at the counter.

"Is Kian coming back for breakfast?" She began her casual interrogation.

"No, mistress, he might not be back until lunch. Very busy man, the master. Lots of work to do. Sometimes he even asks me to bring him a sandwich to the office." Okidu placed the steaming mug of coffee in front of her.

"Is his office in the building?" Syssi sipped on her coffee as she observed the butler, trying to glean more information from his expressions and body language.

Nada. Zip. There was nothing there.

Usually, she was very good at reading people; noting the slight changes in their expressions, the way they held their bodies, what they did with their hands—combining all these clues to form a more complete picture than what their words alone provided.

But the butler gave nothing away.

"Yes, indeed it is," Okidu answered, serving her a plate of divinely smelling waffles, covered with fruit and topped with whipped cream.

"In that case he should be back already. I'm sure his workout is not as long."

Okidu smiled again. "Mr. Shai has an office down in the basement, and the master often works from there."

"Who is Mr. Shai?"

"The master's assistant, of course."

Well, at least the assistant was a guy and not some gorgeous secretary in high heels and a miniskirt.

"I guess he doesn't get out much; working as hard as he does, and his office being right here in the building." Feigning nonchalance, Syssi dug into the waffles.

"I would not say that." The butler turned toward the coffeemaker and picked up the carafe to refill her mug.

So, he knows how to be evasive.

Syssi contemplated the best way to phrase her next question to corner him into a yes or no answer. "Do you get to entertain a lot of ladies up here? Besides myself and family members, that is?" She tacked on the last part to close any loopholes. Concentrating on his face, she gave her perception another go. Maybe this time, she'd discern some minute changes in his expression.

"No, mistress, besides you, only family comes up here, and the master begrudges me entertaining even them. They usually come uninvited."

With that fake plastic smile plastered on his wide face, Okidu's demeanor revealed nothing. Still, she didn't think he was lying.

It was a tremendous relief, knowing that Kian had made an exception in her case. The tightness in her chest eased. She was the only woman he had ever brought home. Well, this home, the butler had said nothing about prior residences.

Still, for some reason it placated her. Even if Kian went out every night and had sex with God only knew how many women, he had treated her differently.

She must've meant more to him.

She was special.

CHAPTER 17: DALHU

Dalhu stared at the empty yellow pad in front of him.

What did he really know about the enemy? Most of his information had come from the Brotherhood's propaganda; admittedly, not the most reliable of sources. And his own experience dealing with the clan had been limited.

To make informed decisions and avoid mistakes, he had to stick to the facts. Things he knew to be true for certain.

That list was frustratingly short.

Starting with what he had learned recently, he filled the first half of the lined page.

First, there couldn't have been more than a few hundred of them, as they were all the descendants of one female and adhered to the old taboos against mating within the same matrilineal line. Which made them desperate enough to search for Dormants descending from other lines among mortals with special abilities.

Second, there was a concentration of them in Los Angeles, the presence of a Guardian Force indicating that there was someone of vital importance here for them to protect. Maybe even their Matriarch...

And wouldn't that make him one lucky SOB.

As he imagined the glory of being the one to lead the final battle over the control of humanity and taking down that abominable female, his chest expanded and he straightened, squaring his shoulders.

Unfortunately, her being here was a speculation and not a fact. Sighing, he slumped back in his chair and looked down at the yellow pad.

Thinking back to what he knew for sure, or at least could make an educated guess about, he flipped to a new page and started a second list.

Most of them weren't fighters; academics, scientists, writers—they didn't pose much of a physical challenge. And in addition to the males who lacked any kind of combat skills, he could completely discount the female half of their small population as well.

The force of Guardians, though, was something to reckon with. These warriors were legendary among the Brotherhood. Part of what had created his impression, that the clan was larger than it actually was, were the myths surrounding them, making them seem like a large and fierce force.

Dalhu wondered how many Guardians the clan actually had. Not that it made a difference, he seethed, even if their numbers were small, they had still decimated almost half of his men with ease.

But then, he had no intentions of seeking out Guardians. He definitely didn't need any more proof to convince him that he stood no chance against them—not with the inferior fighters at his disposal.

The rest of the clan was up for grabs, and he didn't need to catch a Guardian to lead him to their nest. A civilian would do. He just needed to figure out where the rest of them hung out.

There were things all near-immortals had in common; sharper senses and reflexes, stronger bodies that required only a few hours of sleep, and most notably—one hell of a sex drive. Lacking suitable partners in their community, the clan males, just like Navuh's troops, had to rely on mortals to satiate their ferocious appetites.

His brethren, himself included, used hookers, and so had the enemy in days past. Stumbling upon a near-immortal in a whorehouse accounted for the few kills the Brotherhood had scored.

But nowadays, living in the West, women were available to them everywhere. The males were probably prowling the nightclubs and bars, looking for hookups. The corrupt, western females, the willing and easy sluts, made themselves available like whores in those places without even asking to be paid for their services.

Dalhu reclined in his chair and smiled as an idea began forming in his head. Nightclubs and bars; that's where he'd find his targets.

Except, the obvious hitch in his brilliant plan was the fact that there were probably hundreds, if not thousands, of those in a city this size.

CHAPTER 18: KIAN

"What do you think?" Ingrid asked as Kian followed her into his new informal conference room.

"I'm impressed."

Ingrid's tense shoulders relaxed. "I'm glad. You didn't give me much time."

"I have to hand it to you and William. You've done a spectacular job without my input or interference."

She beamed, straightening her back, suddenly looking a couple of inches taller. "I don't think you complimented me like that even after I'd done your penthouse, or any of the other spaces I've decorated for this building. I remember you grunting 'good job' and shooing me out."

Kian scratched his stubble. Had he been so callous? He didn't remember what he'd said to Ingrid, but he didn't doubt her words. He wasn't normally generous with praise. If it meant so much to his people, maybe he should make an effort. The thing was, it didn't come naturally to him. He expected top notch performance from everyone around him and took it for granted when things were done to his satisfaction.

"When I'm not happy about something, you'll know it. So when I say nothing it means you've done a great job."

Ingrid grimaced. "I'll remember it for the next time I walk out with tears in my eyes."

"If you don't want this to be the last time you hear a compliment from me, don't try to guilt me into it. I have a mother and three sisters, I'm immune to female manipulation."

She smirked. "If you say so."

Was he that easy to read? Her words had managed to penetrate his thick skin, bringing on an uneasy feeling. He'd kept his expression neutral by going on the offense. She was right, he was an ass.

"I like the clean contemporary lines of the furniture. Are they made of wood? Or is it some composite material?" A useful trick he'd learned to use with the other females in his life—change the subject and have them talk about something they were passionate about.

Worked every time.

"It's not fake. They are made from several varieties of highly polished woods. Cost a fortune, but I saved on the art. How do you like it?

I wasn't sure about the black and white, but I thought it would be less distracting for a business environment."

Kian glanced at the large still-life photographs adorning the walls, their unobtrusive lack of color providing some interest without calling too much attention to themselves.

"Good call."

"Thank you." Ingrid bowed her head a little. "I could stay longer and wait for more of your rare words of praise, but I'm sure you have work to do, and so do I. I'm still up to my eyeballs in the other project you assigned to me. Furnishing apartments for all the people coming down from the Bay area is one hell of a task. But it came in handy for getting this office done so quickly. I dangled the huge order in front of my supplier to have him deliver your stuff as soon as possible. He must've given us someone else's order and made them wait instead."

Kian shrugged. Throw enough money at a problem and things happened the way you wanted. "Do you need help? I can assign you an assistant." For a moment, he considered giving the job to Syssi. Decorating wasn't architecture, but it was closer to her field of study than working at Amanda's lab. Except, he had to remind himself that she wasn't staying, and the more memories he would have to scrub, the more damage her brain would sustain. During Syssi's brief stay at the keep, it would be better to keep her as isolated as possible.

Ingrid shook her head. "Thank you, but I'm managing just fine. A little less sleep at night, but it's not like this madness will not end soon."

"For you, yes." For him, not so much. He was stuck in the insane rat race with no exit in sight.

Ingrid nodded. "I'd better get to it. See you later, Kian. Enjoy your new office."

"Thanks."

He waited for her to close the double French doors behind her, and walked over to the massive desk facing them. It was already set up with a desktop and a laptop, no doubt hooked up and ready to go. Behind it a credenza, just as massive, was topped by a huge screen that took up half of the wall above it. The screen would be useful for presentations. That way everyone would be able to watch in comfort instead of cramming together around a laptop.

His favorite was the long conference table with a top made from some beautiful, exotic wood. With six large chairs on each side and one at each end, it could accommodate the smaller meetings of either the Guardians or the council members or both.

He wasn't sure, however, that the fully stocked bar on one side and the serving buffet on the other were such a hot idea. With food and drinks being served, the meetings might drag on forever.

Nonetheless, he liked it.

Sitting behind the desk, Kian smoothed his palms over the glossy surface, contemplating doing his work from down here instead of his home office upstairs.

It was true that he would miss the magnificent view he had from his penthouse, but on the other hand, it would solve the problem of Guardians intruding on his privacy and barging in on him at all hours of the day. And what's more, with Syssi there, he really didn't like the idea of the men sniffing around his woman.

No, wait, she wasn't his... Couldn't be.

Propping his elbows on the desk, he let his head drop onto his fists. What was he going to do with her? Should he offer her the same deal he'd offered Michael? Somehow that seemed inappropriate. Cruel.

Hey, honey, I'll be ~~fucking~~ screwing and biting you for the next couple of weeks or months. But if you don't turn, I'm going to erase that memory and send you on your way.

Except, what other options did he have? To keep thralling her daily was just as cruel—as well as deceitful. And harmful.

The only decent thing to do was to let her go. Yet, he knew he wouldn't do that.

Couldn't.

She was too important to the clan...

Hell, who was he kidding? She was too important to him.

But what could he offer her that would make it okay? Ease his guilt?

And what about her family? Did she have any siblings? If she had, then they would be in danger as well.

Sighing, he leaned back in the chair and let his head go lax on the padded headrest behind him. Kian wanted the lie off his chest. But that too was selfish of him.

On the other hand, he'd believed he had been protecting Lavena when he had concealed who he was from her. And look how well that had turned out...

~~Fuck~~ Crap! Kian banged his head against the headrest. He had completely forgotten about the addiction. They all had—that little ditty of their ~~fucked~~ messed-up biology being irrelevant to their revolving-door style of sex partners.

The bloody venom was addictive—ensuring mated couples stayed faithful to each other.

At least in theory.

He hadn't known that when he had run away to be with Lavena. Enlightened by his mother upon his return, he'd learned that in addition to becoming a widow at eighteen, Lavena would also suffer from withdrawal.

Apparently, being repeatedly injected with the venom of the same sexual partner created an addiction in his mate. She would be physically repulsed by the sexual scent of other males and crave only him.

Supposedly, it took a long time for the addiction to set in, and just as long for it to wane.

Annani had laughed at his naive assumption that as a result mated couples in their society must've been very faithful to each other.

"To the contrary," she had said.

To avoid getting addicted to one person, some had made sure to be with several partners. Mixing it up. Being such a lustful species, monogamy hadn't been at the top of their highly valued morals. More like near the bottom.

The males hadn't escaped unscathed either; eventually, the addiction had gotten them as well. As the scent of the female had changed with her growing attachment, she had become as irresistible to her mate as he had been to her.

For some, it had happened sooner than for others; Annani and Khiann becoming attached within weeks. She had claimed it had happened so fast because they had been so in love.

Kian wondered, though, what came first: the chicken or the egg. The love or the addiction…

Still, he had to consider the possibility that he and Syssi might be of the sooner variety. Which meant that if they were forced to part, in addition to the mental agony, they would suffer painful withdrawal.

Damn, the thought of him taking other partners as a preemptive measure sickened him. Worse, the thought of Syssi doing the same enraged him to the point of turning homicidal.

CHAPTER 19: SYSSI

"Is there anything else madame requires?" The butler bowed his head.

Someone to talk to, Syssi thought. She was bored out of her mind. "No, thank you."

"I have to leave, but there are plenty of snacks and various beverages in the refrigerator. Please, Madame, feel free to help yourself."

"I will."

The butler retreated with another slight dip of his head.

Great, now she was totally alone in the penthouse. Not that Okidu had been much of a company, but at least she'd known someone was there.

Having nothing better to do, Syssi poured herself another cup of coffee. She even hazarded reading the headlines of the *Los Angeles Times* that Okidu had left for her on the kitchen counter. Luckily, there had been no new disasters reported.

With the butler gone, all alone in the big, empty penthouse she felt even more restless and bored. Kian must've gone to work straight from the gym, and he hadn't even bothered to call.

Kind of disappointing. And disheartening. The night they had spent together had been monumental in the effect it had on her. That didn't necessitate, though, that it had been even remotely meaningful to Kian.

It made sense. She was young and inexperienced and being with Kian had been like a discovery—a perception-altering one. He, on the other hand, had most likely already experienced the full gamut of things. It had been nothing new for him.

With a sigh, she walked over to the couch, sat down and let her head drop on her fists. All that self-doubt was killing her, and it was made worse by the oppressing quiet of the apartment and having nothing to do to keep her busy. It wouldn't have been so bad if she at least had something to distract her like surfing the Internet. Kian had left his tablet on the coffee table, and not really expecting it to work for her, Syssi reached for it and turned it on. But it was passcode protected just as she'd known it would be. So that was out. And to use her laptop she needed the access code to the internet, which, of course, she didn't have.

That left only the boring neuroscience papers Amanda wanted her to read. She had them downloaded already, but her brain felt too scattered to concentrate on such heavy reading.

She should call Andrew. In fact, she should've done it as soon as Kian had disposed of her cellphone. If her brother tried her at home or on her cell, not finding her would freak him out. He would think something had happened to her and might mobilize a taskforce to look for her. She'd better let him know that she was alive and staying with Amanda.

Well, she was... kind of.

Shit. She definitely wasn't expecting to find the kitchen phone blocked as well. Who did a thing like that? This was a private residence, not a public office. Had Kian thought that she would make long-distance calls?

The thought was ridiculous. The guy threw money around as if it grew on trees, phone charges would be the last thing he would've been concerned with.

Maybe it was just the one in the kitchen.

With the coffee mug in hand, she walked down the hallway, checking the phones in every bedroom and finding each and every one blocked.

The last door to the right led to what must've been Kian's home office. And though it was neat and tidy, it didn't look like the kind a decorator stocked with shelves full of leather-bound books no one ever read—for the sake of appearances.

It was obvious Kian worked here.

A stack of correspondence was piled next to the keyboard, with colorful sticky notes peeping between the pages. Behind the desk, a large cabinet housed a multitude of name-tagged folders—their crumpled edges indicating that they were frequently used.

Curious, Syssi tilted her head to read some of the labels.

It was an interesting assortment of enterprises. The information the folders contained must've been on companies comprising an investment portfolio, as it didn't make sense that Kian's family business was that diversified.

Some of the names sounded like biotech companies, software firms, building projects, ore and coal mines. Others had been marked by acronyms that bore no meaning she could decipher. He'd told her about the real estate and the drone factory, but apparently Kian was investing heavily in other industries as well.

Taking a seat in his executive swivel chair, she checked the phone on his desk. It was blocked like the rest of them, and so was the desktop.

Seriously annoyed, she considered leaving.

As far as she knew, she wasn't a prisoner and could come and go as she pleased… unless the elevator was code blocked as well, and she'd have to take the emergency stairs to get down to the lobby. For a moment, she actually contemplated trudging the many floors to reach the street level.

Exasperated, Syssi returned to the living room and took to pacing it in circles. The longer she paced, the angrier she got at Kian.

The nerve of this man, leaving her without any means of communication. And where was the new cellphone he had promised her?

Evidently, he was just as thoughtless and clueless as the rest of his gender. Only, being gorgeous and sexy, he was more likely to get away with it.

As her next round brought her to the glass doors, she paused to look out, pining for the outdoors like a caged bird.

Well, she wasn't really caged… she was free to roam the terrace… Har-har, hardy-har-har.

With a strong shove, she sent the glass panels into their concrete hiding place and stepped out. The distant sound of the city hustle and bustle was a welcome intrusion after the solitude of the inside, and standing in the light breeze, she felt it waft across her face and carry some of her ire away.

Taking a calming breath, she walked over to where she had eaten her solitary dinner last night, and sitting down, noticed Kian's forgotten pack of cigarettes.

It had been years since she had smoked as a rebellious teenager pushing at her boundaries, but here and there she still craved it. Especially when she got seriously pissed off. Like now.

What the heck, why not, she thought, it wasn't as if she was planning on making it a habit.

Pulling one out, she held it between her thumb and forefinger and moved to lie down on the lounger. Lighting up, she was careful not to inhale too much, letting most of the smoke out.

The point was to enjoy the little sinful pleasure without getting dizzy, which was what would happen if she inhaled too much too fast. She needed to ease into the tobacco's effects.

Still, as careful as she was, she got a little light-headed and closed her eyes.

Funny, how this forbidden pleasure made her feel naughty. Or how ridiculous it was that she felt grateful that there was no one around to witness her crime.

Most of her friends smoked pot, which she refused to touch, but they frowned on cigarettes. Kind of hypocritical. But whatever, people justified their own vices anyway they could, but they didn't extend the same courtesy to others.

Hannah claimed it was the smell that was offensive, but Syssi thought pot smelled way worse. Like mold and dirty socks. Ugh. How could anyone put it in their mouths?

She chuckled. They probably thought the same thing about tobacco.

Pulling small drags then exhaling them, she felt herself relax, and with each pull her tight muscles released more of their tension.

It wasn't long before her mind wandered back to last night. Syssi felt changed by the experience. What was hidden and repressed even from her own psyche, had gotten loose. And instead of being terrified, she found it liberating.

Whether there was a future for her with Kian or not, she'd be forever grateful to him for helping her get rid of her suffocating inhibitions.

Taking another drag on the cigarette, she let the carnal scenes replay in her mind. Embracing them, owning them, feeling empowered by them... getting aroused.

CHAPTER 20: KRI

Food; someone was cooking something that smelled delicious. Kri stopped in her tracks as the appetizing smells hit her nose. The thing was, no one ever cooked in the basement. Curious and rather hungry, she followed her nose to the kitchen.

"What are you doing here?"

It wasn't every day that Kian's butler roamed the lower levels of the basement in general, or visited the big commercial kitchen that no one ever used for anything other than storing beer and dried goods in particular.

"I am cooking for our new guest, Madame," Okidu said.

"Could you stop calling me that? It gives me the creeps. The humans call old ladies Madame."

He quirked an eyebrow. "Would you prefer mademoiselle?"

"I would prefer Kri. That's my name."

"I cannot oblige you, Madame, or if you prefer, Mademoiselle."

Yeah, he probably couldn't. If it had been hardwired into his programming, nothing could change it.

"Fine, the other one. At least it doesn't sound like you're addressing an old lady."

He dipped his head. "As you wish, Mademoiselle."

Kri got closer and peeked to see what was in the pot. Some kind of stew that didn't look very appetizing but smelled divine. The good news was that there seemed to be enough in there to feed the entire Guardian force, including Anandur and Bhathian, which was saying a lot. Okidu was using one of the commercial sized pots.

"Is it ready?"

"It is, Mademoiselle."

"Can I have some?"

"Naturally, I cooked enough for twenty-seven people."

Kri chuckled. "Which means it's just enough to feed the Guardians."

"If you say so, Mademoiselle. The Guardians and Master Kian and his two guests and several others."

Right, she'd heard about Amanda's assistant staying at Kian's. Not something Kri appreciated at all. Even though there was no chance that there could ever be anything between Kian and her, she certainly didn't want to see another female sharing his penthouse. Too cruel.

Well, if Kian was entertaining one of the guests, she could entertain the other.

"Okidu, would you mind if I bring our guest his lunch?"

"Not at all, Mademoiselle. Let me prepare a tray for you."

"Thank you."

When it was ready, Kri hefted the thing and carried it down the corridor. Standing outside Michael's room and listening to the sounds coming from behind the closed door, Kri's lips curled in a knowing smile.

Machine-gun fire and exploding grenades accompanied by a litany of expletives could mean only one thing—the kid was putting the PlayStation to good use. And by the sound of it, he was playing Call of Duty—her favorite game.

Holding a tray with one hand and balancing it on her hip, she entered the numbers into the room's code-protected lock and pushed open the door.

"Room service!" she called out, snapping Michael's attention from the game.

"Oh, hi." He looked up from the couch, his eyes widening as they traveled up and down her body.

"I've got your lunch, kid, where do you want it?" She stifled a grin, glancing away from his blushing face to the coffee table which was littered with open covers of DVDs and video games, a half-eaten bag of potato chips, and two empty bottles of beer.

"Just give me a moment to clean up this mess." Michael got busy stuffing the games and movies back in their cases and putting them away, then threw the rest of the stuff into the trash container.

"Here we go!" He straightened to his full height and pointed to the table.

Nice. The kid was tall and built like a linebacker. And that cute, shy smile was… yum.

Shooting him her crooked smile, Kri lowered her butt to the couch and placed the tray on the table.

"Come, let's eat." She moved two plates off the tray then patted the spot next to her. "I figured that being stuck here all by yourself you'd like some company. By the way, I'm Kri." She extended her hand, which he shook.

CHAPTER 21: MICHAEL

"Nice to meet you... Thank you. That's really nice of you..." Michael sat down next to Kri.

Wow, that is one helluva woman.

He'd been surprised by the strength of her handshake. Hell, he'd been surprised by the whole package. It wasn't often that he met a girl that was almost as tall as he, had more pronounced biceps than most guys, and looked like she could kick some serious ass.

Catching a glimpse of her impressive cleavage as she bent down to scoop rice onto her plate, his eyes got stuck staring, and he salivated a little.

She was so damn hot...

"Eyes up here, kid!" She pointed with two fingers at her clear blue eyes.

His ears heating up in embarrassment, he quickly lifted his eyes to her face.

Up close, Kri was very pretty.

Her smooth, creamy skin was clean of makeup, and the peach shade of her full lips was all her own. A few wayward strands escaped the thick braid of her wavy, light-brown hair, or dark blond, he wasn't sure what to call it, softening the tough impression of her tall, muscular build.

She was tough, but she didn't look any older than he was. So why the hell was she calling him "kid?" Maybe she thought he was younger than he actually was. Not that he could blame her for the misconception, not after the way he stared at her breasts. Like he was some stupid teenager who had never seen boobs before. Well, he hadn't, not like hers. Kri's belonged on a sculpture.

"Sorry, my bad." Michael looked down, busying himself with loading rice and stew onto his plate.

"Nah, it's okay. I get that reaction all the time. Apparently, guys do not expect such a lovely set of double Ds on an athletic female like me." She cupped the bottoms of her breasts, hefting them up for emphasis.

Michael almost choked on a mouthful of rice, spewing some of it out across the tray and spraying it all over their food. Some of it ended up going down the wrong pipe. He coughed, trying to get it out.

Kri's powerful pat on his back didn't help much with the coughing, sending his whole upper body in the same direction instead.

"Stop… please… I'm okay… really…" Michael coughed out the few remaining grains of rice. He'd made a mess of things, but that didn't mean that he deserved broken ribs. The girl was freakishly strong.

"I'm so sorry that I've ruined your lunch. I'm such a klutz…" He looked at the rice-sprinkled food. What the hell was he supposed to do now?

"Don't worry about it. I'm not some delicate, dainty doll. I'll eat it if you will." She took another forkful from her plate, chewing deliberately to make her point.

She certainly wasn't dainty… or girly… or like any other woman he had ever met. His first impression of her just got reinforced. She was a hot, strong, no-nonsense warrior chick.

"Are you married?" he asked, hoping she wasn't.

"Why would it be any of your damn business?"

"Because short of a husband, I don't care who I have to fight for you. You're amazing."

Now it was Kri's turn to do the whole choking, spewing, spraying routine, and Michael offered the back patting.

"You're joking, right?" she finally croaked. "You got me good for my boob stunt, didn't you?" She laughed, slapping his shoulder. Hard.

"Yeah, it was a joke… But no, it wasn't revenge. I meant it as a compliment. I like your style. You're a Guardian, right?"

"What do you know about Guardians?" She narrowed her eyes.

"Yamanu spent some of the morning keeping me company, then Arwel showed up with the beers and the chips. We watched some, played some, talked some. They told me some stuff. I know that they are Guardians, a kind of internal police for your people. Last night I got to see them in action, kicking some serious Doomer ass. It was ████████ epic. If I turn, I definitely want in. Yamanu thinks I have what it takes, so does Arwel." Michael pushed out his chest and squared his shoulders, looking at Kri for affirmation.

Chuckling, she patted his shoulder, gently this time. "We'll see about that. First, you need to turn, and there is no guarantee you will. And then it takes years of training. It's not an easy path. Before deciding that you want to sign up for this kind of life, you need to be sure you want it above all else."

He shrugged. "If I have what it takes then I want in. The way the guys talk about it, it's obvious that they love what they do."

"So, what did they tell you about me?" Her lips pressed into a thin line and she narrowed her eyes again, evidently expecting some snide comments from the guys.

"Nothing, they didn't mention you at all. It's just that you look like a soldier, move and talk like one too. A mighty Amazon warrior..." Michael demonstrated, flexing his biceps.

By the smug look of satisfaction on her face, Kri took it as the compliment he'd intended. "Good. Even though they are well aware of my amazing skills, they still treat me as if I'm a little girl they need to protect. I hate it."

"Maybe it's because you're the youngest recruit?" He understood her frustration, but he also understood the guys. He would've been protective of her as well, even though she seemed perfectly capable of taking care of herself. It was something that was hardwired into his psyche.

"That's part of it, but I'm sure the old timers still think that a girl can't do what a guy can."

Michael knew he was treading on thin ice, but for some reason he felt like he needed to explain the guys' reasoning. He didn't want her to be angry at them, because he didn't want her to be angry at him for thinking the same thing. "I'm sure you are stronger and more capable than most guys, and in a situation where it's you and some average Joe against some thugs, you'll do better. But faced with the same situation with a male Guardian by your side, who is at least as well trained as you are, he will do better for the simple reason of having more muscle power. So the same way you feel protective of those who are not as strong as you are, the guys are protective of you."

She pinned him with a hard stare. "I know. Doesn't mean I have to like it. Eat your lunch, kid, before it gets cold so you can grow and become a big, strong, male Guardian." Kri sat down to polish off her plate.

Great, she was pissed.

Idiot, you should've kept your mouth shut.

CHAPTER 22: KRI

It wasn't his fault, and Kri shouldn't have felt angry, but it was a sore point with her. She trained harder than any of the guys, was faster than most of them and more flexible, which she believed compensated for her lesser muscle power.

She could hold her own.

The thing was, none of the men had ever gone at her the same way they'd gone at each other. So how the hell was she supposed to know if she could handle an opponent as strong as a Guardian if they never gave her a chance?

Couldn't they get it through their thick male skulls that they weren't doing her any favors? What would happen when she faced a Doomer? Would he take it easy on her as well? Not likely.

It might not have been Michael's fault, but she was going to take it out of his hide anyway.

"How about a game of Black Ops?"

He arched a brow. "You play?"

"You bet your ass, I do. And I'm going to show you how it's done."

Michael snorted. "Not likely. I beat all of my friends hands down."

"Prepare to lose, kid."

"Let's do it."

As she'd expected, he held back for a little while, probably thinking that he'd let her win a few rounds before he obliterated her, so she wouldn't feel too bad about it. But as she kept winning round after round, the kid began taking her seriously.

"Damn, you're good."

"Told you."

By the time she called the game over, there was a sheen of sweat on his forehead.

"It was fun." Kri patted Michael's shoulder. "You're good, kid. Just not good enough." She winked.

"Yeah, it was. Though next time, I'll be ready for you, and your ass will be mine... Sorry, it came out all wrong... You know what I meant... in the game."

"Aha, sure, whatever you say. I'll come back tomorrow. Be ready." She pointed a finger at him.

Pushing up to her feet, Kri picked up the tray of dirty dishes and headed for the door. Then caught him checking her ass as she turned to say goodbye.

Well, what do you know… Kri smirked. Walking out, she gave him a nice, exaggerated saunter to admire.

Cute. Obviously, he was into her. But was she into him?

Nah, he was still a pup; handsome, eager, but too young.

Maybe… She shrugged.

He was a nice kid.

Michael was young and fresh, and his eyes were still hopeful, innocent, still excited about life, so different from the jaded expressions of her companions—of Kian's. Old eyes that had known too much, had seen too much—the spark of excitement extinguished long ago.

Or perhaps, the only reason the boy had piqued her interest was because he was there? A male she was not related to?

She had been pining for Kian since she had been a little girl—long before she had reached the appropriate age for her mother to explain that clan members were forbidden to each other. But by then it had been too late. She had developed a crush and it wouldn't go away no matter how many hookups she tried to distract herself with. None of those guys interested her beyond what it took to seduce them. Once her lust was sated, she felt nothing.

But Michael had managed to stir something inside her.

Maybe… She smiled. It was a definite maybe.

CHAPTER 23: SYSSI

Out on the terrace, Syssi stubbed out her cigarette in the ashtray and seriously contemplated lighting another one. What she'd hoped would be a relaxing experience had unexpectedly turned into nothing but.

The trouble with having a vivid full-color imagination was that it had hijacked her memories, turning them into a stream of X-rated scenes that had been no fun to watch by herself.

And as hard as she'd tried to think about something, anything else, it had been as effective as resisting the pull of a black hole.

Syssi ran a shaky hand over her prone body, wishing Kian would be back already, so she could bite his head off not only for abandoning her with no means of communication, but for turning her into a sex addict as well.

Yeah, it was that bad.

She needed a distraction.

With Okidu gone, she could commandeer his kitchen and make lunch. If she prepared something complicated, it would keep her busy for at least an hour.

The butler would be mad as hell, but she could feign innocence and claim she didn't know kitchen access was restricted.

Her Nana's lasagna recipe was the only fancy dish Syssi knew off the top of her head. It was delicious, unique, and labor-intensive. She hardly ever made it because it involved too many pots and pans that she later needed to clean, and it took over an hour to make. Perfect.

Hopefully, Okidu kept his kitchen well stocked and had all the ingredients she needed.

As she stepped inside, Syssi turned to close the sliding door panels behind her, and it wasn't until she turned back that she realized she had company.

Sitting on the living room's couch, Anandur and Brundar were eyeing her with matching smug smirks.

Just peachy.

They must've witnessed her little adventure with the cigarette, and were now giving her their version of the hairy eyeball.

I'm being ridiculous... acting as if smoking was a criminal activity. Although as shunned and ostracized as it was, she probably wasn't the only one made to feel like a felon for lighting up.

"Hi, guys, I'm afraid Kian is not back yet." She smiled politely, though in truth, she wanted them to leave, so she could run to the bathroom and get rid of the smelly evidence before Kian showed up.

A toothbrush and plenty of perfume were in order.

"And hello to you too, pretty lady." Pushing up to his feet, Anandur uncoiled his massive bulk from the couch and took hold of her hand, planting a kiss on the back of it.

In a perfunctory bow, Brundar lifted slightly off the sofa.

"We'll wait for him," Anandur whispered, looking both ways as if letting her in on a conspiracy. "You see, Syssi... we are here to mooch off Okidu's cooking. He'll be serving lunch soon... Shh..." He winked. "Don't tell anyone..."

If that were the real reason for them sitting uninvited in Kian's living room, she could get rid of them easily. "Okidu isn't here, and there is no lunch."

Anandur smirked. "Not yet, but there will be. I bet he will walk in any minute now, carrying a huge tray. There is no way Okidu wouldn't have lunch ready for Kian. At half past twelve, like clockwork. That's how we knew exactly when to show up."

"I see," she said. "And I guess Kian is not too happy about you guys joining him?"

"Nope, but we don't care. Okidu's cooking is worth the pain of Kian's ranting and raving."

"What if he kicks you out?"

"He hasn't yet—and my brother and I have been pulling this stunt for years."

Unfortunately, it seemed there was no getting rid of them. The good news was that Kian would be back soon for his lunch. Glancing at her watch, Syssi estimated she had another twenty minutes or so until lunch time, but there was a chance he would come home earlier, which meant she should hurry up and cover the cigarette stink.

"Okay then, I'll leave you boys here and go freshen up, I'll be back in a jiffy."

Feeling awkward, Syssi headed for her room. It had been on the tip of her tongue to offer them refreshments while they waited, but it had seemed inappropriate. She was even more of an interloper in Kian's home than they were, and it wasn't her place to offer them anything other than her company. Besides, if it weren't outright rude, she would've preferred to avoid entertaining them as well. Right now, the only company she wanted was Kian's. Though she wasn't sure what she wanted to do first; clobber him over the head with a frying pan, or jump his bones.

CHAPTER 24: ANANDUR

"Did you smell that?" Putting on a lecherous smile, Anandur turned to Brundar as soon as he heard the door closing behind Syssi. "My favorite bouquet; a female in need of shagging."

Brundar shrugged, ignoring him, but Anandur knew his brother well enough to know he hadn't been unaffected. Hell, no male immortal could've remained indifferent to a powerful attractant like that.

"Which of us do you think it was for?"

"Neither, you dimwit, I smelled it as soon as she slid the doors open—before she even noticed we were here."

Anandur smirked. Brundar saying two whole sentences, or even bothering to answer his taunt in the first place, was a clear sign that he'd been right. His brother had been just as affected by the irresistible call of the female's arousal.

"So what, you think someone parachuted onto the terrace and turned the heat on? No one can come up here. Unless it was another Guardian."

"How the hell should I know? Maybe she was having phone sex with her boyfriend, or watching porn."

Man, this is going to be fun... "Did you see a phone anywhere on her? With those painted-on jeans, and a white, thin T-shirt I could see her bra through. She couldn't have been hiding a tube of lipstick. And she wasn't holding anything in her hands either."

"Maybe she left it outside. Could we please drop the subject? It makes me uncomfortable." Brundar wiggled, adjusting his pants.

"I still think it was for me." Anandur kept pushing.

"You think every female has the hots for you—you arrogant bastard."

Brundar's normally stoic face was getting red. One more push and he would snap.

"Because they do... son of my mother but not my father. And as you are well aware, we are all bastards in this big happy family. Some of us are just sexier than others, and you're jealous." Anandur ran his hands over his big body and began singing and undulating his hips to the tune of "I'm Sexy and I Know It..." Until the throw pillow that Brundar chucked at him smacked him in the face, shutting him up.

For a moment.

CHAPTER 25: SYSSI

Back from the bathroom, Syssi sat across from the brothers, fidgeting with her bracelet in the uncomfortable silence. For some unfathomable reason, the guys seemed antsy, with Anandur alternating between scratching his beard and the back of his head, and Brundar crossing and recrossing his feet at his ankles.

Both were regarding her as if they were waiting for her to do or say something.

"Did you leave your phone outside, Syssi?" Anandur finally spoke, his eyes darting for a split second to his brother.

"No, why?" she asked, puzzled.

"I thought I heard you talking to someone on the terrace, and as there was no phone in your hands when you came back in, I assumed you left it out there." Anandur wasn't even trying to conceal the smirking glance he shot at Brundar as if saying I-told-you-so. And when Brundar rolled his eyes in response, he confirmed her suspicion.

What the heck was all this about? Was it the cigarette? Syssi got pissed. "Okay, so you caught me. I had a smoke outside. Big deal!"

"Must have been one hell of a cigarette. I wouldn't mind having one myself, love…" Anandur chuckled.

"I don't know what you mean, but be my guest. They are Kian's anyway. He left them there." She motioned toward the terrace.

"Kian's… I see… No, thank you, Syssi, I'm not into that brand." Anandur turned to Brundar, who nodded his head in agreement with a little knowing smile blooming on his austere face.

Why did she feel as if they were having two separate conversations? An overt one she was having with Anandur and a covert one between the brothers.

"What's going on, guys? Are we talking about the same thing here?"

"I don't know what you mean."

Anandur's feigned innocence didn't impress her at all. What's more, he was too… something she couldn't put her finger on. Too cocky? Too happy with himself?

Without Kian around to keep him in check, she had a feeling the guy would start flirting with her, which would put her in the uncomfortable situation of having to tell him no thank you. Anandur was a good looking guy, and she had no doubt he had no lack of female attention, but a rejection was a rejection and she hated causing anyone unnecessary hurt feelings. The best strategy was to avoid the situation in the first place.

"It seems Okidu is a no-show. I think I'll go to the kitchen and start working on the lasagna I'd been planning to make before you guys showed up." Syssi pushed up from her chair. She would pretend to be getting ready while waiting for Okidu or Kian to get back. In the meantime, she could munch on whatever Okidu had left in the fridge for her.

Pushing off the couch, Anandur got in her face and gripped her hands. "I'm sure Okidu wouldn't want you working in his kitchen. A beautiful woman such as yourself should be kept pampered and spoiled, and her delicate hands kept safely away from the hazards of hot pots and sharp cooking utensils." He lifted her hands and kissed the back of each one before letting her pull them out of his grip.

Shit, it was exactly what she'd been afraid of. Without Kian around, Anandur was allowing himself to get too friendly.

She was about to give him the only friends speech when Kian's icy tone took them all by surprise.

"Oh, really? I wasn't aware that you had experience keeping beautiful women, your usual fare being more of the disposable kind."

Syssi had no idea where he had come from. They had been sitting in the living room this whole time, in full view of the front door. "Oh, hi, Kian, I'm so glad you're back. I told the guys you weren't home."

"Right." Kian lowered the tray he'd been carrying onto the counter and wiped his hands on a dish towel.

He hadn't smiled at her, hadn't even said hello. The guy was so mercurial. "Is there another entrance to the penthouse? I didn't see you come in."

"Obviously," he barked back.

What is his problem? Kian looked furious, his tone sarcastic and accusatory.

Anandur took a step back away from her. "Hi, Boss. We just got here. And we found the lovely lady waiting for you. She was really disappointed it was us, and not you. I told her we came for Okidu's cooking, nothing else."

Whatever Anandur was trying to hint on was falling on deaf ears. Kian wasn't paying attention to a word that left Anandur's mouth. Holding his fists tight by his sides, he looked like he was a breath away from pounding Anandur's face into a pulp.

Syssi held her breath, waiting for Kian to release the punch that would come smashing into Anandur's face. Kian's anger and barely contained aggression was frightening.

"Yeah, it's like he said. We got here, and here she was like that..." Brundar was obviously trying to communicate something to Kian and avert the brewing storm by backing his brother.

But why? What was he so angry about?

It must've had something to do with her; both brothers were acting as if Kian had caught them with their hands in the cookie jar, or rather the bone stash—cowering before the alpha dog and crawling on their bellies.

Was this about Anandur's flirting? That little thing?

It was ridiculous.

It was insulting.

It reminded her of Gregg.

Fits of ungrounded, irrational jealousy—she was well acquainted with those.

Any man glancing her way had been a suspect. Any guy she had happened to mention, regardless of the context, had been a suspect as well. It had been even worse than the constant complaining because his accusations implied that on top of what he had perceived to be her many other flaws, he had also deemed her untrustworthy.

For Syssi, it was a deal breaker.

Overcome by bitter disappointment, she felt the bile rise up in her throat. Her Prince Charming, the man that had rocked her world only the night before, had just turned into a slimy toad.

Ugh!

Talk about naiveté...

"You boys go on playing your wolf-pack power games and growl at each other's throats to your hearts' content. I'm out of here."

Turning away and marching to her room without looking back, Syssi hoped she'd sounded as disgusted as she'd felt. In truth, though, she was fighting back tears.

The last thing she wanted was for Kian to see her cry and realize he had disappointed her. Because it would imply that she'd entertained unwarranted expectations. After all, for Kian she was probably nothing more than a convenient lay, and an easy one at that.

A woman he believed would jump on any attractive pair of pants that crossed her way.

CHAPTER 26: BRUNDAR

Brundar cringed. Kian looked like he was hanging by a thread, and if he snapped... well... it was hard to tell who would have the upper hand in this fight. Though Brundar had a strong suspicion, it wouldn't be his brother.

Coming up in the service elevator with Okidu, Kian was helping the butler bring lunch up from the basement kitchen. He must've smelled the girl's arousal as soon as its door opened. Her scent was sure potent enough to overpower even the strong aroma of the freshly cooked food. Then walking in on the big jerk flirting with Syssi, he surmised what had gotten her so aroused, or rather who.

"Get the hell out!" Kian barked at Anandur as he whipped around to follow Syssi.

"Don't be a jerk, Kian, it had nothing to do with us. She came in after smoking outside and that scent was already there..." Anandur tried to explain.

Turning his head with just a slight twist of his torso, Kian pointed his finger at Anandur, staring him down. "If I ever catch you flirting with her again or even looking at her with anything other than courtesy and respect, I'm going to pound the living daylights out of you. Are we clear?"

"Crystal!"

"Good! Now, get out of here before I change my mind and beat the hell out of you just to make sure you got it!"

"Yes, Boss!" Anandur dipped his head and headed for the front door.

Behind him, Brundar threw an apologetic glance at Kian before following his brother out.

It wasn't really Anandur's fault. How were they supposed to know Kian felt so possessive about Syssi? It wasn't as if he'd ever acted this way before. There was no way for them to recognize the signs.

Although thinking back, they should have.

The way he had been frantic to get to her before the Doomers had. The way he'd snapped at Anandur and him for checking her out. Staying at the hotel with her though keeping his distance. It had been more than a simple concern for a mere acquaintance that he happened to like.

Standing next to his brother as they waited for the elevator to come up, Brundar accused, "You really did it this time."

"What? You were just as surprised as I was that he called dibs on her."

"Yeah, but you kept on going even after we figured it out."

"I know... Just couldn't help myself. You know how I get." Anandur shrugged. "No big deal. He'll get over it. You know how Kian gets all worked up. And anyway, he couldn't have done any serious damage to me even if he tried." Anandur stretched to his full height and pushed his massive chest out.

"You're so full of crap." Brundar shook his head, doubting Anandur had it right. Kian wasn't as big and didn't seem as strong physically, but he was, after all, Annani's son.

A direct descendant of the gods.

CHAPTER 27: KIAN

Rushing after Syssi, Kian reached her room in a few long strides. But then, standing in front of her door, he hesitated before knocking.

Not because he sensed she was angry, that would've been fine. He could've dealt with that. But because the dark scent reaching his nose was laced with disappointment and regret.

Crap ~~Shit~~! Can you say overreact?

What had gotten into him?

When the elevator's door had opened, the scent of Syssi's arousal had hit him head-on, making him instantly hard. With a big grin spreading across his face, he marched toward the siren call of Syssi's aroma, passing through the kitchen with the tray he had been carrying. But then, hearing Anandur's come-on lines and realizing what had gotten Syssi so aroused, or rather who, he had been gripped by intense jealousy. He dropped the tray on the kitchen counter and turned around.

Blinded by fury, Kian strained the limits of his hard-won self-control, keeping himself from leaping at Anandur and ripping the jerk apart. Or maybe it had been the nagging feeling in the back of his mind that there was no way a girl like Syssi could've been attracted to Anandur.

Even if the guy was known as an irresistible female magnet.

If nothing else, the way she had stormed off had convinced him that he had gotten the situation all wrong.

Way to go, asshole... Kian felt like banging his head on the closed door.

He had to fix this somehow. The prospect of Syssi looking at him with anything other than her sweet, wide-eyed adoration was killing him.

Rapping his knuckles on the door, he probed, "May I come in?" hating that he sounded like a wayward child begging for forgiveness. But then, if it came down to that, he knew he would beg—on his knees if that were what it took. And it pissed him off that he found himself needing to apologize.

Again.

It wasn't something he found easy to do. Truth be told, even when an apology was in order, he rarely did. Maybe it was a personality flaw.

~~No~~ *maybe!*

It was a flaw.

Each time he had been forced to make amends, getting the words out had felt like chewing on shrapnel.

CHAPTER 28: SYSSI

As she stuffed her few possessions into her travel bag, Syssi's anger gave way to disappointment. She was forced to recognize her mistake for what it was.

She shouldn't have come here in the first place, and definitely shouldn't have stayed with Kian at his home. She knew next to nothing about him. And evidently, being great in bed did not equate to him being a nice guy. Trouble was, she had chosen to trust him when she should've been more careful and guarded.

It appeared that contrary to the way she saw herself, she was still naive.

Damn Kian for giving her a beautiful illusion and then shattering it. Except, she had only herself to blame.

Stupid! She was so bloody stupid!

Kian's rap on the door came too soon, and she wanted to tell him to go away.

She didn't want to face him, or the drama that was sure to follow when he'd see that she was packing to leave. But something in his voice tugged at her stupid soft heart, and she invited him in. "Sure, it's your home…" And anyway, she figured refusing to talk to him would only postpone the inevitable.

"Why are you packing?" Kian pointed at the bag the moment he stepped in, his angry face belying his apologetic tone from a moment before.

Well, surprise, surprise. That's what she got for being a softie…

"It was a bad idea for me to come here. I should've stayed at my brother's. I would've been just as safe with him as I am here," she said in a flat tone that could've made Queen Amidala from *Star Wars* proud, while pretending to rearrange her bag so she wouldn't have to look at Kian.

It was all a front, though, and on the inside she was falling apart, struggling to keep breathing through the choking in her throat. Berating her own stupidity for making what was nothing more than a tryst into something meaningful, she was trying to reignite her anger in order to fortify her resolve.

I'm such a girl, she thought, *tearing and choking instead of lashing out and giving him a piece of my mind.*

But what would've been the point?

The disappointment would still be there, and venting her anger would not make that sour feeling go away.

He was who he was, and not who she wished him to be, and that didn't give her the right to penalize him. Only to walk away.

"I'm sorry." He surprised her. "Please don't go."

She lifted her head from where she was bending over the bed and turned to look at his pleading eyes.

He had gotten her attention.

Not making demands or pounding his chest with his protector routine, he had said the only thing that had any chance of changing her mind.

With a sigh, she sat on the messed up bed and faced him. "Do you even know what you're apologizing for? Or is it a blanket statement meant to absolve you of whatever I might find objectionable?"

It had crossed her mind that he might be clueless as to what had offended her, and she had no intention of making it easy for him.

"I don't know what came over me. I felt this insane surge of jealousy... It never happened to me before, and I didn't know how to deal with it. I'm sorry if I acted like a jerk..." He pinched his forehead between two fingers. "And for being rude," he tacked on.

"Why?"

"Why was I rude? Because I'm an uncouth brute? What do you want me to say?"

Yep, clueless.

"Why were you jealous?"

"Isn't it obvious? Anandur was flirting with you, and the big oaf has a reputation as an irresistible ladies' man..." Kian rolled his eyes. "And you seemed to like him. A lot... That incredible smell you gave off—" He stopped mid-sentence.

Looking up at Kian, Syssi felt profound sadness. He had no idea that it wasn't his rude behavior that had hurt her, but his misguided belief that there was anything to be jealous about.

"What?" Seeing her resigned expression he raised his hands in defeat.

"Don't you get it? How offensive and degrading it feels? Your lack of trust in me? Your belief that I might be tempted by any attractive man that passes my way? Like some floozy? Maybe you have some justification to feel this way; as it sure as hell didn't take you long to get me in your bed. But rest assured it's not something I often do, or ever…" Unable to hold back the tears anymore, she felt them slide down her cheeks. It took all her willpower just to stifle the sobs that were stuck in her throat and pushing to get out.

"Oh, sweet girl…" Kian dropped to his knees in front of her and hugged her to him tightly. Stroking her hair, he pulled her head to rest in the crook of his neck. "I'm so sorry, baby. If it's any consolation… I wasn't thinking rationally at all. It was pure animal instinct. If I had stopped to think for a moment, I might've realized how stupid I was. Can you forgive me? Chuck it to 'the-clueless-male-defense-plea'? Please?"

"I don't know…," she croaked, smiling behind the tears that were wetting his skin.

Shaking her head, she couldn't believe she was contemplating giving him another chance. But the feel of him, and dear God… his scent… were scrambling her brain.

"What's going on?" Amanda said from the doorway. "What did you do to the poor girl?"

Walking in, she sat on the bed next to Syssi and pushed Kian away. Then tugged on Syssi's shoulders to bring her into her own arms.

"What did this meanie do to you?" Amanda patted Syssi's hand while glaring daggers at Kian.

"Nothing, I just need some time to figure things out. I need to call Andrew. If he calls and does not get a hold of me, he is going to freak out."

Syssi looked at Amanda, beseeching her with her eyes to stop the questioning. They could have a girls' talk later. As it was, letting Kian glimpse her vulnerable underbelly, she was already feeling too exposed.

CHAPTER 29: KIAN

Glaring at Amanda, Kian was infuriated with her for poking her nose where it didn't belong. This intrusion on his privacy was becoming intolerable. "Go home, Amanda. Everything is under control," he dismissed her, trying to pull Syssi back. Amanda didn't let go, though, and the tug of war was becoming ridiculous.

"Yeah, I can definitely see that. Crying girl and all... Syssi, would you like to stay with me for a while? It's only across the hallway, but I promise you it's way more fun than here... We can do each other's nails and gossip about Kian... Play with makeup and trash talk Kian... You know, all the fun things we girls do."

He hated to admit it, but Amanda's attempts to cheer Syssi up were working. She chuckled and dried her tears with the comforter, thankfully ignoring his furious expression that had nothing to do with her and was directed at Amanda, who couldn't care less.

"Thanks, I would love to. I think the last time I had a sleepover at a girlfriend's house was in middle school."

Pretending to be excited by Amanda's invitation, Syssi was putting on a good show. Except, he wasn't sure who she was trying to convince: them or herself. But he wasn't fooled. She looked as if she would do just about anything to get out of there as quickly as she could, and Amanda's offer just provided her with a convenient excuse.

As if to prove him right, she got off the bed and shoved whatever was still strewn about into her duffel bag. "I'm good to go. Packed and everything." She slung it over her shoulder and headed for the door.

He just couldn't let her go like that. Not without setting things right between them first. But as he reached for Syssi's arm to stop her, he felt Amanda's hand on his shoulder.

She shook her head at him. "Syssi needs some space. Let her go," she whispered so quietly only he heard her.

Nodding reluctantly, he let Syssi pass and followed them to the front door.

"I'll see you later." Syssi said her goodbye with a slight tilt of her head, without even looking at his face.

"Don't worry. I'll take good care of her," Amanda mouthed before shutting the door behind them.

Standing at the threshold of his apartment, Kian looked at Amanda's closed door. Just a few steps across the vestibule, it was so near, and yet as far as his welcome went it might have been in a different zip code.

Sighing, he stepped back inside and closed the door, then headed for the kitchen to eat his lunch by himself.

Alone, sitting at the counter, the irony of his situation was not lost on him. Finally, he got his wish and none of his relatives were there to bother him.

So why did he feel like shit?

CHAPTER 30: SYSSI

Amanda's place was a mirror image of Kian's. Same layout, same placement of furniture—the decor and colors a slight variation on the same theme. Clearly, both apartments were done by the same interior designer.

"Come on, sweetie, I'll show you to your room." Amanda led the way down the corridor and opened a door to the left. "Just drop your bag on the floor. Let's go and have something to eat. I can hear your belly rumbling from here." Throwing her arm around Syssi's shoulders, she turned on her heel and walked her toward the open terrace doors.

"Onidu, honey, we have a guest. Would you be a dear and serve us lunch on the terrace?" Amanda called out before stepping outside. "It's such a beautiful day. The sun is out but it's not too hot." She pulled out a chair for Syssi and sat down across from her.

"Onidu? Is he related to Okidu?" Syssi asked.

"Yes, my darling butler is the same as Kian's; a present from our mother."

Perplexed by Amanda's peculiar choice of words, Syssi asked, "Your mother gave you butlers as presents?"

Amanda smiled and waved her hand dismissively. "It didn't come out right. You see, the Odus were trusted members of her own staff for years, and she wanted her kids to be well taken care of by someone she could count on. So she assigned one to each of us. I grew up with Onidu as my companion, and when I left home, naturally, he had to come with me. Without him, I'd be a complete mess. He does everything for me. And he keeps me safe. Don't you, sweetheart?" She smiled at her butler as he arrived with the tray of food.

"Whatever you say, mistress." Onidu bowed before placing the tray on the glass table.

"Wow, they look like twins." Syssi glanced at Onidu's retreating back. Both men had similar height and build with just slightly different hair and eye color. "Are they brothers? And by the way, do you and Kian have more siblings? You said each one... sounded like more than just the two of you."

"We have two more sisters. And about the Odus... yeah, it's kind of obvious that they come from the same stock." Amanda lifted her sandwich with both hands and took a bite.

"Older? Younger?"

"Who? The Odus?

"No, silly, your sisters, you never mentioned them before. I'm curious."

"Older, I'm the baby. Alena is the oldest, Kian is next, then Sari."

"And…?"

"And what?"

"Where are they? Where do they live? What do they do?"

"Alena stays with our mother, and Sari is in Europe, heading the family business over there."

"And your father? Is he still around?"

"No, he passed away a long time ago."

"I'm so sorry to hear that." Syssi lowered her eyes. She knew how hard it was to talk about a lost loved one. Sighing, she took a forkful of the delicious apple crumble Onidu had served for dessert.

"Nothing to be sorry about. I never met him, so I couldn't really feel sorrow at his passing." Amanda shrugged, a shadow darkening her expression.

"Did he die before you were born?" It was so unlike Syssi to be asking all these personal questions. Still, she felt compelled to keep it up and find out more about Kian and his family.

"No, but it wasn't the poor schmuck's fault either. He didn't even know I existed. Mother had never told him. And I never got to meet him."

"How about Kian and your other sisters' father, did your mother divorce him? Or did he pass away as well?" Syssi made the logical assumption that Amanda had been a love child, arriving later in her mother's life.

Amanda paused with her sandwich suspended in front of her face. A moment of contemplation later, she sighed and lowered the thing back to the plate. "Fathers, as in plural. We each have a different father, and not one was married to our mother or informed of becoming a father." Amanda picked up her sandwich and took another bite.

Uncomfortable, Syssi looked down at her hands. That was somewhat unorthodox, but who was she to judge someone else's choices in life?

To each her or his own.

Life's twists and turns made for different paths for different people. She wondered, however, what was the story behind this one. "It must have been hard for your mother to raise four kids on her own. Not financially, as it seems she didn't suffer for a lack of means, having a staff of servants and all. But why did she choose to do it this way. Didn't she love any of the men?"

Amanda wiped her hands on the napkin before dabbing it at her lips. "She was married once when she was very young and deeply in love. When her husband died, she vowed to remain faithful to him in her heart and never love another man again. But she wanted children, and she loved sex, so here we are."

Amanda smiled her radiant smile, but then her eyes narrowed with a wicked gleam. "Speaking of sex... You and Kian?" She arched one of her perfectly shaped brows in question. And yet, judging from her smug expression, she had already known the answer to that.

Syssi almost choked on a mouthful of cake, feeling a blush spread all the way up to the roots of her hair as she swallowed it. "He's your brother, for God's sake, how can you ask me that?"

"Oh, please. We are all adults here. If I can talk about my mother's sex life, you think Kian's is off limits?" Amanda laughed. "There is nothing to be bashful about. Remember who you're talking to; the self-proclaimed queen of sluts." She pointed at herself. "And proud of it."

"Yes... happy?" Syssi blurted and immediately dropped her eyes to her plate.

"Ecstatic!... But what did the stupid goat do to make you cry? And don't you dare try covering up for him." Amanda crossed her arms over her chest, waiting. "Well?"

Syssi sighed and folded her napkin, smoothing it next to her plate. "Anandur and Brundar showed up for lunch when Kian wasn't there, and when he came back and saw them with me, he went bonkers, threw a jealous tantrum and kicked them out." She shrugged as if the whole thing hadn't been a big deal.

"That's all? That's what got you so upset? I think it's sweet that he got jealous over you. That means he cares for you. What's wrong with that?"

"It's disrespectful to me, don't you think? Assuming I'd even show interest in another man after spending the night with Kian. He made me feel cheap, like he thought I was some kind of floozy." Cue the quivering chin.

"Oh, sweetie, I forgot how inexperienced you are with men. You assume that he was thinking and analyzing what was going on because women overthink everything. Men don't. He went ape-man territorial when he found another virile male sniffing around his female and felt threatened. If anything, it shows his own insecurities, not his opinion of you."

"Look who's covering for Kian now. I thought I was the one who was expected to do that." Syssi filled her cup from the steaming pot of coffee and stirred in the cream and sugar. "And the fact that I only had one boyfriend doesn't make me inexperienced. Well, maybe variety-wise it does... But be that as it may, Gregg and I were together for four years, during which I got my share of irrational, unfounded accusations. In the beginning, I dismissed them the same way you just did, feeling flattered. But believe me, after a while I got so sick of them, I felt like he was pounding another nail into the coffin of our relationship with each new onslaught. Kian's behavior today was a very unpleasant déjà vu. It made me want to throw up." Syssi pretended to gag, and sticking out her tongue, made a face like she was about to puke.

Amanda didn't respond for a while. Sipping on her coffee, she picked apple-crumble crumbs off her plate and placed the tiny bits on her tongue one at the time.

"Are you sure it's the same? Maybe you're just projecting your ex on Kian. Knowing Anandur's antics, he was probably flirting with you shamelessly, so the jealousy wasn't completely unfounded. Am I right?" she asked.

"So what if he was flirting. I wasn't responding to him or anything!"

A flash of understanding crossed Amanda's eyes. "Were you thinking naughty thoughts about Kian before the guys came in?" She looked pointedly at Syssi.

Her cheeks began burning again, and the heat was spreading all the way to her earlobes. "So what if I did? What does that have to do with anything?" How on earth could Amanda have known that?

With a wide grin spreading over her face, Amanda lifted her hands as if it was self-explanatory. "It has everything to do with it... I'll run by you the scenario from Kian's point of view. He walks in, sees you all flustered from your earlier carnal musings, while Anandur is putting his moves on you. Reaches the wrong conclusion, thinking your arousal is the other guy's doing, gets crazy jealous... Sounds plausible?"

"How would he know I was... you know...?"

"You have a very expressive face, and Kian is very perceptive."

Was he? Syssi didn't notice that about him. In fact, he was just as oblivious as the next guy. "Even if you're right, he still should have known better."

"Oh, really? Picture the same scenario with different players. You walk in, Kian is in the company of two gorgeous women, one of them flirting with him unabashedly, and a hard-on is tenting his pants. Would you be all smiling and thinking rationally? Or would you want to strangle all three of them?"

"I wouldn't get physical... Just imagine it... Very, very, vividly..." Syssi chuckled. "Okay, you made your point. I forgive him. But I'm not going back to his place. You promised me a sleepover and I'm holding you to it."

"I wouldn't let you go even if you begged, you're all mine for tonight. We are going to go out, and we are going to party hard. I need to teach you how to live a little."

"Fine. But first I need to call Andrew and let him know I'm okay, and that I'm staying with you. Maybe he can even help us in some way. After all, he deals with these kinds of situations in his line of work. I told you he used to be Special Ops, didn't I?"

"No, you didn't. How fascinating... And now that you did, I want to meet him. Can you introduce us? I have a thing for dangerous boys... grr..." Amanda did her cougar imitation, growling and swiping the air with pretend claws.

Syssi laughed. "I wouldn't call him a boy. Andrew is pushing forty. But sure, I would love to introduce you guys." Then getting serious, she added, "I think tomorrow I'll go to his place. I should have done it from the start, instead of coming here. But everything happened so fast, and Kian kind of took control of everything and it was easy to just let him. He managed to convince me that I would be putting Andrew in danger if I go to stay with him, but the more I think about it the more ridiculous it sounds."

Amanda frowned. "I trust that Kian knows what he is talking about. You shouldn't dismiss what he said. If he thinks it's not safe for you to stay with your brother then he is probably right."

Unless he is lying about it to keep me here.

"I think it would be better for everyone if I kept my distance. We got too close too fast. It cannot be healthy for a new relationship. If it is a relationship... Shit! I don't know what to think." Syssi ran her fingers through her hair.

"Is Andrew listed as your next of kin anywhere?" Amanda suddenly looked worried.

"No, because of his job I couldn't. I listed my parents. Why?"

"It's a remote chance, but if they can't get you they might decide to go after other family members. Special abilities sometimes run in families. Any other siblings?"

"No... my other brother died four years ago in a motorcycle accident." Syssi tried to swallow as her throat convulsed with the familiar choking sensation.

"I'm so sorry, sweetie. How about your parents? Still in Africa?"

"Yeah, still there."

"Good. I don't think the lunatics will venture that far."

Looking down at her plate, Syssi chased the scattered crumbs of cake with her fork, struggling to regain her composure. "What are the police doing about this mess, did you check with them?" she asked.

"They took pictures of the damage at the lab, but they're not taking the incident seriously. They're convinced it was a prank. Drunk students, maybe someone who got a bad grade. I don't think they are going to do anything about it."

"Did you tell them about the people chasing after us? They should investigate that group."

"Yeah… about that. First, I have no evidence; just my suspicions. Second, it's a shadow organization no one knows about. It's a dead end."

"So, what are we going to do? I can't keep hiding forever, and we need to resume our work. Besides, how do we know they even came looking for me? Maybe we overreacted and they are already gone?"

"I wish. We didn't want to alarm you, but Michael Gross got jumped last night. He escaped and is fine, but I think that proves that we weren't paranoid. The goons really went after him."

A cold chill ran up Syssi's spine. "But if he was attacked, isn't it proof enough for the police to get serious about investigating these people?"

"He was attacked at night, outside a night club. They assume it was a drunk brawl." Amanda looked apologetic as if any of this was her fault. "Look, Kian had a surveillance camera installed at your place, and our security is monitoring the activity there. If nothing suspicious happens over the next couple of days, you can go home. Deal?"

"I guess… I need to call Andrew, though. And by the way, why are all your phones code protected?"

"Mine are not. I don't know why Kian's would be." Amanda shrugged, though for some reason looked like she was still feeling guilty over something. Leaning with her elbows on the table, she kept fidgeting with her fork when she added, "Listen, when you call your brother, don't tell him exactly where you are and why. I know it sounds a bit strange, but we need to keep a low profile. Our family has enemies—vicious business competitors that will stop at nothing to bring us down. Okay? Can I count on you to keep us a secret?" She looked into Syssi's eyes.

"Of course." Syssi thought it was beyond strange; talk about paranoia. But whatever, if she was asked to keep a secret, she would.

"And I don't want to hear another word about you staying elsewhere. Did you forget that you are supposed to do some work for me while you're here?"

"If it's only a couple of days then I'll stay."

"Good!"

CHAPTER 31: SYSSI

"You must be kidding, right? You dropped your phone in the sink?"

Syssi grimaced. Not surprisingly, Andrew sounded suspicious of the story she had concocted.

Damn, how she hated having to lie.

"Yeah, I answered a call while washing the dishes. It just slipped and fell right in. Died on the spot." Syssi looked at the ceiling, hoping he'd drop the subject. "Anyway, as I said, I'll be staying at Amanda's for a couple of days, just until they are done repainting the lab. We have a paper we need to rush and finish by the end of the month, so I will probably be staying here overnight until we are done. I'll call you as soon as I get my new phone."

"Are you calling from her place? The number is blocked."

"Yes."

"And where is that?"

Okay, that would be tough to wiggle out of... "It's somewhere downtown. Amanda was driving and I didn't pay attention, so I'm not sure exactly where. All I know is that it's a fancy penthouse apartment."

Well, it wasn't a complete lie... after all, she didn't know the exact address. Still, she had a feeling he wasn't buying any of it, or maybe it was just her guilty conscience talking. She wished she had never made that promise to Amanda.

The loud music suddenly blasting from the direction of the living room rescued her from having to make up any more lies.

"What's that racket?" Andrew asked, providing the opening she needed.

"It sounds like Amanda's idea of background music. I'll better go and tell her to turn it down before the neighbors complain. I'll call you later."

"You do that."

Hanging up, Syssi exhaled a relieved breath and got up.

The music got louder as she crossed the few feet separating the office from the living room, and what was worse, Amanda began singing along. Out of tune.

So there was something the woman was not good at... what a relief...

Well, if you can't beat them—join them. Syssi added her own voice to the cacophony.

Dancing and singing along with the hard rock blasting from the powerful speakers, Syssi had more fun than she remembered having in ages. From good old Van Halen and Led Zeppelin to Aerosmith and Metallica, the playlist kept going strong long after they had gotten tired of dancing and switched to painting each other's toenails on the living room's couch.

With Onidu pushing at them one margarita after the other, Syssi lost count of how many she had, although she was pretty sure Amanda had way more.

By the time it got dark outside, Syssi was hoarse from singing and very drunk. "Wow, Amanda, I forgot how wonderful it feels to do things just for the fun of it," she slurred and tried to lie down on the couch. Immediately, her head went spinning, and she sat back up, resting her neck against the upholstered back.

Oh, boy. Was she in trouble.

Every time she tried to close her eyes, the feeling of vertigo forced her to snap them open, but keeping them that way was a struggle. "I swear not to touch another margarita for as long as I live," She moaned, clutching her head.

"Onidu! No more margaritas!" Amanda called out and turned off the music with the remote.

Syssi sighed in relief. "Thank you!"

Sounding a little slurred herself, Amanda patted her shoulder. "Don't you worry, by the time we're ready to go, you'll be fine."

"I don't think I'm in any shape to go anywhere. What a bummer, I haven't been to a club since before Gregg."

"No worries. We're going to fix this." Amanda headed for the kitchen and beckoned Syssi to follow. "Onidu! We need food and coffee. You got us drunk, and now it's up to you to sober us up!"

Sitting at the kitchen counter, they gulped several cups of water before moving on to the coffee.

"I'm glad you enjoyed yourself. You've been all work and no play for far too long, and the night is still young. We have lots of partying left to do." Amanda's eyes sparkled mischievously.

"Are we going by ourselves?"

"Two is not enough for a girls' night out. We need reinforcements. I'm going to call Kri, my cousin."

"What's she like?"

"Muscle…" Amanda snorted, the twirl of pasta on her fork shaking along with her body.

"Okay… that tells me a lot… not… What do you mean—muscle?"

"When you see her, you'll get it. She's the kind of gal you want to watch your back, in case some jerk gets too frisky, uninvited, that is, some you'd actually want to get frisky with you." She winked. "That girl can inflict some serious damage, and that's just a bonus to being way cool and lots of fun to hang out with." Amanda stuffed the twirl of pasta into her mouth.

"All I have are two pairs of jeans, some T-shirts, and a semi-okay blouse… but I can wear my platforms to spruce up the look. You think that will do?"

"Don't be silly. You can borrow some of mine. Wait till you see what's in my closet. Poor Onidu schlepped half my wardrobe over here." Ignoring Syssi's panicked expression, Amanda rubbed her hands together in glee.

CHAPTER 32: ANDREW

As he drove home through the quiet residential streets of his middle-class neighborhood, Andrew thought back to his phone conversation with Syssi.

She was so full of crap.

Careful, cautious Syssi would never drop her cellphone in a sink full of water. She wouldn't even have the thing in the proximity of anything wet.

Who did she think she was fooling?

Lucky for her, he couldn't observe her through the phone—then there would've been no doubt—no one could lie to his face.

He wasn't sure how he did it, but he was better at detecting lies than the machine. The only caveat being that he had to be face to face with the person to be certain.

He was never wrong.

And the story of staying at Amanda's to finish a paper while the lab was being repainted? Right... At the least she should've thought of something more plausible.

Syssi was such a straight shooter. She couldn't lie convincingly if her life depended on it. Andrew smiled as he recalled the few times she had tried to put one over him.

He'd have to coach her to become better at it.

Lying was an important skill that had saved his butt on several occasions. Being an open book the way she was, was a luxury for either those who had nothing to fear or those who had nothing to lose.

Neither applied to his baby sister.

Still, he wondered what the real story was. Did she finally meet a new guy? He certainly hoped so.

That douchebag Gregg had ruined her confidence, turning his vivacious sister into a pitiful hermit. Not for the first time, Andrew wished he could beat the shit out of the jerk, or at least make life really difficult for him.

His lips lifted in a sinister smile as he imagined the possibilities. A few incriminating items could find their way into Gregg's file, making finding a job or obtaining credit impossible. He could envision the asshole squirming, trying to figure out who was ruining his life.

It could've been so satisfying.

Unfortunately, guessing his intentions, Syssi had forbidden Andrew to touch the guy, physically or otherwise. He would have done it anyway, but the jerk still called her from time to time, and she would've found out and figured right away who was behind her ex's misfortune.

Damn it! Why did she have to be such a softie?

After easing his car into the garage, Andrew waited for the garage door to close before exiting, then walked in through the kitchen, disarmed the alarm, and turned the lights on. On his way to the spare bedroom that he had converted into a home office, he dropped his keys on the counter and grabbed a water bottle from the fridge.

Sitting at his desk, Andrew booted up his satellite laptop and brought up the sophisticated tracking software: courtesy of Uncle Sam. For his peace of mind, he needed to find where Syssi was staying.

Let's see where this mystery guy lives. Andrew took a long gulp from his water bottle as he waited for the program to pinpoint the signal.

Hopefully, she kept her promise to always wear the pendant he had given her on her sixteenth birthday. The one with the tracking device he had installed.

It was a beautiful piece of jewelry, a small gold heart surrounded by diamonds that he had inscribed with *You're always in my heart.*

Syssi had vowed to never take it off. He made sure she made good on that promise whenever he saw her. It was always around her neck.

Andrew felt a twinge of guilt for deceiving Syssi for years, but he was glad he had done it nonetheless. At the time, he had felt compelled to do it because he hadn't been around anymore to keep her safe. And considering how spacey and self-centered their mom and dad were, he had wanted to be able to keep track of her.

Now that she was an adult, he still liked the idea of being able to find her.

With their parents always too busy with their careers, with each other, with their social circle—he had practically raised his two younger siblings.

God bless them, his parents were good people. Even before they had retired, they had routinely volunteered their time and resources to charities for children, doing it now full-time in Africa.

Funny, how they took care of so many but had neglected their own.

When he had confronted them about that, his mother's reply had been that the three of them were capable, intelligent people and didn't need their parents to hover over them.

"You'll be just fine taking care of yourself and each other," she had said.

And they were. Fine.

There had been the nannies and the housekeeper and grandma and grandpa who had lived nearby. And yet, as much as he hated to fess up to any lingering resentment, he could've used some more help. The truth was that he had been the one in charge. Making the numerous day to day decisions that had been needed to run the household, he had been forced to become a part-time surrogate parent at fourteen.

Right. Water under the bridge and all that.

Thank God, the red dot showing the tracking device's location wasn't at Syssi's home, so he was reassured that she hadn't left the pendant behind. It was blinking over where she'd said she was staying; somewhere in downtown Los Angeles.

Zooming in on the building the signal was coming from, Andrew whistled as it came into focus and he recognized the lucrative address.

Nice. A wealthy boyfriend... Not bad, Syssi.

That was one fancy place. It was one of those new trendy residential towers, built for those who craved the Manhattan lifestyle and could afford it. But then, he had to wonder where his sister had met someone with that kind of money, given the way she was always hanging around campus.

Right, he shrugged. Probably a student or a teacher at the university that came from money.

Make it a lot of money. A penthouse in a building like that must cost a small fortune. Okay, next step. Let's see who owns the top floor residence.

Rubbing his hands gleefully, he pulled up the tax assessor records. Ah, the things he could learn from all the information his employer made available to him.

His job didn't pay enough to make him wealthy, but it sure as hell provided him with a wealth of information.

CHAPTER 33: SYSSI

Amanda hadn't been kidding about her closet, the contents of which could've made up the entire inventory of a high-end boutique. Or two.

Finally, after trying on at least a dozen outfits, none of which Amanda had deemed hot enough, they had compromised on a short, gray silk dress.

On Amanda, the dress probably bordered on indecent, barely covering her bottom; on Syssi it reached mid-thigh.

One hand on her hip, the other propping her chin, Amanda regarded the outfit critically. "I wish we had time to adjust the hemline. This dress is too long on you."

"It's perfect, and it even matches my shoes." Syssi twirled to demonstrate how well the dress hugged her curves, praying Amanda would let it go and wouldn't make her try any more outfits.

"I guess it'll have to do… Don't get me wrong—you look gorgeous. I just wanted you to look a bit more daring. But never fear, a little makeup and you're going to knock them dead anyway." With a wave of her hand, Amanda dismissed any further discussion and moved to examine her own reflection in the mirror.

Wearing a very short, off-white skirt, topped by a loose, sparkly, silver blouse that left most of her back exposed, Amanda was daring enough for the both of them. And with the spiky-heeled, silver sandals that completed the look, she was sure to tower over most of the club goers. Next to Amanda, there was little chance anyone would spare Syssi a glance.

"I'm glad you're wearing heels. They make you so tall, there is no chance I'll lose you. I'll be able to spot your head above the crowd."

"You'll only have to follow the line of drooling males to zero in on my location." Amanda smirked and sauntered to the makeup table. "Come, let's see what we can do about that innocent-looking face of yours." She patted the stool facing the mirror.

"Oh, boy. I think I'll close my eyes for this. Please don't make me look like a streetwalker," Syssi pleaded with a cringe.

"Trust me, you're gonna look amazing. Don't open your eyes until I say it's okay." Amanda commanded, brandishing the brush like a cudgel above Syssi's head.

"Yes, mistress," Syssi parroted Igor, Dracula's servant.

Amanda laughed, exposing her somewhat overlong canines. "I look the part, don't I? Black hair, fangs…" She made a hissing sound.

That she did.

"You should audition for it. You'd make a perfect vampire—beautiful, scary, bossy…," Syssi ribbed.

"Yeah, not in the cards, regrettably. Now close your eyes. I want it to be a surprise."

"You can look now," Amanda announced after fussing endlessly with Syssi's hair and makeup. Looming over Syssi, hands on her shoulders, she smiled with satisfaction at both their reflections in the mirror.

Syssi gazed at herself in wide-eyed amazement. "Wow, who is that girl, and what have you done with plain old me?" The makeup made her look beautiful and sophisticated without being obvious.

Pushing up, she got closer to the mirror, then retreated, examining herself from different angles.

"Thank you. It's perfect!" She cheerfully hugged Amanda.

"Careful on the makeup! No kissing!" Amanda tilted her head backward, avoiding Syssi's enthusiastic, gloss-covered lips.

"I see the party started without me." A tall, muscular woman sauntered into the room and tossed her heavy leather jacket on the bed.

"Kri, this is Syssi. Syssi, meet Kri." Amanda made the short introduction.

Syssi offered her hand for a handshake only to be pulled into a crushing hug.

"Don't you dare ruin her makeup!" Amanda shrieked.

Letting go, Kri took a step back. "You two look awesome!" she said, admiring their outfits. "I feel underdressed… And don't even think about offering to dress me up," she forestalled Amanda, then turned to Syssi. "Did she torture you for hours?"

"Not for hours, but long enough." Syssi snorted.

Amanda wielded the brush like a weapon again. "Let me at least do something about your hair."

Taking Syssi's place in front of the mirror, Kri straddled the small stool. "Okay, give it a shot."

Watching Amanda unbraid Kri's long wavy hair, Syssi observed that there was something both intimidating and vulnerable about the girl.

She was big. And even though not much taller than Amanda, she dwarfed her not so small older cousin.

Kri's outfit, of black leather pants and heavy combat boots, made her look like a serious kickass. But then the pink rhinestone heart on the front of her black muscle shirt, with Girl Power printed over it, seemed to say; hey, I might be tough, but I'm still a girl.

She looked to be about twenty. Powerfully built with wide shoulders and pronounced biceps that bespoke of many hours spent at the gym. And yet, reflected in the mirror, the girl's face was surprisingly feminine. The loose waves of her waist-long tawny hair framing gentle blue eyes and clean, smooth skin.

"Okay, girl, what do you think?" Amanda fluffed Kri's hair, creating more bounce. "Is there any chance I could convince you to put on some lip gloss?" Looking at Kri in the mirror, Amanda waved the small tube above the girl's head.

"No way, I hate the way the stuff tastes." Pushing up to her feet, Kri flipped her long hair back and raised her chin as she examined her profile's reflection. "I'm hot enough without it. Just look at me. You think any guy could resist all that?" She ran her hands over her curves.

"I'm sure none would dare." Amanda smirked with a wink at Syssi.

"Are we ready, ladies?" Kri picked up her leather jacket and swung it over her shoulder.

"Let's go. I just want to stop by Kian's on our way out." Amanda grabbed her sequined clutch and headed out the door.

Syssi felt a flutter of excitement at the prospect of seeing Kian again. Or rather, of him seeing her—all decked out and looking fab. Clutching the purse she borrowed from Amanda, she crossed the vestibule behind the two tall women.

"Wait here. I'll just let him know we're leaving." Amanda started down the hallway toward Kian's office.

"I heard you come in. Though next time, I would appreciate it if you knocked..." Kian intercepted her and together they returned to the living room.

He looked so good. An old pair of faded jeans hung low on his hips, and a thin, worn-out T-shirt stretched over his chest, showing off all those incredible muscles. Barefoot, even his feet looked sexy.

Who knew feet could be so enticing? Or was it the whole man she found irresistible. Every little bit of him.

It wasn't until Kri moved aside that Kian got an unobstructed view of Syssi. And when he did, his expression was priceless. With his eyes traveling the length of her body, he made her feel beautiful. Desired.

Rubbing his hand over his sternum, it took him a moment to

compose himself before he approached her. "You look beautiful," he stated simply as he took both of her hands in his. "Where are you going?"

"We are heading to the Underground; just us girls." Amanda spoke to his back.

Kian ignored his sister—his sole focus on Syssi. "Give me a minute to change, and I'll join you."

"Hello? Girls. Night. Out. No boys invited... Sorry, bro." Amanda headed back to the vestibule.

"It's not safe. I should go with you," he tried, his eyes staring into Syssi's as he held on to her hands.

"Don't be silly, we have Kri with us. And don't wait up; we're gonna party until late... Ta-ta..." Amanda pressed the elevator button, turning around and motioning for the girls to hurry out.

Syssi pulled her hands out of Kian's grip. "Don't worry. We're going to be fine." She stretched up to place a quick kiss on his cheek.

"Be careful!" he called after them as they entered the elevator.

"Night, Kian." Amanda waved goodbye as the doors were closing.

On the way down to the parking level, Syssi thought back to the way Kian had looked at her and wondered; had jealousy been the reason he had wanted to join them? Had he been worried about her going to a club looking like that?

Would he show up there despite Amanda's veto?

Did she want him to?

CHAPTER 34: SYSSI

The Underground, as the name suggested, was a basement. From the outside, the only indication that there was a club in the building was the long line of people hoping to get in.

Roped off with a thick red cable, the line snaked all the way to the parking lot of the industrial complex.

Going straight for the door, Syssi felt like a red-carpet celebrity as the three of them bypassed the gawking, roped-off cattle.

Shocked by some of the outrageous outfits on the girls standing behind the rope, she did a little gawking herself—watching them shift from foot to foot in their uncomfortable sky-high heels and tiny, tight skirts.

It seemed Amanda had been right about Syssi's dress being a little too long. But then again, it wasn't as if Syssi cared to blend in with the rest of this crowd.

They were let right in, with the bouncer holding the door as he nodded respectfully at Amanda. Once inside, they got the same royal treatment from the guy in charge of the elevator.

Evidently, in this place, Amanda ruled.

It took no longer than a few seconds for them to reach the basement, and as soon as the elevator doors opened, Syssi was blasted with the club's deafening music and nauseating smells.

Sticking her fingers in her ears, she tried to block the onslaught. And yet, it still felt as if everything in her abdominal cavity was thumping to the pounding of the beat. She grimaced, wishing for two extra hands so she could shield her belly and protect her insides as well.

She should've remembered how loud and crowded clubs were, and brought earplugs... and a nose clip...

Breathing through her mouth to ward off the cloying smells of perfumes, sweat, booze, and God-knew-what-else, she didn't dare inhale through her nose until they cleared the crowd, climbing the stairs to the VIP balcony.

Up there, the music was just as loud, but at least the air was fresher and it wasn't as crowded.

Out of the five round granite-topped tables by the railing, only two were occupied, with most of the balcony's exclusive clientele preferring the privacy of the intimate, dark booths lining the back wall.

Sitting down at the table next to Amanda, Syssi peered over the railing at the packed dance floor below, watching the dancing crowd as it appeared and disappeared in between bursts of throbbing strobe-lights.

She wondered if the couples and sometimes threesomes, writhing against each other, touching and fondling, were aware of the fact that they were providing a peep show for those sitting above them on the balcony.

Most likely, though, as tightly packed as everyone was on the smoky and dim platform, they must've assumed they had some measure of privacy.

Or maybe they didn't care.

"Amanda, haven't seen you in here for a while. How're ya doing?"

"I'm doing great. How about you, Alex?" Amanda replied.

Shifting her attention away from her voyeuristic fascination with what was going on below, Syssi looked at the man pulling a chair from a nearby table and parking it at theirs.

The guy was so well put together, she wondered if he was gay. Very few of the straight men she knew paid that much attention to their looks.

His blond hair was perfectly styled, and although he wore nothing fancier than jeans and a white, button-down shirt, both looked like expensive designer items that had been custom tailored to his exact fit.

Still, she wouldn't have thought much of that getup if not for the row of three diamond studs in his right ear and the matching set of a diamond watch and bracelet.

The guy had more jewelry on him than her and Amanda combined. Kri wasn't even wearing a watch.

But then, the leering glance he sneaked Syssi's way was all heterosexual.

"Alex, sweetheart, meet my friend Syssi. It's her first time here, so be a doll and take good care of her." Amanda smiled at the guy.

"Syssi, this is my good friend Alex, the owner of this fab place."

"A pleasure to make your acquaintance." Smiling with the confidence of a man who was well aware of how handsome he was, Alex lifted her hand for a kiss.

As he held onto it way longer than was polite, his dark eyes bored into hers, sending strange shivers up her spine. The guy was making her very uncomfortable—and not in a good way. And yet, she couldn't force herself to look away or pull her hand out of his grasp.

"Back off, Alex, she is Kian's. And I'm sure you would rather avoid tangling with him," Amanda warned with a wink.

As if suddenly burnt by it, Alex let go of Syssi's hand so fast it remained suspended in front of her face for a split second before she shook off the stupefied sensation and retracted it to her lap.

What was that? Syssi wondered at her peculiar reaction to him.

The shivers and the mesmerizing effect he had on her didn't make any sense, as she didn't find him attractive at all. There was a lascivious quality to his demeanor, and although handsome, he looked too slick and kind of sleazy; like a pushy salesman or a campaigning politician.

"What can I get you, ladies?" He pushed up from his chair, and his smile was so genuinely friendly that she thought for a moment that the whole thing had been a product of her imagination.

"The usual for me. Kri, the same?" When Kri nodded, Amanda turned to Syssi. "What would you like, darling?"

"Club soda for me, thank you." Syssi offered Alex a perfunctory smile.

"You sure?" Amanda cocked a brow.

"Absolutely, I had enough to drink for one day." Syssi grimaced. It took almost two hours before the vertigo sensation from earlier had dissipated, and there was no way she was subjecting herself to that kind of misery anytime soon.

After a quick kiss on Amanda's cheek, Alex left for the bar.

Her companions began to chitchat, and Syssi tried to join in but gave up when her voice got hoarse from straining to be heard over the music. And yet, it deterred neither Amanda nor Kri. Oblivious to the noise, they kept at it as if they were sitting in Amanda's living room.

How they could hear each other was beyond her. Even trying to listen in on their conversation was proving too much of an effort. Which left her with nothing better to do than watch the sexually charged dancing scene below.

If not for the clothing that provided some small barrier between the writhing bodies, it would have looked like a mass orgy.

Had it always been like that?

She didn't remember it being so bad. Had things changed so much in only a few years? Or was it possible she just hadn't noticed it before?

Be that as it may, it was kind of depressing to think that she had gotten either too old for the club scene or had been too clueless to notice what had been going on around her before. Or both.

"Come on, Syssi. Let's go dancing." Amanda tapped her shoulder, diverting her attention from the pseudo porn show below.

"Go ahead. I'm going to stay here. It's way too crowded down there for me, not to mention stinky." Syssi strained her voice, trying to be heard without actually shouting.

"You sure?" Amanda asked, exchanging looks with Kri.

"I'll stay with you." Looking disappointed, Kri sat down.

"No way! Go have fun. I'll watch you guys from up here. Go!"

Amanda glanced at Kri and nodded, apparently deciding it was safe to leave Syssi on her own.

Heading down, Amanda stopped by the upstairs bar to talk to Alex, and with a hand on his shoulder said something in his ear. When both of them briefly glanced Syssi's way, she waved and smiled, letting them know she was on to them.

Doubtless, Amanda had asked Alex to look out for her *little friend*.

CHAPTER 35: KIAN

Once the girls had left, Kian paced restlessly for about two minutes before pulling out his phone and calling Onegus.

"What's up, Boss?" His chief of Guardians answered after several rings.

"I know it's late, but I need you to grab Bhathian and go to the Underground. Amanda is heading there with Kri and Syssi, one of the potential targets for the Doomers. I want them guarded."

"Amanda will have our heads for following her. She doesn't like us snooping around her hunting grounds."

"I don't care. If she gives you any crap, tell her to take it up with me." Kian slowed his agitated pacing only to kick the couch, making the whole thing slide and hit the coffee table.

"Yes, Boss."

"Thank you, and try not to get in her face. I just need you to keep an eye on them."

The easing of pressure he had expected after ensuring the girls' safety never came.

As much as he hated to admit this even to himself, his motives hadn't been all that noble. The truth was, he loathed the idea of Syssi in a club teeming with lustful males—without him by her side to scare them off.

Just imagining the men leering at her made him see red.

Since when did he develop such a possessive streak?

Sending the guys to basically spy on Syssi was almost as bad as stalking her himself.

Damn, he wasn't that kind of guy... or was he?

The kind of man he wished to be would trust Syssi and give her all the space she needed without obsessing like a lunatic the moment she got out of his sight.

But this wasn't about him not trusting Syssi. This was about the men that would be lusting after her, their dirty thoughts touching her, somehow contaminating her.

He knew the sort of things men would be fantasizing about doing to her, not because he was a mind reader, but because he had been guilty of the same.

Men are pigs... each and every one of them.

Taking a deep breath, Kian ran his hands through his hair and tried to calm down. *Come on, buddy, every attractive woman would be the source of male fantasies, it's harmless... most of the time...*

Yeah, trouble was, he couldn't help feeling as if those supposedly harmless fantasies were sullying his Syssi.

CHAPTER 36: SYSSI

Syssi watched Amanda and Kri weave through the dancing floor, each dragging a hunky guy behind.

That didn't take long, she thought as they started undulating and rubbing against their partners in an overtly sexual way.

It was kind of shocking to see Amanda behave like that. Despite all of her prior proclamations of wantonness, Syssi couldn't believe her boss would get randy, with a stranger, on a dance floor, in a crowded club.

The distinguished professor, Dr. Amanda Dokani, was indeed a slut.

Syssi chuckled, admitting that she shouldn't be surprised. Amanda had made it abundantly clear—on numerous occasions—that she was ruled by a ferocious appetite for sex. The fact that Syssi had believed her boss had been greatly exaggerating for dramatic effect and had been proven wrong was her problem and not Amanda's.

And her young cousin was even worse.

By the way Kri was grabbing her partner's butt, grinding against him and shoving her tongue into his mouth, it was obvious the girl was cut from the same cloth as her cousin. Except, she was more aggressive about it. Not that the guy had a problem with her dominance. Judging by his stupefied expression, he was loving every moment of it.

Amanda and her guy were a step further. He had his hand under her loose blouse and was fondling her braless breast while she had her palm pressed between their bodies. And it didn't require X-ray vision to imagine what was going on down there.

Too embarrassed to watch, Syssi turned her back to the railing and reached for her soda glass. But it was empty.

Symbolic of her situation, that seemingly insignificant fact unnerved her more than it should have. With nothing to hold in her hands and no desire to keep watching what was going on below, there was nothing to distract her from the awkwardness of sitting alone in a club that was bursting at the seams with people.

Looking for the waitress, she spotted the young woman taking an order from one of the booths, and as soon as the girl turned, she waved her down.

Watching as she sauntered over in her high heels, Syssi pitied the poor girl's feet at the end of the shift. Not that she thought the waitress had a choice in the kind of footwear she wore on the job.

The black pumps, as well as the really short black shorts and tiny white halter top, seemed to be a uniform of sorts for all the hostesses serving drinks—with only slight variations in style and make.

With a boss like Alex, Syssi was willing to bet that the girls were required to buy their own version of the uniform. Not only would it be in line with his sleazy character, but it would also explain why the outfits were not identical.

"What can I get you?"

"I'd like a sangria, but very light on the wine, please. And some nuts or tortilla chips if you have them." Syssi wasn't hungry, but the snack would keep her hands busy while she waited for Amanda and Kri to come back.

This outing was turning out to be not as fun as she imagined it would when Amanda came up with the idea. Not by a long shot. Instead of sitting alone, nauseated by the noise, watching others making out, and feeling like she didn't belong, she would have rather been snuggling with Kian at his place. Or doing other things...

But then, the whole point of going out had been to get away from him, so she could think clearly and rationally without the hormonal haze of being around him clouding her head.

Which proved to be an exercise in futility.

Without something to distract her, she kept obsessing about him anyway.

Mercifully, it didn't take long for Amanda to come back. Syssi smiled at her friend and the guy she was dragging behind her; the same one she saw her getting busy with on the dance floor.

Except, instead of returning to the table, Amanda stopped at the bar, and after exchanging a few words with Alex and a little hand-wave in Syssi's direction, she and her partner disappeared through a door hidden behind a thick velvet curtain.

Forgetting the club was underground, Syssi had assumed that the thing was covering a window to the outside, not a doorway to God-knew-where or what. When a few moments later Kri pulled the same stunt, Syssi struggled to see what was behind the curtain. But it was too dark.

As if lying in wait for just the right opportunity, Alex showed up the moment the curtain had dropped behind Kri and parked his butt in the chair next to Syssi.

Sitting way too close to her, with his arm on the back of her chair, he was invading her personal space.

"It's hard to hear above the music," he explained, but the hunger in his eyes and his leering smirk made it clear he had more than talking on his mind. "So, how do you know Amanda?" he asked in her ear as he pretended to absentmindedly play with a lock of her long hair, winding it around his finger.

Was this the special attention Amanda had asked him to show her? For some reason, Syssi didn't think so...

Shaking her head a little, she tried to free her hair without being too obvious about it. "We work together," she answered in the coolest tone she could muster, which was only a shade away from outright rude.

"Ah, the university... must be exciting," he continued in the same seductive tone.

"Where did Amanda and Kri go?" Syssi tried to divert his attention. And regretted it as soon as his expression turned from leering to pure lust.

Oh, boy... She diverted his attention all right... In the wrong direction...

"We have some private rooms in the back, reserved for... special guests... with special needs... Come, I'll show you." With each pause, he wound a little more of her hair on his finger until he reached her scalp. Not pulling on it or causing her pain, he was nonetheless holding her immobilized as he slowly closed the distance between their mouths.

With his smug face no more than an inch away from hers, she was about to tell him to stop, and if that didn't do the trick, to kick him where it would count, when he suddenly let go of her.

Following his gaze, she saw what or rather who had given him pause. Walking toward them were two very large men; the kind that made the bouncers up front look like accountants.

"Hello, Alex old man. Have you seen Amanda and Kri? They and another girl, Syssi, were supposed to be here. Kian sent us to check up on them." The guy seemed friendly enough, easygoing. And yet, judging by Alex's tensed body, he made him nervous.

"Bhathian, Onegus, always good to see you guys. I guess that you haven't met Syssi yet because she's right here. I'm keeping her company while Amanda and Kri are doing their thing in the back."

The men seemed oblivious to the implied activity that was taking place in the rooms behind the curtain, as well as to the way Alex had been all over her when they'd walked in.

Apparently, Kian hadn't specified the kind of checking up he had in mind.

"Syssi, nice to meet you. I'm Onegus." The pretty blond one offered his hand, smiling a smile that could melt ice.

"Bhathian." The tall, serious one shook what was offered.

"Nice to meet you too, would you care to join us? *Please, please say yes...* Syssi pleaded with her eyes, hoping their presence would keep Alex's tentacles at bay.

But apparently, being male meant that they sucked at reading facial cues. "We would love to, but Amanda is not going to be happy about us showing up on her turf. We'll just go and sit over there at the bar; give you gals your space." Onegus smiled politely.

"I'm sorry, but I can't stay either. After all, I have a club to run." Alex made it sound as if she had been keeping him there.

Whatever, she wasn't about to correct him. Syssi was just glad to be rid of him, and as far as she was concerned, he could keep his damn pride and shove it.

Alone at the table again, she glanced at the men. Sitting at the bar, the two were hard to ignore, drawing the attention of the few single females there, and even some covert wistful looks from those accompanied by a partner.

Onegus... Bhathian... What peculiar names. Come to think of it, so were Anandur, Brundar, and Kri. Even Kian was unusual. The only one with a common name was Amanda.

Maybe they were foreigners? But where were they from? They had no accents that she could discern. Except, sometimes their choice of words and some of their gestures seemed out of place, or rather from a different era.

The way Brundar lifted off the sofa when she came in, bowing a little... Come to think, both Bhathian and Onegus bowed slightly when shaking her hand. Maybe the bunch spent some time in Japan, absorbing the local penchant for bowing.

Still, that didn't explain the names. If she had her phone, she could have Googled it while waiting for the girls to come back. But Kian hadn't provided the replacement he had promised yet. She would have taken care of it herself if given a chance to get out. But as Kian and Amanda were determined to keep her prisoner, she was forced to rely on her jailer.

"Hey, you." Amanda plopped down next to her, looking spent and relaxed until she noticed Kian's men at the bar. "What are they doing here?" she hissed.

"They said Kian sent them to watch over us. Who are they? Do they work for Kian, or are they friends of yours?"

"More like family."

"More cousins? You must be kidding."

"What? I told you it's a family business. We are big on employing our own." Amanda waved the waitress over and ordered more drinks. Then went back to glaring angrily at her cousins. "But it pisses me off that they are here. Like they have nothing better to do than follow me around."

CHAPTER 37: KIAN

After pacing around his living room like a caged animal for what seemed to him like hours, Kian pulled out his phone.

Update! he texted Onegus.

It took the guy forever to answer. *They are fine, nothing interesting going on, besides Alex pestering Amanda's friend.*

~~Crap fuck~~, that was it. He was going to that club whether Amanda liked it or not. And if Syssi accused him again of unwarranted jealousy, so be it.

Kian could barely tolerate the thought of all the other males in the club sniffing around Syssi, and Alex was a sleazeball bastard to top them all.

There was a limit to what Kian was willing to suffer in the name of gentlemanly conduct.

Even though Alex managed to run his club skirting around clan law by not breaking any clan specific rules, he was breaking plenty of the human ones.

The prostitutes, Kian had to grudgingly accept as their services were needed for some of his men. But he abhorred the drugs. Alex claimed he didn't deal; just turned a blind eye to the stuff changing hands in his club, but Kian had his doubts.

The guy was living a lifestyle that even a successful club like the Underground couldn't support. To make that kind of money, Alex must've been doing something illegal.

Hell, he had just bought a new super-yacht; a luxury Bluewater beauty that must've cost over twenty-five million.

For some inexplicable reason, Amanda liked the guy and considered him a friend. A bad judgment on her part. But she was a big girl and he couldn't tell her who to be friends with.

Syssi, on the other hand, he would keep as far away from that scumbag as possible.

Without bothering to change, Kian slid into a pair of loafers, grabbed a jacket, and heading for the garage, called for Okidu to drive him in case he decided to stay and indulge in more than a couple of drinks. Not that drinking would have been enough to impair his driving, but the last thing he needed was to be pulled over and fail the breathalyzer test.

CHAPTER 38: SYSSI

Syssi couldn't help but notice that Kri's expression upon returning from her back room activities was very different from Amanda's. She looked irritated. Walking behind her, her partner looked kind of lost and confused. And as Kri took a seat at their table, the guy went downstairs without even waving goodbye.

Come to think of it, Amanda's partner hadn't joined them either. Strange. The club scene must've changed a lot in the six years Syssi hadn't been part of it; and not for the better.

"I feel like dancing some more. Anyone care to join me?" Kri said and finished her drink.

"I will!" Amanda chirped, shooting up from her chair.

The woman sure bounced back quickly.

"I'm good. You go ahead." Syssi shooed the two away.

They kept staring at her as if she was nuts.

"You didn't dance even once. What's the point of coming here if all you do is sit up here? You have to come with us... at least one song." Amanda reached for Syssi's arm.

Syssi leaned away. "No, really, I'm fine here. Watching you guys is enough entertainment for me," she said, failing to hide the slight note of sarcasm in her tone. Though with all the noise, she doubted the girls could've heard it.

Exchanging looks with Amanda, Kri shrugged and headed for the stairs. A moment later, Amanda shook her head at Syssi and followed Kri down.

Sorry to be the disappointing prude...

Syssi was angry with Amanda, for the head shaking, for dragging her here and then behaving the way she did.

It wasn't that Syssi condemned their promiscuity; they were big girls and could do as they pleased. She just wished they wouldn't do it while she waited awkwardly alone.

Sighing, she glanced at the bar. Maybe she could join the guys. But they were gone. Turning to look at the dance floor, she spotted them not far from Amanda and Kri, watching the girls dance.

Observing them, it struck her that there was a military flair to their demeanor. It manifested in the way they held their bodies and the alertness with which they were scanning the crowd. Come to think of it, Anandur and Brundar, and even Kri were the same.

Bodyguards. It was so obvious she wondered how she could've missed it before. For some reason she'd thought the brothers were Kian's assistants. It didn't make sense to have family as bodyguards. Yes, they could be trusted more than strangers, but who wanted to risk their own cousins' lives?

Apparently Kian had no such reservations.

The question begging to be asked was what kind of business were Kian and his family in that it produced so much competition and animosity and required that level of protection?

Mafia! It has to be.

Suddenly, she saw it all clearly; recent events creating a pattern and all the puzzle pieces fitting together to form one scary picture.

All that money.

The big family business…

It hadn't been a group of zealots that Amanda and Kian had been running from that evening at the lab. They'd been ambushed by a hostile competitor. And the goons after them had belonged to another mafia. Unable to strike at their targets, they had returned at night and ransacked the lab to send a message.

Probably turf wars…

Was Amanda dealing drugs? On campus? Here at the club?

The guards Kian had sent had mentioned she didn't like them showing up on her turf. Was that what she and Kri had been doing behind the curtain? Selling drugs to those guys? That would explain why their partners hadn't hung around, scurrying away quickly once the deed had been done.

Oh. My. God. I had sex with a mafia boss! Syssi inhaled sharply as panic threatened to cut off her air supply.

Pushing her chair back, she grabbed her purse and was about to flee when Alex stuck his sleazy face in front of her, blocking her escape.

"Where are you running off to, sweetheart?" He reached for her arm.

Twisting away, she clutched her purse with both hands. "Ladies' room? Can you point me toward one?"

"There is one behind that curtain. I'll take you there." His eyes gleaming dangerously, he grabbed her bicep, digging his fingers into her flesh.

"Let go of her! Before I rip off your ████damned arm!" came the hissed command from Kian.

Relief and panic warred for dominance in Syssi's frantic mind. The Lion King was rescuing her from the clutches of the hyena. Unfortunately, he just looked like Mufasa but was really Scar...

"Come dance with me." Kian clasped her hand as soon as Alex dropped it, ignoring the jerk's resentful glare as the guy sauntered off.

Afraid to say anything, Syssi let him pull her down the stairs and onto the dance floor. But at the same time, her mind was going a thousand miles per hour, calculating her options. If she could somehow get away, she could run to Andrew for protection. But then what? They knew where she lived, and she'd lose her job. Which was a big problem, as finding a decent one in this economy was next to impossible.

Oh, well, there was always the option of joining her parents in Africa, but she really didn't want to do that. And anyway, as well guarded as Kian had her, her chances of escape were nil.

She had to face facts. As long as Kian wanted her around, she was trapped. Like in the movies, the wife or mistress of the mafia boss was a captive—never allowed to leave... alive!

Oh! My! God! What a mess.

And yet, as he held her close she didn't resist—powerless against her need to cling to him. Burying her nose in the fabric of his shirt, she inhaled his unique scent, getting high on it like some junkie.

The pathetic truth was that, on some irrational level, she felt safe in his arms despite who she believed he was and needed him so badly that it hurt.

She was driving herself crazy; the feelings of trepidation and disappointment clashing with the intense longing, conflicting and augmenting each other and wreaking havoc on her mind.

CHAPTER 39: KIAN

Holding Syssi close as they swayed to the music, Kian had no trouble reading her emotions; even without his enhanced senses. Though for the life of him, he couldn't fathom what caused her such distress. Or how the hell could she be so afraid of him and at the same time cling to him like he was her lifeline.

You'd think that he'd know a thing or two about women after almost two thousand years, but evidently, he still had a lot to learn.

"Don't be upset, sweet girl, I meant what I said before. My jerky behavior had nothing to do with my opinion of you. I think you're a rare treasure, my sweet Syssi…," he whispered in her ear while rubbing gentle circles on her back.

Syssi didn't respond and remained tense and rigid in his arms. Then, as he waited for what seemed like forever for her to say something, anything, it dawned on him that with her limited mortal hearing, she couldn't have heard a word of what he had said over the excruciatingly loud music.

Taking her hand, he pulled her behind him up the short flight of stairs and led her out the back door, where Okidu was waiting with the limo.

Syssi didn't resist, but he was painfully aware that she followed him with the enthusiasm of a prisoner led to her own execution.

"I need to let Amanda know that I've left with you," Syssi whispered as Okidu pulled the limo out from the alley behind the club.

It hurt watching her sit glued to the limo's opposite side, as far away from him as she possibly could in the confined space. She was gazing out the window, clearly to avoid looking at him.

"Don't worry about it. I'm texting her right now." Kian was truly baffled by Syssi's emotional storm and the mixed signals he was getting from her.

Earlier, when he had made an ass of himself, she had been upset and disappointed. Now she was way worse.

If he didn't know better, he would've thought Syssi had just lost a loved one. Micah had projected a similar scent when he'd brought her the devastating news of her son's death.

Grief.

What a ▓▓▓▓▓ mess.

Something else must've been going on. It didn't make sense for her to be that distraught over his petty jealous tantrum.

But what did he know.

If she was anything like Amanda, she might've twisted the whole thing in her head, blowing it into monstrous proportions.

"I'm really sorry for hurting your feelings. If it's any excuse, I'm terribly inexperienced in dealing with these kinds of emotions. It's all new to me." He reached to take her hand but then reconsidered—afraid she'd pull away.

"It's okay. You don't have to explain. I understand. I'm sorry that I overreacted," Syssi said in a flat voice, looking out the window and pretending nonchalance.

Except, she kept playing with her purse, tugging the magnetic clasp open and letting it snap back into place—over and over again.

"You still look upset. Please tell me what I can do to make it better. I'm going out of my mind here." Kian wasn't exaggerating; he really was becoming desperate, hating the helpless feeling of not knowing what to say or do next.

Was it just him? Or were all males completely clueless about women and how to deal with their peculiar emotional states? It seemed a man had to tread carefully through the minefield of a female's psyche to avoid unwittingly stepping on a land mine. Kian would've paid good money for someone to draw him a map and help him navigate safely through these dangerous grounds.

"It's nothing."

Nothing? It was the worst kind of answer. He could've dealt with accusations, with anger, even with tears. But nothing, gave him nothing to work with.

All he wanted was to pull her onto his lap and kiss her senseless; until she forgot all about whatever it was that was causing her to be so upset and so remote.

He didn't.

Sadly, he didn't think he'd be welcomed.

After what had felt like an endless silence, Syssi turned away from the window and looked straight into his eyes. "I need to ask you a question, and I need you to answer me honestly." She sounded dead serious.

"Anything, I'll answer any question you might have." And he meant it. Even if she guessed what he was, he would admit it.

"Are you a mafioso? Is that what your family's business is all about—dealing drugs?"

"What!? That's what you wanted to ask? Why would you think something so absurd?" Out of all the questions he had anticipated, this one completely threw him off.

"Not absurd at all. One, you guys seem to have shitloads of money." She lifted a second finger. "Two, everyone I meet is family. Three, the men and Kri are very obviously bodyguards. Four, the attacks on Amanda and then her lab stink of retaliation or a warning strike by another mafia. Most likely, one that is competing with you for drug territory. Five, Amanda asks me to keep your location secret. Did I miss anything?"

Unable to hold back, Kian burst laughing. "Oh, baby, I'm sorry. You're right. I totally get it how you could reach the wrong conclusion putting it all together like that. That's not why I'm laughing." Holding his hand over his heart, he took a moment to calm himself. "I'm just so tremendously relieved that this is what got you upset. I was racking my brain, trying to figure out what landmine I had stepped on."

He made a move to pull her to him, but Syssi stopped him with a hand to his chest. "You still didn't answer my question. Are you, or are you not, a mafioso?"

"I swear on everything that's dear to me, neither I nor any other member of my family is in the mafia or has any connections to any kind of organized crime. As far as I know. Okay?"

Scrunching her forehead she looked at him with narrowed eyes, scrutinizing his face for any signs of deception, then frowned. "Not yet, you need to tell me more than that."

With a sigh, he acquiesced. "Our family owns a large international conglomerate of enterprises that I assure you is all perfectly legal and has nothing to do with organized crime. Actually, our main objective is to benefit humanity by encouraging scientific innovation in a variety of fields, cultural shifts toward more freedom and equal opportunity around the world, women's rights, eradication of prejudice and oppression, etc…"

"So why the bodyguards? The secrecy? And what about the attack? It all seems so clandestine," Syssi interrupted.

"I'm getting there. We have enemies, those who hate what we do and what we stand for. They're ruthless, hateful people who will stop at nothing until they annihilate my family and destroy all the amazing progress our work has accomplished."

"Why?"

"It's an old and complicated story. I don't want to go through all the long and sordid history of it. All I can say is that it's an ancient feud that started eons ago with a scorned suitor that didn't take the rejection well, to say the least. He swore himself and his descendants to an eternal vendetta. His progeny is very powerful and influential, and they pose an existential threat to us. Bottom line, we have to hide; operating under shadow corporations, always in a defensive mode. That's the reason behind the bodyguards, and why only family can be trusted in our inner circle."

Syssi seemed dumbfounded.

Did she believe his tale?

He had done his best, being very careful with how he phrased it, attempting to give her all the main points without divulging too much or twisting the truth. But was it enough? Were her instincts telling her he had been genuine despite being forced to omit the things he couldn't tell her? Searching her eyes, he was seeking reassurance that she was willing to accept what he had told her.

She looked at him for a long moment, her brows drawn together as if deliberating whether she should believe him or not. Then taking a deep breath she seemed to come to a conclusion. "I believe you. Though you're not telling me everything, but that's okay. I'm still a stranger to you, and you don't know if you can trust me, despite how close and intimate we got. It all just happened too fast. I understand that your family's safety must come first. I respect that."

Was this woman something else or what? One in a million... Scratch that. One in a billion!

Relieved that she'd believed him and grateful she hadn't pushed him to reveal more than he was comfortable with, Kian pulled her into his arms for a soulful kiss. She didn't resist, but although her body had lost its stiffness, she was still far from truly participating.

Holding her close, luxuriating in the sensation of her soft body pressed against his, he felt buoyant. With the relief of finally touching her, knowing he had her back, the heaviness that had been weighing him down, had lifted.

It didn't take long for the kiss to morph from something sweet and gentle into something hungry and wild. With his hand cradling the back of Syssi's head, he wedged the one on her back under her bottom and lifted her onto his lap.

As if a dam had burst inside her, Syssi's passive acquiesce turned into wild abandon. With her hands finding their way under his T-shirt, she caressed his pecs frantically then clawed into his skin as if she couldn't get enough of him. Moaning into his mouth with what sounded like desperate longing, she undulated her hips, rubbing her soft behind against his shaft.

"God, I missed you." She groaned when they came up for air, grabbing at his shoulders and going for his neck, licking and sucking on his skin.

"You have no idea." He looked at her neck hungrily while snaking his hand under the hem of her short, loose-fitting dress. With his palm on the inside of her thigh, he kept caressing it, slowly going up to where it met its twin, taking his time.

He didn't want to overwhelm her—wasn't sure she was up to taking their passion further yet. But it seemed he had nothing to worry about.

Syssi welcomed his touch, and spreading her legs a little, let him in. He hissed as he pushed her panties aside and inserted a finger between her wet folds, finding her already drenched.

As another strangled moan escaped her throat, she glanced nervously at the half open partition, recalling they were not alone.

"Okidu," she whispered, gesturing with her head toward the driver.

Not willing to let go of his prize, Kian leaned with her still impaled on his finger, and with his other hand punched the button that raised the partition.

"Better?" he whispered.

"Yes," she slurred and closed her eyes.

In the limo's dim interior, her beautiful face was bathed in the lambent light cast by his glowing eyes. He kept pleasuring her, his finger going in and out, slowly, deliberately, carefully kindling her fire so it would burn steadily; getting gradually hotter before bursting into one big flame.

Feeling his glands swelling with venom, Kian dipped his head to suckle on her nipple through the thin fabrics of her dress and bra. Pulling on it carefully with his lips, he swirled his tongue around the turgid peak, creating a big wet spot on the silk.

Oh, how he loved the little tortured sounds she made when he turned her mindless with pleasure; they were sweet music to his ears. But even more, he loved the sounds she made when she climaxed. Adding another finger to his in-and-out motion, he pressed his thumb to her clitoris, and rubbing it gently, brought his masterpiece to its grand finale.

Syssi erupted, falling apart on his lap and making the loud keening moan he loved. Man, he would never tire of hearing that. Prolonging her pleasure, he kept his hand pumping and rubbing while his lips and tongue took care of her other nipple, producing another big wet spot.

It took momentous effort not to sink his fangs into the nipple he was working on. Dropping his forehead to her chest, he breathed in and out slowly, trying to regain control—commanding his throbbing erection and his fangs to let off.

Syssi lay so limply in his arms, he would have thought he had killed her with bliss, if not for her chest gently rising and falling with her shallow breaths.

Kian lifted his head, and as he looked at Syssi's blissful face—the long lashes fanning out of her closed lids, her flushed cheeks, her red and swollen lips—a tide of tenderness that he was afraid felt too much like love washed over him. Cradling her head, he brought her cheek to rest on his chest, and as he held her nestled against him, Kian suspected he would never be able to let her go.

Too soon, though, Okidu parked in the underground garage and Kian had to reluctantly release his treasure. With a sigh, he helped her up to a sitting position and straightened her dress.

As Syssi glanced down at the two wet spots, her cheeks reddened in embarrassment. "I can't get out of the car like this," she whispered, smiling her shy little smile.

He shrugged out of his jacket and handed it to her. "Here, you can wear this over your dress."

After wiggling her arms inside the sleeves, she held the two halves clutched in her hand, waiting for Kian to exit and help her down.

"As you have my jacket, you'll have to walk in front of me to provide cover." He smirked, glancing down at himself.

Syssi giggled, positioning herself with her back to his front.

It was sly of him. He wasn't worried about Okidu noticing his bulge, and the chances of anyone else arriving right then were slim. But it was fun holding her in front of him as they made their way to the elevator.

Waving them off, Okidu began wiping dirt off the limo's windshield.

Good man. Kian smiled at the butler's unexpected subterfuge. Evidently, Okidu had learned a few things during his long existence. Though Kian had a strong suspicion that this newfound knowledge was gained mainly from watching shitloads of television.

With a wicked smirk, he followed Syssi inside the elevator, and the moment the doors closed, pressed her against the mirrored wall, his body enveloping hers from behind. She was wearing high heels, and her sweet little butt was perfectly aligned with his groin, providing delicious friction for his aching shaft.

Rubbing himself against her, he glanced at his reflection in the mirror and was alarmed by what he saw.

His eyes were glowing brightly even in the well-illuminated elevator, and with his lips pressed tightly over his elongated fangs, he wondered how was it possible for Syssi not to be terrified of him.

He didn't look human even to himself.

At that thought, something snapped inside him. Forgetting he'd been in the doghouse just moments ago, he was seized by an overwhelmingly savage impulse to make Syssi his, to possess her.

And he wanted her to watch him do it. Holding her eyes in the mirror, he grabbed her long hair and tilted her head to the side, exposing her neck as he bared his fangs.

Her eyes widened in fear, but he gave her no time to process what was happening. With a snakelike hiss, he struck, sinking them deep into her smooth, creamy neck.

As he pumped her full of his venom, he was all animal, the tremendous relief of it triggering his other long overdue release.

Spent, he sagged boneless against her back, braced his hands on the mirrored wall, and closed his eyes. Now that it was all over, he was mortified by his behavior; afraid to look at Syssi in the mirror and see the horror and disgust on her face.

CHAPTER 40: SYSSI

Oh, my God! What is he?

Syssi had a moment of pure terror as Kian flashed a pair of monstrous fangs and sank them into her neck. The sharp burning pain of the twin penetrations had lasted no more than a few seconds before a euphoric pleasure swept through her, wiping away everything but its own mind-blowing effect.

Yes! Don't stop!

Her knees buckling, Kian's bruising grip on her hips was the only thing holding her up.

Dimly aware of Kian's fangs still embedded in her neck and his lips forming a tight seal on her skin, the pain failed to register.

She couldn't think. Just feel pleasure.

So good...

That too didn't last long, as a wave of powerful lust washed over her content haze, contracting and focusing all of it into her sex.

Her already wet nipples tightened into two stone-hard aching points, and her channel spasmed, creaming, begging to be filled.

Please...

She was about to do exactly that—beg Kian to impale her from behind—when the mere image of him doing so triggered an orgasm so powerful, her whole body shook with its aftershocks.

She blacked out.

The intense pleasure coming on the heels of such a terrifying experience must've been more than her body could take.

A moment later, as Kian's fangs retracted and his grip on her loosened, Syssi came to.

What had just happened?

Though still drugged and euphoric, she managed to crack her lids open and look at Kian's terrifying reflection. His intense blue eyes were glowing. The light wasn't coming from some outside source; the illumination came from inside. And those fangs, those monstrous long fangs of his, were tinted red from her blood. "What are you? What have you done to me?" she whispered.

Kian licked his fangs clean, his expression changing as they slowly shrank to an almost normal size. With guilt written all over his handsome face, he let go of her and took a step back.

Without him to hold her up, Syssi's knees buckled and she crumpled down to the elevator's floor.

CHAPTER 41: KIAN

I'm despicable. Kian cursed as he picked Syssi up and carried her inside. *I should get whipped for what I've just done.* What was I thinking?

He wasn't... Succumbing to an instinct like a ▓▓▓▓ animal...

Getting a thrill out of terrifying her? Coming in his pants? Where was all that self-control he prided himself on?

Shot to shit; that's where.

With Syssi, he was starting to think he had none.

Laying her gently on his bed, he was about to rectify the situation and thrall the memory away when her lids fluttered open.

Syssi looked at him and smiled seductively, her expression languid and satisfied from the euphoric effect of the venom. "You didn't answer me," she said with a purr, sounding as if she was talking about something carnal.

"I'm still Kian, the ass who momentarily lost his mind but is going to fix it right now." Kian focused on her eyes, attempting the thrall again.

Shifting her eyes away, she leveled them at the wet spot on his pants and giggled, breaking his concentration.

"Did I do this to you?" Shifting back to his face, she sighed contently. "Holy shit, that was amazing. I never knew I could actually black out from an orgasm." She giggled again. "But what kind of a vampire are you? Aren't you supposed to suck my blood out or something? Not pump me with some aphrodisiac... Oh, God, I still feel so loopy... But soooo gooood..."

She must be still high on the venom, that's why she is not panicking. Yet...

It was so tempting to just tell her the truth. What was the point of repeatedly thralling her anyway? He could always do it at the end of it; if and when she turned out not to be compatible. The best time to tell her was now when she was too hazy to freak out.

"I'm not a vampire." He sighed. "Vampires don't exist. At least as far as I know, although the stories about them most likely originated with my kind."

"Your kind?" Syssi's eyes seemed to get a bit clearer and more focused as she studied him closely.

"We are immortals—a more accurate definition would be near-immortals. We age extremely slow, we don't get sick, and we heal very quickly if injured. But we can still be killed, it's just harder to do." Kian observed her reaction, waiting for either disbelief or alarm, but there was none.

Instead, she frowned. "What about the fangs, the biting, what's the story with that? Not that I'm complaining, mind you..." She fluttered her long-lashed eyelids.

Kian smiled and sat down on the bed beside her, then hesitated for a moment before taking her hand—afraid she'd pull away.

Amazingly, she tightened the grip reassuringly as if sensing his apprehension.

"The males of my kind produce venom when aroused sexually or provoked to aggression by other males. During sex, it's a powerful aphrodisiac for the female, as you have experienced yourself, and a euphoric. In a violent struggle, it serves to incapacitate an opponent, the drugging effect weakening his ability and resolve to fight, paralyzing him. In large dosages, the venom can be lethal, stopping the heart."

Syssi took a moment to mull over what he had told her, then sounding more curious than worried, she asked, "How do you make sure you don't accidentally overdose your partner... You know, get carried away in the throes of passion and all that..."

"It cannot happen unintentionally. I'm not sure if it's biology controlling the amount and the potency of the venom produced, or if it's driven by intent. I've never heard of any male harming a female this way. But I'm not qualified to say if it's physically impossible or not. Although it makes sense that different emotions trigger the production of different hormones, which in turn determine the appropriate quantity and composition of the venom required for the particular situation. In any case, you're safe with me. Despite what just happened in the elevator, and I'm so sorry for losing it and frightening you, I'd never harm you... you must know that." He caressed her cheek, flabbergasted by how calmly she was accepting all of this.

Turning her face into the caress, she kissed the inside of his palm, the sweetness of the gesture sending a wave of tenderness through him.

"I know," she said. And yet, she didn't sound as if she truly believed that.

"At first, when I saw your fangs, I was terrified. And when you bit me, it hurt like hell, but only for a few seconds, and then the pain got washed away by what I assume was the aphrodisiac in the venom. What I felt after that... is just indescribable... A girl could get addicted to that." She smiled sheepishly.

You have no idea… It was eerie the way her random shots hit home.

"Was it the first time you bit me?" She frowned, her tone suggesting she suspected it wasn't.

"It was the second time," he admitted, feeling like a scumbag. Second bite, third thrall. But he wouldn't mention it if she didn't ask.

"How come I don't remember it? And how come there are no marks on my neck? I can't feel anything different there." She touched the smooth skin where he'd bitten her, running her fingertips over the area and searching for the puncture holes that should have been there.

"You won't find anything. My saliva carries healing properties. The wounds close in a matter of seconds." He hoped she'd be satisfied at that and let go of the other part of her question.

"And the memory?"

No such luck.

Kian sighed. "I thralled you to forget it. I'm sorry. I know it's unconscionable, but I had no choice. We can't allow the knowledge of our existence to leak to the world. And to answer your next question, refraining from biting is like trying to hold back ejaculation. Eventually, the need becomes impossible to suppress."

Syssi frowned. "What a strange biology… I wonder what the evolutionary benefits were for it to evolve this way." Lifting her arm with marked effort, she caressed his cheek as if to let him know it was okay, and she wasn't mad. But she couldn't hold it up for long and let it plop back down. "I feel so woozy… Am I still drugged?"

"It takes time for the effect of the venom to dissipate, not to mention that it's past two in the morning and you had a long and eventful day. Go to sleep, sweet girl. I'll answer the rest of your questions tomorrow." He brushed back her tangled hair and kissed her forehead.

Syssi struggled to keep her eyes open. "I have so many questions swirling in my head…" But exhaustion and wooziness from the venom were winning. "Promise you will not make me forget…," she whispered.

"I promise." Kian squeezed her hand.

Satisfied, she sighed and let her lids drop.

Kian held on to her hand as he watched her sleep, absentmindedly caressing her palm with his thumb.

Strange biology indeed, he grimaced. And he hadn't gotten to the punch line yet—that there was a chance she was a Dormant carrier of the same biology, or that she was right about the venom being addictive, and she might get hooked and come to crave it like any other junkie their drug of choice.

He had always suspected that their kind was not the product of evolution but the work of genetic manipulation. Some brilliantly deranged ancestor of theirs must have sought to bind their precious females to their mates, counterbalancing the females' stronghold on the race's unique genetics.

Or maybe he had thought to create an antidote to infidelity. Except, if that had been his goal, he had failed miserably. His people had found a way to circumvent it by methodically doing exactly the thing he had been trying to prevent.

Served the loon right, to witness what a joke his tampering with nature had turned out to be.

CHAPTER 42: KRI

Kri was doing her best to ignore the sounds coming from the backseat of the SUV. Sitting up front with Onidu, she gazed out the window and tried to keep her focus on the deserted streets they were passing by on their way home from the club.

Amanda had decided that one more round was in order and took her dessert to go; snaring another schlump to take home with her and starting on the fun in the car.

Hell, Kian wouldn't be happy with his sister bringing the guy up to her place and ignoring the SOP that no one but clan members was allowed on the top floors.

Never mind that he'd broken the rules himself with Syssi. But then again, the girl was a potential Dormant, and it looked like Kian had claimed her for himself. So in her case an exemption made sense.

But the same could not have been said about the random dude Amanda had picked up. However, trying to persuade Amanda to take her guy to one of the timeshare apartments on the lower level would probably be a waste of energy.

Kri sighed and began braiding her hair.

It was her duty to at least give it a try, and once they got to the building, she would. But at the same time, she knew from experience it would be impossible to reason with the stubborn woman.

Let Kian deal with his obstinate sister.

And good luck with that.

Smirking, Kri snapped the elastic on the bottom of her completed braid.

Man, she could just imagine the tantrum he'd throw finding out. But whatever, it wasn't her problem. She had no authority over the princess. Being a Guardian didn't mean she could just slap handcuffs on Annani's daughter and drag her to a holding cell in the basement.

All she could do was to flap her gums at the female. Uselessly.

In contrast, Kri never broke the rules and never brought her partners home. Not that there had been anyone at that club she had felt like screwing tonight. At home or anywhere else…

She grimaced, thinking about what had happened, or rather had not happened in the back room.

It wasn't that the guy hadn't been good-looking enough or sexed up enough, it was just that she'd kept comparing him to Michael and he'd kept coming short.

Weird, she'd never used to compare the ones she'd picked with Kian.

Maybe being so high up on the pedestal she had erected for him, he'd been in a completely different category, making the comparison irrelevant.

Not to mention the small detail of the taboo.

But Michael, well…

She kept seeing his smiling eyes admiring her in that sweet boyish way of his. He hadn't leered like some guys or tried to front some macho bullshit to impress her. The boy was man enough to admit that he really liked her. Straight out. No bull. And how sexy was that?

In the end, she hadn't done anything with the guy in the club. Couldn't. After some heavy necking that had done nothing for her, she had thralled him and sent him on his way.

Except now, sitting in the car, she debated the wisdom of that move. Still needy and antsy, the backseat activity not helping, she seriously contemplated waking Michael up.

It was such a bad idea, though.

Unless she had some feelings for the kid, it wouldn't be fair to him. He wasn't one of her kind, and with his mortal sensibilities about sex, she would in all likelihood crush his young, vulnerable ego.

Oh, he would love to have her any way he could get her—of that she had no doubt. But how would he feel the morning after when he'd realize he was just a one-night stand? Still having to face her day after day?

Some guys would have had no problem with that, but she had a strong feeling Michael was different. He was a one woman man, and once he found his one, he would look no further.

Unless she planned on being exclusive with him, at least until it was determined that he wouldn't turn and they sent him away clueless, she couldn't do it to him.

But wait… what if he really was a Dormant? If she had a relationship with him prior to his turning, then most likely he would remain hers to keep.

Sweet.

Smiling like the cat that ate the canary, Kri wondered how come it hadn't occurred to her before. She was in a unique position to call dibs on the first potential near-immortal male not of her clan.

What a coup.

And yet, as she had no frame of reference for a long-term relationship, she had a hard time imagining what it could be like having a man of her own.

Feeling a little out of sorts, Kri leaned back in her seat and gazed out the window again. The streets of downtown LA were deserted this late, and tonight, the familiar sight of the occasional homeless vagabond disturbed her for some reason.

Curled sleeping on a street bench, with a shopping cart containing all of his or her earthly belongings within reach, these homeless were completely alone in the world.

With no roots and no one to take care of them in their time of need, they were adrift in a sea of indifferent humanity. Abandoned.

If one died tonight, there would be no one to mourn the loss.

Their misfortune made her feel both guilty and lucky for having a large family at her back. If she ever lost her mind and didn't know who or where she was, there would always be someone to make sure she was all right and take responsibility for her.

Her kind wasn't susceptive to mortal diseases, but that immunity didn't extend to some afflictions of the mind, and there were a few cases of insanity among them.

Some had been the result of post-traumatic stress disorder, others due to God knew what.

Her own mother suffered from a mild case of obsessive compulsive disorder, compelled to keep everything in her house in precise groups of three.

It wasn't a big deal to just go with it and oblige her, but the hysterics when someone forgot and moved things out of their groupings were trying.

Yeah, it was good to be part of a clan; to belong to a community that gave a damn. But how much better would having a mate of her own be?

Someone she could come back to at the end of the day, share her nights with, her thoughts, her memories.

Well, putting it this way, a roommate could provide similar companionship. But the benefits of having one were not worth the compromises she'd have to make.

And in any case, it wasn't the same as someone sharing her bed. Permanently.

All of a sudden she craved it, which was strange because she'd never given it much thought before. But now, she longed for a partner with surprising intensity.

And the one she wanted, was Michael. With his cute smile and his big shoulders and sincere face.

Except, he was so damn young.

CHAPTER 43: SYSSI

Syssi cracked one eye open, not sure what had woken her up. It was either the sound of running water coming from the adjacent bathroom or the sun rays filtering through the parted curtains and shining brightly on her face.

Squinting against the glare, she looked around the unfamiliar bedroom, and it took her a moment until she remembered where she was. Or why...

With the cobwebs of sleep clearing, what had happened last night still seemed like a surreal dream or a drug-induced hallucination.

Yet, she knew it had been neither.

As out of it as she'd been while the whole thing happened, the memory of that bite and the things Kian had told her were too vivid to be a dream. And he'd brought her here last night—to his bedroom.

Well, at least he wasn't a mobster, she chuckled. And he claimed he wasn't a vampire... Though, considering the fangs and the biting, she still had her doubts.

Funny, that this was what was troubling her in light of the bigger picture she was starting to put together from all the bits and pieces he had told her.

The tale was pretty fantastic, but it was hard to argue with the sharp, pointy evidence of Kian's fangs. Apparently, some kind of immortal beings were living hidden among mortals, secretly helping humanity and manipulating global affairs with no one any the wiser. Except, it seemed a faction of them wasn't on board for the humanitarian effort and posed a serious threat to Kian's family.

She was only guessing that other immortals and not humans were the powerful enemies Kian's family was hiding from. But it made more sense than the scenario favored by fiction of some secret order devoted to the elimination of supernatural creatures.

Oh, well, whatever the full story was, the fang thing was strange and scary.

But oh, boy... was it hot.

The way Kian had made her feel, she didn't care if he was a vampire or something else. He was welcome to bite her anytime.

Surrounded by his scent, she snuggled in Kian's incredibly soft bedding, luxuriating at the way it felt on her bare skin...

Bare skin? Syssi realized she was completely naked beneath the duvet.

But for the life of her, she couldn't remember if she had undressed herself or had it been Kian who had taken everything off? Probably Kian... because she would have left her underwear on...

Unless it was wet...

Which it probably was.

Whatever.

Stretching her toes, Syssi felt happy. Which implied that she must be either out of her mind or still affected by the venom.

In light of the bombshell Kian had dropped at her feet, she should've been alarmed, disbelieving, panicking, running for her life; as any normal person would. Instead, all she felt was good.

No way would she let any negative thoughts intrude on her feelings of serenity and wellbeing. She felt healthy, strong, sexy... and pampered.

Kian's bedroom was fit for a king... or a queen... The king-sized bed sat on a raised platform, facing a fireplace with a large screen television hanging above it and a pair of overstuffed bookcases flanking it.

She couldn't see the titles from this far, but judging by their messy and uncoordinated arrangement, the books had gotten a lot of actual use.

Kian must've spent most of his time in here reading, unless he liked watching TV from bed, because instead of facing the screen, the sitting area was oriented toward the wall of sliding glass doors and the terrace beyond.

Syssi loved it. If it were hers, she would've never left this room. She could see herself spending a lot of lazy afternoons here; sitting in one of the comfy chairs, reading a book and drinking a latte as the curtains fluttered in the breeze that blew in through the open patio doors.

Or, she could be lounging lazily in this heavenly bed, preferably with Kian in it...

Naked...

Or almost naked...

Walking in with only a towel wrapped around his hips, and his hair dripping droplets of water down his sculpted chest, Kian took her breath away. There was no doubt in her mind that she would never get tired of seeing him like this, and that each and every time she did, she would be awed anew by his perfection.

Now that she knew what he was, her first impression of him made perfect sense. She was right to think that no mere mortal could look so good because Kian wasn't human. And neither was Amanda.

Oh, boy! Did she have questions for him.

"Good morning, sunshine," he greeted her, smiling a big toothy smile—one she realized she had never seen on him before. His fangs were clearly visible now, but they were nothing compared to the scary things he flashed her in the mirror last night and could easily pass for slightly larger than normal canines.

Did they elongate in response to the triggers he had mentioned? Retracting when of no further use?

"We need to talk," she said, thinking that from here on out, these words that were dreaded by males everywhere would hold a whole new meaning for her.

"I know, and I promise we will. But first... we have some unfinished business from last night..." Growling, Kian let the towel drop as he advanced on her, looking like a mighty jungle cat ready to pounce on his prey.

The effect of seeing his powerful, naked body moving sinuously toward her was like flipping on a switch, igniting a lust so powerful that it had her body trembling with need.

Yeah, talking can definitely wait.

Suddenly, the comforter felt scratchy and too warm on her naked, oversensitized skin, and she threw it off. Framing her aching breasts with her hands, she arched her hips—offering herself like a feline in heat.

CHAPTER 44: KIAN

"So ███████ beautiful..." Crawling on the bed to straddle Syssi, Kian felt feral. And yet, looking down at her flushed body, the few neurons still functioning in his blood-deprived brain managed to process the fact that her level of arousal was alarming.

Syssi's normally pink nipples were red and turgid, and as she spread her knees to welcome him in between them, he found her already wet and swollen. Urging him on, she rolled her hips and cupped her breasts as a needy moan left her parted lips.

Was it even possible for the addiction to take hold only after two bites? He hoped this wasn't the case, and that her wildness could be attributed to plain old lust.

But regardless of the impetus, her explicit carnality effectively slammed down all of his buttons, driving reason and his good intentions away.

Mindless with lust, he was all animal as he drove into her, burying himself to the hilt in one powerful thrust.

Syssi climaxed instantly. And as her convulsing inner muscles gripped him tightly, Kian groaned, straining against the pressure building up in his shaft.

It was too soon.

Slowing down, he was able to hold off for no more than a few strokes before need overpowered his resolve, and he began pounding into her mercilessly, going fast and hard, grunting and groaning like the beast he was.

Somewhere in the back of his mind, a thought was trying to filter through and warn him that he might be hurting her. But its voice was drowned by the turmoil of the blood boiling in his veins.

Growing impossibly hard, he was on the brink of the inevitable eruption, when Syssi turned her head—submitting her exposed neck for his bite.

That was it for him. With the iron links of his self-imposed manacles not so much snapping as crumbling to dust, he bared his fangs and bit her, pumping her full of his venom along with his seed.

Syssi went over again. With her sheath gripping onto him on the inside and her arms holding on tight, she kept his chest pressed against hers as their bodies shook from the exertion and the force of their climaxes.

Long moments passed with them entwined in each other, dazed in a mindless stupor, unable to move, or talk, or even think coherently.

They must've fallen asleep, because when Kian opened his eyes next, the light in the room had changed, indicating that the sun had moved across the sky, changing the angle of its rays.

With his mind clear, Kian felt like scum. He had no doubt some form of addiction had already taken root, and not only in Syssi.

He had never experienced sex like that before, not even close. And looking back at almost two thousand years of it, he could think of only one logical explanation. The one he dreaded most.

"I'm so sorry, baby," he whispered into Syssi's neck, thinking she was still sleeping.

"What the heck for?"

He heard her barely audible whisper, as her hand started a lazy trek up and down his back.

"You make me so wild, cats in heat have nothing on me." She chuckled. "Or you...," she added, nuzzling his neck. "Do you turn all your women into mindless sex maniacs? Or is it just me?" she whispered, blowing hot air in his ear.

Did he imagine it? Or was she attempting to hide her possessiveness and jealousy by pretending to tease? Not that he minded, he kind of liked that she did. And it had nothing to do with satisfaction over the shoe being on the other foot. Nothing at all...

"I'm not sure who made whom more wild. Though I doubt that having the dubious honor of being the only one I've ever rutted on like a crazed animal was good for you. I'm sorry if I hurt you."

"No, you didn't hurt me, you sweet boy. I wanted you exactly like that: mindless with passion, crazed... I'm happy you were just as out of control as I was. I would be dying of shame at my own sluttishness otherwise." Syssi kissed his neck, running her hands over his sweat-slicked body. "I think you need another shower, lover boy." A smirk curled her lips. "We can have one together..."

Later, when the joined shower didn't evolve into another mindless carnal attack, Kian reevaluated his earlier conviction that the addiction was responsible for their crazed sex.

They both seemed comfortably satiated, enjoying some lazy caressing and kissing but not taking it any further than that.

And what a relief that was.

"Oh, damn, I have nothing to wear. All my things are at Amanda's, and I'm afraid the dress I was wearing last night is ruined." Syssi frowned. Sitting on the bed wrapped in a bath towel, she looked at the dress in her hands. "Could you send it to be dry-cleaned? I can't return it to Amanda in this condition."

"Don't worry about it. I'll take care of the incriminating evidence." He chuckled and stepped out from inside his closet with one of his T-shirts. "You can use this in the meantime."

Wearing his plain white shirt, Syssi looked absolutely adorable and sexy as hell—the thing reaching below her knees and providing a semi-decent cover to her otherwise naked body.

The *semi* being the operative word.

With her sweet ass clearly visible through the thin fabric, he kept glancing behind her and ogling it as they walked into the kitchen, holding hands.

"Good morning!" Okidu beamed at them and immediately got busy serving them breakfast.

Once he was done, Kian shooed him away, knowing Syssi would prefer their conversation to be private.

Sitting at the kitchen counter and drinking her coffee, Syssi kept quiet until Okidu left. Then, with her cheeks growing red, she giggled before slanting a quick glance at Kian. "I don't know what came over me. I've never been so out of control before... wouldn't have believed I even had it in me." She lowered her eyes, focusing on the mug she was holding. "Do you think it had something to do with your venom? Did any of the other women react to it like this?"

And here it was again, that jealous note in her tone...

"It might have been the venom. Though I must admit, your reaction was surprising. Don't get me wrong, I loved it. Most intense sexual experience I've ever had. And if you're embarrassed by it, please don't be. I don't think you can top my coming in my pants... twice... That never happened to me with anyone but you either." Kian chuckled nervously. "It seems we're having lots of firsts together, don't you think?"

"I guess... it's just that my experience is very limited. I had only one lover before you. We were together for four years. He and I... we never got that intense. It was kind of lackluster... And since we broke up two years ago, there wasn't anyone I wanted to be with... before you, that is."

Syssi sighed, playing with her mug and looking into her coffee as if the right things to say could be found inside. "I thought I wasn't into the whole thing, the sex thing I mean, couldn't understand what all the hubbub was about. And then you show up. And I burn for you, go wild for you… I never imagined it could be like that." She slanted a tentative glance at him.

Kian pulled her into his arms and hugged her tightly. "Your ex was a moron. His inadequacy, or his confused sexual orientation, influenced the way you thought of yourself because you had nothing to compare it to. Believe me, you're the hottest, most passionate, perfect woman I have ever known. And coming from me it says a lot… I've been around the block… way more times than I care to admit." Tilting up her chin with his finger, he looked into her beautiful eyes. "You believe me, right?" he said in a tone that brooked no argument.

"So, what are you saying? That you're old? Or that you're a slut?" Syssi chuckled, teasing. Still, she looked pleased, her eyes glowing from his compliments.

"Both." He smiled back and kissed her cute little nose. "You got yourself a dirty, dirty old man."

"How old is old? And how dirty?"

Kian took a deep breath, not looking forward to her reaction to what he was about to tell her. "I'm almost two thousand years old, and since reaching puberty, I've been with a different woman almost every night. I'm not proud of it. In fact, I resent my physiology. My kind is driven by a very strong sex drive, probably as a way to counteract our extremely low fertility rate… So yeah, I've been a major slut. I hope that doesn't disgust you…" He searched her eyes, hoping she'd understand and accept.

Syssi was quiet for a moment, mulling over that ditty. "You're two thousand years old, you're serious?"

"In four years I'll be… yeah." If that was the only part that bothered her, he was good.

Well, maybe…

He didn't mind the age difference, but she might have a different take on a disparity measured in centuries as opposed to years or even decades.

"Okay, I think you'd better start at the beginning and tell me the whole story. I'd rather hear it all at once and get over the shock than get flummoxed with every new bombshell." Syssi got loose from his embrace and leaned back, getting comfortable on her barstool.

"There are quite a few more explosive details coming your way, so you better brace yourself." Kian sighed.

Learning the truth, she might decide to leave, wanting nothing more to do with him. But he had no choice. It was the right thing to do.

"My kind had lived among mortals for thousands of years. We don't know if we were a divergent species, remnants of a previous advanced society that suffered some kind of cataclysm, or a group of refugees from somewhere else in the universe.

"In the ancient world, we were the gods of old, worshiped and loved by the mortal societies we were helping to evolve. Besides our remarkable regeneration abilities, we could also control mortal minds quite easily; creating realistic illusions, planting thoughts, thralling... as you had experienced.

"The original number of gods was very small. The limited gene pool, combined with an extremely low conception rate, prompted the gods to seek partners among the mortals. It worked, and many near-immortal children were born. But when those children took human mates, their children were born mortal.

"They discovered a way to activate the dormant godly genes, but only for the children of the female immortals, it didn't work for the children of the males." Kian took a sip of his coffee, giving Syssi the opportunity to ask questions. But she said nothing, looking curious and waiting for him to continue.

"My mother, Annani, a full blooded goddess, was supposed to marry her cousin Mortdh but fell in love with another. According to their code of law or maybe just custom, mating had to be consensual. So she was free to marry her love.

"Mortdh felt betrayed and humiliated and being insane murdered Annani's love. He then declared war on the other gods. That war ended in a nuclear disaster that wiped out the gods as well as a huge portion of the mortal population.

"My mother, alone out of all the gods, escaped the cataclysm, taking with her the advanced knowledge of her people. She made it her mission to continue their work and trickle this knowledge to humanity, guiding it to become a better society.

"Mortdh was killed by the shockwaves of his own bomb, but some of his descendants survived. They carried on his rabid hatred of females, influencing the societies they controlled to eliminate the human rights women had previously enjoyed, plunging that part of the world further into darkness. They took on his vow to eliminate Annani, her progeny, and any progress humanity achieved with her help.

"We, as her children, are helping her with her mission. Unfortunately, there are not many of us, and as we all share the same matrilineal descent, we are forbidden to mate with each other. Annani mated with mortals to have us, and my sisters continued doing the same, as did their daughters, and so on.

"We believe, though, that there are Dormant mortals in the general population, people who carry our genetic code, descendants of the survivors of other lines who we can activate. Potential mates for us.

"We've been searching for them since the beginning, and not finding any, all of us were basically doomed to one-night stands. The females can, at least, have children that are like us, the males can produce only mortal children. Can you imagine how hard it is to watch your children grow old and die while you remain unchanged?"

Kian sighed a heavy sigh. Sensing his sadness, Syssi clasped his hand and held it in silent encouragement.

"Amanda thinks that paranormal abilities could in some cases lead to Dormants. As you know, out of all her subjects, you and Michael are her top candidates. That's why the Doomers want you; the Devout Order of Mortdh Brotherhood, or Doom Brotherhood for short. Our enemies of old."

"So if I'm a potential Dormant, how would you know for sure? How do you activate your Dormants?"

"The venom. Our boys get activated at thirteen, and usually one injection is enough, three at most. The girls change much younger. For them, being nurtured by Annani and exposed to her daily is the only catalyst needed. But we don't know how many injections it takes to activate the dormant genes in an adult. It was never done before."

Syssi frowned. "So when were you going to tell me? Don't you think you should have asked me if I was okay with it?" Syssi's voice quivered. "After all, it is my life you're playing God with. I would think the decent thing to do was to at least warn me before dousing me with your venom." She glared at him; her back straight and her arms crossed protectively over her chest.

"Guilty as charged. You're absolutely right. The thing is, I'm still sure Amanda is grasping at straws, and you're not a Dormant and neither is Michael. Who, by the way, is down in our basement and on board with giving it a shot."

"Oh, this is just getting better and better... So it was fine to inform Michael but not me?"

"We just told him yesterday, and I was planning to tell you as well. It just took me some time to gather the nerve to do it. In some ways, Michael has it worse, but his situation is less complicated."

"Why?"

Kian sighed. "To attempt his activation, he needs to fight one of us just well enough to trigger the aggression needed for venom production. Not a big problem, him being a young, strong guy. The worst that he'll suffer is some pounding—not that much different from other forms of combat training. A young man his age would probably find it an invigorating challenge."

Syssi snorted. "It would seem I have the better deal. I actually find it pleasurable when you pound into me."

"I'm glad you can still find it humorous." Kian raked his fingers through his hair, trying to think of a way to deliver the bad news as gently as possible.

"If Michael doesn't turn, we'll have to thrall away his memory of us, and of him being here, and plant some other plausible scenario in his mind. He might get a little confused from time to time, remembering bits and pieces of things, not sure if he dreamt them or experienced them. Hopefully, this would be the extent of it, and he wouldn't suffer any lasting brain damage." Looking into her eyes, he took her hands in his, waiting for the implications to sink in.

CHAPTER 45: SYSSI

Syssi's eyes widened as the meaning of what Kian was trying to communicate hit home. "Oh, my God, you're planning to erase my memory and send me off, clueless, same as Michael. I can't believe it! And to think I was actually falling for you. Talk about naive."

Pulling away from him, she jumped out of her seat and almost toppled the thing as she stormed into the bedroom she had occupied before—remembering too late that her things weren't there anymore.

Exasperated, she slammed the door behind her, hoping Kian would at least have the decency to stay out.

Not a chance.

A second later, the door banged open and he stormed in. "What would you have me do? What would you have done in my place, huh? I'm listening… Any bright ideas? No? I didn't think so."

The nerve of the guy, venting his frustration and acting as if he was the injured party here. She was the one that would be cast off like yesterday's news. Not him.

It was just too much, and as traitorous tears began sliding down her cheeks, she couldn't stop her chin from quivering. God, why couldn't she be tougher, or at least hold off with the girly emotional display until he was gone. But as there was no chance in hell of him leaving anytime soon, she lashed out. "You're the two-thousand-year-old immortal who should be smart enough to figure something out." Sitting on the bed, Syssi plopped back and grabbed a pillow to hold it over her tear-streaked face.

Kian sat down beside her and tugged on the pillow. "Hiding will not solve anything." Yanking harder, he took it away.

With her temporary shelter gone, she covered her face with her hands—determined not to look at him. "I don't want to talk to you. Go away!" She managed to suppress the quiver in her voice.

Pulling at her arms, he uncovered her teary face. "Please don't cry, you're killing me." Kian leaned to kiss her tears away, planting little pecks all over her face.

Which made it even worse.

"You're such a phony, pretending to care when you knew all along you'd be getting rid of me soon." Syssi turned her face sideways in an attempt to escape his kisses.

"I do care, a lot. It's just such an impossible situation. I'm screwed whatever I do. If you don't turn, and I want to keep you, I'd either have to thrall you repeatedly, which will mess with your brain and might cause long-term damage, or keep you locked up in here unable to leave or get in touch with your family, and you'd grow to hate me either way. The only decent thing I could have done was to let you go. And believe me, I tried. But I couldn't do it, and not only because I couldn't help how much I wanted you. I'm selfish, but not that selfish. This is bigger than just me and what I want, or how unfair it is to you. The slim chance that you might be a Dormant is too important for the future of my clan." Stroking her hair, he leaned into her and waited for her to turn and look at him.

Instead, she grabbed another pillow to hide under.

"Look, let us enjoy the time we have together and see what happens. You wouldn't want me to make promises I couldn't keep, would you? I'm trying to come clean and be completely honest with you. Please don't shut me out."

His pleading tone touched her. And besides, as much as she hated to accept the grim reality, she had to admit he was right.

Discarding the pillow, Syssi shifted her teary eyes to his sad face and opened her arms, inviting him in.

With a relieved sigh, Kian leaned into her embrace and held her tightly to his chest, completely unconcerned with his T-shirt getting wet from her tears. "I'm so sorry. I wish there were more I could offer you." He kissed her forehead.

Syssi sniffled, burying her face in his shirt. "I hate the fact that I need you so much. Just feeling your body against mine calms me down. It's as if I'm addicted to you, craving you even though I know you're no good for me."

Kian's body stiffened and he sat back. "Now that you mention it, there is one last screwed-up detail I haven't told you yet... The venom is addictive. The more your body gets, the more you will crave it, suffering unpleasant withdrawal if denied it."

"What kind of withdrawal?"

"You'll crave only me and get repulsed by any other man trying to be intimate with you. Until it leaves your system, you will not be able to have sex with anyone but me. And that might take a while."

Syssi frowned. She wouldn't want any other man after Kian, regardless of the addiction. No one could take his place, and she wondered if she would ever be able to stop comparing every guy to him and find each and every one wanting.

Still, that wasn't what had gotten her upset. "How about you, will you develop an addiction to me?"

"Eventually, but supposedly it takes longer for males to get hooked. As your body's scent gradually changes, bearing my particular mark, it will both attract me and serve as a repellent to other males of my kind." For some reason, what he had just told her made him frown.

Looking at his hard face, Syssi couldn't decide if he frowned because explaining the compulsory nature of his kind irritated him, or was he secretly yearning for the addiction to shackle her to him... Was his possessive nature once again raising its ugly, primitive head? Except, if it did, she was guilty of the same thing, clinging to what he had said in a desperate hope that he'd get hooked on her... and fast.

Sighing, Kian clasped her hand. "Don't worry, it normally takes a very long time for the addiction to set, probably months. We'll know one way or the other long before it happens," he added, evidently misreading her expression and attempting to assuage her fears.

Syssi wanted to tell him that she wasn't worried, she was disappointed.

Kian had just destroyed the last glimmer of her irrational hope that he would soon come to crave her so much, he would never be able to let her go—regardless of whether she turned or not.

Then, the obtuse man misinterpreted her dejected expression again and made it worse by trying to make it better. "If a miracle happens and you turn, you'll have your pick of clan males before you're compelled to choose one because of the addiction."

Not getting the relieved reaction he had anticipated, he continued to make it worse. "You don't have to commit to one man right from the start. The way to prevent getting addicted to a specific venom is to vary partners and get several different types of it in your system. You can take your time and choose someone that is right for you with the confidence that you aren't compelled to rush into it."

What the hell? Yesterday he was ready to punch Anandur for flirting with her, and today he was okay with her choosing someone else?

Again, she wanted to scream at him to make up his mind. Come to think of it, throwing something heavy at his head would have been way more satisfying.

Men were so frustrating.

Who could understand the twisted way their minds worked... And to think they accused women of making no sense and being irrational. Ha!

Nonetheless, it hurt like hell.

The only way she could make sense of his bizarre behavior was to accept that as long as he considered her his, he didn't want any other males sniffing around her. But evidently, he wasn't planning on anything long-term. He knew he'd eventually tire of her and then pass her on to someone else.

She must've meant so little to him. Just a convenient lay. Another notch on his belt... A very, very, long belt.

Unless she turned...

Then she would be important alright... to the clan. Not him personally, but to all the other males in his family.

Syssi felt so stupid. She had no one to blame for the pain she was feeling but herself. What did she expect? A man like him falling in love with her? Wanting her to be his forever? Forever taking a whole new meaning in his case. He was the freaking son of a goddess, for heaven's sake. Gorgeous, successful...

Syssi wanted to scream in frustration.

She couldn't let him know how deeply he had cut her, though, and regretted even the small glimpses of feelings she had already allowed him to see.

If he could treat their time together as a temporary fling, so could she. Pretending to be just as casual about it, she'd treat him as nothing but a hookup and try to be just as cynical as everyone else.

Too bad, though, that fronting as if it was nothing to her would be hard to pull off. She wasn't that good of an actress.

Pulling her hand from his clasp, she pushed up to her feet. "I need to go to Amanda's place to get dressed."

Kian reached for her as she turned to leave. "Are you okay?" Pulling her in between his thighs, he wrapped his arms around her waist.

"Yeah, sure... I can't spend the day wearing your T-shirt, can I? I have to go." Syssi tugged at his arms until he let go of her. "I also need to put in some work with Amanda, or I'll lose my pay." She tried to smile reassuringly but failed miserably.

Kian seemed reluctant to let her go, catching her hand as she once again turned to leave. "Okay, but I'll come to see you later. Maybe in the afternoon?"

"Yeah, sure, whatever..." She pulled until he let go and walked out.

CHAPTER 46: SYSSI

Standing outside Amanda's door in her ridiculous getup of platforms and Kian's flimsy T-shirt and nothing underneath, yesterday's underwear bunched in her hand, Syssi knocked, then waited a few moments before knocking again, louder this time.

"Let yourself in!" She heard Amanda call.

Syssi opened the door just a crack and peeked in. "Hello? It's me. Can I come in?"

Amanda couldn't answer since her mouth was busy kissing a bare-chested guy. And it wasn't the one Syssi remembered from the club...

The woman was simply unbelievable...

"Here you go, sweetheart." Amanda handed him his shirt and shoes. Without giving him a chance to put them on, she pushed him toward the door.

"Onidu! Where are you? Sam is ready to go. Please drive him back to the club."

Poor Sam looked completely out of it, stupefied. And judging by his unfocused eyes and gaping mouth the guy was probably thralled within an inch of his life.

But what really caught Syssi's attention were the small bite marks on the side of his neck and both of his smooth pecs.

Amanda kissed Sam's cheek, then shoved him out the door with a pat on his butt. As she turned her full attention to Syssi, there was a knowing smirk on her face. "Good morning, stranger, I see you ended up having some fun after all." She tugged on her own long T-shirt down from where it rode up her thighs.

Syssi decided giving being blunt a shot. "How come your guy had visible bite marks, and I don't?"

"I see that Kian has finally spilled... So what exactly did he tell you?" Amanda walked over to the couch and sat down. Tucking her bare legs under her butt, she covered her knees with the long shirt. "Come tell mommy everything." She patted the spot next to her.

"I guess the main points... Who and what you guys are, your enemies, how I might be a potential immortal, and how crucially important it is to the clan if I am, and so on." Sissy stuffed her underwear in her purse, leaving it on the table before settling next to Amanda. Tucking her legs under Kian's long shirt, she mirrored her boss's pose.

In the quiet that followed, Amanda's stare was unnerving. Turning away from those knowing eyes, Syssi grabbed one of the throw pillows strewn on the couch and hugged it to herself, pretending to admire the colorful pattern.

"He did something to hurt you, didn't he... Tell me, so I can go and pummel the fool to the ground." Amanda held her fists up, then chuckled as Syssi arched a brow. "Okay, I'll hire some muscle to do it for me."

"He didn't hurt me. I had like two seconds of panic when he flashed those monstrous fangs of his, but after that, well... it was amazing... It's just that I'm kind of shell-shocked. All of this is a lot to wrap my mind around—to absorb. I need time to think it through—formulate my questions... And speaking of questions; you didn't answer me about the bite marks." For some reason, talking about it helped Syssi get some perspective and organize it in her head, and she felt some of the turmoil inside her subside.

"He told you about the venom, right?" When Syssi nodded, Amanda continued. "Females don't have any. Our small, wee fangs, if you can even call them that, are for decoration only. They don't elongate like the males' do either. I guess it's like the difference between a penis and a clitoris." Amanda snorted. "I bite because I like it and it feels good, not because it can do anything interesting, like activate a Dormant or incapacitate an opponent. Without the venom, it takes longer for the marks to heal... on mortals anyway. An immortal male's body would have healed those in no time, and maybe it's a big turn-on for them. Who knows? I never had one." Amanda looked down at her hands.

"You never had a lover of your own kind?"

"I don't know any immortal men that I'm not related to. So only plain mortals for me. Yay!" Amanda looked up at Syssi with sad eyes.

That's right, Kian had said that they couldn't mate with members of the same matrilineal descent.

Suddenly, the full weight of their plight dawned on her. The lonely existence they were doomed to endure. Being confined to mortal lovers, they had no chance of having lifelong partners, spending their extremely long existence alone.

How sad...

"Have you ever fallen in love? With a mortal?" Syssi probed.

"No, I hardly ever have sex with the same guy twice. None of us do. Even for an idiot, it wouldn't take long to figure out something is not kosher. Eventually, someone that you're close to is bound to notice that you never get sick, heal in seconds from accidental cuts and nicks, that you're stronger and faster than normal and your senses are sharper. The males have it even worse; kind of hard to explain the fangs away. And there is the addiction factor. Did Kian share that little morsel with you?"

"He did." Syssi grimaced.

"It's funny, but we forgot all about it. Mother told Kian a long time ago, but as it wasn't relevant to our situation, one-night stands and all, he forgot. He was reminded because of you."

Syssi rubbed at her chest, the subject sharpening the knives' barely dulled edge and bringing back the pain. "Yeah, not very convenient for a fling... Still, I bet your ancestors had very stable marriages—being forced to be faithful to each other like that."

"Not necessarily, we are a lustful race, as you're surely aware of by now. The way our mother explained it to Kian, mated couples that didn't want to limit themselves were having sex with other partners from the get-go, mixing up the different venoms to prevent being addicted to a particular one. More so in the upper class, where most marriages were arranged and not the result of any great love. Besides, sleeping around was not frowned on. It was an acceptable behavior for both males and females. What do you think the myths of the gods frolicking with one another and with mortals are based on? That's the way they really were."

"So what's the point of having this system if it's so easily circumvented?"

"Kian and I talked about it. We guess, but it's speculation only, that our race was genetically manipulated to have the peculiar traits we have. The scientist responsible for it might have been a romantic at heart, or loved an unfaithful mate. Who knows?" Amanda smiled.

"Kian thinks he was a deranged lunatic, but I think it was sweet. Imagine falling in love, getting married, and during the honeymoon— when everything is still wonderfully exciting and love is fresh—an addiction forms. Voila! Lifelong fidelity. No nasty surprises, no divorces... and an amazing sex life to boot. It could have been a wonderful thing for a true love mating."

"Ha! What if after the honeymoon period—as you call it—they started to annoy each other so much that they grew to hate one another but were stuck together because of the addiction? What then?" Syssi crossed her arms over her chest and switched to sitting with her legs crossed at the knee.

"Well, if it got so bad that they were willing to suffer through withdrawal and abstain from sex for a few months, then they could've gone their separate ways. But it gave them one hell of an incentive to just get along." Amanda laughed, giving Syssi a quick hug.

"I don't know... Relationships are complicated, people are complicated; feelings change, people change, shit happens... You cannot hope to solve all possible problems with good sex." Syssi thought her situation with Kian was a perfect example of that.

Amanda's face turned serious. "Look, I don't know what exactly Kian told you, or how he presented it. I know he can be overbearing and insensitive, and expressing his feelings is not something he is good at. Not much of a diplomat, my brother. That's why we have someone else to do the smooth talking for him at business negotiations. But his intentions are good. He hardly ever thinks about what's good for himself. His life is all about the survival of our clan and ensuring that our work continues to help humanity thrive and evolve. It's such a huge burden to carry. You have no idea how much I admire and respect both Kian and Sari for shouldering that huge responsibility. And how grateful I am for being spared from having to shoulder it myself. I don't think I could've done it."

"Your work is important too. You're trying to find compatible mates for your family. I'm sure they appreciate it, especially if you actually succeed." Syssi sensed that Amanda felt overshadowed by her older siblings and wasn't used to getting praise.

"Yeah, after two centuries of being a selfish party girl, I'm finally trying to make a contribution."

Yep, Amanda definitely wasn't used to praise… And she was two hundred years old? Wow!

"So, does that mean you don't party anymore?" Syssi asked, thinking Amanda partied plenty.

"Of course I do, silly. I just put some work in as well."

CHAPTER 47: KIAN

Kian stared at the small box sitting on his desk, fighting the urge to grab it and use it as an excuse to go see Syssi.

Almost an hour had passed since she left for Amanda's, and during all that time he kept churning over their conversation in his mind, ignoring the paperwork stacked on his desk.

All along, he had been afraid that once she realized what was in store for her, she would react exactly the way she had. Grow cold and distant and push him away.

But then again, he couldn't really blame her, could he.

It was exactly as she had said. He was a jerk. He had lied to her, hadn't asked her if she wanted to be changed, and in the end, he would be forced to send her away.

And that wasn't even the worst of it. The truth was, he hadn't been thinking about changing her when he had sunk his fangs into her lovely neck. During those intense moments, he had thought of nothing but the sex.

It had been all about his need and his craving...

He wondered what Syssi would've thought of him if she had known that the supposedly noble intentions he'd been fronting were nothing but a cover for him being a beast. Or that the little speech about letting her choose whoever she wanted had been total crap.

In fact, even though he'd lied through his teeth about giving her a choice, the mere act of verbalizing the lie had him almost pop a vein. He had a feeling he would not hesitate to annihilate any male who would dare try to take her away from him.

Family not excluded.

Snatching the box with Syssi's new phone, Kian pushed out of his swivel chair, shoving it so hard that the thing hit the bookcase behind him and rolled sideways as it bounced off.

In several determined strides, he crossed the short distance between the apartments, but then as he stood in front of Amanda's door, he hesitated.

Given the laughter percolating from the other side, it sounded as if Syssi and Amanda were having a good time, and he wondered if he hadn't blown things out of proportion.

There was only one way to find out, and he sure as hell wasn't going to do it by standing outside and eavesdropping like a coward.

He rapped on the door and walked in without waiting for an invitation. "I brought you your new phone as soon as it was delivered," he said, smiling at the domestic scene of Syssi and his sister sharing a couch in their oversized T-shirts. "You can call anyone you want and give them your new phone number. The phone uses our own satellite, and the line is untraceable and secure."

With a quick look at Amanda, he searched his sister's expression for a clue as to Syssi's mood. But her impassive face gave nothing away.

"Thank you, I was feeling lost without a phone." Syssi took the white box and tore at the wrapping, eager to get to her new toy.

Using her momentary distraction, Kian looked at Amanda again, this time gesticulating his question.

"Jury still out," she mouthed, shrugging her shoulders, then made a shooing motion urging him to leave.

"I'd better go. See you later, ladies." He excused himself but remained glued to his spot, waiting for Syssi to look up; hoping she'd smile at him or, at least glance his way. But to his chagrin, her head remained bowed over the phone's instructions as if he wasn't even there.

Swallowing a bitter sense of disappointment, he said, "Goodbye then," and beat feet to the door.

"Goodbye," Syssi called after him.

He whipped around, hoping to catch her looking his way. But she didn't—killing his small spark of hope.

Standing outside Amanda's apartment, Kian ran his hands through his hair and sighed. It would be a waste of time to go back to the office. He was too agitated to be able to concentrate on anything.

Instead, he took the elevator down to the basement.

At the gym, Kian found Brundar and Michael training, with Kri watching them from the sidelines. It seemed Michael's training session had been going on for a while. The kid was tired and frustrated. Not that Kian could blame him, Brundar had Michael practicing the same three moves over and over again.

Detect, block, deflect... detect, block, deflect.

"Again!" Brundar ordered and launched another mock knife attack. With a rubber stick in each hand, he kept slashing relentlessly at Michael, cutting through his ineffective defense and hitting him time and again.

Bundled as he was in protective suiting, Michael no doubt felt the blows, but besides his ego, he wasn't really getting hurt. Nonetheless, he was sweaty and exhausted and looked ready to call it quits.

Except, Kri was watching him from her spot next to the punching bag. Jabbing perfunctorily at it, she seemed more interested in Michael's training session than her own. And given the quick glances he was sneaking her way, it was obvious that as long as she kept watching him, the kid would keep pushing until he dropped.

Kian smirked, turning away quickly before Kri caught him observing her, then went back to watching Michael.

The kid was inexperienced and somewhat clumsy, but Kian had to admit that there was raw potential there. What he lacked in endurance and discipline, he made up in brute strength and youthful enthusiasm.

Brundar was driving him hard, but then again, no one got good by watching how it was done from the couch. At his current level of skill, Michael wouldn't stand a chance against a trained opponent, and the sooner he got the basics, the sooner he'd be able to defend himself.

"Okay, kid, take a break. You did well." Brundar clapped Michael on the shoulder.

"Thanks. But when are we going to move to something else?"

"When those moves become second nature, when no matter when, or from what angle, I come at you—you'll execute them perfectly. Then... we can move on, and not before." Brundar walked over to the fridge and took out a water bottle.

Kri abandoned her post next to the boxing bag and sauntered to stand next to Michael. "You better listen to him. Brundar is our weapons master and there is no one in the world that's better. Consider yourself lucky he is training you." She patted his cheek, but the pat sounded more like a slap.

"Yeah, I feel very lucky..." Michael groaned, wiping the sweat from his face with a towel. "Any luckier, and I'll be dead... He is killing me!"

"Wuss." Kri snorted. "He is teaching you how to stay alive. And just between you and me..." She leaned to whisper in his ear conspiratorially, "I'm surprised he volunteered to train you. He is not exactly the friendly, giving type if you catch my drift. And he only trains experienced fighters. Taking on a newbie... Damn! He must really believe in you." She punched Michael's shoulder. "Go get yourself some water. It's important to stay hydrated during training." She smiled and sauntered away, swaying her hips.

Kian rubbed his hand over his chin. There was definitely something going on between Kri and Michael.

Good, it was about time for her to shed the immature fascination she had with him and move toward something more appropriate. For Kri's sake, as much as for the good of the clan, Kian hoped Michael would turn.

Which raised the issue of choosing an initiator for the boy. The honor of accepting the role carried with it some serious responsibility. The male Michael would challenge to a fight would not only be the one to induce his transformation but also assume the role of a lifelong honorary big brother.

The coming of age ceremony usually involved two boys: a thirteen-year-old Dormant and a transitioned boy—if possible no more than a year or two older. The friendship encouraged by the ritual benefited both boys, as it created between them a brotherly bond similar to the one between real brothers.

Siblings were a rarity in their community, and even if one was lucky enough to have a brother, chances were that they were separated by hundreds of years in age. Having an adopted one, certainly beat growing up alone.

Kian walked over to the center of the gym and stood on top of the rubber mats delineating the wrestling area. "Listen up. I want you all in the small conference room in half an hour. Go shower and change. We'll be choosing Michael's initiator."

"What? Now? I'm completely beat!"

"At least you got a good warm-up." Kian clapped Michael's shoulder. "Don't worry about it. You've got about an hour to recuperate, and then you only need to provide some kind of a challenge. No one is expecting you to remain standing for more than a couple of minutes. You'll be fine."

"In that case, I'd better hurry and shower... Phew!" Michael grimaced as he began stripping off his protective suiting and smelled the nasty coming out of it. "I would rather not show up for my own ceremony smelling like dirty socks."

* * *

Later, once everyone made it to the conference room, Kian stood at the head of the table and motioned for Okidu to serve the ceremonial wine.

"I'll have to change the traditional wording a little to allow for Michael's age, so don't try to correct me when I cut out the whole thing about a boy becoming a man." Kian nodded at Michael.

Looking nervous and excited, the kid stood at the other end of the table, presenting himself to the assembled group as required by custom.

Kian cleared his throat. "We are gathered here to present this fine young man to his elders. Michael is ready to attempt his transformation. Vouching for him are Guardian Yamanu and Guardian Arwel. Who volunteers to take on the burden of initiating Michael into his immortality?"

"I do." Yamanu stood up.

Kian nodded his approval.

"Michael, do you accept Guardian Yamanu as your initiator? As your mentor and protector, to honor him with your friendship, your respect, and your loyalty from now on?"

Michael had sneaked a quick glance at Kri before he answered. "I do."

The ritual demanded that Kian, as the leader of this group, verify that everyone agreed it was a good pairing—regardless of it being unnecessary in this case. "Does anyone have any objections to Michael becoming Yamanu's protégé?" When no one did, Kian raised his wine glass. "As everyone here agrees it's a good match, let's seal it with a toast. To Michael and Yamanu."

Once the Guardians were done with the cheers, Yamanu pulled Michael into a crushing bear hug. "Always wanted me a little brother." He rubbed his knuckles against Michael's skull.

"Ouch! And I always wanted a big brother, but now I'm not so sure." Michael laughed and twisted free from Yamanu, only to get caught by Kri.

Now, that hug he didn't seem to mind at all. And as he lifted her off the ground and twirled her around, the mighty Kri squeaked a very girly squeak.

As he held her plastered against him, it might have been the squeak or the Guardian's brouhaha, or maybe both that had given Michael the courage to plant a sloppy kiss smack on her lips.

Kri, on the other hand, didn't need any encouragement, and not being shy by any stretch of the imagination, kissed him back for all he was worth without the slightest regard for her cheering comrades.

Kian felt his face stretch into a wide grin.

Like a proud father, he was glad to see his people excited and happy. It had been a long time since anything new and positive had happened in their stronghold.

It was about bloody time.

CHAPTER 48: SYSSI

"I'm in the mood for a run, but as you guys will not let me out..." Syssi cast a look askance at Amanda. "Do you have a treadmill I could use?"

"Do we have a treadmill? We have the mother of all gyms down in the basement. Go get changed. We'll go together and I'll give you a tour."

"Good... By the way, when are we going to do some work? Not that I mind lazing around all day, but I do need to earn my keep."

"First, I'm going to introduce you to William, our computer guy, so you'll know who to turn to in case you run into programming problems. In fact, we can stop by his lab on our way to the gym."

"I hope he won't mind dealing with someone as technologically challenged as I am."

"Don't worry about it, William is a sweetheart, you're going to like him, you'll see."

And she did. Later, when they reached his cluttered domain, Syssi was surprised to find William looking nothing like the rest of his hunky cousins. He was chubby and bespectacled, and boy did he love to talk...

"Will—" was all Amanda managed to say before he interrupted.

"Hi, you must be Syssi, I'm William." Leaving Amanda with her mouth open, he took Syssi's hand and shook it vigorously. "Don't ask me how I know. I know everything that's going on around here, and not because anyone bothers to tell me anything." He cast Amanda an accusing glance. "Sorry, I tend to blabber. Which might explain why no one comes to visit me."

The poor guy was out of breath, either from excitement over the unexpected visit, or talking at the speed of a firing machine gun. With an awkward glance at Syssi, he took off his glasses and wiped them on his billowy Hawaiian shirt.

"And now you know why we nicknamed him Uzi, after the machine gun." Amanda chuckled. "William, darling, you know we all love you." She patted his shoulder. "I brought Syssi over so she'll know you're the go-to guy with everything concerning tech stuff."

Syssi offered him a bright smile. "It's really nice to meet you, William. My programming skills are nonexistent. I would be grateful for any help you'd be willing to offer."

"Whenever you need me, I'm at your service. And if you want, I would be more than happy to teach you all you need to know. Amanda's research might be complicated as far as the tests she runs, but it requires only basic programming skills."

"That would be wonderful. Are you sure you can spare the time?"

"Of course, I have the time. And when you come," he whispered conspiringly, "I'll show you the underbelly of this monster. Even for a non-techie, the technology I've implemented in this building is fascinating. I showed some of it to Ingrid the other day when she came for help with her interior design software. She was very impressed. Did you meet Ingrid? Everything that looks nice was designed by her, and—" William stopped mid-sentence as Amanda raised her palm.

"I'm sure Syssi would love to hear all about it later, but we need to go."

"Yeah, sure, see you later, Syssi." William's shoulders sagged.

"Wow, he certainly talks fast," Syssi said once they were out of his earshot. "I like him, though. Is he working all by himself down here? The way he is hungry for someone to talk to, I guess he must be lonely."

"Yeah, I guess he must be. Though on Tuesdays and Thursdays, he teaches programming to a group of our kids."

Walking the rest of the way in silence, Syssi observed that the belly of the beast, as William had called the underground levels, had more of a utilitarian look to it than the public areas above. Wide, well-illuminated corridors with plain office-style carpeting and unadorned white walls, lacked even the motivational posters or reproductions of famous art one would find in most office buildings.

Evidently, Ingrid the interior designer hadn't gotten to wield her magic here. Syssi wondered if it was intentional, or if the designer just didn't get to it yet because she was busy elsewhere; the building looked to be relatively new.

"I would like to meet Ingrid," she told Amanda as they stopped in front of the bank of elevators. "I love the way she furnished your place and Kian's, and I'm curious to see some of her other work."

With a ping, the elevator doors opened, the opulent interior a sharp contrast to the drab corridor they were leaving.

"Ingrid has her hands full at the moment. She is helping settle the evacuees from the Bay Area and needs to prepare apartments for clan members trickling in from all over Southern California. It'll be a while until she has any free time."

Exiting the elevator at the gym's level, Syssi noted it was just as plain as the one they'd left.

"Did you say, evacuees?"

"Yeah. Tragically, a few days ago, the Doomers murdered one of our top programmers in that area. Kian ordered everybody out of there. Having a small force of Guardians, we can only protect our people in here. They are not happy about it. It's hard to just get up and go, and Ingrid's job is to make them as comfortable here as we can."

"I'm so sorry for your loss... I don't know what to say." Syssi dropped her eyes. Amanda looked so pained it was clear she knew the victim and mourned his loss.

"There is nothing to say. Mark was one more casualty in this endless war of good versus evil. He wasn't the first and won't be the last. That's just the way it is." Amanda's strides got faster and longer, betraying her anger and determination.

It was a sad reality. No matter how strongly you wished for a peaceful existence, if your enemies were the kind that would not rest until they killed each and every one of you, you had to go on fighting, and make damn sure you were smart enough and strong enough to prevail.

Syssi sighed and followed Amanda into the gym.

The woman had been right; this was the mother of all gyms, with rows of top-notch equipment of every imaginable kind lining the walls of the cavernous room.

At its center, standing on top an arena of blue matting, Michael and a stunning dark man were embracing in a brotherly hug. Surrounding its perimeter stood a group of who she now knew were the Guardians.

Syssi recognized most of them: Kri, Onegus, Bhathian and the brothers, Anandur and Brundar. The only new faces belonged to the tall guy on the mat with Michael, and a pleasant-looking blond standing next to Kian.

For some reason, there was a palpable air of excitement in the gym. And even though it looked like nothing more than two guys in simple gym clothes about to engage in a training exercise, she had a strong feeling that a monumental event was about to take place.

"What's going on?" she whispered in Amanda's ear.

"Michael is about to fight Yamanu, who I assume was chosen to be the one to initiate him. By accepting this role, Yamanu promises to be Michael's guide and protector, becoming his surrogate big brother. Embracing before they begin the fight symbolizes their new bond of friendship."

Nice way to give a caring twist to a brutal coming-of-age ritual, Syssi reflected. "The sentiment is beautiful, but that guy is huge. He's going to pulverize the poor kid." The man looked formidable. Yamanu had several inches on Michael, and although slim, he was all sinewy muscle.

"If you don't have the stomach for it, maybe you shouldn't be here. Even a friendly match may seem rough to someone that didn't see one before. We could go and come later when it's over and done with." Amanda grasped Syssi's elbow with the intent of turning her around.

Syssi crossed her arms over her chest and planted her feet firmly on the concrete floor. Someone had to look out for Michael, and as the only other mortal around, she felt it was up to her. "No, I want to stay and make sure he's okay. I know he is strong, but compared to these guys he looks like the little kid who got caught in the big boys' playground."

Amanda sent her a measuring look. "As you wish. And anyway, if I pull you out, you're probably going to imagine things being way worse than they actually are." She shrugged, crossing her arms over her chest as well. "Just promise not to scream or faint on me."

Syssi slanted her an affronted look. "Don't hold your breath…"

Are you ready for some ass whooping, little brother?" Yamanu smiled, flashing a gorgeous set of gleaming white teeth.

Michael grinned, his eyes sweeping over the faces of his witnesses as he crouched in a fighting stance. "Bring it on, big brother."

Watching the Guardians' expressions as they stood around the blue mat, Syssi was moved by the unexpected fondness and encouragement they showed Michael. It dawned on her then that taking part in this ritual, this coming of age ceremony, symbolized more than Michael's transition from one state to another.

These people were welcoming him into their club—into their family.

Someone sounded a whistle and the match began. Trading kicks and punches, Michael used his bulk to topple the taller man to the mat and even managed to get out of Yamanu's choke holds a few times. But he was seriously outclassed, and a minute into the fight the poor kid was sporting a bruised eye and a bleeding lip.

On the sidelines, Kri was making a fool of herself shouting and cheering Michael on. "Yeah! Go Michael go!" She jumped up and down excitedly, ignoring her fellow Guardians' amused expressions.

At first, it was obvious that Yamanu was going easy on Michael, but as it became evident he was not as easy to subdue as Yamanu had expected him to be, the guy got serious and in short order had the boy pinned face down on the mat.

With a knee between Michael's shoulder blades, Yamanu twisted the boy's arms painfully behind him, keeping Michael's struggling body immobilized as he bared his venom-dripping fangs. With a loud hiss, Yamanu sank them deep into Michael's neck.

Michael's body tensed and arched off the mat before going lax as the venom hit his system. Slowly, as his grimace morphed into a euphoric smile, his eyelids slid shut and he passed out.

"Is he all right? Should we call for help?" Syssi made a move to run for the mat.

Amanda caught her arm. "Easy, girl, everything is all right. He'll shake it off in a few moments."

"Are you sure? Is this normal?"

"Yes, darling, this is a perfectly normal reaction for males. You have nothing to worry about. I've seen my thirteen-year-old nephews and grandnephews go through this ceremony. The boys get knocked out, black out and shake it off in no time. Our big guy is in no danger."

Coming back from the adjacent facilities with several wet washcloths in her hands, Kri knelt beside Michael's prone body. "I'll take care of him," she said, and turning him a little, began wiping away the blood from his busted lip and bruised knuckles.

With a wicked smirk curling the side of her mouth, Amanda leaned into Syssi and pretended to whisper. "It's usually the mother that does the aftercare, and although technically, Kri could be his mother, I don't think she's acting from a motherly place right now."

Kri flipped Amanda the bird and sat down on the mat. Cradling Michael's head in her lap, she wiped his sweaty forehead with a clean washcloth. "Jealous?" she taunted.

"Already fighting over the prize, ladies?" Anandur teased them over the catty exchange, then looking to his comrades for support, he chuckled as the guys attempted nonchalance.

Evidently, fearing Amanda's wrath, they tried to hide their amused faces and pretended like they heard nothing. Standing at the edge of the mat and huddling close, they did their best to avoid looking at either Amanda or Kri.

Instead, they began discussing the match.

"The kid did well," Brundar stated, his austere face showing the slightest nuance of pride.

"He's a natural fighter," Anandur agreed with a quick glance at Kri, making sure she had heard him, apparently trying to get back in her good graces.

"Yeah, Yamanu, you didn't expect him to get away that first time, did you?"

Arwel's comment had Yamanu grimace. "He surprised me, that's all. I didn't know he had any wrestling training, otherwise, I would have held on properly." Yamanu crossed his arms over his chest with an affronted expression on his handsome face. "Didn't want to hurt him unnecessarily, you know."

"Yeah, suddenly you're a ██████ Mother Teresa. Give the kid some credit, you arrogant ass." Arwel punched Yamanu's shoulder. "Like we don't know you're a merciless bastard."

"All right, I have no problem admitting he has potential, but today he just got lucky. Maybe if I spent some time training him, he could become a decent fighter. At least against mortals."

"He'll do better with my weapons training. Until he turns, he'll need the advantage they provide," Brundar said.

With an amused grin, Kian interjected, "No need to fight over the bone, boys, you could both train him. Think how well he'll do, getting two great teachers instead of one." He glanced at Syssi, and smiled with a slight nod.

Syssi smiled back before averting her eyes. Kian wasn't the only one uncomfortable with acknowledging the thing that was going on between them. Except, right now she wasn't sure there was even anything to acknowledge.

From the corner of her eye, she saw him look at her for a brief moment before turning to Onegus. "That's actually not a bad idea. The men are on to something."

"What do you mean?"

"The two fighting over who should train Michael gave me an idea. We could bring more young men to be trained by the Guardians. And young women…" Kian seemed to remind himself that times had changed. "With this new threat looming, the clan needs more Guardians, and the men seem hungry for some new blood in their ranks. I never gave it much thought before, but it makes sense that they would like to impart the knowledge and skills they've accumulated throughout the centuries to a new generation. With no sons or daughters of their own, I can understand their need to validate the importance of what they know how to do best."

"You're awfully philosophical today." Onegus chuckled. "You have a point, though. And I think something along the lines of a basic self-defense course for all members of the clan would be even better. It wouldn't hurt if everyone had some skill at defending themselves. And from the ranks of trainees, we could choose the best for more advanced training and eventually the Guardian force. What do you think?"

"I like it. We should do it, and the sooner, the better," Kian said, then glanced at Michael. "I think our boy is coming around."

Michael's eyes fluttered open, a huge grin spreading across his battered face as he saw Kri smiling down at him. Except, with his head and shoulders cradled in her lap, her heavy breasts were hovering barely an inch away from his nose, and it seemed he was having a hard time focusing on her pretty face.

As his tongue darted to his lips, Syssi smirked, imagining what must've been going through his head. And if she needed additional proof, the loose gym pants he was wearing were not much in the way of hiding what was going on down below.

Face gone red, Michael sneaked a quick glance at his audience. Realizing they were all watching him, he jerked up to a sitting position and bent at the waist in an attempt to hide the evidence. "That wasn't so bad... Ouch!" He winced in pain as he tried to get up.

Kri offered her arm. "Take it easy, big boy. Slow down... I'm going to help you up."

"I'm good, thanks." Michael made another go at standing on his own, but swayed, having to hold on to Kri's shoulder to regain his balance.

"Hey, Yamanu! Next time I won't go so easy on you!" Michael attempted some bravado.

Yamanu grinned. "Yeah, I want to see you try... Come here." He pulled Michael into a hug and clapped his back. "Not bad. Not bad at all, kid."

"Let's go, tiger. I'll take you to your room." Kri wrapped her arm around Michael and helped him limp out of the gym.

CHAPTER 49: DALHU

About thirteen miles away, in a rented Beverly Hills mansion, Dalhu woke up to the sound of light snoring. Turning to look at the call girl sleeping beside him, he braced on his elbow and traced his finger over her puffy red lips.

Allowing a hooker to stay the night wasn't like him, except, after what he had put her through, the girl had been in no shape to go anywhere.

Not that she had voiced any complaints.

She sure hadn't expected to enjoy what he'd done to her so much. After he had sunk his fangs into her neck, the girl had orgasmed so hard her voice had become hoarse from her screams. And then he had her again... and she'd screamed some more.

He smiled. She sure looked like a woman well satisfied; her pretty face flushed and her bleached-blond hair tangled and sticking wetly to her rosy cheeks. What a shame he couldn't allow her to remember any of it.

Still, even though she was a pro, she had passed out way before he'd been ready to be done with her. Unfortunately, there was a limit to what a mortal female could take.

Not for the first time, Dalhu wondered what sex with an immortal female would be like. For all he knew, she might be able not only to match his stamina but tire him out...

Or even bite him back...

Dalhu closed his eyes as the image sent a shiver of lust through his body. His palm found his growing erection and he began stroking it in leisurely up and down strokes, building on that image. She would go wild for the pleasure he would bring her, remember every wickedly sensual thing he would do to her, and beg for more.

Nice fantasy... But it was not to be.

The only immortal females he knew of were Annani's descendants—his sworn enemies—and even though he had no problem overlooking that small detail, he didn't know where to find one.

Deflated, Dalhu lost his good mood along with his erection.

Pushing off the bed, he trudged to the master suite's luxurious bathroom, stepped into the waterfall shower and turned all of the jets on. With his arms braced on the marble wall, he closed his eyes and tilted his head back. The water sluicing down his hair, he once again allowed his mind to conjure the elusive phantasm of an immortal female of his own.

As pointless as it was, it felt incredibly good to indulge in the fantasy, and as he tried to envision his perfect female, the face he saw belonged to the beautiful woman in the framed picture he kept by his bed.

The professor...

He would hold onto a woman like that forever. There would be no more whores for him to share with his brothers; he'd never soil himself like that again. It would be just her for him, and needless to state the obvious, only him for her.

She'd bear him a son, maybe more than one. Or even a daughter...

With her, he could have the kind of life he only caught a glimpse of in the mortal world. The only thing he ever envied humans in their wretched existence was having a family.

Smiling, he imagined himself a proud patriarch; admired, respected, surrounded by his children and grandchildren. The head of his own clan. He would be a good leader, providing for and protecting his own.

Honorable. Appreciated...

Yeah, right.

With a heavy sigh, he leaned his forehead on the wet shower wall, his hold on the illusion crumbling—the beautiful picture he had created dissolving into the mist.

He was old.

And his over eight hundred years of life felt pointless. The endless and senseless wars he had fought in. The meaningless sex with meaningless women he had shared with his fellow soldiers. Even the hating got old.

Lately, he couldn't summon the energy to loathe his enemy with the same passion he had used to.

He didn't really care about anything anymore.

If Annani continued to corrupt the West with her immoral and loose ways, so be it, they could all go to hell as far as he was concerned.

Let someone else take up the hating.

He was tired.

If he could only find an immortal mate, he wouldn't give a rat's ass if she belonged to the enemy's clan. He'd grab the woman and run. Hide somewhere, where no one would ever find them—neither her people nor his.

He needed to fulfill his own godforsaken dream—a family of his own.

With no money and no source of income, he'd have to start from scratch. But he'd manage, selling his collection of valuable jewelry to hold him over until he found another job. Killers for hire were always in high demand and the pay was good. Dalhu doubted there could be more than a handful of professionals who could match or surpass his level of skill. He was very good at what he did.

Indeed...

A ~~fucking~~ wonderful role model he would be for his hypothetical progeny.

Chilled from the inside by the ugly reality of who and what he was, the cold spread from the center of his chest to his extremities, and he shivered despite the shower's humid heat.

Who was he kidding? A doting patriarch? A loving mate and father? These kinds of fantasies befitted a naive, young boy with hopes for the future still fresh in his heart; not an ancient soldier hardened by life's cruel reality.

A killer for hire.

Turning the water off, Dalhu stepped out of the shower, wrapped a towel around his hips, and reached for another to dry off his beard and the rivulets of water streaming from it down his chest.

With the wadded towel in hand, he moved over to the vanity and wiped the vapor off the mirror, then took a good look at his face. He looked hard and old—more so with that dark beard and mustache covering most of his suntanned skin.

It had to go.

The few young men that he had seen on the streets with his kind of full-on beard were mostly the unattractive ones. The better-looking males had been either clean-shaven or sported a couple of days worth of growth but no more, and they had it stylishly trimmed.

Rummaging through the vanity's drawers, Dalhu found the scissors he was looking for and proceeded to snip away the bulk of the hair.

Once he was done, he examined his face again.

At first, he had planned to leave a short stubble. But now, as he stared at his reflection in the mirror, he had the urge to just get it all off.

When he was done, he felt as if a weight had been lifted off of him. For the first time in ages, he felt a cool breeze on his newly exposed skin, and even though it was only the recirculated air blowing through the air-conditioning vent, it felt damn good.

Dalhu hadn't seen his own face without a beard since he had been fifteen. When it had finally gotten dense enough for him to feel like a man, he'd been so proud of the damn thing. But now, looking at himself clean-shaven, he decided he looked much better without it. Quite handsome, in fact, younger, if one didn't look too closely at his deadened, dark eyes.

Splashing water on his face, he removed the last of the shaving cream and bits of hair still clinging to his skin, then dried it off with the towel.

When he got back to his bedroom, the hooker was still sleeping. He moved to stand near the bed and shook her shoulder. "Wake up. It's time to go!"

As her eyes flew open, he gripped her chin firmly, forcing her to look into his. She had a brief moment of fear and confusion before he entered her mind and thralled her to forget him, the sex, the mansion. Instead, he gave her new memories; of a plain-looking middle-aged man, in a plain-looking hotel room, and plain, boring sex.

Exchanging the extraordinary and unusual for the normal and mundane. Except, he regretted erasing the memory of her incredible orgasms and gave them back.

Even a whore deserves to have some pleasure in her miserable life, he reasoned his uncharacteristic kindness.

Rubbing his neck, Dalhu wondered if his mother and sister had ever been granted any, but suspected they had gotten none. No one cared for a whore's pleasure or any of her feelings for that matter. They were treated as objects, not as human beings. As if they deserved being despised and mistreated for choosing to be what they were. Except, most of the wretched women didn't have that choice.

Come to think of it, the attitude toward women in general in his part of the world wasn't much better. They were at the mercy of the men in their lives, be it fathers or husbands.

Even here in the West, where women were free to make their own choices for the last eighty years or so, he suspected very few sold their bodies voluntarily.

A wrong turn somewhere, an abusive boyfriend, drugs, poverty... Most probably thought it was only temporary—just until things got a little better. But things seldom did.

They usually got worse.

Blurry-eyed and stupefied, the woman got dressed clumsily and brushed her hair with her fingers. Dalhu gave her a few moments to clean up in the bathroom before leading her to the mansion's grand vestibule.

Still hazy, she stared myopically into space as she sat on the dainty chaise by the massive entry door, waiting for the taxi that would take her home.

CHAPTER 50: SYSSI

Heading for the row of treadmills, Amanda winked at Syssi. "Aren't you glad the process is so much more pleasurable for females?"

"Yeah, I don't think I could've gotten Yamanu even slightly worked up with my fighting skills."

"Oh, I'm sure you could get him worked up all right." Amanda chuckled. "Just not with your fists... Well, maybe you could do something with them..." She laughed a deep throaty laugh.

"Amanda!"

"What? I'm just saying... It's true!"

Syssi rolled her eyes and decided to change the subject before Amanda embarrassed her even more. "By the way, I was wondering about how different it is for the girls. Kian said that being around your mother was enough to facilitate the change in them. What about the boys? Why doesn't it work the same for them? Was it tested?"

"Of course it was tested. It doesn't work for the boys. My guess is that it's easier to turn the girls because they are the ones that can actually transmit our specific traits to their offspring; they might have a stronger predisposition. But I can't say for sure that's the reason. It just works this way.

"Our children are born and raised at my mother's place, with the expectant mothers traveling to be with her as their time grows near. It's beneficial for the boys as well as the girls to spend their early years with Annani. And besides, she loves having them there. It's not like there are that many, and sometimes decades pass with no children at all, even centuries. So when they arrive, her greatest joy is spending time with the little ones, hugging and kissing the babies, taking care of the mothers.

"Her place is amazing, a real heaven—like a miniature Hawaii. The same perfect temperature year round. Pools and streams of warm water, waterfalls with slides... It's beautiful. The kids have a wonderful time with her and they are safe, protected." Amanda paused, a sad shadow crossing her beautiful face.

"The boys are mortal until they reach puberty and are able to put up a decent fight against a transitioned boy. Until they are turned, they're just as vulnerable to injury and disease as any other mortal. In order to keep them safe, most mothers choose to stay at Annani's place until their sons are old enough to transition. We've lost several of our precious little boys to accidents and illness over the generations. It's always tragic to lose a child, and we have so few." Amanda whispered the last sentence, struggling to breathe as tears glistened in her eyes.

Oh, God! No! The anguish in her friend's eyes could've meant only one thing. Syssi felt her chest tighten, Amanda's pain cutting straight to her soul. "I'm so sorry," she whispered.

"He was such a beautiful boy." Amanda's lip trembled as tears trickled down her cheeks. "I don't want to talk about it. I can't. It happened over a century ago, but it still hurts like hell... as if it had been only yesterday." Wiping her face with her hand, Amanda turned the treadmill on, and without bothering to warm up began running as if the hounds of hell were on her tail.

Turning her own machine on, Syssi began with a brisk walk. She knew how it felt. She didn't lose a child, which must've been even more devastating than losing her brother had been, but four years after the tragedy she still couldn't think about his death without a choking sensation constricting her throat and her eyes burning with tears.

After about fifteen minutes of running at a breakneck speed, Amanda finally slowed down, gradually coming to a stop. Fighting to bring air into her lungs, she bent at the waist, supporting her upper body with her hands on her thighs. "Hard to run when you're choking," she huffed.

Syssi understood all too well. Slowing, she brought her machine to a halt and stepped down. With a ragged sigh, she touched her hand to Amanda's shoulder, and choking on her own emotions, she whispered, "We carry our pain buried deep within our hearts, hidden away and securely locked, and when these raw emotions escape the prison we've built for them, it feels like acid is eating us from the inside. It burns... burns so bad."

There was nothing more she could say, no magic words that could ease Amanda's pain. Instead, she pulled the taller woman into her arms and ran her hands soothingly up and down her back. Sharing her body's warmth with her shivering friend was really all she had to offer.

Mortal or near-immortal, it didn't make a difference. The pain of loss was the same, and physical contact provided the only comfort to be had.

For a few moments, they commiserated in silence, holding on to each other, with Amanda leaning into Syssi and resting her head on her shoulder. Then heaving a shaky sigh, she disentangled from the embrace and drew in a calming breath.

Looking up into Amanda's eyes, Syssi saw in their depths the dark shadows of the woman's grief and her valiant effort to push against the pain. Tragically, Syssi often saw the same miserable expression staring back at her from the mirror.

And even though the loss they had shared had brought them closer than ever, it was a pity that what had helped strike this new kind of communion between them had been the result of anguish and grief.

Nevertheless, given the fact that she still had a hard time dealing with her own loss, Syssi was glad Amanda hadn't wanted to talk about it. So maybe she was being selfish and wasn't such a good friend after all, or maybe she was weak, or cowardly. But she just didn't have the strength to take that on; couldn't handle the added dose of grief.

"I'm okay now, I can breathe again..." Amanda shot Syssi a sad, thankful smile. "Let's run." She climbed back on the treadmill and resumed her breakneck speed.

Syssi maintained an easier pace on her own machine while going over the conversation in her head.

She wasn't thinking about what had made them both sad. Since her own tragedy had struck and changed her forever, keeping her mind off the depressing subject became a mental exercise she was getting better and better at as the years went by.

Instead, her head was buzzing with all the questions she was dying to ask Amanda, mainly about her mother—the Goddess.

What did she look like? What kind of a person was she? How powerful and in what way? What was their relationship like? And where was that heaven Amanda had described?

Except, now was not the time for it. With Amanda pounding away on the treadmill, trying to outrun her demons, Syssi figured she'd better save her questions for later.

CHAPTER 51: DALHU

Dalhu left the hooker sitting on the bench and headed for the mansion's dining room, which served as their makeshift headquarters. His six remaining warriors were waiting for him there.

As he entered the room, he glanced at the large street map of downtown Los Angeles and its adjoining neighborhoods, which he'd tacked last night onto the tapestry covering the room's east wall. The thing was covered with colorful pins, marking the locations of the numerous nightclubs and popular bars he planned on scoping once the reinforcements he had asked for arrived.

Tonight, he'd start with what remained of his original team. The same bunch that was now staring at him as if he had sprouted horns. At first, he didn't understand their dumbfounded expressions, but as he ran his fingers over his smooth chin and realized what had caused their moronic reaction, his face pinched in anger.

What a bunch of mediocre simpletons. But what could he expect? A full beard was considered a sign of potency and virility, and it was expected from fearsome warriors to sport one. These guys knew nothing other than what had been drilled into their heads. They were incapable of thinking independently or observing their environment and then adapting accordingly.

They knew only what they had been told, and questioned nothing. Brainwashed since birth by Navuh's propaganda, their deeply ingrained hate made them into well-sharpened weapons with which he delivered death and vengeance to those he considered his enemies.

The way of true zealots, they were ready to die fighting for Navuh's cause without really understanding what they were willing to sacrifice their lives for.

Not that Dalhu could really blame the morons. It had taken him long enough before he had begun questioning what he had been told, and even longer for the supposedly holy cause to lose its luster in his eyes.

But then, he was smarter than most, and with how easy it was to obtain information in this new, Internet-connected world, he was better informed.

It all boiled down to the quest for power and wealth. Who had it, and who did not. Dalhu preferred to be on the side that had it—regardless of its moral underpinnings.

It was all crap anyway.

The whole world was corrupted, and those who believed differently were stupid and naive and deserved being led like cattle to the slaughter.

Dalhu was as far from naive as it got.

For real, though? All he needed from his men were their muscle, fear, and blind obedience. The thinking and strategizing he could manage himself.

In the cutthroat world of the Brotherhood, having idiots for foot soldiers was a necessary evil; a smart ass, capable underling was liable to challenge your position, take you out, and seize leadership of your unit.

Dalhu should know. Realizing early on that he didn't want to spend his long life as a foot soldier, he had cunningly disposed of his first immediate commander. Though in his defense, he had believed he had no choice; as no one ever retired willingly or left to vacate a spot, it had been the only way to advance in the Brotherhood's ranks.

To become a leader, he had to oust his predecessor.

The men were still shooting quick glances at his face when the elderly cook and her rolling cart, loaded with their breakfast, granted them a short reprieve.

For a few blissful moments, they gave their undivided attention to wolfing down the huge stacks of eggs, toast, and hash browns onto their plates. Once they were done, and the cook cleared the table, Dalhu pushed up from his chair.

"I have a plan," he began. "The colored tacks on the map mark the locations of nightclubs. Each night, you will go out and scope for immortal males in the clubs you'll be assigned to. For now, it will be one man per club. When reinforcements arrive, we'll scope a larger area, and you'll be working in teams of two. But even with the reinforcements, we'll be stretched thin covering such a large city."

Given the guys' clueless expressions, it was obvious they had no idea where he was going with this, and he explained. "In the past, we managed to snag a few of the clan's males in whorehouses. Their biology being the same as ours, they need a constant supply of mortal females. Except they are not as lucky as we are, with a built in brothel at our disposal; courtesy of our exalted and brilliant leader, Lord Navuh."

He paused for them to finish their chuckling and saluting. "They are forced to constantly prowl for females. As we all know, given the rampant corruption of the West, willing women come to the clubs and bars looking for males to screw them. Therefore, it stands to reason that we'll find what we are looking for in those places."

Dalhu waited, giving the men a moment to process what he had told them, then assuming his most severe expression, delivered the instruction that would trouble them most. "Your beards have to go; they are not popular here in the West, and you need to call as little attention to yourselves as possible. Consider it a sacrifice for our holy cause."

"But, sir, we'll get ridiculed upon our return," one of the men protested.

The panicked expressions of his comrades should have warned him that he had made a huge mistake; questioning your superior was not something a subordinate Doomer dared to do. Their lives belonged to their leader to do with as he pleased and to question his orders was to court dangerous retribution.

"Come here!" Dalhu called the soldier to him. "You worthless dog! You do not think! You do not question! You obey!" he hollered and sent his fist flying, at the last moment aiming lower and instead of the guy's jaw, punching his middle. The powerful punch had the guy double over on the floor, retching his food. Still, the man had been lucky; Dalhu needed his face to remain pretty for tonight.

Taking a steadying breath and then another, Dalhu tried to rein in his rage. It was becoming harder to do lately—the anger would rise at the slightest provocation and linger, poisoning his mood and impairing his thought process. But at least he retained enough self-control to change the trajectory of that punch...

Thank Mortdh...

The bastard had a point, though. The few unlucky men born without the ability to grow facial hair were ridiculed and humiliated for not being real men. And to add insult to injury, the poor bastards were not allowed to join the warrior ranks, becoming servants in the barracks or the brothel—a truly disgraceful existence.

Cowering in their chairs, his men were trying to ignore the sight of their comrade wiping his vomit off the rug, but their troubled expressions spoke of all the unanswered questions they still had.

"I know what you're thinking, but don't worry, I've thought of everything. You're asking yourselves how are you going to catch and extract the males, without getting too close for them to realize what you are. Right?" Dalhu pulled a small plastic bag with white powder out of his trouser pocket. "You'll thrall the bartender or the waitress to slip this powder into the male's drink. The drug will make an average-sized immortal male sleepy, but although he'll be too fuzzy to talk or offer resistance, he'll still be able to walk with your assistance. To the mortals, the male will appear drunk while you'll look like the good friend taking him home. With the thing being tasteless and odorless, the male will not suspect he is being drugged until it's too late. Good plan, huh?" Dalhu smiled smugly. The drug connection the Brotherhood had in Los Angeles was proving once again to be a most valuable resource.

"You'll bring them here for me to interrogate. If you value your own lives, they'd better be alive and well enough to talk when they get here. So make sure you don't accidentally overdose any. Even if your intention is to knock the male out, don't use more than two packets." Dalhu looked around making sure they got it. "We go out tonight. I'll text each one of you the address of the club you'll be scoping. Before you leave, check the map to orient yourself. Make sure to get all clean and scrubbed by eight this evening and dress appropriately. Jeans are okay, a dress shirt, and don't forget the cologne. No playing with the females until it's closing time, and then only the willing ones. No thralling until after the deed. Am I clear?"

"Yes sir!" the men acknowledged.

There was really no way for him to ascertain if the thralling occurred before or after the sex, but hopefully, the men feared him enough to follow his orders.

CHAPTER 52: AMANDA

Out of breath and drenched in sweat, Amanda stepped off the treadmill and glanced at Syssi. "I'm done. Are you ready to go up and put in some desk work?"

After an hour-long run at a speed that could've put an Olympic athlete to shame, Amanda at last felt as if she was done exorcising her demons. For the time being at least... Walking over to the paper-towel dispenser, she pulled one and used it to wipe the sweat off her face.

"Thank God! I thought you'd never stop. I'm exhausted from just trying to keep up at a fast walk," Syssi said, following behind her.

Being the last two at the gym, the sound of their voices echoed off the walls, making the place feel like a crypt. Hurrying out and stepping into the elevator's welcoming interior, Amanda was relieved to leave behind the empty gym and the bad memories that had surfaced there.

Syssi was quiet and somber all through the ride up to the penthouse, and Amanda wasn't in the mood for small talk either. Which was okay. The silence didn't bother her, and at this point she hoped that Syssi was comfortable enough in their friendship for the quiet to feel companionable as opposed to oppressing.

Be that as it may, it was time to do something about Syssi's bad mood and to fix the mess Kian had made.

At the penthouse, Amanda showered, changed, and then spent a good ten minutes applying her makeup. Feeling like herself again, she walked into her office and smiled as she saw her best girl already at the desk. "Ready, sweetie?"

"Show me." Syssi rolled her chair sideways and pulled another one for Amanda.

It didn't take her long to introduce Syssi to the proprietary software that was developed by none other than William. The thing was years ahead of what they had in the lab which, of course, meant that any significant trend they'd discover could not be used in the official research papers. But it would save them time by identifying, quickly and efficiently, which of their assumptions were correct and which were not. That way, they could focus their efforts and use the official program, which was a slow and inefficient monster, on what was more likely to work.

"I have to leave for a little bit. Are you okay here on your own?" Amanda asked once Syssi got the gist of the new program and began uploading the research data they had accumulated over the past several weeks.

"Yeah, I'm good. With this software, I'll probably be done in a couple of hours. If you're not back by then, I'll text you when I have the results so you can decide what you want to do next."

"Good deal. I'll check on you later."

Letting a few minutes go by, Amanda peeked into the office to make sure Syssi was immersed in her work, then snuck out her front door, closing it soundlessly behind her.

In several strides of her long legs, Amanda crossed the vestibule and entered Kian's place without knocking.

Too much was at stake, and she wasn't going to let Kian blow it.

CHAPTER 53: KIAN

"We need to talk," Amanda said as soon as she entered Kian's office.

Lifting his head, Kian's lips twisted in an involuntary grimace. An angry expression marring her pretty face, she looked ready for battle. Bracing for the attack that was sure to follow, he eased back in his chair and folded his arms across his chest.

Amanda halted in front of his desk and placed her hands on her hips, tapping her shoe on the hardwood floor. "What did you do to her this time?" she accused.

He really didn't have the patience for the scene she was making, and her offensive behavior was getting on his nerves. And what's more, once it dawned on him that he was the one assuming a defensive posture, his temper flared hot. The little hellcat was the one who was supposed to bow to his authority and answer to him. Not the other way around. He was cutting her way too much slack and forgiving her impudence out of love. But enough was enough.

Uncrossing his arms, he placed his palms on the glossy surface of his desk and pinned her with a hard stare. "What do you want, Amanda?" he barked back, letting some of his anger leak into his voice.

Amanda winced. Plopping down on the chair facing him, she continued in a softer tone. "Syssi is upset and unhappy. You must've either done something or said something to hurt her."

"I know. But I'll be damned if I know what it was. I hoped she would tell you." Kian ran his fingers through his hair. Now that Amanda had abandoned her combative attitude, his anger gave way to frustration.

She frowned and straightened in her chair. "Syssi told me she was overwhelmed with all the stuff she had to wrap her mind around, but I know there is more to it. The way she was holding her arms around her middle she seemed almost in physical pain." She was watching him carefully, and Kian knew Amanda was searching his face for signs of guilt.

What the hell was she thinking? That he had gotten too rough with Syssi? Except, what if he had? What if Syssi had only pretended to be okay? Kian winced uncomfortably.

It didn't escape Amanda's notice. Suspecting the worst, her intense blue eyes began glowing from under her clenched brows.

The hellcat looked ready to tear him a new one.

But then he shook his head. "No, she was fine after we... after we made love... It was only after I told her our story that she clamped down."

"Tell me everything exactly as it happened. You may not know what you've done wrong, but I might."

"Everything?" Kian cocked his brow with a little smile tugging at his lips.

Amanda waved a hand in front of her face. "Ugh! I don't need the steamy details! Too much information. Just the sequence of events, and what you said to her, or rather how you said it. We both know you tend to be somewhat uncouth."

Kian sighed. Maybe she had a point. As a female, Amanda might have the insight he was apparently lacking. Except, he had a feeling that as a near-immortal, her way of thinking would be very different from Syssi's. But be that as it may, it was worth a shot even if talking with his sister about his relationship with Syssi felt uncomfortable. But what choice did he have?

There was no one else.

"Okay. So last night, after we came back from the club, I didn't thrall her after the sex. She was spacey from the bite, and I figured it was the perfect time to tell her what was going on; while she was still in a receptive mood and wouldn't freak out. It just didn't feel right to keep thralling her and lying to her. I decided to come clean the way we did with Michael. I told her some of it last night and the rest this morning. She didn't freak out, didn't panic, but she got upset. Mainly because she figured out that I would have to erase her memory if she didn't turn. But then it looked as if she understood why it was necessary and seemed better, then got upset again and wouldn't tell me why."

"Tell me exactly how you explained it to her."

"Why?"

"Just humor me. I have a feeling your presentation lacked finesse, and since I wasn't there, the only way I can figure it out is to hear it word for word." Amanda tapped her long fingers on her biceps, nailing him with her blue stare.

"I told her everything, pretty much the same way we explained it to Michael. Our history, the unique biology, how important both Michael and she might be to the future of our clan. Then I elaborated a little more about the venom and how it works. The first time she really got upset was when she realized she'd be sent away if she didn't turn. The second was when I explained about the possibility of her getting addicted to the venom. Instead of alleviating her concerns, the more I explained how it could be circumvented by having several different partners, the more cold and distant she became. I think I did the best I could to make it clear that she wasn't trapped in a relationship with me because of it, and would be free to choose anyone she wanted." Kian felt his face twist with rage. Just imagining Syssi being approached by another male made him want to shred the hypothetical bastard to pieces. "And believe me, it cost me to get the words out of my mouth," he growled the last sentence.

"Suave, Kian... really suave, almost two thousand years old and clueless." Amanda shook her head. "I'm amazed that an intelligent and experienced man like you can be so blind."

Blind? Who was she calling blind?

She was the one who, oblivious to his state of mind, was fueling his rage with her insolence, instead of offering to calm him down. Breathing hard, he fisted his hands until his knuckles turned white; feeling like anytime now smoke would start coming out of his nostrils and horns would poke out from his forehead, making him look like one of his demonic illusions. "That's enough, Amanda! I will not tolerate this tone of voice from you. You're my sister and I love you, but that doesn't mean I'll allow you to talk to me with disrespect."

True to form, instead of cowering before him, Amanda bowed her head with mock penitence. "My apologies, Regent, you're right of course. This era is not very respectful toward its elders." She smirked.

And just like that she had him disarmed.

"You're forgiven. Now talk... respectfully..." Kian looked at her sternly, but a smile was tugging at his lips. She'd gotten him there. Was he really too old and rigid? Clinging to some outdated notion of propriety? He didn't think so.

Kian considered himself an easygoing ruler, far more forgiving and lax than his mother ever was. Amanda would have never dared to use this tone of voice around Annani, even when not addressing her directly.

Amanda straightened her back and clasped her hands before her on his desk, looking like a chastened schoolgirl in the principal's office. All that was missing were pigtails and a naughty schoolgirl uniform to make her performance good enough for a comedy skit.

It was a shame, really, that she couldn't pursue an acting career... With her looks, natural talent, and predisposition for drama, she would have made it big. Despite himself, Kian shook his head and chuckled.

Except, Amanda had no intention of being funny. Using her teacher's voice, she asked, "How do you feel about Syssi? Think about it for a moment before you answer. I want you to get a clear picture in your head."

Looking at Amanda's beautiful face wearing an expression that was composed and serious for a change, Kian was startled by the resemblance she bore to their mother. Most of the time it was masked by the marked differences between them. Amanda was tall as opposed to the diminutive but formidable Annani, and her mischievous and lively demeanor was very different from their mother's regal composure. Except, right now, the similarity of their features was striking. And for some reason it made it easier for him to open up to his sister.

Still, long seconds passed as he tried to come up with an honest answer. "She is sweet. I like how unassuming she is. She is definitely smart, and not prone to dramatics or exaggerations like some people I know..." Kian looked at Amanda pointedly as she rolled her eyes. "Syssi is beautiful, lush, sensual... lustful... I can't get enough of her, and she responds in kind... We are definitely in serious lust with each other." Kian smiled before taking in a hissed breath as memories of their wild lovemaking assaulted his body.

"Are you sure it's only lust?" Amanda probed gently.

No he wasn't, but he wasn't ready to admit it either. To himself or to Amanda. "What else could it be? We've known each other for less than a week." Kian avoided Amanda's smiling eyes. He was a lousy liar and she knew him too well. Hiding the truth from her wasn't easy.

"So you didn't become a jealous monster when another male was sniffing around her, or turn practically demonic just at the thought of her with another guy?" Amanda sounded smug.

Bracing his elbows on the desk, Kian dropped his head on his fists. "I did. Big time." He sighed. "I was ready to pound Anandur to a pulp, and barely held myself from breaking Alex's arm when the scumbag touched her. I don't know what came over me. I've never been the jealous type, not even with Lavena, whom I loved... had a child with... I don't understand what's happening to me."

Kian felt guilty.

Why the hell had he never gotten jealous over Lavena? Was it possible he hadn't loved her enough? For some reason, questioning what he believed he had with her brought on a despondent feeling.

Over the years, he had cherished the memory of the short time he had with Lavena as a precious nugget of good. A taste of normal— knowing that he would never have that again. But with what he was now feeling for Syssi, he was forced to question the authenticity of those memories.

Amanda watched him with pitying eyes—as if he was slow-minded. "Yet, you've told Syssi that she is important *to the clan*, that she should not fear addiction because she can choose *some other male* for her mate."

Kian's anger flared anew. "So? It's true! I wanted her to know she is important to us, and I didn't want her to feel trapped or forced. She has the right to know what her options are."

Amanda palmed his tightly fisted hand and held it in both of hers with an expression so somber, he was afraid she was slipping into her dramatics again. "You lied, Kian; lied to yourself, lied to Syssi, and by doing so you hurt both of you."

Yup, she did... Delivering her statement in a perfectly modulated tone to maximize the dramatic effect.

Kian tried to pull away from her, but she held on. "Listen to me! She is important to you, and you want her to choose you because you want her for yourself, not for the clan. That's what she wanted to hear, needed you to say, and it also happens to be the truth."

When he didn't try to refute her, she continued. "Syssi is not like us. She is not someone who has casual sex. This thing with you means the world to her. The poor girl had just one lover until now and went without for two years for goodness' sake... And the way you explained things made her feel like she is nothing to you. Way to go, Kian." With a last disapproving look Amanda finally let go of his hand.

"I'm an ass..." Kian dropped his head and rubbed at his temples. It was so obvious when Amanda had put it like that. How come he hadn't realized that before?

"I'm such a moron..."

"No, my dear sweet brother, you're not a moron, just inexperienced; shagging thousands of women notwithstanding. You don't know how to deal with your own emotions, let alone someone else's. You never had to woo a female, so you don't know how to go about it. But all is not lost. I'll help you romance her back." Amanda squared her shoulders and pushed her chin up.

Kian chuckled. "You, Amanda? What do you know about wooing or romance? What do any of us know? We use and discard partners like dirty underwear or used condoms."

"Okay, Kian, now you're being crude. As regent, you're not allowed."

He dismissed her with a wave of his hand. "In here, I'm just your brother."

"Could have fooled me... Watch your tone, I demand respect, Amanda..." She emulated his haughty tone, crossing her arms over her chest and jutting out her chin.

"Cut the crap. What do you suggest I do, Miss-Know-It-All?"

"I do have some human female friends, and I've read a few romance novels, so I do have some idea of what mortal females want—besides the shagging, or in addition to it, that is. You should take her out on a date, make it several dates, to some classy, romantic restaurant, or a show, or the theater. Take her dancing. And gifts—I think mortal females expect that from their suitors. Shower her with attention, but it has to be outside the bed... or the wall... or the closet... or the shower..." Amanda couldn't help herself and was trying to make him squirm a little. But he just smirked. "Make her feel she is the most important person in the world to you. Tell her how you feel, show her; give yourself to her and make her yours." Amanda sighed, her little speech evidently making her wistful.

"But what if she is not compatible, and I'll have to let her go, erase her memories? It's going to hurt like hell..."

"Letting her go is going to hurt like hell regardless of what you do. You're already head over heels with her. But at least, this way, giving it all, letting this thing between you bloom, you'll get to sample a little bit of wonderful. The consequences of not admitting the truth and following your heart would bring a whole new world of hurt—much worse than just letting her go." She shivered. "I hate to think what that will do to you."

"What do you mean? What could be worse?"

"What could be worse? Think of it this way; she turns immortal, but wants nothing to do with you, chooses another male... one you cannot kill because they are all your nephews."

"You're right, this is worse..." His eyes flashed dangerously as his imagination ran rampant with disturbing possibilities. Unbidden, an image of Anandur smirking at him while holding Syssi with his arm wrapped around her shoulders made Kian see red. Tamping down his fury, he pushed out of his chair and began pacing the length of his office.

"Take a risk, Kian. I have a really good feeling about Syssi. Michael too." Amanda's eyes followed him as he paced back and forth the thirty feet or so.

"You had good feelings before," he said sarcastically as he stopped to glare down at her.

"This time it's different. You've never acted like that with anyone. And besides, I was just reminded of a talk I had with Mother a couple of months back. She said something I didn't pay attention to at the time, but I think you'll find it intriguing. You know how she sometimes makes those cryptic remarks that do not make any sense at the time, but then are crystal clear in hindsight?"

"What did she say?"

"She called me. We talked about my research, and she said; 'Finally you have found what the soul eternally craves.' I thought she just misused the language—you know, the way she sometimes translates from her native tongue and it comes out weird. I thought what she meant was that I found my heart's desire—something I like to do. But thinking back, she didn't say your soul, she said the soul, meaning that I found something not for me personally but in general. What do all of our souls eternally crave, Kian?" Amanda gazed up into his eyes.

"A mate—an immortal, true love mate," he said quietly.

"Bingo!"

CHAPTER 54: AMANDA

As she gazed at her brother's stunned expression, Amanda struggled to keep a big grin from splitting her face.

Another milestone had just been achieved, and it had happened much faster than she'd hoped. Which in her opinion indicated that the third and final milestone was going to be achieved as well.

Kian had admitted he was falling in love with Syssi, and for this to happen that fast must've meant that they were indeed true love mates. Which in turn must've meant that Syssi was a Dormant and that she would turn.

True love pairing couldn't happen with a human.

Of course, none of it was guaranteed, but with each passing day, Amanda felt more and more certain that she was right. Everything was progressing in the right direction and at an amazing speed.

Still, a little prayer couldn't hurt.

Lifting her eyes to the ceiling, she beseeched the merciful fates to bestow on Kian this ultimate reward for his many sacrifices. The man was selfless to a fault, dedicating his life to his family and to humanity at large. If there was anyone who deserved his happy ending it was her brother.

Please, I'm not asking for myself this time, and therefore my prayer should be heard. Please let Syssi turn, not only to reward Kian for his sacrifices, but to bring new hope to our clan.

DARK STRANGER
IMMORTAL

CHAPTER 1: KIAN

The silence that followed was interrupted by Okidu's light knock on the door. "Master, Dr. Bridget is here to see you."

Tearing his gaze away from his sister's hopeful face, Kian frowned. Amanda was so excited, her deep blue eyes were glowing. Unfortunately, she was reading too much into their mother's words, grasping for meaning where there was none.

In his opinion, false hope was more dangerous than the baser emotions people scorned. A cruel and powerful mistress, hope obscured common sense and made random occurrences appear as meaningful signs, prompting those who followed its misleading trail to take questionable actions. Mindlessly disregarding the well-being of others and their own sense of self-preservation for hope's illusive promise, more often than not, they were rewarded by nothing but chaos and pain.

"Show her in," he told Okidu. "On second thought, never mind. I'll go to her."

In the living room, Bridget was pacing the small distance between the front door and the edge of the rug, looking agitated.

Great. His lips pulled into a tight line. Another female ready to tear into him over something he had supposedly done wrong.

Take a number and stand in line.

"Good afternoon, Bridget, what a nice surprise." Kian wondered if she heard the thinly veiled sarcasm in his tone.

The doctor wrung her hands nervously. "Good afternoon, Kian, sorry to come up here without calling ahead, but this is urgent."

"Think nothing of it, everyone else does…" He placed his hand on her shoulder, conveying the reassurance his tone didn't. "What can I do for you, Bridget?"

"I've just learned that you have two potential Dormants here, and frankly, I was appalled I had to hear it from William. How come you didn't check with me before initiating the process? I need blood samples before and after each venom injection. It's the first time I have adult Dormants who I could test as we are attempting to activate them, and there might be a chance that their blood will provide the clues I need. You know how important this is." By the time she finished her rant, her temper had painted her cheeks red to match the color of her hair.

"You're right. With everything that was going on, it didn't even cross my mind. But my oversight aside, I don't want you to get your hopes up. I don't believe they are really what we are looking for, but just in case..."

"Yeah, just in case... Hi, Bridget." Amanda gave the petite woman a hug. "Don't listen to him, he of little faith. They. Are. It," she whispered in the doctor's ear, making sure it was loud enough for Kian to hear.

He rolled his eyes. "I'll make sure they'll be at your lab shortly."

"Thank you." Bridget smiled a tight, nervous smile and hurried out.

Closing the door behind her, Kian turned to Amanda. "I assume Syssi is at your place?"

"She is in my office. I've sat her down to do some work."

"Good, I'll get her. Call for someone to escort Michael to the lab, unless you want to do it yourself?"

They walked out together.

"Remember! Be nice... Woo her!" Amanda slapped his back before punching the button for the elevator.

Woo her, right.

What the hell did it mean? Kian wracked his brain trying to come up with something that would qualify as wooing. Should he quote poetry? He chuckled. He didn't know any. Didn't like it, and in his opinion, it was a lot of pretentious crap. If one wanted to convey an idea, one ought to do it in a way that would be clearly understood and not mask it in vague wording. Whatever. His opinion on poetry notwithstanding, he needed something more concrete than that word.

Woo.

Being serious and pragmatic wasn't going to help him woo anyone, besides business associates, that is, not that he was any good at that either. Kian thought of himself as courteous and polite, and he was... most of the time... unless his temper got the better of him. Other than that, the extent of his social skills was limited to business dealings and seducing women in bars and clubs.

It wasn't much to work with. In comparison, even bloody Anandur seemed like a witty charmer.

I'm so screwed...

With his footfalls making almost no sound on the hallway's soft rug, Sissy didn't hear his approach. She didn't even lift her head when he peered into Amanda's office.

For a moment, he observed her unawares. She looked adorable; scrunching her little nose in concentration, her wild multicolor hair all over the place—cascading down her back and front, covering her left breast while leaving the other outlined perfectly against her white, low-necked T-shirt.

She was so damn sexy it hurt.

Did she wear those T-shirts on purpose to taunt him? How was he supposed to get his head out of the gutter when she looked so tempting? Kian heaved a sigh. It would be next to impossible to follow Amanda's advice and interact with Syssi in a nonsexual way.

She looked up from her work. "Hi, Kian... What was the heavy sigh for?"

For a moment there, he was tempted to yank her out of her chair and show her. Instead, he raked his itchy fingers through his hair. "Bridget, our in-house doctor, wants to take some blood samples from you and Michael. She needs to run tests before and after each venom infusion..."

On the wooing scale of one to ten, that was probably a minus two.

With an inward curse, Kian's brows drew tight. "Come, she is waiting for us in her lab." He offered his hand.

Yep, I'm Mr. ~~Suave~~ Debonair.

CHAPTER 2: SYSSI

Here he goes again. Syssi winced.

In a heartbeat, Kian went from looking wistful to grumpy, his darkening mood casting an unpleasant, oppressive shadow.

Syssi swallowed past the hard lump in her throat. Was he suddenly reminded of the dismissive way she had treated him before?

Okay... two could play that game. She could be aloof and grumpy as well...

Yeah right...

Holding onto Kian's hand as they headed for the elevator, Syssi struggled just to keep herself from plastering her body against his and rubbing all over him—like a cat on a scratching post.

But a quick glance at his grim, agitated face was enough to kill that impulse.

As they stood side by side, waiting for the elevator, there was an awkward silence between them, and if not for his hand holding onto hers almost crushingly, she would've thought he didn't want to be with her.

As soon as the doors slid shut behind them, the tension got even worse. With the memory of last night's momentous ride slamming down hard, the already small space shrunk around her, constricting her air supply.

"Screw that!" Was all the warning she got before Kian shoved her against the wall and smashed his lips over hers with a low guttural sound reverberating deep in his throat. He held her in place with his hand on her nape, his tongue invading her welcoming mouth.

She moaned.

Her small needy whimpers must've urged him on, and he bent his knees to align their bodies, gyrating his hips and grinding himself against her.

Testing, she pushed her tongue past his lips and thrust into his mouth. He let her, groaning as she went on swirling and licking at his fangs' extended length.

"More..." Kian growled when she left his mouth to kiss and nip at his throat, pulling her back to his lips, "... my fangs, I never knew it'd feel so damn good..."

Was she the first to give him this pleasure? Floored by his admission, Syssi's heart swelled with satisfaction. Kissing him long and hard, she swirled her tongue round and round his fangs until he groaned with bliss.

Once again, they were on fire, their need for each other insatiable. But unlike last night, acting on it was not an option. As the elevator chime announced that it reached its destination, Kian released her, and a moment later she let go of him as well.

Panting breathlessly as Kian held the door from closing, Syssi took a moment to compose herself before exiting into the wide corridor.

"Hold on!" He grabbed her arm as she stepped out. "I need another moment here." He leaned his back against the hallway's wall, holding onto her bicep as if afraid she'd bolt. "Between my fangs and what's going on down below, I'll make quite a spectacle of myself if I walk into Bridget's lab like this."

"Need me to talk about gross, disgusting stuff? I can help you deflate in no time…" Syssi giggled, not at all sorry for his predicament.

Kian cocked a brow. "What gross stuff?"

"Once, when I was at the mall, I saw this little kid in a stroller eating a hamburger. He choked on a larger piece and puked, but kept eating the puke-covered hamburger as if nothing happened. Meanwhile, his mother was chatting with a friend and pushing the stroller, bewildered by the horror-filled glances of passers-by, oblivious to what was happening, until a saleslady ran out from one of the stores with a roll of paper towels."

Kian chuckled. "Only you could think of telling a story like that. I was expecting guts and gore, and here you go, talking about little kids and puke." He caressed her cheek tenderly. "My sweet Syssi." He bent to kiss the top of her head.

"But it worked, didn't it?" She smirked.

"Yep, only partially, but it will do. Let's go." He took her hand and led her toward the lab.

Whatever it was that had him all twisted up before seemed to have ebbed, and Kian was once again affectionate and easygoing with her. She wondered if their kiss in the elevator had been responsible for Kian's mood change.

Yeah, that was probably it.

Smiling up at him, she asked, "You know the saying that the way to a man's heart is through his stomach?"

"What about it?"

She joggled her brows. "In your case, it's not the stomach."

"I have a newsflash for you, baby..." Kian snorted. "Unless a guy is gay or impotent or otherwise compromised, I don't care who he is; sex would always trump a full stomach." Pulling her tightly against his side, he gave a little squeeze.

As they walked into the lab, Bridget was tying a rubber tube around Michael's bicep. Sitting on one of the metal tables, Michael winced and turned his head away. "I hate needles, can you make it quick, Doctor?"

"Don't be a big baby. You're just like my son. Watching gory horror movies that make me cover my eyes and ears is fine, but a drop of his own blood makes him faint." Bridget plunged the needle in one swift move.

Syssi sat on the table beside him. "Hi, Michael, how are you feeling?" She took his right hand to distract him from what was going on with his left.

"Nauseous... faint..." he admitted with a grimace.

"I mean, how are you feeling after the match, anything hurt?" She kept talking, drawing his attention to herself and away from the needle and the number of glass vials Bridget was filling with his blood.

"Oh, that? Nah, it's all good. That venom is a miracle drug. Most of the bruises were gone in a couple of hours, and the pains and aches even before that. I wish I had the stuff after football practice or games, or when..."

As he kept talking, Bridget finished filling the vials. "All done, big boy, you can hop down now." She removed the tourniquet and pressed a gauze square to the crook of his arm, attaching it with an adhesive tape. "Want a lollypop?"

"Sure, I'd love one. What flavors you got?"

"Cherry, apple, and caramel."

"I'll take the apple. Is it sour?"

"I don't know..." She smiled. "Here you go." She handed him two apple-flavored lollypops.

"It's your turn, young lady. How is your relationship with needles?" Bridget finished sticking labels on the tubes she had filled with Michael's blood and pulled out a new tourniquet to tie around Syssi's bicep.

"Don't love them, don't hate them... I'm not squeamish." Syssi held out her arm.

Michael walked over to where Kian was leaning against another lab table and eased back beside him. Sucking on his pop, he offered Kian his spare one. "Want a pop?"

"No, I'm good, kid. Keep it for later."

"So, Doctor Bridget, what exactly are you going to do with all that blood?" Michael asked, waving the pop in the direction of the test-tube rack.

"Well, I'm going to run a bunch of tests. Genetic tests mostly. First I'm going to check your mitochondrial DNA to establish your matrilineal descent and make sure you and Syssi are not from the same line, or ours. Then I'm going to be checking for anything and everything that might give me a clue. Unfortunately, the knowledge rescued from the cataclysm did not include medicine or genetics, so we are just as clueless as mortals on those subjects." She sighed, placing another ampule of Syssi's blood in the rack.

Alarmed by the possibility, Syssi glanced at Kian. By the grim expression on his face, so was he. "Is there a chance we might be of the same line as you guys?" she asked.

"It's a very remote chance. Annani was an only daughter to her mother, who was also an only daughter. The gods started mating with mortals only after Annani's mother came of age and not before. So as far as we know, there weren't any other descendants from that line besides Annani. But we need to make sure. We take the taboos very seriously. In-line mating might have disastrous genetic implications that we couldn't even fathom. As promiscuous as the gods were, there must have been a good reason for such a strong taboo."

"Well, let's hope for the best. I'm positive you'll find Michael and I are from two completely different lines…" Syssi smiled, trying to reassure Kian, or maybe herself.

"Yes, I certainly hope so." Bridget finished with the last test tube.

"Hope springs eternal for the young and naive. Personally, I hate the bitch," Kian spat as he pushed away from the table. "In my experience, hope is often groundless. Fairy tales have happy endings—real life seldom does." He lifted Syssi off the table as if the one-foot jump down could be hazardous to her health, or perhaps just used it as an excuse to hold her tightly for a moment.

Whatever his reasons for the gallant gesture, at the contact, her skin prickled with awareness. And as he held her close, she breathed in his unique musk, getting intoxicated by it. Syssi had to briefly close her eyes. The man smelled absolutely delicious. When he reluctantly released her, she opened her eyes slowly, swaying on her feet a little before turning to Bridget. "When will you have something for us?"

Fidgeting with her equipment, the doctor seemed uneasy with their open display of affection. "The mitochondrial DNA testing will be done probably today. The rest will take as long as it does. I have a slew of tests I'm thinking of, and probably will come up with some more as I go."

"Don't you need to send it out to a genetics lab?" Syssi didn't know what exactly was required, but the small lab they were in certainly didn't have anything looking even remotely sophisticated.

"Oh, this?" Bridget followed Syssi's appraising eyes. "This is just my examination room. I have all the best equipment available in the lab proper, a level down from here. Besides this room, I also have an operating room and several recovery rooms. I'm a whole hospital and research facility of one." Her chin went up. "I have everything a girl like me could ever dream of." She blew a kiss at Kian. "All thanks to our very generous regent."

"Flattery will get you everywhere." Kian blew her a kiss back. "You'll let us know as soon as you have the initial results?"

"You'll be the first to know," Bridget promised.

As they made their way back to the elevator, Michael was a step behind them. "Do you guys really need to keep me locked up? Can't I at least enjoy the freedom of the basement? Syssi gets to, so why can't I?"

Michael seemed to be happy and excited about the opportunity he had been given, and Syssi doubted he would bolt. But apparently, Kian wasn't ready to take the risk.

He glanced back at Michael, appraising him.

"Okay, kid. I'll take you to William and have him encode the elevator with your thumbprint. However, I'll have you wear a locator cuff. And just to make things clear, the thing is impossible to remove by anyone but William. Not without cutting off your hand. Still want one?"

"Hell, yeah! Sure I want it! It's not like I have any desire to leave or anything. " Michael shook Kian's hand vigorously. "Thank you. I hate being locked up."

"You're welcome."

"How about me? Don't I get a thumbprint pass to the elevator?" Syssi hadn't thought to ask before, but now with Michael getting it, she saw no reason why she shouldn't have access to the elevators as well.

"You don't have one yet? I thought Amanda took care of it. How did you get around?"

"There was always someone escorting me. I never used the elevator by myself. Frankly, at one point I even considered taking the endless stairs down. I'm getting claustrophobic being cooped up in here."

"Both of you are coming with me to William right now to take care of this." Kian led them toward another turn in the endless labyrinth of the underground.

"If I'm to navigate it on my own, I'd need a map of this place. Otherwise, I'd get so lost, it will take you days to find me." Syssi wasn't joking. Besides the place being huge, there were no distinguishing signs between one corridor and another. They all looked the same; same industrial carpet, same concrete walls, and the same metal doors leading to various rooms. With her nonexistent sense of direction, she would be lost in no time.

A wicked gleam in his eyes, Kian bent to whisper in her ear. "I'll slap a locator cuff on you as well, my sweet."

"Aren't you the big bad wolf." She stretched up on her tiptoes, pretending to go for his lips. But instead of the kiss he'd been expecting, she nipped his nose.

"Oh, I'll get you for that..." Kian growled.

"As I see it, I owed you a bite... or two... you had it coming..."

"You're lucky we have company..." Kian pinched her butt.

Michael chuckled.

"Shut up, kid. You haven't seen a thing..." He twisted back, pinning Michael with a hard stare.

"I see nothing, hear nothing... I'm not even here..." Michael saluted solemnly, his face pinched in an effort to suppress another chuckle.

"You and I are going to get along just fine, kid..." Kian winked at Michael, then wrapped his arm around Syssi's waist, pulling her closer against his side.

CHAPTER 3: SYSSI

Back at the penthouse, Syssi examined the wide metal cuff on her wrist. It didn't look too bad. The highly polished metal gleamed like a fine piece of jewelry, and the cuff's unbreakable locking mechanism was so cleverly concealed that no one would ever suspect the thing housed a sophisticated tracking device.

Except, regrettably, the pretty cuff would trigger an alarm as soon as she tried to leave the compound.

And here she thought she would be free to roam the streets whenever she pleased.

With that thought, Syssi slanted a suspicious glance at Kian, who was sitting beside her on the couch, busy going through his emails on an iPad. "How come you have these cuffs in the first place?"

Lifting his head, he deposited the device on the coffee table and leaned toward her. "For house arrests. If a clan member broke one of our laws, he or she might be sentenced to house arrest. Or in the case of restriction—allowed to leave only for school or work. The cuff ensures compliance with sentencing."

"Interesting, it didn't occur to me that you need to govern yourselves separately from the mortal population. Although it makes sense. With your special abilities, someone needs to keep things in check, right? So is it like a monarchy or a democracy? And who makes the laws? Who enforces them? And who is the judge?"

Pausing to take a breath, she smiled apologetically at Kian's amused expression. "I'm sorry for blasting you with so many questions, but this is so fascinating. Oh, and how are your laws different from ours?"

"Our laws are not that different. The two clan specific issues are; keeping our existence secret and the use of thralls and illusions. The teenagers are the most difficult to control. Imagine being able to thrall the bartender to sell you a drink, your teacher to raise your grades, or the pretty girl in your math class to get intimate with you. Even good kids might be tempted. And as in any society, we have our share of bad apples. The adults are less problematic. Not because they are all well-behaved angels, but because they are better aware of the consequences." Kian shrugged.

"We maintain a small police force, the Guardians, all of whom you've already met. Arrests are made and the perpetrators are brought before a judge or a panel of judges: depending on the severity of their crime. For the most severe cases, the whole clan has to vote. Sentencing varies from monetary fines to house arrests, to incarceration here in the underground, etc."

Syssi was impressed. "Wow! You guys are like a country within a country. With your own laws, police force, judges, jails... So, do you get a lot of unlawful behavior?"

"Not a lot, but enough, mostly minor infractions. If you're really interested, I can arrange for you to meet Edna. She is our legal expert, attorney, judge... Everything you want to know regarding clan law, she'll be more than happy to tell you all about it in excruciating detail. She loves the law, and she loves talking about it even more. But what I want you to do now is come with me to the kitchen and eat something. You look pale."

"I'm a little hungry... come to think of it, I didn't have lunch yet." Syssi followed Kian to the kitchen and took a seat at the counter, not sure if she should offer to make something or let him play host.

"Let's see..." Kian poked his head into the refrigerator. "No worries, Okidu left us lunch." He pulled out a container of pasta and a large bowl of salad. After warming the pasta in the microwave for a few minutes, he brought both over to the counter.

"By the way, where is Okidu? I'm surprised he is not here to fuss around us like we're a couple of helpless children who need to be fed."

"Probably went grocery shopping." Kian stuffed a large swirl of pasta into his mouth.

"You're so lucky to have him. He is an outstanding cook, everything he makes is delicious." Syssi ate slowly, taking small bites to savor the taste.

"Yeah, he is great... Though speaking of delicious food... I was wondering if you'd like to go out with me to a restaurant tomorrow night. If you think Okidu's is good, the food there will blow your taste buds. I thought dinner and some dancing would be nice. What do you say?"

"That sounds wonderful." *He is actually taking me out on a date!* A spark of hope shimmered in her heart. "I'd love to go out with you." *A romantic outing...* "But just to a restaurant, not to a club. I don't like the scene. Last night, I was very uncomfortable. I'm not in the mood to repeat that experience anytime soon."

"No, not a club, I don't like them either." Kian twisted toward her and swiveled her stool, bracketing her knees between his thighs so they were facing each other. "The restaurant I'm talking about has live music and dancing. It's not loud, and the clientele is very exclusive. Just to get in you need to be a member, or be invited by one. It's a bit snobby, but the upside of that is an atmosphere that is posh and romantic, not vulgar like the club's. I guarantee you're going to love it."

"What is it called?"

"By Invitation Only."

"Seriously? That's the name? It's like naming your dog, Dog." She snorted. It wasn't really that funny, but she was giddy. *I'm such a fool, it's only a date.* "I've never heard of it."

"Of course not. Those who are willing to spend that kind of money on a membership do so as much for the privacy as for the exclusivity. It would defy the whole purpose of the place if the paparazzi got a whiff of it and descended on it like a pack of hounds, hunting for the celebrities."

"You've got a point... So, should I assume you're a member? Or did you pull some strings to get us invited?"

"I'm part owner of the place. After graduating from the culinary institute, a nephew of mine came asking if I would be willing to loan him the money he needed to open his own place. I liked the concept, not to mention the taste of what he had prepared for me to try. So, I made it an investment instead of a loan. He runs it, and I collect a share of the profits. Win-win for both of us."

"Is everyone in your family a member?"

"Definitely not, just the ones we invite and who are willing to pay for membership..."

"What about those you don't invite? They must feel left out."

"What they don't know won't hurt them. Anyway, the place was not intended to be a family hangout. The concept was to provide a top-notch place for the rich and famous—the movers and shakers of society—to mingle and have fun away from the public eye."

"And you want to take plain me to hang out with those kinds of people? I'll stick out like a sore thumb. What will I wear? I don't know how to dress for a place like this." She cringed, some of her initial excitement ebbing. "Can't we go somewhere less intimidating?" As much as she was intrigued, she couldn't help thinking of how awkward she'd feel amongst such a crowd.

"Nonsense, Amanda will take you shopping and get you everything you need. You know it's her favorite pastime... Well, maybe second favorite... Anyway, just leave it to her and you'll be fine; she is a pro when it comes to fashion. And besides, you need to get out of here and get some fresh air, even if it's the somewhat polluted type that hangs over Rodeo Drive. I'm certain you'll have fun on an outing with her."

Syssi was sure she would, but the idea of spending a small fortune just so she could fit in with the patrons of a snooty place for one night, didn't sit well with her pragmatic nature. And shopping at a place like

Rodeo Drive? Not going to happen.

Maybe I could borrow something from Amanda—that makes much more sense.

"Okay, I'll go... Just for once, I'm curious to see how the elite parties. But I'm not sure about buying new expensive stuff that I'll probably never wear again."

"Don't worry about the money—it's my treat."

"I have the money. I just hate spending it frivolously."

"Please, do it for me. I feel so bad for turning your life upside down. Getting you something you would never buy for yourself will bring me much pleasure. Be a good girl and say yes."

"I'll think about it. First, I'm going to see if I can borrow something from Amanda." It was hard to say no to him, but she didn't want to accept presents from Kian just so he could ease his conscience. This had been exactly what her parents had done every time they had neglected her or her siblings. They had bought expensive presents; after a long absence, or for not showing up for teacher conferences, or school plays, or sports games, or graduations... It had been nothing but a bribe.

"There is nothing to think about. If I'm dragging you to this expensive place, I think I should be the one to provide you with whatever you need to feel comfortable going there. Case closed." Kian really wasn't used to anyone saying no to him, and with the way his brows were tightening, Syssi realized he was getting impatient with her.

"My big bad wolf... You can huff, and you can puff, but this little piggy will not bow down." She leaned to nip at his nose again.

"We'll see about that..." On a surge, he gripped her at the waist and pulled her up, then tossed her over his shoulder. With his arm locked over her thighs, he strode down the hallway toward his bedroom, playfully smacking her upturned behind.

"Put me down, you brute!" Laughing, Syssi pounded her fists on his back.

"Oh, I will... as soon as we reach the bed. Then I'll put you down... over my knee to finish what I've started." He delivered a stronger smack that actually managed to sting a little.

"Oh, no you will not. Put me down this instant!" Giggling hysterically and fighting to catch her breath, she was barely able to get the words out. But secretly, she was incredibly turned on and wondered how far Kian would take this game... Or more to the point... how far she wanted him to take it...

CHAPTER 4: KIAN

Kian smiled smugly as he inhaled the intoxicating aroma of Syssi's arousal. The minx was turned on by the little scene he was enacting, and he wondered how far she would like to be pushed.

The truth was, that even though his predatory nature attracted those with spicier tastes, he had never had the urge to test his partners' limits before, and during the short interludes he was accustomed to, mostly followed their cues.

Except, that was with women he hadn't been emotionally invested in and hadn't really cared how they had felt about him. It was different with Syssi. With her, he had an overbearing craving to push the envelope and see how far she was willing to go.

On some level it disturbed him; he wished he didn't have these kinds of urges. But given the predatory nature of his people, there wasn't much he could do about it. ████████, most of the males of his kind were beasts, and even the females were rapacious. Only those further away from the source seemed to get their genetically preprogrammed impulses somewhat diluted.

In his case, however, he was as close to the source as it got.

Being dominant and aggressive had been an advantage in the era he had been born into; as a natural leader and fighter he had what it took to safeguard his family. But as times had changed, and what had been required of him had shifted toward the diplomatic and managerial, he had learned to keep these impulses on a tight leash.

It was a constant struggle.

Growing up without a father, or any other male of his kind to look up to and emulate, he had chosen as his role models the few mortal men that over the years had gained his respect. And the type of man he admired and believed he ought to be, wasn't the fierce warrior or the ruthless commander.

It was the cultured gentleman: polite, lenient and accommodating.

Civilized.

Except, with Syssi it seemed his civilized facade was cracking—the fissures getting wider—and last night, in that damned elevator, the false veneer had shattered completely.

That being said, he was all too aware that Syssi liked this side of him—at least to some degree. But the thing that gave him pause, the reason he strained to rein in the beast was that he might cross the line and scare her off.

He wanted to bring her nothing but pleasure; to be the one and only to fulfill all of her wildest desires. And by doing so, some of his own.

Sitting down on the bed, he lowered her down over his knees, just as he had promised. And as he caressed her denim-clad bottom, his other palm resting between her shoulder blades and holding her down gently, he waited to see if she'd try to get free.

She didn't. Turning her head sideways, Syssi laid her cheek on the comforter, holding her breath in strained anticipation.

"You know it's only a game? That I would never hurt you?" he asked quietly, his voice raspy with his arousal.

"Yes," she answered, her throaty whisper betraying how much she wanted this.

CHAPTER 5: SYSSI

Why? Syssi had no clue. She had never done anything like that before. Hell, she had never even thought about it. Up until she had met Kian, she had been convinced she was purely vanilla: and a very boring flavor of vanilla at that. What could be so damn arousing about a spanking?

Something must've been really wrong with her to be so turned on by the prospect of what she should find at least degrading, if not scary and completely wrong.

On some level, she hoped she would hate it—that it would hurt and prove to be a big turnoff—because that would make her normal.

Not kinky and weird.

As Kian yanked down her jeans with her panties coming along for the ride, she bit down on her lower lip, and feeling the cool air on her exposed bottom, fought the urge to giggle and make him stop. But she forced herself to stay put. Resolved to find out once and for all what it was like. To have the experience so she could put that demon to rest—one way or the other.

With his hand lightly caressing her bottom, Kian inhaled sharply through his clenched teeth, making the kind of hissing sound that she came to expect before his bite. Syssi tensed, bracing for his fangs. Instead, she felt his soft lips, kissing each cheek before he went back to caressing them.

"You have a gorgeous ass, Syssi, small and perfectly plump...," he said with that same snakelike hiss as his finger stroked over her drenched folds. "And you're soaking wet... my sweet girl."

Syssi groaned. Then she almost climaxed when he brushed lightly over her sensitive, throbbing bundle of nerves.

Between her fearful anticipation and his light caresses, Syssi was so turned on she felt like crawling out of her skin. "Please..." she pleaded, not knowing what exactly she was pleading for. At this point, she would've done just about anything to get what she needed to hurtle over that strained edge.

Answering her plea, Kian's palm descended, landing with a light smack on her upturned behind. But it was not enough, she needed more. The next three landed in quick succession, but he was still being too gentle with her, and she was getting antsy. Pushing her bottom up with a little wiggle, she tried to communicate her need for him to do better without having to say a thing.

"Greedy little minx, aren't you?" He smacked her bottom harder, finally bringing on the sting she craved. After five more delicious smacks, the small ache pulsing in her behind was almost enough to send her over the precipice. She groaned again, waiting. But he stopped.

"Not yet, sweet girl, I want to be inside you when you come," he growled. With a quick surge, he moved her over, pulling up her hips so she was propped on her knees with her cheek still pressed down to the mattress.

While caressing her warmed-up bottom with his palm, Kian struggled to pull down his pants with the other. He ended up only pushing them down past his hips, and with a grunt, thrust inside her from behind.

Syssi felt as if a tight rubber band had snapped, and as she was flung over that cliff, she flew apart. Kian kept his hold on her hips, preventing her from being shoved forward as he kept pounding into her and prolonging her climax.

As his pelvis kept slapping against her tender behind, the explosive combination of the submissive pose and his forceful thrusts had her orgasm two more times. Though coming one on the heel of the other, they felt like one long rapture crashing to shore in several powerful waves.

Drained to the point of passing out, Syssi thought she couldn't take it anymore. Except, Kian wasn't done yet. Pulling on her hair, he brought her up so she was kneeling with her back pressed against his chest. His arm holding her in an iron grip around her middle, he tilted her head and with a loud hiss sank his fangs into her exposed neck.

Syssi found she still had some hidden reserves, climaxing again when Kian's venom and his seed flooded her body.

With a keening moan that sounded more like a weak sob escaping her dry, hoarse throat, she collapsed—utterly drained yet completely sated.

CHAPTER 6: KIAN

With Syssi still cradled in his arms, Kian plopped down on his side and smirked.

At this rate, they were going to drain each other dry until there was nothing left of them but two shriveled husks.

Oh, but what a way to go.

Feeling oddly at peace, he stroked Syssi's damp hair and wrapped himself tighter against her back, letting sleep slowly claim him...

Kian found himself in the small, one-room house he had shared with his wife all those centuries ago. He snuggled closer to the woman sleeping in his arms, dimly aware that he was dreaming and that the warm body he was spooning didn't belong to Lavena.

Rubbing his erection against her naked bottom, he buried his nose in her hair. "Hmm... You smell so good, love," he whispered in her ear before nuzzling her neck.

She turned in his arms, lifting her sweet lips for a kiss. "Good morning, my love."

"Morning?" The rooster crowed outside. "Good morning it is, then." He took her mouth, his tongue parting her lips.

She pulled away. "No French-kissing—morning breath."

"I don't care." He pulled her back and covered her with his body, pinning her to the bed. Catching both of her wrists in one hand, he stretched her arms over her head.

Her body went soft, surrendering, and she closed her eyes. Kian took his time exploring her mouth at leisure. Syssi parted her legs, cradling him.

"I love you," he whispered in her ear as he sank into her wet heat.

"Don't leave me..." she whispered back, a tear sliding down her rosy cheek.

"Why would I ever leave you? I love you. You know it, right?" He looked into her sad eyes.

How could she ask him that? Why on earth would he leave her?

Everything was perfect. He was making love to his beautiful woman in the home they'd built together.

What more could a man want?

CHAPTER 7: SYSSI

With Kian's warm body enveloping her from behind, and his heavy arm draped over her middle—palm resting splayed-fingered against her belly—Syssi felt a delightful, inner quiet.

She opened her eyes. It couldn't have been long since she'd passed out because the sun, shining brightly through the glass walls of the terrace doors, was still pretty high in the sky.

They were both a mess; still dressed, their pants bunched around their ankles, and Kian's groin was sticking wetly to her behind.

Evidently, he had been too wiped out to perform his cleaning routine. Funny, how this little thing made him seem more human to her—proving that he wasn't Superman after all.

Although in her humble opinion, he came pretty damn close.

Smiling contently, she lifted his hand to her lips and kissed the inside of his palm, then rubbed it against her cheek.

I love this man. She sighed.

There was no point in denying it. She didn't want to fall in love with him, knew it was going to break her heart, but to keep pretending wasn't doing her any good either.

She'd be deceiving no one but herself.

Oh, God, she felt like crying.

But if she cried now, it would be as good as admitting that there was no hope, nothing she could do, and Syssi wasn't ready to throw in the towel yet.

Accepting defeat without a fight wasn't something she was capable of—even over a losing battle like her relationship with Gregg. She should've ended it long before it had fizzled and died on its own. But not willing to admit failure, she had kept fighting for it when it would've been smarter to let him go.

It wasn't the same, though. In this case, the end was beyond her control. But what she did in the interim wasn't. Pulling her resolve around her like a suit of armor, she made up her mind to be grateful for whatever she could have with Kian and not succumb to despair over what was not to be.

Still, it was easier said than done.

With another sigh, she gently extracted herself from Kian's embrace. After wiggling out of her pants, she tiptoed bare-assed to the bathroom, washed up, then soaked some washcloths in warm water for Kian.

Sleeping like a dead man, he didn't stir as she wiped the sticky residue from his groin. Though true to form, her ministrations got him instantly hard.

Yep, Superman indeed. Syssi chuckled.

After tossing the washcloths in the laundry bin, she returned to the bed and snuggled back into Kian's arms.

His striking face was peaceful in sleep, and she realized that when awake, he had always looked strained. *Poor baby, shouldering the weight of the world, literally.*

Stroking his cheek, she felt her heart overflow with love, and unexpectedly, a sense of gratitude. It was a strange emotion to have after the bit of naughty they'd played. And yet, it was how she felt. Grateful for the incredible pleasure—for the freedom to experience things with him without the fear of ridicule or rejection.

In the few days they had known each other, he'd never criticized her, had never implied she was anything less than perfect in his eyes.

Kian accepted all of her the way she was. Even her little kink...

Syssi smiled as the gleam from her cuff caught her eye. Kian was pretty kinky himself. The obvious thrill he had gotten from locking the thing on her wrist gave her an inkling to his own twisted desires. She'll have to pry them out of him—curious to see what tickled his fancy.

Confident in the reassuring safety of his care... or was it his love? She was willing to try new things.

Except, how long did she have?

Closing her eyes, she tried to hold back the tears, but her imaginary coat of armor was crumbling under the onslaught of the dark shadows cast by the reality of their situation.

If she still believed in a benevolent God, she would have prayed reverently for a fairy-tale ending to their story; her turning immortal, the two of them spending eternity together... raising children...

The whole happily-ever-after thing.

But after her brother's death, she had lost her faith in happy endings. If there was a real deity somewhere, it didn't listen to prayers or care about the individual parts of the multitudes of its creation.

Chaos ruled, and bad things happened to good people all the time. At any moment, all of this could be taken away from her, without even the memories to sustain her.

Then again, maybe it was a blessing in disguise.

If she didn't remember any of it, she wouldn't have to live with the pain of losing it. Except, what was worse? Never to know what she was privileged to experience, or remember and mourn its loss?

Feeling Kian's gentle finger wipe away the traitorous tear caught in her lashes, her lids fluttered open.

"What's the matter, baby?" he asked, then kissed her eyelids. "Was it too much? I thought you liked it…" He frowned, looking apprehensive.

"No, it's not that. I did like it…" Embarrassed, she felt her face heat up. "It's just that I don't want us to end…" she whispered, and a few more tears escaped despite her valiant effort to hold them back.

"We will not…" Kian pulled her tightly against his chest. "If you don't turn, I'll just chain you naked to my bed and keep you as my sex slave forever." He kissed her forehead, stroking her back in small soothing circles.

She chuckled. "You'd like that, wouldn't you?"

"We'll figure something out. I don't think I could let you go, no matter what." He sighed and bent his head to kiss her lips.

"Even if I stay on as your sex slave…" Syssi smiled a sad little smile. "The cold reality is that I'll grow old while you won't. And that's the biggest obstacle in this wishful fantasy. As much as I hate to admit it, you were right. If I don't turn, you'll have to let me go."

His eyes were so sad, she knew she was going to flay him with what she was compelled to say next. "I just wish you could leave me my memories, so I could relive our time together in my mind and know that I lived to experience something wonderful and treasure it forever… despite how torturous knowing I had this and lost it will surely be."

"Oh, baby." He choked as he held her close—his pain echoing hers. "All we can do is hope. I know hope is for fools and children, but I have nothing else."

"I know… neither do I." She kissed his chest through his T-shirt, a few more tears wetting the soft fabric. And yet, there was comfort to be had in the knowledge that he was just as pained by their dim prospects as she was. Which in turn, as absurd as the notion was, made her want to be strong enough for both of them.

The irony, of an almost twenty-five-year-old mortal thinking she could shore up an almost two-thousand-year-old superbeing, wasn't lost on her. Nevertheless, she went on to imagine her armor snapping back into place—this time extending over Kian as well.

With a big brave smile plastered on her face, she kissed his warm lips. "Well, I for one am done moping around. There is no point in lamenting that which cannot be changed. We just have to take it one day at a time. Right?" She glanced down at her watch. "Anyway, I need to get back to work, it's late."

"What time is it?" Kian asked.

"It's ten past four."

"Oh, damn, I have a meeting scheduled for four-thirty."

"I need to go too. Amanda must be wondering why I'm not back yet." Syssi scooted off the bed and grabbed her pants off the floor, then pulled them on. "Ugh, yak! My panties are wet!" She pulled them back down. "Can I borrow a pair of yours? I hate wearing jeans with no underwear. Too rough on my sensitive girl parts..." She waggled her brows.

"Sure, I'll trade you a clean pair of mine for yours." His tone promised something wicked was to follow. "I'm going to carry your sweet-smelling panties in my pocket, and whenever I miss you, I'll take sniffs of your essence."

Syssi laughed. "You're a pervert, you know that? Catch!" She threw her panties at his face.

"Ah, Syssi..." Kian caught the little scrap of satin and lace and crushed it to his nose, taking a loud sniff. "Delicious..." He sniffed again, taunting her while she ran into his closet to get a pair of his boxer briefs.

"You should really get your stuff back in here. It's kind of pointless to leave it at Amanda's when you keep ending up here anyway." He stuffed her panties in his back pocket.

"I will. Now give me back my undies, I need to put them in the wash." She extended her arm.

"Ah, ah, ah... a deal is a deal. I'm keeping them." He pulled her in for a scorching kiss.

Coming up for air, she said, "I thought you needed to be somewhere..."

"Yeah, how unfortunate..." He let her pull out from his arms. "You'll be at Amanda's?"

"Yes, and if you miss me, you can call me on this brand-new, wonderful phone I got instead of sniffing my panties..." Syssi pulled out the device from her pocket, caressing its sleek surface. "Precious...," she whispered coarsely like Sméagol from *Lord of the Rings.*

"Let's go, Sméagol." Kian tousled her hair. Outside Amanda's door, he kissed her hard before letting her go. "I'll see you later."

CHAPTER 8: SYSSI

"Lucy! I'm home!" Syssi called as she opened the door.

Rushing out of the kitchen and waving her hands in a damn good imitation of the legendary Lucy, Amanda chirped, "Oh, Ricky, darling!"

The woman was a born actress.

"Sorry I took so long, I'll get to work right away."

"Rubbish, it's not important. Come, talk to me. Tell me what you've been up to. You should have been done with Bridget hours ago." Amanda dragged her by the hand to sit beside her on the couch. "I see that Kian cuffed you." She lifted Syssi's forearm to examine the cuff.

"Yeah, I have access to the elevators now, and so does Michael. Now both of us can spy on you guys and uncover all of your dirty little secrets."

"Very funny... So, what else have you been up to, besides having your blood drawn and getting... cuffed..."

"Kian asked me out on a date for tomorrow night. He wants to take me to this very posh restaurant..." Syssi was pretty sure Amanda was a member, but just in case, she skirted around the name of the place.

"He's taking you to *By Invitation Only*? That's wonderful!" Amanda squeezed Syssi in her arms as if she had just delivered the best of news.

"That's the one... but why are you so excited?"

"How could I not be? It's the first time that I know of, that is, Kian has asked anyone on a date! I'm going to have to drink to that. Margarita?" She walked up to the bar.

"Yeah, why not, bring it on..." A drink actually sounded wonderful.

"How is it possible he has never done that before? What about all the women he shagged?"

"You've seen me in action. Would you call what I do dating?" Amanda handed her the drink and took a sip of her own.

"No, I guess not... So that's all you guys do? Pick up random strangers for hookups?"

"Yep, told you it sucks... The sex is okay, though, most of the time..." Amanda grimaced.

"I couldn't have lived that way. Now I understand what Kian meant when he said he hated it." Syssi took a big sip of the cold drink.

"Hey, we need to go shopping!" Amanda's eyes lit up with excitement. "I'm thinking a whole morning of girl fun. We'll go for a facial. A manicure and pedicure are an absolute must, then the hair salon complete with professional makeup. And then... Ta-Da! Rodeo Drive!"

"I can't afford all that!" Syssi laughed at Amanda's enthusiasm.

Dismissing Syssi's monetary concerns, Amanda waved her hand. "Don't be silly. I'm going to charge it all to Kian's card."

"You can't do that! I don't want him spending a small fortune on clothes I'll use for only one night. Where will I wear stuff like this? Starbucks?"

"He doesn't care about the money. You know he can afford it. But he cares about you, and you're not going to be selfish and refuse. You're going to let him do this small thing for you, just to make him happy. *Capisce*?" Amanda arched her well-defined dark brow and took another sip from her drink.

That shut Syssi up, effectively making any farther arguments seem petty. She realized Amanda was right. Kian had made it clear that it would please him to pamper her.

So why was she still making waves about it?

Was it pride?

To some extent... But mostly it was about who she was and what she believed in. Spending obscene amounts on clothes or shoes seemed vain and frivolous to her. Still, she had to consider that what seemed obscene to her was perfectly reasonable to Kian and Amanda. And if she wanted to hang out with them at places like that fancy restaurant, she had to fit in with the rest of their rich friends.

"Okay, you win...," she conceded.

"Yay! I'm so happy!" Amanda hugged her again. "We're going to have so much fun."

"You're going to have fun. I, on the other hand, am not such a big fan of beauty salons and shopping. I lose patience real quick."

"Don't worry. With me by your side... there won't be a dull moment."

"Oh, I'm sure you're right... there is never a dull moment when you're around." Feeling the margarita's effect, Syssi laughed. "That's what I'll miss going back to Kian's... He asked me to bring my stuff back to his place."

"You do that, as you never actually sleep here... But no worries; we'll have plenty of good times together. It's not like I'm a long commute away, right?"

"Right… Well, I'm going to pack my stuff and then finally do some work." Syssi walked over to the kitchen to rinse out her glass.

"Okay, party pooper. Now you've guilted me into doing some work as well." Amanda pushed up from the couch and sauntered over to the bar. Making herself another drink, she turned to Syssi. "Want one?" she asked.

"No, thank you, I don't want a repeat of what happened the last time you kept pushing margaritas at me…" Syssi grimaced and headed for her room to pack.

It didn't take long until most of her belongings were neatly folded and packed into the duffle bag. But when she got to the velvet pouch containing her modest collection of jewelry, instead of adding it to the rest of her stuff, she turned around and dumped its contents on top of the dresser.

Sifting through the small pile of earrings, she sighed. None would work for her date with Kian. The diamond studs were okay, but they were as good as invisible beneath her full, wavy hair, and the rest of the stuff was just too plain for the occasion.

The same was true for the necklaces and bracelets. None of the bracelets would look good matched with the gleaming silver cuff on her right hand. And as for the necklaces, she didn't feel like taking off Andrew's pendant for something flashier even if the gold didn't go with the silver of the cuff.

"Oh, well…" Syssi returned everything to the pouch. Turning around, she found Amanda leaning against the doorjamb and sipping from her drink.

"I'll be right back," Amanda said. Leaving her goblet on the dresser, she stepped out and headed down the hallway.

A few minutes later, she returned with an ornate jewelry box. Placing it on the dresser, she lifted its lid with marked reverence.

Inside, nestled in black velvet, was a gorgeous set of platinum and diamond earrings and a matching necklace. Syssi had never seen jewelry as beautiful as this. And even though she knew next to nothing about the styles or designer names of the fine-jewelry world, she had no doubt it was a one of a kind masterpiece.

"I want you to wear this tomorrow." Amanda put her hand on Syssi's shoulder. "Go ahead… try it on…," she urged.

"Are you serious? Would you really let me borrow this for tomorrow? It's stunning! Where did you get it? It must be one of a kind."

"It is. It was a present from my mother for my two-hundredth birthday. I have no idea who she commissioned to make it, but I'm certain she ensured it was the only one made." Amanda ran her fingers over the surface of the beautiful necklace.

"It must be very special to you. I will feel weird wearing it… even for one evening." As much as Syssi was tempted, she knew she would be constantly stressed and worried that something might happen to it. The set was priceless, irreplaceable.

"You mean a lot to me, Syssi." Amanda's tone got so uncharacteristically serious, it compelled Syssi to pry her gaze away from the jewelry and look up at her friend's face.

Amanda still wore that reverent expression, except, it wasn't directed at the masterpiece in the box. She was looking at Syssi.

Syssi's eyes misted with emotion. "You mean a lot to me too." She wrapped her arm around Amanda's shoulders and pulled her into a hug.

Amanda leaned into her for a moment, her soft hair brushing against Syssi's neck. Then pulling back, she placed both hands on Syssi's shoulders and pinned her with her intense blue stare. "In the short time I've known you, I've come to think of you as a sister. I'm not that close to my real sisters, who are much older and busy with their own responsibilities, and I only became close to Kian when I moved here and he took me under his wing. But regardless of how things will turn out for the two of you, my feelings for you will not change. I want you to have the set, not only for tomorrow but to keep—as a symbol of our friendship."

Touching a finger to Syssi's lips, Amanda shushed her protests. "Hear me out. I want to give you something that has a special meaning to me and is close to my heart. And I can't think of anything else that will better fit the bill. Money means nothing to me, so anything I may buy for you wouldn't be special enough. Don't say no, let me have the pleasure of knowing you are carrying on your person a token of my love."

Syssi was moved to tears. At some point during the last several days, she'd grown to care deeply for the complicated woman; there was no way she was going to jeopardize their nascent bond by being callous with Amanda's feelings. And as she saw no way to refuse without offending her friend, she was left with no choice but to accept.

But she'd have to gift Amanda something of equal value back. Except, the value would have to be in the sentiment it carried since she didn't own anything even remotely close to the monetary worth of that set. Syssi suspected that even her car, which had been pretty expensive, wasn't worth that much.

This left only one thing she could think of. Grasping at the necklace Andrew had given her on her sixteenth birthday, she opened the tiny clasp and took it off.

"If I'm to accept this gift from you, then you have to accept this from me. This necklace was a gift from my brother Andrew, and since the day I got it I never left home without it. It's not nearly as valuable as what you gave me, but if you believe objects get imbued with their owner's essence, then this necklace has the most essence I have ever imparted on any one thing. I regret the fact that it isn't worth even a fraction of what your gift is. My only consolation is that when you wear it, you'll carry some of me with you." She took Amanda's hand and pressed the delicate chain with its small heart pendant into her palm.

"Thank you. I'm going to wear it always, just the way you did..." Amanda wrapped the chain around her neck and closed the clasp. When she was done adjusting the diamond-encrusted heart to lie in the hollow of her neck, she swiped a finger under each of her teary eyes. "Come here..." She opened her arms, inviting Syssi to step into another embrace.

Standing in each other's arms, they were both sniffling. It felt good, though, to acknowledge this bond between them.

Syssi wondered what was it that had brought them so close together in such a short time. Was it the love they shared for Kian? Or was it the fact that they were both survivors of similar tragedies?

Or maybe it was the attraction of opposites?

On the surface of things, they had nothing in common; different looks, different temperaments, different values. They didn't even belong to the same species for goodness' sake. Except, it seemed like they were both in desperate need of a good friend.

CHAPTER 9: ANDREW

Ready to be done for the day, Andrew closed the Maldives case file when his phone rang.

He frowned. An unknown caller? No one besides a select few that were already on his contacts list was supposed to have this number. On an impulse, he accepted the call instead of letting it go to voice mail. "Yes?" he barked.

"Is it a bad time? You sound busy."

"Syssi, I thought you were a wrong number... No, not busy at all, what's up?"

As it was, Andrew still had no new leads on that damned case. He had searched everything he could think of; going through the registration records of every hotel, motel, and inn he had access to. Which, unless they were not connected to the internet, meant everything with rooms for rent in the greater Los Angeles area. He had even gone as far as checking every group of four men or more registering at the same time, and when that had produced zilch, he'd narrowed it down to three.

The twelve had disappeared without a trace. If they were still somewhere around LA, they were most likely staying at someone's private residence. Unless they got themselves into some kind of trouble, he would have no way of locating them.

"Just wanted to give you my new cell phone number and tell you that I'm still at Amanda's, working on that report."

"I thought you were calling from a blocked landline. Why didn't you keep your old cell number?" Andrew's bullshit radar switched on, its red alert light blinking like crazy. "What aren't you telling me, Syssi?"

The sigh she'd heaved had him jack upright in his chair and tighten his grip on the phone. What kind of trouble had she gotten herself into?

"I didn't want to worry you... but Amanda's lab was ransacked a couple of nights ago. That's why we are working at her place instead of the lab."

"We'll get to why you didn't tell me about this before, after you explain what the hell this has to do with you changing your phone number." Pushing up from his chair, Andrew began pacing around.

When instead of providing an explanation she sighed again, he felt like punching someone. Except, with no ready candidates lined up, he ended up smashing his fist into the concrete wall and bruising his knuckles instead. "Talk!" he grated. If she sighed one more time, he was driving over there and shaking the truth out of her.

Did she think to coddle him?

"It was a hate crime. A group of religious fanatics that think Amanda's research has some occult ramifications. They stole a list of her test subjects; the ones with paranormal abilities. I was at the top of that list, and Amanda was afraid they'd come after me, as well as one of the other high ranked talents. That's why both of us are staying at her family's place. I had to get rid of my phone so they will have no way of tracking me…"

"And it didn't cross your mind to call me? Who's better equipped to protect you? Amanda or me? I can't believe you acted so irresponsibly. And what are the police doing about it?" Striding back to his desk, Andrew sat down and booted up his terminal.

"The police are investigating, but they think it's just a malicious prank. And I didn't come to you because there was no need. Amanda's place is in a highly secure building, as in Fort Knox secure. You have nothing to worry about. And besides, if I stayed with you, I wouldn't be able to continue my work with her, and as you are well aware, I do need to work for a living." Syssi huffed as if to say, "You see? I was completely reasonable."

"Even so, you could have let me know. You know the resources available to me…"

"I know, I'm sorry. But really, there is no need for you to get involved in this. I'm sure the whole thing will blow over in a few days."

"I'll look into it and see what I can do. Bummer, though…"

"Yeah, I know. There are some crazy loons out there."

"That too, but that's not what I'm bummed about. I was hoping you were shacking up with a guy and covering it up… It's about time you got something going on."

CHAPTER 10: SYSSI

Syssi took a fortifying breath before plunging headfirst into the deep. "Amanda does have a brother…"

"I knew it!" Andrew chuckled before switching into his interrogator mode. "And how is that brother of hers?"

"He is fine, like in *really* fine. But there's nothing for you to get all worked up about. There is not much to tell." Syssi cringed. *If lightning indeed struck liars, I would be a smoking husk right now.*

"I want to meet him." Andrew got that resolute tone that meant he wouldn't take no for an answer.

"I just met him, for God's sake. Perfect way to scare the guy off… Oh, by the way, my big brother wants to give you the third degree… Really, it's nothing to worry about, just an interrogation from hell—the kind reserved for suspected terrorists and serial killers… Not going to happen, Andrew. I don't want it to be over before it even begins."

I'd better step aside to avoid that lightning when it strikes me where I stand…

"Okay, okay… You've got a point…," he conceded. "So, how about you introduce me to this Amanda I keep hearing about? I can question her instead… You were nagging me to meet her anyway, true?"

He got her there. Now she couldn't refuse.

"I can arrange something with Amanda, but no questions! And I mean it! You're not going to embarrass me in front of my boss who happens also to be my best friend." Syssi was surprised by her own words. It was true, though, and a warmth spread through her at the realization.

"I'm glad you are BFFs with your boss. I promise I'll be discreet. You can kick me in the shin if I cross the line."

As if summoned by being the subject of their conversation, Amanda walked in. "Who are you talking to?" she asked.

"It's Andrew. He wants to meet you…"

"I would love to meet your fascinating brother." Amanda sat down next to Syssi and opened her laptop. "How about lunch, tomorrow, after our shopping spree? There is this great little Italian café not far from Rodeo, Café Milano. Ask him if he can meet us there at around three."

"Did I hear right? Shopping on Rodeo Drive? You never even pay retail, let alone visit high-end boutiques." Andrew sounded amused.

"I know… don't ask…" Syssi snorted.

"Tomorrow at three, Café Milano, tell your boss I'll be there."

"See you there." Syssi ended the call and shook her head at Amanda.

Typing away on her laptop, the distinguished professor, Dr. Amanda Dokani, was quietly singing, "Bad boy, bad boy, whatcha gonna do, whatcha gonna do when Amanda comes for you…"

CHAPTER 11: KIAN

On his way to the meeting, Kian reflected on the fact that although he had never resented his work before, he did now. Damn, he would've loved to stay in bed with Syssi and cuddle, or maybe go for another round... But then, she had work to do as well.

Screw that.

He would've just told her to stay.

If it were up to him, he'd make sure that unless Syssi wanted to, she wouldn't have to work another day in her life. Though, knowing Syssi, she would not have liked him managing her like that, and besides, she seemed to love her work.

Kian sighed. This whole train of thought was pointless. Even if he could persuade Syssi to slack, there was no escaping his responsibilities, and the Guardians he was scheduled to meet were awaiting him in his new office. And what's worse, with the way he'd been neglecting his duties lately to be with Syssi, he probably would have to pull an all-nighter to catch up on his work.

Normally, that wouldn't have bothered him, except now, his obligations were eating away at what little time he had left with the woman he loved.

He loved her. No ifs, ands, or buts about it.

Earlier, right after admitting he never wanted to let her go, he'd almost blurted those three monumental words. But letting these words loose when their future was so unclear would've been unkind to Syssi, even cruel.

Choking down that compulsion, his throat had clogged with the unvoiced confession, but he'd covered it well, goofing around with her panties.

When he arrived at the meeting, his sour expression must've forewarned the guys, for once thwarting their usual smart-ass remarks.

Thank God.

As he sat down at the table, Onegus took one look at Kian's face and cleared his throat, while Shai busied himself with rearranging the neat stacks of paperwork in front of him. Bhathian only frowned, but that had nothing to do with Kian. A scowl was the guy's regular expression.

"What do we have for today?" Kian asked.

"Carol is back to her old tricks." Onegus pushed his phone over to Kian. "See for yourself; play the recording."

Palming the device, Kian watched the scene playing out on the small screen. Carol, drunk or high on something, sat on a stool with her back propped against the bar, facing a sizable audience. Encouraged by their rapt attention, she went on and on about her adventures as a highly sought after courtesan in eighteen-century Paris.

Kian sighed. Poor, misguided Carol.

Clearly, it had escaped her notice that as fascinated as her audience had been by the tale she'd been spinning, they had also looked amused. And the fact that they hadn't believed any of it and had thought she was either a nutcase or drunk had been obvious to everyone but her. Nevertheless, she'd broken the law by exposing her impossible age.

"Did you thrall them?" Kian asked Onegus.

"I did. But as she told the same stories the night before, the damage was done."

To most ears, the stories were harmless, too fantastical to be taken as anything but tall tales. But there was a remote chance that their adversaries may hear of it and easily figure out what she was, putting her and the rest of the family in danger.

"Bring her in. The first time she pulled that stunt, I let her off with a warning. But this time, she will stand trial. Let Edna decide what to do with her." Kian sighed, regretting the necessity.

Carol wasn't malicious—just disturbed and not too bright. But he couldn't let her endanger everyone with her behavior. Hopefully, some time spent alone in a small cell would be just the wake-up call she needed.

"Okay, this is settled then." Onegus took his phone back and searched for the next item on his agenda. "Evidently, someone believes that Jackson, son of Mira, is thralling girls in his high school into giving him blow jobs. We got this anonymous email last night." He handed the phone to Kian to read for himself.

Bhathian snorted and crossed his arms over his chest. "After the whipping this will earn him, I'm sure blow jobs will lose some of their appeal."

"Jackson is innocent until proven guilty. It may as well be someone who holds a grudge against him. You know how boys are... and this email was clearly written by a teenager. How old is he anyway? And who does he go to school with?" Kian needed more information before bringing the kid in for questioning.

"He is sixteen, and he is a student at Zelda Mayer's school. We have two more high schoolers there. It is a very prestigious institution, and some of LA's most prominent families send their kids there." Onegus sighed. "It's just getting better, isn't it? What if it was the mayor's daughter or some other public figure's kid? Not to imply that it makes a difference morally, but if she remembers anything and presses charges, it might make the evening news. The cleanup will be a nightmare."

"We'll need to bring our kids in for questioning, all three at the same time. Don't tell them the reason; I don't want them to be able to prepare for it. And what's more important, I don't want Jackson's name smeared because of a rumor. We need to interrogate each one separately to get to the bottom of this." Kian raked his fingers through his hair. If what the email claimed was true, Jackson would stand trial for rape. If proven guilty, he would be sentenced to a whipping.

This kind of punishment seemed barbaric in this time and age, especially when administered to someone who was considered a minor in mortal terms.

But this was their law.

Kids were responsible for their actions as soon as they reached puberty. But although the punishment was just as excruciatingly painful for an immortal as it was for a mortal, the difference was in how fast and fully an immortal healed.

"You know, I got whipped when I was that age. Since then, I've made damn sure that a girl wanted what I was doing to her and never assumed anything again." Bhathian's face contorted in a grimace. "It was a tough lesson, though. I never knew anything could hurt that bad, and I got only two. I hated my mother for a very long time after that; couldn't forgive her for reporting me for something I thought was trivial. She said it was the principle that mattered, and it was better I learned it before doing something worse and earning a more severe punishment."

Hearing this story for the first time, Kian asked, "What did you do?"

"I didn't even thrall the chit. I was kissing her and the kiss got us nice and steamy. She was moaning and clinging to me, so I got cocky and palmed her breast. I thought she was ready for second base, as they call it today. Imagine my surprise when she slapped me and ran to complain to my mother. When I tried to explain that I thought the girl wanted this, my mother saw red. 'Did you ask permission?' she asked. I was dumbfounded. 'Is this what a man is supposed to do? Ask before every move?' I challenged her. She looked me in the eyes and said, 'Yes. You don't have to ask with words, but you ask with your actions. Did your hand linger near her breast, giving her the opportunity to brush it off? Or conversely encourage you to continue? Or did you just go for it?' She was right, of course. Being honest with myself, I knew I didn't want the girl to have the chance to say no, hoping she would like what I was doing and maybe even let me pull up her skirt. So I admitted my guilt, never expecting to get a whipping for my honesty. I was angry for a very long time, but eventually, I understood and internalized how important the law of consent was—mainly after a very embarrassing lecture from my uncle, explaining in graphic detail everything concerning sex. He also explained that my mother was afraid I would not adhere to the law fully unless it were branded into me. I forgave her. But I lost my trust in her. I left home as soon as I was old enough and enlisted in the Guardian force." Bhathian looked down at his hands, his perpetual frown turning into a deep scowl.

Onegus put his hand on Bhathian's shoulder. "We've all done stupid things as kids or gotten punished beyond what we thought was fair. But there is no point in dwelling on past mistakes or the pain suffered, if we learned our lessons and moved on, becoming better people as a result. We are not human, but we are not infallible gods either, regardless of what our ancestors wanted everyone to believe." Onegus squeezed Bhathian's shoulder. "And neither are our mothers. Call your mom, Bhathian. Tell her you love her. It will make you feel better."

"Oh, yeah?" Bhathian arched a brow. "When was the last time you talked with yours?"

Onegus looked down his nose at his friend. "I talk to her every day."

"Seriously, man? You call your mom every day? Isn't that a bit excessive?" Kian blurted.

"You're damn right it's excessive. She calls *me*... several times a day, wants a report on every damn thing I do, keeps me on the phone forever, and gives me a guilt trip when I say I'm busy... You'd think I'm five, instead of five hundred years old..."

Bhathian laughed so hard, his eyes teared. "I didn't know our illustrious commander was a mamma's boy..."

Kian laughed as well, thankful his mother wasn't the intrusive, controlling type. On the contrary, at times when he might have lingered under her protective wing, she had pushed him to become independent, to take more and more responsibility and become the leader she needed him to be.

"Do you think I should talk with Edna about changing the definition of rape in light of your experience? A whipping for getting a feel of a girl's breast seems extreme." Kian had mixed feelings on the subject. Teenage immortals were very hard to control, their new powers lending themselves to feelings of superiority and entitlement. Combined with the impulsiveness and hormonal havoc of their changing bodies, they needed a strong deterrent to keep them from becoming dangerous monsters. Yet, he wished there was an alternative that wouldn't involve such brutal measures.

"And what would you suggest? Not considering nonconsensual oral sex as rape? Sternly scolding offenders for abusing their powers as punishment? Where do we draw the line?" Bhathian surprised them by defending the existing law.

Kian conceded, "You're right. Although I would have loved to have a more civilized alternative."

"These laws have served us well for thousands of years. Yes, the whipping is brutal, but the pain starts to recede almost as soon as the punishment ends. The memory of it, however, stays forever, ensuring the perpetrator never dares to repeat the crime. I don't think anything else will work on our kind. The power we have over mortals is too corrupting and too tempting for us not to take advantage of." Bhathian crossed his massive arms over his wide chest.

"He is right. What's the alternative? Keeping teenage offenders locked in the basement for years? I personally would prefer to get whipped and be done with it." Onegus shrugged.

"Let's just hope the accusations are groundless. But if this is the case, we'll need to deal harshly with whoever made them... Anything else on the agenda, Onegus?"

"No, that's all." Onegus got to his feet.

Once the Guardians had left, Kian got up and walked over to the bar, pouring himself a drink before sitting down with Shai to go over the files on his desk. "What's the progress with the resettling?" he asked.

"It's going pretty well, considering the haste. We have all of the Bay Area folks already settled. I hired several services to pack their homes and ship everything to various self-storage facilities around town. The locals are coming in at a slower pace. I estimate at least a month before we are able to drag them all here." Shai smiled apologetically—his initial estimate had been to have everyone settled in less than two weeks.

"The locals are less urgent; it's more of a long term plan. I'm more concerned with the adverse impact of us pulling our programmers out from their respective software firms. We need to figure out a way to enable them to continue their work from here. I need to have a meeting with the programmers and William to work out the logistics."

"I'll schedule it for tomorrow." Shai began fidgeting and rearranging the files, clearly stalling as he gathered his nerve before bringing up the next subject. "As all the council members are already in residence, I thought it might be a good idea to invite them to a nice big dinner. It will be good for morale, a show of unity. I'll take care of all the details. You wouldn't have to do anything other than show up..." Shai was well aware of how much Kian hated entertaining.

"Good idea. When do you have in mind?"

Surprised, Shai looked up. "Tonight... if it's okay with you. It would be best if it looks like something spontaneous that you've just thought of—give the impression that you're actually glad to have them here. I'll have Okidu and Onidu on it. We can use this room, or we can use your dining room; it's up to you." Shai's hopeful expression clearly indicated his preference.

"Having it at my place will be better received. Inform the council members. I also want Syssi and Michael to attend. Let's schedule it for eight. We need to give Okidu enough time to prepare."

Kian heaved a sigh. He was going to hate it. And yet, as regent, this was something that was expected of him, regardless of his lack of skill or enthusiasm for this particular part of the job. And what's more, at a time like this, his family needed to come together.

Pulling out his phone, he texted Syssi and then Amanda, informing them about the dinner.

"Okay, what else do we have?" He glanced at the pile of files Shai had stacked on his desk.

Damn, this was going to take a while.

CHAPTER 12: SYSSI

Peeking into the dining room, Syssi exhaled in relief. No one was there yet.

Talk about stressful.

As if the prospect of dinner with Kian's posse of Guardians and members of his council wasn't bad enough, he texted her saying he and Amanda were going to be a few minutes late and to go ahead without him.

Great.

It was like inviting your boyfriend's parents to dinner... only worse... because he wouldn't be there with you to greet them.

Imagining the looks and the questions and the judgments passed, Syssi cringed. If she could've thought of any way to wiggle out of it, she would've. Unfortunately, there was a doctor in the house to disprove any pretend maladies she could've come up with. And though the idea of hiding somewhere until Kian showed up crossed her mind, she dismissed it. That would mark her as a coward. Not going to happen. Even though in truth, she was one.

Oh, well, she'd survive.

Shoving her insecurities aside, she turned her focus to the beautifully set table. There was only one way to describe it. Wow.

Okidu had outdone himself preparing for this dinner. Though if that was supposed to be casual, she wondered what possibly more could've been done for a formal affair.

Maybe the butler just didn't get the memo... or got it and ignored it...

He certainly went all out.

Set with fine china, crystal goblets, and what seemed to be real silver silverware, the table looked like something from a period movie. It held the kind of old-world splendor that implied evening gowns and tuxedos. Not jeans.

Everything gleamed, the sparkle bouncing between the expensive-looking stuff on the table and the crystal chandelier above it. Even the artfully folded, pristine white napkins seemed to shine. And the silver goblets, with their tiny though elaborate flower arrangements, must have been delivered fresh from some exclusive florist. No way Okidu could've made those as well.

With a quick look behind her, Syssi pulled out her phone from her back pocket and snapped a picture. The table was so beautiful, she just had to preserve the image.

"Good evening." Onidu startled her as she returned the phone to her pocket.

"Hi, I was just admiring the magnificent table. Was it you or Okidu who had set it up so beautifully?"

"It was a joint effort, Madam. And I thank you kindly for your praise. Please, let me show you to your seat." He bowed at the waist and proceeded to pull out a chair for her. The one to the right of Kian's place of honor at the head of the table.

"Thank you." She smiled at him.

As Syssi sat down, the tablecloth's heavy, luxurious fabric brushed against her plain blue jeans, as if to point out that she was underdressed for the occasion. Not that she had much choice in the matter. Besides jeans, her only other option was the black yoga pants she had been wearing when Kian had whisked her to safety. Luckily, she'd at least put on a nice blouse and exchanged her flip-flops for heels.

Good thing she hadn't listened to Amanda's reassurances that it was a casual affair and she didn't need to change.

Yeah, right, casual. Maybe for the queen of England it was!

But then, as the guests began trickling in, dressed just as plainly, she might have relaxed if not for the way they looked at her—as if she was a strange exhibit.

Fidgeting with her napkin, she returned their nods and hellos with a strained, fake smile plastered on her face—all the while secretly plotting revenge on Kian for abandoning her like that.

Except, was it possibly all in her head?

Between the Guardians' friendly, familiar smiles and easy banter, and William's whining about not being seated next to her, she loosened up a bit.

Yeah, it must've been.

And yet, casting a sidelong glance at Michael, she envied the ease with which he seemed to fit in. Calm and confident, his handsome young face smiling, he was chatting with Yamanu and the other Guardians as though they were his lifelong friends.

He seemed happy, excited.

But maybe his good mood had less to do with the camaraderie he felt with his new friends and more with Kri's palm resting possessively on his thigh—publicly staking her claim on him.

Smiling, Syssi looked away from the young couple... Well, one of them was young. Kri, supposedly, was old enough to be Michael's mother.

Oh, well, Syssi shrugged. With an almost two-thousand-year-old boyfriend, who was she to pass judgment.

Boyfriend... the term kind of didn't feel right... whatever... But where the hell was Kian?

Glancing at her watch, Syssi frowned. What was keeping him and Amanda? Most of Kian's guests were already there and waiting for them to show up. Besides theirs, there were only two other vacant spots at the table.

And then even those last two arrived.

One was a frumpy, plain-looking woman; the other a very stylishly dressed, good-looking man. The woman had to be Edna, the judge, but Syssi had no idea who the guy was.

As she contemplated the dichotomy in their appearance, the woman turned her gaze on her, piercing Syssi with pale blue eyes that could only be described as otherworldly—nailed by that penetrating stare, what Edna or anyone else was wearing became inconsequential.

As she gazed into those unfathomable eyes, everything else in the room seemed to dim and recede into the shadows. Deep, soulful, and wise, they probed her like some alien device, and Syssi had the odd feeling that the woman was reading her thoughts, looking at her memories, and brushing ghostly fingers against her feelings. Unable to look away, powerless against the woman's hold, she was being weighed, measured, and judged.

It wasn't that she felt threatened, there was nothing malevolent in that stare, but she felt violated.

Syssi's distress must have shown on her face because it prompted Edna's companion to come to her rescue. He tapped the woman's shoulder to divert her attention, and as Edna turned to him, he winked at Syssi over her head and smiled.

Released from the woman's hold, Syssi took a deep breath and then another, trying to shake off the uncomfortable tightness in her chest.

But her reprieve was short-lived; the two were heading her way.

"I'm Edna." The woman extended her hand.

Syssi pushed up from her chair. "Hi," she answered coolly. Taking Edna's hand, she concentrated on the woman's neck, avoiding the freaky eyes.

"Sorry about the probe, I know I made you uncomfortable, but it's a knee-jerk reflex." Edna held on to her hand, willing her to look at her face.

"Yeah, well... It was very disturbing to say the least." Syssi took the risk of looking into the woman's eyes again, daring Edna to see how wronged she felt.

Edna held her gaze without flinching and without a hint of remorse. "You're a stranger brought into our fold, and you seem to have our regent ensnared. I had to know what you're about, but I do regret making you uncomfortable."

Syssi's face flushed red. "Find anything interesting?" she asked sarcastically, imagining the kinky stuff the woman had been privy to as she probed her memories.

Unexpectedly, Edna laughed and patted her shoulder. "You're as sweet and as pure as they come, Syssi. But I'm not a mind reader, all I sense are feelings and the purity, or conversely taint of the soul. For whatever it's worth, you have my stamp of approval. I just hope the fates will treat you kindly." Edna released the hand she was holding and her brief smile wilted, replaced by a look of melancholy contemplation.

"Brandon." Her rescuer offered his hand as Edna left them.

Consumed and shaken by her encounter with his companion, Syssi had forgotten all about him. With a hand over her chest, she exhaled through puckered lips before taking his offered hand. "Hi."

"Just imagine how an accused offender feels under that probe." He chuckled.

"I don't want to. She is scary." Syssi shivered, promising herself to learn and follow every last nuance of immortal law. She never wanted to be judged by those eyes again.

"She is not that bad... after you get used to her soul-searching stare, that is. She is actually an amazing woman. A very harsh and unforgiving one, but a fair judge nonetheless. Not to mention one of the greatest minds you'll ever encounter. Edna is brilliant." He smiled in a disarming yet somewhat overdone manner, making Syssi wonder what he was really like.

"So, what do you do, Brandon? I know everyone else's job here apart from yours."

"I'm the media consultant. The one responsible for our agenda being delivered to the public in enticing pretty packages. Movies, plays, novels... I make it happen. Like an invisible puppet master." He lifted his hands, pretending to be pulling invisible strings with his fingers.

"And what is your agenda?"

"Democracy, equal opportunity, education, human rights, promoting science and technology. To fight evil in all its mired guises; prejudice and discrimination, hatred and ignorance, etc., etc..." Brandon smiled broadly, his white teeth gleaming in a Hollywood-worthy smile that didn't reach his eyes.

Suspecting that under all that easygoing charm, Brandon was a shark in an elegant playboy's disguise, Syssi felt a little wary of him. But then again, she couldn't really fault the guy for having what it took to survive in show business—where the waters were infested with predators.

Good thing that he was using his sharp, shark teeth for the home team. Sharp teeth indeed... Choking on the giggle that was threatening to bubble up, she saluted him. "Well, good for you," she said quickly. "Keep up the good work."

"Will do, ma'am." Brandon grinned.

Finally! She spotted Kian entering the room.

As Syssi's eyes shifted to look at him, Brandon turned around to follow her gaze. "Oh, good, they're here. I'd better take my seat. It was nice chatting with you, Syssi."

"Good evening, everyone," Amanda said as she entered the room with Kian. "Sorry we are a tad late." She took her place to his left.

Kian remained standing at the head of the table, and after a quick smile at Syssi, turned to his guests, waiting for them to hush down. "Good evening, I wasn't planning on making a speech, but I don't want you to get the wrong impression and think this is a party. It seems Okidu and Onidu got carried away in preparing what I intended to be a simple dinner, using this as an excuse to take all this fancy stuff out of storage and finally put it to good use. But this is not a celebration, as it would be inappropriate in light of our recent loss. My plan is to start a new tradition of casual gatherings, once or twice a week, for us to enjoy each other's company as a family, and not just a bunch of individuals working toward a common goal." He paused.

"But as I'm already standing, I would like to take this opportunity to introduce you officially to Michael and Syssi, whom most of you have already met. The credit for finding these two special people belongs to Amanda, who researches mortals with unique paranormal abilities under the assumption that they might be potential Dormants. Syssi has a very strong precognition ability, and Michael is a good receiving telepath. Both agreed to attempt the activation process, which we have already begun." Kian smiled at Michael before resting his eyes on Syssi.

"I would like to propose a toast to a successful outcome of this brave attempt, and the new hope Syssi and Michael bring to our future." Kian raised his goblet, waiting for the others to join in.

Syssi watched with interest the order in which each of those present pushed to their feet to join the toast. Amanda and the Guardians were first, followed closely by William and Bridget. It took a few seconds longer for Edna and Brandon. Evidently, these two still had mixed feelings about the strangers in their midst.

"May the fates shine kindly upon us and grant us that which our hearts desire." Kian winked at Amanda. With a light squeeze to Syssi's shoulder, he continued. "To all of us—a long, peaceful and prosperous life." He took a long sip of his wine.

"Amen to that!" Michael exclaimed, then looked around the table, puzzled when no one echoed his affirmation. "What?"

"Not many are aware that the term amen actually stems from Amun, the Egyptian god of Thebes," Edna supplied. "With time, his name became synonymous with justice and truth, and hence saying Amen after a prayer or a proclamation served as joining in it and affirming its truthfulness. However, by using his name in this manner, you're implying that you're an Amun worshiper, which I'm sure you're not." She smiled at him apologetically. "I know this tidbit of information tastes sour to most mortals accustomed to saying Amen in their various modes of worship."

"I didn't know that." Michael looked down at his plate.

"Very few do, and even fewer care. It's akin to non-Christians saying, Jesus, or Christ, or atheists saying God. It became just an expression."

Thankfully, the sound of the pantry door swinging open broke the uncomfortable silence that followed.

"Oh, good, I'm definitely ready for some food." Edna unfolded her napkin and draped it over her trousers.

"Dinner is served," Okidu called from under the huge platter of soup bowls he was carrying. With the grace of a seasoned acrobat, he held the enormous thing with one hand while placing the bowls in front of each person without spilling a drop.

How is he doing that? Syssi wondered as she took the first spoonful, closing her eyes when the exquisite flavor hit her taste buds.

For a few precious moments, everyone was quiet, busy with the first course. Then, clearing her throat, Edna addressed Kian. "I don't want to be the Grinch and spoil this festive mood, but aren't we taking a great risk, exposing ourselves this way? I'm not implying that Syssi or Michael's intent is to harm us, but what happens if they don't turn? It will be next to impossible to suppress this many memories. They'll be bound to remember some of it."

"It'll be nothing more than tidbits of hazy dreamlike recollections. I gave it a long and thorough consideration and took a calculated risk, Edna. The alternative is to thrall them repeatedly, which in my experience compounds the damage. And besides being deceitful and cruel, it borders on violating the law of consent, which I'm sure you of all people should find objectionable." Kian held Edna's gaze.

Eventually, she lowered her eyes, reluctantly accepting the logic and moral underpinnings of his decision. "Okay, I agree. I don't like it, but I guess it is a risk we must take."

"Hey, everyone! I have an idea for a movie!" Brandon snapped the tense quiet stretching across the table. "It will be called, *My Immortal Lover*—a love story between an immortal woman and a mortal mercenary soldier who was left for dead and she saves with a small transfusion of her potent blood." With a smug smile, he cast about the dinner guests for support.

"It's so cheesy, I could puke!" Kri didn't hesitate to shoot it down. "I'm so sick of the whole vampire, slash blood thing. How about a bunch of kickass immortal female warriors taking down a drug cartel in Mexico?" She elbowed Bridget, who winced and rubbed her side instead of supporting the idea.

Brandon nodded. "That's actually good... I can see it." He crossed his open palm in front of his face as if painting a picture. "Twelve, tall, scantily dressed, gorgeous women—glistening with the sweat of the hot and humid Mexican air, slaughtering evil drug lords and their merciless minions. They uncover an imprisoned, badly injured group of American commando fighters who had crash-landed in the jungle and been captured by the drug traffickers. They save their lives with injections of their blood, and together they continue the commandos' mission of uncovering and killing an even greater evil: sex slavers, trafficking in young girls."

Brandon flashed Kri his practiced Hollywood smile. "Want a part?" He dangled what he knew she wanted but would never get.

"Hell, yeah! I want a part!" Kri banged her hand on the table. "I can rock a role like that!"

Syssi had to agree. Kri would be perfect portraying an Amazon warrior. "You may have something there. A movie featuring beautiful, scantily clad women bringing justice to the wicked and saving the innocent could become a big box office hit," she said.

"Who would you cast as the main kick-ass girl?" Anandur asked from across the table.

Brandon answered without pause, "There is only one actress I could envision for that part... Charlize Theron." He leaned back in his chair, taking his wine goblet with him.

Anandur's eyes sparkled with excitement. "That's one helluva woman. You can count me in for the lead commando. I want a piece of that..."

"Nice fantasy, children." Kian broke their happy, excited banter. "No one is auditioning for any parts."

"Why not?" Kri whined. "We are all good actors by default; we could pull it off…"

"Don't be stupid, Kri, this whole discussion is absurd."

"It was a fun dream while it lasted." Kri exchanged wistful looks with Anandur.

"By the way…" Kian turned to the doctor. "Do you have any news for us, Bridget?"

"Oh, yes, there is no matrilineal connection. Michael and Syssi are unrelated to us, or each other."

Bridget's announcement should have been good news, and it was. But it was like getting all excited about guessing just one lottery number out of the five—no closer to winning the jackpot than if guessing none.

With that sad realization sinking in, Syssi lost her appetite. Pretending to be busy with the food on her plate, which for all intents and purposes could have been some fast food junk instead of the gourmet meal it was, she tried to swallow. But it tasted like sawdust, clogging her tight throat.

Hiding her somber expression behind the mass of her hair, she hoped Kian wouldn't notice. Sick of her own bouts of sadness, she imagined he was as well.

No one enjoyed the company of a whiny, sad woman.

"It will all work out. You'll see," Amanda said quietly from across the table. "Chin up, Syssi… You too, Kian. A little optimism wouldn't hurt."

The rest of the meal went by quickly, with Kian's palm intermittently finding its way to rest on Syssi's thigh.

After dinner, with everyone stuffed to their limit, Amanda pushed away from the table and rubbed her flat tummy. "Who's up for watching a chick flick with me down at the theater?"

Kian got to his feet and offered Syssi his hand. "You go and have fun, Syssi. I wish I could join you, but, unfortunately, I only made a small dent in the pile of work still waiting for me." He kissed the top of her head.

"Would you be back before I fall asleep?" she whispered, hating the thought of being alone in his big, empty bed.

"The pile waiting for me could take all night to go through, but I don't intend to. Two hours tops. If you're asleep by the time I get there, I'll wake you up… Deal?" He smiled suggestively.

Syssi dipped her head, blushing into his shirt. "Deal."

Kri, Michael, Anandur, and Arwel joined her and Amanda, and together the small group headed for the private theater down in the basement.

With its eight rows of eight plush reclining chairs each, the theater was much larger than Syssi had expected it to be. But then again, this home theater didn't serve an average-sized family; it served a clan.

Sitting down, she engaged the chair's reclining mechanism, turning her viewing experience from merely comfortable to decadent. As the movie Amanda had selected started playing, the quality of picture and sound rivaled that of an IMAX. And that wasn't all. In case someone got hungry or thirsty, a full bar and a popcorn machine were housed in a curtained-off alcove behind the last row. Which was the row Kri and Michael chose, snuggling and kissing like a couple of teenagers.

The romantic comedy had Anandur and Arwel bored in no time. So it was no big surprise when Anandur tapped Amanda's shoulder. "We are leaving to go clubbing, you want to come?"

"No, I'll stay and keep Syssi company," Amanda answered, sounding resigned to her babysitter role.

"Don't be silly, go! I can watch a PG-13 movie all by myself. I promise I'll call you if I need adult supervision to watch an R-rated one." Syssi pushed at Amanda to go.

"Are you sure it's okay?"

"Yes! Go!"

"Okay. Tomorrow at nine, my place. We have a nail appointment scheduled for ten."

"Yes, ma'am!" Syssi saluted and faced the screen, pretending to be absorbed in the movie.

She waited until they left, and then contemplated staying or going up to bed.

The movie was nice enough, but the problem was her acute awareness of the couple necking in the back row. It was hard to ignore their muffled sounds of passion while being the only other person in the theater. She felt like a Peeping Tom, or rather an eavesdropping Tom.

Few moments and several hushed moans later, she pushed up from the comfortable chair, leaving it in the reclining position so the sound of it retracting wouldn't disturb Kri and Michael, and draw their attention to the fact that she was leaving.

CHAPTER 13: SYSSI

As she rode the elevator to the penthouse, Syssi dreaded how empty the place would feel at night. She hoped to at least find Okidu there, except chances were that he was done with the cleanup and already gone.

She wondered where the butler was going each time he disappeared. Was there a girlfriend somewhere? Or maybe he was spending his free time with his brother?

It was hard to tell with Okidu; the man was strange, kind of flat, two-dimensional, like an elaborate caricature instead of a real person. She was saddened by the thought that it might've been the many years of servitude that had painted a permanently false mask over his true self, only allowing him the expressions expected by others.

Syssi sighed. As if she needed another reason to be sad...

Just as she had feared, Kian's penthouse was dark and quiet. Flicking the lights on, she peeked into the dining room and then the kitchen. Amazingly, there was no sign left of the big dinner which had ended only an hour ago.

Walking down the corridor to Kian's room, she paused by each of the closed doors and listened carefully for any kind of sound. But Okidu was either asleep or not there.

The place felt deserted.

Once she reached the master bedroom, a quick glance at Kian's big empty bed convinced her she didn't want to be there alone. And anyway, as strung up as she still felt after that stressful evening, there was no chance she'd be able to fall asleep.

Deciding some quiet time while waiting for Kian was a better plan, Syssi kicked off her shoes and plodded barefoot back to the living room.

As she slid the glass doors open and stepped out onto the terrace, the cool, soft breeze caressing her heated face was refreshing, and with a soft sigh, she sat down on her favorite lounger.

Sprawling comfortably, Syssi took a deep breath and gazed at the clear, cloudless sky, its darkness relieved by the lambent glow of a full moon and tiny sparkling stars. It was peaceful, with the city quiet below and the distant hum of traffic lulling her with its monotone drone. But a few quiet moments later, a tinge of a familiar craving had her glance in the direction of the side table; where she had left Kian's cigarettes.

The pack and his gold-plated lighter were still there, neatly aligned next to a sparkling clean ashtray. Evidently, Okidu had no problem with her little transgression, eliminating the incriminating evidence of the stubbed-out butt, but leaving the pack out there to tempt her.

She looked at it with longing. *Should I? Or shouldn't I?*

It took a few moments of internal struggle, but in the end, she couldn't help herself.

Ah, what the heck...

With a guilty little smile, she reached for the pack, pulled out a cigarette and lit it quickly before her conscience had a chance to talk her out of it. Breathing in carefully, Syssi closed her eyes.

She felt the tension ease out of her with each pull.

Such a decadent pleasure. If only it weren't stinky and unhealthy, she could've enjoyed it guilt-free. The health concern would become a nonissue if she turned, but it wouldn't solve the problem of the clinging stench.

Well, whatever.

Right now, she didn't care. She was alone on the terrace and in her solitude felt free to do as she pleased. That feeling of freedom, the element of rebellion she associated with smoking, was what made the whole thing so delightful—beyond the obvious chemical reaction to the nicotine.

Later, she would just rinse her mouth and spray herself with perfume, and no one would know...

"Hi, gorgeous..." Kian startled her.

Caught red-handed with the cigarette in her hand and smoke coming out of her nose, Syssi felt mortified. How did he get out here without her hearing the sliding door open?

Kian leaned to kiss her.

"Oh, don't kiss me! I stink!" She made a move to stub out the thing.

"No, don't stop on my account!" Smiling, he caught her wrist. "You're obviously enjoying yourself, and I don't mind the smell. They are, after all, mine..." He winked and plopped on the lounge beside her, then pulled a cigarette for himself. "Now we're going to stink together..." He lit the thing and took a long, grateful pull.

"I wasn't expecting you so soon... you said you'd be working late..."

"That was the plan. But a memory of a certain beautiful, sexy lady was distracting me..." He pulled her panties out of his pocket and brought the crumpled scrap of fabric to his nose. "And these didn't help either..." Kian made a production of inhaling her scent and pretending bliss.

"You're such a pervert..." Syssi laughed.

CHAPTER 14: KIAN

"**I** know..." Kian slanted Syssi a lascivious look. Then remembering Amanda's admonition, stuffed her panties back in his pocket and decided to change topics before their sexual banter got them in bed.

"Did you enjoy dinner?" he asked, then took a puff, exhaling it in a ring of smoke.

"Besides Edna's probe? I guess so."

"Edna probed you? When?"

"Before you and Amanda arrived."

"Shit! I'm sorry, baby, I know how intrusive that feels. What did she say?"

"She liked me, I guess... Gave me her stamp of approval. Not that it mitigated how violated she made me feel. I kept thinking of what she must've seen in my memories—us together, intimate—despite her claim that she can't read thoughts, just emotions. Still, lust is an emotion, isn't it?" Syssi's cheeks reddened all the way up to her ears.

"Whatever she saw, she must have liked it. Don't forget, we don't share mortals' inhibitions about sex. As long as it's consensual there is nothing embarrassing or shameful about it."

"I'm in no way ashamed, but I would like my sex life to remain private. I'm not into exhibitionism." Syssi stubbed out her cigarette and crossed her arms over her chest.

Kian pushed up from his lounger to sit beside her. Looking at her pouty face, he just couldn't resist her sweet, puffed-up lips and bent down to kiss them. "Imagine you had Edna's ability and were faced with the same dilemma. Would you have acted differently?" He caressed her cheek gently, rubbing his knuckles over her sensuous mouth and along her jawline.

Syssi closed her eyes, kissing his knuckles as they passed her lips, her expressive face flushed with the simmer of arousal stirring up inside her. Then, as if forcing herself to think past her awakening libido, she looked up with hooded eyes as she conceded, "I would have done the same."

Damn, with Syssi responding to him the way she did, it was hard to stick to that whole nonsexual interaction thing. He needed to put some space between them if he had any hope at all of sticking to that plan.

With a sigh, Kian moved to sit on the nearby side table. Facing Syssi, he continued from the safer distance. "Edna is the smartest person I know. I have great respect for her. Actually, she is my second."

"What does it mean, a second, like second in command?" Syssi asked, looking a little hurt, no doubt wondering why he moved to sit away from her.

"No, it's more like a Vice President. She takes over if something happens to me. It should have been Amanda, but she is not ready for that kind of responsibility. Not yet anyway."

Syssi nodded in agreement. "Definitely not... Amanda would have hated it. She told me she was grateful you and Sari spared her the burden."

"That's why I chose Edna. I know she can handle it. Edna is tough, strict, and incredibly capable. Though it's a pity that she is not well liked. Most are wary of her because she seems harsh, and that probing stare of hers doesn't help her popularity either. But I know she is a fair and decent person. A little low on compassion and forgiveness, but nobody is perfect, right?"

"Well, I don't know about that... How about your mother? Isn't she perfect? As a goddess, she must possess incredible power and wisdom..." Syssi's eyes sparkled with curiosity.

Kian chuckled. "Oh, she would like everyone to believe that. She is the ultimate drama queen. I guess that's who Amanda gets it from, though next to our mother, she is an amateur. Annani is incredibly powerful, but she tends to be frivolous, more passionate than contemplating. She might be as smart as Edna, but she is definitely not as wise. Trusting her gut, she acts on impulse, thinking with her heart and not her mind. Surprisingly, it has never stirred her wrong, yet. So maybe wisdom is overrated?" He tilted his head, arching his brows.

"What does she look like? Is she majestic and regal?" Syssi was still bursting with curiosity.

"She is. Her power is so palpable, she radiates it." Kian chuckled fondly. "It's funny, though, that all that splendor is housed in a tiny package of a little over five feet, weighing maybe a hundred pounds, half of it probably contributed by her long hair. She could blend at a high school, posing as a teenager. With her power suppressed, she could pass for a seventeen-year-old girl."

"I have a hard time imagining a childlike goddess inspiring that much awe. Does she believe that she really is a goddess?" Syssi asked.

"Yes and no. She misses the way mortals worshiped her kind and thinks she deserves it. And in a way she does. She is personally responsible for much of humanity's progress. Not to say that mortals wouldn't have eventually done it on their own, but it would have taken them thousands of years longer, and if the Doomers had their way, never. So she deserves her semidivine status. But of course, we all know that she is not the creator of the universe if such an entity even exists in some form."

"So basically, your kind has no religion? You don't believe in a god?"

"We have no formal religion. There are some festivals and rituals we observe as part of tradition, and we have some informal beliefs. But mostly we are agnostic. Just as mortals, we have limited capacity for understanding the underlying principles of material and nonmaterial existence and, therefore, refrain from making statements regarding things we know next to nothing about. It would be too presumptuous of us to do so based on our infinitesimal knowledge. How about you? What are your beliefs?" Kian asked, despite being afraid of stumbling upon another land mine.

In his experience, mortals clung with irrational ferocity to their faith, no matter how misguided or ridiculous, and felt offended when it was challenged in any way.

"I'm a confused agnostic. I don't believe in a personal, benevolent God who hears our thoughts and answers our prayers. I used to. It was comforting to have that kind of an imaginary friend who was privy to my thoughts, who was always on my side and would always protect me from harm. But as I got older and lost the naive hopefulness of childhood, I could no longer hold on to that belief in the face of reality. I realized that good doesn't always prevail, and very bad things happen to very good people all of the time. Humanity's sordid past and present, the sheer magnitude of suffering, inflicted by both men and nature, does not indicate a benevolent, caring deity. So instead of being constantly angry at that indifferent, or even cruel entity, I prefer to think that we are left to our own devices." Syssi paused.

"On the other hand, there is my precognition. How can I get glimpses of a future that didn't happen yet? Or that sometimes I have the feeling that things are fated to happen in a certain way? Or the entire plethora of experiences that could not be explained? Near death visions, messages from beyond the grave... There is just too much of it to be ignored and dismissed as quackery. Do I make any sense?"

Kian pushed up from the small side table to sit back next to her. "Yeah, you do. Amanda believes in fate, and so does my mother. Myself, I'm an old skeptic. But what I know is not to shrug off anything as impossible and conversely not to take anything on faith. There is so much misinformation out there and so little is truly known, regardless of what scientists or religious leaders would like us to believe." His hand was back to caressing her soft cheek, his thumb swiping gently over her tempting lips. He just couldn't stand being near her and not touching her.

Syssi leaned into his palm and placed her hand over his, holding it to her cheek. "Edna said she hoped fate would be kind to me," she whispered. "I have to cling to that hope." She reached with her other hand and pulled him down for a kiss.

Kian bent, twisting his torso so he could press his chest to Syssi's, seeking as much contact as he could from his sitting position.

There was hunger—a desperation—to his kiss that went beyond the physical need relentlessly clawing at him.

He yearned to fuse their kindred souls and cleave to Syssi with the certainty that together they would form something that was better and stronger than the sum of its parts. But at the same time, he suspected that once fused, they would shatter to pieces if forced apart—no longer able to survive on their own.

CHAPTER 15: SYSSI

As she held Kian close, running her hands up and down his strong back, a flood of endorphins washed over Syssi, bringing about a profound sense of relief. Clinging to his warmth, inhaling his scent, feeling his familiar hands roaming over her body, she felt as if he was her home, and without him, she was just drifting. Rudderless.

It scared her.

Was it just her? Or was falling in love terrifying for everyone? If Kian didn't feel as strongly for her, she'd be crushed. But it was too late to shield her heart.

She was a goner.

Still, to let herself go with that feeling—to revel in it—required the kind of trust she believed existed only between child and parent, and sometimes not even there.

Her body, though, enraptured by the carnality of Kian's kiss, had no problem ignoring the turmoil going on in her head. As he plundered the cavern of her mouth, retreating to nip at her lips then plundering again, the tiny zings stoked the flames of her desire. And as he moved to the column of her throat, the gentle scrape of his fangs was so damn erotic, it pulled a ragged groan from her chest.

With need unfurling in her belly, she welcomed the familiar tightness in her breasts and the contracting and wet warming of her sex. To abandon herself to her body's cravings felt good, uncomplicated.

Easy to fulfill.

It didn't leave room for doubts or fears.

"I'm taking you to bed..." Kian hissed through his fangs, swiftly snaking his arms underneath her and scooping her up effortlessly.

Curling into his solid body, Syssi smiled. "What took you so long?"

Kian chuckled and dipped his head to kiss her again. "All good things come to those who wait."

"If you say so..." Without realizing it, Syssi had spent the last two years waiting for Kian. She was done waiting, and impatient.

He carried her to his bedroom, stepping inside through the open terrace doors, and put her down on his bed. Taking his time undressing her, he kissed and caressed every inch of skin he was exposing—driving her absolutely crazy.

"Patience, my sweet girl." He pulled her hands away from the jean button she was fumbling with. "I don't want to rush it." He placed her arms at her sides, then kissed her belly before tackling the same button.

Slowly, he unzipped her pants, his lips trailing kisses down her lace-covered mound, but as he stopped right above the juncture of her thighs, Syssi voiced her protest with an angry groan.

Kian lifted his head and smiled an evil, fanged smile before peeling her tight-fitting jeans all the way off her legs.

As her pants hit the floor, Kian paused for a moment to admire what he'd just unveiled, but then as his gaze climbed up to where her pink lace panties were soaked with the evidence of her desire, his eyes lit up and he sucked in a harsh breath.

With hands that trembled with his effort to keep the slow pace he was dictating, he caressed, kissed, and nipped his way up, starting at her toes and culminating at that sweet spot.

Panting with anticipation, Syssi lifted her hips to meet his lips, but Kian would have none of that. Spreading her thighs wide with his hands, he anchored them to the bed, preventing her gyrations. Blowing gently on her hot sex, he cooled it a little, taking his sweet time before finally placing his lips over her small greedy nubbin and kissing it gently through the wet lace.

Syssi was hanging on the precipice. Being held down was turning on the heat, as were his teasing lips, but it was not enough. She needed more and Kian knew it, torturing her with his soft, gentle touches.

He kept alternating between kissing and blowing air on her burning core, denying her what she desperately wanted.

But besides panting, Syssi did nothing to hurry him on. Sensing his determination to go slow, she yielded to his will. And as before, that surrender added another dimension to her pleasure.

Finally, Kian pushed her panties aside and slipped one long finger inside her, groaning when she clenched around it. But his finger didn't move. Holding her still, he pinned her down with his other hand, preventing her from writhing and providing the friction she needed.

Syssi bit down on her lip, struggling to stay still and not plead for him to make her come. But she couldn't stifle the desperate, keening moan that escaped her chest. She was so close. Just a little bit more, and she would go flying.

And still, Kian denied her.

Smiling wickedly, he pulled his finger out and pushed up to kiss her parted lips. "I want you on edge when you take me in your mouth." Climbing higher, Kian straddled her head, then pulled off his shirt and unzipped his pants.

Freeing himself from their confinement, he braced his hand on the headboard above her, looking at her lips as he teased them with the velvety head.

"Open for me," he commanded.

Yes! Syssi closed her eyes, his tone and his words sending a bolt of fiery arousal straight to her sex.

She surprised herself with how much this turned her on; how much she craved taking him as deep down her throat as she could and pleasuring him into oblivion.

Kian went slow, pushing just the crown past her lips. She licked, savoring his taste and the smooth texture of his shaft. He pushed a little deeper, then retracted for several shallow thrusts before going a little farther; careful not to overwhelm her.

When he reached as deep as he could go, he once again pulled out, feeding her just a small portion of his length, making sure she didn't gag.

Syssi moaned around him, in part because she was so turned on, but also because she knew the vibrations would add to his pleasure. No longer restrained, she sneaked her hand to rub at her clit, her hips gyrating in sync with Kian's thrusts.

She was so close, needing just a little more to combust, but the edge eluded her. Kian was getting close as well, hardening and thickening the way he did when his seed was about to burst. And as she prepared for it to flood her mouth and go down her throat, her moans became frantic. Not because she was afraid of how it would feel or taste, or if she would be able to swallow it all, but because she was hungry for it, and the crescendo leading up to the grand finale was driving her wild.

Kian stopped and pulled out.

In seconds, he shucked his pants while she watched—waiting for him with parted lips and heaving chest.

With a growl, he plunged deep into her wet heat.

Syssi was so ready for him that his impressive girth slid effortlessly through her dripping wet folds, denying her the little bite of pain she needed to careen over that elusive edge. Still, the way he filled her felt amazing. Arching her back, she urged him to move.

Kian remained still. Buried deep inside her, he waited. "You're not up there with me, yet." He hissed through gritted teeth as he looked into her questioning eyes.

She had no idea what he was talking about. The pleasure was so intense that her eyes rolled back in her head.

But then, as he began rolling his hips, thrusting in and out slowly and forcefully, the pleasure became almost unbearable, and the imaginary rubber band holding her back got pulled taut, reaching its utmost limit.

But Kian held onto his steady pace, not letting it snap.

Bracing on his forearms, he looked down at Syssi's pained expression as he held her mercilessly on the edge—not letting her fly. "I know, baby. I know how much you want to come. But not yet, just a little longer and you'll fly higher than you have ever flown before. And when you come down, I'll be right there to catch you."

Syssi looked up at Kian, her focus splitting between the pulsing and throbbing of the steady push and pull going on below, and the fierce expression on his handsome face. With his eyes glowing again, and his lips peeled back from his elongated fangs, he looked like a monster.

My beautiful monster.

Not letting go of her eyes, he increased the force and tempo of his hammering thrusts and closed his fingers around her taut nipples, gradually increasing the pressure.

Syssi squeezed her eyes shut. It was almost too much, and yet not enough.

But then, as she heard him hiss and felt his fangs pierce the skin of her neck, her eyes flew open and she screamed. The exquisite agony of the twin pricks finally snapping that rubber band.

The orgasm that exploded over her kept coming in wave after wave of pleasure so intense, she felt herself catapult into a different plane.

Coming down, Syssi had no idea how long she'd been out, or which cloud she'd been on while there. Not that it really mattered. She felt at peace, lying encircled in Kian's arms with her face tucked into the crook of his neck, his familiar, masculine scent grounding her in this reality.

"Welcome back to earth, sweet girl." Kian's chuckle reverberated from his chest.

"How long was I out?" Syssi whispered hoarsely, her throat parched and scratchy. She must have been screaming for a while but couldn't remember if she had.

Kian took a water bottle from the nightstand and brought it to her lips. "Here, drink this."

She drank greedily, the water cooling and soothing her sore throat.

"My sweet girl." He kissed her damp temple.

Handing Kian the empty bottle, she curled into his embrace and closed her eyes.

CHAPTER 16: DALHU

Sitting in a darkened corner of the nearly empty pub, Dalhu glanced at his phone. It was after two in the morning, and still no word from his men.

After trolling four clubs, he had given up, finding reprieve in this modest establishment. Here he could breathe, as opposed to those bastions of depravity where he'd found the stench of mortals packed tightly like sheep in a pen hard to endure.

It wasn't only the occasional nasty odor of a sweaty, unwashed body—that he could've handled easy. It was the cocktail of other smells mortals produced that had gotten to him—the hormonal outpour of their various emotions—lust and anxiety, greed and envy, rejection and despair, fear...

Nauseating.

And the ogling looks he'd gotten from the females, and some of the males, had disgusted him. No decorum, no modesty. It was Western fetid decay at its worst.

The clubs were brothels and drug dens combined. Except, unlike the brothels, money didn't exchange hands for sexual favors granted or received. The money bought the drugs, and sometimes the drugs also bought the sex. But mostly sex was free.

Except, when it was not. He had spied a few prostitutes working the crowd.

Dalhu took another sip from his drink and shifted in the booth, trying to find a comfortable position for his long legs. The damned thing wasn't built for someone his size.

As it turned out, he didn't have to wait long till texts from his men began coming in, admitting defeat.

Truth be told, he hadn't expected them to succeed. There were hundreds of clubs throughout the big city, and finding an immortal with only seven men on the job was like sifting through rocks at the bottom of a stream—hoping to find gold. Even with the reinforcements due to arrive in a few days it would be more of a miss than hit game.

Where the hell did the bastards go hunting? There must be a way to narrow the search.

Think, damn it.

Where would the privileged sons of bitches hang out? What kind of clubs would appeal to their spoiled sensibilities?

The *fuckers* were filthy rich—capitalizing on their stolen knowledge and amassing untold fortunes. They claimed it was all in the name of helping humanity. As if getting obscenely wealthy in the process was just a byproduct of their *noble cause*. And as the lucky bastards were known to play nice with each other, everyone got to share in the loot.

They are so full of shit...

They claimed they wanted to bring progress and freedom to the mortals. Freedom from oppression, freedom from hunger, hard labor, discrimination...

What an idiotic and naive notion.

Mortals were not designed to be free. With their herd mentality and the ease with which they were brainwashed by their own leaders and their misguided, blindsided media, it would only take one insane and charismatic ruler to end their world.

Which the bleeding-heart idiots made entirely possible by providing mortals with nuclear know-how.

From Annani's clan perspective, it had been a last resort, desperate move.

The forces of evil, as they had called the Nazis and their cohorts, had been winning the war. Navuh's clever machinations had finally been working, and about to bring humanity's age of enlightenment to a crushing and devastating end.

The clan-sponsored Industrial Revolution, together with the new ideas and philosophies they had promoted, had been threatening to catapult mortals into a new era.

That progress had to be arrested and crushed.

Navuh had maneuvered the events that brought on World War I, and when that war hadn't achieved the desired results, he had easily manipulated the weak and appeasing Western leaders into allowing World War II to go on unchecked while millions had perished.

Humanity had been on the verge of being plunged back into the Dark Ages.

The cataclysmic losses and devastation would've pushed humans back into the arms of their various religions. And those, influenced by Navuh's propaganda, would've blamed the brutal blow on their followers' immoral behavior. They would've zealously shunned their newfound ideas and technology as ungodly and greedy, blaming them for earning their God's wrath.

It had been a beautiful and simple plan that had worked time and again in both enlightened and backward societies.

Humans were so gullible.

But the clan had intervened. They had done the unthinkable, supplying the Allied forces with the tools to develop a nuclear bomb.

For a while, the technology had been closely guarded by the West, but eventually others had gotten their hands on the secret, and now even Navuh's protégés had it.

Funny, how it had come back to bite Annani and her progeny. Their stupidity now threatened to bring their own annihilation.

The virus that had helped bring down Iran's nuclear facilities had only slowed production, as nothing short of a full-out invasion could've brought it to a halt. But by interfering, they had tipped their enemies off.

He had their location. Sort of.

Think! Dalhu commanded himself again. What kind of clubs would the rich go to?

Motioning the waitress over with his empty glass, he placed a hundred dollar bill on the table and pointed to the seat across from him.

"Sorry, honey, as tempting as the offer is, I'm not allowed to sit with customers..." She leaned to wipe the table, offering him a glimpse of her ample cleavage. "It's almost closing time, though. If you can wait, I'd love to, but I don't take money for it..." she whispered throatily.

"The money is for information I need. It will only take a couple minutes of your time... though I'll gladly take your offer for later," Dalhu said quietly, his words coming out somewhat hissed.

She was a pretty little thing, and the thought of screwing her shoved against a wall behind the pub, with his fangs embedded deep in her neck, had his erection and his fangs throb and elongate in unison...

Yeah, that would be very nice... Dalhu readjusted his uncomfortably hard shaft in his pants.

Enjoying his heated reaction, she smiled at him brightly, then turned toward the bartender and lifted two fingers. "Okay, ask. You've got two minutes." As she took the seat across from him, she leaned forward as if to prevent anyone from overhearing their little chat.

"I need the names of the most exclusive nightclubs in LA," he said.

She looked surprised, probably had been expecting something more exciting, but he didn't offer an explanation. It was none of her business.

Scrunching her nose as she tried to come up with the names, she looked cute and very young. Too young to be offering quickies to strangers behind the pub. The thought momentarily tugged at what remained of Dalhu's conscience, only to be shoved aside. She offered herself freely, expecting nothing but pleasure in return.

Dalhu smiled a tight-lipped, cruel smile. That, he could definitely give her, and then some.

It seemed the girl found his nasty smile concupiscent. As the heady scent of her arousal wafted up into his nostrils, her nipples grew visibly taut beneath the flimsy fabric covering her breasts.

She shifted in her seat. "I heard talk about a club named the *Basement*. Personally, I've never been there, nor has anyone I know. It's way, way… out of my league, or yours… Only the rich and famous go there, it's not for regular folks like us." She snorted derisively, crossing her arms over her chest.

"Why would you assume it's out of my league?" Dalhu had taken offense at being bundled in the same category as her. She might be regular people, but there was nothing regular about him. He was one of the finest male specimens of a superior race; the progeny of gods. He wished he could show her. And maybe later he would, just to see her reaction before erasing it from her memory.

"No offense, honey, you're gorgeous… But your Levis and Nikes don't peg you as a potential customer for *The Basement*. These people wear thousand dollar jeans and designer watches that cost more than a new luxury car, not the imitation crap you're flashing." She snorted again, waving a dismissive hand at his Rolex.

"And anyway, you need an invitation from an insider or a lot of grease money to get in. And I mean; a lot of money," she emphasized.

"I guess you're right, it sounds like it really is out of my league. Thanks for the info." He let his lips curve in a tight smile.

"No problem… sorry I wasn't much help. It's just that the clubs I go to aren't fancy, they are for regular people. I could ask around tomorrow, maybe there are some nice clubs that are not that snooty." She pushed up from her seat, hesitating for a spell. "Would you still wait for me? Closing time is only like half an hour away…" Waiting for his answer, she held her breath.

"Sure will, sweetheart…" He winked at her. She was pretty enough, and a free screw was a free screw. He was in no hurry.

Watching his little waitress cleaning tables and stacking chairs, he made his plan for the next day. He'd need to go shopping for the type of designer apparel she described and make a bunch of phone calls to see which of his contacts could get him into that club.

Having drug lords and arms dealers as business associates had its fringe benefits. They were exactly the type of people who would value the glamorous scene of a club frequented by the rich and famous.

After all, they happened to be some of the richest people around.

Dalhu grinned, feeling he was on the right track. He shifted to readjust himself again. His damned erection wasn't showing any intentions of letting off, throbbing painfully in the confinement of his jeans. The thing was, he wasn't sure if his hard-on was for the waitress, or for his prey. Though, in truth, he had kissed a lot of pretty girls before, but he had never been as close to his coveted prize as he was now.

A little after three in the morning, the girl took her purse, waved the bartender good night, and walked out the door. Dalhu, the only remaining customer, pushed out from his seat and followed her out.

As soon as the doors closed behind them, he had her in his arms, kissing her hard. She moaned and clung to his shoulders as he picked her up and carried her to the alley behind the pub.

Finding a dark recess, Dalhu shoved her against the cold stone, and holding her up with a hand under her ass, pinned her to the wall with his body. Kissing her and licking his way into her mouth, he reached down the top of her flimsy blouse. One at a time, he pulled her breasts out of her bra cups and above the neckline. With both plump globes exposed and pushed up, he took a moment to admire the creamy white flesh, topped by lovely large nipples that were just begging to be sucked. Happy to oblige, he dipped his head, and taking one erect little nub between his lips, lashed it with his tongue.

Panting, the girl closed her eyes and let her head loll back, hitting the wall behind her.

As he feasted, Dalhu groaned in pleasure, sucking, licking and nipping, making sure to give each sweet nipple equal attention. Until it became too much and she pushed at his head. With one last soothing lick to each of the sensitive peaks, he lifted his head to gaze at her pleasure-suffused face. Smug, he then turned to kiss and lick the column of her throat.

She moaned, and her arms slid around his neck, pulling him closer.

He reached under her skirt and pushed her little thong aside, then gently circled her wet folds with his fingers. She almost came when he slid two of them inside, her inner muscles clamping and rippling around his invading digits.

Dalhu stilled, holding her impaled, but not moving them inside her. "Not yet, sweetheart, you'll wait for me," he whispered into her ear, nipping the soft lobe for emphasis.

"Ouch!" she complained, but her sheath stopped spasming. Then as Dalhu pulled out his fingers to free his shaft, she began writhing against him and closed her eyes in breathless anticipation.

He ripped off her thong and shoved himself inside her with a grunt.

She froze. "Condom! You forgot the condom!" The accusation came out in a loud shrill.

Dalhu froze as soon as she did, but he was actually relieved when she shrieked her accusation, realizing it wasn't pain that caused her alarm.

Looking into her eyes, he released a little thrall, just enough for her to believe that he had taken the necessary precaution. He wanted to keep her lucid for as long as he could.

She relaxed, but her sudden fear had dried out her channel, making it painful for him to move. He forced himself to stay still and take his time kissing her and gently fondling her breasts until she was ready for him again.

Starting with easy, shallow thrusts, he stoked her fire, building it up before letting loose and fucking her with wild abandon.

As she neared her climax again, he grabbed her hair and tilted her head to the side, exposing the expanse of her creamy white neck. Licking and kissing the soft skin, he waited for her to reach her peak so he could sink his fangs into her neck while she came. But she was taking too long, and the damned things were throbbing painfully, dripping venom into his mouth and down her neck. He couldn't wait any longer.

With a loud hiss, he struck hard.

As she felt the sharp pain of his fangs slicing through her skin, she gasped and tried to push him off. But it was as effective as shoving at a wall.

Dalhu held her head in an iron grip, keeping it completely immobilized to prevent her from tearing her throat on his embedded fangs.

It took only a few seconds for the venom to do its thing, but it was long enough for the girl to emit the acrid scents of fear and pain.

Damn. He hated when that happened, cursing himself for forgetting to thrall her before biting her.

Now, it wasn't needed anymore.

As the venom triggered her orgasm, the girl began convulsing around him, and the rippling and squeezing of her tight passage triggered his own happy ending. But the intensity of his climax was diminished by his anger.

Pulling out, he let her down gently, smoothed down her short skirt, and rearranged her breasts inside her bra and blouse.

The lingering euphoria kept her docile and weak. If not for his hand holding her up, she would've crumpled to the alley's floor like a rag doll.

"Look at me," he commanded, curling a finger under her chin and tilting her head up so she was forced to look into his eyes. Very carefully, Dalhu sifted through her most recent memories, changing and erasing only the small portion needed to protect his identity and the memory of the bite. Fortunately for her, he was old enough and experienced enough not to do the hatchet job a younger immortal would have done.

Still, the girl looked dazed.

He had to make sure she arrived home safely.

There was no way he was just going to leave her in her dazed and confused state alone in the dark alley. A woman alone in the middle of the night was vulnerable, even with all her faculties intact.

If anything should happen to her, someone might remember him leaving the pub with her. And that wouldn't be good.

Glancing at her parted lips, Dalhu suddenly felt a need for one last taste and dipped his head to kiss her. He had forgotten how damn good it felt to have a woman because she wanted him, and not because he paid her to pretend she did... "I'll walk you to your car." He wrapped his arm around the girl's waist and led her toward the pub's parking lot.

Holding her tightly against his side, as they crossed the short distance to her car, Dalhu wanted to feel contempt for her, and to some extent he did. She was a slut—offering herself like this to a complete stranger.

He was taught to believe that decent women were only supposed to service their husbands, with prostitution being a necessary evil that was tolerated only for the sake of single men like him.

Except, he found he couldn't harbor negative feelings for the fragile and vulnerable girl leaning on him for support.

She fumbled with her key, having a hard time inserting it into the handle of her old, beat-up car. He took them from her, helped her get in, and buckled her seatbelt around her, then dipped his head and kissed her swollen lips for the last time.

"Wait until you feel okay to drive," he said before closing her door.

Walking over to the only other car still parked next to the pub, Dalhu folded his six-foot-seven-inch frame into the driver seat of his rented Mercedes. The luxury car engaged automatically, but he didn't drive off, waiting for the girl to exit the parking lot first.

She wasn't safe yet. Some scumbag might be lurking in the shadows, just waiting for Dalhu to leave her unprotected.

He hated those kinds of worms.

It was ironic really; on a battlefield, he was a cold-blooded killer but wouldn't let harm come to a female if he could help it. Only cowards and scum preyed on women and girls, and when facing someone like him, the same maggots who relished the power of abusing the weak and defenseless would cower and piss themselves.

They didn't deserve to live.

Tightening his hands on the steering wheel, he felt the familiar rage rising and wished like hell for one of the worms to show himself so he could kill the bastard. His eyes glowing with his seething anger, he scanned the area for any signs of a potential perpetrator, letting his senses spread out over everything in his surroundings. But besides the two cars idling in the parking lot, the place was deserted.

Great. Now he was stuck with his rage engaged and no one to take it out on.

A few minutes later, the girl finally pulled out into the street and drove away. As her car disappeared around the curve and he shifted the transmission to drive, Dalhu realized he hadn't even asked her for her name.

CHAPTER 17: KIAN

"Kian! Are you even listening?" Onegus asked.

The morning meeting had been going on for some time, but Kian was barely paying attention to Onegus or any of the other Guardians present.

Ever since waking up before sunrise and reluctantly extracting himself from Syssi's warm embrace, he'd been preoccupied with thoughts of her.

Despite the mountain of work he'd planned to catch up on before the meeting, he'd spent most of the time leaning back in his chair and ignoring the stuff on his desk.

He found himself grinning like a fool, recalling pieces of their conversations—her smiles, the desire in her eyes, the way she responded to him. The sexy sounds she made. But most of all, he cherished the way she would on occasion look at him adoringly, as if he was the most wonderful man in the world. And in those moments, he could almost believe it.

She made him happy.

He loved her.

And imagining life without her was unbearable.

Kian's smile wilted, and as a tidal wave of emotions swept over him, grabbing at his heart and squeezing hard, he clutched at his chest— the hoping, the wishing... imploring the fates and the gods and whoever else might heed his plea...

She had to turn. He'd go insane if she didn't.

Then it hit him.

If he waited until after her transition to tell her he loved her, she would always doubt his sincerity. Becoming the most valuable asset to him and his clan, she'd believe he would do and say just about anything to keep her—regardless of his true feelings.

He needed to tell her now. Even if it meant more pain down the road if she didn't turn. Syssi deserved to hear him say it, out loud. His love not just implied but voiced clearly and emphatically.

Decided, Kian felt almost giddy with anticipation. He'll tell her tonight at dinner; the exclusive restaurant providing the perfect romantic setting. And what's more… he'd get to say it out of bed. The last thing he wanted was for her to think he said the words in the throes of passion without giving it real thought.

If he was to proclaim his love, he wanted to do it right, without leaving even a shred of doubt in Syssi's mind as to how deep and encompassing his love for her was.

"Kian?" Onegus snapped his fingers in front of Kian's face.

"Sorry, could you repeat what you've said? My mind was elsewhere."

"Was it by any chance preoccupied with a certain young lady? The one peeking at you from behind the glass doors?"

Kian looked up, and there she was, his sweet Syssi. Standing outside the conference room's closed doors, smiling at him and doing the little wave thing with her hand.

"Please excuse me for a moment. I'll be right back." Kian pushed out of his chair and in long, urgent strides hurried toward his love.

CHAPTER 18: SYSSI

Unnerved by Kian's intense gaze and stalking stride, Syssi took a step back. Was it a mistake to come here uninvited and intrude on his meeting? Was he angry with her?

She just wanted to see him and say goodbye before leaving for her shopping trip with Amanda.

But then, as soon as the French doors closed behind him, he lifted her in his arms and kissed the living daylights out of her.

Lost in the passionate kiss, she closed her eyes until the sounds of catcalls percolating through the closed doors reminded her they had an audience.

Kian was kissing her in clear view of everyone in the conference room—as if staking his claim in a public declaration of ownership.

Her embarrassment cooling some of her fervor, Syssi pushed ineffectually at the solid wall of his chest.

Growling at her in warning, he tightened the grip on her nape and deepened his kiss.

Their audience forgotten, Syssi felt like any moment now Kian would tear off her clothes and have his wicked way with her right there on the floor. But instead of alarm, the thought sent delicious shivers of desire through her, and she clung to him, moaning into his mouth.

Kian broke the kiss only when their oxygen ran out; he then turned to look at the Guardians' smirking faces behind the glass doors, giving them a look that sent a clear message.

This is my woman!

Holding Syssi in his arms, he took two steps to the right and out of the Guardians' line of sight. With a big grin on his beautiful face, he pressed her against the wall next to the doors.

Syssi giggled. Kian looked kind of conceited—like a warrior returning victorious from battle and claiming his reward by ravishing his woman.

Heck, yeah, he is welcome to ravish me anytime.

Wrapping her legs around him, she clung to him, and holding on like a monkey, peppered his neck and his chin with urgent kisses before attacking his lips.

With his hands freed from holding her up, Kian brought his palm to her cheek, caressing it tenderly until she relinquished his mouth to look into his eyes.

They were glowing, and the ferocity she saw in them would've been scary if not for his tender caress.

"You're mine," he growled, a shadow of trepidation crossing his eyes.

Did he think she would object? Wasn't it obvious?

Then it dawned on her. The sweet man wasn't sure and needed to hear her acquiesce.

Pulling her courage around her, Syssi gave him what he seemed so desperate for. "I'm yours," she whispered, her voice shaky with her own fear of baring her soul. "But are you mine, Kian?"

"Body and soul, my love." Kian's eyes shone with tender emotion, their fierceness softened by his feelings.

"What are you saying?" Syssi whispered, her throat tight as she struggled to hold back the emotional storm threatening to erupt.

"I'm saying that I love you, my sweet Syssi." He sighed. "I had it all planned... wanted to tell you tonight over a romantic dinner... But instead, I had to blurt it out here, in the drab corridor of our basement, with you pushed against the wall. I'm such a ██████ moron." He dipped his head and touched his forehead to hers.

"I will not allow you to talk this way about the man I love. You hear me?" Syssi pretended to scold him while her heart was overflowing with feeling. Stroking his silky hair with both hands, she waited until he chuckled softly.

"I don't need romantic gestures, Kian, or fancy dinners to charm me into loving you." She cupped his cheeks with her palms and pulled his head up so he could see the truth in her eyes. "Those are nice, and I appreciate the thought and the effort, but I don't need them. This... raw and true, in its naked, unadorned essence... this feels right. Something perfectly timed and staged, but lacking in ferocity just can't compare. I love that you feel so strongly about me that you couldn't hold it inside for a moment longer. You couldn't have done it better if you'd tried."

Kian smiled, his whole face brightening. "You must truly love me to think so." He shook his head in disbelief.

"You really love me..." he repeated in a whisper.

Didn't he know? Or was he just happy to hear her say it?

"Of course I love you, silly boy. Didn't I show you? Couldn't you tell?"

"Yes, but I had to be sure. Under this guise of confidence, I'm just as insecure as the next guy." He chuckled, pretending to exhale a relieved breath and wipe some imaginary sweat from his forehead.

"I love you... I love you... I love you..." Syssi laughed, planting sloppy kisses all over his face between one I-love-you and the next. "Now let me go before Amanda blows a gasket. She's been waiting in the limo this whole time. We can continue later over that romantic dinner you promised me..."

"Okay." Kian let her slide down his body, making sure she didn't miss the bulge in his pants on her way down. Then held on, not ready to release her yet. "You're mine, don't forget it..." He kissed her until her toes curled and she forgot all about Amanda.

CHAPTER 19: SYSSI

"**Y**ou very pretty lady, still no husband?" the tiny Vietnamese asked in heavily accented English, her old face scrunched in a disapproving grimace.

Sitting on her stool at Amanda's feet and applying bright red nail polish to her toes, she somehow managed a regally condescending attitude from her low perch.

The small nail salon wasn't at all what Syssi had been expecting. Instead of an elegant and snobby Beverly Hills spa, Amanda had taken her to this everywoman's place, smirking at Syssi's surprised face.

"They are hilarious," Amanda said in a hushed voice. "It's like watching a comedy show while having your nails done. I love it here. The women are all from the same family and they entertain themselves by poking fun at each other and at the customers. They are shameless, especially when they think no one understands what they are saying…"

"Where did you learn Vietnamese?" Syssi whispered back. "And what the heck for?"

"I know a little, just enough to converse. Or eavesdrop. I pick up languages easily…" Amanda trailed off.

"She so pretty, no man good enough, huh?" The younger woman buffing Amanda's nails arched her eyebrow like a scolding schoolmistress, then winked at the old crone at Amanda's feet.

"Maybe I don't like men?" Amanda taunted.

The woman's jaw dropped. And with her brown eyes peeling wide in mock shock, she snorted, saying something in Vietnamese that had all the others guffaw. A fast exchange and more laughter followed.

"What are they saying?" Syssi asked the young woman massaging lotion into her hands.

"Oh, they say she lie, she a man-eater. Like the tiger say he no like meat. They say, one man no enough food, she need many." The girl smirked.

"Wow, Amanda, they got you pegged. I wonder what tipped them off?" Syssi slanted a look at her friend.

"I'm telling you, they are witches… They're probably hiding a smoldering cauldron somewhere in the back, and every time they disappear over there, they toss our nail clippings into the pot and chant spells to spy on our lives and discover all of our secrets…"

"Maybe a husband for you in pot, I go see, maybe tell you if he handsome, maybe no." The old crone cackled.

"You see why I love them? They have a sense of humor and are not afraid to use it." Amanda blew a kiss at the old woman who was smiling smugly at her toes.

"Next, Rodeo Drive," Amanda said as they exited the hair salon, which in contrast to the nail place had been just as fancy and snobby as Syssi had been worried it would be. But she had to admit, her hair had never looked better. Without shortening it, or changing its natural wave, the hair designer with delusions of grandeur had made it look sophisticatedly tamed.

The makeup job, however, had been what really had blown her away. Armando, the self-proclaimed makeup artist to the stars, was a magician. Looking at herself in the mirror, she'd followed his magic taking shape on her face with a wide-eyed stare. He'd made her look stunning. Examining herself from various angles, Syssi had grinned at her reflection in the mirror. Kian's jaw would drop down to his chest when he saw her tonight.

"You're gorgeous, darling. Go get 'em, girl." Armando had shooed her up from the chair, making room for his next customer. "Kiss, kiss." He'd kissed the air next to her cheeks and hurried to escort to his station a very elegant lady, whom Syssi could've sworn she'd seen somewhere before... Maybe on TV?

"Wait till you see the outfits Joann picked for you to try." Amanda had called ahead, giving Syssi's measurements to the proprietor of her favorite boutique. "She has excellent taste and connections in all the top designer houses. Prepare to be wowed."

"Don't get your hopes up. I have a real hard time with dresses. They never seem to fit right." Syssi made a pouty face. "I usually end up with a skirt and top."

"Don't worry, they make fabulous alterations. Everything is going to fit perfectly." Amanda opened the door to the exclusive boutique, motioning for her to step in.

"Amanda! Syssi! Come in. I have your selections in the back room." Joann gave each a perfunctory hug before ushering them into the large, private changing room.

Mirrors everywhere, the room was furnished with two white couches, probably provided for those who wished to watch the clothes being modeled on the small raised stage.

"Wine? Cappuccino? Mineral water?" she asked, striking a well-practiced pose. At one time, Joann must've been a model—rail-thin, perfectly groomed, and beautiful—she made quite an impression.

"Wine sounds good." Amanda walked over to check out the outfits Joann had prepared for them to try.

"Syssi, this must be for you. The thing is too short to cover my butt." Amanda handed her a tiny dress.

"Is this supposed to be a dress? It looks like a swimming suit." Syssi pulled the stretchy fabric, trying to figure out how it could cover her.

"Yeah, it looks kind of small... But I trust Joann. Just try it on."

Amanda had been right. Every dress, skirt, and blouse Syssi had tried on looked amazing on her. It was difficult to narrow it down to one outfit.

"I need help, Amanda! I'm going crazy trying to decide which one looks the best. You've got to help me choose," Syssi beseeched, looking over the large selection again.

"Easy, we take them all. Joann, can you find shoes to go with Syssi's outfits?" she addressed the proprietor, ignoring Syssi's vigorous side-to-side head shaking.

"No way I'm taking all of it! That's tens of thousands of dollars in merchandise! Are you out of your mind?" Syssi's voice rose with each word, becoming shrill.

"Ignore her protests." Amanda waved the perplexed Joann away and turned to confront Syssi.

Syssi's face felt so hot, she was certain she was flushed all the way from her chest to the roots of her hair. And the way she was hyperventilating got her so choked up, she couldn't speak.

Which, of course, Amanda took advantage of, plunging right ahead with her campaign. "Look, sweetie, don't get so upset. You cannot continue prancing around in your plain T-shirts and jeans that you bought at Macy's on sale. Not after what Kian did today; it would reflect badly on him. You have no choice."

Amanda succeeded in stunning her out of her anger. "How do you know what he did today? You weren't there... And anyway, what does it have to do with what I wear or don't wear?"

"Kri texted me and probably every other female in the clan. It's huge news and it travels fast when our regent not only falls head over heels in love but makes it public. I'm so happy for you both, I could cry." She wrapped her arms around Syssi, hugging her tightly and sniffling. "It's so romantic..." She sighed dramatically, adding another sniffle for effect before letting go.

"I can't believe you knew and said nothing until now. And how the heck did Kri hear us? We were outside in the hallway and the doors were closed..." Feeling exposed, Syssi crossed her arms over her chest.

"You forget how exceptional our hearing is, everybody heard. And I didn't say anything because I waited for you to fess up. Some best friend you are—not telling me right away." Amanda pouted and folded her arms over her chest as well.

"I can't believe everyone heard, it should have been private." Syssi let her chin drop, disappointed at having her cherished moment shared with a crowd. Then a suspicion had her pin Amanda with a hurt look. "Kian knew, didn't he? This whole thing was some caveman-like display of ownership to warn off the other guys, wasn't it?" she asked, her doubts and insecurities raising their ugly heads.

"No, sweetie, don't you dare belittle what transpired between you two, just because it was witnessed by people who happen to care a lot about Kian and about you. I don't think it even crossed his mind." She chuckled at Syssi's arched eyebrow. "Not the toe-curling kiss, that he wanted everyone to see. He was making a statement... I mean the things he said after... when you were alone and out of sight. He got carried away, forgetting he had an audience. Give him some credit, would you?"

"Yeah, you might be right... It's just... I feel like something was stolen from me... I was so happy..." Syssi wiped at the traitorous tear sliding under her eye.

"I'm so sorry, darling. I should have kept my big mouth shut. The last thing I wanted to do was to upset you. You know that I love you, right?" Amanda dipped her head to peek into Syssi's downcast eyes.

"I'm sorry too. I don't know why I'm so emotional..." Syssi heaved a breath and tried to crank up a smile.

"Are you kidding me? You are taking it all like a trouper. Your whole life has been turned upside down. You fall in love, and you're facing the possibility of becoming immortal... I'm surprised you didn't crack till now. I would if I were you." Amanda embraced her once more, caressing her back in small circles.

"Thank you. You're a really good friend, you know?"

"I know... but wait till you see how I do as a sister-in-law..." Amanda chuckled and started singing quietly in Syssi's ear: *Love and marriage, love and marriage go together like a horse and carriage. This I tell you brother, you can't have one without the other.*

"What's next? You'll start going around singing; *Kian and Syssi, sitting in a tree?*" Syssi laughed, feeling better despite herself.

"I just might..."

CHAPTER 20: ANDREW

Andrew was early—the precaution of arriving ahead of time to stake out a place a deeply ingrained habit he saw no reason to forgo just because of his shift to civilian life. Selecting a table facing the front, he watched the glass door, waiting for his first peek of the infamous professor.

He had expected Dr. Amanda Dokani to be good-looking—Syssi mentioned the woman was stunning... once or twice... or a hundred times—but nothing could have prepared him for the sight of the most beautiful woman he had ever seen, on-screen or off, walking in behind his sister and towering over Syssi's slight form.

She must've topped six feet, all of it exquisitely shaped and expensively dressed. And her short, almost boyish haircut did nothing to detract from the perfection of her beautiful, feminine face.

His jaw literally dropped before he willed it shut and swallowed the drool that had gathered in his mouth. Pushing up from his chair, he smoothed his hair and pulled on the lapels of his suit jacket, making sure they lay flat—suddenly mindful of his appearance.

For the first time in his life, Andrew felt inadequate and it pissed him off.

He managed a smile for Syssi, who left her gorgeous boss behind and rushed to give him a hug with a big grin on her face. He was thankful for the reprieve his sister's hug was affording him, using it to collect himself as he waited for Amanda to catch up. Glancing over Syssi's shoulder, he watched her saunter with a sensual sway to her hip, carrying her body with the confident glide of a graceful predator.

She caught him staring at her and held his gaze with a small, devious smile curling one side of her full, luscious lips.

Letting go of Syssi, he extended his hand and forced a well-practiced smile on his face. "Hi, it's a pleasure to finally meet you, Amanda. Syssi told me so much about you." Andrew smiled, satisfied that his tone hadn't betrayed how nervous she made him feel.

"The pleasure is all mine, Andrew," she purred, her incredibly blue eyes twinkling with coquettish amusement as she took his offered hand, leaving her elegant, long fingers in his grasp.

Andrew was intrigued. He had little experience of being pursued; his severe demeanor discouraging most women, to the exclusion of the gutsy or the clueless, from making a move. And as he wasn't a rich man, and in his own opinion not that good-looking, there was hardly a reason for any to make an effort. Which meant that he was used to being the hunter and couldn't decide whether he liked this reversal of roles or not. On the one hand, he was flattered and turned on. On the other, he felt uncomfortable and suspicious when a woman like that gave him this kind of attention. Not that he had ever met a woman like Dr. Amanda Dokani.

As they waited for their food, Andrew felt Amanda's eyes watching him and pretended not to notice, keeping his gaze firmly on his sister while they chitchatted about their parents' recent adventures in Africa.

He feared that once he shifted his eyes to her, he would get stuck gaping at her beautiful face like an awestruck, pubescent boy.

Later, when their lunch arrived, he waited for Amanda to focus her attention on her food so he could ogle her without being observed. But somehow, the damn woman ate without looking at her plate and kept pinning him with that sexy gaze of hers. And if that wasn't enough to make him sweat, she was driving him nuts with the way she ate, each sensually infused bite sending a signal straight to his groin.

She was toying with him, tantalizing him, and deriving wicked satisfaction from his discomfort.

Experiencing this new and unexpected chink in his armor was making him angry, which in turn helped him regain control. He was nearly forty, and a Special Forces veteran for fuck's sake, not a goddamned horny teenager.

Time to switch things around and shift the direction this campaign is going.

Placing his napkin over his plate, he lifted his glass of mineral water and leaned back in his chair, staring straight into Amanda's deep blue eyes.

"I have a few questions for you, Amanda. I hear Syssi is involved with your brother, and as she refuses to let me check him out, she leaves me with no other choice but to grill you instead. What could you tell me about him? What kind of a man is he?" Andrew ignored Syssi's sharp kick to his shin.

Amanda looked surprised by his question, evidently not expecting him to be able to focus on anything other than her magnificent self. As she mulled over her answer, a couple of moments passed before she said, "He is smart, loyal, hardworking and cares a lot about Syssi... Does that answer your question? It's all true. But how can you trust my word? After all, he's my brother and I'm biased..." She smiled innocently and took another tantalizing bite of her sandwich.

"I have no reason to doubt you. All I wanted was your honest opinion... Any negatives you'd care to share?" Andrew smirked smugly, noting her questioning eyes. She'd anticipated he wouldn't take her word at face value, but he always knew when people were lying to his face, and Amanda was telling him what she believed was the truth.

"Well, not many... He works too hard, is way too serious, doesn't know how to let loose and enjoy himself, and has a short fuse... probably because he works too hard and doesn't let loose... So although I love him, I find him somewhat boring and sometimes overbearing, but Syssi's opinion of him differs, doesn't it, sweetie?"

Amanda glanced at Syssi fondly, her whole face softening. Impossibly, she became even lovelier as she momentarily dropped her seductress act, and some of her true self shone through the facade she was projecting.

Andrew smiled. Amanda regarded his sister like a cougar would regard her cub. Which was funny—such motherly, protective expression coming from someone so young.

Syssi's face reddened as she tried to come up with an answer, probably afraid to sound like she was waxing poetic about her new boyfriend. "I find him fascinating, charming, and sweet." She dug into her food with gusto, refusing to look Andrew in the eyes.

By the deepening crimson of her cheeks, he could just imagine the things she'd left unsaid.

Chuckling at his sister's obvious discomfort, he shared a knowing look with Amanda—feeling an odd affinity with her. She seemed not much older than Syssi, but there was something about her that made him think of her as someone closer to his age. Maybe it was life experience, or perhaps her title, that made her seem older, more mature... or maybe it was his wishful thinking. He needed Amanda to be at least thirty so he could lust after her without feeling like a dirty old man.

Later, as the topic of conversation shifted to what had happened at the lab and then to Amanda's research, she dropped her femme fatale persona for good, becoming the consummate scientist instead. And the passion she had for her work impressed Andrew in a way her previous antics did not.

CHAPTER 21: AMANDA

The change in Andrew's guarded demeanor had not escaped Amanda's notice, and she realized that her earlier efforts to make him squirm had been the wrong approach.

She'd been coming on too strong.

Some men were just strange that way; offended instead of grateful for being pursued by a beautiful woman. Or maybe he wasn't used to this kind of attention. Except, if that were the case, she couldn't understand what kept her competition away. He was very attractive in his own ragged and brooding way.

Tall and broad, his handsome if not pretty face was adorned with two small scars; one slicing diagonally across his chin, and a smaller one over his left brow. In her opinion, the scars only added character to his irresistible bad-boy allure. She wondered if there were any more of these cruel testaments to the battles he'd fought and survived hidden beneath the cover of his clothes. It was despicable of her, but she hoped so. It would make him even yummier...

There was nothing like a fierce warrior to whet her appetite...

Now that she'd eased up on the sexual innuendo, he seemed to be really taken with her, the scent of his arousal intensifying as he let down his guard. The dear man was attracted to her intellect and not just her looks.

How sweet. It made her like him even more.

It was a shame she couldn't just drag him off somewhere private and show him how much. But there was something she needed to do away from Syssi and her yummy brother.

Amanda sighed. "As much fun as this is, I have a few more errands I have to run. You two stay. No reason to cut your time together short on my account." Pushing up from her chair, she collected her handbag. "Onidu is parked in the back and will take you home when you're ready."

"What about you?"

"I'll call him when I'm done to come and pick me up, or I maybe I'll just take a cab home." Amanda leaned to kiss Syssi goodbye. "Andrew, it was a pleasure. Once the lab is up and running again, I would love to run a few tests on you as well, if you're willing of course."

Andrew stood up and offered his hand. "Sure, it would be my pleasure. Just let me know when. I had a really good time... You're a fascinating woman, Amanda."

Ignoring his offered palm, Amanda pulled him in for a quick hug and kissed his cheek. "We're family now, shaking hands is for strangers." Flashing him her megawatt smile, she chuckled as a blush crept up his rugged face.

Once out of the café, Amanda walked the short distance back to the shops, heading for a jewelry store.

She planned to have a duplicate made of the small heart pendant hidden behind the collar of her blouse—the one Syssi had given her. There was no reason for Andrew to get upset upon discovering that Syssi had given away his gift. With both of them having identical pendants, chances were he would never find out.

CHAPTER 22: DALHU

Dalhu stuffed his shopping bags in the trunk of his rented car, still outraged at the obscene cost of the few items they contained. Two pairs of designer jeans at over a thousand dollars each, and a dress shirt at close to eight hundred—insane—he'd bought three.

Not to mention the custom tailored suit he'd ordered for six thousand four hundred dollars. And this was supposed to be a great deal. After over an hour of bargaining, he'd managed to get it at half the price he'd been quoted, the timid tailor probably giving in out of fear.

That still left the shoes.

Damn! He hated shopping.

It seemed as if all the high-end apparel for men boutiques were operated by faggots. And not the kind that kept their sexual orientation to themselves. No, he had to be served by the flamboyant types; getting drooled on in one store and fondled, *accidentally,* in another.

The guy was probably still nursing the offending hand… It had taken supreme effort on Dalhu's part to refrain from crushing it to dust.

The things he had to endure for his job…

Leaving the car parked behind the restaurant he had lunch at, Dalhu headed back to the war zone of the shopping jungle.

With the shoe store across the street in mind, he walked over to the crosswalk and waited for the lights to change at the intersection when a tingling at the back of his neck made him turn his head and look to his right.

His attention was immediately drawn to a tall, exquisitely shaped female walking away from him. And as he kept staring at her retreating back, Dalhu felt a shiver of awareness and a hint of recollection.

Everything else forgotten, he hurried to shorten the distance between them, careful not to get too close.

He needed to see her face.

There was something familiar about her tugging at his memory. Perhaps she was a movie star, or a model he recognized from the screen or from a magazine. Either way, he had to find out.

The woman stopped in front of a window display, and he had no choice but to pass her by. Pausing to stand beside her would have been too conspicuous. There weren't that many people walking down the street, and with his height and build it was impossible for him to blend in—even in a crowd.

Passing several stores, he ducked into the first one that wasn't exclusively geared toward women and displayed a decent selection of luxury watches for men. Pretending to look around, he had his eyes on the street, waiting for her to walk by.

A few minutes later, he grew anxious. She'd either turned back or had gone inside the store with the window display she had been admiring before. But as he stepped out, intending to backtrack and pick up her trail, he was relieved to see her a couple of storefronts down, looking at another display.

Good, she was still heading his way.

Glimpsing her profile, he was certain he'd seen her before. Something about this magnificent creature made his stomach churn with excitement. And it wasn't just a male's natural response to an attractive female. For some reason, he had a feeling about her...

A very good feeling...

With his muscles coiled and ready to pounce, Dalhu retreated into the darkened interior of the watch store and waited.

It was his lucky day...

She walked in.

As her eyes landed on him, she froze, the rising terror on her beautiful face indicating that her mind had just finished processing what she had already felt in her gut.

In that moment of recognition, two lighting-quick realizations hit him at once. First, he knew who she was. She had cut her hair short and colored it black, but there was no mistaking the stunning face he knew so well from the framed picture he kept by his bed. Second, he was going to grab her and run.

Fate had granted him this one chance to have a shot at fulfilling all of his impossible dreams, and he was going to take it. But he had to act fast.

The professor was about to bolt.

CHAPTER 23: AMANDA

Amanda was paralyzed with fear. Aside from one girl behind the counter, she was alone with a huge Doomer in the jewelry store.

There was no doubt in her mind as to what he was—the scent of his arousal was distinctly that of an immortal male... and not one of her clan.

Run, she commanded her feet, but they took too long to respond.

She was too late.

As she turned to flee, her fight-or-flight response finally kicking in, he lunged for her and grabbed her neck.

"Don't move, and don't make a sound if you want that girl to live," he whispered in her ear.

"Is everything okay?" hesitantly, the girl asked from behind the counter—hopefully, with her finger hovering over the panic button.

"Everything is all right. Don't worry about it. It's just a game my girlfriend and I play." He projected influence with his voice, which Amanda prayed wouldn't be enough to thrall the girl without him looking directly into her eyes.

Obviously not possessing the strongest of minds, the girl said cheerfully, "Okay then." She shattered Amanda's last sliver of hope.

Desperate and scared out of her mind now that she realized the Doomer could also affect a powerful thrall, Amanda began shaking in his grasp.

"Don't be afraid," he whispered, his mouth so close to her ear, his breath tickled. "I mean you no harm." He slackened his grip on her neck and blew warm air on the bruised area. Moving his large hand around, his strong fingers closed over her throat and chin.

Tilting her head, he struck quickly, sinking his fangs into her neck.

I'm going to die, was the last coherent thought Amanda had before the venom-induced pleasure took over her body and mind.

She leaned back into the strong male behind her, marveling at how nice it felt to be held by someone so much taller than her for a change. He smelled delicious, all male and fresh scent of soap. And as her body flushed with powerful arousal, she wanted him to touch her all over.

Arching her back, Amanda mentally willed him to bring his big hands up and cup her aching breasts. She pressed her behind into his groin, rubbing against his erection. "Just touch me before I die," she whispered as he retracted his fangs and licked the small wounds closed.

"You're not going to die, and although there is nothing I want more than to have my hands all over you, I'm not going to. I want your sober consent when I do…" the Doomer whispered in her ear, encircling her waist with his arm and tucking her against his big, strong body.

As he led her outside, she rested her head on his shoulder. Her arm going across his broad back, she delighted in the feel of all those incredible muscles flexing under her roaming palm—dimly aware that they must've looked like a couple in love to the few pedestrians they were passing by.

With her legs too wobbly to support her weight, the Doomer was propping her up and holding her glued to his side. She moved because he wanted her to move: the venom making her uncharacteristically docile and submissive.

Somewhere at the back of her mind, Amanda caught wisps of random, disconnected thoughts.

So that's the real purpose of the venom.

Who needs seduction and foreplay when all a male has to do is grab a female by the neck and bite her for her to welcome him between her thighs…

Who knew it would feel so damn good…

Why is that insufferable man refusing to touch me?

I'm so wet…

Is he going to kill me?

He said he wouldn't.

Didn't he?

CHAPTER 24: DALHU

As they walked the few blocks from the jewelry store to the restaurant where he'd left his car, Dalhu was counting the seconds. He wanted to take her as far away as he could, as fast as he could, fearing that any moment someone would come running to her rescue. Someone like a Guardian... or two...

And the scent of her arousal wasn't helping either. He was so painfully stiff, he could barely walk. When they finally reached his car, he stifled a relieved breath.

They were alone in the parking lot behind the restaurant; nevertheless, Dalhu was glad Amanda was still too woozy to resist him as he helped her inside and buckled her seatbelt, or when he pulled out a pair of handcuffs from the glove compartment and secured them around her wrists. Using a second pair, he closed one cuff on the chain connecting her shackled wrists and attached the other one to the door handle. That way, once her lucidity returned, she wouldn't be able to grab the steering wheel or jump out from the speeding car.

"Kinky..." she purred, squirming in her seat.

"No, sweetheart, just careful and prepared." Dalhu chuckled, shaking his head.

The poor girl will be mortified once she sobers up and remembers her wanton behavior.

He'd have to explain that it had been the venom's fault, not hers. How else would she know? It must've been her first bite.

Pulling out of the parking lot, Dalhu debated what to do next. First priority was to get his other watches from the mansion so he could sell them for some cash. There was no way around it. They'd need lots of money on the run, and using his credit cards or hers was not an option.

But she couldn't be seen by his men because then he'd have to kill them all, and that would look even more suspicious than him just disappearing without a trace.

It would be better if they assumed he had a misfortunate encounter with Guardians and was taken out.

Actually, he realized, that would be the perfect cover-up.

CHAPTER 25: SYSSI

"**Y**ou look a little flushed, is everything okay?" Andrew cast Syssi a measuring look.

She brought her palm to her forehead. Ever since Andrew's embarrassing questioning session with Amanda, her face had remained warm, but she thought nothing of it. Except, it was getting worse. *Damn, why now?* "I feel a little feverish. I'm probably coming down with something, and it couldn't have come at a worse time."

"Why? What's special about today?"

"Kian made a reservation at a very fancy and exclusive restaurant. I was really looking forward to spending a romantic evening with him, and even went to all this trouble to look nice." Syssi pointed at her face and shook her head to show off her new hairdo. Then lifted her hands and wiggled her fingers, showing him her manicure.

"Yes, I was wondering why you look different today. I thought it must be love…" he teased.

"That too…"

"Seriously? You're in love with the guy? You just met him, for Pete's sake…"

"I know, but I can't help the way I feel. I love Kian…"

"Kian who? Now, I really need to do a thorough background check on him."

"I don't know." Syssi felt stupid. She'd never bothered to ask.

"You claim to love the guy, and you don't even know his last name…" Andrew shook his head, his expression disapproving.

"I assumed it was the same as Amanda's, but later I found out they had different fathers. So I'm not sure anymore, okay? It's not such a big deal. I'll ask him tonight. And no… I'm not going to tell you so you could dig into his background. You can forget about it." Syssi crossed her arms over her chest, ready to butt heads with her stubborn brother. God only knew what Andrew could discover if he were to snoop into Kian's business.

Surprising her, he just smiled. "As you wish… Don't come crying to me, though, when later you discover things you wish you'd known before; previous marriages, illegitimate kids, prior incarcerations… Small things like that…"

"Oh, just drop it, Andrew, there is nothing like that lurking in his past." *His very, very long past...*

"Okay, okay..." Andrew raised his palms in mock surrender. "You know I'm doing it out of love. Someone has to look after you. You're just too nice and trusting."

"I love you too, Andrew. But I'm a big girl now, and you need to start trusting my judgment. You cannot protect me from everything and everyone at all times. I can take care of myself..." Syssi was starting to feel even worse. Forcing a weak smile, she said, "I think I'd better go. I feel really crappy." Trying to get up, she got dizzy and had to grab the back of her chair to steady herself.

"I'll walk you to the car." Andrew wrapped his arm around her so she could lean on him as they made their way to the limo waiting for her in the back.

"A limousine... Nice... Now, I'm really curious," Andrew taunted.

With no energy to keep it up, she didn't respond. Casting her a worried look, Andrew dropped it. Still, she had no doubt he'd go snooping around—regardless of her asking him not to.

Pulling her into his arms, Andrew kissed the top of her head, then helped her inside. "Take care of yourself, and call me if you need anything. You hear?"

"I will. It's probably nothing."

CHAPTER 26: DALHU

It took Dalhu about ten minutes to find a motel. As he stopped and got them a room, he couldn't care less that it seemed questionable. With Amanda already looking a lot less dazed, he was running out of time.

With a quick glance, he made sure there was no one in the parking lot before he uncuffed her, scooped her up in his arms and carried her inside. Kicking the door closed behind him, he didn't waste any time before gently laying her out on the bed and securing her wrists to the slatted wooden headboard.

"Ohh, I feel like a bride on a bondage honeymoon..." she giggled and swiveled her hips in invitation.

Taking a moment to look her over, he was struck again by how beautiful she was. "You're magnificent..." He rubbed his mouth with his hand, wanting her so bad, it hurt. But he couldn't have her, not yet, because sure as hell, she was still very much high on his venom.

Amanda didn't appreciate his efforts one bit. "Would you put us both out of our misery and fuck me already? Is this your idea of torture? You're such a jerk! I'm going insane with lust, and with my hands cuffed like this I can't even do anything about it myself..." she hissed at him, stunning him speechless.

Apparently, he had a lot to learn about immortal females, or maybe just this one. Defying his expectations, instead of cussing him out for abducting her, she was mad because he refused to have sex with her...

Go figure...

Sitting beside her on the bed, he was careful not to touch her as he looked into her eyes, checking for the glazed look he was expecting to find. Amanda's eyes seemed clearer, though her pinched expression made it obvious that she was suffering for real. Evidently, there was another thing he hadn't known about immortal females—their needs were just as overpowering as the males'.

Dalhu sighed. "I have to go and get us some money, but I'll give you something to make you sleep, making it easier for you until the venom leaves your system. And if you still feel the same when you wake up... then I promise, I'll take care of you..." Gently, almost reverently, he touched his palm to her cheek and caressed it lightly. "I'll always take care of you..."

"What do you want from me?" she whispered.

"A future..." He sighed again. "A life partner, a family, everything..." Gazing at her stunned expression, he held his palm to her cheek for a moment longer. "I know you don't want this with me right now. But I promise I'll do everything I can to earn your love. You shall want for nothing..."

Dalhu pushed off the bed, walked over to the dresser, and took one of the motel's two complimentary water bottles. Reaching into his pocket, he pulled out a plastic packet and emptied its powdery contents into the water, then shook the bottle lightly.

"Drink!" He touched the bottle to her lips. "It'll only make you sleep, nothing else."

Amanda pressed her lips tightly closed and shook her head from side to side.

"We can do it the easy way, with you being a good girl and drinking it all up, or the hard way, with me pinching your nose and forcing it down your throat. Your choice." Dalhu didn't want to scare her again, but he didn't have the time nor the patience to play games, which, unfortunately, made him sound harsh.

When she opened her mouth to drink, the fear in her eyes as she looked up at him was something he hoped never to see again.

Dalhu tried to be as gentle as he possibly could, supporting her head and making sure she had time to swallow before he gave her more. But in the end, he had her drink it all.

"Good girl," he praised, caressing her cheek as he waited for the drug to do its thing.

"I don't even know your name," she mumbled.

"Dalhu," he told her before her lids fluttered down over her eyes.

CHAPTER 27: KIAN

"Master, I'm sorry to bother you, but I think you should come up. Mistress Syssi just returned from her excursion and asked me if we have any Advil. She said she is not feeling well and is going to lie down. I called the front desk and they are sending someone up with the medication, but I thought you would want to know."

"I'm on my way, Okidu." Kian ended the call and rushed to the elevator. *It's probably nothing.* A mortal coming down with a cold or the flu wasn't something to worry about... or was it?

As he entered his bedroom, he found Syssi in bed, shivering, looking flushed and sweaty, the down comforter pulled all the way up to her chin.

"What's wrong, sweetheart?" He sat down beside her and brushed sweaty strands of hair away from her forehead.

"I'm so sorry..." She sniffled, a tear running down her flushed cheek.

"Whatever for?"

"For ruining our plans... I got all pretty for tonight... and now I'm sick... I never get sick... why today?" she whined, looking miserable. "I hate it... I hate feeling weak and useless like this... Did you bring me the Advil?" She wiped a shaky hand across her tear-stained face.

"It will be here in a moment, but I think we need to get Bridget to take a look at you before self-medicating." Heading to the bathroom, Kian texted the doctor on the way, then got two wet washcloths to clean Syssi's face with.

After wiping off her smeared makeup, he grabbed a clean one and patted her face to cool it down. "Don't worry about a silly thing like us going out. We'll do it some other night. Just concentrate on getting better. Something tells me you're going to be a very fussy patient." He forced a smile in an attempt to cheer her up.

"I know, right? Who gets all teary-eyed over a little fever?" She smiled a little smile and took a shaky breath.

"Master, Dr. Bridget is here." Okidu let the doctor in. "And I also have the Advil Mistress Syssi requested, and a glass of water for her to wash it down with." He placed the items on the side table.

"May I trade places with you, Kian?" Bridget motioned for the bed, dropping her doctor's bag on the side table next to the Advil.

"So, what exactly is going on?" Bridget asked as she wrapped the blood pressure cuff around Syssi's bicep.

"I feel crappy. I'm cold and sweaty at the same time. I think I have a fever."

"Any aches and pains? Sore throat? Runny nose?" Bridget removed the cuff and touched the thermometer to Syssi's ear.

"I feel weak and my bones hurt... can bones hurt? No sore throat, though, and no runny nose... I'm sniffling because I've been crying...," Syssi said in a small voice, dropping her eyes to look down at her hands.

"Well, your blood pressure is a little high, and your temperature is a hundred and one. It's elevated, but not dangerous. Let me take a blood sample as well." She pulled a syringe and a packet of antiseptic gauze from her bag.

"Any nausea? Stomach cramps?" she asked as she took Syssi's blood, quickly and efficiently.

Syssi didn't even cringe. "No, just general discomfort."

"Well, that rules out food poisoning," Bridget mumbled, returning the tools of her trade to her bag.

"So what do you think?" Kian stuffed his hands in his back pockets, forcing himself to stay put and not pace like a caged animal.

"I think we should bring Syssi down to my clinic. I want to hook her up to the monitors. I'll send one of the guys with a gurney." Bridget pushed up from the bed and lifted her doctor's bag off the bedside table. Standing, she looked first at Kian, then at Syssi. "I'll know more when I take a look at your blood, Syssi. For now, it doesn't look like a cold or the flu, or food poisoning... It might be some other viral or bacterial infection... Or it might be the start of the change." Bridget dropped the bomb.

CHAPTER 28: DALHU

Dalhu made the drive from the motel to the mansion in exactly eight minutes, and left the car idling in front of the entry as he rushed in and up the stairs. Taking them two at a time, he ignored the men greeting him as he passed them by on the way to his room.

Once there, he opened the safe and emptied its contents into a duffle bag. There wasn't much, just his two other watches and what remained of the money he was entrusted with for the mission's cash expenses.

His weapons were in a fireproof lockbox in the master walk-in closet. Crouching over the open lid, he pulled out the semi and the nine-millimeter handgun, loaded them, and then double-checked the safety before screwing the silencer on the SIG.

The knives were next.

Dalhu strapped two of them to his biceps and one on his calf, and four more went into the duffle bag. Whatever space was left, he filled with boxes of ammunition. Zipping the bag closed, he slung it over his shoulder, then grabbed a jacket on his way out.

Taking a look around the master bedroom, he scanned for anything else he might need. His laptop was on the nightstand, next to the picture of his beautiful woman. He took both, reshuffling the contents of the bag to make room.

The last items he decided to add didn't require a lot of space. Opening his desk drawer, Dalhu took out a bunch of plastic packets and shoved them into the side pocket of the duffle bag. Who knew how many more times he'd have to drug his beauty to sleep?

And besides, they might prove useful in other situations. He needed all the resources he could put his hands on.

As he slipped on his jacket over his personal arsenal, Dalhu quickly decided on a probable cover story to tell his men—one that would explain his rush and buy him some time.

On his way out, he grabbed the first man on his path. "I've identified an enemy male entering a restaurant less than one mile away from here. A Guardian. I came back for my weapons." Dalhu clapped the man's shoulder before dashing down the stairs.

"Need backup, commander?" the man called after his retreating back.

"No, the sucker is mine." Dalhu slammed the door behind him and ran the short distance to his car.

CHAPTER 29: KIAN

"Have you ever witnessed a transition start like this?" Kian's voice faltered as dread squeezed his heart like a vise.

"It's rare, but there were instances where a transitioning boy, in addition to the normal pains of growing venom glands and fangs, developed a fever accompanied by skeletal pains. So it's a definite possibility, although all the girls transition smoothly with no side effects."

"Is there anything we can do?" Kian ran a shaky hand through his hair.

"Unfortunately, there is nothing that can be done other than waiting. That's why I want Syssi monitored. I have no idea how severely the transition could affect an adult female." Bridget gave them an apologetic look. "I'll send the gurney up."

Kian sat back on the bed and took Syssi in his arms. "I love you so much," he said, hating how desperate he sounded.

"Why are you so sad? This is exactly what we were hoping for," Syssi whispered, trying to return his embrace. But holding her arms up proved to be too much of an exertion in her weakened state and she let them drop.

Kian sighed. "I'm scared shitless. Not knowing what's going on and powerless to do anything to make it better for you is driving me insane." His body sagged in defeat.

"Don't. I need you to stay strong for both of us," Syssi whispered. "Can you hand me that water?"

"Of course, my love." He brought the glass to her lips, propping her head with his hand as she drank.

A knock on the open door was followed by Anandur and Brundar's worry-lined faces peeking in. "We brought the gurney. How is Syssi?" Anandur asked.

"Not so good, you can leave the gurney out in the hallway. I'll carry her out." Kian pushed up from the bed and walked over to close the door. "Thank you, guys. I'll keep you informed..."

As he turned around and faced Syssi, Kian squared his shoulders and plastered a smile on his face. "Would you like to change into a nightshirt before I take you to the clinic?" He peeled the comforter of off her.

"Can you help me shower first? I'm sweaty and sticky." Syssi was shaking so hard that her teeth chattered.

Kian felt like crying. But Syssi was right, he had to man up and be strong for both of them. She needed him to take care of her and not fall apart like a wimp...

What the hell was wrong with him anyway?

When did he become so weak?

"Sure, let me prepare a bath for you, I'll be right back."

To keep her warm, Kian pulled the comforter back up to Syssi's chin, then hurried to the bathroom and cranked the thermostat all the way up before running hot water for her bath.

CHAPTER 30: DALHU

Finding Amanda still fast asleep when he returned, Dalhu sighed in relief. The drug was supposed to keep a mortal out for a couple of hours. But even though the whole round-trip took him less than half, which should've left him with plenty of time to spare, this kind of thing wasn't a precise science.

And more to the point—his captive wasn't mortal.

He still couldn't believe how lucky he was. He had done the impossible, snagging himself an immortal female—and not any immortal, but the stunning professor. Now that he had her, he would do everything in his power to keep her, and the last thing he needed was her waking up and sounding the alarm.

On the way back, he'd gotten rid of her cell phone, smashing and dumping it in a big trash bin next to a strip mall he'd passed. And had done the same with his own for good measure, despite it being the prepaid kind. It was vital for both of them to disappear from the grid.

If captured, he was a dead man, regardless of who found them first; her clansmen or his fellow Doomers. He had to find them some deserted place—somewhere far and secluded so his captive would have nowhere to run... and no one to hear her cries for help. After all, he couldn't keep her drugged and chained to a bed—that would certainly not endear him to her. He needed a safe place where he would have at least a shadow of a chance to win her heart.

His best option was to find a remote cabin—a winter retreat unoccupied during the summer months. Before going there, he would need to gather supplies to last them a couple of weeks. Hopefully, by the time they ran out and needed to go for more, she'd warm to him, and he'd figure out what to do next.

Dalhu pulled out his laptop and typed in the motel's Wi-Fi password, connecting to the Internet, then opened Google Maps and started his search.

Let's find us a nice place to hide.

CHAPTER 31: KIAN

Kian pulled out a chair and sat next to Syssi's bed in the clinic, holding her limp hand as he listened to the rhythmic sound of her heart monitor. Covered in the warmed blankets Bridget had supplied, she had thankfully stopped shivering and fallen asleep.

He heard Bridget's light footsteps coming up behind him. "I have Syssi's blood results," she said quietly.

"And?"

"I'm still not sure what's going on. It's definitely not a bacterial infection, and I'm pretty sure it's not viral. My best guess is that she is going through the transition."

"Be honest with me, is she in danger?" Kian pinned Bridget with an uncompromising stare.

"I honestly don't know. Her heart is doing all right, and the fever is not high enough to be dangerous, and it's holding steady. But her blood pressure is climbing."

Kian shook his head. "I feel so helpless, wishing there was something I could do. I have no idea how mortals deal with things like that, watching their loved ones get sick, not knowing if they'll pull through. Their existence is so short and full of misery."

Mortality.

Kian was no stranger to death claiming loved ones. He had watched generations of his descendants live their lives and die. But most managed to live to an old age, in no small part thanks to his discreet help. And he had been away when his brother Lilen had fallen, finding out about the tragedy only after the fact. But never before had he felt as helpless and useless as he was feeling now. With all of his clan resources—the money, the advance technology—he was forced to watch, powerless, as the woman he loved fought for her life.

Bridget patted his shoulder. "They deal because they have to. If it would help, you might try praying. Mortals find it calming and reassuring at times like that."

CHAPTER 32: AMANDA

Amanda woke up with her arms stiff from being pulled over her head. Still groggy, she had a moment of confusion trying to figure out why she couldn't bring them down.

Dalhu, the name popped into her waking mind—the lunatic Doomer who wanted to make her his wife. Concentrating, she tried to remember everything he had said and done so she could figure a way out of this mess. Taking a peek from under her lashes, she looked around the dingy motel room, finding him hunched over a laptop.

First thing first, however, she needed out of these handcuffs. Her arms hurt too much to think clearly.

"Hey you, Dalhu, how about removing these cuffs. My arms hurt."

Startled, he jumped. "You're awake." Dalhu walked over and unfastened the cuffs, then sat down beside her on the bed and began massaging her stiff muscles.

Amanda said nothing, watching the Doomer as he worked at her kinks with surprisingly gentle hands. He was quite handsome: dark short hair, dark big eyes, and a classically structured face. Not to mention a big, powerful, yummy body…

It was such a shame that he was broken…

"What are you planning to do with me?" she asked.

Looking at her as if she were a hard-won prize, Dalhu kept massaging and bringing circulation back to her arms. Then, when she thought he wouldn't answer her, he took hold of her hand and brought it to his lips for a kiss. "We are going to run—away from your people and mine. I found us a place to hide for a while. We will get to know each other… get close…"

His eyes were so full of hope that she felt sorry for the delusional bastard. "A modern time Romeo and Juliet running away from their families, with just one small twist: Juliet doesn't want to run, she is happy where she is…"

"Are you happy, Professor? With no mate? And no hope of ever finding one? Just going through your life alone? I know I wasn't happy. I just existed, not really living through the long centuries of my life until I found you and grabbed a chance. We are each other's only hope. Face it, there are no other compatible mates for us. It's either this or a very long and lonely life. I'm willing to do whatever it takes to make us happen. How about you give us the same chance?" The besotted look was gone, replaced by iron determination.

Amanda was speechless for a moment. The lunatic actually made sense... or maybe she was just losing it, succumbing to the Stockholm syndrome. "Could you bring me some water, please?" She bought herself a few moments to gather her thoughts.

Sipping slowly from the fresh water bottle he had handed her, she speculated that he'd found out her name and title by going through her purse. Probably had gotten rid of her phone as well, eliminating the only chance of anyone locating her. It was up to her to convince him to let her go...

Yeah, right, as if that is going to work.

Except, with no other options she had to at least try.

Okay, here goes nothing...

"I understand your logic, but it's flawed." Amanda assumed her teacher's voice, preparing for a lecture. The Doomer was crazy but not stupid, maybe she could make him see the light. "We come from very different worlds, different values, different beliefs, opposing beliefs actually, conflicting goals. We are each other's worst enemies. These kinds of differences could never be reconciled, and you cannot build a house on such shaky foundation, for it will crumble and fall. I'm sorry, but this will never work between us." Amanda actually reached for his hand in an effort to comfort him.

He caressed the back of her hand with his thumb, smiling at her as if she were a misguided fool. "Didn't I tell you I'll do whatever it takes? You want me to take up your clan's humanitarian mission? I'll do it. You want me to forsake the Brotherhood? Already done. I don't give a flying fuck about either. All I want is a little piece of heaven with you, and I'll do whatever it takes to make you happy." He looked triumphant; there was nothing she could say to that.

"It's not that simple," was all she could manage on the spot.

"It is. Unless you can honestly say that you find me repulsive, ugly..." Dalhu arched a brow.

Damn, remembering how she'd begged him to fuck her, she knew she couldn't lie about this. "No, I can't say that... You're not completely unfortunate in the looks department." Amanda shrugged dismissively.

"That's the best you could do? Come on, Professor, I'm sure you have something better up your sleeve." Dalhu lifted her hand up for a kiss, moving his thick, firm lips back and forth over the back of it, sending shivers down her spine.

Did he have to be this sexy? Really? Bad guys were supposed to be ugly and mean. It just wasn't fair. "I'll think of something. I promise." And she meant it. There must be something that would burst his hopeful bubble.

She just had to find what it was.

CHAPTER 33: KIAN

"Master Kian, may I bother you for a moment?" Onidu asked from beyond the threshold.

Kian tensed, knowing that Onidu would never disturb him unless it were important. Releasing Syssi's hand, he laid it gently on top of the warming blanket, then stepped out of the room and closed the door quietly behind him. "What's going on, Onidu?"

"It is Mistress Amanda. She is not back yet, and I suspect something is wrong. She told Mistress Syssi that she had a few errands to run, and would call me when she was done or take a taxicab home. But it is already after eight, and Mistress Amanda is not back yet."

"Did you call her? She might have gone to a club or dinner somewhere. You know how she is."

"I called, but she did not answer."

"Amanda might be in a noisy place and didn't hear the ring." Kian pulled out his phone and selected Amanda's contact. The call went straight to voice mail.

He started worrying in earnest. It wasn't that Amanda hadn't done this type of thing before, she had, plenty of times. But she usually answered her phone—her immortal hearing sufficient to hear the ring even over a club's deafening noise.

Except, it was entirely possible that she was busy with some guy in a back room, and though it was a bit early for that, it was still the most likely explanation.

Hell, he really didn't need this on top of what was going on with Syssi, but knowing that doubt would keep eating at him till he made sure Amanda was all right, he got Onegus on the line. "We have what might be a situation. Amanda hasn't returned home yet, and she is not answering her phone. Could you send the guys to check her usual hangouts? Better yet, get William to track her phone signal."

"I'm on it, boss." Onegus ended the call.

CHAPTER 34: DALHU

After leaving the motel, Dalhu found a large shopping mall and turned into its underground parking.

"Are you taking me shopping?" Amanda asked as soon as she realized where he was heading. "So nice of you," she mocked.

He glanced her way, a smirk curling his lips. "I promise I will take you shopping later, but not now, and not here."

"Really?" She looked surprised.

"Really." What he had in mind was breaking into some store later at night and grabbing provisions for the mountains. But for now, he'd let her think what she would.

Waiting for the right opportunity to present itself, he slowly drove around the parking garage. Going down a few levels, Dalhu eventually found what he was looking for. A young man was exiting his car, and there was nobody else around. Not wasting any time, Dalhu stopped and got out of his Mercedes.

Thralling the young man to trade his old, battered Honda for Dalhu's rental took only a few seconds. Hopefully, it would take the Brotherhood some time to track the Mercedes to the guy and start looking for the Honda.

Dalhu was taking every precaution he could think of.

Amanda made a face as he rushed her to the passenger seat of the small car. "You are really taking me slumming. At least the Mercedes was something I was comfortable being driven in. This car is just blah, and it smells." Amanda resumed the nonstop complaining she had started as soon as they left the motel, probably hoping he would grow sick of her annoying company and decide she wasn't worth the trouble.

Oh, man, she had it wrong. He couldn't imagine anything that would detract from how much he wanted her. She could've sung for hours, off key, while farting, and he would've found it charming.

"It's not going to work, Professor. I know what you're trying to do." Dalhu smirked.

"Stop calling me Professor. Why do you do that anyway?"

"Because I can't believe how lucky I got. My woman is gorgeous and smart—a professor no less—it makes me proud to say it."

"Well, I don't like it. Call me Amanda, you sound condescending when you say, professor."

"How do you figure that?"

"You say it as if I'm stupid despite being well educated."

Dalhu glanced her way before returning his eyes to the road. "Guilty as charged. You are being stupid if you think this constant nagging will change my mind. I just tune it out."

"Insufferable man…" she spat.

CHAPTER 35: KIAN

"**W**e checked all of the clubs; she wasn't at any of them. And William couldn't get a signal. He said her phone is history." Onegus delivered the dire news.

Kian was going slowly insane.

Syssi had gone from sleeping to losing consciousness, and now this. Frantic with worry, he paced the small room, feeling like his world was crumbling around him and he was powerless to do a damn thing about it.

Maybe I should pray. Kian's face twisted in a sardonic grimace. *If only I could think of a deity I could pray to...* He stopped in his tracks and pulled out his phone.

"It's Kian, put my mother on the line, please. It's urgent." He resumed his pacing.

"What happened?" Annani came on line, her melodic voice instantly providing him with a measure of relief.

Sighing, he felt like a small boy again, when sharing his troubles with his mother had always managed to make him feel better. "I met a girl, Syssi, and she is a Dormant."

"I know all about her." Kian heard the smile in his mother's voice.

"How?" he asked, awed by her astounding powers.

"Nothing profound, Kian, we do get texts and phone calls up here. The news traveled through the grapevine." She chuckled at his misconception.

"I see... Anyway, Syssi is transitioning and is not doing well. She lost consciousness a little while ago, and we don't know what to do. And to top it off, Amanda is missing." He waited for Annani to say something.

"I am flying over. I will be there in a few hours," she said after a short pause.

Kian was torn between wanting his mother's support and keeping her safely away. "No, Mother, you can't come. It's too dangerous. With the Doomers here in LA, we can't risk your safety like this."

"My daughter is missing, my future daughter-in-law is unconscious, and you think I will stay here twiddling my fingers? I am coming, whether you like it or not. Have the helicopter ready to pick me up from our airstrip." She waited for him to say something. "Kian, this is where you say yes, Mother," she supplied.

"Yes, Mother… but it's thumbs. Not fingers."

"What?"

"The expression is twiddling my thumbs."

CHAPTER 36: DALHU

"So, now you added stealing to your list of crimes, along with kidnapping." As soon as Dalhu was done loading the car with the last of the supplies, Amanda resumed her incessant nagging.

Driving on a dark and deserted mountain road, he'd found a small shopping center. Closed for the night, with no soul for miles around, the decrepit wooden building housing a general store and a donut shop looked creepily like something one would expect to find in a ghost town. But it was exactly what he'd been looking for.

The simple lock had posed no real challenge for Dalhu, and as he'd suspected, the store had no alarm system.

He'd piled on canned foods, loaves of bread, and drinks. Looking around for more items that were not too difficult to prepare, he'd grabbed several packages of ramen noodles and, some spaghetti, along with canned spaghetti sauce. His own expertise in the cooking department was limited, and he had no illusions as to Amanda's willingness to prepare food for them.

There were a few racks of garments for both men and women at the back of the store, and he'd picked sweats for Amanda and himself. Luckily, he'd found some XXL sweats. They were cheaply made, not to mention too short, but beggars couldn't be choosers. They would have to do.

Despite her loud protests, he'd left Amanda cuffed in the car while he'd gathered the supplies. She'd retaliated by making him go back time and again for towels, blankets, toiletries, and other things she'd figured they would need.

She was right, of course. They had no way of knowing what they would find in the deserted cabin he planned on breaking into, wisely making sure that they would at least have the bare necessities. So why the hell was she suddenly throwing that in his face when only a few minutes ago she was sending him for more things?

His gaze cut to her. "If that was the sum of my crimes, I would be a happy man," he grated then, seeing her shrink away from him, added in a softer tone, "If it makes you feel any better, I left three hundred bucks on the counter to cover what we took. I may be many things, but I'm not a thief."

CHAPTER 37: AMANDA

Reminded of who and what her kidnapper was, Amanda's bravado faltered. He was a Doomer, for goodness' sake, by definition a cold-blooded, professional killer. She must've been out of her mind pushing him the way she had. She should tread lightly around him and shut up, instead of antagonizing him.

The smart thing to do was to wait patiently to be rescued. Except, how would anyone find her? Had they even noticed that she was missing? Kian and Syssi were probably still on their date, oblivious to her fate. Only Onidu would know something was wrong. It was sad, really, that the only person waiting for her to come home wasn't really a person.

Stop feeling sorry for yourself.

Kian and Syssi would be worried sick about her just as soon as they found out. And so would be the rest of her family. They'd do everything in their power to get her back.

"Why are you so quiet all of a sudden?" Dalhu studied her face in the dim illumination of the dashboard lights.

"I thought my nagging was annoying you," she said without looking at him.

"Nah, I like the sound of your voice… even with the whiny undertones."

Forgetting her newfound resolve of only a moment ago, she hazarded, "You sounded like you have regrets, are they for all the killing you have done?"

Stupid! Stupid! Stupid! Why can't I keep my mouth shut?

Dalhu pinned her with an unreadable look before turning his eyes back on the road. "Regrets are for those who had a choice and made the wrong one. I didn't have a choice. So no, I have no regrets. That doesn't mean, however, that I'm happy with the way my life has turned out." Dalhu paused as if deliberating whether to tell her more.

Amanda's silence eventually prompted him to continue. "My mother was a slave and a whore with no say in her life either, and yet she loved me despite the way she came to have me. Which could not have been said for the rest of the women at the harem; some hated the children that were forced upon them. After all this time, even though I can't recall her face anymore, I still remember her crying when I was torn from her arms and taken to be activated and raised as a warrior in a cold and cruel military training camp. That camp and its teachings of hate and war became my whole life, and I never saw her or my sister again. I could feel sorry for myself and indulge in wishing that my life's circumstances were different, but that's all it would be—wishing. It would change nothing."

Chewing on her lower lip, Amanda reflected on what he'd told her. He was right. She grew up pampered and sheltered, never having to face the things he had since he'd been a young boy. Could she blame him? Judge him? Not really. But the fact remained that after a lifetime of hatred and killing, Dalhu was no doubt broken beyond repair, and to think differently would be wishful and naive. It was exactly as he had said; wishing would not make it so.

Glancing at his hard profile, Amanda felt a mixture of pity and grudging respect for him. Somehow, through all that he'd done and all that had been done to him, he'd managed to keep a tiny bit of himself out of the darkness, and with that flickering flame, he still hoped and struggled to feel something other than hatred and rage. It made her curious. The scientist in her hankered to discover how he was able to do it after centuries of living in what must have been a damn close approximation of hell.

"So what now? Did you really leave the Brotherhood just for me, or did something change?"

Dalhu didn't respond right away. Staring at the dark, winding road ahead, he tightened his grip on the steering wheel. "A lot has changed. I'm almost eight hundred years old, Amanda. I got tired of the fighting and the killing... and I learned. This new era of easily accessible information opened my eyes and made me realize that we were being brainwashed and lied to; pretty much about everything. From the moment I figured it out, I began planning an exit strategy and buying this ridiculously expensive jewelry so I would have something to trade for money when the time was right..." He lifted his hand off the stirring wheel, showing her his Rolex and his ring. "When I saw you, I knew I'd never have another chance like that. It was time to take the plunge and run. And here we are..." He smiled and patted her knee.

"That's nice, Dalhu, but what happens when the money runs out? What then?"

"I'll worry about it when the time comes. There is always a market for my kind of skills. I'll find something. Don't worry, I'll take care of you." Dalhu squeezed her knee reassuringly.

"I bet you will." Amanda could just imagine the type of skills he'd been referring to. "I guess you're not talking about becoming a lumberjack, or a professional wrestler." She chuckled with a sidelong glance at him.

"If that's what turns you on, why not? But for some reason, I can't imagine a woman like you managing on a lumberjack's pay or coming to cheer me on at a wrestling match..." He gave her outfit an appreciative look-over. "Even I know that what you're wearing must have cost thousands."

"Seeing you shirtless and covered in sweat might be worth the slumming..." Amanda just couldn't help herself. She was used to saying whatever was on her mind, and once the image had formed, she hadn't stopped to think before blurting it out.

"Happy to oblige, ma'am. I'll gladly take my shirt off right now." He chuckled. "If that's all it takes to turn you on, I'm a lucky, lucky man."

"Nah, it's too cold for sweating, and it's not the same without." Amanda shrugged, her lips twitching in an effort to suppress the urge to smile.

"I can think of a surefire way you can make me sweat... you can take *your* shirt off." Dalhu regarded her with a leering grin.

CHAPTER 38: DALHU

Dalhu was enjoying the lighthearted banter they had going on. He'd never experienced that with a woman before, and besides providing a pleasant respite from the shit-scape of his mind, it was turning him on.

Tonight, he hoped she'd let him take care of her the way she had begged him to do before. She might need a little coaxing, but he had a feeling it wouldn't take much to seduce her. Amanda was forward and lustful, and she'd already admitted that she found him attractive.

Testing, he slowly moved his hand across her knee to caress the inside of her thigh. Her sharp inhale was muffled. Dalhu's smirked, she shouldn't have bothered to hide her reaction—she forgot he could smell the spike in her arousal.

Well, what do you know? He had been right. Dalhu smiled and returned his hand to her knee.

Distracted by carnal thoughts, he almost missed the turn onto the dirt road leading up to the secluded cabin. As he slammed on the brakes, the car swerved as he made a sharp turn, skidding on the loose gravel before coming to a full stop.

"Nice driving," Amanda grated.

He shrugged and got out.

The rusted lock securing the simple metal gate at the bottom of the hill required only minimal manipulation to open, and he relocked it behind them before driving up the heavily wooded mountain trail.

It was a little past midnight when he finally parked the car at the end of the long, private driveway.

The place was perfect, just as he had known it would be from the close-up Google image he had pulled up at the motel. With no other dwellings for miles around and no power lines leading up to it, the cabin was completely off the grid. A solar array and a decent sized-wind turbine provided its power. And a water well equipped with an electrical pump took care of the water supply.

The chances of anyone being able to track them to this remote, isolated location were slim to none, as were Amanda's opportunities to run or get help.

Flipping the light switch on, Dalhu was relieved to find that the power was working just fine. He took an appraising look at the cabin's plain interior. The downstairs was one big room, with a simple L-shaped kitchen and a narrow wooden staircase leading up to an open loft-style bedroom. Both rooms were sparsely furnished with old, well-worn pieces that were currently covered with a thick layer of dust.

A massive brick fireplace, flanked by windows going all the way up to the gabled ceiling, was the cabin's one redeeming grace. He liked the simple, homey feel, but he had to admit that it was definitely not up to his woman's standards.

With a grimace that conveyed her opinion louder than words, Amanda clutched her purse close to her body as if to prevent it from touching the grime. "I'm going to pee and take a bath. You go ahead and start cleaning. This place is filthy." Without sparing him a second look, she took the stairs up to the loft and strode into the cabin's only bathroom, locking the door behind her.

"Pampered brat," Dalhu mumbled under his breath.

"I heard that!" she said, flushing the toilet.

"Good!" He answered loudly this time, following her up the rickety stairs and dropping the bags he had carried up on the dusty bed cover. In need of the facilities himself, he waited for her to get out.

But then, a squeak of an old faucet, followed by the sound of water hitting the bottom of a tub, made him realize that the selfish woman had started a bath without considering that he might need to use the bathroom as well.

No big deal; he could take care of business outside.

Once that most pressing need was satisfied, Dalhu finished unloading the Honda and drove it off the driveway, hiding it in the thicket. He made sure it was well covered with heavy greenery, in case someone thought to do an aerial search for the missing car. The keys went under the floorboards of the porch, safely hidden, and out of Amanda's reach.

Back in the cabin, Dalhu took a calculating look at the thick layer of dust covering every exposed surface and the spider webs hanging from ceiling corners and between furniture legs. No matter how dirty the place was, it was small enough for him to have it cleaned before the spoiled princess finished taking her bath. And hopefully, by the time he was done, he would manage to work up a little sweat…

Imagining Amanda's lustful response to his half-naked, glistening body, he felt a surge of arousal. Now that he knew her weakness, he planned to exploit it.

"Game on, Professor." With a wicked smile tugging at the corner of his mouth, Dalhu took off his shirt and went to work.

CHAPTER 39: KIAN

Outside Syssi's room, Kian found most of the Guardians keeping vigil, sitting or sprawling on the hallway's thinly carpeted floor. The only two absent were on their way to escort his mother when she arrived.

"Any news?" he asked Onegus.

"William is still working on hacking every relevant security camera in the area that's connected to the web. He even mobilized his geek squad to help."

"His geek squad?"

"You know, the class he's teaching. You should see it, it's like a ██████ war room down in his lair."

"What about the police; did you talk to the chief?"

"Yeah, I impressed upon him that our continued contributions are contingent upon the level of attention he's going to dedicate to this case. Every cop in the state has Amanda's picture by now and is searching for any possible clues. Someone must've seen something, it's not like she could've disappeared into thin air or went unnoticed. Amanda doesn't exactly blend in."

"That's why I'm so worried. She could disappear into thin air if someone thralled everyone who had seen her getting nabbed. If the Doomers got her..." Kian couldn't finish his sentence. The horrific implications of that eventuality were just too much for him to bear.

He knew he was starting to crack, the fissures becoming longer and deeper with every passing hour without a shred of good news on either front. He held on because he had to; because there was no one else to shoulder the responsibility and relieve him of his burden.

It was absurd, but Kian had the feeling that the moment his mother arrived, he would just let go and shatter to pieces.

And how ██████ pathetic was that?

CHAPTER 40: AMANDA

The racket Amanda heard coming from beyond the bathroom door sounded as if Dalhu was tearing the place apart instead of cleaning it up.

She heard him hauling the mattress outside and then beating the hell out of it with what sounded like a bat. Wincing, she imagined the clouds of dust that were billowing out of the old, dirty thing. Then came the sound of the noisy, cheap vacuum going on and on as Dalhu battled the dust on the rest of the stuff.

Soaking in the bathtub that she had to clean with her own two hands—Amanda had to admit Dalhu had been right to call her a spoiled, pampered brat. This was the first time she had done anything even remotely domestic. Ever. Unfortunately, there had been no way around it if she wanted to use the deep, but dirty claw-foot tub.

Now, as the water was cooling, she also realized she'd forgotten to bring in the toiletries and a towel. At her home, Onidu was the one who made sure they were on hand for her. She never had to bother with something so trivial herself.

She was stuck.

Okay... her options were to either run out naked and dripping or call Dalhu for help. Both sucked.

She was about to make a run for it, when the vacuum's incessant drone stopped, replaced by the sound of Dalhu's heavy footfalls going up the cracking wooden steps.

Forcing the door open, he walked right in. "Hello, princess." He grinned like the cat who was about to swallow Tweety Bird.

When she didn't gasp or try to cover herself as most women would, the surprised look on his face was priceless. But why would she? She was nothing like what he was used to.

Not even close.

Amanda was the daughter of a goddess, for fate's sake.

Her naked body, boldly displayed in the bath's clear water, rendered Dalhu speechless and drooling. He wasn't the only one affected, though. As he devoured her with his hungry eyes, her body responded, her small nipples growing taut under his hooded gaze.

Wiping the drool off his mouth with the back of his dirty hand, Dalhu ogled her, looking just as awestruck as one of her students. But that was where the resemblance ended.

Dalhu was a magnificent specimen of manhood, and in comparison, all her prior partners were mere boys. Shirtless and sweaty, he looked just as amazing as she had imagined he would.

He was big, not even Yamanu was that tall, and Dalhu was more powerfully built. Nevertheless, his well-defined muscles were perfectly proportioned for his size with no excess bulk; he looked strong, but not pumped like someone who spent endless hours lifting weights at a gym.

Following the light smattering of dark hair trailing down the center of his chest to where it disappeared below the belt line of his jeans, she wasn't surprised to find that he was well proportioned everywhere. And as he kept staring at her, mesmerized, his jeans growing too tight to contain him, she held her breath in anticipation of her first glimpse of that magnificent shaft poking above his belt.

Oh, boy, am I in a shitload of trouble.

There was just no way she could resist all that yummy maleness. Amanda knew she was going to succumb to temptation.

She always had.

Except, this time, she would be stooping lower than ever. Because she could think of nothing that would scream *slut* louder than her going willingly into the arms of her clan's mortal enemy…

CHAPTER 41: KIAN

Annani arrived.

The large helicopter landing on the stronghold's rooftop carried in addition to the goddess, her two servants Oridu and Ogidu, and the two Guardians Kian had dispatched to pick her up from the clan's private airstrip.

Kri exited first, bending her head under the chopper's rotating blades, and offered her hand to help the small, black-robed figure down and away from harm's way.

Kian rushed forward to embrace his mother's slight form, shielding her with his large body from the whirlwind created by the helicopter's slowing blades.

The great, formidable Annani was so tiny and light, he'd been afraid she might get blown away.

Once inside the rooftop vestibule, he let go of her and went down to one knee, kneeling so he wouldn't tower over her.

Annani pulled back her hood, the mass of her red, wavy hair spilling forward and cutting some of the lambent light cast by her luminescent, pale face.

Looking at Kian with eyes full of mother's love, she clasped his scruffy cheeks in her warm palms and bent slightly to kiss his forehead. "I have not seen you in such a long time, I forgot how handsome you are, my beautiful boy."

Ignoring her shameless effort to lay a guilt trip on him, Kian sighed with relief; her tender touch and the sound of her soothing, melodic voice were a salve on the growing fissures of his psyche. "I missed you too, Mother. I should have visited more often. I allowed myself to get distracted by all things mundane, forgetting what's really important in this miserable life. Forgive me." He hung his head, the truth of his words adding to his despondent mood.

His whole life was work. He neglected his relationships with his sisters and mother, got angry when other family members dared to disturb him, and for what? So he could spend more endless hours bent over reports and contracts? It all felt so meaningless now as his world was falling apart.

"Get up, Kian, and stop that self-flagellation you have got going on. I raised you to be a strong and capable leader. You cannot allow yourself to wallow in self-pity when fate challenges you. Let us go and help your girl pull through." Annani patted his cheek and waited for him to rise.

As he got to his feet and looked down at his tiny but formidable mother, Kian had to smile. She was the strongest, most willful person he knew. Letting nothing bring her down, she relentlessly pushed forward when others would have given up.

Later, in Syssi's room at the clinic, Annani removed her heavy robe and handed it to Kian, then sat on the hospital bed next to Syssi.

Her long, sleeveless, black silk dress was plain, but it clung to her body in a way that made the lack of a bra quite conspicuous. She never wore one. And though his sisters had tried to convince her it was unseemly, she had retorted that as gravity had no effect on her never-aging body, she saw no reason to bother with something so uncomfortable in deference to the transient sensibilities of others. Why should she? After all, she was the goddess, and it was everyone else's duty to show deference to her. Not the other way around.

And who could argue with that?

"She is so lovely," Annani said quietly, running her fingers through Syssi's thick, multicolored hair.

"On the inside as well." Standing next to his mother, Kian was tormented by gut-wrenching worry.

Taking Syssi's hand and holding it between both of hers, his mother asked, "Does she feel as strongly for you as you feel for her?"

"She does."

"And if she pulls through the change, do you plan to mate her for life?"

"Yes, I've never felt like this about anyone. I thought I loved Lavena, but I'm not sure anymore. I know it seems improbable and maybe even foolish for me to feel this way about a woman I've known for such a short time. But I've known Syssi was the one from the first moment I laid eyes on her. Since then, all I've done is prove to myself that my initial gut response was right. I've yet to find even one thing that I don't like about her. I love everything. Even the little snoring sounds she makes when she sleeps—they soothe me." He chuckled, but then his smile wilted, and he rubbed the place over his heart.

"I get crazy jealous and possessive over Syssi, I never did with Lavena. I don't know why... she never does anything to encourage these feelings. It's just me, acting like a caveman who's guarding his turf, all primal instinct and no brains." Glancing at his mother's satisfied smirk, Kian raked his fingers through his hair.

"You react this way because your immortal body and your soul recognize the one woman who completes you, and you would do just about anything to guard her and keep her safely to yourself. It is as it should be for a male of our kind. I am so happy that against all odds, fate—with a little help from Amanda—has granted you this rare fortune of a truelove match... But are you sure Syssi feels the same way about you?"

"Yes, why do you keep asking? Do you have a reason to doubt it?" It was disconcerting the way his mother double-checked. Did she think he was not lovable? Or worse, that Syssi was some kind of opportunist? Seeking to gain something other than his love and devotion?

"Close the door, Kian." Annani gestured toward the open door, where the Guardians keeping vigil in the corridor outside were listening in on their conversation.

He had completely forgotten that they were not alone. Now everyone would know how out of control he was.

Whatever... let them.

As he felt a soundproofing shield snap into place, Kian figured his mother wished to guard their conversation. Couldn't she have done it before asking him all those personal questions? Annani was the only one whose power was strong enough to block other immortals, affecting them as easily as they affected humans.

"I kept asking to make sure I am not bringing you in on my most guarded secret without a very good cause." She sighed, gesturing for him to take a seat on the chair beside the bed.

"What I am going to reveal, I shared out of necessity only with Alena. And now I am sharing it with you... The way we turn our girls is not the way we led everyone to believe we do. They cannot turn just by being exposed to my magnificent self." She smiled sheepishly as she paused for effect. "I give them a small infusion of my blood to facilitate the change."

Kian was speechless for a moment. "No wonder you kept it secret. I assume only your blood works? Obviously, if anybody else's had, it wouldn't have been such a big deal."

"Now you understand why I cannot risk it leaking out. I will become even more of a target than I already am. This information must not fall into the wrong hands by someone blurting it accidentally, or it being tortured out of them."

"Yes, you were right to keep it a secret. So how does it work? Was it always done like that with the girls?"

"No, it was not needed when there were enough boys from different matrilineal descent to facilitate the change. The girls were turned at around the same age as the boys, at puberty. It was such a lovely ceremony, similar to an engagement party but not as binding. The girl's family would choose an older transitioned boy, or her future intended if there was one, and throw a big party with lots of food and entertainment. Scantily clothed dancers would put on a show to arouse their audience with their erotic and enticing moves. And at the end of it, the young couple would be escorted to a secluded room for the girl's first kiss and her first bite. Nothing more was allowed, and knowing the consequences, no boy ever crossed the line. A paid substitute was provided for him if later his need became too pressing. And it wasn't because premarital sex was allowed for the boys and not for the girls or any such nonsense; it was just discouraged for those not yet seventeen. In most cases, one bite was enough, but occasionally the boy was called for a repeat performance." With a wistful smile on her lovely face, Annani gazed blankly at the wall.

"So how did you come up with the idea of giving them your blood? Was it ever done before?"

"No. Desperate times called for desperate measures, and I was desperate. We could not use our boys to turn the girls; it would have been considered incest, and as far as we knew, it would carry disastrous consequences. I remembered my uncle mentioning that even a small amount of a god's blood could bring miraculous healing to a mortal, and I figured it was worth a try. The first Dormant girl child was born, of course, to Alena, so obviously I had to ask her permission before trying something potentially dangerous on her daughter. She agreed that we had to try; otherwise, we would've been doomed to extinction and her female children to mortality. Luckily, by the time her first son was born, you were old enough to be his initiator. And the rest is history. We decided to keep it to ourselves, and concocted the story of my amazing ability to bring about the change by my godly presence alone. Truthfully, I did not think anyone would buy it, but they did." Annani shrugged her bare shoulders.

"That's the real reason you came." Kian stated the obvious.

"I would have come regardless, but yes. Your girl should have been fine with your venom alone, but she is not. I figured I could increase her chances of survival by giving her a boost with a tiny infusion of my blood. If she makes it… when she makes it… Syssi could become the mother of a new line, and her descendants could mate with mine. There will be no more need for my blood. She is the key to our future, Kian. I am happy you love her and she loves you back, but I think I would have done it even if that was not the case. She is just too important."

Kian nodded. "Do you know what to do? I'm not good with needles."

"Do not worry about it, by now I am an expert, and I have everything I need with me. Hand me my robe and go stand guard outside. I do not want Bridget catching us in the act. I will knock on the door when I am done."

Kian handed Annani her robe and leaned over Syssi, kissing her lightly on her parched lips. "I love you," he whispered before leaving the room and closing the door behind him.

Out in the hallway, Kian was greeted by eight worried, questioning faces. All of the guardians and Michael were still there. The trays of half-eaten food and the blankets strewn out on the floor were a testament to their resolve to stay.

"There's still no change," Kian told them as he leaned his back against the closed door and crossed his arms over his chest, waiting until a discreet knock from inside the room signaled it was okay for him to come back.

"It is done. Syssi should start getting better now. Take a seat, Kian. It might take a while."

As he plopped tiredly onto the chair and stretched his long legs in front of him, Kian wanted to feel elated at Syssi's increased prospects of making it through the transition, but thoughts of Amanda were keeping him grim.

"I know you are worried about your sister, but I have reason to believe she is not in danger," Annani said softly as she brushed her knuckles over Syssi's flushed cheek.

"What makes you say that?" Kian straightened in his chair.

"I dozed off on the plane and dreamt of her. Amanda was lying in an old-fashioned bathtub and smiling. She did not look worried or afraid." Annani turned back to Syssi and placed her palm over Syssi's forehead. "I think she is cooling down."

"How can you be certain of this? It was only a dream."

"I know the difference between a regular dream and a remote viewing, Kian. You should know better than to doubt me."

"I'm sorry, you're right. I shouldn't. You've certainly proven some of your dreams are more than just dreams. It's just hard for me to rely on visions… But even if Amanda is fine at the moment, and I'm tremendously relieved that she is, there is no guarantee she will remain this way. We still need to find her as soon as we can."

"We will."

CHAPTER 42: MICHAEL

"Kri." Michael kissed the sleeping girl's warm cheek.

"Yeah? I'll get right on it..." she mumbled with her eyes still closed.

"Wake up, sweetheart, you're dreaming."

She lifted an eyelid. "What?"

"I just wanted to tell you I'm going to look for some Motrin. I'll be right back. I didn't want you to wake up and wonder where I am."

"Why, what's wrong?" She sat up.

"I've got a headache, and my gums are bothering me." He had been trying to brave it out for the last couple of hours, but the pain was becoming unbearable.

"Ask Bridget, she might have some... and if not, the guys in the lobby will surely have it..." Kri waved him off and plopped back down onto the blanket, letting her eyelids slide shut.

Bridget had her hands full with Syssi, and the last thing Michael wanted was to bother her with his inconsequential toothache.

Taking the elevator up to the lobby, he stood in front of the mirrored wall and tried to see what was going on in his mouth. Stretching his jaw as far as he could, he checked his teeth. But he saw nothing besides some swelling that he wasn't even sure was actually there.

I need a dentist.

But as far as he knew, other than Bridget, there were no other doctors at the keep. And he was pretty sure that leaving to see a human dentist was out of the question.

Shit, I hope they have Motrin.

The guy at the front desk gave him a pitying look and pulled out a packet of pills from his drawer. "Here you go." He handed Michael the square plastic packet, then added a bottle of water. "Hope it helps, kid."

"Thanks, man. Appreciated."

On his way back down, Michael emptied the whole packet of Motrin into his mouth and washed it down with the bottle of water.

When he got to the clinic's level, he didn't go back to sit next to Kri. Instead, he paced the winding corridor, waiting for the pills to kick in.

CHAPTER 43: KIAN

When Kian shifted once again in an effort to find a more comfortable position on the rigid chair, Annani frowned. "You should ask someone to roll a gurney in here and catch a few hours of sleep. I will wake you if there is any change."

"It'll be of no use. I'm too worried to fall asleep, but there is no reason for you to suffer as well. I'm sure you'd appreciate a comfortable bed after your long plane ride. Though, don't take it the wrong way; I'm not kicking you out. You're welcome to stay."

"I will stay and keep you company for a little longer. I am not tired at all. The nap I took on the plane was very restful. Did you know it was my first time using the new jet? And I must say, it is a wonderful little thing. The two main seats recline and turn into beds. Can you imagine that on such a small airplane? It even has a shower in addition to the standard facilities. Now that I know I can fly in such comfort, I might visit Sari, Amanda and you more often." Annani glanced at him, checking to see if he liked the idea.

Funny, how she'd done it in a roundabout way, as if not sure of her welcome.

"I wondered when you'd begin to venture away from your sanctuary and travel a little farther than the nearest populated town. I, for one, am always happy to see you, as are the rest of our people. You literally brighten our world..."

"You know I love it there. Why would I want to leave my own paradise? And anyway, I cannot bear to be away from my little ones for long. They are the joy of my life, and I will miss them too much. It has been so long without any children at my place, and now I have two new sweet babies and a toddler boy. You should come visit me and spend some time surrounded by their adorable sounds and smells. It would do you a world of good."

"I wish I could, but my workload is becoming impossible. I have so much to do, I feel guilty every time I steal a few hours to be with Syssi. It's ridiculous." Kian pushed out from the chair and started pacing again, his fingers raking his messed up hair.

"My darling, sweet boy, that is because you are still doing things the way you were doing them two hundred years ago. It was okay to do everything by yourself when things were simpler, and we were not as diversified. But thanks mainly to you, we've become huge. You have to hire professional help, have a team of directors to manage each arm of our holdings separately and report to you. It would free a large chunk of your time to do as you please. You may even decide to study business management at a university." She looked at him hopefully.

It was a conversation they had before; his mother suggesting he should get some form of formal education and him maintaining that he didn't need it and didn't have time for it.

Kian had never gotten to study in any learning institution, higher or lower. What he knew, he had learned from Annani and on his own, and in his opinion, it was enough. If he wanted to learn something new, there were books available on nearly every topic, and the few times he'd needed further explanations, he'd found a leading authority in the field to teach him.

Less time-consuming and way more efficient.

The main advantage of going to any kind of school was socializing, which was fine for the young with no responsibilities on their shoulders. But that didn't mean that graduating from some college or university made them experts or necessarily qualified them for the job.

Only experience did that.

"I don't know if I can trust others enough to relinquish control to them. And anyway, I don't know where to find qualified people. That undertaking alone will take time I don't have." He paused his pacing to look at her stubborn expression and knew she wouldn't let it go.

"We have several young clan members who have graduated with honors from top universities. Two with Masters in business management, one with a degree in industrial management, and one with a law diploma specializing in business. And those are just the top ones. There are others who may be not as studious but are just as qualified. I can send them your way for interviews."

"How do you know all that?"

"I keep tabs on my progeny. They all spent their early childhoods in my sanctuary, and I care about them and what they do with themselves after they leave." She smiled. "Being called the mother of the clan means more to me than just an honorific or a figure of speech," Annani added with pride.

"In that case, sure... Maybe the time has come to let the younger generation show what they can do..." Kian plopped down on the chair, letting his head drop on his fists.

Annani went on, "Another advantage of hiring the young professionals will be quelling the simmering disquiet in the ranks. Many are frustrated, thinking that our top management positions would always be unattainable to them. You need to demonstrate that you are willing to share the spotlight with others and let more of the clan members climb up and have important jobs."

Annani seemed to have the thirty-thousand-foot view he lacked, and evidently, was much better informed. He should have known what was going on under his nose; should have been more connected to his people. But be that as it may, right now he was too depleted to get energized by the prospect of doing things differently, or to plan a shift in his management style.

"I gave you a lot to think about, so you would not be bored when I leave. Let me know if anything changes. I will be up at Amanda's penthouse." Annani slid down from the hospital bed. "No, do not get up; it is easier for me to kiss you when you are sitting." She took his face in her small, delicate hands and kissed him on both cheeks.

Kian covered her hands with his. "I want to keep your presence here a secret from everyone but the Guardians and council members. So make sure to use only the dedicated penthouse elevator, and if you need anything, send Onidu for it. I don't want someone noticing your servants and figuring out you're here. Keep them at Amanda's place. Please." Too used to issuing orders, he checked himself at the end. This kind of tone wouldn't do with his mother. Even under extenuating circumstances.

Annani nodded at him imperiously and headed for the door.

Once she'd left and he was alone again with Syssi, Kian moved the chair closer to the bed, and holding her hand, rested his cheek on her soft palm. Comforted by the touch he closed his eyes, and in no time, the monotone sounds of the monitoring equipment lulled him to sleep.

It couldn't have been more than a few minutes when the sense of someone creeping around the room woke him up. He jumped, alarmed and ready to pounce on the intruder. But as the cobwebs of his dreamless slumber cleared and his mind registered who had made the sounds that woke him up, Kian slumped back into his chair and blew out a relieved breath.

"You scared the crap out of me, jumping like that!" Bridget held her hand over her racing heart. "I thought you were asleep."

The spike in adrenaline used up what little boost he'd gotten from his few minutes of sleep, and Kian felt just as exhausted as he had been before. "I was…" He sighed.

"I brought you your breakfast—courtesy of Okidu. It's on the rolling tray behind you, but be careful when you reach for it; the coffee is hot."

"Thank you."

Pulling the cart to him, Kian lifted the coffee mug to his lips and took a few sips of the hot brew. "How is Syssi doing? Any improvement?"

"Much better. Her fever is almost back to normal, and her blood pressure has stabilized. Heart is doing well; brainwaves are fine... By the look of it, she is dreaming. She should be waking up any time now. Just as soon as her body is done accommodating the main changes that are taking place."

Turning away from Syssi, Bridget looked him over, and with a hand on her hip, cast him a disapproving look. "Kian, you need to eat, drink, wash your face... No offense, but you look like shit. I have toothbrushes in the bathroom cabinet. Use one!" she ordered, pointing a finger at the bathroom door and waiting till he returned from freshening up, then scowled at him until he took several bites of his sandwich.

Satisfied, she opened the door to leave just as William poked in his flushed face. "I've got it!" he exclaimed, and pushing past Bridget shoved a tablet at Kian.

Frowning at the guy, Kian whispered, "Slow down and keep your voice down... What is it?"

"Sorry," William continued in a hushed, breathless tone. "I checked the security camera recordings from all of the stores I could hack... on and around Rodeo Drive... Amanda's last known location... My boys helped... It was really hard to find all of them... and then it took a long time... to go through all that footage... But we got it... Press the play arrow on the tablet... and see for yourself... I just wish there was an audio... but at least we have the face... of her kidnapper." William's relatively short explanation was delivered between one pant and another. Evidently, the guy had exerted himself running all the way from his lab with his exciting news.

With Bridget and William hovering behind his shoulders, Kian braced for what he was about to see.

It began with what he immediately recognized as a Doomer entering the store, up until the hulking guy had left with Amanda. Kian replayed it two more times, starting with Amanda's terrified expression when she had seen the Doomer, through the disturbingly sexual way she had reacted to his bite, and ending with her leaning her head on his shoulder when they had left the store. It wasn't her fault, Kian kept reminding himself, sickened by the overtly sexual display—she had been high on the venom and had no control over her reactions.

"Interesting..." Bridget commented from behind his back before quickly turning away.

"Interesting? That's what you have to say about it?" Already livid from what he had seen, Kian lashed out at her for what he considered to be a grossly inappropriate response.

"I apologize. I know how disturbing it must have been for you to watch this. It's just that it was the first time I had an opportunity to observe the way it works between an immortal male and female, and couldn't help but be fascinated by the physiology of it. I wasn't commenting on the fact that Amanda was kidnaped, and that we fear for her safety... Of course, I'm distraught over it."

"What the hell was so fascinating?"

"You've experienced women's reaction to the venom, Kian. But I haven't... I... just wondered how it would feel... I'm sorry..." Bridget blushed and turned away.

Her discomfort finally clued him in. The woman had been aroused by what she had seen. Rationally, he could understand her yearning for that which she couldn't have, but emotionally he was repulsed by her response. Afraid his disgust would show on his face, he turned to William.

"Good job, William, give Onegus a good close-up of the fucker's face, and have him distribute the picture to each of the Guardians and the police."

"I will. Is there anything else I can do?"

"If there is, I cannot think of it now. Go get some sleep, you look beat." It was already late morning, and judging by the guy's red eyes, he had spent the whole night staring at computer screens.

CHAPTER 44: YAMANU

Propped against the clinic's hallway wall, Yamanu glanced up from the book he had been reading to see Michael winding between the bodies of Guardians sleeping on the carpeted floor.

The kid was heading his way.

"Yamanu, I need your help, man." Michael's pained voice grabbed his mentor's immediate attention.

"What's wrong?"

"I think I need to see a dentist, and I'm not allowed to leave. Is there anybody you could bring in here? I wouldn't ask, but I can't take it anymore. I took Motrin and it did nothing for the pain... I don't know what else to do..." The poor kid looked tortured.

"Let me see... Open your mouth..." Yamanu took a peek. "Don't be a wuss...," he said as Michael flinched away from his finger, then gently probed the guy's swollen gums. "Just as I thought..." Yamanu grinned and clapped Michael's back. "Welcome to immortality... You're growing fangs and venom glands, and it hurts like a son of a bitch. I know, still remember it as if it happened last week though it was ages ago. It was that bad."

Michael remained speechless, his mouth still gaping as he stared at Yamanu's happy face in shocked disbelief. "You're shitting me, right?" he finally said.

"No, I'm not. But let's ask the good doctor's opinion if you don't trust mine." Yamanu took Michael by the shoulders and turned him toward Bridget's office.

"Hold on, I want Kri to come with us..." Michael walked over to where she was sleeping on the floor.

"Kri... wake up, sweetheart. I have great news." Michael brushed his hand over her arm.

Kri sat up with a start. "Did they find Amanda? Did Syssi wake up?"

"No, unfortunately not... But Yamanu thinks I'm transitioning, and we are going to see Doctor Bridget to confirm it. I would really like for you to be there with me."

With a surge, she got up and hugged him tightly. "Oh, Michael! This is wonderful. I can't believe it… I'm so happy for you."

"I'm happy for *us*…" The kid grinned.

Puppy love. Yamanu rolled his eyes.

CHAPTER 45: KIAN

Nauseous with fatigue, Kian finished his coffee and took a few more bites of the sandwich, making an effort to shove some food down his tight throat and into his empty stomach. But swallowing was a pain, and he dropped it back on the plate.

With a grimace, he kicked the rolling cart away.

Turning back to Syssi, he enfolded her small hand with his own, and closing his eyes, rested his forehead on her open palm.

For a moment, he wasn't sure whether what he'd felt was real or his imagination playing tricks on him, but he could've sworn he had felt Syssi's finger brush lightly over his cheek.

Slowly, he lifted his head, hopeful, and yet afraid it was just a phantasm.

Her eyes were open, and as a profound sense of relief washed over him, the small, pitiful smile she managed for him was the most beautiful sight he had ever seen.

She lifted her arm with marked effort, reaching for his cheek. "Wha..." She tried to talk but managed only a croak.

"Hold on, baby. I'll get you something to drink..." Kian rushed over to the tray and poured a glass of water from the pitcher. "I need a straw..." Frantically searching through the cabinets, he found what he was looking for in the one above the sink.

"Here you go, sweetheart..." Kian lifted the head of the bed and brought the straw to her lips. "Slowly, I don't know much about this, but I don't think you should drink a lot at once... Where the hell is Bridget when we need her?" He looked for the call button.

"I'm here." Bridget knocked once before barging in.

"The monitors in my office sounded the alert. Welcome back, Syssi." She smiled.

"Back from where?" Syssi whispered around the straw.

"You've been unconscious since yesterday afternoon, and we've been worried. I'll run some tests and take a blood sample to see where we're at."

Syssi drained the glass. "Did I transition?" she asked hopefully.

"That's what the tests are for. We'll know in a moment." Bridget pulled a syringe and a small surgical knife from the supply cabinet, placing them on her tray.

Kian grabbed her wrist. "What's the knife for?"

"I'm going to make a small cut to see how fast it closes. It's a crude but conclusive test. We'll know right away." She looked at him pointedly, waiting for him to release her.

"It's okay, Kian. I want to know. Let her do it." Syssi extended her arm, offering her palm to Bridget. Then she motioned for Kian to refill her glass with the other.

"Make sure it's tiny and doesn't hurt!" He released Bridget's wrist to pour Syssi more water. Holding the glass with the straw to her lips, he grasped her free hand. "Squeeze my hand if you feel pain."

Bridget rolled her eyes and quickly slashed with her knife.

A line of bright red blood formed over the cut, more of it welling as the seconds ticked away with the three of them watching and holding their breath.

"It's not working…," Syssi whispered, a few tears rolling down her cheeks.

"No, look!" Bridget lifted Syssi's hand, bringing it close to her eyes. "It's closing!" She took a small gauze square from her tray and wiped the blood away. The skin underneath it was already knitting back together, and the small scar faded right before their eyes. In less than a minute, there was no sign of the incision.

"Welcome to immortality, Syssi. To completely transition will take up to six months, but the major change has already taken place. Your body heals itself fast, and it will just keep improving." Bridget smiled at Kian and Syssi's relieved faces. "You're the second one I've welcomed today."

"What?" Kian eyes shot to her.

"I have Michael in the next room, suffering like a trouper through growing venom glands and fangs. I offered to knock him out and spare him the pain, but he refused. Told me he wants to witness his change. I wonder how long he'll hold out on the painkillers when he realizes it may take up to a month for these beauties to grow." She beamed proudly—as if she had just delivered two new lives into the world. And in a way she had.

"I'm so happy…" Syssi sniffled, returning Kian's gentle embrace.

"Can I take her upstairs now?" Kian asked. If he never had to see the cursed sick room again, it would be too soon.

"Let me just take a few blood samples, and then you're free to go, Syssi. But take it easy until you feel stronger. Small liquid meals to start with, and then nothing heavy for the next twenty-four hours. After that, eat as much as you can stuff into your stomach. You'll need the fuel."

Kian brushed his hand over Syssi's hair. "I'm going to step outside for a minute and tell everybody the good news. They all kept vigil for you, sweetheart. None of the Guardians left this corridor unless they absolutely had to..." He smiled at her and kissed her hand. "It looks like they all have fallen under your spell..." He paused. "My mother flew over to be with you as well, and she wants to meet you as soon as you're up..." He stopped when he saw Syssi's terrified expression.

"She is here?" Syssi whispered. "I can't see her now! I must look like a wreck... Oh my God! She already got to see me looking like this, didn't she?"

"You're being silly. She said you're lovely..."

"I don't care. I want to shower and get dressed before I meet her. Please, Kian, don't let her see me before I do..." Syssi pleaded.

"I won't. I promised to let her know as soon as you were awake, but I'll tell her you want to freshen up... Deal?"

"Thank you!"

Later, after Bridget was done with her tests and released Syssi into his care, Kian carried her all the way up to his penthouse, despite her protests that she was okay to walk on her own.

Then when he let her down in the bathroom, she shooed him away like some annoying pest. For some inexplicable reason, the mulish woman refused his offer to wash her, insisting she was well enough to do it by herself.

As if that had anything to do with it.

He wanted to take care of her... needed to...

Eventually, he dropped the argument only because he didn't want to upset her so soon after all she had been through.

Waiting, Kian sprawled on his bed, stretching his stiff body as he listened to the sounds percolating from under the bathroom's door; ready to jump to her rescue in case she needed him after all.

But his worry for Amanda pressed heavily on his chest, preventing him from getting any measure of rest, and as his cell phone vibrated in his pocket, he quickly fumbled to pull the thing out; hoping for some good news. "What do you have for me?"

"Kian, we have a situation down at the lobby," Onegus told him. "Martin, the dayshift's security supervisor, called. There is a guy down there, Andrew Spivak, claiming to be Syssi's brother. He demands to see his sister or either Amanda or you. He is making a scene and threatening to bring a SWAT team to storm the building if refused. What do you want me to do?"

"I'm on my way. Tell Martin I'll be there in a few minutes." Kian dropped his legs down the side of the bed and hung his head for a moment. He was so depleted that he couldn't even bring himself to be angry with Syssi for disclosing their location to her brother.

Just another situation for him to handle, he sighed. What else could go wrong? Pushing off the bed, he trudged to the bathroom and opened the door. At the sight of Syssi's delicate body wrapped in a big blue towel, and her long wet hair dripping on the floor, his frustration flew out the window. She looked even smaller and more fragile than before.

With a muted curse, he took her in his arms, and a sense of profound gratitude washed over him as he realized that despite how frail she looked, she was here, alive, and practically indestructible.

Oddly, though, as he held Syssi he felt as if her small, soft body was infusing him with renewed energy, and instead of him lending her his strength, she was his power source.

He kissed the top of her wet hair, filling his lungs with her unique fragrance. "I don't want to rush you, but I just got a call that your brother is down in the lobby and is demanding to see you. I'm going down to talk to him," he said softly.

Syssi seemed just as surprised as he'd been. "How did he find me? Had he had me followed? He must've… after I left the restaurant. I'm so sorry…"

"Well, somehow he has found you. The question is, why is he here? What does he want?"

"He is probably worried about me. I began feeling sick at the restaurant, and he must have called to ask how I felt, then had a conniption when I didn't answer his calls. He is very protective…" Syssi chewed her lower lip, looking troubled. Though Kian wasn't sure what disturbed her more; being the cause for the breach in security or the source of Andrew's angst.

"Don't worry about it, sweetheart. I'll deal with him. Everything is going to be all right." Kian wasn't sure how exactly he would accomplish that, but while she was recovering from her ordeal, he didn't want her upset over anything.

"Maybe I should go down and reassure Andrew that I'm fine. He wouldn't rest until you let him see me anyway. Don't underestimate him, Andrew has his resources. He is an undercover government antiterrorism agent, and before that he was Special Forces."

"In this case, I'd better not have him wait any longer…" Kian smiled at her. "Get dressed. If he wouldn't be satisfied with talking with you on the phone, I'll bring him up here."

"Thank you, I know he'll want to see me."

CHAPTER 46: ANDREW

Down at the lobby, Andrew paced restlessly, shooting murderous glares at the security people watching his every move. He was beside himself with worry after calling Syssi nonstop for the past two days and leaving urgent messages on her voice mail—to no avail. How sick could she be not to answer any of them, or check her messages? Did this new boyfriend of hers do something to her?

And where was Amanda? He was so sure the woman would take care of Syssi. Why didn't she pick up Syssi's phone?

Andrew's hand went to his concealed weapon.

Don't be an idiot. He dropped his hand back to his side and went back to glaring at the bank of elevators, waiting for the boyfriend to show up, so he could tear him a new ass.

As he waited, several loads of people got out of the elevators. It didn't escape his notice, however, that only two out of the three served the general public. And as soon as the doors of the third one opened, revealing an extraordinarily good-looking man, Andrew knew it was his guy.

It wasn't that Kian and Amanda looked alike, they didn't; Amanda being a brunette and this guy being a reddish, dark blond. But it was the towering height and the level of physical perfection they shared that made it obvious the two were related.

His good looks aside, the man appeared tired, and his haggard appearance made Andrew's gut clench with worry. Dispensing with polite introductions, he pounced on the guy. "Where is my sister? Is she all right?"

"Syssi is fine. She was unwell, but it is all over now, and she is getting better. I'm Kian." The man offered his hand.

"I know." Reluctantly, Andrew shook what he offered. "Andrew Spivak, as I'm sure you were informed by your goons. But although I'm happy to hear Syssi is feeling better, I need to see her with my own eyes..."

CHAPTER 47: KIAN

As Kian assessed Andrew, taking in the steely determination and the barely contained aggression wafting off him, he realized Syssi had been right. Her brother would never back off or be placated with a mere phone call. And what's more, Andrew Spivak didn't seem like the type to issue empty threats he had no way of backing up either. Kian had no doubt that if denied audience with his sister, the guy would come back with a SWAT team and storm the building.

"I sympathize. I have three sisters of my own... Come, I'll take you to see her." Kian led the way toward the elevators.

He couldn't believe he was allowing a practical stranger into his sanctum sanctorum.

Well, whatever. He could always thrall the man to forget the place later. And besides, this was Syssi's brother, which made him part of the family... Sort of.

And yet, even though these were all valid excuses for his easy acquiescence to Andrew's demands, Kian suspected the real reason behind his caving in so quickly was his fatigue. He was just too tired to argue.

As soon as the doors closed, Andrew pinned Kian with a hard stare. "Sorry about the goon remark, I know your people were just doing their job. But why the high level of security? What kind of business are you running that demands it?" he asked, his eyes holding Kian's with relentless scrutiny.

Kian countered, leveling Andrew's unflinching stare with a hard one of his own. "I assure you there is nothing nefarious about our conglomerate, besides enemies who wish to destroy it and my family along with it." Kian crossed his arms over his chest, his hard frown daring Andrew to further his insulting insinuations.

"Okay then." Andrew nodded his acceptance of Kian's brief explanation, then mirroring Kian's pose, leaned against the elevator's wall and crossed his arms over his chest and his legs at the ankles.

"That's it? No more questions? I would've expected more from someone like you." Kian exited into the penthouse's vestibule, holding the elevator's door open for Andrew.

"For now, it will do... I know when people lie to my face, and you were telling the truth..."

Kian opened the door to his home and motioned Andrew to go ahead. "That's a very useful talent to have."

"I know." Andrew looked around the place with appreciative eyes. "Nice place you got."

"Thank you." Kian closed the door behind them. "Please, make yourself at home while I get Syssi." He pointed to the couch.

Andrew was about to sit down when he got caught with his butt in midair as Syssi rushed in at full speed to hug him fiercely. "I'm so sorry I had you worried. They held me for observation down at the clinic, and my phone was up here. Kian was with me the whole time I was sick, so no one heard it ringing. We just came back up here a short time before you showed up and didn't have the chance to check yet..."

"That's okay; I just need to know how you're doing now."

"I'm all better. It was just a nasty twenty-four-hour bug."

CHAPTER 48: ANDREW

Syssi had lied.

Though looking her over, Andrew had no idea why, and about what. He was there when she had gotten sick, and it was obvious that she was recovering from something. But aside from looking tired and thinner, Syssi seemed fine. There were no visible bruises or other signs of injury he could detect.

"By the way, Andrew, how did you find us? Syssi tells me that she didn't share with you where she was staying..." Kian sat down on the couch and stretched his arms on its back.

Shit. I'm screwed.

Rushing over, worried and angry, he hadn't thought of coming up with a plausible story.

Fuck! Syssi was going to blow up. Except, there was not much he could do about it now. He was cornered into admitting the truth.

"I checked your location, Syssi, right after you called me with that story of working from Amanda's place. There is a tracking device in the necklace I gave you for your sweet sixteen. The one you swore you'd always wear." Andrew frowned. "The one I don't see around your neck. Where is it?"

Syssi gaped at him, then as the implication of what he had told her sank in, she narrowed her eyes and flushed red.

Andrew winced. Syssi looked so furious that he wouldn't have been surprised if she grabbed something and threw it at him.

"You always do stuff like this. I'm really sick of it. When are you going to start treating me like an adult?" Syssi pushed up from the couch and turned her back to him.

Andrew suppressed a smile. Ever since she'd been a toddler, Syssi would always do that; refuse to look at him when he made her mad. "I don't know why you're so angry with me... It's just a location tracker. And it's not like I'm spying on what you're doing or listening in on your conversations. In my opinion, everybody should have one. Even I have a tracker on me at all times... It's a perfectly reasonable precaution." Andrew pushed up from where he was sitting and placed his hands on Syssi's shoulders.

She shrugged them off.

"Some help here?" He shot Kian a pleading look, hoping the boyfriend might hold more sway.

"Andrew is absolutely right. I wish I had Amanda wear a tracking device. I wouldn't be sitting here helpless if I had." Kian grimaced.

Syssi turned to Kian, her face suddenly lined with worry. "Why? What happened to Amanda?"

"Yes, where is Amanda? What's going on?" Andrew echoed, his gut clenching.

Kian's pained expression confirmed his fear. "After she left the restaurant where you three had lunch yesterday, she was abducted. We found a recording from a surveillance camera at the jewelry store she was taken from, so we know it was one of our enemies who took her. But that's all we have. We don't even know where to begin looking." Kian sank into the couch cushions, hanging his head on his fists.

The distressing news sliced through Andrew like a serrated blade, tearing up his gut. He knew all too well what could befall such a beautiful woman in captivity—the images, unfortunately, made vivid by the many others he had witnessed during his time on the force.

"Oh my God. Oh my God..." Syssi repeated frantically, her hand flying to her throat.

"Oh! My! God!" she exclaimed more forcefully as her eyes popped wide open.

Bewildered, Andrew glanced at Kian, whose questioning expression echoed his own.

"Amanda has my necklace, Andrew! My sweet, overprotective brother! You're my hero! She was wearing my necklace! You can find her!" Syssi jumped on him, hugging him with all she had.

It took a few seconds for her words to sink in, and as they did, Andrew felt Kian's hands on his shoulders, twisting him around and pulling him into a brief embrace.

"I'll be forever in your debt for this. Thank you!" Kian sounded hoarse.

Overwhelmed by Kian's infectious hope, Andrew took a step back. "I haven't found her yet..." A hope he was loath to disappoint. Unfortunately, experience had taught him that not every rescue mission ended with success.

"I'll assemble a team with some of my buddies from my old unit. That was what we did, hostage retrieval. I will get her back for you," Andrew offered, praying he would be able to deliver on that promise: more for Amanda's sake than Kian's. But it had to be handled with extreme care. In a situation like this, even a seemingly insignificant mistake could have fatal consequences.

Kian placed a hand on Andrew's shoulder. "I truly appreciate the offer, but all I need from you is her location. My men and I will handle the rest. We have reason to believe her kidnapper is acting on his own behalf, and no one else is involved. It's not like we have to invade another country or storm a stronghold and need a trained commando unit to do the job. He is just one man."

Andrew's anger bubbled up like hot tar. Was the idiot concerned with honor or appearances when his sister's life was on the line?

"You listen closely now, as I'm going to say it only once." Andrew got in Kian's face. "I'm heading the rescue with my people, and you can tag along... if you can follow orders. This is not a job for amateurs, regardless of any combat training you might have, or how much you care about Amanda, nor how easy you believe it would be. My men and I are trained and experienced in exactly these kinds of situations. If anybody has a chance to bring her back in one piece, it is me. Don't you dare indulge in playing power games when the stakes are this high. Do we have an understanding?"

CHAPTER 49: KIAN

Kian gritted his teeth, knowing Andrew was right and resenting him for it. It was irrational, even stupid, to feel this way about the man with the means and know-how that were crucial for Amanda's rescue. But he loathed the necessity to relinquish control over the situation to an outsider.

"Fine! You lead, and you can bring two of yours. But I'm coming with two of mine... You need us; there are things only we know about our enemies," Kian growled, and pulled out his phone. "Tell me what you need and I'll arrange for it."

"I'll call my friend, have him swing by my place and bring my laptop. Once we know more about where the perp is holding her, we can form a plan of action. We'll need a private room for our people to meet and plan the mission."

"Have your guy come to the lobby. I'll have a room ready by the time he gets here."

"Good."

As Andrew stepped out to the terrace to make his calls, Syssi tagged behind him. "I need a cigarette..." She grabbed the pack that was still out on the side table next to the chaise.

Andrew arched a brow but said nothing. Turning his back to her, he kept talking with his man in a hushed voice.

Joining Syssi on the lounger, Kian wrapped his arm around her shoulders. "It must've been difficult to grow up with a badass like him." He smirked. "Compared to Andrew's raging bull style, I'm merely a housebroken bulldog. Not that I'm not grateful beyond words for his help..."

"I know, right? Now you know why your he-man antics have no effect on me. I have lots of experience dealing with that." Syssi playfully bumped his shoulder with her head.

"Imp..." Kian cupped her neck, and holding her pressed against him, buried his nose in her hair.

Syssi sighed. "Andrew had to take charge. With our parents always busy elsewhere, he practically raised my younger brother and me. But he is a great guy, and I love him. I bet once you're done with your macho posturing, you guys will get along great... He cares about Amanda, you know... Yesterday at that lunch there was definitely something going on between them."

"You know Amanda. She would flirt with a wooden post… It doesn't mean anything." Kian sighed, missing his sister with all her little annoying habits and her never-ending drama. He would never admit it, but he enjoyed all that brouhaha she created around her. She was fresh, and fun, and lively… Oh hell, he really hoped his mother's vision was true…

"Perhaps…" Syssi said. "I had a feeling it was more than that, though. It looked like they really liked each other. Found each other interesting, beyond the physical attraction. It wasn't just Amanda's usual act." Syssi took a drag on her cigarette, collecting her thoughts. "I want to tell Andrew the truth. He has to have all the facts if he is to bring Amanda home safely. Besides, as my brother, he is also a Dormant. You should offer him the same deal you offered Michael and me."

Kian ran his fingers through his hair and grimaced. "You're right. He should know. Although I hate to do it under these circumstances. What if he refuses the offer? I can't thrall him until after the mission without compromising him, and in the meantime, he'll have us by the balls."

"You can trust Andrew. He'd never do anything to endanger my safety, and I'm one of you now."

"I can just imagine his response…" Kian chuckled. "Who is going to lay it on him?"

"I'll do it. But you'll have to supply the details and the proof. Regrettably, I don't have fangs to show him or the ability to create illusions. Or do I?" Syssi looked at him hopefully.

"I don't know. You might. I'll try to explain how it is done once things get back to normal." Kian leaned into her, taking her mouth in a hungry kiss. "I can't wait for us to enjoy ourselves with each other without some calamity hanging over our heads…" he whispered once he let go of her lips.

"Me either," Syssi whispered throatily.

"I can't believe you two are making out at a time like this!" Andrew snapped. "Can't you control yourselves?"

Syssi and Kian exchanged knowing glances.

"Take a seat, Andrew. There is something I need to tell you, and you'd better be sitting for this." Syssi gestured toward the lounger across from them.

"Don't tell me you're pregnant and running off to Vegas to get married…" Andrew looked them over, his expression only half-joking.

"No, I'm not pregnant. Not yet, anyway…" Syssi smiled at Kian and winked, teasing Andrew for sounding like an old prude. "But I did go through an interesting change recently… a change you might consider for yourself."

"What are you talking about?" Andrew frowned. "Let me guess... A fanatic cult? Self-help nonsense? New health diet?" He taunted his sister with his absurd suggestions.

"No, and stop it. You're not playing nice. But anyway, back to what I was trying to say. I wish I could tell you all of this under less stressful circumstances, but we decided that it is important for you to know what you're dealing with on this mission. So here it goes..." Syssi took a long breath, bracing for what she was about to reveal.

"Kian, Amanda, and the rest of their extended family, as well as their enemies, including the one that abducted Amanda, are the descendants of the gods of old. They are near immortal, immune to all mortal diseases, and can regenerate from all but the most severe injuries, which makes them almost indestructible. Also, some of them have the ability to cast very convincing illusions; fooling mortal minds into believing whatever they project. Their own minds are resistant to that kind of manipulation, so they cannot fool each other... Do you understand now why a team of mortals would fail against this kind of an opponent? That's why you need Kian and his men with you."

Andrew stared at Syssi as if she had lost her mind, then turned to Kian with what looked like an intent to harm. "What kind of drugs have you been feeding her?"

"Would you like a demonstration? Hand me the knife you have strapped to your calf, and I'll prove it to you."

"Are you nuts? I'm not going to give you my knife..."

"If I wanted to do you harm, it would have been already done. I need the knife to cut myself. I think what you'll see will convince you."

Still shaking his head, Andrew pulled the knife from the holster strapped to his calf and handed it to Kian. "Knock yourself out..."

Kian ran the sharp blade over the inside of his forearm, watching the blood well. The cut closed itself almost as soon as he made it, the small scar disappearing a few seconds later.

"Wow, you healed much faster than I did. Is it because your blood is purer?" Syssi looked amazed at the speed with which his body had regenerated.

Kian nodded, affirming her assumption. "Do you need more proof?" He turned to Andrew. "I can project Godzilla, or Spider-man, or anyone else you could think of... Take your pick."

"If it weren't my own knife, I would have thought it was a trick... I've never seen anything like that... But just for kicks... humor me with an illusion." Andrew shook his head. "What you claim is so out there, I feel I need more to be convinced it's for real."

"Anything in particular?" Kian smirked.

"Surprise me…"

"Okay, that's one I haven't done in a while…"

Andrew's eyes almost popped out of their sockets at the sight of the huge Phoenix bird that appeared in Kian's place. Syssi, on the other hand, was still looking at where it perched on the chaise as if she was waiting for something to happen.

"You can't see it anymore, sweetheart. Your mind is now immune to thralls and illusions. But if you close your eyes and focus, you'll see it." Kian smirked at Andrew's shocked expression when the guy heard him talk out of the bird's beak.

"Okay, you can drop the bird. I believe you… Explain why Syssi couldn't see it?"

So the guy wasn't completely stupefied and noticed their telltale exchange.

"That's because she was turned into one of us. She, and you as her brother, are rare possessors of our dormant genes, which we can activate. You are only the second Dormant male we've discovered, with Syssi being the first and only female, and as the rest of us are all related, that makes you a very valuable asset, especially to the females of our clan. Until now, their only choice of partners were mortals, with all the limitation that entailed. I'll spare you the history and the complicated explanation. When we get Amanda back, she'll fill in the details. It's her field of expertise."

"So what are you saying? Syssi is immortal now, and you intend to turn me as well?" Andrew frowned.

"No one will force you to do it. It's your choice. But why would you choose not to? Are you so tired of living that you would refuse near-immortality?" Kian arched his brow.

As he regarded Kian, Andrew's expression revealed his skepticism. "I need to know more. I'm sure there is a catch somewhere. Like selling my soul to the devil or something like that. There is never something offered for nothing."

"You'll get all the info after the mission and will have time to decide. The transition is not easy on the body, and it seems that the older the body, the harder it gets. So you cannot attempt it now. You have a team to lead. But after…" Still holding the blade, Kian raised his hands in the air to indicate the open possibility.

Andrew took it back and returned it to its holster, then pushed up from the lounger. "We have a rescue to plan… Or do you lovebirds need some more time alone?" He grimaced at the sight of their entwined hands.

"We do, but time is not on our side..." Kian kissed Syssi's hand and leaned to whisper in her ear. "Tell Okidu when you're ready to see my mother. You don't want to offend her by making her wait too long. And by the way, only the Guardians and council members know she is here, and, of course, the Odus. I want to keep it this way. So don't mention it to anyone besides them." He kissed her cheek before pushing off to stand.

"I'll be back to fill you in on the details after we formulate the plan." Kian cast one last glance at Syssi's concerned face before heading out with Andrew.

Once Kian had closed the door behind them, Andrew pinned him with hard eyes. "If I can trust my judgment about you at all, after that little demonstration of yours, I think you love my sister. And in that case, you have my blessing. But if you ever hurt her..."

"Yeah, yeah... You'll chop me into small pieces. I get it... No worries, Andrew. I'm going to spend my very long life loving Syssi and protecting her from all harm. You have my word."

CHAPTER 50: SYSSI

Nothing could have prepared Syssi for Annani's splendor. The goddess's radiance and palpable power were so overwhelming that she had an urge to curtsy.

Instead, she reclined her head respectfully.

"Oh, my dear girl, you look so much better already. Poor Kian was going out of his mind with worry. He loves you very much... Come, sit with me." Annani took Syssi's hand, leading her to sit on Amanda's couch much in the same way her daughter had done.

"So, how do you feel? Anything different?" She patted Syssi's hand in a motherly gesture that belied her much-too-young appearance.

It was really disconcerting, this dichotomy between the goddess's youthful looks and the ancient power and wisdom of her eyes. But surprisingly, there was also mischief and liveliness in them—more so than in the eyes of her much younger progeny.

"There is nothing truly significant. I feel healthy and vital, and my senses are sharper than they used to be. I hear and see better and smell... that's actually the weirdest part; I think I can smell emotions. Am I imagining it?"

"No, my dear, you are not imagining the smells. The body secretes different hormones for different emotions and each has its own unique smell, some more pungent than others..." Annani chuckled and winked at her.

Syssi peered down at their entwined hands. *What do I say next? How do you conduct a conversation with a goddess?*

Annani was friendly and her smile was genuine. But it was impossible to forget what she was. She was freaking aglow! And not in the metaphorical sense!

"Come on, Syssi, you must have thousands of questions. Ask away. You are going to become the mother of a new clan—our best hope for the future of the last five thousand years. I am here to guide you and help you, so you do not have to do it all on your own. My vast experience is at your disposal." Annani gave Syssi's hand a reassuring squeeze.

"Oh, my God, when you put it like that, it terrifies me. I'm not ready to become this queen bee. I pray Amanda finds more female Dormants, so I can share this burden with others. I don't think I can handle that much responsibility on my own." Syssi kept her eyes downcast, ashamed of her cowardice.

"I hope there will be more like you too, but it is beside the point. When I started on this journey, I was an immature, spoiled girl with no idea of what would be required of me. I stepped up to the plate, and so will you, but with the added benefit of my guidance and help. I am older than most civilizations, you know. There is very little I have not seen or done..." She joggled both brows suggestively.

Syssi had to smile, Annani reminded her so much of Amanda with her outrageous persona. "How do you do that? After all this time and all you have seen, you still have your sense of humor and a glint of excitement in your eyes. I get depressed reading the headline news... There is so much suffering and misfortune out there... I find it hard to stomach. It weighs me down."

"The answer to that is multifaceted." Annani's demeanor turned serious. "You read the news and feel powerless to do anything to make it better. You can only bear witness to all that suffering, and that helplessness depresses you. I, on the other hand, am fortunate to have the means to change this world for the better. And although we suffered many setbacks through the millennia, and the progress is slow, things are getting better. As my efforts bear fruit, I feel fulfilled. I have hope. My dream lives. That is the major source of my happiness, the knowledge that good will prevail in no small part because of me..."

Annani paused, and a bright smile enlivened her perfect face as she continued. "And there are my little ones, my great-grandchildren. I am surrounded daily by their innocence and their unconditional love. I see them grow and blossom into wonderful people... well, most of them anyway... They fill my heart with love and pride. And last but not least, I make sure to have fun... if you know what I mean... lots of fun..." Annani's voice dropped an octave, her demeanor reverting to playful and mischievous.

Then she smiled like an old sage and squeezed Syssi's hand. "So you see, my darling, what I was trying to do with my long-winded speech about my fabulous self—was guide you to your new destiny. You are not helpless anymore; you are no longer a powerless witness to evil; now, you are part of the force for good. But as wonderful as having a purpose and working toward your goals is, the heart needs more to thrive. You have a wonderful man to love, to look after and to guide. I know you think you are too young and inexperienced and wonder what guidance you could possibly provide someone like Kian. But he needs you more than either of you realize. My darling son feels like poor Atlas, carrying the weight of the world on his shoulders, and he needs you to lend him yours."

"I'll do what I can… I have a minor in business and could possibly take over some of his less important tasks. Though I don't think I'll be much help really. I have a lot to learn before I'd be of any use."

Annani dismissed Syssi's concerns with a wave of her hand. "Oh, I am not talking only about his work. I have already talked him into hiring some of our young professionals for that. But you, my dear, could help him choose the right people for the job. What Kian needs assistance with the most is creating a cohesive team. My son is a natural tactical leader and does great as a commander-in-chief, which served him well in the past when an autocratic style of leadership was the norm. Except, he has never developed the skills necessary for diplomacy and building a strong business team. You, on the other hand, with your sweet nature and humble disposition, could be the glue that binds them together. Everyone likes you; you are approachable."

"Except, I'm not assertive, and I shy away from confrontations. Not exactly the traits of a leader…" Syssi tried and failed to pull her hand out of Annani's grasp.

"Bah, but that is exactly my point. You will balance Kian's excess of those traits. As a cool, logical seer, you will probably hold more sway than my hotheaded, obnoxious son."

Syssi regarded her with wary eyes. "I'm not exactly a seer, and Kian is not that obnoxious…"

"So, I have exaggerated a little… Your precognition ability is a very rare gift, even among my kind. And in all likelihood, it will grow progressively stronger now that you have transitioned. And as to my son… Kian takes after me. Being obnoxious runs in the family." Annani laughed, the musical chimes sound of her laughter so beautiful it raised goose bumps on Syssi's arms.

She chuckled. "If you say so…"

"Yes, I know what they say about me: the good and the bad. Anyway, back to what I was trying to explain. You have to have balance in your life and not forget to have fun. Those who neglect that crucial ingredient, in the long run, become more dead than alive. So make sure to make fun a priority for you and my son." Annani winked and squeezed the hand she wouldn't let go of.

"I hope Kian and I will be happy with each other. Though I don't know how we are going to keep our love and passion fresh. With so many years ahead of us, is it even possible?"

"This is the beauty of our peculiar physiology. You will crave each other above all others and always find bliss in each other's arms. But that is only the physical part, the rest is up to you. Tragically, I lost my love at the start of our lives together, so I do not have personal experience with long-term relationships. But I was fortunate enough to witness some wonderfully fulfilling truelove matings, and even some of the arranged marriages blossomed into love and thrived. So to answer your question; yes, it is definitely possible."

"I hope you're right. I love Kian passionately, but we have only just met, and it scares me to think things might change—that I'd make mistakes and ruin it somehow…"

"Do not fret. If the foundation is strong, it will withstand some rattling. It may even provide some spice… after all, making up after a fight is fun…" Annani smiled a knowing little smile.

"Again, I hope you're right…" Syssi sighed.

"Come here, sweet child…" Annani pulled on Syssi's hand with surprising strength for someone so small and seemingly fragile, embracing her tightly. "If my son ever does anything to upset you, he will have me to deal with." She kissed Syssi on both cheeks then leaned back a little and looked into her moist eyes. "As of now, you are my daughter, and I want you to think of me as your second mother. I will always be there for you, even if it means boxing Kian's ears or kicking his posterior occasionally… You hear?"

"Thank you…" Choked up with gratitude at the wholehearted acceptance, Syssi sniffled as tears slid from under her lashes. Never, not in a million years, would she have expected that kind of pledge from the goddess.

From Kian's mother.

CHAPTER 51: SYSSI

"**D**id you complain to my mother about me?" Kian asked as he stepped out onto the terrace.

"No, of course not… Why?" Puzzled, Syssi looked up at him.

After leaving Annani, she had gone back to the terrace outside of Kian's penthouse and sat down to smoke another cigarette. Now that health was no longer a concern, she was really letting herself indulge with a promise to quit later once this crisis was over.

Except, she had a strong feeling that it was just the beginning and more trouble was lurking on the horizon. With all the recent turmoil, she had been too preoccupied to let her mind wander aimlessly, and the cursed premonitions had been held at bay. But the moment things returned to normal and resumed a slower pace, she had no doubt her foresight would come rushing back. Perhaps even worse than before, as Annani had predicted.

Oh, the joy.

As obscure as her premonitions tended to be, they were pretty useless, serving only to darken her mood.

"Oh, I don't know… I stopped by Amanda's place to update my mother on the rescue plan we came up with, and she threatened to kick my butt if I ever dared to upset you… Care to explain?" He plopped next to her and kissed her heated cheek.

"Oh, that… It's nothing. Well, not nothing. Your mother has done the sweetest thing; she made me feel so accepted and so welcomed, that I teared up. She pledged to always have my back. Even against you. Can you believe it? I hope that doesn't hurt your feelings…" Syssi gazed up at Kian's tired, smiling face.

"I'm actually elated that she has made such a promise to you. It makes me a happy man to know that my mother cares so much for the woman I love." Kian pulled Syssi close to his body and kissed her with tender, soft lips. "I love you," he whispered into her mouth.

"I love you so much." Syssi sighed. She felt guilty even thinking it—but it was so unfair. Instead of celebrating her successful transition, preferably by making love, Kian was heading for a dangerous rescue mission. The fates Amanda believed in must've been cruel and capricious, amusing themselves by messing with people's lives.

"Make love to me before you go," she whispered, tugging on Kian's shoulders as she leaned back.

Slipping his arms around her, he held her up and kissed her again. "I can't. Not until I come back."

CHAPTER 52: KIAN

There was nothing Kian wanted more than to lay Syssi down on that lounger and cover her body with his. Unfortunately, he couldn't allow himself that sweet indulgence. If he made love to Syssi in his exhausted state, he would be worthless for tonight's mission.

"I'm running on fumes."

"And here I thought you were Superman." Syssi chuckled.

"I'm sure even Superman needs a few hours of sleep once in a while."

"Don't look so hurt, I was just joking." She kissed his nose. "You'll always be my Superman."

"I wasn't hurt." *Well, maybe just a little...*

"Aha... sure..." Syssi narrowed her eyes. "Men and their egos. Just promise me you'll be careful and not pull any macho stunts out there. I need you..." Her voice quivered a little. "When are you heading out?"

"We are leaving at midnight," he said, touching his forehead to hers. "The Doomer holds Amanda at a remote mountain cabin, so we cannot risk landing the helicopter anywhere near the place—even with the silent blades. We'll have to trek several miles through the forest for a surprise attack."

"How long do you think it will take?" Syssi whispered in a failed attempt to hide the growing tremor in her voice.

"We estimate it will take us at least two hours to get there on foot. The rest should go down quickly. We'll probably be back before three."

Syssi's worried eyes were getting moist with unshed tears, but she said nothing.

"There are six of us going and only one of him. The Doomer doesn't stand a chance. You have nothing to worry about. Andrew knows what he's doing. His plan, at least on paper, seems fail-proof." Kian did his best to sound more assured than he really was. Even the best of plans sometimes failed. There were always surprises, and unforeseen obstacles could derail the whole thing. It was impossible to account for everything, and the help of the capricious Lady Luck was needed.

"Just bring Amanda home, safely," Syssi whispered. "The lives of the most important people in my life are on the line tonight. I will lose a millennium of my new immortal life until I see all of you safely back," she said with a lone tear sliding down her cheek.

"Oh, baby… Don't cry. I promise we will all come back." He hugged her close.

I'm such a ██████ liar, promising what I can't guarantee to deliver.

CHAPTER 53: SYSSI

At midnight, Syssi accompanied the men to the rooftop helipad. Outside, dark clouds obscured the moon, casting ominous shadows on the dimly illuminated platform and the large craft perching on top of it. Syssi suppressed a shiver.

It's not a premonition, don't read anything into it!

"Come back home safely, all of you!" She briefly hugged Anandur and Brundar, then crushed Andrew in a desperate hug while choking back tears.

If I lose him too, it will destroy me. I'd rather die than live with that pain again. My new immortality may as well become a curse instead of a blessing.

"Don't worry. We'll be back with Amanda in no time at all." Andrew kissed her forehead, then dislodged himself with effort from her tight embrace. "Damn, you're strong now..." He gave her hands a reassuring squeeze before running under the helicopter's blades to board the craft.

The moment Andrew let go, Kian took her in his arms. "Stay with my mother. You could use each other's support..." he said before kissing the living daylights out of her. "That was just an appetizer. Later tonight, we feast..." Wiping her tears away, he commanded, "Smile!" then shook his head at her pitifully miserable attempt at one. "I think you need another kiss..." He took her lips again.

She held on as he tried to pull away. "Just a little longer..." she whispered.

"Everything is going to be fine, sweet girl," he murmured against her lips as he kissed her again, softly, then with one last squeeze extracted himself from her arms and hurried to the waiting helicopter.

"Good luck!" Syssi called after his retreating back.

Hugging herself against the night's chill, she watched as the helicopter carrying the two men she loved most in the world took off, then banked north. Her vision blurred by tears, she followed the craft's blinking lights until they disappeared in the distance. "Come back safely to me... Please!" She cast her prayer on the cold, indifferent wind.

Amanda's Story Continues In
DON'T STOP HERE
AMANDA'S STORY IS ONLY GETTING STARTED

Dark enemy taken

Dalhu can't believe his luck when he stumbles upon the beautiful immortal professor. Presented with a once in a lifetime opportunity to grab an immortal female for himself, he kidnaps her and runs. If he ever gets caught, either by her people or his, his life is forfeit. But for a chance of a loving mate and a family of his own, Dalhu is prepared to do everything in his power to win Amanda's heart, and that includes leaving the Doom brotherhood and his old life behind.

Amanda soon discovers that there is more to the handsome Doomer than his dark past and a hulking, sexy body. But succumbing to her enemy's seduction, or worse, developing feelings for a ruthless killer is out of the question. No man is worth life on the run, not even the one and only immortal male she could claim as her own…

Her clan and her research must come first…

EXCERPT

As she heard Dalhu exhale a relieved breath from behind the bathroom door, Amanda smirked with satisfaction.

Dalhu's surprised expression when he'd burst into the bathroom had been priceless. Seeing her in all her nude glory with her body boldly displayed in the bath's clear water—not gasping or trying to cover herself as most women would—the guy had been rendered speechless.

But then she was nothing like what he was used to.

Not even close.

Amanda was the daughter of a goddess, for fate's sake.

He hadn't been the only one affected, though. As he'd devoured her with his hungry eyes, her body had responded, her nipples growing taut under his hooded gaze.

Ogling her, he'd wiped the drool off his mouth with the back of his dirty hand, looking just as awestruck as one of her students. But that was where the resemblance ended.

Dalhu was a magnificent specimen of manhood, and in comparison, all her former partners looked like mere boys. Shirtless and sweaty, he'd looked just as amazing as she'd imagined he would.

He was big; not even Yamanu was that tall, and Dalhu was more powerfully built. Nevertheless, his well-defined muscles were perfectly proportioned for his size with no excess bulk; he looked strong, but not pumped like someone who spent endless hours lifting weights at a gym.

Following the light smattering of dark hair trailing down the center of his chest to where it disappeared below the belt line of his jeans, she hadn't been surprised to find that he was well proportioned everywhere. And as he kept staring at her, mesmerized, his jeans growing too tight to contain him, she'd held her breath in anticipation of her first glimpse of that magnificent length.

Oh, boy, am I in a shitload of trouble.

There was just no way she could resist all that yummy maleness. Amanda knew she was going to succumb to temptation.

She always had.

Except, this time, she would be stooping lower than ever. Because she could think of nothing that would scream SLUT louder than her going willingly into the arms of her clan's mortal enemy...

Shit, damn, damn, shit... she cursed silently.

It had taken sheer willpower to kick him out. She so hadn't wanted to...

But she would've never been able to look at herself in the mirror if she'd succumbed to the impulse and had dragged him down into that bathtub to have her wicked way with him.

Hopefully, he'd been too busy hiding his own reaction to have noticed hers.

What was it about him that affected her so? Yes, he was incredibly handsome, and she was a lustful hedonist... but, come on, she had been a hair away from jumping the guy...

Was she one of those women that got turned on by bad boys?

Yep, evidently I am.

How shameful...

Her hand sneaked down to the juncture of her thighs, and she let her finger slide over the slick wetness that had nothing to do with the water she was soaking in. But after a quick glance at the door that wouldn't close, she gritted her teeth and pulled her fingers away from the seat of her pleasure.

She couldn't let Dalhu know how he affected her if she hoped to have a chance of keeping him off her.

And herself off him...

Damn!

She had to keep telling herself over and over again, repeating it like a mantra until it sunk in, that there was nothing that would scream SLUT louder than her going willingly into the arms of a Doomer.

Oh fates, I'm such a slut...

But wait… this was it…the solution to her predicament…

If there was one thing that was sure to shatter Dalhu's romantic illusions, it was to find out that the woman he wanted for his mate had been with a shitload of others before him.

She was well acquainted with the Doomers' opinions about women and their place in society. Someone like her would be probably stoned to death in the parts of the world they controlled. And though Dalhu seemed smarter and better informed than the average Doomer, he no doubt believed in the same old double standard. It was perfectly okay for him to ~~screw~~ a different woman every night because his body demanded it. But it was not okay for her.

She was supposed to suffer the pain like a good little girl because decent women were not supposed to want or enjoy sex…

Well, she not only wanted it and enjoyed it but needed it to survive, just like any other near-immortal male or female.

But try explaining it to a Doomer…

Stupid. Blind. Deaf.

Members of the brotherhood of the "Devout Order Of Mortdh*"* were brainwashed to hate women and believed them to be inferior and unworthy. It was sad, really, how easy it was for Navuh and his propaganda to affect not only his followers, and not only the male population of the regions under his control but also the women living there. They succumbed to the same beliefs, accepting that they were inferior, that being abused was their due, and that that was what their God wanted for them.

The poor things didn't know any better.

If a girl heard all throughout her life that she was worthless, and her education was limited to basic literacy at best, she was going to believe it, buying into the label she'd been given and perceiving herself that way.

Thinking back to her own youth in Scotland and even later in their new home in America, the situation for women had been only slightly better. Though they were not as badly mistreated as their counterparts in Navuh's region, the prevailing attitude, sadly, had been similar up until recent times. Women had been considered not as smart and not as capable as men, but at least their mothering and homemaking skills had been appreciated. For most of her life, women had accepted these beliefs as immutable truths, treating the few that had tried to rise above them as bad mothers, misguided individuals, and an undesirable influence on their daughters.

Thank heavens this was changing. There was still discrimination in the workforce, with men getting better pay and faster promotions, but at least the West was on the right track.

Oh, well, her mother and the rest of their clan did what they could. But where Navuh had his clutches deeply in the hearts of mortals there was nothing to be done.

They were lost souls.

As was Dalhu.

The guy struggled against what he was, though, she had to hand him that. But could he break free after the centuries of brainwashing he'd suffered?

As a scientist, Amanda knew there was no hope for him. But as a person, as a woman... well... hope was for children and fools—as Kian was fond of saying.

She wasn't a child... so that left being a fool...

Still, hopeful or not, how was she going to get the guy disillusioned with her without getting him so enraged that he would chop her head off?

Dalhu was unstable, going from rage to affection in a heartbeat, and she was afraid of what he'd do if she told him the truth about whom he was planning to spend his life with.

Perhaps the smart thing to do was to bide her time and wait to be rescued.

But how would anyone even know where to look for her?

Damn. What to do... what to do...

Wait... but what if she let Dalhu have her...

Just so he wouldn't kill her... of course...

That wouldn't count as her going to him willingly, would it?

And if she didn't suffer horribly in the process... well...

Now that she'd come up with a semi-moral excuse for sleeping with the enemy—only if it became necessary of course—her mood improved, and she hurried to finish soaping, shampooing, and conditioning before Dalhu got tired of waiting and decided to jump in the tub with her.

Having the option didn't mean she should court that particular outcome, did it?

She finished drying off with the cheap, coarse towel and wrapped it around her body with a grimace. It was way too short, barely covering her butt.

Clutching the shitty towel so it would cover at least her nipples on top and the juncture of her thighs on the bottom, she walked out of the bathroom.

"Not a word, Dalhu. Not a ███████ word..." she hissed at his ogling smirk, the cuss word feeling foreign and vulgar on her lips.

He arched a brow but said nothing. Grabbing a pair of gray sweats, he tore off the price tags and ducked into the bathroom she'd just vacated.

There was another set of sweats folded on top of the bed... pink... and plain cotton panties... also pink...

Her lips twisted in distaste. "Oh, goody, that must be for me."

With a quick glance behind her, she made sure the bathroom door was closed, or as well as it could be, before dropping the towel. With a sigh, she reluctantly shimmied into the cheap panties and then pulled on the shapeless, polyester-blend sweats.

Her bare skin had never before touched anything as disgusting, and a glance at the mirror hanging over the bathroom door proved that she'd never before wore anything as ugly as this either.

She looked positively... well... blah.

The good news was that no one she knew was going to see her in this humiliating getup. Unfortunately, though, she was pretty sure that it didn't make her look ugly enough for Dalhu to lose interest either.

The bad news was that she had no idea how she was going to sleep with the horrible synthetic fabric irritating her skin. And sleeping naked was not an option—even if she made Dalhu sleep on the couch downstairs.

Sifting through the bags, she found the bedding she'd had him bring from the store. One scratchy sheet went over the naked mattress, then pillowcases over the two pillows, and another sheet under the comforter that, surprise, surprise, was also made from polyester...

Had there been nothing else in that store? Or had Dalhu chosen the worst stuff to torture her with...

Well, payback is a bitch.

Grabbing a pillow and a woven blanket, she hurried down the stairs and dropped them on the couch. The thing was too short for Dalhu's huge body, and hopefully, it was lumpy as well...

"Sleep tight... hope you get lots of bedbug bites..." she singsonged as she walked over to the kitchen.

The food supplies Dalhu had stolen from the store were on the floor, still in their paper bags, and as she began taking the stuff out and arranging it on the counter, her spirits sunk even further. Apparently, Dalhu's idea of nutrition was mostly canned meat, canned beans, a few cans of vegetables, sliced white bread, and peanut butter.

The only thing to brighten her mood was a can of ground coffee, but only momentarily—there was no coffeemaker.

Putting together a peanut butter sandwich was something even she could do, but making coffee without the benefit of a coffeemaker was above the level of her meager culinary skills.

A quick search through the cabinets yielded nothing more exciting than some pots and pans, but at least, thank heavens, she found a can opener.

Scooping some of the coffee into a pot, Amanda filled it with water and turned on the electrical stove. Trouble was, she had no idea what the ratio should be, or if it was even possible to make stovetop coffee.

Hopefully, it would be drinkable...

She was desperate for it.

As she arranged the rest of the supplies in the cabinets, the aroma wafting from the cooking coffee smelled delicious, and once it looked like it was done, she poured it into two cups and began making peanut butter sandwiches for Dalhu and herself.

The Children of The Gods

DARK STRANGER THE DREAM

DARK STRANGER REVEALED

DARK STRANGER IMMORTAL

•••

DARK ENEMY TAKEN

DARK ENEMY CAPTIVE

DARK ENEMY REDEEMED

•••

MY DARK AMAZON

•••

DARK WARRIOR MINE

DARK WARRIOR'S PROMISE

DARK WARRIOR'S DESTINY

DARK WARRIOR'S LEGACY

•••

DARK GUARDIAN FOUND

DARK GUARDIAN CRAVED

DARK GUARDIAN'S MATE

CPSIA information can be obtained
at www.ICGtesting.com
Printed in the USA
LVHW081544180420
653961LV00015B/1181

9 781548 399